JUSTICE IN MANHATTAN

. . . is the brand-new collection from The Adams Round Table—the acclaimed authors who brought their uni
Big Apple in the
Manhattan!

WARREN MURPHY reveals how the dead can haunt the living in "A Cry from the Heart."

JUDITH KELMAN shows how the high cost of living in New York forces a woman to use her wits in "Check Mate."

LUCY FREEMAN uses a high-priced psychoanalyst to analyze the killing instinct in "Rehearsal for Murder."

JUSTIN SCOTT examines the law of the streets in "An Eye for a Tooth."

JOYCE HARRINGTON shows in "Betsy's Butterfly" that for a small-town couple, making it together in the big city is no day in the park.

DOROTHY SALISBURY DAVIS tells of the sins of the father—and the suffering of a child—in "Now Is Forever."

The members of The Adams Round Table, which was founded in 1982 by Mary Higgins Clark and Thomas Chastain, meet every month to discuss their craft—plotting murders, finding a motive, and creating some of the best-loved mysteries of our time. Collectively, they have produced over a hundred novels, including bestsellers and Edgar Award winners.

Also by
THE ADAMS ROUND TABLE

MURDER IN MANHATTAN
A BODY IS FOUND
MISSING IN MANHATTAN

JUSTICE IN MANHATTAN

The Adams Round Table

MARY HIGGINS CLARK
JUSTIN SCOTT • LUCY FREEMAN
JUDITH KELMAN • STANLEY COHEN
WARREN MURPHY • MICKEY FRIEDMAN
THOMAS CHASTAIN • JOYCE HARRINGTON
DOROTHY SALISBURY DAVIS

Created by Bill Adler

BERKLEY PRIME CRIME, NEW YORK

JUSTICE IN MANHATTAN

A Berkley Prime Crime Book / published by arrangement with Longmeadow Press

PRINTING HISTORY
Longmeadow Press edition published 1994
Berkley Prime Crime edition / December 1995

For information address: Longmeadow Press, 201 High Ridge Road, Stamford, CT 06904.

ISBN: 0-425-15102-6

Berkley Prime Crime Books are published by The Berkley Publishing Group, 200 Madison Avenue, New York, NY 10016.

PRINTED IN THE UNITED STATES OF AMERICA

10 9 8 7 6 5 4 3 2 1

In memory of Tom Chastain

CONTENTS

INTRODUCTION

The concept of justice is ancient. Humans have yearned for justice since before the days of the pharaohs and the Olympian gods. Modern justice is portrayed as a woman, blindfolded and balancing a scale. Emerson said, "One man's justice is another's injustice. . . ." Our courts attempt to deliver justice, often with quite the opposite result. Justice is not infallible. And sometimes people take justice into their own hands.

When our Round Table agreed that the theme of this book was to be justice, most particularly a Manhattan brand of justice, we were all thrilled with the possibilities. You could see the stories taking shape even as we discussed the project. After three previous books, we knew that we would each come up with a yarn quite different from all the others. And with the incredible diversity of

Manhattan for our background, each writer's vision of justice would be unique.

The Adams Round Table has been meeting once a month for almost ten years. Its members now include Mary Higgins Clark, one of the founders of the group, as well as Stanley Cohen, Dorothy Salisbury Davis, Lucy Freeman, Mickey Friedman, Joyce Harrington, Judith Kelman, Frederick Knott, Warren Murphy, Justin Scott, and Whitley Strieber. We have dinner together at an East Side Manhattan restaurant owned by a man named Adam, who provided us with a round table in a private room. (That's how we got our name, from Adam.) There we discuss the craft and the business of writing. We report on our works in progress, and, very often, we are able to help each other over the difficult spots.

From time to time, we commit to a book of stories together. This is our fourth. Two members of our group are absent from this collection. Frederick Knott is a playwright, and Whitley Strieber was up to his ears in book commitments.

In *Justice in Manhattan* you will find many kinds of justice, with only a few of them delivered by way of a courtroom. There's a very expensive kind of justice and there are such exotic varieties as the multicultural vengeance, the heart-to-heart, the who-gets-the-kids custody battle, the resolution of the unsanctified, the psychological-theatrical, and the downwardly mobile yuppie sorts. There's meddlesome justice in spite of itself, and there's Emerson's variety—injustice visited upon the head of the just.

We've had a lot of fun writing these stories. We hope you'll get as much pleasure reading them.

Joyce Harrington
FOR THE ADAMS ROUND TABLE

JUSTICE IN MANHATTAN

Mickey Friedman

BAD HAIRCUT

IT WAS THE WORST HAIRCUT JOELLE HAD EVER HAD.

Rex, the stylist, was distracted. The tenants in a building he owned were suing him. "The ingratitude," Rex said, as the scissors snicked. "The unbelievable ingratitude."

Joelle, too, was distracted. The executive editor, Mr. *New York Scoop* himself, wanted to see her at three that afternoon.

"I put in a new boiler just last October. What do they want from me?" Rex said, with a particularly vicious *snick.*

What does the boss want from me? Joelle wondered. The other member of the newspaper's investigative reporting team, Joelle's mentor, Marty, had also been summoned. The boss never handled anything personally unless it was big.

Rex kept cutting. To Joelle, he was a fuzzy blob in the mirror. She'd rushed out without her contact lenses, and her glasses lay on the marble counter. She couldn't see Rex's florid features, his rapidly moving fingers. Her own face was equally blobbish. Only guesswork told her those brown blurs were her eyes and that rapidly diminishing chestnut corona was her hair.

Why should she worry? Rex was the most sought-after hairdresser in New York. The elite of politics, society, and show business gathered at Salon Rex for expensive trims. Joelle's salary at the *Scoop* was barely large enough for indulgences like haircuts by Rex himself. They were reserved for special occasions such as meetings with the boss.

Rex whisked the cape from Joelle's shoulders. Joelle put on her glasses. Rex said, "The *gamine* look. It suits you, I think."

Joelle didn't answer. Beyond speech, she stared at her reflection. Rex, perhaps sensing trouble, said, "*Ciao,*" and disappeared. Joelle glanced at the floor, where detached wisps of chestnut were lying ready to be swept up. She left Salon Rex in shock. Down the street, a man at a sidewalk table was selling fake Hermés scarves. Joelle bought one and tied it around her head, pulling the knot very tight under her chin.

"What's with the scarf?" Marty asked.

Joelle settled the wheel of black straw more firmly on her head. "What's wrong with wearing a hat for a change?" she snarled.

Marty and Joelle were sitting on the sofa in the boss's

outer office, waiting to be summoned. The pale skin on Marty's neck and above his ears showed that he, too, had had a haircut. Marty was a grizzled, husky man twenty years older and half-a-head shorter than Joelle. A legend in his own time, Marty had worked on all the crucial stories of the past decades. Marty had been covering Elizabeth Taylor since the second time she married Richard Burton. Marty had covered Bigfoot. As a cub reporter, Marty had covered Elvis when Elvis was actually alive. Since they started working together as the *Scoop* investigative reporting team, Marty had been teaching Joelle trade secrets: how to get hold of someone's trash and what to look for when you've got it; how to pretend to be a friend of the family; how to duck when an infuriated celebrity goes for your eyeballs.

Marty squinted at Joelle. "What happened to your hair, anyway?"

Joelle clenched her teeth. "Never mind."

The boss's secretary told them to go in.

The boss was wearing his usual black suit and shades, lounging in his chair of mouse-colored plush. He wasn't alone. The stranger who rose to greet Joelle and Marty was a tall, slim young man with a sharp face and unruly dark hair—more hair, Joelle noted, than she herself had at the moment. The boss waved a languid hand and said, "Joelle, Marty, meet Antoine Despard, our European correspondent. You probably remember the impressive think piece Antoine did on Princess Stephanie last month. Antoine just arrived from France. The three of you are going to work together on a story."

Joelle and Marty exchanged a flicker of a glance. They were a team. What did they need with Antoine Despard?

They shook hands and settled down to hear what the boss had to say.

What he had to say was sensational. "We've found Frost."

Frost! Joelle swallowed. Her mouth had actually started to water.

"I should say, Antoine found him," the boss went on. "Tell them about it, Antoine."

Antoine touched his tie. He was, Joelle noted, extremely good-looking. "For a year I've been searching for Dwight Frost," he said with a pleasant French accent. "Finally, I located him in a villa in the hills above Nice. I alerted the police. We were about to move in when he bolted. The *café au lait* was still warm in the cups when we got in, but Frost was gone."

Marty mumbled something under his breath. Joelle thought she heard, "Amateur night."

"Recently, I picked up the trail again, here in New York," Antoine continued. "This time, he must not escape."

Marty gave a faint snort. Joelle said, "Why would Frost risk coming back to New York? It doesn't make sense."

"It makes perfect sense if you're 'Dapper Dwight' Frost," said the boss. "He came back to see his plastic surgeon. Our information is that he's had his face completely made over this time."

Joelle nodded. It did make sense. Dapper Dwight Frost, wealthy man-about-town, socialite, and fugitive from justice, was famous for two things: ruthlessness and vanity. Frost's relentless drive had led him, as CEO of a conglomerate called Amalgamated Industries, to cheat widows and orphans, bankrupt several companies, put employees out of work, and loot assets to live in luxury on the French Riviera.

The same drive had pushed Frost to endless experimentation with his appearance. Originally an unremarkable-looking businessman, Frost had been known to seek, with determination bordering on frenzy, the perfect tan, the perfect biceps, the perfect jowl-free jawline. Certainly he would risk returning to New York, where his disappearance had been a sensation and his name still evoked heated conversation at the best dinner parties, if he could have his regular surgeon do his makeover.

"So when do we break the story?" Marty asked. He did not add, although it was surely on everyone's mind, that once Dapper Dwight was in custody those who had helped put him there were eligible for a substantial reward, put up by the Amalgamated board of directors.

The boss nodded approvingly. "You're a real shark, Marty. We'll break it very soon, I hope. As soon as we figure out who Frost is."

Joelle and Marty looked at each other. *Who Frost is?* It wasn't, after all, going to be so simple. Frost had already been made over before Antoine picked up his trail again. The stack of glossy portraits in the *Scoop* files no longer bore any resemblance to the new improved Frost. "We can't talk to the surgeon, for fear of alerting Frost that we've found him," the boss said. He took a photo from his "In" basket and passed it around. "Take a look. Antoine managed to shoot this yesterday."

The picture was a blurry shot of three men having a drink at a sidewalk café. One had a dark ponytail, a gold hoop in one ear, and a heavy black beard; one had thinning light hair, a scar on his cheek, and a crooked nose; and one had a brush cut, a receding chin, and heavy-rimmed glasses.

"That's the new Dwight Frost, accompanied by two bodyguards," the boss said. "Your job is to figure out which of the three men is Frost himself. Once you've done that, we break the story. And then—"

He didn't go on. He didn't have to. Frost in custody. Fame. Reward. And, incidentally, justice.

"Antoine said Washington Square, didn't he? So where is he?" Marty, behind the wheel, craned his neck.

Joelle pulled the brim of her baseball cap lower and peered out the car window at the skateboarders, dog-walkers, drug dealers, NYU students, street musicians, panhandlers, and hangers-out populating the Square on this sunny midsummer afternoon. "I don't see him."

"What exactly did he say when he called?"

"He said he'd left the three of them drinking espresso at Dante, and he'd meet us here to change shifts."

"So why isn't he here?" Marty sounded irritated. Joelle could see that five days of fruitless surveillance of the three Dwight Frosts were telling on his temper.

For convenience, they had christened their quarries Tom (beard and earring), Dick (broken nose), and Harry (glasses). The three men were staying in a rented Greenwich Village town house, and showed every indication of enjoying summer in New York. Always as a trio, they went to the movies, hung out in coffee houses, ate pasta in little Italian restaurants. They triple-dated frequently, but never with the same women. Once, Joelle had managed to strike up a conversation with Harry's date in the ladies' restroom at Nadine's. The woman had said she'd met Harry at a health club the same afternoon and knew little about him except that he claimed to be, despite everything, a loyal fan of the Mets.

The car crawled along at the edge of the park. Behind them, a taxi horn hooted.

Joelle sat up straighter. "Wait a minute. There he is." Antoine was across the park. He wore faded jeans, sneakers, a John's Pizzeria T-shirt, and Ray-Bans, and still managed to look like a Frenchman. Joelle waved, but he didn't see her. "I'll get him. Meet you at the corner," she said.

She jumped out of the car and jogged along the baking sidewalk. When she was close enough she called, "Antoine! We've been looking for—"

Antoine turned toward Joelle. *"Chérie!"* he cried. He scooped her into his arms and planted his lips firmly on hers.

Joelle grabbed for her baseball cap, but it fell off anyway. Antoine's lips were warm and his kiss—for he was definitely kissing her—was expert without being showy. Vaguely she wondered how she would reprimand him for this breach of professional etiquette. When the kiss finally ended, before Joelle could get her breath, Antoine whispered, "They're on a bench over there. I just saw them myself. I had to keep you quiet."

Joelle opened her eyes, which had been closed for some reason. On a bench across the way sat Tom, Dick, and Harry, deep in conversation. "Oh. Right," she said, feeling curiously let down. She stepped back from Antoine, who was looking at her in a dazed way. She remembered her haircut, snatched her cap up from the sidewalk, and jammed it on her head. She stomped off toward the car with Antoine hurrying behind.

"Did you overhear anything interesting?" she flung over her shoulder.

"Only their dinner plans. They will eat tonight at the Rainbow Room. A celebration, they said."

When they told him Marty said, "Yeah. A celebration of outwitting us. They're jerking us around. I hate being jerked around."

"What does that mean, 'jerked around'?" Antoine asked.

Marty sighed.

Joelle, Marty, and Antoine sat around a table at a bar near the *Scoop,* drinking seltzer with lime.

"Three guys," Marty said. "Same height, weight, general body type. One of them is Dwight Frost. How do we tell which one?"

After an extended silence Marty went on, "Let's try this. Choose the man you think is Frost and say why. You first, Joelle."

Joelle had thought about the question already. "Tom. The one with the beard," she said. "A beard is the best camouflage. Tom is artsy-looking, a completely different type from the businessman Frost used to be. That would appeal to Dapper Dwight."

Marty nodded. "Antoine?"

Antoine rubbed his chin. After a minute he said, "I'll take Dick. A broken nose can change the appearance almost as much as a beard. Dick looks tough, and I think Frost would enjoy pretending to be a thug." As he finished speaking, Antoine caught Joelle's eye. He smiled shyly. She felt herself flush.

"So I'm left with nerdy Harry, the chinless wonder," Marty said. "That's fine, because he's my choice. He's the least likely candidate, and Frost is smart enough to go for an unlikely alternative. I take Harry. So where does this leave us?"

He looked around the table. Neither Joelle nor Antoine answered. What was the point of saying that it left them nowhere?

The lights of Manhattan, visible through lofty windows, were spread like a galaxy far below. Waiters in tuxedos carried trays laden with silver-domed platters. The orchestra was playing "Begin the Beguine." Joelle, Marty, and Antoine followed the Rainbow Room *maitre d'* to a table beside the slowly revolving dance floor. At a nearby table, also next to the dance floor, Tom, Dick, and Harry were sipping flutes of Pol Roger.

Joelle was wearing a cream-colored silk slip dress and a lacy *cloche* crocheted of silk ribbon. When they met downstairs in the lobby, Marty had said, "What's that on your head? My grandmother used to put those on the backs of her armchairs."

Joelle ignored him. As they moved toward the elevator Antoine had murmured, "You look charming, Joelle."

Antoine looked good too, sophisticated in his navy suit, his abundant curls neatly brushed. *If only,* Joelle thought, *we could've met under normal circumstances, circumstances when my hair looked halfway decent.* Fate hadn't wanted it that way. Rex had butchered her hair and made it impossible for any man in his senses to find her attractive.

Joelle shook herself. She was here to work, not to mourn lost opportunities for romance. A waiter appeared. She ordered a *kir royale.*

Earlier that day, after their fourth round of lime

seltzers, Joelle had formulated a plan. When she explained it, Marty said, "That's the dumbest thing I ever heard," and even Antoine had looked dubious. But nobody had come up with anything better, so they were going with it.

They were under the gun. The boss had used his pull to get them a dinner reservation at short notice, but he had let it be known that he wasn't pleased. His exact words, according to his secretary were: "If this meal is going on expenses it had better be worth it."

The orchestra played "I Get a Kick Out of You," "Mountain Greenery," "Willow, Weep for Me." Across the way, Tom, Dick, and Harry ordered another bottle of Pol Roger to accompany their tournedos of beef. The Latin band took over.

Joelle had had only a few bites of her salmon when the band began to play "La Cumparsita." Marty pushed his chair back and said to Joelle, "Ready to tango?"

Marty was a fabulous dancer. His mother had run a ballroom dance studio in Brooklyn when he was growing up. Dancing with Marty was such a joy, Joelle didn't care that she was so much taller. Smoothly, they tangoed across the floor. Joelle's evening bag, a glittering concoction of gold chain and crystal beads, swung from her shoulder. Marty said, "You want some advice? Watch out for Antoine. I've heard what Frenchmen can be like."

Joelle gave a bitter laugh. "There's no need to worry."

"No need to worry? His tongue is hanging out every time he looks at you."

"Don't be absurd, Marty." They moved into an open promenade, directly approaching the table where Tom, Dick, and Harry were being served chocolate seven-layer cake.

Joelle looked down at her evening bag. The clasp was undone. She caught a glimpse of the embossed white card balanced precariously in the opening.

"Here goes," Marty said, and initiated a progressive side step reverse turn. Joelle's bag swung out and somehow, perhaps with help from her fingers, the embossed card slipped out of her bag and sailed under the chair of Dick, who was sitting closest to the dance floor. Joelle and Marty danced away, and Marty said, "Bingo."

Joelle and Antoine were sharing an order of profiteroles when Tom, Dick, and Harry got up to leave. Marty stopped eating his passion fruit sherbet to watch. Under his breath, he said, "Yeah, there it is, Dickie Boy. That's right, check it out, show it to your pals. *Uh-huh.* Put it right there in your breast pocket, fella."

When the three men had left the room Marty said, "Okay. So far so good. He took it."

They all sighed. Then Antoine said, "Forgive me, but I wonder—"

"Wonder what?" said Joelle.

He grimaced apologetically. "Dwight Frost has been in hiding, away from New York. Will he know that this *coiffeur*—this Rex—is so terribly chic?"

"Believe me, Dapper Dwight will know," Joelle said.

Exactly according to plan, Tom, Dick, and Harry had left the Rainbow Room in possession of one gift certificate from Salon Rex, entitling the bearer to a haircut by Rex himself. Joelle had bought the certificate that afternoon. It would go on expenses, along with the Rainbow Room tab. When the *Scoop* broke the Dwight Frost story, the boss would know it had been worth it.

They sat back and ordered espresso. Marty said, "Hey, Joelle. Want to samba before we get the check?"

* * *

Drinking coffee in the office the next morning, Joelle said to Antoine, for the hundredth time, "The man who uses that gift certificate will be the real Dwight Frost. Dapper Dwight is too vain to resist a fancy haircut."

Joelle and Antoine were alone. Marty was in the Village, staking out the town house. Antoine said, "I'm sure that's true. But—"

"But what?"

"Frost is a ruthless criminal. If something should go wrong, it could be dangerous."

"Nothing will go wrong," Joelle said. "The minute Frost gets in the chair, we call the police. They'll have him before anything can happen." Besides, Joelle had to admit to herself, she wouldn't mind if Rex had a bad moment or two. After the misery he'd caused her, spoiling her chances with Antoine, it would be poetic justice. She adjusted her Greek sailor cap, picked up her bag, and said, "I'm off. Time to relieve Marty."

Antoine said, "Wait, Joelle." He reached out and removed her cap. She stiffened as he bent and gently kissed the top of her head. "Such pretty hair. You shouldn't keep it covered all the time," he said tenderly.

Joelle's face was burning. She jerked her cap from Antoine's fingers and said, "You're out of line, Antoine. I don't have to put up with ridicule from you. Back off." She stormed out, carrying with her the memory of Antoine's shocked face, the hurt in his eyes.

There was a street fair in progress on West Fourth. Joelle was to meet Marty at the Italian sausage booth nearest to Perry.

West Fourth Street was lined on both sides with booths

and teeming with street fair customers. Joelle found Marty eating grilled sausage with peppers and onions and drinking lemonade. "So where are they?" she said.

His mouth full, Marty nodded across the crowded street. Tom, Dick, and Harry were at a T-shirt booth, chuckling over a shirt with the outline of a dead body on it and the legend, "New York: Another Satisfied Customer." Marty said, "So far, they've bought twelve pairs of cut-price sport socks, two Ecuadorean sweaters, a used Billie Holiday CD, and a pair of batik Bermuda shorts. Are you ready to take over?"

"I guess." She stared glumly at the trio. "Nobody's gone for a haircut, huh?"

"Not yet. Oh, and be careful they don't spot you. They might remember us from last night."

Elbowing her way through the crowd, Joelle tried to keep up with the three men as they wandered through the fair. A group of Andean folk musicians began to play, the music throbbing in her ears. She couldn't get Antoine's face out of her mind. *Pretty hair.* What an outrageous insult!

She had to forget Antoine, get hold of herself. She took off the stupid Greek cap she was wearing and blotted her face.

A voice near her ear said, "Who do you think you're kidding with the hats?"

Through the thin cotton of her blouse, Joelle felt something chilly against her ribs. Slowly, she turned her head and looked over her shoulder. Chinless Harry, his eyeglasses glittering, was standing behind her. A linen sports jacket was draped over his arm. Under cover of the jacket, he was holding the gun that was pressing into her back.

"Of course we spotted you. Changing hats! How bush-league can you get?" Harry said with an evil chuckle. He pressed the gun harder. "Keep moving."

Furious with herself, Joelle did as he ordered. After a moment or two, Dick joined them. But where was Tom?

Harry and Dick were conversing in low tones. Joelle could pick up only snatches of what they were saying over the noise of the fair. She heard, "tie her up," and "Frost," and "back from his haircut." She heard, "out of here tonight."

Her heart was drumming. Tom had gone for the haircut! Bearded Tom was Dwight Frost, just as she'd thought! Her plan had worked!

And there was nothing she could do about it. Frost's henchmen were going to take her somewhere and tie her up. Frost would get his haircut and escape. "Keep moving," Harry said nastily. She plodded forward.

Then, she saw Antoine. He was standing by a display of straw hats for sale, looking anxiously over the crowd. She bobbed on her toes, hoping he would catch sight of her cap. He didn't seem to notice. Joelle was frantic. What if she screamed? Would Harry really shoot?

He might. She kept quiet, her eyes on Antoine.

Antoine had stopped scanning the crowd, and was now inspecting the straw hats. Joelle saw him reach for his wallet.

Joelle wanted to scream. Here at the crucial moment, all Antoine could think of to do was buy a hat?

They were approaching the corner of Charles Street. At Charles, Joelle guessed, the men would force her to turn off toward their rented town house. There, they could tie her up—or worse.

She wouldn't think about worse.

Anyway, surely Antoine and Marty would find her eventually, but in the meantime Dwight Frost would escape.

Suddenly she felt jostling behind her. She heard Harry say, "Wait just a—" The gun was no longer pressing into her back. She whirled to see Harry with a very large straw sun hat pulled down over his eyes. Antoine, behind him, pushed the blinded Harry into Dick. As the two bodyguards staggered together he cried, "Run, Joelle!"

Joelle ran, dodging through the crowd. She heard feet pounding behind her and risked a glance. It was Antoine. Harry and Dick were half a block back. Antoine grabbed her hand and dragged her around the corner, where the investigative team car was double-parked. Joelle jumped behind the wheel and Antoine flung himself into the passenger seat. As they took off, Joelle saw Harry and Dick in the rear-view mirror, watching them go. Harry flung the straw hat to the pavement in disgust. "Hang on," she told Antoine.

They screeched around corners, scattering pedestrians in their path. Maybe they could make it to Salon Rex before Frost got away. Joelle lay on the horn, terrifying a group of schoolchildren. Antoine said, "Joelle, I couldn't let you go like that. I had to come find you. We have to talk. I must tell you how I feel. Oh, Joelle—"

Joelle patted his knee. "Later," she said.

When they were within blocks of Salon Rex, traffic became impossible. They left the car at a hydrant and sprinted along the sidewalk, threading across streets through the nearly touching bumpers of major gridlock. A block away, the focus of the problem became apparent. Police cars, their lights flashing, television crews, hordes of milling people—all in front of Salon Rex.

Joelle and Antoine elbowed through the throng. As they emerged at the front of the crowd, a phalanx of police came out of the salon. The man they were guarding—could it be Dapper Dwight Frost, also known as Tom? The beard was intact, but the once-luxuriant mane of black hair was now a bristly, uneven disaster. Faced with the jeering crowd, Frost scowled. He spoke to one of his escorts, and the policeman pulled his jacket up over his head. He was shoved into the back seat of a police car. Frost was in custody!

But why? How?

As the police car drove away, the television lights shifted. A gabble of voices began screaming questions: "Weren't you frightened?" "What made you suspicious?" "How does it feel to be a hero?"

Joelle stood on tiptoes. Amid a crowd of screaming journalists stood Rex the stylist, looking completely self-possessed. Rex bent toward the thicket of microphones. "That tacky black dye job didn't fool me for an instant. I never forget a head of hair."

"You'd cut Dwight Frost's hair before?"

"When he left the country, he still owed me for a styling and three trims."

"Can you tell us what happened, Rex?"

Rex smirked. "I recognized Frost immediately. I thought he deserved a haircut to end all haircuts. When he began causing a scene, I sprayed him in the eyes with Ever-Hold Styling Mousse from the Salon Rex product line and called the police."

Joelle caught sight of Marty, standing to one side taking notes. She and Antoine worked their way over to him. He growled, "Not exactly an exclusive for the *Scoop.*"

"I don't understand," Joelle said. "What happened?"

"My guess is, Frost got too cocky. He was so proud of his makeover he thought he could fool his own former hair stylist. That gift certificate gave him the push he needed to try it."

Joelle sagged against Antoine, and felt his arms close around her. "But it was my idea! He went to Rex because of me!" she cried.

"Never mind, Joelle," Antoine whispered in her ear.

"Rex, are you aware there's a substantial reward offered for the capture of Dwight Frost?"

Rex spread his hands wide. "I need no reward to do my duty as a citizen. However, if a sum has been offered—" His eloquent shrug said he would not be so rude as to refuse.

Rex would get the reward. He would be more famous than ever. He would raise his already exorbitant prices. All because he had given Joelle a bad haircut.

From within the warmth of Antoine's arms Joelle burst out, "It isn't fair! It's completely unjust!"

Marty gave her a look. "Justice? There is no justice in Manhattan."

No justice. But still—Joelle turned to Antoine. "Now, what was it you wanted to tell me?" she asked.

Justin
Scott

AN EYE FOR A TOOTH

HAGOPIAN WAITED FOR THE SHOOTING TO STOP BEFORE HE ventured out of his Amsterdam Avenue Luggage Repair. On the sidewalk, lay one body only: Ramos, selling crack, cheating his supplier. Hagopian—who was thirty-eight, looked a wizened sixty with three days' beard on his sunken cheeks, and felt seventy—was astonished at how long it had taken someone to shoot the fool.

A small boy knelt over the body, weeping. He scrambled into the crowd as the first of many police cars came screaming like artillery shells. Enormous blue-coated officers demanded to know who'd seen it happen.

Hagopian hesitated, torn between his instinct to hide and a powerful fear that if the police came into his shop to interrogate him they might discover his illegal apartment. If only he had a green card. The eight thousand he had already paid the immigration lawyer—who also happened to be his landlord—bought no peace of mind when a huge policeman asked, "Wha'd you see, Pop?"

Hagopian froze. His English, not yet reliable, failed him under pressure. He couldn't remember "Pop." His first language was Armenian; his second, the Russian they'd beaten into him in the Soviet Army; his third and fourth, the Afghan people's Peshto and Dari. The lawyer-landlord had laughed, "You sound like a Polack."

"You see anything? . . . Hey, Pops? Wake up! This your store?"

"Inside, I am fixing," Hagopian managed at last.

"You saw out the window."

Hagopian shook his head. The window of the basement shop was barred, the glass filthy, with luggage heaped behind it.

"What happened when you heard the shots?"

Hagopian gestured at the body. "Is kill-ed."

"Hey, detective?" the cop called. "Got a live one here."

Hagopian felt his blood congeal. Uniformed militia were one thing, detectives quite another. But he got a pleasant surprise when a pretty blonde flashed her badge and said, "Detective Dee. How are you doing, sir? A little shook up?"

"Shooking," Hagopian agreed.

"What is your name, please?"

"Hagopian," Hagopian admitted, swiftly re-assessing his predicament. Detective Dee spoke gently, but she had eyes like a blizzard in the Hindu Kush.

"It would appear this gentleman was shot right outside

your shop. I wonder if you can help me in my investigation. This *is* your shop?"

Hagopian nodded.

"You repair luggage," she prompted, reading the signs on the railing and the door.

"Luggage. Handbags. Zippers. I am fixing zippers many times."

"What's a 'trank'?"

"Trank? Ah!" Hagopian smiled and for a moment he looked more like the young man he might have been had he made it to Manhattan a decade earlier. "I am drawing—writing—sign when I come-ed," he explained. "Old sign." He pointed at the yellow sign on the stair railing he had hand-lettered in black print. Then he directed the detective's attention to the nearly identical sign on his battered tin door. "New sign. I am meaning 'trunk.' No 'trank.' You get?"

She smiled. But Hagopian was soon back in the ice fields. "Do you know the name of the victim?"

He was careful to first look at Ramos, who had bled into the gutter.

"No."

"Never seen him before?" she persisted.

Conditioned by a lifetime of dodging officially generated misery, Hagopian hunched deep inside the quilted jacket he wore indoors and out, and commenced a drift into anonymity. His body seemed to shrink. His eyes emptied. His cheeks sunk deeper.

"Mr. Hagopian, did you see who shot that man?"

"No."

"Did you hear the shots?"

"No."

"Mr. Hagopian, five shots were heard blocks away.

Are you *sure* you didn't hear them ten feet in front of your shop?"

The detective misinterpreted Hagopian's cringe as a shrug. "Let's see some ID, sir. Driver's license? Visa?"

Hagopian swept an apologetic arm over the front of his shop, the barred window blocked by luggage, the bent tin door, the yellow signs with block lettering. "Trank" was the only misspelling. Although every time he saw the squeezed-in "HANDbags," he was reminded that he was no longer a man who planned ahead.

She wrote his name down in her book and lectured him like a school teacher: "This isn't a bad neighborhood, yet. But it's gonna get worse until people like you help cops like me. Now come on, Mr. Hagopian. You're a neighborhood businessman, after all, and . . ."

As she scolded and cajoled, Hagopian stared at his feet. He watched from the corner of his eye the body, the ambulance attendants, the cops questioning his neighbors. For relief, he allowed his attention to settle on Consuela, the round and lovely Spanish woman who belonged to Eduardo, dispatcher of the Bolívar Car Service. Consuela tossed him a kind smile. Sadly, Eduardo carried a knife.

"Urban violence won't be stopped until good people stand up and be counted," Detective Dee was going on.

Hagopian almost smiled. Urban violence? One body? Urban violence was a Russian tank shelling the ground-floor supports of an apartment building until the people upstairs were spilled into the street. Urban violence was a gunship strafing city buses. Urban violence was . . . many things this pretty little American would never know.

She droned on. He let his mind wander to happier

things—to the pleasures of his new home. He could buy cooked food from a dozen nationalities in this one block. Bookstores sold tens of thousands of books. The library lent them for free.

Around the corner, ballerinas served as waitresses in the Café Lalo. He could splurge three dollars for a cappuccino, heap it with sugar, steep himself in the warm talk around him, the music, the bakery smells, celebrate the winter light streaming in and pretend he was in Moscow, inside a Party-only café he had only seen through the window.

Too skinny, the ballerinas. Better this voluptuous policewoman. Or Consuela. Best, the beautiful daughter of the proprietor of the Amsterdam Afghanistan Restaurant. He couldn't bear to go in, but through the window he admired her long black hair and violet eyes—exactly like the girl he had married in the war.

"Oh, god," said Detective Dee, patting Hagopian on the arm. "Please don't cry."

"Excusing, please," he asked, and struggled in a trembling voice to explain. "A person remembered."

Detective Dee looked like she wished she hadn't reported to work that day. "Here's my card, Mr. Hagopian. If you remember anything about the dead gentleman shot outside your shop, please call me immediately."

Hagopian promised he would, to make her go away, and escaped at last into his shop. It was dim as a cave, ten feet wide and twelve feet deep, heaped floor to ceiling with bags repaired, bags awaiting repair, and bags forgotten—some by his customers, some by Hagopian.

Through these leather and vinyl mountains twisted a narrow ravine. Hagopian followed it past his workbench and through a curtain into his living quarters, a windowless storeroom that contained a single bed, a hotplate, and a humming refrigerator he had found on the sidewalk.

He set his tea kettle on the hotplate and shuffled out to his sewing machine. The boy who had grieved for Ramos was crouched in the shadows of the shop with tears in his eyes and a gun in his hand.

Robbery? Hagopian looked without looking. His money was safe in the scuffed backpack that seemed to be waiting its turn at the sewing machine.

The gun—a cheap and serviceable rust-pitted 9 mm auto pistol, Hagopian noted—looked enormous in the little hand. But it pointed so steadily at his face that gun, hand, and the scrawny child himself might have been stamped from the same metal.

Wire-thin arms poked from a dirty red sweatshirt that read "Ralph Lauren POLO" and hung like an empty garment bag. His skin was gray, his nose as aquiline as a Spanish grandee's, his hair black and shiny as that of the South American Indians who delivered for the Korean liquor store. His eyes were red rimmed, wet, and determined.

Hagopian recognized him from the neighborhood and attempted a cautious smile. "Are kite boy? Yes?"

His little jaw dropped. His eyes narrowed. "Say what? How you know that?"

"Is not pointing gun . . ."

"Why you call me kite boy?"

Hagopian explained that he had seen him flying kites on Eighty-third Street.

"I got no money for kites."

Hagopian asked the boy's name. It was Hector.

". . . Gun, I am thinking . . ."

The gun stayed right where it was, while Hagopian explained how much he had admired the kites little Hector made from plastic straws and tissue paper. The other children had kites from the stationery shop. Hector's flew higher. "Like eagle. Great airplane engineer when grown. Gun is pointing—"

"I got business when the cops split."

"Cops . . . Perhaps I am locking door. Perhaps pointing gun elsewhere."

"Don't move!"

"Please, Hector. I am not telling. I am locking door so cops aren't walking in."

"If you run I'll bang holes in your back."

Hagopian promised that would not be necessary and walked slowly down the ravine, carefully keeping his hands in sight, and turned the massive Fox Lock. "All safe. See? Safe."

"Stay where I can see you, man. *What's that?*" Hector jumped down from the bags, and leveled the weapon at the whistling behind the curtain. Frightened, he looked even younger.

"Tea boil-ed," Hagopian assured him. "Wanting tea?"

"Got any food?"

"Perhaps we are looking inside refrigerator."

"You got candy?"

"Cookies."

"Get 'em."

Hagopian edged past the gun, poured boiling water on a tea bag in a mug and grabbed the boy a half-eaten bag of Oreos, rustling the plastic first to rout the roaches.

Hector finished the cookies before Hagopian's tea had cooled enough to drink. "What business you are having?" he asked.

"Justice."

"Justice? What is this justice? Police?"

"Not cops. *Justice.* Do right from wrong."

"What wrong?"

"The son-of-a-bitch Luis shot Ramos."

Hagopian covered his ears. "No, no, no. I am not hearing." Hot-tempered Luis Carbona, the most vicious thug in the neighborhood, was a customer. Hagopian was holding a fancy leather bag he had repaired for him.

"I saw him. Luis shot him in the back. Ramos didn't even get to pull his gun."

"That gun?"

"I took it off Ramos before the cops came. So I can bang Luis."

"Why you?"

"Ramos and me, I think we have the same father."

"Wait, wait, wait," said Hagopian. "You're a boy, you can't—"

"Who's going to stop me? You?"

The contempt in his eyes mirrored a helpless old man, but Hagopian persisted. "That not justice. What do you call it? Reverse—? No. Revenge."

"You got it, man."

"Eye for eye, is saying in my country."

"Same here."

"Now everybody blind."

Hector shrugged. "Here, guy bangs you, you bang him back."

"No, no, no. Here—" Hagopian could hardly believe the thought he was about to express; he expressed it anyway because, as much as he feared government, chaos was worse—"Here, seeing murder, you tell cop."

"No way. Cops'll lock him up, two years he's out. I got

a cousin, shot in the Bronx? They catch the guy on video? Security camera? Cops a plea? Judge gives him two years in Rikers. He's out in nine months 'cause they got no room. Killed my cousin and he's back on the street. I got another cousin? Amelia? Customs catches her with a little coke at Kennedy Airport. Federal offense. Ten years. Hard time. My mom said she won't get out of jail 'til she's *thirty*. For a little coke? And the guy who kills my cousin, he gets out in nine months?" He stroked the gun. "Luis ain't gonna get out of *this* in no months."

Hagopian shook his head, struggling to explain that even if revenge was justice, it was not practical. "This Luis is very bad?"

"He kills for the drug dealers."

"He has friends?"

"Yeah?"

"Maybe they are coming to you for 'justice'?"

"I don't care, man. They come after me, I'll bang them too."

"How old are you?"

Hector claimed to be twelve. Outside on Amsterdam a police siren whooped. The boy looked out that way and Hagopian took the opportunity to snap the gun out of his hand.

"Hey! You bastard. You fucker. Hey, what are you doin', man?"

Hagopian's fingers flew and before the boy's astonished eyes the gun disintegrated into a tidy heap of metal parts.

"How you do that?"

"Practice."

Hagopian could have added, but hadn't the English,

that skills mastered at night, in the rain, while people were shooting, were never forgotten. Just as he would never forget a child, lost on such a night. Shuffling sear spring, main spring, and recoil spring, he emptied the magazine and poked disdainfully at the dirty slide.

"Rust-ed." Hagopian snapped his fingers. "Behind you. WD-40!"

Hector, round-eyed, passed him the spray can Hagopian used to free corroded zippers and snaps. Quickly, methodically, he cleaned the gun and reassembled the now-glistening parts.

It was the first gun he had touched since 1991 when he abandoned his own in the men's room of De Gaulle Airport—a weapon he had carried four years in Afghanistan, home to Armenia, through the Azerbaijan War, all the way across Europe to Paris, fifty feet from the airport security metal detectors.

He wished he could tell Hector how frightening that last fifty feet had been, walking like a naked man. Then maybe the boy would know what "justice" cost.

Suddenly, a fist pounded the tin door. "Hey, open up! You got my bag, man. It's Luis. Open up or I'll kick the door down."

Hector whipped the gun off the worktable.

"No," said Hagopian.

"I'll bang that fucker right through the door. You try and stop me, I'll bang you too."

"Already you are stop-ed."

"Say what?"

Hagopian held up a tiny steel stud. "How you call? Fire pin."

"You fucker."

"You hiding."

"I'll get another gun, man. You can't stop me."

"Yes, yes, yes. But first, hiding . . . There!" He shooed Hector through the back room curtain. Luis resumed pounding, but Hagopian paused at his work-bench before he shuffled to the door. He unlocked it and blinked out at Luis Carbona, a Latin with the dead gaze of a mountain wolf.

"Yes?"

"My bag, man. Give me my bag."

As usual, he had left his BMW with the door open and the motor running— a contemptuous dare that Hagopian likened to the custom in his part of the world of massing tanks at the border to remind neighbors who was dangerous.

"Receipt, please?"

"Screw that, man. You know my bag. Black leather. Strap come loose."

Hagopian cast a dubious look into the darkness behind him, then shuffled through the bag mountain, returning with Luis's many-zippered carry-all dangling by the broken strap.

"Is not ready."

"*What?*" He seized Hagopian's collar and lifted him off his feet. "I tole you a week ago. You tole me she be ready."

"Is very hard fixing inside. Putting down, please. I show." Luis flung him down and stood over him, his eyes hot, as Hagopian demonstrated how the strap had to be sewn from within. "Is good bag."

"Shit! I'm on a eight o'clock outta Kennedy. I'm leaving *here* at five-thirty. You got two hours or"—he shoved Hagopian against the stack of luggage—"or mine won't be the only bag 'is not ready.' "

Hagopian believed him. Drugs, of course, paid for Luis's airline tickets between North and South America—not that he carried himself, Consuela had assured Hagopian during one of their chats in the morning sun. She called Luis a "mule driver," an overseer of the peasant women so often arrested at Customs, like Hector's cousin. *"Muy malo,"* the liquid Spanish had poured like honey from her lips. *Malo,* for sure. Ask Ramos on the sidewalk.

Cursing his impulse to save Hector from himself, Hagopian hurried to his workbench. He had no illusions about children—not in a world where eleven year olds rolled hand grenades into markets—but he did have hope.

Had his son survived, he'd have been Hector's age. And yet the connection he felt with this little boy ran deeper, into his own childhood, when the world had still seemed boundless. Was it possible, he wondered grimly, that Ramos was not the only fool on Amsterdam Avenue?

"Is gone-ed," he called.

Hector pushed through the curtain. "Fix the gun."

"Later."

"I told you, you don't fix it, I'll get another. I know where."

Hagopian did not look up from his sewing machine. "Later."

"When?"

"Eight o'clock. In airport."

"Say what?"

"So neighborhood not seeing you shooting. Yes?"

"Yes!"

Hagopian told him to find out what airplane Luis Carbona flew on. Hector hesitated in the doorway.

"What are you doing?"

"I do what I do." He hunched over his machine.

"Don't forget the firing pin."

Two hours later, Luis Carbona slung his bag on his shoulder, told Hagopian he'd pay him when he got back to Manhattan, and raced off in his BMW. Hagopian hurried next door to the Bolívar Car Service. He fidgeted nervously behind a customer who asked for a receipt, and finally reached the bulletproof window that protected the dispatcher's desk.

"*¿Cómo está,* Eduardo? I am hiring car."

"Got any money?"

"How much?"

"Where you goin'?"

"Kennedy Airport."

"Twenty-five bucks plus tolls."

"As I am coming both directions, perhaps we are agreeing forty bucks."

"Fifty bucks—plus waiting—plus tolls."

Hagopian had sixty in his tattered change purse. The zipper stuck. Eduardo sneered.

Hagopian apologized: "How you say? 'Shoemaker's children get no Adidas. . . .' Ah, here! We go now."

"You gotta wait. Rush hour. I got no drivers."

Hagopian snatched back his money. "No waiting. Taking taxi."

"I'll drive him," said a honey voice, and there was Consuela, all round and dark, shiny white smile, red lips and fingernails, lush hair like a twist of night. And there was Eduardo, caught between greed for the fifty dollars and his suspicions. "Gimme the money."

As he followed her tight jeans to the car, Hagopian felt

years slide from his body like melting snow. Hector ran from Caesar's Pizza clutching a greasy bag.

"Where you going?" demanded Consuela.

"I'm with him."

"Hector, if Eduardo finds pizza on his seats, you're dead meat."

"Where's the gun?" Hector whispered.

"Gun fine. Where's change?"

Hector returned fifty cents. As soon as he finished his slice, he started whispering to see the gun, despite Hagopian's warning nods in the direction of Consuela, who was cursing a fluent stream through the rush-hour traffic. To shut him up, Hagopian asked, "What is Uncle Sam?" He explained how the customer ahead of him at the car service had needed a receipt for "Uncle Sam."

"Don't you know nothing? IRS. Taxes."

Hagopian, ignorant of much in his new land, and glad of any means to distract Hector from out-loud outbursts of "Bang that fucker," asked, "Eduardo pay tax?"

Hector laughed. "You joking, man?" He repeated this absurdity in Spanish. Consuela giggled. Finally, as they passed under the Long Island Expressway, God smiled: Hector, lulled by food and the warm car, fell asleep.

"So where you going?" asked Consuela.

"American Airlines."

"I *know* that. Then where? Who you meeting?"

"We are seeing sights."

"Okay, don't tell me." She pouted, prettily, and Hagopian racked his brain for things to say. But whenever he hit on a subject, he couldn't come up with the words, and they drove mostly in silence into the airport and up to American departures.

Hector woke up fast, eyes glittering. He tried to dip his tiny hands into Hagopian's pockets. "Gimme the gun."

"Later," Hagopian whispered, slapping his hands away, terrified that Consuela had heard. She looked perplexed.

"You wait?" said Hagopian.

"Not here. They'll bust me. I'll park and wait for you inside."

"No, no, no. We find you in parking." He looked around the moving maze of cars and buses and hurrying people and spotted the walkway to the parking lot. "By there!" he said, suddenly firm.

Consuela looked surprised. "Okay, if that's what you want."

The car clock read seven-twenty. "Coming," he said to the boy. "Hurry!"

Through electric doors and up the escalator Hector kept pestering him for the gun. But while repairing Luis's bag, Hagopian had rehearsed what he would tell the boy at this point, and had cobbled together some unusually coherent sentences.

"You are knowing what is hit man?"

"Me. Soon as you give me the gun."

"You know how hit man work?"

"I'll bang the fucker second I see him. We split up. Meet at the car."

"No, no, no. This is not rap video. Real hit man is having . . . uuuhhhhh . . . what you call—*teammate.* I am being teammate. Hit man *not* carrying gun. Teammate carrying gun. See target, teammate giving hit man gun."

"Then you watch my back while I bang the fucker."

"Very good, Hector. Now we are finding gate."

They perused a departures screen and located Luis's flight.

"Gate six. Gimme the gun."

Hagopian strode off, following signs. The boy scampered after him, pleading for the gun. Hagopian watched for Luis. He felt his skin begin to crawl, his heart speed up. People rushing with bags, a thousand shoes—clinking, scuffling, rustling—voices from the ceiling, all hurled him back to Paris, back to those last fifty feet.

Blocking the corridor was a security checkpoint, beyond which only passengers with boarding passes were allowed. It funneled the passengers through X-ray machines and metal detectors. Agents stood in front, directing the flow. Others frisked those who set off the detector. Those studying the X-rays stopped the machines for closer looks, and opened bags that didn't pass. In addition, Hagopian noticed a plainclothes agent, an apparent passenger, whose shoulder bag, he would have bet a night with Consuela, contained an assault weapon.

"Gimme the gun."

Hagopian led Hector into the foyer of the men's room, which gave them a clear view of the checkpoint. Hector gasped. Luis came striding out of the men's room, running a comb through his hair.

Hagopian whirled to the wall, lifting one foot as if to tie a shoelace, and enveloped the boy in the folds of his quilted jacket. Luis brushed past them. His shoulderbag skimmed Hagopian's arm, but he did not turn to apologize and the next instant he was on the line forming at the checkpoint.

"Gimme the gun."

"Here."

"Hey, what are you doing?"

Hector tried to squirm away from the barrel pressing

his belly, but Hagopian jammed his other hand behind his back, holding him hard against the weapon.

"You are not moving, or you are gut shot. You know what is gut shot? Maybe crack spine."

Hector looked up into the deadest eyes he had ever seen.

"But, but—You son of—But why? Luis buy you off? He pay you to stop me?"

"You want justice?"

"Yeah, man. You said you'd help."

"Watching."

"Hey, no fair, you banging him. *I* bang the guy who killed my brother, not you."

"Watching."

Luis's turn had come. A seasoned traveler, he laid his shoulderbag on the X-ray conveyor and passed through the metal detector, after first depositing his keys and coins in a tray. Flashing a smile at one of the prettier agents, Luis went to retrieve his shoulder bag. But as Luis's bag emerged, an agent took it and beckoned Luis to a table.

"What's he doing?" asked Hector.

Another agent ducked his head to speak into a shoulder mike.

"Watching."

The agent opened Luis's bag, zipper by zipper. Luis Carbona checked his watch. A second smile to the pretty agent got a look of stone, and now, as Hagopian held the boy, a swiftly moving cadre of plainclothes agents approached the checkpoint, while uniformed police officers suddenly appeared to steer passengers away.

"I can't see," Hector protested. To his amazement, Hagopian pocketed the penlight he had been pressing to his belly and hoisted Hector in a swift, sure motion to his shoulder.

"Watching."

He saw Luis arguing, refusing to face the wall, until two burly agents turned him around and slammed him against it.

"What do you see?"

"He had a gun in the bag. It has a false bottom. The X-ray machine nailed it."

"And more?"

Hector watched the agents remove the gun. "Hey, that's Ramos's gun—Wow, Luis tried to get away. This huge cop banged his face on the wall. There's blood all over. Excellent. They cuffed him."

Hagopian lowered him to the floor, stretched his aching back, and headed quickly for the escalator. "We gone-ed. Now!"

From the Triboro Bridge, it appeared as if every light in Manhattan was burning. Hagopian remembered the Milky Way pierced by ice-capped mountains.

"Man, that was great! The Feds'll lock him up forever."

Not so great, thought Hagopian. It would have been greater for him if the hot-blooded Luis had fought to the death.

"Better justice than nine months, yes?"

For the rest of the drive, Hagopian and Hector discussed the possible penalties for the Federal crime of smuggling a gun onto an airliner. If cousin Amelia got ten Federal years for a little coke, it stood to reason that Luis would receive many more.

Suddenly Hector said, "He's gonna get you, man. He's going to know you put the gun—"

"Jail-ed."

"He's got friends. They know where to find you."

Hagopian had already concluded that he had put too much hope in Luis's fighting back. Worse, he had mistakenly assumed that American security agents would open fire like Russians.

"Better justice than small boy killing man. Yes?"

Hector said, "Watch your ass on the street, man."

"No kites in jail," Hagopian persisted. "No airplane engineer. Yes?"

"You better get a gun."

"I don't want a gun." Drained, Hagopian tipped Consuela two dollars and went to bed in the back of his shop.

The next day he jumped whenever the door opened. Luis's arrest was on page two of both the *News* and the *Post*. He was pleased to see that his and Hector's estimates of jailtime had been conservative. But of course Luis had friends. Sadly, wishing he didn't have to, he asked Consuela if she knew someone who would sell him a gun.

From the many offered, he chose a man-stopping .45 automatic, discounted for a frozen slide which he easily repaired. It was a big weapon, but he had room in the folds of his quilted jacket. No one saw it when he had his cappuccino. But Café Lalo didn't feel the same.

That night, as he was closing, the door swung open.

"Close-ed," Hagopian called.

"It's me."

Hector's little face was round in smiles. "Boy, is Luis pissed. He's so mad he's banging his head on the bars."

"How are you knowing?"

"They got him down at Manhattan Correctional. My cousin's uncle is in there. I sent Luis a message."

"What message?"

"Told him I put the gun in the bag when you weren't looking."

Hagopian was appalled. "Why?"

"For Ramos."

"But we make-ed justice for Ramos. Now Luis's friends are hunting you."

"Hey, man, it weren't justice 'til Luis knew I banged him."

Joyce Harrington

BETSY'S BUTTERFLY

IT WAS THE BUTTERFLY THAT DID IT. OH, IT WAS A FINE butterfly. Pretty, you know? Like all butterflies. Did you ever see an ugly butterfly? Well, okay. So in the city, you don't see a whole lot of butterflies. Except maybe in Central Park, but you don't notice them so much because of all the people and the softball games and the dogs playing Frisbee and so on. And, believe me, people and dogs do come in the ugly variety. It was mid-summer in the city, and all the ugly people and dogs were on display everywhere you went.

Betsy was pretty and so was her butterfly. Small and delicate, just like she was. But, as I said to her when I saw it, "Betsy, what did you go and do that for?"

She was eating a burrito at the time—Betsy sure does

like Tex-Mex—and she mumbled something around a big mouthful that sounded like, "Stick it in your ear, Charlie."

I couldn't believe she said that. So I said to her, "What?"

She swallowed and repeated slowly and distinctly as if I were a particularly dimwitted two year old, "Stick-it-in-your-ear-Charlie. If you can find it. I got tattooed because I wanted to get tattooed."

"Well, okay," I said. "Don't get upset. I was just asking. It's a fine tattoo. I don't know anybody else who has one. How much did it cost?"

"It's my money," she said, chomping into another mouthful of burrito.

"Just curious. I've heard tattoos cost a lot. Costs even more to have them removed. I think they use lasers. But that's a very nice one. Looks great on your shoulder. Aren't you cold? Don't you want to put a sweater on?"

She sighed. "Charlie," she said, "it's ninety-two degrees. And the air conditioner is broken. I'm not cold. I'm not even cool. I'm so hot, in fact, I think I'll take all my clothes off. Then you can see the other one. Cheeky little thing."

"What other one?" I think I shrieked. "Where is it? No. Don't tell me. You mean you exposed your butt to a sleazy tattoo artist? Are you crazy, or what?"

"Or what," she said. "That's what I was. A great big 'or what.' A living, breathing attribute of Charlie the Magnificent. A prize possession. A pretty little object for Charlie to show off to his friends. Not a real person at all. And now I'm the tattooed lady. That's pretty real, isn't it? Think I should join the circus?"

So there we were, sitting across from each other at the little table in the dining room end of our studio apartment in Chelsea having a little late lunch on a Saturday afternoon, me ignoring the White Castle hamburger on my plate, her mopping up the salsa and sour cream and the unidentifiable brown stuff that came inside her burrito. Betsy didn't cook. She just defrosted and microwaved.

"Eat, Charlie," she said, scarfing down more of her repulsive mess.

"I can't. My stomach's on the blink."

"Poor you. Want to go to the movies? Schwarzenegger's at the Cineplex."

She knows I love big Arnold. She knows I'd love to *be* big Arnold. She lets me have it every time I work out with my barbells or ride my bicycle to nowhere. I decided to sulk. "No."

"Let's go over to the Y and swim a few laps," she suggested. "At least we can still afford to do that."

Sure, Betsy, so you can show everybody your butterfly. "I don't feel like it."

"How about renting some Rollerblades? You said you wanted to."

"Not today. Today I'm sure I'd get knocked over by a speeding beagle."

"Ooh, funny," she said. "The man's a real comedian. Well, how about something real safe? Let's see if we can find a street fair. Somebody must be having one. We don't have to buy anything."

"Betsy, I'm not going anywhere with you until winter. I'll go rent a video and we'll watch it here." I bit into my White Castle. It was still semi-frozen inside.

"What are you talking about?" She pushed her chair back and almost knocked over the fifty-year-old snake plant my grandmother left me in her will. That was all she left me because she was so proud that I was doing well in New York and didn't need her money while my poor sister had been left in the lurch by her rotten husband and had three kids to raise on her own. So she got Granny's life savings and I got the snake plant, which was now teetering on its rickety stand.

"Watch it!" I shouted, grabbing for the plant with one hand and steadying the stand with the other. And right away, I knew I should have kept my mouth shut.

She grabbed her fork. "You don't like my tattoo!" she screamed. "Then see how you like this!" She started jabbing the fork into the fronds of the snake plant. "The tattooed plant!" she shouted. "This plant is gonna be tattooed from head to foot." With each word, she forked the plant until all its fronds were oozing a milky sap. "Die, die, die, you ugly sucker!" she cried. And she really was crying, the tears slopping all over her face and dripping off her chin.

I got up slowly and edged around the table. "Betsy, honey. It's all right. I didn't mean what I said. About not going anywhere until winter." Very, very carefully, I put one arm around her shoulder. I didn't want that fork penetrating any of my vital or even non-vital parts. The butterfly nestled right there in my armpit and I could almost feel it fluttering its wings. The plant drooped and oozed pitifully. Betsy was right. It was an ugly sucker. "I'm sorry, Betsy. I think your butterfly is beautiful. How about letting me see the other one?"

"Oh, sure. Why not?" she sobbed. "Indoor sports. So you don't have to go outside with me. Until winter, huh? Then I'm cutting you off until the snow falls. And furthermore, I'm gonna have my whole body tattooed. I don't care how much it costs. Even my face! You can just forget about lasers. Unless I decide to use one on you! Beam it off, Scotty!"

As I tried to calm her down and wipe her face with my paper napkin, she jabbed the fork into the palm of my hand. I'm afraid I shoved her away. Rather roughly. She kicked me in the shin with one of her Doc Martens and then ran into the bathroom screaming, "Wife abuse! Wife abuse!" at the top of her lungs. I heard the lock click home.

I wasted a few minutes whispering endearments and apologies outside the door. She responded by flushing the toilet after each poignant plea for forgiveness.

My shin was a wasteland of agony and my palm was bleeding from four little red dots in a row. I sucked on the wound and then spit the blood into the napkin. That's what you do for snakebite, and I wasn't taking any chances with the possibility of deadly venom from a snake plant. If we had any antiseptic, it was locked in the bathroom with Betsy. So I scrubbed my hand with dish detergent and bleach. And then I limped out to walk around the block a few times to cool off and try to figure out what to do about Betsy.

Betsy and I had met at college back in Ohio, lived together during our senior year, and agreed that we both wanted to tackle New York City after we graduated. I was on the MBA track and Betsy was studying art history. We got married as soon as I got my first job as an assistant account executive in a big, big, very, very big advertising agency. There weren't a whole lot of jobs in the art history field so she worked at whatever she could find, but nothing seemed to last very long. Mostly, she hung around the Soho and Tribeca galleries. Getting acquainted, she said. Getting to know the scene. Meeting all the right people. But not making any money at it.

That didn't matter as long as I kept getting raises and bonuses and promotions. And she always came up with invitations to great, weird parties. Life was terrific. We were young, we had enough money to really enjoy the city, and we were in love. The future looked positively brilliant so we didn't think about it very much.

That lasted for about four years. And then I lost my job. A lot of people in advertising lost their jobs. The future didn't look quite so brilliant anymore.

First thing we had to do was move out of our wonderful, high-floor, great view, wood-burning fireplace, eat-in kitchen, large closets, luxury apartment with terrace on the trendy upper West Side. My unemployment checks didn't even approach covering the rent. Then we had to give up testing all the fine restaurants in the city. That was when I discovered Betsy couldn't cook, couldn't even scramble eggs, and wasn't about to learn how. No more ski vacations to Vail or Chamonix. No more impromptu long weekends in the Caribbean. No more snuggling by the wood-burning fireplace, congratulating ourselves on the splendor of our lives together. I sold my Rolex and replaced it with a Swatch.

Betsy was lucky to get a part-time job selling cosmetics in Bloomingdale's, but regarded the pittance she earned as her own. My unemployment check was supposed to cover everything else. And there were about two zillion other people like me panting after every advertising job that opened up. We'd used up our credit cards and the overdue notices were getting fairly terse. For about two minutes I considered applying for food stamps, but decided I'd rather starve first. Life was dreary in the extreme.

True love has a tendency to wither in an atmosphere like that. At least, Betsy's seemed to. And me? I admit I was preoccupied most of the time and quick to find fault with her. Her quirkiness that I had once found so appealing began to pall. I wished that she could be a little practical once in a while. I wished that she could be more like my mother, at least in the cooking department. No. Not really. My mother is a lousy cook, much given to lumpy mashed potatoes and extremely well-done shoe-leather steaks. I loved Betsy the way she was. Tattoos and all. Didn't I?

The first time I wished that she would get mugged to death by one of the hundreds of crazed drug addicts that swarmed the streets, I began to take my wishes seriously. That was after the first time she stayed out all night and refused to tell me where she'd been.

"I could lie to you," she said. "But why bother?"

So I started following her. As soon as she left the apartment I was after her, day and night. I forgot about looking for a job. There weren't any anyway, at least any that I would consider taking. Me, a former vice president in charge of a major toothpaste account, hawking magazine subscriptions over the telephone? Telemarketing, they call it. Ridiculous! Besides, I'd had enough of the so-polite interviews that led nowhere.

I followed her to Bloomingdale's and cruised the nearby aisles, always keeping an eye on her until her shift was over. More than once, I imagined I was being followed myself, by a store detective. Or maybe I wasn't imagining that. The glitzy mirrors on the first floor showed me that I had become somewhat lax about my personal grooming. But I could no longer afford my usual sixty-dollar haircuts or having my clothes dry-cleaned after each wearing. The daily shoeshines went the way of the white rhino.

I followed her on the subway, wasting precious tokens or sometimes, if I thought I could get away with it, leaping over the turnstiles. I rode between the cars, my eyes glued to the window of the car she was in. As soon as she headed for the door, I did the same, waiting until I actually saw her on the platform to get off. I lurked outside of movie theaters, restaurants, galleries, boutiques, even the tattoo parlor in Coney Island where she went to add to her body art collection. As the weeks and months went by, she acquired a rose on her neck, a snake twined about her left wrist and God knows what else in places she refused to reveal to me.

Sometimes I lost her. She'd be walking along and then suddenly hail a taxi. Or I'd wait for hours outside a beauty salon or a dance club only to realize that she'd left by the back door.

Oh, she knew what I was doing, all right. I made little attempt to conceal myself. I *wanted* her to know I was watching her. But she never mentioned it. She just continued to lead me on a long chase all over the city, usually alone, but sometimes with some of her flaky friends. And almost every night she would head for home. Late, of course, and full of stories of her escapades. "You should have been there, Charlie," was her favorite refrain, accompanied by a knowing smirk. But on the subject of our life together, she was silent.

We still slept in the same bed. There was no other. And I refused to bed down on the floor. But that's all we did.

Sleep. It was as if a wall, invisible but quite impenetrable, had been erected between us.

Why didn't we get divorced? Well, for one thing, we couldn't afford it. I couldn't afford it. And I didn't want to because it had occurred to me that Betsy was trying to drive me to it. If she wanted a divorce, let her get it. I, on the other hand, wanted the cute, sweet, only slightly kooky Betsy I had married. If I couldn't have that, I wanted her dead.

Yes, I did. She'd always referred to me as "anal retentive." At first, I took it as a joke, but after hearing it almost every day, it began to grate. So what if I liked to hang on to what I had? People as well as things. Didn't mean I was crazy, did it? Just careful. Maybe a little possessive, but not enough to be a problem. Some women might find it flattering. After all, I didn't beat her up or make scenes about her staying out all night. So it was only logical to me that if I couldn't have the old Betsy, then no one else would have the new one.

Little by little, during those long, long jaunts around the city, waiting for the inevitable street crime incident to occur, I began to conceive a plan. When it did happen, when the mugger finally slithered out of a dark alley and attacked her, I'd be right there to rescue her. I began carrying my old Swiss Army knife, the one she'd given me for Christmas back when we were still in college. The way I saw it, the mugger would confront her and I would pounce on him with my knife drawn. He'd struggle a bit. Maybe I'd nick him in the neck or slit a nostril the way they did to Jack Nicholson in *Chinatown.* Then I'd let him go with a kick in the butt. She'd be so grateful, she'd promise to give up her foolish ways. But I would kill her anyway. And blame it on the mugger. Serve them both right.

Plan B was only slightly different. If no mugger appeared, I'd just kill her and make it look as if she'd been mugged. After all, I couldn't wait forever. The strain of the situation was beginning to take its toll on my nerves. I was losing weight, my muscles were going flabby despite all that walking and my skin was taking on a grayish tone. I was beginning to look like a bum.

As it turned out, I didn't have to wait very long. One freezing night in January, I was lurking on a deserted downtown side street, watching for her to emerge from a Tribeca loft party. It must have been around 2:30 in the morning when she came out of the building. Usually, when she left one of these affairs, she was with a group headed somewhere else. But this time she was alone and she looked angry. Must have had a fight with someone.

At first, she looked up and down the street for a cab. "Fat chance," I smirked to myself. I was tucked away in a dark doorway just about half a block away from where she was scowling and muttering to herself. When no cab appeared, she stalked off toward Hudson Street, her shoulders hunched against the cold and her huge shoulder bag swinging at her side like an overstuffed pendulum.

"What a target!" I thought. I would do it now, tonight, and end the stalemate that was ruining my health and destroying my sanity. I slid one foot out of my hiding place. And then I froze.

Somebody else had slipped out of another hiding place a little closer to Betsy and was running after her. He looked pretty big and he was fast. His feet didn't make a sound on the cracked pavement. Must have been wearing

Nikes. But so was I, old and practically worn out, it's true, but still good for sneaking up on people. So I took off after him, but slowly and sticking close to the buildings. I wanted to give him a chance to frighten her thoroughly before I intervened.

Betsy must have heard or sensed something. Before the guy reached her, she whirled around and shouted, "Get lost, Charlie!" Then she apparently realized it wasn't me and began swinging her purse in a wide circle over her head like some demented Olympic shot-putter. The mugger kept on running toward her. A blade appeared in his hand.

This was more than I had hoped for. Betsy would put up a fight and the guy would be so enraged, he'd probably slice her to ribbons—butterflies, roses, snakes and all. Maybe I wouldn't stop him after all. Why should I take the risk of severe personal injury when this vicious felon was willing to do the job for me? I would lose some satisfaction, that's true. But Betsy would be just as dead as if I had done it myself. I congratulated myself on my patience and forbearing. Too bad Betsy would never realize exactly how patient and forbearing I had been.

I crept a little closer. I didn't want to miss a thing. This was better than a Schwarzenegger flick.

The mugger grabbed the strap of the bag on one of its arcs and pulled Betsy toward him. She hung onto the bag with both hands and tried to pull it back. He flashed his knife toward her face and she screamed.

I inched even closer when I saw the dark blood streaming down her cheek. It wasn't like a movie anymore. This was Betsy, my wife, who was bleeding. She was about to die a filthy, rotten death on a crummy street in Manhattan. Did I really want that to happen?

"No!" I shouted, and began running. "Stop that! Leave her alone!" I don't know what came over me. Some inappropriate resurgence of my early Boy Scout training, no doubt.

The mugger's head turned in my direction. Betsy opened her mouth and chomped down on his hand. He dropped the knife. I grabbed his hair, pulled his head back and kicked him behind a knee. He let go of the bag, shoved an elbow into my stomach and took off. When I recovered my breath, I picked up his knife and shouted, "Hey! You forgot something!"

He didn't stop. In two seconds, he was gone, around the corner and far away. I never even got a good look at his face. Betsy had, though. With her art training and eye for detail, I could rely on her to provide the police with a perfect identification.

I felt like a hero. Can you blame me? I'd saved Betsy from certain death, and now everything would be fine. Just the way it used to be. She'd be so grateful, she'd become sweet and loving again. Our pictures would be in the *Post,* and surely such heroism would be rewarded with a great job, once the whole city read about the incident. I wouldn't need to kill her after all. I couldn't wait for her to begin showering me with gratitude.

Oddly enough, she didn't.

She eyed me sourly as I held my slightly soiled handkerchief to her bleeding cheek. Then she started shouting.

"Help!" she screamed. "Police! Call the police! I've been stabbed! He's trying to kill me!" Betsy was very good in the screaming department.

"Betsy! Betsy, it's me, Charlie." I tried to quiet her. "It's all over now. You're safe. I saved you. That guy would have cut you to ribbons. Now aren't you glad I've been watching over you?"

But she kept it up until lights went on and windows opened up and down the street. Well, that was okay. I had thought we could just go to a hospital emergency room and then report the incident to the police. But maybe this was better. If the police came now, they'd be able to see the scene of the crime. They could hear the victim's true story right where it happened.

I tried to put my arms around her, but she shoved me away, not very gently. "Betsy," I said. "It's all over now. I love you and I want you to stop all this silliness. You can have as many tattoos as you want. Maybe we can go back to Ohio and start all over again. Wouldn't that be nice?"

She didn't say a word. Just stood there staring at me. Did I imagine it, or was there just a hint of triumph in her gaze? Or was it contempt?

The first police car, siren whooping, arrived in approximately two and a half minutes, followed by an EMS ambulance and more blue and whites. We were surrounded and the cops had their guns out.

I stepped toward them, holding out the knife. "Glad to see you guys," I said.

"Hold it right there!" one of them barked. His gun was aimed straight at my midsection. "Drop the knife."

I did just that. "But you don't understand," I said in my most reasonably persuasive voice. "It's not my knife. There was a mugger. He cut her with it. He would have killed her. He dropped it after she bit him. Just ask her."

"Is that right, miss?" another one said to Betsy.

"No mugger," she said. "It was him, all right. He did

it. He's been following me for weeks. Isn't that right, Charlie?"

"Well, yes," I said. "But only to keep an eye on you. I saved you from that mugger, didn't I? I chased him off. Tell the truth."

"You!" She snorted. "You couldn't chase off a drunken mosquito." Then she turned to one of the cops. "This is my soon-to-be ex-husband, officer. He attacked me when I came out of that building over there, where I'd been visiting some friends. He's lying. There was no mugger. I'd like to sit down now. I feel a little weak."

The cop tenderly escorted her to the ambulance, while his companions did their thing to me with handcuffs and the speech about rights. They were not a bit tender. They found the Swiss Army knife in my pocket. I'd forgotten all about it and couldn't deny it was mine. For one thing, it was engraved with my name, and for another, Betsy would certainly identify it.

So now I'm here at Riker's Island, awaiting trial for assault with a deadly weapon. No way I could raise bail money, and there's nothing for me to do on the outside even if I could. My lawyer is an overworked, marginally competent public defender. I think he doesn't like me very much, and I'm positive he doesn't believe my story. I don't think I'll get out of this anytime soon.

But I've noticed that a lot of the men here have very intricate tattoos. Some even have butterflies just like Betsy's. They say there's a pretty good tattoo artist on the premises. Maybe I'll get one myself, just to relieve the boredom. A wide-open eye, perhaps, on the back of my right hand. My knife hand. Just to show I'm still watching and waiting.

It has occurred to me that this whole thing could have

been planned. I mean, maybe that "mugger" was a friend of Betsy's and they staged the incident knowing that I was lurking nearby. I wish Betsy would come to visit me. I'd like to ask her about that. But she doesn't answer my letters, and the last one was returned marked "address unknown." It hurts me to think that she might have been cleverer than I thought she was. That she outsmarted me.

But I'll get my chance. First-time offender. Family quarrel. Mitigating circumstances. My lawyer says I might even get off with parole. Even convicted murderers have been known to walk away from doing hard time. I'll get out of this and I'll find her. She won't be able to hide from me forever. Not with those tattoos. I'll find her and this time I won't try to be a hero. This time I'll make sure she gets the treatment she deserves.

Stanley Cohen

HOW MUCH JUSTICE CAN YOU AFFORD?

WHEN MATT GUINAN BEGAN TELLING FRIENDS THAT HE'D decided to dabble in real estate investment and buy an apartment house, his best friend, George Hebner, laughed. "Matt, what the hell do you want to do that for? Why all of a sudden are you crawling out on a crazy-ass limb like that?"

"Why?" Guinan responded. "Because, George, the time is right. That's the reason."

"But, Matt, you're making a bundle in the business you're in. And it's growing like a weed. Given a little time, you're gonna be one of the richest guys I know. Now, from out of nowhere, you're talking about diving headlong into some *real* shark-infested waters. Waters where you've got no experience whatsoever. None."

"What experience did I have when I started my office supplies business? The answer is also none. Right? Absolutely none."

"But, Matt, this is different. Real estate is different."

"You're right. It's quite different. No inventory."

"Where the hell are you going to get the money?"

"I've already been to see my banker. And he likes it. This building I've found is fully occupied. Hear what I said, George? Fully occupied. Using the business for collateral, I can have whatever I want. And the owner's got the building on the market at a very favorable price. Definitely below market."

"Oh?" George chuckled. "It's fully occupied and the owner is giving it away? Doesn't that have a slight smell to you?"

"The man says he wants to retire."

"Is he an old man?"

"Listen. People are retiring younger and younger these days when they can afford it."

"Matt, if I were you, I'd reconsider this very carefully."

"George, just wish your old buddy well. Okay? All I want to do is become the richest man in New York."

"Well, I certainly do wish you luck, Matt, because I've got a feeling you're going to need all the luck you can get."

The year was 1975 and Matt Guinan was right about some of the thoughts behind his planned move into the world of Manhattan real estate. Times were good. The Vietnam thing was over, but all the guilt and recrimination had not yet befallen the country. Nixon had resigned and Ford was president. New York City's financial collapse had not yet occurred, and real estate was considered a very secure investment. A great deal of the city's major wealth was in the hands of the Zeckendorfs, the Helmsleys, and their ilk.

It was also a time when much of the life in the city was still quite laid back, particularly below the midtown area. Cocaine had not yet become a major factor, and pot was enjoyed rather freely within even the more socially acceptable circles of the population. The Village was still the Village.

Matt was forty-three, a burly, easy-going Irishman, a handsome man with a lot of hair swept straight back. He had a quick, self-effacing sense of humor and was slow to anger. He and his beautiful wife, Valerie, who had been "to the manner born" on Long Island, lived in a lovely town house on the best block of St. Mark's Place.

Five days a week Matt wore a suit and tie and ran his office supply company with considerable business acumen. But successful entrepreneur that he was, when Matt returned home from the office, off came the tie and jacket, and he, Valerie, and their many friends enjoyed a laid-back lifestyle that bordered on being Bohemian. One of Matt's favorite pals was a huge black cop, Big Mike to his friends, who often brought the very best grass available to Valerie's little soirées and impromptu gatherings, and on several occasions escorted Matt and Valerie and a few of their friends up to Harlem where they moved around like visiting dignitaries to the best music joints and soul food restaurants.

At the same time, Matt and Valerie enjoyed much of the other side of New York's night life, the "uptown life," so to speak, with its culture and frequent invitations to functions in middle-to-upper social strata. They were on some of the best lists and were once even included in a photograph in *New York* magazine which had been taken at a black tie benefit at the Metropolitan Museum.

The building that Matt had come upon for his first foray into real estate was The Albion, a decent but not fancy middle-class apartment house, a block south of the Flatiron Building. Twenty-four units, six floors, four units to a floor, a single elevator, and a custodian on call, but no doorman. The neighborhood had just begun to undergo revitalization, a face-lift. And all twenty-four units in the building were occupied. Matt reviewed the prospects over and over again. A fully occupied building in an improving neighborhood? At a favorable price? How could he go wrong?

Matt and his lawyer sat across the table from the seller and his attorney. The seller was clearly a very smooth operator who appeared to be about Matt's age. His attorney was a sharpie from a small firm specializing in real estate. The meeting was relatively brief, the crossing of t's and dotting of i's having already been done by the two attorneys, and both parties signed the various documents in all the necessary places. And with those signatures, Matt became the new owner of The Albion, with a serious mortgage, of course.

After the business had been completed, Matt forced a little small talk with the seller, trying to get a handle on why the man was so anxious to sell.

"Let's just say that I've got bigger fish to fry," the man quipped. And that was about all he had to say on the subject.

* * *

Miguel Santana was the consummate New Yorker, a snappy dresser, always decked out in the best that Barney's had to offer, quick enough on his feet to be at ease in any circle, and blessed with more than his fair share of street smarts. He made a nice living as a manufacturer's rep for several electrical equipment suppliers, and had become a salesman's salesman, a highly skilled player in the world of business skip-rope and stoop-tag.

At the same time, Santana was a wily little man who was always looking for an edge, an opportunity to pick up a quick buck, or just have some laughs, to score at someone else's expense by applying a little heat of some kind, within the law, of course. He was sharp-witted and could be quite funny at times, usually at the expense of others. Beneath the humor, his mind was always looking for that little chink in the protective armor of any existing or potential adversary.

Santana's oily brow sloped back from his dark, deeply set eyes, so that in profile, the line of his nose seemed to flow rather continuously up his brow and into his receding hairline, giving his face a ratlike appearance. Along with this look, he had a pudgy, roly-poly body. Thus, his presence was that of a fat mouse. A fat but scheming mouse. His eyes were in constant motion, giving the impression that his mind was never at rest.

Santana and his wife were among the newer tenants in the apartment building in which they lived, having only been there a year or so, and when he received the very friendly letter from the building's new owner, announcing the change in ownership, he decided to test the man, to see how he was put together.

He reviewed the letter and dialed the phone number. The flushing mechanism on the toilet in one of the bathrooms in his unit had a tendency to occasionally stick and cause water to dribble continuously. And since water is much too valuable a commodity to waste, the toilet needed attention. Right? Right. Even though the slightest jiggling of the handle on the toilet put a quick end to the dribble.

After a receptionist answered, he asked for Mr. Guinan.

"Matt Guinan here."

"Mr. Guinan?"

"Yes."

"This is Miguel Santana calling. Number 4-D."

"I'm sorry. What's number 4-D?"

"Apartment 4-D. Do you recall sending out a letter to us poor, miserable tenants, telling us you were the new owner of our building. That ring a bell?"

"Oh, of course. Of course." He laughed. "Sorry, Number 4-D. And what did you say your name was?"

"Santana. Miguel Santana."

"Nice to hear from you, Mr. Santana. Sometime soon I'm having a separate phone line put in just for real estate work, but I don't have it, yet. Maybe then I'll take the time to call and say hello to all the people in the building. Try to know everybody by name. A bit of personal touch. I thought that would be nice."

What? Personal touch? What kind of a total asshole have we got here? With a soft chuckle, Miguel said, "Yeah. That *would* be nice. Very nice."

"Anyway, how can I help you, Mr. Santana?"

"Well, we've got a toilet here in the apartment that needs a little attention. It's wasting water. Besides being a pain in the butt. You can hear it all over the place. It's kinda like Chinese water torture, if you know what I mean."

"Have you called Mr. Landini, the custodian? He should be able to take care of that."

"He's been up here a couple of times. Frankly, Mr. Guinan, I don't think the old guy's able to fix this or much of anything else. He keeps the lobby swept, but that's about it. We're going to need a real plumber up here. And I frankly think we'll need a new toilet. Or at least a whole new set-up inside the thing."

"I'll see if I can get somebody up there. Anything else?"

"Yeah. The intercom's not working very well. You can't make out who the hell's down there."

"Did you tell Mr. Landini?"

"You're going to have to get a professional, Mr. Guinan. That old guy. . . ."

"I'll look into it, Mr. . . . You said your name was . . . ?"

"Santana, Mr. Guinan. Santana."

"Okay, Mr. Santana, I'll look into these matters. I want all my tenants to be happy with things. Okay?"

You want to keep us happy, Mr. Guinan? You're going to be one busy sumbitch. "Thanks, Mr. Guinan. Sounds like having you as our new landlord'll be a definite change for the better around here."

Guinan made a few calls and found a plumbing firm that specialized in maintenance in residential real estate in the city. He dispatched them to the Santana apartment with instructions to do whatever was necessary to satisfy the tenant. It took Guinan even longer to find the right firm to deal with the intercom system in the building, but he finally did, and he sent them over with the same basic message he had given the plumbers.

He was a little startled when he got the plumbers' bill, and shaken when he got the one from the electrical contractors. The profit margin between his monthly notes on the building and the total income from the rents was rather substantial with full occupancy, but he'd be losing money on the Santanas' unit for a couple of months.

But of even greater importance, he'd wasted an afternoon fooling around with this problem, time he could ill afford away from his business. Would he have to hire a manager to handle his modest entry into real estate? Or possibly make a deal with some realty management firm? What would *that* do to the margins?

As he sat, pondering these questions, his receptionist put another call through to him, a Mr. Redelsheimer, in 4-A.

"What can I do for you, Mr. Redelsheimer?"

"Mr. Santana said we should call you, that you'd take care of a problem here. We have a window that won't open if we should need some air. And the door on one of our closets, the hinges have come loose from the wall."

"Did you call Mr. Landini, the custodian?"

"Long ago. He couldn't fix. He scratched up the window trying to get it open. He even cracked one glass."

"I'll see what I can do."

The phone kept ringing. The wave of complaints picked up momentum. Guinan received calls from the other two tenants on the fourth floor, with Santana's name being dropped, and then calls began coming from tenants up and down the building, with Santana's name often being mentioned. What was the man trying to do?

Guinan began to feel the effects of this rather strongly. He was spending all his time and lots of money responding to these calls, making him afraid to pick up the phone, sending him home in a foul mood, pushing him into long periods of brooding, both at the office and at home—a condition Valerie found very irritating. This wasn't his style. And this change impacted their way of life.

He began to drink more, and to lose interest in living their free-spirited social life. His venture into real estate was fast becoming a losing proposition, and all his negative thoughts about it seemed to focus on a single word: Santana.

The clincher came in the form of a letter, signed by all tenants, with Santana's name first, practically demanding that the "corridors" on all floors be redone, with improved lighting, new wallcoverings to replace what was there but was still in good condition, and carpeting over the lovely old imported tile floors to reduce the noise of traffic. What corridors? With only four units to a floor? And what traffic? With only four tenants to a floor, going in and out, maybe once or twice a day?

He tried to satisfy this one by simply having old Mr. Landini put larger bulbs in the antiquated fixtures. He quickly received another letter, signed by all tenants, assuring him that this was not an acceptable improvement. And once again, lo, Santana's name led all the rest.

Guinan contacted his lawyer, Dave Goldman. Did he

have to respond to this barrage of demands he was getting from the tenants in the building? Goldman reviewed the lease agreement form and advised him as to which demands he had to meet and how much time he was allowed in complying. There was certainly nothing in the leases that required him to refurbish and carpet the elevator landings.

Guinan looked up the number and dialed. Santana's wife answered and told him that Santana would not be home for two days, that he was away on a business trip. Guinan impatiently waited the two days and called back at around five in the afternoon. Santana wasn't home yet, but should be arriving from his office shortly. Guinan decided to go over and confront Santana, to try to find out what the hell the man was trying to do.

He took a taxi from his office to The Albion. He entered the lobby with his passkey, rode the elevator to the fourth floor, and knocked on the door for 4-D. Santana opened the door cordially, inviting him inside.

Guinan glanced quickly around, finding the decor distinctly Southwestern, about as Mexican as was possible within the limitations of a typical two-bedroom unit in an old New York apartment house. The furniture was of a good quality "ranchy" character, and a large, authentic-looking Indian rug covered the living room floor. A huge sombrero hung on the wall above the sofa. The several paintings in the room all contained cactus.

But if the room smacked of Old Mexico, Guinan noted that Santana, although a bit Mexican in facial appearance, was very much corporate American in manner and dress. Tassel-tie shoes, flannel slacks, a button-down shirt and a repp-striped, silk tie. A veritable Ivy Leaguer.

With an infectious smile, the man grabbed Guinan's hand and shook it vigorously. Mrs. Santana entered the room. She was definitely not Mexican, but WASPish in appearance, attractive and seemingly charming. She smiled and greeted him.

"Well," Santana said, grinning, as he looked Guinan up and down, "now we see the man that goes with the voice. A big, good-looking Irishman, just as I expected. Can I fix you a drink? Big, good-looking Irishmen usually like a drop or two this time of day. Right, Matt?"

Guinan might have liked accepting the seemingly good-natured offer, but he sensed that he was being manipulated. "Thanks, no."

"You sure, now? Don't get the impression that our liquor cabinet is limited to tequila, our national poison. Matter of fact, I'm not even sure I have any on hand at the moment. Who can drink the stuff? But we do have single malt Scotch, Beefeaters, Stoli, even Bushmill's for you Irish types, in fact, most anything you'd want. Or how about a cold Heineken?"

God, I'd love one. "Thanks, no." But he smiled, something he hadn't intended doing on this visit. He hadn't expected Santana's personality to be so disarming, and wondered how he was going to be able to say what he'd come to say.

"Well, let me tell you, Matt—mind if I call you Matt?—we all think you're doing a great job here. A great job. First class all the way. Keep up the good work, and with my help, pretty soon you're gonna have one of the nicest buildings in the neighborhood."

That did it, you son of a bitch! "Keep up the good work, and with my help. . . ." "That's what I came to speak to you about, Mr. Santana." Guinan felt the heat rising under his clothes but concentrated on remaining outwardly calm. "I came to ask you to stop helping me. And the rest of the tenants. Don't help them, either. You're creating a problem for me."

"Come on, Matt, baby, we all got your letter telling us what a stellar landlord you wanted to be. I've just been trying to be a good Samaritan. What's wrong with that?"

The grin on the fat little face was no longer an engaging, playful grin. It was something entirely different, and Guinan's temperature continued to rise. He suppressed a very strong urge to take a swing at that face. "Mr. Santana, my phone is ringing off the wall with tenants calling about all sorts of nitpicking little things. Things they should take care of themselves. As well as outrageous requests—no, not requests, demands—for stuff not covered in the lease. I want you to stop creating this problem for me or I'm going to be forced to take some sort of action. . . ."

"Just what sort of action do you have in mind, Matt?" Santana interrupted.

"I'll talk to my lawyer. I hope I've made myself clear, Mr. Santana." He studied Santana's face. A faint smile persisted, but it wasn't a real smile. It was a look of challenge, of picking up the gauntlet. Guinan glanced in Mrs. Santana's direction, but she had disappeared. He turned and let himself out. He walked across the tiled landing to the elevator.

A few days later a call came in from Mr. Landini, announcing that the elevator wasn't working. Guinan phoned Goldman, his lawyer, who advised that this was a complaint he should act upon at once, but Guinan decided to drag his feet for a few days. Let Mr. Santana and the rest of them walk up and down the steps a couple of times. It would do them good. But when the complaints persisted throughout that day, particularly from an elderly tenant on an upper floor, Guinan felt a strong sense of urgency about getting it fixed quickly. He got the name of the company that routinely serviced the elevator in the past and dialed.

The next day he heard from them. "Mr. Guinan?"

"Yes."

"Mr. Guinan, I'm John O'Reilly, the service manager here at Standard Elevator. My guys checked out the elevator in your building yesterday, and they brought me out there today, and, well, to tell you the truth, there's something a little funny about your elevator problem."

"My first question is, were you able to get it fixed?"

"Oh, I'm afraid it won't happen that fast. Not this one."

"I hope it won't take too long. We need it fixed right away."

"That's an old unit in there, Mr. Guinan. It's going to need a whole new controller, and that could take some time. And some serious money. I felt you oughta be warned about this."

"How much time is it going to take?"

"Well, we've got to locate a suitable replacement controller and prepare a proposal, and get you to sign it, and then order the unit, get it shipped, and schedule a team over there to install it and check it out."

"Mr. O'Reilly, we've got to get it fixed. Some of the old people in the building are prisoners there without that elevator. How long are we talking?"

"Probably three, four weeks. Maybe a little less."

"Jesus! And offhand, how much is it going to cost?"

"Hard to say 'til we price out that controller. But like I said, we're talking a whole new unit, and it won't be cheap."

"Ballpark figure?"

"Probably around thirty thousand."

"Shit! And Mr. O'Reilly, what's so funny about this situation?"

"Sir?"

"A few minutes ago you said there was something funny about the problem with our elevator. What's funny about it? I can't find anything to laugh about. I feel more like crying."

"Oh. Sorry. I certainly didn't mean funny that way. . . . Mr. Guinan, do you know of anyone who'd have any reason to want to . . . how should I say this? . . . who'd want to sabotage that elevator?"

Santana! "Are you serious?"

"Well, lemme tell ya', it's an old unit, but it's been running just fine for a lotta years. But listen to this. When I went up top to the motor room with the mechanics, they opened the controller cabinet and showed me some small traces of water inside there. And as I'm sure you know, the last thing you're wanting to find in one of those cabinets is any water. You understand that."

Santana! "You found water? Jesus H. Christ! Anyway, go on."

"Well, after going over the unit with them, it looks to me like someone who knew what he was doing simply went in there and threw a bucket of water on the wiring and stuff so it shorted everything out."

Santana! "Are you serious?"

"That's the way it looks. And then I guess he must have turned off the main power switch and tried to towel up all the water, because it looked like someone had wiped around in there. You could tell from the way the traces of dust inside the unit had been wiped up. But not all of it. And he didn't get all the water. Because, as I said, we found a little in places he wouldn't have been able to reach with a towel. And the guts of that unit is a mess. It's an old relay logic unit. Nothing but relays. No solid state. And everything's burned up. You know how you can look at wires and tell they've been arcing? You know how the ends of wires can look burnt and melted?"

Santana! "Sure. Of course I do."

"Well, I don't have any proof of anything, and I know this sounds a little far-fetched, but I'm just telling you, I think somebody's been into that controller with a bucket of water. At least that's the way it looked to us."

Santana! "Well, regardless of what happened, we've got to get the thing running again. Will you work on it and get back to me as soon as you can?"

"We'll get on it, Mr. Guinan."

"I mean, soon. Absolutely as soon as possible. I can't leave those people without an elevator."

Guinan had received the call from the elevator company several days before the end of the month, when rent checks were due from the tenants, and by the fourth day of the following month, no checks had been received in the office. Usually, the checks began to trickle in a few days before the end of the month, and most were in by two or three days into the new one. A reaction to the elevator problem? Possibly, from a few tenants. But from all of them? It just wouldn't happen from top to bottom in the building unless there was something going on beneath the surface. *Santana!*

Guinan had rushed a letter out to all the tenants, apologizing for the inconvenience, and assuring them that the elevator service company was working diligently to get the thing back into operation as quickly as possible after its total and unexplainable shutdown. But, still, nobody was paying the rent. Nobody. This called for at least a couple of phone inquiries.

He scanned the list of tenants and called a family named Abelson in 2-B. Second floor. Only one flight up. And what's walking up one flight? Why, hell, most of the houses in the world were two-story houses out of choice! He called and Mrs. Abelson answered, and she seemed embarrassed when he identified himself and explained why he'd called.

"Tell me, Mrs. Abelson. Is having to walk up one flight of stairs sufficient justification for not paying your rent? Just one flight, for a short time, while the elevator is being repaired as a result of its strange ailment? You'll recall when I took over the building that I wrote you and told you I wanted to do a good job of keeping everybody happy. But I can't afford to just sit around and do nothing if people don't pay their rent."

"To my husband you should probably talk. He did it to help the people on the upper floors."

"What? Help them how?"

"Well, from upstairs a man came around and asked everybody to help. He said it would get the elevator fixed a lot faster if everybody held back the rent money."

"Tell me who the man was."

"Well, I guess it's all right to say. Santana, I think his name was. Santana, or something like that. Fourth floor."

"A very persuasive man. Right?"

"I guess you could say that. Yes."

In his mind's eye, as he spent the rest of the day brooding, Guinan repeatedly watched Santana, wearing rubber gloves, creep up the stairs in the middle of the night, slip inside the motor room, which should have been locked, open the door to the cabinet, toss in the bucket of water, and then jump back and sit on his fat haunches and stare with his playful smile at the fireworks as wires and switches and relays sparked and fumed and sputtered, shorting out everything in the box. In some of his run-throughs of this fantasy, he had Santana even wearing the huge sombrero from his living room wall.

Then he watched Santana pick up a towel and meticulously wipe around, taking pains to get all the water. But he couldn't get it all. It's impossible to get every trace. And while he was sopping up water, he was also leaving wiping patterns in the accumulated dust inside the unit.

But, so what? Accuse the man? How could he establish that Santana had done such a thing? Tell the police to check for fingerprints? There would be fingerprints, possibly quite a few, from mechanics over the years, but none of Santana's. Santana would be too smart for that. So what could he tell the police? What would his story be? Santana didn't like me and didn't want to pay his rent, so he wrecked the elevator and then organized a rent strike because the elevator didn't work. How would the police react to a story like that?

He watched the second hand on a wall clock move slowly around. It was almost four and he'd wasted the whole day doing nothing, just staring at the clock and replaying the fantasy about Santana. He finally decided he had to have a showdown with his friend Mr. Santana. Face to face. He'd go over there at around five-thirty or six. Santana should be home by then. And he wouldn't call Dave Goldman first. Dave would only discourage him from going, and he was in no mood to be discouraged.

He walked out of his office, down to the street, and across to the dark stillness of his favorite little watering hole. He needed a bit of reinforcement before cabbing over to The Albion.

"You're awfully quiet today, Mr. Guinan," Paul, the shiny-domed bartender said to him.

"Yeah. I got a problem."

"And you don't wanta talk about it?"

"No." He'd planned to nurse just one double Scotch the whole time he was there waiting, but found he needed at least one more. And then, one more after that. But no sweat. He'd had some of his most productive afternoons after three doubles at lunch. Then he went out and hailed a taxi.

When he arrived at the building, he realized that he needed someone to buzz him in. He'd left his passkey at the office. Should he go back for it? No! Let Santana buzz him in. He pressed Santana's button on the intercom system.

"Who is it?" Mrs. Santana answered.

"Mrs. Santana, I need to talk to your husband."

"Who is this?"

"It's Matt Guinan, Mrs. Santana. Could you buzz me in?"

A short delay, and then, Santana. "What do you want, Matt?"

"I want to talk to you. Will you please buzz me in?"

"I . . . don't think so. I don't think I like the way you sound, right now."

"Santana! Press the goddamn button!"

"I'm afraid that doesn't seem like such a hot idea to me."

At that moment an elderly couple walked into the vestibule and eyed him apprehensively as the husband used his key to unlock the door. Guinan quickly stepped through the door with them, muttering that he'd forgotten his key, and forcing a friendly smile. He made small talk about the weather with them as they walked up the steps together. They went into a door on the third floor and flipped the deadbolt behind them as he continued up the steps.

He reached Santana's door and knocked.

"We don't need any, today." Santana.

"Mr. Santana, would you open the door? I'd like to talk to you." As he said it, Guinan realized his voice was a little louder and a little stronger than he'd meant it to be.

"Well, I've got nothing to say to you. If you've got something you just have to tell me, write it in a letter and I'll take it under advisement." There was a trace of a chuckle in his voice.

"Santana, open the goddamn door! I want to talk to you."

"The feeling's not mutual. Go away."

"OPEN THE GODDAMN DOOR, YOU HEAR?"

The door to another apartment opened and a middle-aged couple walked out and toward the stairs. They paused, looked at Guinan, and then quickened their pace.

Guinan wanted to say something credible and friendly to them, but he was too far gone. He just stared back, and as soon as they had turned the corner and started down the steps, he pounded on the door with the side of his fist. "SANTANA, OPEN THE FUCKING DOOR! YOU HEAR ME?" The footsteps on the stairs paused for a prolonged moment and then resumed at a slower pace.

"We just left by the back door," Santana yelled. "See you around."

"THERE IS NO BACK DOOR! NOW OPEN THE FUCKING DOOR!"

"We're using our parachutes."

"OPEN THE DOOR! NOW!"

"Bye-bye."

Guinan threw his shoulder against the door, and it didn't give way, but he felt a slight splintering. He threw his shoulder again and did more damage. Then again, and again, and the upper panel gave way. He pushed through it with his hand, and saw Santana in the middle of the room. He reached inside and turned the doorknob, but the door didn't open. He fumbled upward from the knob and found a deadbolt. He turned it and the door opened, allowing him to stride into the room.

"You dumb knocker," Santana said, "you're gonna be going to jail. You know that? You just broke and entered."

"That's not all I'm going to break." He moved toward Santana. "Just who the hell do you think you are?" he yelled. "Wrecking the elevator and then organizing a rent strike because there's no elevator service. Is that your idea of some kind of a joke?"

"What *is* wrong with the elevator? Matter of fact, that's something I've been meaning to call you about. But you certainly don't expect us to pay rent when the thing's not working. This is not exactly some el cheapo, rent-controlled building you've got here. . . . Hey, Matt, cool it, man. What the hell's with you? What are you doing coming at me? I wouldn't suggest coming any closer. You wanta be in real deep shit?"

"You slimy little bastard! I can't believe you'd fuck up that elevator like that!" Guinan kept coming, his eyes focused on the grin that was beginning to fade from the fat little face. Out of the corner of his eye, he saw Santana's wife standing in the doorway at the end of the room, looking frightened, but he kept coming, in short but deliberate steps.

And when he got close, he yielded to an uncontrollable need and swung out with one of his clenched fists, hitting Santana flush on the side of the face. Santana's wife screamed as he staggered and cried out in pain but didn't go down. He swung at Santana's stomach with his other hand, doubling him over, and then hit him in the face again, knocking him to the floor.

"You stupid asshole!" Santana yelled, gasping for breath from the shot to his belly. "You're in real deep shit now, sucker! Now you're really gonna be going down."

Guinan looked apologetically at Santana's horrified wife but couldn't manage to say anything. He turned, and as he walked out the door, he heard Santana yell, "Your ass is mine now, sucker!" He'd made a bad mistake. A truly bad one. In all his adult life, he'd never struck another person. He hardly ever raised his voice. Suddenly trembling, he hurried down to the street and hailed a cab.

He knew exactly who was at the door when he heard the bell. He'd been home for a little over an hour and had had several more drinks. To Valerie's dismay, he'd recounted his afternoon's experiences and then started drinking. He walked uncertainly to the door and opened it.

"Mr. Guinan?"

"I'm Guinan."

"Mr. Guinan," the plainclothes cop said, looking at thc glass in his hand. "I'm Detective Barone from the Thirteenth Precinct, and this is my partner, Detective Heinrich. We have a warrant for your arrest." Both cops flashed their shields. "We'd like to ask you to come to precinct headquarters with us."

"Don't I get to tell my side of the story, first?"

"Sure. If you've got a side to tell. We'll want to take your statement, whatever it is, when we get there."

Valerie walked into the room to see what was happening, and a look of shock crossed her face when the second cop pulled out a set of handcuffs.

"What the . . . ?" Guinan said. "Hey, guys, come on. Put those away. I'm not going to run or anything." And as he said it, even he could hear himself slur the words. He was sloshed.

"It's the usual routine," Barone said. "We might have made an exception in your case, but considering the charge, and considering the condition you're in, let's stick to the routine."

"Can I call my lawyer to meet me there?"

"You can call him from there."

"How long will I be there?"

"You're guaranteed arraignment within twenty-four hours. Maybe tonight. Tomorrow, the latest. At that time, you should be able to post bail, or whatever. It'll be up to the judge."

"You mean you're going to . . . lock me up 'til then?"

"For this charge, I'd say you'll be retained until your arraignment. Yes."

Guinan looked helplessly at Valerie, who stood watching in total disbelief. He set his glass down. "Please, guys, do you really have to use handcuffs? Come on. I've got neighbors."

"I think we'd better stick to the routine."

"Shit!" Guinan held out his wrists.

"In back, please." Heinrich said. He grabbed Guinan's hands, pulled them behind him, and snapped on the cuffs.

As they led him toward the door with Valerie watching, he tried to think of something funny to say but couldn't come up with anything. He finally said, "Call Dave and tell him to come to the Thirteenth Precinct. Right, guys? You said the Thirteenth?" Then, he just listened as Barone began reciting the Miranda.

Guinan sat in front of the huge, clear desk and studied the face of Alexander Hammond, the ultra-prominent criminal defense lawyer, as the man quietly scanned the one file in front of him.

"Your attorney, Dave Goldman, said you wanted to retain me to represent you," Hammond said.

"Yes."

"Dave and I reviewed the case at length. I hope you know that you're in serious trouble."

"What about *my* side of the story? Are you sure you're familiar with everything Santana did?"

"Organizing a rent strike is not a criminal act. You should have let Goldman help you deal with that through the various legal options open to you."

"What about the elevator?"

"If it could have been established that Santana did in fact do intentional damage to that elevator, that might have helped your case. But the police did investigate your claim that Santana was responsible for the elevator and could find absolutely nothing that tied him to it. You may as well face the music, Mr. Guinan. You're on the hook for an aggravated assault charge."

"Well, I want to fight the charge, anyway, Mr. Hammond. Anyone who looks at all aspects of the case has got to get the picture. Do you know what that elevator control system cost?"

"The prosecution has an open and shut case against you, Mr. Guinan. You broke the man's door down, you forced your way into his home, and you attacked him. In front of his wife. And they have other witnesses to your violent state who heard you screaming profanities in front of his door and who heard you start to break it down. And the cops who picked you up shortly afterward reported that you were heavily intoxicated. Here. Take a look at this. One of their exhibits. You probably haven't seen it." He handed Guinan a photograph from the file.

The photograph was of Santana with one side of his face bruised and swollen. Guinan winced and tossed the photograph back. "I still want to fight this. He's a rotten son of a bitch for doing what he did, and I want justice."

"Weren't you listening, Mr. Guinan? You're on the hook. My advice to you is to plead guilty and let me get you the best deal I can in negotiating with the prosecutor. You're obviously not a criminal type. You're a prominent businessman, a tax-paying citizen with an absolutely spotless past. You should get a very minimal, and probably even a suspended, sentence."

"But I'll still have a criminal record. Right? I don't deserve that. I want justice."

"What do you want to do? Go to trial? I can't guarantee that you'll be cleared. Dealing with a jury is always a crapshoot. And it'll cost you a lot more money."

"Mr. Hammond, Dave sent me to you because he said you were the best around, and I had the best chance of being cleared with your help. For what he did, Santana deserved a hell of a lot more than what he got from me, and I, at the very least, want justice for myself."

Hammond shrugged his shoulders, and then his demeanor changed, taking on a sudden intensity as he studied Guinan. "Well, it might not be impossible that I could get you your justice. But there's a major question involved here."

"Which is?"

"Mr. Guinan, just how much justice can you afford?"

Guinan stared at him in confusion. "What? What do you mean?"

"How much justice can you afford, Mr. Guinan?"

"I'm not sure I understand the question."

"Assuming you want *absolute assurance* that you will be cleared of all charges, and would not be satisfied with a brief or suspended sentence, or a little community service, your defense could cost a great deal of money. How much are you in a position to pay for that defense?"

"I want to do whatever's necessary to be *cleared* of all charges. Which I'm confident will happen with your help."

"Well, what can you afford? Give me a number."

"If it means going to trial, okay, I want to go to trial."

"A number, Mr. Guinan."

Guinan shrugged. "What do your services for handling my kind of case usually come to?"

"A number, Mr. Guinan."

Guinan sighed. "Oh, I don't know. Forty thousand? Fifty? Maybe sixty? Maybe a little more? That's about the limit of what cash I can raise, I suppose. You know. Without some kind of nasty lien on the business."

"And if I suggested that it might take three to four times that amount? Maybe more, for the kind of assurance you want?"

He studied Hammond. "Is that what your fee would be for defending me in a court trial? Or are we talking . . . something . . . else?"

"What I'm talking is my estimate of what it would cost to be absolutely sure we'll get you off scot-free. Do you understand? And there'd probably be no need for a court trial."

"You're talking something else." Guinan took a breath. "I think I get the message . . . well, I can't afford that, Mr. Hammond, but I still won't plead guilty. I want to go to trial, and win, and with your reputation for handling cases like this, I'm convinced that we've got a chance. I still believe no court would convict me once they have all the facts. Can I afford you for that?"

"To go to trial? I would think so. As long as you understand that I can't guarantee you the acquittal you expect. You're sure this is the course of action you'd like to take, despite the fact that it does *not* follow the advice I've offered you?"

"I want justice, Mr. Hammond, and what I need is your representing me and all the facts known. Then, I'll get it."

Hammond studied Guinan at length before speaking. Then with a shrug, "Well, it's clear you don't 'get it.' Considering the case the prosecution has, I think you're more than a little optimistic. But it's your decision, and if you wish to move ahead on that basis, I'm willing to give it my best shot."

Guinan grew increasingly relaxed as the brief trial moved along in the sparsely occupied courtroom. The jury seemed benign enough. And no question about it, Hammond was *good.* He had a natural flair for the dramatic. He drove his points home with force: Matt Guinan was anything but a criminal, or even a violent person, but instead a highly respected member of the business community who had been goaded into a brief act of passion by the mean-spirited wiles of an unconscionable individual clearly intent on causing Guinan great trouble and expense. The aftereffects to this individual were minimal, a few well-deserved bruises which were gone in a matter of days. No permanent damage whatever.

On the other side of the room the prosecutor went about his work in a totally undramatic, strictly business manner, calling Santana and the other witnesses to the stand, and interrogating them quietly to establish the factual details of the case. Nothing more. The judge charged the jury and sent them out after reviewing the applicable details of the criminal code.

Guinan felt very much at ease as the jury went out, and he even looked forward to their return so that he could turn and smile at Santana, sitting near the back of the room. During the trial, he'd studied the prosecutor and the judge, wondering if they would have been the recipients of the pay-offs alluded to by Hammond. Obviously, this wasn't needed.

The jury returned within an hour and the judge was called back to the bench. Guinan was almost grinning when the judge asked for a verdict and the foreman got to his feet. When Guinan heard the word, "GUILTY," he felt as if he'd been kicked in the pit of his stomach. He looked in anguish at Hammond who returned his stare without comment.

As Guinan was led out of the room, Santana walked over to the aisle, and when Guinan passed, he grinned and playfully jumped back, saying to the cops escorting him, "Be careful with him. He's dangerous."

Guinan's sentence was set at six months and he served four at Rikers Island before being released. During that period, Valerie returned to her family out in the Hamptons, and only came to visit him once, an event she found very distasteful.

Fed up with New York because of all that had happened, Guinan quickly sold the apartment building at a loss and moved his business to New Jersey. He bought Valerie a lovely home and fully expected life to return to normal. But she soon found life in Jersey painfully dull, considerably less than to her liking after the fun years in the city, and as a result of this, along with the fact that their relationship was already badly strained because of the ugly stigma of what had happened to him, she left him.

And so much for life and affordable justice in the Big Apple.

Judith Kelman

CHECK MATE

"THAT'S IT, BABY. NOW, I'M GONNA KILL YOU."

"No!"

"Rip your rotten liver out and feed it to the rats."

"Please, no, Davey. I didn't mean it!"

Stiffly, she backed away. She had to make it to the door. Had to run before he grabbed her.

Fury mottled his face. His hands were balled in bloodless fists. He kept edging closer. His looming shadow was slithering up her legs, swallowing her alive.

"Stop! Leave me alone."

Fear squeezed her throat, making it hard to breathe, to think.

"You're dead meat, baby. Finished," he hissed.

Her back was pressed to the wall. Blindly, she groped

for the doorknob. Another few steps, and he'd have her. The guy was crazy. No telling what he'd do. She had to get away!

Yes!

Finally, her fingers struck the cool metal knob. A quick turn, and she'd be safe. He wouldn't dare touch her out there. Way too risky.

One more second.

Suddenly, he lunged at her and clamped her wrist in a vise grip. She was caught. Trapped.

"Now you're dead, baby. Cooked."

Her mind was reeling. Desperately, she cried out: "Mommy! Davey's fret'ning me!"

"David, honey. Don't threaten your little sister."

"Stupid baby's lying, Mom. You know how she gets."

"Janny? No fibbing, sweetie."

"Was not."

"Were too," David snarled. "Little brat's a head case, Mom. Probably needs a shrink."

"Do not."

"Do so, you dopey little rug rat. Bet you don't even know what a shrink is."

"Do too. Mommy! David called me a Shrinky Dink. Make him stop."

"Cut it out, you two. Hurry and get ready for breakfast now."

Linda Barasch drew a measured breath and frowned. The bathroom mirror had nothing pleasant to report. Months overdue for a trim, her once luxuriant auburn hair hung on her shoulders like a mass of lifeless worms. Her green eyes were dull and set in dusky troughs. Her skin looked pasty, her face drawn.

She'd lost weight. Ten pounds or more, she estimated.

And without even trying. Her noose-tight food budget didn't allow for much variety. The very thought of another tuna or macaroni casserole was enough to kill her already listless appetite. So was her schedule. Between the kids, the job, the apartment, and the teetering mountain of bills, Linda had precious little time for frivolities like food.

Ironic.

For most of her fifteen-year marriage, she'd struggled to shed those vexing extra pounds. Back then, in what seemed another lifetime, she could afford diet plans and exercise classes. There was time for fretting about cellulite and twitchy triceps. For years, Linda had deliberately avoided all but the most essential clothing purchases. Once she reached her figure goals, she'd planned to reward herself with the purchase of an extravagant, new, size-eight wardrobe.

But she'd never come close. Before the separation, Greg had insisted they dine out several nights a week in fancy, fattening restaurants. Though he knew she was struggling to reduce, he always pushed her to view the dessert cart and order something "to play with." At home, he frequently tempted her with gifts of her favorite cheesecake or chocolate truffles. Claiming he hated to waste food, he urged her to finish the kids' leftovers as well.

When Linda bemoaned her burgeoning Jell-O belly and the butt that was spreading beneath her like marshmallow fluff, Greg was quick to reassure. "There's more of you to love, Lindy-poo," he often said. What he failed to mention was the part about there also being more of her to cheat on and still more to divorce.

Hard to believe that was only three years ago.

So much had changed. Linda had experienced so many rude awakenings.

Though they'd been sweethearts since junior high school, Linda discovered she still had much to learn about Greg Barasch. It turned out the man had countless hidden talents. In a blink, he could shed his skin, change his stripes, rewrite family history. Above all, Greg was quite the accomplished magician.

Poof! He made their savings and investments disappear. Alakazaam! Bye-bye checking and charge accounts. Hocus pocus, and Linda and the kids were transported from their posh, four-bedroom co-op on Central Park West to a cramped one-bedroom, third-floor, walk-up in the Bronx.

And that was just for starters.

Mumbo jumbo, and Greg's six-figure income from his family's thriving piece goods firm vanished. As fast as you could say "abracadabra," Linda's beloved volunteer efforts at the children's hospital were transformed into a deadly six-day-a-week drone in the aerobic shoe department at the Shorts & Sports in Riverdale.

Before her very eyes, Linda's prince turned into a frog. And the frog, warts and all, hopped off smug and self-satisfied. Linda was caught between a schmuck and a hard place. If she formally accused Greg of concealing his income, the IRS could wipe him out. She could ill afford to lose the meager, but essential, child support checks her ex eventually got around to sending, when he felt like it.

Linda kept battling for an increase in those absurdly low support payments, though her chances for a victory were slim. Her well-meaning but inexperienced legal aide lawyer was no match for Greg's crack team of barracuda barristers from the venerable midtown firm of Dewey, Cheatam, & Howe.

For Greg's grand finale, with a couple of thrusts of his magic wand (which, to be honest, Linda had never found all that enchanting), Greg had replaced her with a frightfully young step aerobics instructor named, of all things, Bambi.

"You look perfect," Linda told herself firmly. "Way better than that bimbo of Greg's, I bet."

She mused about the magic potion recipe for a Bambi. Probably two parts plastic, one part silicone, liberal sprinklings of jiggles and giggles, and just the teensiest pinch of brains.

Squaring her shoulders, Linda puffed pink blusher over her hollowed cheeks. She patted pale concealer under her eyes and applied a tasteful trace of lip gloss. After brushing her hair vigorously, she bound it at her nape with a bow. Finished, she stepped back to assess the overall effect.

"Perfectly awful," she pronounced.

Frowning harder, she cinched the gaping waistband of her gray skirt with a safety pin. She spotted a stain on the collar of her best blouse, a teal silk number she saved for special occasions. Gently, she dabbed at the blotch with a dampened washcloth, but the dye started to run. Her mother's old cameo brooch camouflaged the damage. Luckily, Linda hadn't pawned it with the rest of her jewelry to cover the down payment on Davey's orth-odontia.

Greg agreed that the boy's teeth needed straightening, but braces weren't covered in their separation agreement. Neither, for that matter, was the thousand-dollar stereo component set Greg bought for Davey's last birthday or the genuine shearling coat and hat set he had made for Janny's, though the child predictably outgrew the expensive ensemble by mid-December. Buying those things gave Greg "pleasure," he explained. He considered it only just for Linda to experience similar bliss when she made the monthly dental payments.

Rage made Linda's eyes sparkle. Her cheeks flushed. She looked better.

"Janine? David? You guys almost ready?"

No answer.

Linda's black pumps needed half soles. Actually, she needed new pumps. The left heel wobbled like a three-legged piano. Hopefully, she wasn't out of Krazy Glue. When Linda wasn't looking, Davey liked to use the stuff to fuse his fingers together and flap around imitating a pterodactyl.

"Kids? Let's go!"

Silence.

Kicking off the rickety shoe, Linda limped to the bedroom. Splayed on the floor in Batman boxer shorts, ten-year-old David was happily absorbed in a game of nuclear holocaust. With his curly red hair and squashed features, the boy resembled Raggedy Andy on speed.

"Rrrrrr—booom! A million dead. Fifty zillion wounded. Limbs flying. Heads bashed. Blood everywhere. Look outtttt! Here comes another warhead. Oh noooooo!"

Still in her ruffled nightie, five-year-old Janine was curled on the bed in fetal position. Her opal eyes were vacant. Absently, she sucked her thumb and twirled a ribbon of white-blond hair.

Linda kept the lid on her temper. After the weekends they spent with their father, the kids were always like this. Daddy dearest brought them home pumped on junk food and dangerously low on sleep. For two heady days, he let them watch, play, and say whatever they pleased. Greg indulged them in extravagant toys and grossly inappropriate entertainments. Five days of Linda's firm socializing proved no match for forty-eight hours of shock jocks, sugar highs, shoot-'em-ups, and Wrestlemania.

"Come on, you guys. I need you dressed and ready in fifteen minutes."

"RRRRRR—Booom! Oh no! Watch it. Don't trip on the eyeballs!"

"Davey, please. I'm in a hurry."

Linda hefted Janine to a sitting position, tugged off her nightie, and worked her limp arms into a pink sweatshirt. The child stood as placed while Linda pulled up the matching sweatpants. Seated again, she allowed her feet to be shoved into ruffled socks and lavender sneakers.

David was charging around the room now, totalling up the body count.

"Eleventy zillion bodies. Eleventy zillion and four."

"Come on, Davey," Linda coaxed. "Please get dressed."

"Ker-bloom! Oh no. I'm hit!"

Suddenly, the boy stiffened, made a constipated face, reeled backward clutching his bony chest, and crumpled to the floor.

"I'm not kidding, David. Get ready for school. *Now!*"

"Jeez, Mom," he groused. "Can't you see I just croaked?"

"I'll count to three. One . . ."

David puffed his contempt. "I got news for you, Mamacita. School's not for dead guys."

"Two—"

"You think Mrs. Battleax is gonna want me in class

with my organs all hanging out and crawling with maggots? Old witch'll probably puke her guts."

"Two and a half—!"

He raised his hands in surrender. "Okay. I'm getting up. You don't have to make a freaking federal case out of it."

Janny's silken hair refused to hold a braid. Brushing it out again, Linda sliced a center part for pigtails.

"Watch your mouth, David. You know I don't like that kind of language."

The boy huffed. "I said *freaking*, Mom. Not f–u–c–"

"That will be quite enough," Linda added hastily. "There now, Janny girl. You're all set. Breakfast is on the table. Go start eating while Davey puts on his clothes."

The little girl emerged from her waking trance and looked herself over.

"I wanna wear my red dress."

Linda kept her tone level. "You're all ready, sweetheart. You can wear the red dress tomorrow."

The rosebud mouth quivered. "I have to wear it *today*!"

"Please, Janny. Mommy has an important appointment this morning. I don't want to be late."

Janine opened her mouth and made a sound like a car alarm. Rivers of grief overflowed their banks and coursed down her cheeks. "Red dress," she wailed. "Red dress and tights!"

With a slow cleansing breath, Linda removed the screeching child's sweatsuit and went to the cramped closet. After a frantic search, she found Janny's favorite dress crumpled under David's broken brick collection. Protecting the filthy fragments from carpet lint, no doubt. Linda brushed off the soiled garment, smoothed it with a palm, and slipped it over Janny's tear-streaked, puffy face.

"There. All set. You look like a princess."

"It's all dirty," the child snuffled.

"That's magic dust," Linda improvised. "Very lucky stuff. Quick, make a wish."

After a beat of open skepticism, the little girl shrugged, hefted two of the dozen gigantic stuffed bears Greg had bought her, and slogged down the hall.

One down.

Taking full advantage of the diversion, David had donned his favorite tattered jeans and the hideous mud-colored T-shirt Greg bought him at a recent Snot Rockets concert.

Linda sighed. "You know I don't approve of your wearing those things to school, Davey. You look like a hoodlum."

Striking a pose, the boy fixed her with a heavy-lidded look of contempt. "But these are *cool,* Lindy-dude. They don't suck, you know what I'm saying?"

"David Norman Barasch, have you been watching *Beavis and Butt-head* again?"

The green eyes rolled. "Chill out, lady. Cool your jets."

This time, Linda did a silent ten count. "Just go, David. Eat your breakfast and get your things ready. And step on it!"

He swaggered out of the room, pausing only long enough to slip on his baby Doc Martens and slap a fake spider tattoo on the back of his neck.

Linda tossed the beds and herself together. *David and Janny were terrific kids,* she thought. Bright, healthy little souls with a healthy complement of quirks and foibles.

The standard Monday morning misbehavior was Greg's fault, not theirs. The man had no interest in teaching or disciplining his children. Shameless spoiling was so much easier, especially when you didn't have to live with the consequences. No doubt Bambi found his Peter Pan parenting style simply adorable.

Linda hadn't met Bambi, but she had a pretty clear picture from David's wide-eyed description. "Bambi's like a kid, Mom." Cupping his hands a honeydew's distance from his chest, he added, "a great, big, *tremendous* kid."

"He means she's very, *very* fancy," Janny added somberly. "Bambi doesn't have flat boobies like you and me, Mommy. Hers are like balloons."

"Mom's aren't flat, you little turd bird. They're just saggy."

Pushing the memory aside, Linda went to the tiny kitchen for a cup of instant coffee. Passing the table, she saw that Janny hadn't touched her juice or cereal. David was busy drowning his Cheerios in the milk.

"That'll teach you to rat on Blackie. Heh, heh, heh," he snickered. "See how you like playing shark bait, you dirty creep."

Linda shovelled a few spoonsful of cereal into Janny's slackened mouth. Pressed by time, she tossed the rest into the garbage.

"Okay. Let's hit the road, chickies. Don't forget your math homework, Davey."

The boy's face told the whole sorry tale.

"You didn't do it?"

Recovering quickly, David flipped up his palms.

"What's more important, dude? Stupid math or *American Gladiators*?"

Linda kept her calm. "Fine, David. No problem. You want to do fifth grade again, that's your prerogative."

"What's a parogative, Mommy? How come Davey has one and I don't?"

"It means making choices, sweetie. Which you certainly do."

Janine's devilish smile revealed the gaping space where her two front teeth should have been. She'd knocked them out a month ago when David was chasing her around the dining table in Greg's riverview duplex penthouse.

At the time, Greg and Bambi were in the master suite. They were taking a Jacuzzi and playing "tickle," as Janny termed it. Fortunately, as Greg was quick to point out, the table, which cost him a bundle at Sotheby's, wasn't scratched.

More fortunately, the missing pearly whites were baby teeth and soon scheduled for replacement. But their loss still saddled Linda with several days of whining and the need to purée Janny's food for a week.

Linda didn't blame Greg for the tooth incident. It wasn't possible to watch the kids every minute. What irked her was his cavalier attitude. Sure, he loved the kids in his way. But his way was to take the cake and frosting and leave Linda with the desiccated crumbs.

Still grinning, Janny nodded firmly. "Okay, I make a choice to take Feffer and Regent and Marcus and Alexandra to school with me today."

"Janny, honey. You know the rules. The giant bears have to stay home and watch the apartment."

The lip started quivering again. "You said I could

make my own parogative, Mommy. Davey gets to. It's not fair."

Linda eyed the clock. If every bus, train, drop-off, and transfer went perfectly, there remained the slimmest possibility that she could make it to the hearing on time. Greg had filed for a modification of the terms of their separation agreement. She had to get there and plead her case against the unthinkable change.

"Okay, one bear. But only if you get your coat on extra fast. We're late."

Hurrying down the bright corridor at Little Flower Elementary, Linda thanked the stars that Janny loved kindergarten. The little girl had taken to plump, reassuring Mrs. Itzkowitz immediately. Linda suspected that the teacher, whom all the children called Dot, reminded Janny of her Grandma Lorraine. Whatever the reason, while many of the other kids clung and cried, Janny always accepted the woman's hand and strolled off toward the story corner without a backward glance.

At the door to room one, Linda smoothed Janny's hair and kissed her forehead. "Okay, sweetheart. You have the best ever day."

"Wait, Mommy. You forgot to say goodbye to Feffer."

"Silly me." Linda faced the giant bear. "Be good, Feffer. Don't make noise during rest time."

Linda turned to leave.

"Mommy," the child mewled. "Feffer wants a kiss."

As Linda was kissing the bear, a lanky man with thinning brown hair and thick tortoise glasses emerged from room one and waggled his fingers at Janine.

"Hi there, dearie. I'm Mr. Robertson. I'll be teaching you today."

Janny recoiled. "Where's Dot?"

"Out with a cold. I'm the substitute. And you are?"

"I am going home. Mommy, I'm not staying with him. No way."

Nearly ten minutes later, Linda gave up trying to mollify the little girl. Janny's piercing screams trailed her down the corridor like a volley of poison darts.

"She'll be all right," Linda said, echoing the substitute's empty promise. "She'll be fine."

The hearing was in twenty minutes. At best, the trip took twenty-five. Of course, that wasn't counting the waiting ambush at the door.

Mrs. Battlesby, David's teacher, had the longest tenure of anyone at Little Flower. The woman was an institution, like Alcatraz. She had the face of a beetle, the body of a sixteen-wheeler, and the temperament of a pit bull. From all indications, she'd been born without a sense of humor. David, prone to pranks and high energy, was in no danger of being her pet.

Linda literally ran into Mrs. Battlesby at the door. The teacher came at Linda like a tidal wave. "That boy of yours is a problem, Mrs. Barasch. A serious problem. We need to talk."

"I understand, Mrs. Battlesby. Why don't I call and make an appointment?"

"You're in luck. I've got first period free. Come."

"Sorry. I'm in a rush this morning. Got to run."

The beady eyes glared. "Nothing's more important than the boy's education, Mrs. Barasch. Maybe that's the trouble. Boy sees you don't care, why should he?"

Linda flushed. "Of course, I care. But I'm running late."

The old witch strolled away muttering. "Typical. Predictable. Lousy mother, lousy kid."

Cheeks burning, Linda raced out of the building only to see her bus pulling out two blocks down. No way she could wait for the next one. Instead, she jogged a mile to the subway station at Gun Hill Road and caught the downtown Lexington Avenue express.

As the train chugged out of the station, the teacher's condemnation reverberated in her head: *Lousy mother, lousy kid.*

Damn it, she was a good mother. She did her level best to instill positive values, especially the critical importance of school. She was the one who insisted the kids finish their homework before they turned on the TV. Her holiday and birthday gifts were books and modest educational toys.

Greg was the one who stressed big-ticket goodies and nonstop fun. What did he know about bad report cards, dire pronouncements, and nasty notes? He showed up for pageants and parents' nights, when the kids and classrooms were at their shining brightest. On such occasions, even Mrs. Battlesby doled out nothing but praise and pleasantries.

When Linda tried to explain David's difficulties in class, Greg refused to take her seriously. "You always were a gloom-and-doomer, Lindy-poo. Lighten up. The kid's fine."

"He's failing math, Greg."

"Math, shmath. I'll buy him a calculator."

"Mrs. Battlesby tells me his behavior is terrible."

"Oh yeah? So how come last week she said this is the best class she ever had?"

"That was an open house speech. They all say that."

Linda knew she was wasting her breath. As a weekend and holiday dad, Greg would never understand what it was like to be truly responsible for shaping the children into respectable, responsible, capable adults. He thought the whole business was a snap. Done with mirrors.

And now, he was determined to prove his point the hard way.

As the subway rumbled toward her destination, Linda felt a chill of apprehension. This time, she couldn't let Greg beat her. The stakes were too critical. Much more was at risk here than orthodontia or support payments. David and Janny's future hung in the balance. So did Linda's.

For the past week, since she was served with Greg's motion to amend their agreement and the summons to appear in court, Linda could think of little else. This time, Greg had gone beyond sleight of hand and gamesmanship.

Way beyond.

Her ex-husband was threatening to take the kids. Sole custody. Linda would be restricted to limited visitation. Alternate weekends, holidays, birthdays, two weeks in the summer.

When she recovered sufficiently from the shock, Linda had called to demand an explanation. In typical fashion, Greg acted as if his incredible new demands were no big deal.

"It's simple, Lindy-poo. I'm sick and tired of your bitching at me. You keep nagging that the support check's late. Then, when I send it, you carry on that you need more. You're forever crabbing that I send the kids home tired and cranky.

"So I figured, if the little ones are too much for you, I'll simply take them off your hands. Either you agree to back off and stop your carping, or I'm taking custody."

"You wouldn't."

He chuckled. "Oh, yeah? Watch me."

"Come on, Greg. Be serious."

The chuckling stopped. "I am, Linda. For once, I'm dead serious. I want it in writing. No more nagging. No more complaints. No more filing for amended support payments, or I'm taking Janny and David. My legal team has more than enough to get you declared unfit."

"Unfit? What are you talking about?"

Greg puffed his impatience. "For starters, there's David's lousy school performance. Our people have an affidavit from the teacher stating that she's gotten inadequate cooperation from home."

"I don't believe this."

"Then there's the matter of all Janny's injuries. The knocked-out teeth, those stitches on her forehead. Not to mention the broken wrist last summer."

"All those things happened when she was with you, Greg."

"Prove it. You're the one who took her to the doc and dentist, isn't that right, Lindy-poo? I guess it'll come down to your word against mine. And Bambi's."

Linda was speechless.

Greg had no such difficulty. "Like I said, it's simple, Lindy-poo. You show up before ten and sign the modification agreement my lawyers have prepared, and I'll call off the custody hearing. Otherwise, you can see your precious darlings by appointment."

Linda still had the yawning pit in her stomach that opened when the line went dead. If she didn't go along with Greg's outrageous proposition, her children would move in with Dad and Bimby. Greg and Ditsy would be the ones to see them through their colds and nightmares.

Supervise their baths and homework. Comfort them when they were cranky or angry or hurt or disappointed or scared. Eventually, Janny and David would probably start calling Bambette, "Mommy."

Meanwhile, Linda would come home from work every night to an empty apartment. She tried to imagine the bristling silence. The overwhelming solitude. She tried to picture eating alone and going to sleep without the company of her sleeping angels.

How could this be?

She'd given her life to those kids. And now Greg was threatening to turn her into a weekend mommy. Either she relinquished her fundamental human right to carp and complain about the world's injustices, or she gave up her children.

By the time the train lurched to a stop at the Brooklyn Bridge station it was six minutes to ten. Linda raced the two blocks to the Supreme Court Building on Foley Square. As she charged up the imposing stone steps, her glued heel broke off. Hobbling the rest of the way, she started to sweat. She dabbed her face with a tissue, blotting off the makeup. Straps of hair escaped the ribbon and stuck to her clammy face.

Three minutes to ten.

The elevators were all on high floors. Racing up the stairs, Linda popped the safety pin cinching her waistband. Moments later, she emerged breathless and disheveled on the fourth floor. Trying to settle her jangling nerves, she hastened toward the Part V hearing room, where Greg's custody demands would be weighed.

Greg and his lawyers were huddled outside. They looked like an ad for Giorgio Armani suits. Spotting Linda, Greg sniffed.

"Quite a sight, Lindy-poo. Hope you're ready to sign our modification agreement. The judge gets a load of you looking like that, he's likely to insist on supervised visitation only. Very fetching style. What do you call it? Geriatric grunge?"

Linda was gasping. No sign of her legal aide lawyer. As if he'd read her mind, Greg said, "Your mouthpiece waited around for twenty minutes. Said she had to run and file some motions. She'll be back, eventually."

Desperate, Linda searched the corridor. She poked her head into the ladies' room and called the lawyer's name.

No answer.

Instead, there came the booming voice of the bailiff. "Next case: Docket number three-four-one-six-six. Barasch vs. Barasch."

Out of time, Linda limped into the courtroom. Poised behind the massive mahogany bench was Judge Edgar Culligan, widely reputed to be a wife-eater.

Linda's mouth parched. Her heart stammered. Court was so damned intimidating.

"Ready for the plaintiff?" the judge growled.

"Ready, Your Honor," crooned Greg's lawyer.

"Is the defense ready?" Culligan regarded Linda as if she were a cockroach he'd found crawling up his arm.

"My lawyer's not here, Your Honor. Can we please wait?"

"No, we can not wait. This is a courtroom, not a bus station." He thwacked his gavel, killing the roach in spirit. "Get on with it."

"Of course, Your Honor," Greg's other lawyer preened. "If the court will indulge us in a five-minute recess, I believe we may have a settlement in this matter."

Thwack! "Five minutes." Culligan lumbered up from

the bench and slipped out toward his chambers. Greg's henchmen swaggered over to Linda like dueling bandits at high noon.

"Sign on the dotted line, and we can all get the hell out of here, Mrs. Barasch."

Linda scanned the modification agreement. Basically, it ordered her to cut out her tongue and sew her lips together when it came to Greg. She couldn't ask him for anything, couldn't question him, couldn't burden him with any further complaints.

In exchange, Greg would do exactly whatever he pleased with, for, and about the children. And he would withdraw his petition for sole custody, at least, for now.

Numbly, Linda eyed the signature line. How had it come to this? Greg was forcing her to give up her children or her rights.

Where was *her* prerogative?

Opening her purse, she dug around for a pen. She finally found one from Shorts & Sports under the payment coupon book for the orthodontist.

The five minutes were up. The bailiff stood and hollered: "All rise for the honorable Judge Culligan."

With a shaky hand, Linda took the papers. Greg's lawyer smiled. "That's the way, Mrs. Barasch." His other lawyer held up a victory sign.

"So, have you cleared things up or not?" Culligan barked.

"We have, Your Honor," Greg's number-one lawyer chirped.

"Have not, Your Honor," Linda hurried to add. Clicking out the pen point, she flipped through the modification agreement. On each page, she scrawled a giant X.

"What do you think you're doing?" Greg whined. "Are you nuts?"

Linda kept crossing out the heinous terms of the extortion notice. "Actually, yes, I think I am. I guess it's all the stress. The noise. The crowding and the bills. They've finally made me snap, Your Honor."

"All right, Mrs. Barasch. That's quite enough," Culligan said.

Linda kept crossing and crossing. "But that's not all of it, Your Honor. There are all those fresh remarks from David. And his wars. Dead guys, blood, eyeballs. It's all from the movies and TV shows Greg lets him watch. 'I'll kill you, you creep. Rip your rotten liver out and feed it to the rats.' "

Culligan whacked his gavel. "Enough, I said!"

"—And Janny's whining. Not to mention her picking at her food and carrying on about her bears and her clothing. Red dress. Blue pants. Frilly socks. No socks. Kid gets cranky when she's exhausted. And he lets her stay up 'til all hours. What does he care if she's in a coma on Monday? What does he care if I have to lug a whiny kid and a giant bear on the subway?"

"Order! I'm warning you, Mrs. Barasch."

"Plus Mrs. Battlesby. Let's not forget her. Woman's face alone is enough to send me to the funny farm. David doesn't do his math, and I'm the one who hears it. Lousy mother. LOUSY MOTHER, my foot!"

"Order!"

Linda kept marking the pages. "Four thousand dollars for orthodontia. Twenty-six dollars for purple sneakers. And tuna is up to a dollar ninety-six. A dollar ninety-six for goddamned tuna! And I can't even stand the stuff."

"Bailiff. Remove that woman. Mr. Barasch, this court

grants you full custody of your minor children, Janine and David. Mrs. Barasch is ordered to undergo a full psychiatric evaluation immediately. If she's found capable, she will be granted visitation every other weekend, two weeks in the summer, alternating holidays, and birthdays. Court stands adjourned."

At the final shot of the gavel, Greg's eyes bulged. "What the hell was that?"

Linda crumpled the marked agreement and tossed it in the trash. Turning, she smiled pleasantly. "That was the court granting your wish, Greggy-poo. Janny and Davey are all yours—to play with."

"That's ridiculous. Come on, Lindy. You don't mean it."

Her smile broadened. "Have them ready Saturday at nine, will you? I think I'll take them to Mickey D's and a flick. Maybe catch the new Stallone. I hear there are bodies all over. Davey'll love it."

"Okay, Linda. Enough. I'll give you the damned twenty-buck-a-week increase."

"Oh, and make sure David has his homework done before the weekend, will you? I've only got a couple of days with the tykes, and I'm not wasting them on junk like math problems."

Greg's grin was a rictus. "All right. Thirty bucks, and I'll pay for the stupid orthodontia."

"That's true. As custodial parent, it happens to be your responsibility. Never thought of that one. But you can keep the thirty bucks, Greg. Without the kids, I can do just fine on my salary. Better than fine."

Linda started to giggle. She hadn't felt this light and airy in years. "See you, Greggy-poo. Say 'hi' to Bambi for me."

Greg looked stricken. "Come on, Linda. Bambi won't put up with this. You're kidding, right?"

Linda stopped and looked her ex-husband hard in the eye. His expression was somber. Responsible and mature. No doubt he'd make a fine custodial parent. All the guy needed was the opportunity.

Meanwhile, she'd have the time and distance necessary to truly enjoy her kids. When she saw them, it would be pure pleasure, real quality time. What could be better?

"No, Greg. No kidding. From now on, I'll be doing hardly any kidding at all."

Lucy Freeman

REHEARSAL FOR MURDER

WHEN THE PRIVATE LINE IN BILL AMES'S CONSULTING ROOM rang, the doctor thought it must be his answering service with a message from a patient in distress or, perhaps, even a cancellation. Few people knew his unlisted number—the service, his wife, and several close colleagues. And they all knew his schedule well enough never to call when he might be seeing a patient. After all, Dr. William Ames was one of the city's foremost psychoanalysts.

Ames had just returned from a lunchtime stroll in Central Park to clear his mind for a heavy afternoon of listening to the largely self-induced emotional traumas of New Yorkers who could no longer cope with their lives but didn't know what to do about it. Still wearing his overcoat, he sat at the desk in his consulting room and picked up the phone, notepad and pen at the ready. "Dr. Ames here," he said.

"Hi, Doc. Am I interrupting anything?" said a familiar voice.

"Jack! How the hell are you? It's been a long time."

"Working hard as usual. It never stops. Seems to get worse all the time. How about you?"

"I suppose I could say the same. Only I deal with the killers inside the mind. You have to deal with the reality."

Lt. Jack Lonegan, homicide detective in New York City's Midtown North Precinct, chuckled. "I can recall a few times you got into the real thing. And did pretty well, for a shrink."

It was Bill Ames's turn to laugh. "Yes. And each time, I vowed never again." His voice took a sober turn. "Don't tell me . . ."

"You guessed it," said Lonegan. "I've got a case that's right up your alley. Accusations flying right and left. Too many suspects, not enough facts. Somebody's lying, maybe a lot of somebodies, and they're doing a first-class job of it. Maybe you read about it in the paper? A young actress killed right on stage in an empty theater."

"Afraid not, Jack. My reading these days is mostly psychiatric journals and the occasional thriller for a change of pace. It's amazing how often the two coincide."

"Am I tempting you at all, Bill? Do you think you could help me cut through the bullshit?"

Ames fell silent, gazing out the window of the Central Park South apartment where he maintained his office. In early March, spring had not yet visited the city and the day was cold and overcast. He longed for the first baseball game of the season. A Mets fan since 1962, he never missed opening day at Shea Stadium. And while he liked Jack Lonegan and often wondered how he managed to stay sane amid the daily carnage of his life, Ames was not at all sure he wanted to get involved in helping him solve yet another killing.

"Hello? Anybody there?" Lonegan's voice penetrated the doctor's reverie.

"I'm here, Jack," Ames answered. "Just mulling it over."

"Suffering from ambivalence, are you, Doc? See! I can sling your kind of jargon too. I had a good teacher."

Ames had to laugh. "You got me, Jack. Yes, I want to and I don't want to. I've been through this with you three times in the past eight years. Don't you think you're getting a little too dependent?"

"Zinger!" Lonegan exclaimed. "But you have to admit, we're a helluva good team when it comes to figuring out what makes people do what they do to other people. You get at the hidden motives and I get the facts to back up your insights. Unbeatable! Why don't I come over and fill you in on this? Then you can decide whether or not you want in."

Ames glanced at his desk clock. Almost time for his first appointment of the afternoon. He could say "no, thanks" and that would be that. But curiosity was niggling at his mind. He'd first met Lonegan when one of his patients, a prominent publisher, had been murdered in his midtown office. He'd been able to point the detective in the right direction. Now, he faced up to the self-knowledge that it had pleased him immensely to see justice done.

"Come to my office at six," he told Lonegan. "Maybe all you need is to talk the case over objectively. You might come up with your own insights."

"Deal," said Lonegan. "Be prepared to be hooked. This one is a real psychological riddle. See you later."

Bill Ames hung up the phone with mixed feelings. Lonegan was right. He'd always been ambivalent about participating in the detective's puzzling cases. On the one hand, he enjoyed probing for the answers to why some people kill. On the other, he felt oddly guilty about using his knowledge and skills to trap the killer. Perhaps it was something he ought to take up with his own psychoanalyst and mentor. He still saw Dr. Hendricks two or three times a year.

The automatic buzzer sounded, announcing the arrival of his two o'clock appointment. Quickly, he took off his coat, hung it in the closet and opened the door to his waiting room.

All during the afternoon, he had to discipline himself to pay more attention to his patients than to speculation about what Lonegan would tell him at the end of the day. He knew he was "hooked," as the detective had put it. Lonegan had told him just enough to pique his vanity. Pride, one of the seven deadly sins, had taken precedence over common sense.

His last patient of the day, a young woman fashion designer trapped in an abusive marriage, had almost conquered her fear of leaving her brutish husband although she didn't yet realize it. The dreams she reported were all of flying, soaring blissfully alone in a cerulean sky dotted with fluffy white clouds. Although her dreams were happy, she always awoke in a panic.

Soon she would recognize the message her subconscious mind was trying to send her—that she had nothing to fear and everything to gain from breaking away and flying on her own.

As she was leaving, she said, "You know, it's funny, doctor. I'm scared to death of airplanes, and yet I keep having these flying dreams. They're almost as if I had died and gone to Heaven. Maybe they're a premonition. I'm scheduled to fly to Rome in a few weeks. Should I cancel my trip? What do you think?"

Ames smiled at her. "Do you believe in premonitions?" he asked.

"Not really. But I don't know what else to make of these dreams."

"We'll talk about that next time," Ames answered. He walked with her through the waiting room, reminding her, "Call me if your husband threatens you again. You know you don't have to endure that."

When she had left, Ames returned to his consulting room to wait for Jack Lonegan. It was five minutes to six and the sky over Central Park was just beginning to darken. Although he stood absolutely still, gazing out the window at the ever-fascinating view, his mind was in a whirl of impatience. Each of the previous cases he'd worked on with Lonegan had yielded him new insights into the turbulent emotions of those who solve their problems through murder. Perhaps this one would as well.

At six o'clock exactly, the buzzer signaled that the outer door had been opened. Ames hurried from his consulting room to greet his old friend.

Lonegan strode toward him, a square, bulky man,

bundled into a rather shabby tweed overcoat and a trilby hat. He ripped off his gloves and gripped the doctor's hand with the bruising strength of a boxer or a stone mason, both of which he'd been in his younger days.

"Hey, Doc!" he exclaimed. "You don't get a day younger!"

"Good to see you, Jack," Ames replied. "Your clients haven't exactly been a fountain of youth for you either."

The two men beamed at each other, the tall, debonair doctor towering over the solid, pugnacious detective. They were both in their late fifties, both at the peak of their professions. But they were as unlikely a pair as a basketball sneaker matched with a patent leather dancing pump.

Ames locked the outer door and led the way into his consulting room. "Take your coat off, Jack. Make yourself comfortable," he said. "And tell me everything."

When Lonegan was settled in the armchair opposite the doctor's desk, he pulled out his notebook and flipped through a few pages. "I hardly need this," he commented. "I've been working on nothing but the Laura Graham case since Monday night."

"That's the dead woman's name?" Ames asked.

"Yeah. Twenty-eight years old, beautiful, successful, and stone cold dead. Somebody sure didn't like her."

"Are you close to arresting anyone yet?"

"Nope. Got plenty of suspects, though. Just not enough evidence to arrest any single one of them. I figure it had to be just one killer. Probably someone she knew and trusted. I've questioned all of them—the theater people, her mother and father, and the guy she was going to marry. Each of them has a theory. The only thing wrong is that there's nothing to back any of it up. That's where I hope you'll come in. I'd like you to go over the same territory and tell me what you think."

Ames nodded. "Tell me more about Laura Graham," he said.

Lonegan glanced at his notebook. "In a nutshell," he said, "struggling young actress finally lands leading role in a Broadway show. She's determined to make good. Spends extra time rehearsing her part. Very serious young lady. A bit stand-offish. Lives with her parents. Mother hysterical. Father angry as hell. Boyfriend in a deep funk." He looked up at Ames. "Does this mean you're gonna give it a whirl?"

"How can I resist?" Ames asked. "You've hit all the right psychological buttons. Where do I start?"

Lonegan grinned. "Are you hinting that I've been plying you with carrots?"

"You're a first-class manipulator and you know it," Ames responded. "But I don't mind." He swiveled his chair around to gaze out the window. "I think I've got a touch of cabin fever. I'll regard this as a kind of sabbatical." He swung his chair back again. "Fill me in on a few of the crucial details—where, when, how."

"Okay!" Lonegan drawled. "You know the Imperial Theater on 46th Street?"

Ames nodded. "Been there a few times."

"That's where. The play, something called *Hearts Transplanted,* was scheduled to open in three weeks. Laura was in the habit of staying on for a while after rehearsals to do a little work on her own. Sometimes other members of the cast would stay to work with her. That's what happened last Monday night."

"You said she was killed in an empty theater," Ames interrupted. "How was she killed? And what happened to the others? How many people stayed on after rehearsal?"

"Four. Two men and two women. They all left after about an hour or so," Lonegan answered. "At least, that's what they say. After they left, Jimmy, the stage doorman, slipped out to get some supper. He found Laura, stabbed in the chest, when he got back a little after nine. I'd like you to talk to all of them. See what you make of their stories."

Ames consulted his desk calendar. "I'm booked up solid all day tomorrow, but I'm free in the evening. Will that be soon enough?"

"It'll have to be," said Lonegan. "I'll make the arrangements and let you know. Hope I can reach them all."

"Do you want them to come here?" Ames asked. "Or shall I meet them at the precinct house?"

Lonegan thought for a moment. "Neither," he said finally. "I'll set it up for the theater. Being right on the spot where it happened might shake something loose for you."

Ames made a note in his calendar. "Fine," he said. "I've never been backstage before. This'll be something new for me. Now, what about the others? Her parents, her boyfriend? Do you want me to see them, too?"

"What do you think? As far as I'm concerned, they're all suspects. Until you tell me otherwise."

Ames smiled. "You're putting far too much faith in me, Jack. What if I come up dry?"

"You won't," Lonegan answered. "Can you see the others on Saturday?"

"Nancy won't like it. She was planning a trip to the Botanical Gardens to see the spring flowers."

"Nancy?" the detective queried. "Somebody new in your life?"

The doctor felt his face reddening. "Ah, yes," he said. "I've remarried since the last time I saw you."

"Well, congratulations! Nothing like marriage to keep a guy steady, I always say. Louise doesn't like my hours much either, but after twenty-five years, she knows it'll never change. At least your Nancy is only going to lose you for one afternoon."

"And tomorrow evening," Ames reminded him.

Lonegan rose from his chair and reached for his coat. "I'll call to confirm everything. And thanks a lot, Bill. When this is over, we'll have to treat ourselves to a celebration. Just like the old days. What do you think?"

"That would be nice," Ames answered, wondering how his new wife would react to his involvement in a criminal investigation. There hadn't been any reason, in the two short years they'd been married, to tell her about the earlier cases he'd worked on with Lonegan.

The following evening, Ames arrived at the Imperial Theater at seven o'clock. He went to the stage door as Lonegan had instructed him and rang the bell. The door was promptly opened by a husky young man with a mop of flaming red hair and a round, cheerful face covered with freckles. His grin was as warm and inviting as a cup of hot tea on a rainy day.

"You're Dr. Ames, right?" he exclaimed. "That cop told me to let you in. Am I glad to see you! We need a nut doctor here. Anybody would have to be crazy to kill

Laura. She was just the nicest person in the world. Always said please and thank you when she needed something, not like some of these Broadway types who think they're too high and mighty to mind their manners with the help. It had to be one of that crew inside. That's what I think. I'll name no names, though. You'll figure it out for yourself."

"I hope so," said Ames. "Will you be around for a while?"

"Sure. The name's Jimmy Johnson. I practically live here. My father had the job before me. It sort of runs in the family."

"Then maybe you'll give me a few minutes of your time after I finish with the others. I'd like to know more about what you think."

"Be happy to help out," said Jimmy Johnson. "I really liked that kid. This was her first big break. She told me all about how hard she had to work for it. The rest of them are here already. They're out on the stage. I set them up with some chairs and turned the worklights on. Nothing fancy. Come with me."

He led the doctor through the dim warren of canvas flats and stored furniture, dangling ropes and wires, until they came to the wings of the broad stage where Laura Graham would have achieved her heart's desire. The doctor paused for a moment before joining the others who were grouped in a small semi-circle on the empty stage. The curtain was raised on the darkened auditorium. It was a lonely and somewhat eerie scene. He could almost see the young actress going through her paces here, alone after the others had left, determined to make the most of her chance at success. With that image in his mind, he walked out onto the stage.

Jack Lonegan spotted him immediately and hurried over to greet him. "Thanks for coming, Doc," he said. "Everybody's here. I think they're kind of intrigued at meeting you. A couple of them are seeing shrinks of their own. I guess acting's a pretty unsettling kind of business."

The four people seated on the stage had all turned to stare in their direction. There were two men and two women, all dressed casually and seeming at ease. As he and Lonegan crossed the stage toward them, one of the women turned to whisper to the man seated next to her. They both laughed. Ames wondered what the joke was.

The man who had laughed got up and said, "I'm glad to meet you, Doctor. I've played plenty of psychiatrists, but I've never met one before. My name is John Morgan." His voice was deep and vibrant, matching his authoritative figure and silvery gray hair. "I was Laura's father in the play."

Betty Greene was next, a trim, tiny young woman with a head full of glistening black curls. "I still can't believe Laura's gone," she whispered. "I've known her since we both appeared in *The Cherry Orchard* off Broadway. That was about three years ago."

The woman who had joked with John Morgan said that she hadn't known Laura at all well. "For a relatively inexperienced actress, she had remarkable depths. I'm Susan Langer," she added. Was there just a hint of sarcasm in the woman's statement, Ames wondered.

He noticed that Betty Greene seemed about to say something, then thought better of it.

"Ed Grey here." The fourth member of the group gave a mock salute. "Edward to my thousands of rabid fans."

"Don't you wish," murmured Susan Langer.

"Kidding aside," Grey added, ignoring the jibe, "I'll do anything I can to help. Laura was a very special person. I never knew anybody who worked as hard as she did."

Ames was intrigued by the undercurrents among the group. There was definitely tension between the two women, and Ed Grey, an extraordinarily handsome young man, was doing his best to distance himself from Susan Langer. Was it possible she knew something damaging about either of the two? John Morgan seemed oblivious to the submerged enmity. Was he completely self-absorbed or just putting on a very good act? With this group of actors, what you saw was definitely not what you got.

"Thank you all for coming," he began. "This shouldn't take very long." He turned first to Morgan. "John, please tell me why you stayed late and what time you left."

Morgan frowned. "This is difficult to say, especially about someone as talented as Laura. She was having some trouble establishing a believable relationship with me, as her father, of course. She was stiff as a board when she should have been relaxed and trusting. I thought that if we did some improvisation, it might help. We worked on that for about a half hour. Then I had to leave. It was about seven o'clock. You can imagine how shocked I was when I picked up the paper the following morning."

"Were the others still here when you left?" Ames asked.

"Oh, yes." He lowered his voice. "And so was Jimmy Johnson. I saw him on my way out. I'd have a talk with him if I were you. He was always hanging around Laura. She complained about him once or twice."

"Indeed," said Ames. He wondered if it was Morgan himself who had been importuning the young actress.

He turned to Betty Greene next, deliberately saving Susan Langer for last. "Betty, would you answer the same questions? Why you stayed and when you left?"

"Sure, Doc," she answered in a breathy whisper. "But before I do, I just want to say that this play would have put Laura on top of the world. She was good, very good, no matter what John says. It's just a damned shame."

"I didn't say she wasn't good," Morgan interrupted hotly. "Just that I was trying to help her over a difficult spot."

"Yeah," said Betty. "And get your groping paws all over her. She was too nice to tell you to bag it. I guess she was being respectful of your advanced age."

Morgan looked ready to explode. "I'd thank you, young lady . . . if I may call you a lady . . ."

Ames broke into the spat. "If this has some bearing on Laura's death, please continue. Otherwise, let's get back to the subject, if you don't mind."

"Sorry, Doc," said Betty Greene. "No, I don't think John had anything to do with it. I just couldn't stand him building himself up at Laura's expense when she's not here to shove it back in his teeth. Not that she would have." She took a deep breath and calmed herself. "Where were we? Oh, yeah. Why I was here that night. Laura had asked me to run some lines with her. There's a big scene that we had together and she wanted to be sure we both got it perfect. I asked her if she wanted to have supper with me, but she said she was meeting Gary when she finished. Gary's her boyfriend." She made a rueful face. "He's not an actor. He doesn't understand how the cast of a play becomes your family while you're working together. I think he was jealous of the time she spent with us."

"Was Gary going to meet her here?" Ames asked.

"No. He didn't like to come here. She was going to meet him at Lindy's around nine o'clock. So I left. I'm not exactly sure what time it was. Probably about seven-thirty."

She settled back into her chair and glared across the semicircle at John Morgan, who affected a kind of supercilious disinterest.

What a crew! Ames reflected. Betty had one thing right, though. It was exactly like the internecine warfare carried on in any dysfunctional family.

Ed Grey was slouched in his chair, his long legs extended, his eyes half closed, taking it all in. When Ames addressed him, he pulled himself upright and came to vibrant life.

"Why am I here? Why am I living?" he sang in a rich baritone, his arms outstretched to encompass them all. "Let me tell you all about that," he added in a normal speaking voice. "I needed the extra work even more than Laura. My role isn't large and it sure isn't going to make me a star. But it's a step in that direction. I asked Laura, as long as she was staying late, if she would mind going through our love scenes. And no, Betty, it wasn't just an excuse to get next to Laura, in case that's what you're thinking."

"Never entered my mind," Betty murmured. "We all know you're faithful to your true love."

The young actor flushed a bright red and silently mouthed the word "bitch." Then he continued. "When we were finished, I sat down in the front row. Laura'd asked me to stick around while she worked on her monologue. There's a scene where she was on stage alone for almost fifteen minutes. It's crucial to the whole play. I left about eight and went straight home."

Susan Langer stood up and draped her mink coat around her shoulders. "I don't think I have anything much to add to this charade," she said as she moved languidly across the stage. She stopped to lean against the proscenium arch. "I sat through all that earnest nonsense on Monday night because I wanted to see for myself just what Laura was up to. It wasn't much. The kid was an amateur. Everybody knows that part should have been mine. But don't get me wrong. I wouldn't kill for it. I left when Ed and Laura started working on the love scenes. Neither one of them knew what they were doing. I could have showed them, but why bother."

She swept toward the wings, then dramatically turned back to them. "That means Ed was alone with Laura, doesn't it? And by the way, Doctor Ames, I think psychiatry's a crock, too. Goodbye all. Happy trails." She was gone.

Ames stood up and stretched. "I guess that does it," he said. "For now, anyway. Do any of you want to add anything?"

The remaining three looked at each other and mutely shook their heads.

"Can we go now?" Betty asked.

Lonegan, who had been silently observing the interplay among the players, said, "Sure. Appreciate your cooperation. I've got your phone numbers in case the doctor needs to get in touch."

Ames said, "On your way out, would you please ask Jimmy Johnson to see me for a few minutes?"

When they had left, Lonegan asked, "Could you tell which two of the four are seeing shrinks?"

"My guess is Ed Grey and Susan Langer," said Ames.

"Bingo!" said Lonegan. "That's fantastic! How'd you know?"

"It was only a guess," Ames protested. "Ed's emotions are very close to the surface and Susan protests too much. I'd say she's at a very crucial point in her analysis."

"Another question," said Lonegan. "Did you learn anything that might help us? I listened to the whole thing, but outside of figuring out who's got a gripe against who, I'm no closer to the answer."

"Straws in the wind," said Ames. "A few things I need to think about. I'd like to see Laura's boyfriend before I talk to her parents."

"Yeah. Gary Weston. He's a philosophy professor at Columbia. Bright guy. Quite a bit older than Laura. That's all set for early Saturday afternoon. He'll come to your office, if that's okay with you."

"Perfect," said Ames. "But I'd like to see the Grahams in their home. I want to get a better sense of who Laura was. And why a grown young woman was still living at home with her parents." John Morgan's words had made a deep impression on him. Laura, according to him, had been unable to portray a normal father-daughter relationship.

"You wanted to see me, Doc?" Jimmy Johnson slouched onto the stage, a can of beer in his hand. "I'll be getting overtime pay for this, so I don't mind how long it takes." He slumped into one of the chairs and swigged at his beer can.

"It won't take long," Ames assured him. "You liked Laura Graham, didn't you?"

"Oh, yeah. She was a good kid. Shouldn't have died like that. Did you figure out who did it yet?"

"Not yet, Jimmy. Tell me, did you ever try to date her?"

"Who, me! Nah. Not my type. I got plenty of girls who like to party. Give 'em all a chance, if you know what I mean." He snickered and drained his beer can.

"You said before that it had to be one of the cast. Who?" Ames asked.

Jimmy shook his head. "Ah, Doc, I was just shootin' off my mouth. That Langer babe really frosts me. And I know for a fact that she hated Laura. I heard her telling Morgan once that she wished Laura would drop dead. But, hey, I'm not saying she did anything to help it along. That would be wrong, wouldn't it?"

"I'm afraid so, Jimmy. Unless you actually saw her do it."

"Well, I didn't. Is that all?" He started to rise from his chair.

"No," said Ames. "After all the others left, Laura was alone on the stage. Correct?"

Jimmy nodded.

"And where were you?"

"Well, like I told the detective," he looked over at Lonegan for approval, "I was hanging around backstage, waiting for her to finish. But I got kind of hungry so I went out to grab some dinner."

"And when was that?"

"Oh, I dunno. About eight-thirty or so. I told Laura I was going and she said okay."

"Did you lock the door behind you?"

"I sure did. What do you think I am, crazy? You don't leave nothin' unlocked in this town."

"And when did you get back?"

"It was after nine, about ten or fifteen minutes. Something like that. I just had a quick sandwich down the street. The cops already checked all that out."

"Was the door still locked?"

"It sure was."

"And that's when you found Laura?"

Jimmy's face grew somber. "It was the worst thing I ever saw in my life. I went onto the stage to let her know I was back, and there she was, stretched out on the floor, blood all over everything." He gestured toward stage left. "That's where she was. They cleaned it up pretty good. I didn't touch her or anything. I could see she was dead. I called the cops right away."

"And you're sure she was alone when you left?"

"Sure I'm sure. The whole place was locked up. Nobody could get in unless they went by me."

"Then Laura must have let someone in while you were away."

"Hey! That's right!" Jimmy's face brightened. "I never thought of that. Maybe one of them came back. Is that what you're thinking, Doc?"

"It's a possibility," Ames answered. "Or it could have been someone else she knew."

"I guess." Jimmy seemed to discount that idea.

"Thanks, Jimmy," Ames said, getting to his feet. "We'll be going now."

"Is that all?" Jimmy asked. "I thought you were gonna talk about psycho stuff."

"I have been, Jimmy. I have been."

After they left the theater, Ames and Lonegan stopped in a nearby bar for a drink.

"What do you think, Bill?" the detective asked.

"I think that for a nice girl, Laura Graham was at the center of a storm of rage and jealousy. But I'm not sure yet whether any of the people I've seen so far was angry enough or jealous enough to kill her. All of them, including Jimmy Johnson, are artful dissemblers. I guess it goes with the territory."

"See what I mean about this case?"

"I certainly do," said Ames. "I wonder what the boyfriend and the parents will add to the mix."

On Saturday morning, Nancy Ames sat down to the late breakfast her husband had prepared and said, "I had no idea you dabbled in murder. I wonder if that's grounds for divorce."

Bill Ames smiled. "If it's not, I'm sure these waffles are. I'm not a born cook. Entirely self-taught, out of cookbooks. But I'm sorry to miss taking you to see the spring flowers."

"Don't worry about it," said Nancy. "I'll go alone. I've been going for years, long before I met you. And you can go see the Mets alone. Baseball is just not my thing." She took a bite of the pecan waffles on her plate. "Mmm, these are delicious. It's a good thing one of us knows what to do in a kitchen."

Nancy Ames, a tax lawyer with a prestigious Manhattan law firm, was fifteen years younger than Bill. Her busy schedule left her little time for domesticity, but she cherished each moment she could spend with him. And he valued her opinions on just about everything.

"Let me ask you something," said Bill. "How old were you when you stopped living with your parents?"

"Oh, my, that's an odd one," said Nancy. "I was in and out. Away to college and back home again. First job, first apartment. When the job didn't work out, back again. That sort of thing. My parents were very patient. I must have left and gone back at least four times. I think a lot of young people are doing that these days. The chicks keep coming home to roost. Why do you ask?"

"Curiosity more than anything else," Bill answered. "The murdered woman was twenty-eight years old, yet she still lived with her parents. I'll be seeing them later this afternoon."

"And you were wondering if there was some psychological significance in it."

"That's right," said Ames. "What do you think?"

"Well," Nancy mused. "I suppose there could be. But I can't believe that all those grown-up kids living with their parents are crazy. Or that they're driving their folks around the bend."

"It's not a question of crazy, my love," said Ames. "Although murderers often do their work when their minds are unbalanced. Laura Graham did pretty well for herself. Lonegan told me she'd done off-Broadway, TV commercials, even a few months' work in a soap opera. She was pretty serious about getting married. Why did she still live with Mommy and Daddy?"

"You'll find out this afternoon," said Nancy. "Maybe she really liked them. Maybe she just found it convenient."

"I'll find out exactly what Mommy and Daddy want me to know." He finished his coffee and reached across the table to take Nancy's hand in his own. "Sorry you married me?" he asked.

"You bet I am. If you keep on feeding me pecan waffles I'll get fat as a pig, and then you'll be sorry." She glanced at her wristwatch. "You'd better get going. Didn't you say Laura's boyfriend was coming to your office at one?"

Ames sighed and rose from the table. "I was really looking forward to the flowers. I've never been to the Botanical Gardens."

"Off with you. As far as I know, spring comes every year. We could even go tomorrow if you want to. The Conservatory is always beautiful in any season. It's my version of a vacation when I can't take a real one."

"Sounds good to me. I hope this whole thing is cleared up by then." He bent to kiss the top of his wife's head, then tilted her face up to kiss her mouth. "Yum. Maple syrup. Sticky but good. See you later."

When Ames reached Central Park South, he found Gary Weston waiting for him in the lobby of the building.

"I know I'm early, but I've been at loose ends ever since it happened," Weston explained. "I walked all the way from Columbia but I still had time on my hands when I got here. I feel like the rest of my life is going to be like this. Empty, without purpose."

As they rode up in the elevator, Ames estimated that Weston was quite a bit older than Laura Graham—unless the tragedy had aged him beyond his years.

Once settled in Ames's office, Weston began asking questions. "Isn't it unusual for a psychiatrist to be investigating a murder? How come that detective can't figure this out? I gave him plenty of hints about where to look."

"Oh?" said Ames. "And where was that?"

Weston pulled a battered pipe out of the pocket of his tweed jacket. "Mind if I smoke this?" he asked. "You'll probably think it's some kind of emotional crutch. I suppose it is."

"Go right ahead," said Ames. "Used to smoke one myself." He slid a crystal ashtray across the desk. "Where did you tell Lonegan to look? Or should I say, at whom?"

"It's a long story," said Weston, lighting his pipe. "I'll have to go back a bit. I met Laura about a year ago. She was between roles and was taking a weekend seminar in philosophy that I was teaching. I was quite impressed with her. She asked good questions and seemed quite bright. I didn't realize at first that she was an actress. I didn't see her again after the seminar until one day I received a note in the mail. She was in a reading of original one-act plays at a small theater uptown, and she invited me to be her guest. Of course, I went. I was curious."

"I've been told that you and Laura were planning to marry," Ames prompted.

"That's true," said Weston. "I never thought I would marry again after my first wife died. But Laura was just so full of energy and happiness, she made me believe that even I could be happy again. It was months before I understood her well enough to get a glimmer of the dark side of her life."

"The dark side?" Ames felt a chill run down his spine.

Was this man going to hand him the answer? Or was it going to be yet another false lead? Weston seemed much more plausible than Laura's theatrical colleagues.

"Maybe that's an exaggeration," said Weston. "What I mean is that she had a deep well of unhappiness that she kept covered up very, very expertly. I think it had something to do with her parents. Have you met them yet?"

"Not yet," said Ames. "I'm seeing them later this afternoon."

"They don't like me," said Weston. "They did everything they could to turn Laura against me. They said I was too old for her. I'm forty-two. Laura was twenty-eight. And we loved each other. I don't think fourteen years is too great a difference."

Ames thought about the difference in age between himself and Nancy. It didn't seem to matter at all.

Weston continued. "Laura was a different person around her parents, particularly around her father. With me, she was a charming, intelligent young woman. But with him, she was childish and even sullen sometimes. He would become angry with her, and then make up by giving her expensive presents. It was a very strange relationship. Sometimes, I felt that he regarded me as a rival."

Ames decided to come straight to the point. "Do you think he might have killed her?"

Weston was obviously shocked. "That would be obscene!" he gasped.

"Yes, it would," Ames agreed. "I thought, perhaps, that's what you were leading up to."

"No! No, it never entered my mind." Weston dropped

his face into his hands as if ashamed of what he was thinking. When he spoke, his voice was muffled. "I thought . . . I thought that maybe . . . just maybe . . . her father might have sexually abused her."

When Weston raised his face, Ames offered the box of tissues that was never far out of reach in this room.

When Weston had recovered himself, he said, "Don't get me wrong. Laura never said a word against her father. In fact, she seemed to idolize him. Maybe it's just that there's so much in the news these days about child abuse. I could have been reading something into their relationship that simply wasn't there."

"Do you believe that?" Ames asked.

Weston groaned. "I don't know what to believe. And that's the truth."

"Then let's deal with facts for a while," Ames suggested. "Where were you on the night Laura was killed?"

"I was going to meet Laura around nine o'clock at Lindy's on Seventh Avenue. It's just a few blocks from the theater. I got there about a quarter to nine. When she didn't show up by nine-thirty, I decided to walk over to the theater to meet her. When I got there, I found . . . well, you know what I found. The police wanted to know everything about me."

"They thought you might have killed her?"

"That they did. Fortunately, the waiter at Lindy's remembered me. I was the guy who got stood up."

"But that still leaves fifteen minutes unaccounted for. The stage doorman left Laura alone at eight-thirty."

"I took a cab from my apartment on Riverside Drive to the restaurant. The cabbie and I got into a discussion about Nietzsche, the old superman argument. He thought he was one, but it all boiled down to racism. He couldn't see that and I got out just in time. I think he was ready to explode. He remembered me, too."

"So you have an airtight alibi," Ames remarked.

"I guess I do. I didn't think of it that way. To tell you the truth, I haven't been thinking straight at all since it happened. Please forget what I said before. About Laura's father. I've just been groping for answers. There are no easy answers, are there?"

"If there were," Ames replied, "I think you and I might be out of jobs. I want to thank you for coming here. I know it's been difficult for you."

Weston rose and reached for his trenchcoat. "Actually, it's been a bit of a relief to get those terrible broodings out in the open. Do you think I might call and make an appointment with you for some help?"

"Wait until after the case is closed. You may feel differently then," said Ames. "I'll go with you. I'm due at the Grahams' in about a half hour."

The apartment building where Laura Graham had lived with her parents was one of the old pre-war treasures of the Upper West Side. But unlike many of its kind, it had not been well-maintained. Rent control, Ames thought as he entered the lobby, had its merits, but it also fostered the decay of buildings like this one.

There was no doorman to announce him, so the doctor went directly to the twelfth floor. The Grahams were expecting him and he was right on time. As he pressed the door buzzer, he wondered what he would find out in this conversation with the last of Lonegan's cast of characters. Would it be a dead end? Or would all the pieces finally fall into place?

The door opened just a crack, held in place by a chain bolt, and part of a woman's face appeared in the aperture. "Who is it?" a voice whispered.

Ames identified himself and said, "Mrs. Graham? I believe you're expecting me?"

The door closed again, the chain bolt rattled, and then the door opened wide. "Forgive me," said the woman. "I always keep the chain on when I'm alone. You can't be too careful these days. Especially after what happened to Laura. Come in, please."

She led the way into a large, cluttered living room. There were green plants everywhere, and between them, on every surface, what seemed a vast collection of small ceramic figurines, mainly of adorable children, with a few puppies and kittens interspersed. There were no books or records, but a large-screen television set dominated one end of the room. Fashion magazines lay strewn across a coffee table.

"Richard's gone out for a bit," the woman chattered. "He just needed some fresh air. We haven't been going out much the past week. Not even to work. We both work at Macy's, you know. I'm a women's fashion buyer and Richard does the same in men's shoes. He should be back soon. Let me take your coat. Would you like some coffee? I've got a pot already made."

As she fluttered around him, Ames wondered if she was always like this or if it was the effect of her grief. Her eyes were ringed with dark circles, as if she hadn't been sleeping well, and her short, gray hair, although stylishly cut, was disheveled.

"Coffee would be wonderful, Mrs. Graham," he answered.

"It's Dorothy," she said. "Please call me Dorothy." She giggled like a young girl, but the laughter didn't reach her eyes. "I guess you'll want me to bare my soul so we might as well be friendly about it. Just sit down anywhere you like, and I'll be right back."

Ames watched her skitter away to another part of the apartment, presumably the kitchen, before he settled down into a worn but comfortable armchair. All of the furnishings had a cozy, lived-in appearance, an aura of middle-class, middle-aged complacency. None of it squared with his mental image of Laura.

Dorothy Graham returned bearing a tray laden with coffee cups, cream, sugar, and a plate of strawberry tarts. "Just help yourself, Doctor," she said, as she set the tray down on the coffee table. "I think Richard's afraid of you. That's why he went out."

"Really," said Ames, reaching for a coffee cup.

Dorothy plumped herself down on the sofa facing him. "Really. But not me," she said. "I'm not afraid. I want to do everything I can to help out. I told that detective you could ask me anything. I'll hold nothing back. You can't imagine what it's like to lose your only child, and in such a terrible way. I can't eat, I can't sleep, and when I do sleep, I have this terrible nightmare, over and over again."

"Oh," said Ames. "Would you like to tell me about it?"

Dorothy shuddered. "I hate even thinking about it. But if you think it would help . . ."

"Dreams sometimes tell us things we can't face in our waking, conscious life."

"Yes," said Dorothy, "I've heard of that. But I've never believed it much. Well, here goes. In my dream,

I'm a little girl again, and my father is taking me to the circus. It's at the old Madison Square Garden. I'm so excited because I've never been to the circus before, but I'm trying to be real grown-up so my father will be proud of me. When we get there, my father suddenly turns into one of the clowns, but he's not a happy clown. His face gets very angry and he has these long, sharp teeth like tusks. He makes me take all my clothes off in front of all those people. I don't want to do it but I have to, because he's my father. Then one of those teeth falls out and he's holding it in his hand, pointing it at me. He says, 'This is all your fault. Now you have to swallow it.' And he shoves it down my throat."

Dorothy stopped speaking abruptly and stared at the doctor. She seemed to be waiting for his reaction. During the description of her dream, her voice had become that of a frightened little girl.

"Is that the end of your dream?" Ames asked softly.

"I always wake up at that point," said Dorothy, her voice once again that of a mature woman.

"Did your father ever take you to the circus?"

"That's the funny part about it," she answered. "I never knew my father. He deserted my mother when I was a baby. And I never saw a circus until Richard and I took Laura when she was five."

There was the sound of a key in the lock. Dorothy leaned across the coffee table and whispered, "That's Richard. Please don't tell him what I said before. About him being afraid of you."

She rose from the couch and hurried across the living room to greet her husband. "Come, Richard, dear. Meet Doctor Ames. I'm sure you'll feel better after you talk to him. I do already." She fussed about him, taking his coat and stroking his wind-tousled hair. "Did you have a nice walk? I've got your coffee ready and your favorite strawberry tarts."

Richard said not a word, but let his wife lead him by the hand to the sofa, where he sat beside her. He ignored the coffee and the doctor, and sat staring glumly at the patterned carpet beneath his feet.

"Richard, dear, you're being just a tiny bit rude," Dorothy murmured. "Doctor Ames is here to help us. The least you can do is say hello."

Without raising his head, Richard mumbled something unintelligible.

Ames decided that shock tactics were in order. "Richard," he said loud and clear, "did you kill your daughter?"

The man's head jerked up. All color had drained from his face, his eyes were tormented, and his mouth worked helplessly.

Dorothy leaped to his defense. She stood over the doctor like an enraged lioness. "How dare you!" she cried. "Can't you see how he's suffering? How could you suggest such a thing?"

Richard reached out and pulled her back down beside him. "It's all right, Dodo," he murmured. "I deserved that." He turned to the doctor. "I've done a lot of things wrong as far as Laura was concerned. I tried to stop her from going into the theater. I thought it was too risky. I found fault with every man she was ever interested in. None of them were good enough for her. I tried to keep her to myself, my little girl. And I realize now how selfish that was. But no, doctor, I did not kill my daughter."

Ames wanted very much to believe the man. He was obviously in great emotional pain. But he sensed there was still something hidden, something Richard was too ashamed to admit.

"You must have loved your daughter very much," said Ames. Although his attention was focused on Richard, he noticed out of the corner of his eye that Dorothy's hand, holding a coffee cup, was trembling.

"I loved her . . . ," Richard began.

Dorothy interrupted, "Sometimes I think you loved her more than you loved me. You certainly spent more time with her than you did with me. All those nights, the two of you up until all hours, talking and laughing, long after I'd gone to bed."

"Yes," said Richard, "I did that. I'm sorry, Dodo."

"It's a little too late to be sorry, isn't it, Richard? And what else did you do to her?"

Ames sat, quietly astonished, as the suppressed rage of years began to pour out of the very ordinary looking woman who sat beside her husband, holding a forgotten coffee cup.

"What else?" said Richard wearily. "You know what else. You've known all along. And you never said a word. You could have stopped it before it started. I think you wanted it to happen. But I don't know why."

Suddenly, Dorothy's cup went crashing to the floor. Coffee splattered all over the rug, the couch, her dress. The accident seemed to restore her to her senses. "Oh, dear!" she exclaimed. "I'll have to mop that up. Excuse me, please. I'll be right back." She hurried off toward the kitchen.

"I'll tell you everything, Doctor," said Richard. "But I'm afraid I can't tell you who killed Laura. The truth is that I . . . I've been the worst kind of father a girl could have. I used Laura as a substitute for a wife I no longer felt any passion for. And every time she tried to break away, I would convince her that things would be different. But they never were. I truly adored her and now I don't want to live without her. But I'll say it once again. I did not kill her."

Dorothy returned from the kitchen with a large tea towel in one hand and a damp sponge in the other. She went directly to the sofa where Richard was sitting. "Don't move," she said. "I'm just going to clean things up here."

She dropped the tea towel, revealing a long, sharp carving knife. "I should have done this long ago," she said. "I should have killed you instead of Laura."

Richard sat still and silent as his wife raised the knife above her head. It was almost as if he welcomed the blade.

"Why don't you scream?" Dorothy demanded. "She did. You should have heard her. But she didn't scream for her daddy. Oh, no. She screamed for Mommy. She wanted her mommy to love her and let her live. Well, I did love her, and I loved you, but you spoiled all that. So she died. And now you. With the same knife."

While Dorothy raved, Ames had gotten quietly to his feet and walked around behind her. Gauging the moment carefully, he grasped her arm just before it began to descend and twisted it sharply down and behind her back. The knife fell from her limp fingers and she collapsed onto the floor.

"You should have let her do it," said Richard.

"Call the police," said Ames. He fished Lonegan's phone number out of his pocket and handed it to Richard. "Ask for Jack Lonegan and tell him to get here as quick as he can. I'll try to keep your wife calm, but I'm not sure how long I can do that."

Later that night, Bill Ames and Jack Lonegan were on their second round of drinks at Jack's neighborhood watering hole, one of the few remaining Irish pubs on Third Avenue.

"Do me a favor, Jack," said Ames, "and don't ever call me to help you out again. This one was a little too close for comfort."

"Ah, you're gettin' to be a real pro at the rough stuff," said Lonegan. "Don't tell me a dust-up with a helpless little woman is going to ruin our friendship?"

"I wouldn't call Dorothy Graham helpless," said Ames. "She would have killed her husband as well as her daughter if I hadn't been there. But if I hadn't been there, probing for answers, he might never have been in any danger. She'd gotten rid of her rival. And she was quite safe. No one would ever suspect her. And even though Richard knew that she'd killed Laura, he would never tell because then his own guilty secret would have to come out."

"You have to admit, Bill," said Lonegan, "this was more exciting than the usual nut-cases you deal with. And if it's any consolation to you, I don't think I could have gotten there without you."

"What will happen to Richard?" Ames asked.

"That's out of my jurisdiction," Lonegan answered. "If it belongs anywhere, it belongs to the Sex Crimes Division. But I don't think he's the sort to go out and start raping teen-aged girls. After talking with him today, I get the impression the guy is living in a hell of his own creation."

"Me, too," said Ames. "And Dorothy will have to stand trial. I've no doubt a good attorney will go for the insanity defense. In a way, it'll be Richard's trial, too. Sometimes, I feel so incredibly sorry for both of them. But then I remember what they both did to their daughter. Sorrow really doesn't help much, does it?"

"I never waste my time with it, Doc. Let's have one more drink and then call it a day."

"Fine with me. And I think that tomorrow, I'm going up to the Botanical Gardens to see the flowers. Nancy tells me it's like a vacation for her. I need a vacation from murder."

Dorothy Salisbury Davis

NOW IS FOREVER

THEY MET IN THE MEDIEVAL SCULPTURE HALL OF THE Metropolitan Museum of Art. It is a vast room through which museum visitors can go off in any of several directions—to galleries for special exhibits, into the wing housing the Lehman Collection, through the Medieval Treasury and on to the Garden Court and the American Wing. It is so vast a room one almost always feels alone, no matter how numerous the company. They shook hands and spoke softly, words that any listener, picking up on them, might interpret as casual. It looked like, and was contrived to look like, an accidental meeting after which, as though there were a discovery she had made recently and wanted to show him, they moved into the small Romanesque chapel with its thirteenth-century stained glass. They stared up at the window from the Lady Chapel of the Abbey of St. Germain des Prés, not really seeing it. They were too absorbed, too overwhelmed by the sudden presence of one another. But when he reached out and touched her hand where it lay on the back of a chapel chair, she withdrew it, and slowly looked around toward a wood carving of mother and child. Beyond the sculpture she could see the hall from which they had come and the people passing there.

"No guilt?" he said in light mockery.

"None," she said, tossing her head in defiance of God knows whom.

"Shall we sit down? You can lecture me on whatever that window's all about."

"The passion of St. Vincent of Saragossa."

"The passion—a word with many meanings," he said, moving a chair to make more room between it and the next one.

"Let's not sit down," she said.

"I understand." Then: "Couldn't sit on these chairs anyway. They're built for midgets."

"There are not many men as tall as you in the countries where you find them."

"Or women as beautiful as you?"

"That is a *non sequitur,* Father Morrissey."

He nodded gravely. They moved beyond the altar-like table supporting a marble bas-relief. When they stood behind it, beneath the St. Vincent window, they could hold hands unobserved from outside the chapel. She squeezed his fiercely and then let go of it. A silence fell between them. She broke it presently to say, "Oh, Dan, what's to become of us?" She again laughed softly at herself, the hackneyed melodrama of her words.

"Before we're old and gray, priests will marry," he said.

"Divorced women?"

"Mmmmm. I have a way of forgetting about your husband."

"So do I when I'm with you."

From the chapel entry a guard spoke. "Step back, please."

Startled, they leapt apart.

"You are not allowed so close." The guard gestured them back to make clear his meaning. His accent was Hispanic.

"We are not touching anything," the priest said, speaking in Spanish. It was a language in which he was almost fluent. He was not recognizable as a priest; he wore a sports jacket and turtleneck sweater.

"It is my responsibility to say," the guard said aggressively, perhaps because he had been addressed in Spanish, calling attention to his accent.

"Let's go, for heaven's sake," Kate said. "I want to see the modern glass."

The guard stood his ground while they walked past him, Kate holding high a very heavy head. "We've been drummed out of paradise." There was not much mirth in the laugh she managed.

"That guy's a bully," Morrissey said.

Kate had it on the tip of her tongue to say that bullies chose their prey carefully. She held her peace and once out of the Sculpture Court felt some restoration of her pride. She ought to have learned, living twenty years with Martin Knowles, how to ignore the tyranny of servants, public or personal. Instead, in a restaurant, for example, where Martin insisted that the service be impeccable, she sympathized with the underdog waiter, however truculently he came to heel. She glanced up at Morrissey. He winked at her and she almost took his hand to swing along with him in the carefree manner of young lovers.

At the heavy glass doors to the Garden Court an odd thing happened: as Kate pushed through, she caught the reflection of a man's face in the glass. His eyes were on hers, sad, questing eyes. She thought she recognized him, but as the glass receded with the door's opening, the image vanished, and when, having passed through, she looked back, there was no one in sight except Morrissey following close behind her.

"The strangest thing," she said. "I saw a face in the glass door, someone I thought I knew, but now it's gone."

"That was me," Morrissey said.

"No, I don't think so."

"Kate, shall we go on to your house and skip the art course?"

"It's too early," she said. "We need to give my housekeeper a little more time to get away."

Katherine and Martin Knowles had been active members of St. Ambrose parish since their marriage. Martin was a convert to Catholicism and, as Kate's mother said crankily at the wedding, it made him more Catholic than the pope. Indeed the Knowles, on their wedding trip to Italy, had knelt before Paul VI and kissed his ring. Kate wished at the time that it was John XXIII whose hand she touched. She could imagine that great hulk of a man with a heart to match, reaching down, taking her by both hands, and saying, "Come, you have as much right to the throne of Peter as I do." Not that she wanted to be pope any more than Betty Friedan did, but she had grown up in the early days of ecumenism and of Women's Liberation and was fiercely partisan. Martin took a dim view of both, and looked in recent years to John Paul II to put both church and women back on course.

Kate knew that the fabric of her faith was thinning before Daniel Morrissey crashed into her life. Martin's was of tougher stuff. Their son and daughter, in college, attended mass with some regularity, but made no secret of their differences with the church in matters they felt should be arbitrated directly between themselves and the Almighty. It was not something, however, they discussed with their father. Kate sometimes would have preferred not to be their confidante herself. She had been somewhat shaken on a recent Sunday when her daughter, visiting home, had gone to mass with her and, meeting Father Morrissey on the church steps afterwards, had declared of the dark-eyed, handsome priest, "What a waste!" On their way home, Kate silent, Sheila had teased her, "Did I shock you, Mother?"

"I agree!" Kate had said.

And Sheila: "Now I'm shocked."

On the day Kate and Morrissey met in the museum, they met again later that afternoon, but not by their own design. Twice a week Kate conducted what she loosely—very loosely—called an art class for youngsters attending St. Ambrose parochial school who, at the end of the school day, might otherwise have been unsupervised until a parent got home from work. St. Ambrose, once a wealthy Upper East Side parish, had become, like the neighborhood, a mix of the moderately rich and the borderline poor, the latter mostly Hispanic. The church had been undergoing extensive renovation at the time; the grime of sixty years was being removed from four large murals that depicted Christ's trial, death, resurrection, and ascension. Much of the original paint came away with the dirt, however, and the restoration became more complicated and costly than the commissioned funds could cover. Martin Knowles made a substantial contribution to allow the work to go forward. Thus it was, Kate felt sure, that Monsignor Carey consulted with her on the work as it progressed. As soon as the restoration crew had closed up shop that day, the monsignor sent Morrissey to ask Mrs. Knowles, in the adjoining building, if she'd mind stepping over to the church for a few minutes. "You won't mind staying a while with the children, will you, Father?"

Morrissey did not mind. Seeing Kate, however briefly, eased the pain of separation that inevitably followed their hasty and furtive lovemaking. The way her eyes lit up when she saw him told of the same quick joy. They touched hands when she put the large scissors in his and told him he was journeyman to her apprentices. The color flared in her cheeks and she avoided looking at him. But very much on the alert was a youngster of eight or nine sitting across the table. His eyes, with the speed of arrows, darted from one adult's face to the other's.

Father Morrissey winked at him. He was a great winker, something that eased him out of many a confrontation. It was a mistake in this case. A little gleam of cunning shone in the boy's eyes. He had intuited something. "What's your name, young fellow?" the priest said.

"Rafael."

"Rafael," Morrissey repeated admiringly.

A pigtailed girl sitting next to the wily youngster said, "His name is José, Father. Rafael is his brother's name."

"José is a fine name, too," Morrissey said, feeling like an idiot, making child's talk.

"She very nice woman," José said. "Smart."

"Who's that?"

"You know." The little demon rolled his eyes toward the door by which Kate had left them.

"Go back to work on whatever you were doing before I interrupted," the priest said.

"She say I'm going to be famous artist." The children were cutting out paper of different shapes and sizes and colors and pasting them together in such designs as they fancied or could manage. "Like Matisse." He said the name with practiced care.

The little girl giggled. "Mrs. Knowles calls all of us her little Matisses."

With lightning speed José grabbed a compass and tore it through the paste-up the little girl was working on. She howled, and Morrissey aimed a slap at the face of José—aimed it, but interrupted his own hand before it touched the boy. His dire intention became nothing more than a clap of noise. José did not even dodge what must have seemed to him an impending blow. The little girl reached over and snatched the collage José had been attempting and tore it apart. Very soon, up and down the long table, a dozen children were caught up in a frenzy of destruction. Those who reached for their neighbor's work too late to get it tore up their own, and shrieked with pleasure.

"Holy Mother of God," Morrissey murmured. "How do I handle this one?" Then, "Come on, you barbarians, let's get some exercise. On your feet and march!" He pushed one youngster in front of him and pulled one after him. He had to hunch down like Quasimodo. The only marching song he could think of was "Onward Christian Soldiers," and he belted out the tune in a sturdy baritone. The other kids fell in and soon they were marching around the room, strung together, hand in hand. Twice around and he called a halt and set them to cleaning up the mess.

José had joined the march, but now he sat, dark and sullen as a stone. When the little mischiefer next to him began to giggle and bite her lip, Morrissey realized something new was going on with José. He was probably peeing where he sat. If he was, his eyes never wavered from the priest's face while he did it.

"I always hesitate to ask you to come 'round and have a look, Mrs. Knowles," the monsignor said. "Ah, now, I'm supposed to call you Kate, Martin says, after all the years we've known each other, but I shy away from that as well. All the Protestants I know are on a first-name basis with their ministers and one another. I suppose it's all right, but I wouldn't want one of those little colts you're kind enough to corral after school, I wouldn't want one of them calling me Timothy to my face. I don't care what they call me behind my back. What was I saying?"

"I'm not sure," Kate said. She could no more call him Timothy than could Dan. Once in a while Dan spoke of him as the Old Man, but with reverence. Monsignor Carey had celebrated his fortieth year as a parish priest and he had trained his curates well. Two of them had been called to parishes of their own, and that, he had once told Martin, was as much as he could do for an ailing church. "It will come back to you," she said of whatever it was he'd been going to say.

"Things do," he said, "and some to haunt me." He squinted at her from under the shaggy black and white eyebrows. "You know, you don't look a day older than when I married you and Martin? He still calls you his bride, you know."

"I know," Kate said. She was sure there was nothing covert in his words, almost sure.

"He's a good man, Kate. There! I've called you Kate, and it didn't hurt a bit. Or did it you?"

"No, Monsignor," she said, more stiffly than she'd intended.

He chortled. "I know when I've been put in my place. Well, as I was saying, I hope I'm not taking advantage of you, asking you to come and see the work in progress." They were standing beneath the scaffolding, before the mural of the crucifixion, the figures lifesize. The garments and much of the background had been vividly repainted, so that the unfinished hands, feet and faces were pale and strangely ghost-like; the heads put her in mind of executioner's hoods. "You don't think the colors are too gaudy?" the old man ventured.

"Monsignor, shall I speak frankly?"

"Would I ask you otherwise?"

"You've put the restoration into the hands of a man the museum recommended. He's far more competent than I am." Kate was several notches above amateur status, but she was keenly aware that if it weren't for her husband's patronage, his financial influence, her standing in the art world wouldn't be much above that of a dilettante. Furthermore, she suspected the monsignor knew it as well as she did. He was courting favor with Martin. But to give him the benefit of the doubt, she said, "We've got to remember the restorer is working toward the original colors, not the faded pictures we've grown used to."

"You must be right. I only know what I like and I like what I'm used to. I'll get accustomed to this if I live long enough—and if I'm not shipped out."

"They wouldn't dare," Kate said.

"Wouldn't they now? Just watch in the next months. It will be me or Father Morrissey. I'll go to pasture, but they have their eye on him as a comer. And it's time. These young priests now—not that he's a youngster—but he goes along with the new generation: to them the priesthood is a profession, not a divine calling."

Kate murmured something. Her lips had gone dry. Her heart had gone dry. Not that she and Dan were unaware of the possibility of his being transferred. She sometimes thought Dan prayed for it, since he still prayed. Or so he said. Now and then they assured one another that they had no guilt, as though it were not bred in their bones. A parish of his own, what he had always wanted before his collision with her. Now it would be a kind of solution, however desperately she dreaded it. She waited while the monsignor stepped carefully over the drop sheets and turned off the floodlights.

"We'll go bankrupt keeping him in light," the monsignor said, returning to her side. "But I don't suppose Michelangelo was bargain basement either."

"I'd better get back and relieve Father Morrissey," Kate said.

"Did you ever meet Melodosi?" the monsignor asked, staying the course of his own thoughts. "It's funny. I thought you knew him, too."

Kate waited for him to let her go, giving no sign of her impatience. The light of day had all but disappeared in the November twilight, the color of the stained glass high in the chancel window all but vanished. A stooped, shuffling, white-haired old man was silhouetted against the glow of many votive lights as he approached the statue of Virgin and child. He selected a taper and lit yet another candle among the glowing bank of them. The monsignor detained her, watching the petitioner. Kate could not remember having ever lighted a candle in church. It was a practice belonging to an earlier time than hers, or to a different class of people of whom, for some undefined reason, she felt envious at the moment.

The monsignor cleared his throat and a few seconds later a series of noisy clangs reverberated through the church as the petitioner dropped coins into the metal box.

The monsignor chortled quietly. "There'll be a few pesos in that lot," he whispered. Then: "Kneel down and I'll give you my blessing."

Kate went down on one knee and made the sign of the cross in unison with his.

The monsignor left her at the door to the passageway between church and school, and went on himself to the vestry and office, passing behind the main altar.

She felt choked, as though something in her chest was blocked. She sucked in the dead air of the passageway. It was such a little distance to the school door and yet the fire light above the door seemed remote. Two low-wattage bulbs caged in ceiling outlets scarcely lit a place already without shadows. No wonder it was called the tunnel. She wanted to hurry, to escape the echo of her own footfalls—if that was what she was hearing—but an inner warning held her back. The last few feet and she crashed into the brass bar that ought to have opened the door, but it did not budge. Again and again she pushed, but it was solidly in place, locked tight. She drew a deep breath and listened for the sound of the children: their room was not far from the door. But she did not hear a murmur. Could Dan have sent them home? And if he had, would he not have come this way himself and waited for her in the passage?

It came to her then that there had been a recent change in the lock-up system. Looters had come through the church and vandalized some of the classrooms. Now, at a given hour, you could pass from the school to the church, but not from the church to the school. Her panic eased and she turned back. She opened the church door to confront a figure palely lighted and seeming about to enter the passage she was leaving. He turned abruptly and went the way the monsignor had gone, passing behind the altar.

"Father?" she called after him. It might have been one of the other assistants. He did not return. She had only seen his face darkly, but she was sure it was the same she had seen reflected in the museum door that morning.

Morrissey was waiting for her, alone in the classroom she was allowed to use for her after-school art class. They both spoke at once, Kate asking where the children were, and Morrissey saying she'd been gone a long time.

"You look terrible," he said then. "What happened?"

Kate shook her head. "Nothing. I take it you dismissed the children?"

"They dismissed themselves, the little villains. I sent the one called José to the boy's room. He'd wet himself. And when he didn't come back, the youngster who sat next to him said he'd gone home. How she knew I don't know. I'm no good with children, Kate, and Monsignor Carey knows it. But every chance he gets, he throws me in with them."

"Daniel to the young lions," Kate said.

"It's no joke. That José or Rafael or whatever his name is a troublemaker."

"He's not," Kate said. "He's full of imagination and his home life is dreadful. He has an older brother he adores, but who beats up on him regularly."

Morrissey remembered how the youngster had not even flinched when he had come near hitting him. It crossed his mind that the boy wanted to be struck. "What did the monsignor have to say? I have to go in a minute."

"The troublemaker is the youngster who tattles on him all the time, Annabelle."

Morrissey was impatient. "Do you think the Old Man suspects us? That's the bottom line, isn't it?"

"No, I don't think he does. If he did, I think he'd come right out and ask what was going on between us."

"Just like that," Morrissey said, mocking her. "And what would you say to that?"

"Nothing, monsignor."

She could premeditate her lies, Morrissey thought. She was more honest than he was, who, at best, could figure out ways to evade the truth. "I must go," he said again. "I can go through the tunnel. You had to go around, didn't you?" She nodded. "Don't hang around here, Kate. These days you never know. Dear God, this place is depressing. No wonder kids grow up hating school."

"You'd better go, Dan. As you say, you never know." The only sound in the building was the pipes, the heat going on or off.

Neither of them had the impulse to embrace, to throw

away caution, as was so often the case. As soon as the heavy door to the passageway closed behind him, he wanted to go back and at least say he loved her as he had never hoped to love a woman. But the day so full of promise in the morning and its brief ecstasy in the afternoon had come to an end in a cold, bleak classroom under the merciless eyes of a too-curious child.

Kate slept with her husband that night. They had gone out to dinner with a client of Martin's. She had offered to make dinner, but Martin preferred a restaurant where, frankly, Kate could carry the principal burden of entertaining a man not easily entertained. She flirted with him openly, flatteringly, or as Martin put it, like a courtesan. It was intended as a compliment. There were not many things Martin liked better than to be the envy of his peers. She took a painful pleasure in making love with him when he was already so greatly pleased with her. She was great at giving pleasure, she thought ironically, and making do herself. The rites of married love had become mostly an agony. She had not reached the peak of self-deception where she could substitute one man for another in her fantasy. Afterwards, when Martin had returned to his own bed, contented and full of sleep, she was free to dream of Dan and a life with him.

Martin soon was breathing with deep regularity, while sleep was beyond her. She got up and went to the adjoining sitting room where, when Martin was away, she used to come up early in the night and read. The house had seemed too big. Now it was not big enough. At one of the deep, high windows with the shutters folded into the wall, she parted the drapes and stared out at the night.

There was no longer the street traffic after midnight in the East Nineties such as used to continue into the early hours of morning. An occasional taxi, a furtive pedestrian, drunk or lost or homeless, with all his earthly goods stacked in a grocery cart headed for a bench along the Central Park wall. What would it be like to be in need, to be among the pitied or among the despised, an object of surreptitious nudges? They had been cast out of paradise, she remembered jesting to Dan in the museum. But suppose they were discovered? They must not let that happen. If there was to be a future for them, they must themselves take the first step at bringing it about. They must salvage some small dignity at least. Theirs was not the first such love in history, only the first for them. The children would understand, Sheila certainly, in time. And Martin: she could name a half-dozen women who would open their arms to him. His hurt would pass, perhaps even his outrage. Dan could make a good confession and petition the archdiocese, the Vatican if necessary, to be released from his vows. They had spoken of it: such release could only happen after a period of separation from her and from the most sacred of his duties. It would not happen, she knew that. Dan would rather wait and pray for the day that priests could marry, so self-persuaded the day was coming he could grant himself premature indulgence. And to tell the truth and shame the devil, she too preferred to wait. Be honest, Kate: now is forever.

Her thoughts became as a thousand tongues babbling half-finished sentences from her subconscious. Try as she might, she could not hold those flashes of memory she wanted most to dwell on now—their first touch, love first spoken, promises, longings shared, such as for the sweet peace they had never known of sleep together after love. She stared at the street lamp beneath her window, to hold onto that longing at least. But it became a halo, then a face: it might have been the image of St. Francis as on the prayer card that memorialized her mother's death. She could not hold to that either: it had become the face as she had glimpsed it in the museum door, the face confronting her at the tunnel door. The pounding in her ears had to be her own heartbeat and not the rhythm of running footsteps. When she closed her eyes, opened them, and looked again, there was only the street lamp and its misty halo.

At dawn, Martin, an early riser, found her curled up in an afghan, deep in a sedated sleep on the divan.

Most Sundays Father Morrissey said the Spanish-language mass at twelve-thirty. The monsignor insisted. He was very proud of him, his non-Hispanic assistant pastor who had learned the language of the growing majority of their congregation. When Morrissey pulled a blooper during his homily, the Old Man said of the barely suppressed giggles, "Never mind. It keeps them alert waiting to catch you up." These Sundays Morrissey had more to overcome than his mistakes in Spanish grammar. He had no choice, he told himself, but to say mass: the people expected it of him, and too, a priest, once ordained, never lost the power of his priesthood, no matter into what delinquency he strayed. He could be forbidden to use the power, but he could not be deprived of it, and the bread and wine he consecrated in the Lord's name became the living presence as truly as if St. Peter himself stood at the altar.

Robed in the purple of Advent, he waited at the back

of the church with the new priest and the readers and servers taking their places for the processional. In the sanctuary, the musicians were tuning up, the choir arranging chairs to their liking. He watched the latecomers scrambling for seats. The youngster José came with his mother. If the boy had not looked around at the assembling processional, Morrissey might have happily missed him. His mother dragged him forward and then pushed him ahead of her into a pew. While she covered her face in prayer, he turned and stared back blatantly at the priest.

To Morrissey's dismay, Kate entered the church. She was alone. He had never seen her at this mass before. She generally attended the eight o'clock with Martin or the ten-thirty if she came on her own. If she saw him, she gave no sign. She sat near the back, but close enough to José for him to see and recognize her. Surreptitiously, his hand half-hidden by his shoulder, he waved at her. The little demon had a crush on her. Whether or not Kate saw him, the priest couldn't tell. She gave no sign of it. He tried then to convince himself that José might well be waving to someone else. Everybody knew everybody in their community, and the latecomers were still scrambling into the church, dodging the barricades set up to protect the restoration riggings. The monsignor himself was routing traffic.

The musicians struck up, the *pandereta,* the *maraca,* the guitars, and the fervent, harsh voices of the choir. As the monsignor had said to him once: if they couldn't beguile you into heaven with their singing, they could scare you half the way. The congregation rose and sang with the choir as the procession got under way, white-robed servers, girls and boys, readers, the new associate just up from Puerto Rico, and the censor-swinging acolyte, laying down a smoke screen before him.

Morrissey sat, three-quarter face to the congregation, the young associate at his side. There was so little for the celebrant to do in the contemporary mass, so much of the ritual given up to the lay participants, with a solacing share to the women. Clouded with incense before reading the gospel, he lost his concentration. *There would be signs in the sun and the moon and the stars . . . the roaring of the sea, men fainting for fear and for expectation . . . they will see the son of man coming upon a cloud with great power and majesty. . . .* He stumbled over the Spanish word, and the new priest whispered it, the loudspeaker picking up his voice as he had not intended.

With the offertory of the mass finally upon him and effort beyond what he had been equal to until that moment, he said the words of the consecration—This is my body . . . this is my blood—words he knew the Lord himself would keep pure.

As far as he could see, Kate was not among those who thronged to the sanctuary steps to receive communion. He would not have expected her to, but suddenly before him was José, his small hands fisted at his side when the priest offered him the bread, his lips, too, tightly closed against it. The boy's mother prodded and scolded him from behind. He had come to the table but he would not partake. His eyes were coals of defiance. Father Morrissey moved to the nearest server and changed places with him. There was only a small disruption until José's mother grabbed her son's arm and flung him away, crying out, "*Perdido! Perdido!*" Lost: it had the ring of a flamenco lament, and it carried through the church. José spat in the direction of the altar and ran from the steps.

Kate could not see what had happened at the altar steps, but those who had seen it were calling out condemnation after the fleeing youngster. She would have been willing to swear that José Mercado was not a bad boy. Troubled, yes, and obviously now in trouble. She left the church, trying to draw as little attention as possible. She was well known as Martin's wife and for her own outreach as well. She squeezed the numerous hands extended to her, and made it to the vestibule before the mass was finished. She ought not to have come to this mass. Besides her own unease, it was not fair to Dan, and encountering the monsignor on the church steps, she tried to think of an excuse for being there at that hour.

The monsignor had something else on his mind. "Did you notice the youngster flying out of the church? I tried to lay hold of him. Slippery as an eel. Do you know what he did? He spat out the sacrament. They're not being well taught, you know. That one should never have made his first communion."

Kate, not about to debate the boy's demeanor with the monsignor, gave a nod to indicate concern and escaped. Someone was following her. She knew an instant of fear before she recognized it was José. She waited for him and they walked in silence for almost another block before Kate finally said, "Do you want to tell me what's the matter?"

José shook his head and they walked on. He was wearing a fake leather jacket, frayed at the cuffs and at least two sizes too big for him; the T-shirt underneath was thin, the red apple on its front badly faded. His jeans were clean and his sneakers had been new at the start of the school year. His dark hair rose and fell as the wind tossed through it.

"Aren't you cold?" Kate asked. She was wishing herself that she had worn a sweater beneath her coat.

Again he shook his head. He wiped his nose on the back of his hand. They walked on.

They had almost reached Kate's building. She wondered if it was wise to let him know where she lived, and then decided, wise or not, it showed some respect for his fiery young person. Once in class she had boosted his ego by calling him a young Matisse and showing him pictures of the artist's windows. He took everything he did in class home with him after that. Or said he did. He liked to please her. He spoke English as well as any of the children. His mother spoke Spanish. His older brother spoke both languages, but beat José if he did not speak English. José loved him, anyway.

Reaching the entryway to the town house where she and Martin lived, she told the boy that this was where she must leave him and proposed to shake his hand. "Where do you live, José?"

He jerked his head toward the north, and ignored the hand she offered him so that Kate quickly withdrew it. "You should go home now and not catch cold," she said.

"Why you don't go to communion this morning?" he blurted out, the first words he had spoken to her all the way home.

Kate was stunned. When she was his age, the lie would have been so simple: I broke my fast. That didn't matter any more. Now all she could do was fall back on authority. "You don't ask questions like that of older people, José. Go home now." As though he were a stray dog. When she turned from him, she saw Martin watching from the window of his study. She waved. He nodded appreciatively, as though he took for granted she would be accompanied by a child or children. When she looked back from the vestibule, José had disappeared.

"I saw it with my own eyes," the monsignor said, waiting in the vestry with Morrissey while he disrobed.

Morrissey removed the stole, touched it to his lips and laid it away in the drawer. "I'm sorry, Monsignor, but the boy didn't receive communion at all. From what I could tell, his mother was insisting that he do, and he was determined not to."

The monsignor grunted. "Everybody wanted to stone him, as though the mass wasn't half circus already. Mind, I'm not criticizing the new liturgy." He waited until Morrissey had pulled the amice over his head. "Was it you or the Almighty he was boycotting, do you think?"

The wild old fox, Morrissey thought. "It might have been me. We had an altercation of sorts when you sent me to sit in for Mrs. Knowles the other day."

The monsignor took longer to respond than Morrissey could handle, uneasy as he was at having even mentioned Kate's name. "I've never been very good with the children, as you know."

"Were you never a child yourself, Dan?"

The use of his name eased Morrissey's discomfort. "I spent most of my youth in fear of my father."

"So you've said. A strapping fellow like you?"

"'Mark my words, laddy,' he'd say, 'I'll bring you down to my size one of these days.' And God knows, he tried."

The monsignor shook his head. "Well, I'm glad it's

you the youngster's mad at and not the Lord. He'll get over it without damaging his faith. But they do hold a grudge, don't they?" he added, presumably of the Hispanic people.

Morrissey was holding a grudge himself against the youngster who, he felt, had deliberately intended to humiliate him. He had brought hate to the altar with him. It shone from his eyes. If he had said it aloud, it could not have been more clear. The priest could be grateful for one thing: if he had not been holding the sacrament in his hands, he'd have been hard put not to shake the boy till his teeth rattled. Even now it was hard for him to thank the Lord for getting in the way. But the monsignor left him, and before he went out of the church himself, he stepped into the sanctuary and said a prayer of contrition.

That afternoon he walked over to the Jesuit parish a few blocks from St. Ambrose. It had been some time since he had gone to confession. Sitting with his confessor, he named as the offense for which he was most deeply sorry his intense dislike for a child in the parish school. The Jesuit wanted to know if he had ever touched the boy. Morrissey told how close he had come to striking him.

"That's not what I had in mind," the other priest said.

"No," Morrissey said, "it's not like that." He completed his confession without ever mentioning adultery or the breaking of his vow of celibacy.

Kate next met with the children the following Tuesday. She had put in for a bus to transport them now that the days were getting short. It would not be available until later in the week, so she decided to drive them home in her own car since she expected to use it later.

Meanwhile, she chided them gently: they ought not to go off on their own as had happened on Friday.

"The padre say 'Get out!'" José said.

"I don't think that's so, is it?" She looked from one child to the next.

A lot of little heads nodded that it was. Annabelle volunteered to explain. "José tore up my picture and Father Morrissey slapped him."

"Right here," José said, pointing to his cheek. "I tell my brother, and he say, 'Next time you tell me, and I take care the *gringo* priest.'"

"He makes us all stand up and march around the room," someone else volunteered.

"He say I don't have to go to boys' room. He makes me piss on floor," José added.

"That's enough," Kate said. If she had been told at the moment that the children were possessed by demons, she'd have believed it. Or was it Dan of whom they'd taken possession? Something had happened in her ten- or fifteen minute absence that day that had thrown them into chaos. She set them to making mobiles, having brought a model from her studio at home.

When she was helping José, she saw that he was looking at her, not at the supposed-to-be mobile. "The priest come today?" he asked finally.

"Not that I'm expecting, José. But then I didn't expect him on Friday either. The monsignor sent him."

"How come?"

"Because the monsignor wanted to see me. Now pay attention or you won't be able to do this by yourself."

José had one more question: "Why you teach us like this?"

"Now let me ask a question, José Mercado: Why are you asking me all these questions?"

He turned his sweetest smile on her. The shyness of it had always beguiled her. "I like you," he said.

She was less than beguiled at the moment. More cunning than beguilement, she thought, and that was distressing. To what purpose? The phrase, *the gringo priest,* stayed with her. "If you really like me, you will make me a perfect mobile."

And with the use of teeth and tongue as well as fingers, he made one that almost hung in balance.

Kate could not make up her mind whether or not to mention Morrissey's misadventure with the children to him. The variation in their stories and his was troublesome. She did not like to ask him outright if he had struck the boy, even though she could not believe that he had done it.

After delivering the children that afternoon she drove around until she found a parking place on the street some distance east. She told Morrissey where the car was when he phoned. They planned to meet there after he had said the rosary at a wake a few blocks away. Martin was in Washington preparing for an early morning meeting. He was not due home until the next evening, but meetings could be canceled and the anxiety of having Morrissey in the house at night was too much. The phantom face, as it sometimes did now, reappeared in her mind's eye after she had given a few minutes' thought to the possible emergency measures if Martin should return to find Dan there. She could pretend, for example, sudden illness so that she had wanted a priest and phoned the rectory. Again she heard her own heartbeat and thought of pounding feet. She tried to stare through the image. It was too bright, featureless, but it would not go away. She finally escaped it by going into Martin's study and re-reading a letter from her son that she had left on her husband's desk. Her forehead was moist. If she could not control her own imagination, what chance had she of carrying off an emergency deception?

Morrissey lingered at the wake longer than he would have chosen to, but the family were longtime members of St. Ambrose, among the few, like the Knowles, who were generations deep in the neighborhood. He knew his popularity among them. More than once he had been told that he was one of theirs. Their generosity and participation in causes he championed recommended him to certain archdiocesan committees and to the occasional chaplainship. Striding along the streets to where Kate was waiting for him, he thought of the jeopardy in which their affair was placing him, and put it out of mind instantly. Once. Once in his life, he told himself, he would know sexual joy, and be the better priest for its denial ever after.

The car was warm when he climbed in alongside her. Their embrace was long and deep. "Oh, my God," he said, after a moment. "I needed that." Then: "Where can we go?"

"I know a place," Kate said.

She drove down and across town to the waterfront in the Twenties, where a few cars were parked, well-spaced apart.

"Isn't this where the gays hang out?" he asked.

"Yes."

He shuddered within his topcoat as he thought about what was going on in those other cars. "Let's get the hell out of here."

"Any suggestions?" Kate asked when they had driven in and around the Village in silence for a few minutes. She parked in front of a fire hydrant.

"Isn't Martin in Washington?"

"He's supposed to be," she said.

"In other words, you'd rather risk us getting caught in a police raid on Sodom."

"It is tacky, isn't it?" Kate said in bitter sarcasm.

Things went from bad to worse as time ran ahead of them and frustration mounted. Morrissey accused her of flirting with the monsignor, something he had only vaguely thought about until now, as her way of diverting the old man from their interest in one another. It opened the opportunity for Kate to ask him just what had happened with the children the previous Friday. "*Did* you strike José?"

"He's a dirty little liar if he says I did. Believe me, I wanted to, and he had it coming, but I caught myself in time. He's a troublemaker, Kate, and you'll be sorry if you coddle him. He's got ideas about us right now—the way some kids his age catch on to people when their prurient little minds are waking up."

"Prurient," Kate repeated.

"You know what I mean."

"Yes, Dan. I think I do. Now tell me what happened in church on Sunday."

"You should know better than to come to that mass, Kate."

"What happened?" she repeated.

"He refused to take communion from me. Made fists of his hands. His mouth was a steel trap. Kate, these Hispanic kids are so far ahead of us in sexual awareness, you've got to be careful with them."

"I will," she said.

But Morrissey was sure she'd take the youngster's side against him. It was incredible that one little black-eyed peasant could destroy something as beautiful as what he and Kate had between them. In no way would he let it happen. He laid his hand on hers. "Kate, could you teach me how to love children the way you've taught me how to love?"

José turned up at art class on Friday showing signs of either having been in a fight or having been abused. The visible marks were a purpling bruise on his cheek and a cut in his lip that bled in his one attempt to smile. Kate's inclination was to put an arm around him. She thought of Morrissey's counsel not to coddle him, but that was not what restrained her. There was a watchfulness about the boy, and she felt that to show concern might put him to flight. The other children shied away from him. They gave him more work room at the table than he needed. In fact, he didn't need work room at all. He simply sat there and did nothing except pluck at the edges of his drawing book with dirty fingernails, as though he could not wait for the class to end.

That afternoon saw the first run of the minibus Kate had arranged for. She shepherded the youngsters onto it herself, a noisy lot, and only at the last minute discovered that José was not among them. It was Annabelle who gave her the clue as to where he might be. Kate sent the bus on and went back into the school building. Sure enough, beneath a closed toilet door in the boys' room, a pair of nearly new sneakers were to be seen.

"José, it's Mrs. Knowles. The others have gone. I'll take you home myself if you like."

Silence.

"José?"

"No."

"No what?"

"No, *grácias*."

"They'll close up the building soon. The custodian will make you leave."

He came out then. "I not go home," he said.

"Let's talk about it," Kate said.

They went back to the classroom and Kate turned on the lights she had extinguished when they'd left. Dan was right. It was a dreary place, especially without the children. Kate sat on the table, positioning herself between him and the door. The boy stood, his hands folded over his fly.

"Is it your brother?" Kate asked gently.

"What you know?" His eyes challenged her.

"I know he hurts you badly sometimes."

She decided that was not what he had feared she might know. She waited.

"You no tell the *padre*?" he said finally.

"Why would I tell him?"

"Because . . . because, you know."

Kate did not follow up. She was remembering his one question Sunday: *Why you not go to communion?* "What did happen to you, José?"

His eyes grew large and round as he began to tell her. "The big old building near my house? The doors . . . boom, boom, boom, boom . . ." He gestured a row of doors such as sometimes line the street where a building is being demolished. "The windows broke."

Kate nodded. She could visualize the building and

knew its approximate location. A new housing project was about to get under way on that whole block.

"My brother, I see him meet his girl, so I no get on the school bus. I follow them. I no come to school today. They go in this building. I go in and listen. Where they go? Then I hear them. I know what they doing. *¿Sí?*"

"Go on," Kate said.

"Then she scream. Terrible, and Raffie swear. He call her bad names. She no scream no more, and pretty soon I hear Raffie come running. I hide so he don't see me, but he no look. He run out. So I run out too. Across the street he look back and see me. When he catches me, he hit me. He say I get hit worse if I tell. I promise to no tell, but he hit me more." José pointed to his lip. "First I go home and hide in basement. Then I go upstairs. Raffie no there. I watch TV till I come here."

"José, do you know the girl?"

"She Rafael's girlfriend."

"Do you know her name?"

He shook his head, but Kate suspected that he did.

Whether it was the right moment or the wrong one, it was the moment at which Morrissey appeared in the doorway. She put one last question to the boy before acknowledging the priest's presence. "Have you seen the girl since?"

José did not answer. He was staring at the priest defiantly.

Kate looked 'round. "Good afternoon, Father."

Morrissey, who had approached the room without making a sound, had been listening outside the door. Without responding to Kate's greeting, he said, "Don't you think we should go and see if she's still there, José?"

"I no want to go there, Father."

"But suppose the police say you have to go?" The priest took a few tentative steps into the room.

"I don't know where. I forget," José said.

Morrissey repeated Kate's question: "Did you ever see the girl again?"

José made a break for the door. Kate almost intercepted him, but Morrissey caught her arm and held her until the boy was gone.

"You have no right to interfere," Kate said. "This is my place."

"So we're talking about rights now. I didn't know they went with a relationship like ours. Kate, that boy was lying to you. He's got you in the palm of his hand and he knows it. You must not get us involved."

"I had no intention of getting us involved."

"You don't know what he'll say he saw or who he'll say it to. Suppose he says he's seen us together in some compromising place or situation?"

"But he hasn't, and who would believe him?"

"You'd be surprised. I didn't strike him, but that's his story, and I think you, for one, bought it."

Kate thought of José's brother; what he'd do to "the *gringo* priest." He had been told something certainly.

"He's a good liar, Kate."

"A better one than you or me? And is that what's important now? We should forget the girl. Is that it? Even if she's lying half-dead in some wreck of a building?"

"Frankly, I don't think there is a girl."

"Do you care?"

"If I thought there was a girl, yes. Then I'd say we should find a telephone right now and call the police."

Kate thought about it. "Do you think that's what he wanted me to do?"

"Oh, no." Morrissey gave a small, dry laugh. "It's what he's afraid I'll do. Kate, ask yourself: Why did he come to you with this story?"

"You tell me," she said.

Morrissey thought for a long moment about what he would say. "I'll give it a shot," he said. "He's made up a story—a street story, common as dirt, as close as he could come to telling you what's in his mind."

"About us?" Kate said, incredulous.

"You asked me to tell you, and now you'll listen to the whole thing. I can't say what triggered his imagination, but he knew from the moment he saw our hands touch when I took the scissors from you that there was something going on between us." Morrissey threw up his hands. "Maybe he's warning you—danger ahead! I don't know."

"Don't be angry, Dan."

"I'm not angry. I'm ashamed, if you want to know."

Ashamed, Kate thought, another word for guilt.

"I was a child just like him," Morrissey went on. "In adolescence I grew in prurience. My father tried to beat it out of me. Instead he beat it in. I fled to the priesthood. I thought it was my penance. It was my salvation."

Kate slipped down from the table and offered her hands, caution be damned. He shook his head, smiled a little and left her. She heard the click of the tunnel door.

She sat again for a few minutes, thinking.

Had their affair been inevitable, a kind of Satanic justice to be satisfied after all these years? And if it was over, was he free now of the demon guilt forever? It was not in the nature of man. Or woman. She thought of the phantom face that had seemed to pursue her, to accuse her. No. That was not its mission. It followed, sometimes with a rhythmic beat, like the Hound of Heaven.

She left the school and went into the church by the side door, the only one left open at that hour of the day. The high-intensity lights were focused on the Crucifixion mural, the artist himself straddling a plank in the scaffolding as he worked overtime. He was almost finished. With the Lord's face and one of the women's restored, Melodosi was studying his work on the other Mary. Even before he looked down at her, Kate knew his half-familiar face to be that of the phantom she had chosen to pursue her.

She moved on to a pew in a darkened place. It had been a long time since she had prayed with her heart and mind, and on her knees. A simple prayer: *Lord, I need help.* She left the church determined to go to the police with José's story, but when she reached the street, she saw two nuns waiting to be admitted at the St. Ambrose convent door. She got to them in time to enter the building with them, and very shortly Sister Josephine Reilly came to her in the parlor. As soon as the nun saw who it was, she said, "I know, it's about José Mercado again."

"I just have a question," Kate said. "Was he absent from school this morning?"

"No," the young nun said. "As soon as I saw him in first class, I sent him to the infirmary, but bad luck that it was, the nurse was out today. I cleaned him up a bit myself between classes."

"Did he tell you what happened to him?"

The nun gave a great rolling shrug. "I think he said his brother beat him up—was it for talking back to their mother? Who knows with José?"

Who knows indeed, Kate thought.

A week passed before she heard from Morrissey. He

called to say he was going upstate to the Trappist monastery on retreat. "Kate . . ." She could hear the deep intake of breath.

"You don't need to say anything, Dan."

"I'm grateful to you for understanding."

"And I to you, Father Morrissey."

Thomas Chastain

TÊTE-À-TÊTE

ARTHUR WHIDDEN WAS EATING LUNCH ALONE IN A SMALL CAFÉ in his neighborhood on the Upper East Side of Manhattan.

He was accustomed to being alone since his wife had died at the beginning of the year and he had retired from his job a month earlier. He had worked as a bookkeeper for thirty years for an import-export company on West Thirty-first Street and after his retirement had moved into a small walk-up apartment on First Avenue.

He always brought with him to lunch the three daily New York newspapers, the *Times*, the *Daily News*, and the *Post*.

On this day in early June he was reading the *Times* when he overheard a conversation at the next table between an elderly woman and a young woman who looked to be in her twenties. The woman appeared to be in her seventies, quite attractive and stylishly dressed; aging had been kind to her, Whidden thought.

He had overheard enough of their conversation to know that the older woman had recently hired the younger to be her companion.

"I think we'll be compatible," she said.

"Yes, ma'am."

"You know, my dear, I've not been lonely for much of my life—until recently. I was lucky in my marriages. Three husbands and each left me well off when he died. I was lucky, too, because all three of them were extremely *virile* men. I'm sure you know what I mean, my dear."

She went on to explain that after her last husband died she decided she didn't ever want to be married again.

"But there was that void in my life. No man, no one to be with me. After a while talking to my widow friends I discovered that the older woman-younger man relationship was now acceptable to society. What's more, that many such relationships came about when the older woman hired the younger man as a companion."

Arthur Whidden was now listening to every word of the conversation at the next table.

The woman said that for the most part this arrangement had worked out satisfactorily. Surprisingly, in addition, more than a few of the younger men actually were attracted to her and were as virile as her husbands had been.

"Now and then," she added, "there were minor problems when the time came to end one of the relationships and the young man didn't want it ended. But an expensive farewell present or a certain, well, termination payment was enough to end the arrangement."

She said she was discussing these relationships because the last young man who had been her companion had become especially difficult to get rid of.

"I sent him on a paid vacation to California and I told him I needed a change and was going to hire a female companion. He went to California, where he is now. But he's been phoning me regularly, saying he doesn't want us to break up. I don't think he'll cause any trouble when he gets back. But I thought you should know."

The conversation ended, the older woman paid the luncheon check and they left the café.

Arthur Whidden watched them go, amused by the conversation he'd overheard and then thought no more about it.

It was a week later when Whidden was having lunch and reading the *Daily News* that he saw the story on page three.

The headline was. WEALTHY WIDOW FOUND STRANGLED.

The story reported that Elizabeth Denise had been found murdered in her luxury apartment on East Seventy-ninth Street. According to the police statement, the woman, a widow, had lived alone. Money and jewels were missing from the apartment and the police had no suspects as yet.

Arthur Whidden immediately thought of the conversation he'd overheard a week or so earlier between the older widow and the new companion she had just hired. He remembered the woman talking about possible trouble from the male companion she had dismissed. He supposed it was possible that the police didn't know about either of these people in the widow's life.

His first instinct was to go to a phone and call the police and give them such information as he had. He quickly put that thought aside, telling himself he simply didn't want to become involved in a murder case at this point in his life. At the very least, after he had told the police what he'd overheard, he'd have to testify later at the trial.

That night he slept restlessly; he was distressed by the knowledge that he wasn't being a good citizen in not talking to the police and yet was still hesitant to get involved in the case.

The next morning he was up early and bought the three newspapers. Both the *Daily News* and the *Post* had accounts of the widow's murder, although there was not much new from the previous day's story. The papers reported that police were questioning other tenants in the apartment building and the doorman. The last line of the story read: "Sergeant Ed Ambrose, Homicide, 19th Precinct, who is in charge of the investigation, asks anyone who has knowledge of the murder to please contact the precinct."

Arthur Whidden knew it was foolish for him to believe that that line had been directed at him, but he did, and it only increased his sense of guilt. He told himself the police would solve the case on their own, sooner or later.

Two more days passed without any mention in the papers about the case. And then on the following day there was a brief story far back in the *Post* stating that police had made no progress in their investigation of the murder of Elizabeth Denise.

Whidden was miserable. He wished he'd never overheard the damn conversation and yet he knew that as long as the police failed to solve the murder, he was going to be torn apart by what he knew was his responsibility to do and by his reluctancy to do it.

Finally, after a long walk through Central Park, he determined the action he was going to take. He decided he would use a pay phone and make an anonymous call to the homicide sergeant mentioned in the newspaper clipping he'd saved, Sergeant Ed Ambrose.

He would call and as soon as Sergeant Ambrose answered, he would make it clear that he wasn't to be interrupted. He would repeat what he'd heard of the conversation that day in the café and then hang up quickly before they could trace the call.

He rehearsed what he would say as he walked through the park.

"Please don't interrupt me or I'll hang up. I think I have information that may help you solve the murder of Elizabeth Denise. I am not involved. But you should look for a young woman who was just hired to be a companion to Mrs. Denise. Also see if you can locate a male companion recently fired by Mrs. Denise. I am just an interested citizen and I don't have any more than I've told you now."

He went over the words a few times in his mind and then sat on a bench in the park and wrote them down on the back of an envelope.

The palms of his hands were wet with perspiration when he made the call from an outdoor phone on Central Park West, and asked for Sergeant Ambrose.

"Ambrose, Homicide. Help you?"

As Whidden started to talk, Ambrose said, "What's your name, please, and phone number."

Whidden's voice was shaking when he said, "Didn't you hear me say if you interrupt me, I'll hang up?"

"All right, all right. Go on."

Whidden read rapidly from the words he'd written on the back of the envelope and dropped the phone back on the hook. He looked around him nervously and then walked away quickly.

All right, he told himself, he'd done all he could do, all he was going to do.

There was nothing about the case in the news for several days. Then, at the beginning of the next week the *Daily News* ran a story on page three reporting that police were questioning a suspect after receiving an anonymous tip from an informer. The suspect's name wasn't given but she was identified as a young woman recently hired by the victim. Sergeant Ambrose was quoted as asking that the person who had anonymously phoned the tip in come forward.

Whidden no longer felt any guilt about avoiding his duty. He had given the police what they needed, now they were on their own. Nevertheless, he still felt slightly sleazy by being even peripherally involved in a murder case and he thought how unfair it was that he had overheard that accursed conversation. He knew it was only mild paranoia that made him feel as if the police were seeking him. Still, he remained uneasy.

Two weeks later, for the first time since that day in the café, he felt relieved. All three newspapers reported that the police had solved the murder of Elizabeth Denise. The young woman who had been hired as a companion had confessed. She had killed the widow and stolen the money and jewels. According to police the woman had been working with a man who had been a male companion to Elizabeth Denise before she had fired him recently. He had then had the woman apply for the job, and the widow, not knowing about the relationship, had hired her. The woman and the man had split the money and jewels between them. Both were indicted for robbery and murder.

Whidden was surprised at the outcome of the murder case but, finally, pleased that he had contributed to the solution. Some months later, when the trial was held, Whidden was tempted to attend the sessions but could never quite get up the nerve to go any closer to the proceedings.

The trial lasted two weeks and the jury returned a guilty verdict. Both were sentenced to twenty-five years to life in prison.

On the day of the first snowfall of the year Arthur Whidden went to lunch alone at the small café in his neighborhood.

He had his three newspapers with him and was reading the *Times* when he felt a sudden chill. He had just overheard part of a conversation at the table next to him. He dropped the newspaper and turned, staring in astonishment at the older woman and the younger woman, the same two women he had overheard talking back in June. The older woman wasn't dead, the younger hadn't killed her.

The murder had been of some other widow in Manhattan, which really probably wasn't all that surprising since there had been other such arrangements, as the older woman had once said.

Ah, well, Whidden thought, even though he had been wrong about this particular widow and her companion, there was a sense of poetic justice in that what he had told the police had helped solve the other murder.

Warren Murphy

A CRY FROM THE HEART

AGE WOULD, IN THE END, SOLVE ALL HIS PROBLEMS. OF THAT, Douglas Brentley had been so certain that he had persevered through all the dark nights of the soul when he was sure that his life was being wasted, being ripped from him one endless day at a time by a woman he neither loved nor liked, but who had nevertheless, through some maniacal quirk of malevolent fate, wound up as his life's partner.

Age.

If I just live long enough, things will somehow work out. She will leave me. She will die. Maybe I will die. Something. Anything.

Years before, during one of his infrequent business trips outside Manhattan, some anonymous face at some nameless bar had asked Douglas Brentley when he had known his marriage was a failure.

"Between the 'I' and the 'do,'" he answered. It sounded flip but he had remembered the exact moment. His wife's family had never seemed to like him and during the wedding ceremony, he had glanced back into the church and seen the bride's relatives, their pale eyes staring at him from their square, stolid faces. *Stop looking at me as if I were an alien,* he wanted to shout. And then he realized with horror that of course he was not an alien. *I am one of them now. I am just like them.*

Douglas Brentley had married Madelaine Stepko because he was thirty years old and lonely. It was only later that he understood there were none so lonely as those who had given up the right to be alone.

Maddie's motive in marrying Doug Brentley was unknown to him but he suspected that she was worried about spinsterhood, he was available and reasonably presentable, and he was responsible and would probably always make a good living, no matter how much he hated being an accountant.

Naturally, though, Maddie would not admit to any such lackluster motive. She had married Doug because she loved him. *Loved* him. She cooked him Hamburger Helper out of love. She did his laundry to prove her love. She submitted to him physically out of love. Love, love, love, love, love, love. It was all love and kissy-poo, loudly proclaimed, incessantly stated until the very word "love" made his stomach churn.

It was all "darling" and "dear" and "honey" and "sweetheart" and for the first few months of their marriage, he had accepted—perhaps even enjoyed a little—being so clearly the center of someone else's life, but that had quickly palled.

It was not that Maddie was a terrible wife. Probably, he once thought, she was average. An average bad cook, average overweight, average not-too-bright, and average no-worse-than-most. His problem with her was that he had expected her to be a human being on her own and she was not. Having recited the marriage vows, she had become a WIFE, and that was clearly how she planned to define herself for the rest of her life. He had not expected that her life would be somehow so empty that she could fill it only with him and then with more of him.

She suffocated him, apparently in the mistaken notion that this was some kind of Rockwellian marriage ideal. He was never free, never away from her. If he traveled out of town, she called his hotel room at odd hours, just to say, "Hello, darling, I miss you," but, in truth, just to check up on who he was with.

He once thought of getting one of the girls from his office to make a sexy tape recording that he could play over the phone when Maddie called. But he never did. There were so many things that he never did.

In the first year of his marriage, he learned that Maddie secretly opened mail addressed to him. He would come home from work at night and find that envelopes had been steamed open and then reglued.

For what, he wondered. The only mail he got was an occasional invitation to a class reunion or somebody trying to get a donation to charity. Still, possessiveness was one thing. Jealousy, too. But this was quite another and quite intolerable. So he bought scented sky-blue stationery, wrote a big question mark on one of the deckle-edged sheets, and mailed it to himself, disguising his handwriting.

A few nights later when he came home, he saw the blue envelope on the table in his pile of mail. He made it a point to take his mail into the bathroom to read. Sure enough, the envelope had been opened and resealed. He locked the door behind himself and took a long time inside. Before he came out, he tore the little blue note up into small pieces and flushed them down the toilet.

"Any interesting mail, darling?" Maddie asked him, rather too casually.

"Usual stuff," he replied and walked away.

Actually, he didn't know what he had expected. Did he want her to admit that she was reading his mail, to justify his losing his temper and yelling? Probably not, he conceded, because then he'd eventually have to confess that he sent himself the question mark on perfumed paper. And while he might win a debating point with that tactic, it would have exposed his impotence, the sad fact being that there was no one in the world who would send him a personal letter.

A week later, he sent himself another letter in a plain white envelope. Inside was a single sheet he had typed on his office typewriter. It read:

> Page 11,
> A Novel in Progress.
>
> "Keep your eyes to yourself, you fat, sloppy beast," he said. "You were born twins and never separated."

That must have galled her because he never did find that letter on the kitchen table in the evening. But she said nothing about it and neither did he.

And after all, why bother? It didn't matter. Nothing mattered. She would keep on opening and reading his mail. He gave up and rented a post office box. He had had it for fifteen years and all he ever got in it was college catalogs from NYU's Extension Division, addressed to "Boxholder."

Nobody wrote him.

Why should they? I am one of the Legion of the Lost, the Squadron of the Damned. Or just yet another man married to a woman he hates.

Confrontation had worked no better than obliqueness. He had embarked on loud noisy arguments but Maddie turned out to have a marked talent for viciously personal dispute and it was in one of those set-tos that he had learned for the first time that his hair was thinning. He stopped arguing for fear of further horrors that might lie ahead.

Finally, he sank into a living coma. He said nothing and did nothing and if he felt anything, he took pains not to let Maddie know about it. He lived. He bathed, he went to work, and always he wished he were somewhere else.

Someday. Someday it will change.

He backed off from his wife. She seemed not to notice, instead choosing to suffocate him with even more affectionate words. But maybe she *had* noticed for it was about that time that her "slight weight problem" became full-fledged obesity and she began to develop the neurotic asthma that had her in the hospital every few months.

Perhaps if there had been children . . . but there had not been. Maddie had been sure it was his fault—after all, her five siblings had managed to spawn a total of seventeen revolting children, without one chin among them—and she had sent him for a series of humiliating medical tests.

When those proved that he was physically capable of fatherhood, Maddie immediately dropped the subject, at least for the time being, although he knew she would hint darkly to their neighbors that there was some indeterminate malady in Douglas's genes that made childbearing out of the question for her.

The neighbors began to look at him sorrowfully, as if he were a leper. Douglas no longer cared. His coma would protect him. And age would make him well again.

Time heals all wounds. He took solace in that and then one day he was thirty-five, and then another day he was forty and now he was almost forty-five years old and age had turned out to be another empty promise, full of everything, signifying nothing.

Finally, Douglas Brentley decided that if age could not be counted on for relief, he would have to do something else.

The big problem was what.

The obvious solution, much favored by sour husbands, was to get himself a mistress but Brentley had no talent in that area. There had been a young woman at work, Annie Jessup, with whom he had been quite taken. She had been kind and gentle to him and several times he had taken her to dinner. At their second dinner he realized that he was truly in love with her. But they had never been lovers. Annie was old-fashioned and would not be a party to cheating on someone's wife. "Growing up in an orphanage makes you honor real marriages," she had said. And he had respected her for it.

She was frail. Some kind of heart problem made her

tired a lot, but she was unfailingly good humored. She listened, really listened, to his silly dreams of wanting to be a cowboy, wanting to travel the world on a tramp steamer, and she topped them with silly dreams of her own, spoken breathlessly in her soft, little-girl voice.

And then one day she did not come to work. When he called her, he learned that her heart problem was worsening and she could not work any more. A few weeks later, he called her again but her phone had been disconnected.

Even now, several years later, he could still picture her vividly, see her white-blonde hair swirling about her face, still remember her warm lopsided smile and he knew that he had somehow lost the only real love of his life. Collecting a mistress would be like cheating on Annie, not just on his wife, and he had no taste for it either. A mistress was not a workable solution.

Just picking up and leaving was out of the question also. He had too many books, too many trinkets laboriously collected over too many years, too many jujus. He liked his rent-controlled apartment very much. Where would he go? His work was in Manhattan. The few things that made life almost tolerable were in Manhattan. How could he leave?

Leaving would inevitably lead to divorce and he had never known any man to survive a divorce with all his faculties intact. He thought this through carefully one night when Maddie had gone to the hospital with her latest psychosomatic ailment. It would never work. His apartment would be gone. As a final indignity, some of her brainless, chinless relatives would move in with her. They would get their paw prints on *his* books, stare uncomprehendingly at *his* prints and paintings. He would be living in some roach motel and Maddie would have riparian rights on his blood until the day one of them died. And she would never die. They were long-lived, her family. Ugly but long-lived. None of them ever died.

They sleep in caskets on a handful of earth from a chicken coop. They eat human beings for lunch. They are the undead.

Maddie had warned him. "You know, darling, I think our organs must be stronger than those of other folks. Everybody in the family lives to be a hundred or more. If you took out one of our brains, I think it'd live on by itself."

You could tell it didn't age because there wouldn't be a wrinkle on it.

So divorce was out and so was suicide. One of his college economics professors had once said that suicide was "just another extreme way of trying to improve one's life condition." That had seemed funny then; everything seemed funny to a twenty year old. But suicide was forever and he refused to give Maddie the satisfaction of knowing that she had driven him over the edge.

No. No matter how he twisted it and looked at it and studied it, there was obviously only one solution.

Murder.

It was so clearly correct that he wondered why he hadn't really considered it before.

Murder. But when? How?

Of course he would not kill her at the hospital where there were too many people trained in bringing others back from the brink of death. No. He would think this one through and do it absolutely perfectly. Maybe the time had come.

* * *

He stood in the hallway outside Maddie's hospital room, dreading the thought of entering. She would call him "darling," he would call her "dear." They would talk meaningless nonsense until the room had filled with treacle. It would rise to his ankles, then his knees, and then it would be up into his nostrils, suffocating him, and he would have to get out of there, at least for a few minutes, and she would be hurt that he had come to visit her in the hospital and had not spent every moment at her bedside, staring lovingly into her eyes.

He was carrying a bag of popcorn. She lived for popcorn, claiming it had great value as part of a weight control program.

Yes. It's called the fat-and-popcorn diet. Call the Mayo Clinic.

"Hello, dear. I have your popcorn."

"You're late, darling. It's 1:05 and they've had visitors here already for ten minutes and I missed you so." Her voice was the usual coarse, guttural whine.

"Traffic," he said. "How are you feeling?"

"How should I feel, hon? My lungs don't work. They always feel like they're bursting. This asthma is terrible. But I want to get out of here. I want to get back to my home. To my husband. I want to be there to take care of you. I just bet you haven't had a good meal since I came in here. If I'm not around, then no one will take care of you."

"I know, dear."

"Come and sit by me, darling. I hate it in this place. I need to see a friendly face."

I'll go out and see if I can hire someone with a friendly

face. My face is the face of the man who's going to kill you.

"Yes, dear," he said, fascinated by her two-handed assault on the popcorn.

Brentley sat. He listened to the stale complaints about the food and the way the nurses always woke you up in the middle of the night to see if you were sleeping, about the way the doctor came in only once a day and then only for ten seconds and for this we have to pay hundreds and hundreds of dollars, and how she was glad the other patient in the semi-private room had been moved out because she had been a terrible snorer and Maddie had not been able to get a wink of sleep.

Then how the hell did the nurses wake you up to see if you were sleeping?

"Yes, dear."

She had figured it all out. If a doctor came in for one minute and his share of the daily hospital bill was $150, then he was making $9,000 an hour and in a twelve-hour day, if he had enough sick patients, he could make $108,000 a day. "Somebody should do something, honey."

If I were the doctor and they gave me the whole $108,000, I still wouldn't spend more than a minute with you because you make me sick.

"Yes, dear."

It must be close to twenty minutes now. Always, at twenty minutes, she closes her eyes, as if she's exhausted just by the act of talking to me. When she does, I'll sneak out for a cigarette. I'll smoke two. I have to get out of here. It doesn't matter if I smoke two or three or ten, when I come back, the reaction will still be the same. "I missed you, darling. I was lying here by myself, all alone, and I missed you so." Good, fatso, but when I come to blow your brains out, count on it, I won't miss you.

On cue, she closed her eyes and Brentley started to count to ten before he moved, but quit at three and ran out the door into the corridor.

Manhattan, he thought, had gotten as lunatic as California so there was no place to smoke inside the hospital building. He went outside, near the emergency room entrance, for a cigarette and to think warm wonderful thoughts about murder.

He was on his third cigarette when an ambulance pulled up to the entrance. Idly, he watched three paramedics spill from the back of the vehicle, drop the wheels on a gurney carrying a patient, and move toward the automatic entry doors.

The blanket slipped back and he saw the back of the patient's head.

The hair.

It was white blonde, thin, long and straight. Annie Jessup. He knew, without seeing the patient's face, that it was Annie.

Brentley tossed away his cigarette and followed the attendants into the hospital. One held an oxygen mask over the patient's face as the other two wheeled it through the hospital corridor.

He still could not see her face. The patient did not move.

The attendants looked at him with disapproval as he walked alongside them and even entered the same elevator with them.

The one holding the oxygen fixed him with a questioning glance.

"A friend of the family," Brentley explained. "How is she?"

"Bad. Real bad."

"Heart again?"

"Yeah."

On the eighth floor, he got off, still following the attendants, until they passed through a door marked Intensive Care Unit and a starched nurse briskly told him that he would have to wait outside.

She pointed him back toward a small lounge, where he waited for a few minutes, then went down to the sixth floor to his wife.

"Where were you, darling? I was awake the longest time and you weren't here."

"Sorry, dear."

I know you've been awake. The bag of popcorn is empty. You eat, therefore you are. At least for a while longer.

Somehow, he managed to struggle through the rest of the afternoon. When he finally extricated himself, he walked up to the eighth floor and sat in the lounge outside the ICU.

After a few minutes, a doctor came through the ICU door and Brentley intercepted him.

"I was wondering if you could help me, doctor. A friend of mine, Annie Jessup, was brought in a while ago. I wondered how she was."

The doctor was young and looked tired.

"Not too well, I'm afraid. She's been here a lot and her heart is just giving out. It's a congenital problem."

"What kind of chance does she have?" Brentley asked.

"She needs a transplant. If she's . . ." He paused and rubbed the back of one hand across his eyes. "Jesus, this is a terrible profession. I was about to say that if she's lucky, somebody'll die in an accident or whatever and she can get the heart. It's strange to talk about someone's good luck in the context of someone else dying."

"Not so strange," Brentley said.

He went to a nearby tavern, one of those shamrock-infested places that New York specialized in, and had four Scotch and waters. He needed time to think.

Annie's going to die. She's suffered all her life and now she's going to suffer some more and then she's going to die. I don't think people are meant to suffer, that some of them are put on earth just for that purpose. I don't think little fish are put in the seas just to feed big fish. I think there's more to life than that. And I think that a human being has to protest. If someone does something, just does something, then he can change not just his life but all the lives around him. That's what makes us all human beings.

He considered all that for a while and then thought: *What a wonderful rationalization for murder.*

He waited until evening visiting hours were almost over before going back to the hospital. He bought a bag of popcorn in a neighborhood market, filled his pocket with loose popcorn, and threw the rest of the bag in a corner trash can.

On the eighth floor, he went to the duty nurse.

"Doctor Johnson told me before that I could visit with Annie Jessup for a few minutes tonight. I'm her friend."

"Just for a few minutes," the nurse said briskly.

Annie was in an oxygen tent but she was awake and she smiled when she saw Brentley through the thick plastic curtain that covered her.

"If I've got to be here, it's good to wake up and see a friend," she said in a voice even softer than he remembered.

He sat in a chair next to her bed.

"I missed you, Annie."

"I missed you, too. We were good friends, weren't we?"

"We still are." He reached out and held her hand in his.

"And how's your wife?"

"Forget her. How are you feeling?"

"It won't be much longer. And then there'll be no more pain."

Brentley shook his head. "No, no. Don't feel that way. I spoke to the doctors. You've got a good chance."

"Not with this heart," she said.

He smiled at her and drew his face close to the tent. "But I'm going to get you a new one."

"They have a special at Gristede's?"

"No, I really am. And then you and I are going to be together. Really together."

She smiled and closed her eyes. "Dreams are nice."

He held her hand while she slept, until the nurse told him visiting hours were over.

Two floors down, the duty nurse was not at her desk. The corridor was empty and no one saw Brentley as he walked into room 6-C. Maddie seemed to be asleep. He glanced at the other bed; they had not yet put another patient into the room and it was still empty.

As he approached, Maddie awoke.

"Darling, you're here."

"It does so seem," he said softly.

"But why? You don't come at night. Of course, it's nice to see you, hon."

"I will be with you until the end of your days."

"You're smiling. I love it when you smile. You have a very nice smile."

"Yes, I do. I'd almost forgotten."

The empty bag of popcorn was still on the end table next to the bed. He told Maddie he would help adjust her pillow.

"It's all right the way it is, dear."

"No, dear, I want everything to be perfect," he said. "It's the least I can do for you after all you've done to me."

"*For* you," she said.

"To," he said as he reached over and pulled the pillow from under her head.

From the lobby of a nearby hotel, he called his wife's private phone at the hospital. He let the phone ring five times, then dialed the number again. After five more rings, he hung up, called the hospital switchboard and asked to be connected to the floor nurse.

"This is Douglas Brentley. My wife is in room 6-C. Is she all right? I've been trying to call her but there's no answer."

"Please hold on a moment."

It took about five minutes, but then her voice came back on. "I'm afraid Mrs. Brentley has taken a turn for the worse. Can you come right over, please?"

"I'll be right there."

A turn for the worse? God, don't tell me that she has been revived from the dead.

But of course Maddie truly was dead. Nurses just didn't have the authority to make death pronouncements over the telephone. That responsibility lay with doctors earning $108,000 a day and one of them dutifully broke the news to Brentley in a small waiting room at the hospital.

"How'd it happen? She seemed fine." Douglas choked back a sob.

"She had popcorn in her mouth. She must have been eating popcorn and some got lodged in her throat. And with her bad lungs, she just choked and suffocated. I'm sorry."

He turned to leave but Brentley stopped him.

"Doctor, there's a patient in the hospital waiting for a heart transplant."

"Yes?"

"I'd like her to have my wife's heart."

Quick, get the damn thing out of her before she comes back to life.

"Are you sure?"

Brentley lowered his eyes in a middling approximation of grief. "Quite sure," he said. "Maddie and I spoke about this many times. We always agreed we wanted to pass on the gift of life."

"That's a fine thing, Mr. Brentley," the doctor said. He almost skipped through the door. "I have to go notify people. Time is critical."

Isn't it, though?

The next week was a blur. But there are blurs and blurs and Brentley knew he would someday regard this as the time of The Happy Blur. He put up with his wife's relatives for a few days, marveling again at their tenacious hold on life despite the overwhelming scientific evidence that mutations almost never survive.

Then there were the nights at the funeral home,

culminating with the appearance of a minister who so eulogized Maddie that Brentley suspected the man had stumbled into the wrong wake.

And then he planted Maddie in the green rolling hills of a cemetery across the river in New Jersey. As he tossed the ceremonial handful of earth onto the casket, he was singing in his mind.

So long, it's been good to know you.

But I've got to be drifting along.

Every night he had called the hospital to ask after Annie's condition. Critical. Serious. Stable. Then satisfactory. He called the surgeon who confirmed that everything was going all right. The operation had been successful; now they must wait to make sure that Annie's body did not reject the heart.

It had better not, after all the trouble I went to to get it.

He had gotten rid of the last in-law, the last pseudo-friend, the last quasi-neighbor. The apartment finally was empty, save for himself. He poured himself a large Scotch on the rocks, congratulating himself on a job well done.

Murder. And he had done it.

It hadn't been age after all. It had been the sudden realization that his life would change only when he changed it. Age was irrelevant.

He could have done it all at thirty; he hadn't had to wait until he was forty-five. But, of course, he hadn't understood that at thirty. Maybe that was the real value of piling up years. Age made you smart enough to realize that age didn't really count.

There was a wonderful paradox in there somewhere but he was too happy to think about it. Paradoxes were for troubled minds to wrestle with, not the happy. He would send it in a note to Bob Dylan. Maybe Dylan could write a song about it.

Hell, maybe a few years from now, he himself would write a song about it. Maybe he'd become a rock-and-roll singer. Maybe he and Annie, free as birds, uncaged as the wind, would take to the road and follow the sun.

Brentley walked to a closet and took out a bag of golf clubs.

I will learn golf. No longer will it always rain when I try to play. Maybe I'll become a professional golfer. If I decide not to be a rock-and-roll singer. Whatever I want to do.

He sang aloud: "There are no strings on me."

No strings. Only freedom.

Freedom for me. Freedom for Annie. Together by choice. Together, but not one. Two who choose to travel the same road.

Tomorrow, he would be allowed to visit her at the hospital. She knew, of course, where the heart had come from. The surgeon had told her. And eventually, Brentley would tell her the whole truth.

But not until later, much later, when I know she can handle it, later when our life together is as important for her as it is for me. She'll understand. There's magic in the air and more magic to come.

He took a practice swing with his five iron. Then another. He would need golf lessons.

Hell, maybe I'll get so good, I'll give golf lessons. I don't have to stay an accountant. I'm free. Free, free, free, free, free, free. My own man, for once.

The telephone rang. He put down the golf club and

reached for the receiver and realized he was more than a little drunk.

He recognized Annie's voice instantly, even though it was darker and deeper than he had ever heard it before.

"Doug?"

"Yes, Annie, I'm here."

"Why are you there, darling? Why aren't you here? I hate it when I wake up and you're not here. Please, dear, come over now."

"I will, Annie. We have so much to talk about. I'll be over right away."

"I want you near me all the time, Doug. Hurry. My heart yearns for you, darling."

Before he left the apartment, he put the golf clubs back in the closet, and as he walked to the elevator he could hear the blood pounding in his brain, thumping loudly with each measured beat of his heart.

Mary Higgins Clark

THE PHONE RANG BUT ALVIRAH IGNORED IT. SHE AND WILLY had only been home long enough to unpack and already the answering machine had picked up six messages. They listened to them but agreed that tomorrow would be time enough to catch up with the outside world.

It's nice to be home, she thought happily as she stepped out onto the terrace of their Central Park South apartment and looked down at the park where now in late October the leaves had turned into a blazing rainbow of orange and crimson and yellow and magenta.

She went back inside and settled on the couch. Willy handed her a manhattan and carried his own to his big easy chair. He lifted his glass to her. "To us, honey."

Alvirah smiled fondly at him. "I have to say all that

sightseeing does wear me out," she said. "I'm going to rest for at least two weeks."

"Agreed." Willy nodded, then added sheepishly, "Honey, I still think riding those mules in Greece was a little much. I felt like a broken-down Hopalong Cassidy."

"You looked like the Lone Ranger," Alvirah assured him. "Willy, we've had so much fun, haven't we? If it weren't for the lottery I'd still be cleaning houses and you'd be fixing busted pipes."

They sat in silence marveling over the wonderful event that two years ago had made a clean sweep of their former life. The dates of their birthdays and their wedding anniversary were the numbers they'd always played, a dollar a week for ten years until the unbelievable moment when the lottery ticket with those numbers was pulled and they'd found themselves the sole winners of the forty-million-dollar prize.

Since then they'd bought this apartment on Central Park South, although they prudently hung onto their three-room, rent-stabilized place in Flushing just in case New York State went broke and quit making their annual two-million-dollar-less-taxes payment.

As Alvirah often said, "Willy, for us, the good life began at sixty." So far among their travels, they'd been to Europe three times, to South America once, had taken the trans-Siberian railroad from China to Russia and now had just returned from a cruise of the Greek Islands.

Alvirah no longer tinted her brick-red hair at home. When she put on that extra twenty pounds she went to the Cypress Point Spa in Pebble Beach where the owner, her friend Baroness Min von Schreiber, got her back into shape. Alvirah was a contributing columnist to the *New York Globe* and along the way had solved several crimes.

Willy, who was the spitting image of the legendary Tip O'Neill, now confined his plumbing activities to repairing pipes and faucets and toilets for people who couldn't afford to pay for repairs.

The phone rang. Alvirah glanced at it. "Don't be tempted," Willie begged. "We need to get our breath. It's probably Cordelia and she'll have a job for me."

Cordelia, the oldest of Willie's six surviving sisters—all of whom had entered the convent at age eighteen—was now pushing seventy and ran the family with a formidable hand. She was the superior of a small convent on the West Side and constantly called on Willy to repair ancient plumbing for the deserving poor whom she watched over.

They listened to the answering machine. It was Rhonda Alvirez, secretary of the Manhattan chapter of the Lottery Winners Support Group. Rhonda, a founding member of the group, had won six million dollars in the lottery and been persuaded by a cousin to invest her first big check in his invention, a fast-acting drain cleaner. As it turned out, the only thing the cousin's cleaner whooshed down the drain was Rhonda's money.

That was when Rhonda started the support group. When she read about how well Alvirah and Willy had handled their windfall, she begged them to be honorary members and regular guest lecturers.

Rhonda had already left one message. Now she got right to the point. "Alvirah, I know you're home. The limo dropped you off an hour ago. I checked with your doorman. Pick up. This is important."

"And you think Cordelia's bad," Alvirah murmured as she obediently reached for the phone.

Willy watched her expression change to disbelief and

concern and then heard her say, "Of course, we'll talk to her. Tomorrow morning at ten, here. Fine."

When she hung up she explained, "Willy, we're going to meet Nelly Monahan. From what Rhonda tells me she's a very nice woman, but much more important, she's a lottery winner who's been shafted by her ex-husband. We can't let that happen."

The next morning at nine o'clock, Nelly Monahan prepared to leave her three-room apartment in Stuyvesant Town, the east side complex that she'd moved into forty years ago as a twenty-two-year-old bride. Even though the rent was now ten times more than the fifty-nine dollars a month that had been the starting figure, it was still a terrific bargain—provided, of course, that you could spend nearly six hundred dollars a month for shelter.

But now that she was retired and living on a tiny pension and her monthly social security check, it had become painfully obvious to Nelly that she might have to give up the apartment and move in with her cousin, Margaret, in New Brunswick, New Jersey.

To Nelly, a dyed-in-the-wool New Yorker, the prospect of spending her final years away from the Big Apple was appalling. It had been bad enough that her husband Tim had walked out on her but to give up the apartment broke her heart. And then to learn that Tim's new wife had produced Nelly's winning lottery ticket! It was just too much. That was when Nelly was put in touch with the support group and now had a meeting with Alvirah, whom Rhonda assured her was a problem solver who got things done.

Nelly was a small, round woman with vaguely pretty

features. Her hair, gray with lingering traces of brown, had a natural wave that framed her face and softened the lines that time and hard work had etched around her eyes and mouth.

With her hesitant voice and shy smile, Nelly gave the outward appearance of being a pushover, but nothing could have been further from the truth. People who tried to take advantage of her soon learned that she had a spunky streak and an implacable sense of justice.

Until her retirement at age sixty, she had worked as a bookkeeper for a small company that manufactured venetian blinds and some years earlier was the one who realized that the owner's nephew was bleeding the place dry. She'd persuaded her boss to make the nephew sell his house and pay back every dime he'd stolen or risk becoming a guest of the Department of Corrections of New York.

And once when a teenager tried to grab her pocketbook as he rode past her, she'd poked her umbrella into the spokes of his bicycle, causing him to go sprawling on the road and sprain his ankle. She alternately shouted for help and lectured the would-be mugger until the police came.

But these episodes paled compared to being cheated out of her share of eighteen million dollars by her husband of forty years and her successor, Roxie, the new Mrs. Tim Monahan.

Nelly knew that Alvirah and her husband Willy lived in one of the fancy Central Park South buildings so she dressed carefully for her meeting with them, selecting a brown tweed suit she'd bought on sale at A&S. She'd even gone to the extravagance of having her hair washed and set.

Promptly at ten A.M. she was announced by the doorman.

At ten-thirty, Alvirah poured a second cup of coffee for their guest. For half an hour she'd deliberately kept the conversation general. From her experience as an investigative columnist for the *New York Globe,* she'd learned that relaxed people tended to be better witnesses.

"Now let's get down to business," she said, touching the lapel of her jacket and turning on the miniscule tape recorder in the gold and diamond sunburst pin that the editor of the *Globe* had given her on her first visit to Cypress Point Spa. He'd assigned her to write an article about mingling with the celebrities there and told her the recorder would help refresh her memory. "I'm going to be honest," she explained. "I'll be recording our conversation because sometimes when I play it back I pick up something that I missed."

Nelly's eyes sparkled. "Rhonda Alvirez told me you used that recorder to solve crimes. Well, let me tell you I've got a crime for you. And the criminal's name is Tim Monahan."

She went on to explain, "In the forty years I was married to him he could never hold a job long because he always found a reason to file suit against his current employer. Tim spent more time in small claims court than Judge Wapner."

Nelly then enumerated the long list of defendants who had tangled with Tim, including the dry cleaner accused of putting a hole in an ancient pair of trousers, the bus company for a sudden stop that he said caused whiplash, the secondhand car dealer for refusing to fix his car after the warranty expired, and Macy's for a broken spring he discovered on a La-Z-Boy recliner Nelly had given him years before.

In her gentle voice she continued to tell them that Tim always considered himself a bit of a ladies' man and would gallantly rush to open doors for attractive women while she walked behind him like Dicky the boob. It had been especially annoying when he sang the praises of Roxie March, the fiftyish caterer he worked for occasionally. Nelly had met her once and knew that Roxie was the type who buttered up her help and then paid them slave wages.

She explained that Tim drank too much, was sloppy, lazy, a chronic complainer and looked particularly silly when he tried to act like Beau Brummell. Nevertheless, he was company of a sort and after forty years she was used to him. Besides that, she loved to cook and always enjoyed Tim's hearty appetite.

Until they did—or didn't—win the lottery.

"Tell me about it," Alvirah ordered.

"We played the lottery every week. One day I woke up feeling particularly lucky," Nelly explained earnestly. "It was the last chance to get in on the lottery for an eighteen million-dollar pot. Tim was between jobs and I gave him a dollar and told him to be sure to pick up a ticket when he bought his newspaper."

"Where was that?" Alvirah asked quickly.

"At the stationery store on Fourteenth Street. When he got back I asked him about it and he said yes, he'd bought it."

"Did you see the ticket?" Willy asked quickly.

Alvirah smiled at her husband. Willy was frowning. He seldom lost his temper but when he did he looked and sounded remarkably like his sister Cordelia. Willy would have no use for a man who cheated his wife.

"I didn't ask to see it," Nelly explained after she swallowed the last of her coffee. "He always held the ticket in his wallet. We always played the same numbers."

"So do we," Alvirah told her. "Our birthdays and our wedding anniversary."

"Tim and I took ours from the street addresses of the houses we grew up in, 1802 and 1913 Tenbroeck Avenue in the Bronx and 405 East Fourteenth Street, the number of our building all these years. That came out to be 18-2-19-13-4-5.

"Tim absolutely told me he'd bought the ticket that day and didn't say one word about picking different numbers. That was on Saturday. The next Wednesday I was watching the TV when our numbers were pulled. You can't imagine my shock."

"Yes I can," Alvirah told her. "I had cleaned for Mrs. O'Keefe the day we won and let me tell you no one could mess up a house faster than that lady. I was bone tired and soaking my feet when our numbers were pulled."

"She kicked over the pail," Willy explained. "We spent our first ten minutes as multi-millionaires mopping up the living room."

"Then you do understand," Nelly sighed. She went on to explain that Tim had been out that night working his occasional job as a bartender for Roxie the caterer. Nelly had sat up waiting for him and to celebrate had made his favorite dessert, a crème brûlée.

But when he got home, a tearful Tim handed her the ticket he was holding. It wasn't the numbers they always played. Every single one was different. "I decided to change our luck," Tim told her.

"I thought I'd have a heart attack," Nelly said. "But he felt so terrible that I ended up telling him it didn't matter, that it just wasn't to be."

"And I bet he ate the crème brûlée," Alvirah snapped.

"Every speck. He said every man should be so lucky to have a wife like me. Then a few weeks later he walked out on me and moved in with Roxie. He told me he'd fallen in love with her. That was a year ago. The divorce came through last month and he married Roxie three weeks ago.

"They'd announced that there were four winners of the eighteen-million-dollar pot and I didn't realize that one of them hadn't shown up to collect. Then last week on the very last day before the ticket expired, Roxie—now the second Mrs. Tim Monahan—showed up at the redemption window and claimed she'd just happened to realize she had the fourth ticket, the ticket with the numbers Tim and I always played."

"Tim was working for Roxie the night your numbers won and he had the ticket in his wallet," Alvirah confirmed.

"Yes, that's the point. He had big eyes for her and probably showed the ticket to her."

"And she's a flirt who saw her big chance," Willy said. "That's disgusting."

"If you want to know what disgusting is, I'll show you the picture of the two of them in the *Post* saying how lucky they were that Roxie happened to find her ticket," Nelly said, her voice quivering into a near sob. Then she got a flinty look in her eye and her jaw moved out an inch. "It's not justice," she said. "There's a retired lawyer, Dennis O'Shea, living down the hall from me and I spoke to him about it. He did some research and learned that there are a couple of other cases on record where one spouse or the other pulled that scam and the court decided that the one holding the ticket is the owner. He said that it was a disgrace and a horror and a terrible shame but legally, I was out of luck."

"How did you happen to go to a meeting of the Lottery Winners Support Group?" Alvirah asked.

"Dennis sent me. He'd read about all the people who throw away all the money they made on the lottery in bad investments and thought it might help me to be around kindred souls."

Righteous wrath in her voice and a certain mulish expression around her mouth, Nelly summed up her luckless saga. "Tim moved out on me faster than you can say Wiener schnitzel and now the two of them will live the life of Reilly while I move in with my cousin Margaret because I can't afford to stay where I am. Margaret only asked me to live with her because she likes my cooking. She talks so much I'll probably be stone deaf in a year."

"There's got to be a way to help," Alvirah decreed. "Let me put on my thinking cap. I'll call you tomorrow."

At nine o'clock the next morning, Nelly was sitting at the dinette table in her Stuyvesant Town apartment enjoying a warm bagel and a cup of coffee. It isn't Central Park, she thought, but it's a wonderful place to live. Since Tim took off, she'd made little changes. He always insisted on keeping that big ugly recliner of his right by the window. But since he'd taken it with him when he moved out she'd rearranged the rest of the furniture the way she always secretly wanted it. She'd made bright new slipcovers for the couch and wing chair and bought a lovely hooked rug for next to nothing from neighbors who were moving. The early autumn sun was streaming through and the place was cheerful and inviting. More and more she'd come to realize that Tim had been a lifelong drag and she really was better off without him.

The trouble was that she couldn't make ends meet, and try as she did, she couldn't find a job. Who wants to hire a sixty-three-year-old woman who can't use the computer? Answer: Nobody.

Margaret had already called this morning. "Why don't you give the apartment up on the first and save a month's rent? I'm having the back bedroom painted for you."

How about the kitchen? Nelly wondered. *I bet that's where you really expect me to spend my time.*

It was all so hopeless. Nelly took a sip of her excellent, fresh-brewed coffee and sighed.

Then Alvirah called.

"We've got a plan," she said. "I want you to go and see Roxie and Tim and get them to admit they shafted you."

"Why would they admit it?"

"Get one of them mad enough to brag that they put one over on you. Do you think you can do that?"

"Oh, I can get Roxie's goat," Nellie said. "When they got married last month I found a picture of him on Jones Beach where he looks like a beached whale and I had it framed and sent it to her. On it I wrote 'Congratulations and good riddance.' "

"I like you, Nelly," Alvirah chuckled. "Here's the plan. One way or another you're going to make a date to see them and you're going to wear a copy of my sunburst pin."

"Alvirah, that pin is *valuable*."

"The copy is only valuable because it has the tape recorder in it. You're going to turn it on, get them to admit that they cheated you and then we're going to get your lawyer friend, Dennis O'Shea, to sign a complaint to Matrimonial Court that you were cheated out of marital assets."

A faint hope stirred in Nelly's ample bosom. "Alvirah, do you really think there's a chance?"

"It's about the only chance," Alvirah said quietly.

For several minutes after getting off the phone Nelly sat, deep in thought. She remembered how when Tim's mother was dying a couple of years ago she asked him to tell the truth. Hadn't he been the one who set the garage on fire when he was eight years old? He'd always denied it, but seeing that she was breathing her last, he broke down that day and told the truth. *I know how to get to him,* Nelly thought as she reached for the phone.

Tim answered. When he heard her voice he sounded irritated. "Listen, Nelly, we're packing to go to Florida for good so what's up?"

Nelly crossed her fingers. "Tim, I've got bad news. I don't have more than another month." *And I don't,* she thought. At least not in Stuyvesant Town.

Tim sounded at least somewhat concerned. "Nelly, that's too bad. Are you sure?"

"Very sure."

"I'll pray for you."

"That's why I'm calling. I have to say I've had some pretty nasty thoughts about you in these couple of weeks since Roxie turned in the lottery ticket."

"It was her ticket."

"I know."

"I mean, I used to tell her how we played those numbers and she tried them for luck that week and I tried some other combination."

"Her numbers?"

"I forget," Tim said quickly. "Look Nelly, I'm sorry but we're leaving tomorrow and the movers are coming in the morning. I've got a lot to do."

"Tim, I have to see you. I'm trying to get my soul in readiness and I've hated you and Roxie so much that now I have to see you face to face and talk to you. Otherwise I'll never die in peace." *More straight talk,* Nelly thought.

From the background, she heard a strident voice yell, "Tim, who the hell is that?"

Tim lowered his voice and said quickly, "We're leaving on a noon plane tomorrow. Be here at ten o'clock. But Nelly, I have to tell you. I can only spare fifteen minutes."

"That's all I want, Tim," Nelly said, her voice even softer than usual. She hung up the phone and dialed Alvirah. "He's giving me fifteen minutes tomorrow morning," she said. "Alvirah, I could kill him."

"That won't do you any good," Alvirah said. "Come on up this afternoon and I'll show you how to work the pin."

The next day at nine o'clock Nelly was about to put on her coat when her doorbell rang. It was Dennis O'Shea, the nice retired lawyer who lived down the hall in 8F. He'd moved there about six months ago. A number of times he'd fallen into step with her when they met at the elevator. He was on the small side, maybe five-seven or so, with a neat compact build, kindly eyes behind frameless glasses and a pleasant, intelligent face.

He'd told her that his wife died two years ago and when he retired from the Legal Aid Society at age sixty-five, he decided to sell the house in Syosset and move back to the city. He split his time between the apartment and his cottage in Cape Cod.

Nelly could tell that like her, Dennis had a strong sense of justice and didn't like the underdog to be pushed around. That was why she'd had the courage to ask him for advice when Roxie turned in the winning ticket.

This morning Dennis looked worried. "Nelly," he said, "are you sure you know how to turn on that recorder?"

"Oh sure, you just sort of run your hand over the fake diamond in the center."

"Show me."

She did.

"Say something."

"Go to hell, Tim."

"That's the spirit. Now play it back."

She pushed the replay button on the back of the pin. Nothing happened.

"I guess you told your friend Alvirah Meehan about me," Dennis said. "She called a few minutes ago and explained what's going on. She said that you seemed to have trouble turning on the recorder."

Nelly felt her fingers tremble. She hadn't been able to sleep all night. Her share of the winnings was just maybe, possibly, within her grasp. But if this didn't work, it was all over. She hadn't shed one tear all this year but right now looking at the concern on Dennis

O'Shea's face she felt her eyes fill up. "Show me what I'm doing wrong," she said.

For the next ten minutes they tried turning the recorder on and off, saying a few words then playing it back. The trick was to snap that little switch firmly. Finally Nelly said, "I have it. Thanks Dennis."

"My pleasure. Nelly, you get them on record saying they cheated you, and I'll have them in Matrimonial Court so fast they won't know what hit them."

"But they're moving to Florida."

"The lottery checks are issued in New York. Let me worry about that part of it."

He waited with her at the elevator. "You know what bus to take."

"It's not that far to Christopher Street. I'll walk one way."

Alvirah had a busy morning. At eight she started vigorously cleaning the already spotless apartment. At eight-thirty she had looked up Dennis O'Shea's phone number and called him explaining her worry that Nelly might not have the hang of using the recorder, and then she got back to polishing the polished. To Willy it was an unmistakable sign that she was deeply concerned.

"What's eating you, honey?" he asked finally.

"I have a bad feeling," she admitted.

"You're afraid Nelly won't be able to handle the recorder?"

"I'm worried about that and I'm worried that she may not be able to get them to say a word and most of all I'm worried that they tell her everything and she doesn't get it on tape."

Nelly was meeting her ex-husband and Roxie at ten.

At ten-thirty, Alvirah sat down and stared at the phone. At ten-thirty-five it rang. It was Sister Cordelia looking for Willy. "One of our old girls has a leak in her kitchen ceiling," Cordelia said. "The whole apartment is starting to smell mildewed. Send Willy right over."

"Later, Cordelia. We're waiting for an important message." Alvirah knew there was no getting off without explaining the problem.

"You should have told me before," Cordelia snapped. "I'll start praying."

By noon Alvirah was a total wreck. She called Dennis O'Shea again. "Any word from Nelly?"

"No. Mrs. Meehan, Nelly told me that Tim Monahan was only going to give her fifteen minutes."

"I know."

Finally at twelve-fifteen the phone rang. Alvirah grabbed it. "Hello."

"Alvirah."

It was Nelly. Alvirah tried to analyze the tone of her voice. Strained? No. Shocked. Yes, that's what it was. Shocked. Nelly sounded as though she was in a trance.

"What happened?" Alvirah demanded. "Did they admit it?"

"Yes."

"Did you get it on tape?"

"No."

"Oh that's terrible. I'm so sorry."

"That's not the worst of it."

"What do you mean, Nelly?"

There was a long pause, then Nelly sighed. "Alvirah, Tim's dead. I shot him."

* * *

Five hours later Alvirah and Willy posted bond after Dennis O'Shea, Nelly's self-appointed lawyer, pleaded her not guilty to charges of second-degree murder, first-degree manslaughter, and carrying a concealed weapon. Nelly arose from her trancelike lethargy only long enough to say in a surprised voice, "But I did kill him."

They took her home. The crumb cake neatly enveloped in plastic was still on the kitchen counter. "Tim always loved that cake," Nelly said sadly. "He looked awful today even before he died. I don't think Roxie cooked much for him."

Alvirah was feeling wretched. All this had been her big idea. Now Nelly was facing long years in prison. At her age that could mean the rest of her life. Yesterday Nelly had said that she could kill Tim. *And I joked about it,* Alvirah thought. *I told her that wouldn't do any good. I never thought she meant it. How did she happen to have a gun?*

She put on the kettle. "I think we'd better talk," she said. "But first I'll make a nice strong cup of tea for you, Nelly."

Nelly told her story in a flat, emotionless voice. "I decided to walk down to Christopher Street to get my thoughts together, you know what I mean? I took the pin off and put it in my pocketbook. It's so pretty I was afraid I'd get mugged for it. Then on Tenth Street and Avenue B I saw a couple of kids. They couldn't have been more than twelve or thirteen. Can you believe one of them was showing the other a gun?"

She stared ahead. "Let me tell you I saw red. Those boys were not only playing hooky but treating the gun like a cap pistol. I marched up to them and told them to hand it over."

"You what?" Dennis O'Shea blinked.

"The one who wasn't holding the gun said, 'Shoot her,' but I think the other kid must have thought I was an undercover cop or something," Nelly continued. "Anyhow, he looked scared and handed it to me. I told them that kids their age should be in school and should play stickball the way boys did when we were growing up."

Alvirah prodded. "So you had the gun with you when you went to see Tim and Roxie."

"I couldn't take time to turn it in to the police station. Tim was only giving me fifteen minutes. As it turned out I didn't need more than ten."

Alvirah saw that Willy was about to ask a question. She shook her head. It was obvious that Nelly was about to relive the scene in her mind. "All right, Nelly," she said softly. "What happened when you were with them?"

"I was a couple of minutes late. They were making a movie on Christopher Street and a lot of people were gawking at the actors. So I was out of breath. Roxie let me in. I don't think Tim told her I was coming. Her mouth sort of dropped. The living room was empty except for Tim's old recliner and he was camped in it as usual. Didn't even get up like a gentleman. Then Mrs. Tim Monahan the Second, bold as brass, says to me, 'Get lost.'

"I was so nervous by then that I looked right at Tim and just blurted out everything I had rehearsed—that I only had a month left and that I wanted his forgiveness for being so angry at him, that it didn't matter about the ticket, that I was glad he had someone to take care of him. But before I died just like his mother I wanted to hear the truth."

"You told them that!" Willy exclaimed.

"You're smart," Alvirah breathed.

"Anyhow Tim had a funny look on his face like he was going to laugh and he said that it always had been bothering him, that yes, he did buy the winning ticket and switched it with Roxie and he had kept it in a safe-deposit box at the bank around the corner here until he took it out and gave it to Roxie to cash last month and he was sorry for my trouble and I was a fine, generous woman."

"He admitted it just like that!" Alvirah breathed.

"So fast that I almost collapsed and he was laughing when he said it. Now I'm pretty sure that he was just making fun of me. I realized I didn't have the pin on and I opened my pocketbook and started to fumble for it and Roxie yelled something about the gun and I took it out to explain and it went off and Tim went down like a load of blubber. And after that it's all vague. Roxie tried to grab the gun and the next thing I knew I was in the police station."

She reached for her cup. "So I guess I don't have to worry about keeping this apartment or going to my cousin in New Brunswick. Do you think they'll send me to that women's prison in Westchester where they keep that woman from Massachusetts who had her husband shot because she wanted to keep the dog when they were divorced?"

She put the cup down and slowly stood up. As Alvirah and Willy and Dennis O'Shea watched, her face crumbled. "Oh, my God," she said, "how could I have shot Tim?"

She fainted.

* * *

The next morning Alvirah came back from visiting Nelly in the hospital. "They're going to keep her for a few days," she told Willy. "It's just as well. The newspapers are having a field day. Take a look." She handed him the *Post*. The front page showed a hysterically weeping Roxie watching Tim's corpse being carried from the apartment.

"According to this, Roxie claims that Nelly just showed up and started shooting," Alvirah said.

"We can testify that she had made an appointment with Tim," Willy said, "but Nelly did say that Roxie didn't seem to expect her." His forehead furrowed as he considered the situation. "Dennis O'Shea phoned while you were out. He thinks it would be a good idea to plea bargain. He said it's like the Jean Harris case. Harris could have been out in a couple of years if she'd copped a plea."

Alvirah flecked a piece of lint from the sleeve of her smartly tailored pantsuit. It was an outfit she usually enjoyed wearing. It was only a size fourteen and she could close the button at the waist without too much yanking. But today nothing could give her comfort. *Nelly may have been cheated out of her lottery ticket but I'm the one who gave her a ticket to prison,* she thought.

"I've been thinking that if I could possibly find those kids Nelly took the gun from it would at least prove that she didn't intend to go there with it. I made her describe them to me."

The thought of action brought a little relief. "I'd better change into some old duds so I can just hang around. That isn't a great neighborhood."

An hour later, wearing ancient jeans, a tired Mickey

Mouse sweatshirt and her sunburst pin, Alvirah took up her vigil on the corner of Avenue B and Tenth Street. The boys Nelly had described were about twelve years old. One was short and thin with curly hair and brown eyes, the other a foot taller and heavyset. They both had duck haircuts and wore gold chains and earrings.

The odds of just running into them were small, and after thirty minutes, Alvirah began to systematically work her way through the neighborhood stores. She bought a newspaper in one, two apples in another, aspirin in the drug store. In each place she began a conversation. It was with the shoemaker that she finally hit pay dirt.

"Sure, I know those two. The little guy is big trouble. The other isn't a bad kid. They usually hang around that corner." He pointed out the window. "This morning the cops were picking up truants and taking them back to school so I guess they won't be here till three o'clock."

Delighted with the information, Alvirah rewarded the shoemaker by purchasing an assortment of polishes, none of which she needed. As he slowly counted out change he explained that he'd dropped and stepped on his reading glasses but that at a distance he could see a gnat sneeze. He glanced past her. "There are the kids you're looking for!" he exclaimed, pointing across the street. "They musta sneaked out of school again."

Alvirah spun around. "Forget about the change," she called as she dashed out of the store.

An hour later she dejectedly related to Willy and Dennis O'Shea what had happened. "When I talked to them they'd just seen Nelly's picture in the *Post* and recognized her. Those little skunks were on their way to the police station to report that Nelly came up to them and asked where she could buy a gun because she needed one right away and offered them a hundred bucks. They claim they didn't know where to get one but later they heard some other kid bragging about selling one to her."

"That's a damn lie," Dennis said flatly. "Just before Nelly left her apartment yesterday morning she checked her wallet. I couldn't help but notice she didn't have more than three or four dollars in it. Why would those kids lie like that?"

"Because Nelly took their gun away," Alvirah told him, "and this is their chance to get even." She realized she did not know why Dennis had been sitting in the living room talking to Willy when she arrived home.

But when he told her the reason she was sorry she'd asked. The autopsy was complete. One bullet had grazed Tim's forehead. The other two had lodged in his heart and from the angle of entry it was clear they'd been fired after he was lying on the floor. The district attorney had called Dennis to tell him the plea bargain was now first-degree aggravated manslaughter with a minimum of fifteen years in prison. Take it or leave it. "And when I spoke to him he hadn't heard from those kids," Dennis concluded.

"Does Nelly know about this yet?" Alvirah asked.

"I saw her this morning just after you left. She intends to check out of the hospital tomorrow and get her affairs in order. She said she has to pay for her crime."

"I kind of hate to bring this up," Willy offered, "but is it possible that Nelly did buy the gun and was mad enough to mean to kill Tim?"

"She pointed the gun at his heart when he was on the floor!" Alvirah exclaimed. "I can't believe it."

"I don't think she did it deliberately," Dennis agreed.

"But she did shoot him. Her prints are on the gun." He got up. "I'd better call and get the plea bargain in motion. I'll see if they'll give Nelly a little time before she has to start serving her sentence."

"He likes Nelly," Willy observed after he'd let Dennis O'Shea out.

"He's the kind of man she should have been with all these years," Alvirah agreed. Suddenly she felt old and tired. *I'm just a meddling fool,* she thought. Once again she could hear herself advising Nelly to go see Tim. And she could also hear Nelly saying, "I could kill him."

Willy patted her hand and she looked up at him gratefully. He was her best friend as well as the best husband in the world. Poor Nelly had put up with a guy who couldn't hold a job, who fought with everyone, who drank too much, and who was the size of a beached whale.

Why the heck did Roxie marry him?

For the ticket, of course.

That night Alvirah could not sleep. Over and over she considered every single detail, and it all added up to one thing: fifteen years in prison for Nelly Monahan. Finally at two o'clock she got out of bed, careful not to disturb Willy, who was clearly in the second stage of sleep. A few minutes later, armed with a steaming pot of tea, she sat at the dinette table and played back the recording she had made of the first meeting with Nelly and then her confession after they bailed her out.

She was missing something. What was it? She got up, went to the desk, got a spiral notebook and pen, returned to the table and rewound the tapes. Then as she played them back she took notes.

When he got up at seven o'clock Willy found her

poring over her notes. He knew what she was doing. He put on the kettle and settled at the table across from her. "Can't figure out what you're missing," he commented. "Let me take a look."

A half hour passed. And then Willy said, "I can't see anything. But reading about Tim's recliner makes me think of old Buster Kelly. Remember he had a recliner too. Even insisted on moving it into the nursing home with him."

"Willy, say that again."

"Buster Kelly insisted on moving his recliner . . ."

"Willy, that's it. Tim was sitting in his recliner when Nelly went to the apartment." Alvirah reached across the table and grabbed her notebook. "Look. Nelly says that the moving men were just pulling away when she got there. Why didn't the recliner go with them?" She jumped up. "Willy, don't you see? Tim wasn't joking when he told Nelly he'd cheated her. I bet you anything Roxie had just told him to go stuff it. She stuck with him until she turned in the lottery ticket and he stood beside her when she explained how she'd bought it last year before they married."

The more she said, the surer Alvirah was that she'd hit the nail on the head. Her voice rose in excitement as she continued. "Tim was trying to keep Nelly from claiming a share in the ticket and never thought that Roxie would double-cross him. His first inkling that Roxie was going to dump him came when she told those moving men to leave the recliner.

"And by admitting to Nelly that he'd cheated her, he thought he'd get the ticket back and have half of it. It makes sense," Willy agreed.

"Nelly never killed Tim. That first bullet just grazed

his head. Roxie didn't grab her hand to take the gun. She was aiming it at Tim."

They stared at each other. Willy's eyes shone with admiration. "Smartest redhead in the world," he said. "There's just one problem, honey. How are you going to prove it?"

How was she going to prove it? Alvirah made a list of where to start. She wanted to talk to the movers who had cleared out Roxie's apartment. Tim had told Nelly that he'd kept the lottery ticket in a safe deposit box in a bank around the corner from Christopher Street. She wanted to find it and see when he took out the box and whose name was on it. Finally she wanted to talk to the superintendent of the building where Roxie and Tim had their little love nest.

Yet even as her brain busily worked away, it was with an overriding sense that she was spinning wheels. The fact remained that it would be almost impossible to prove that Roxie had guided Nelly's hand.

At nine o'clock she called Jim Cross, an editor on the *Globe,* and explained her needs. At ten he called back. Stalwart Van Company had picked up the contents of Roxie and Tim's apartment, he reported. "The three guys assigned to the job were working on East Fiftieth Street today. The Greenwich Savings Bank on West Fourth had a safe deposit box in the name of Timothy Monahan. He had opened it last year and closed it three weeks ago. They're willing to talk to you."

Alvirah wrote swiftly, said, "Jim, you're a doll," then hung up and turned to Willy. "Come on, honey."

Their first stop was at East Fiftieth Street where the Stalwart Van movers were dismantling an apartment.

They hung around the van until the three movers returned, struggling under the weight of a nine-foot breakfront.

Alvirah waited until they hoisted it onto the cavelike back of the truck then introduced herself. "I won't take but a minute of your time with a few very important questions." Willy opened his wallet and displayed three twenty-dollar bills.

They cheerfully explained that Tim hadn't been in the apartment when they got there. In fact, when he did come back just before ten, they could tell he wasn't expected. Roxie had yelled, "I told you to get a haircut. You look like a slob."

The burly mover chuckled. "Then he said something about having an appointment at ten that she wouldn't like, and she said, like, 'What appointment, to fix yourself a drink?' "

"We were on the way out the door and the guy yelled for us to come back and get his recliner and the wife told us to just get going," the smallest mover, the one who had carried the heaviest part of the breakfront, volunteered.

"And in court it wouldn't prove anything," Willy reminded Alvirah an hour later when they left the Greenwich Savings Bank, having confirmed that Tim Monahan rented the safe deposit box a year ago—the morning after the disputed winning ticket was drawn—and visited it only once, the day he closed it three weeks ago. That day he'd been accompanied by a flashy looking woman. The bank clerk identified Roxie's picture. "That's the one."

"He went into the vault and closed that account half an hour before they showed up at the lottery office to turn in the ticket," Alvirah said, every inch of her frame tense with frustration and determination.

"I know they did," Willy agreed, "but . . ."

"But legally it doesn't prove anything. Oh, Willy it may not do any good but let's try to get a look at the apartment they lived in."

They turned the corner and were treated to a crowd of spectators pressing against police barriers as they watched Tom Cruise catch up with a fleeing Demi Moore and spin her around.

"Nelly said they were filming a scene here the other day," Alvirah commented. "Well, we've got better things to do than gawk."

She was at the door of 101 Christopher Street when a familiar voice yelled, "Aunt Alvirah."

She and Willy spun around as a thin young man with half-glasses on the end of his nose expertly made his way to them.

"Brian, as I live and breathe."

Brian was the son of Willy's deceased sister, the only one of his seven siblings to marry. Raised in Nebraska, he was now a successful playwright and to Willy and Alvirah, the son they never had.

"I thought you were in London," Alvirah breathed as she hugged him.

"I thought you were in Greece. I just got back and they wanted some additional dialogue. I wrote the screenplay for this epic." He nodded to the cameras down the street. "Look, I've got to get back over there. I'll catch you later."

An overhead camera anchored to a van was being positioned down the block. Subconsciously Alvirah made note of it as she rang the superintendent's bell at number 101.

Ten minutes later she and Willy were being shown the three-room apartment where the late Tim Monahan had met his fate. "You're in luck," the superintendent informed them. "Roxie just called yesterday to say she didn't want the apartment anymore so nobody knows it's available. And you're the kind of tenants the management wants," he added virtuously as he thought of Alvirah's check for a thousand dollars nestled in his hip pocket.

"You mean she wasn't going to give it up when she moved to Florida?"

"No. She said it might be needed but she'd switched it to Tim's name."

The battered recliner of the late Tim Monahan caught the morning sun. The rest of the room was empty except for the chalk marks drawn on the floor by the police to indicate where his body had lain.

A shadow passed over the chair. Startled, Alvirah turned and was treated to the sight of the Mirage Film cameras passing outside. "That's it," she breathed.

The next morning Nelly Monahan sat on a chair in her room in Lenox Hill Hospital waiting to be discharged. On her lap she had a lined pad and was making notes of everything she had to do before she went to prison. She had started the list after a saddened Dennis O'Shea had told her that the district attorney would only let her plea bargain if she would accept fifteen years in prison without the possibility of parole.

"It's only justice," she'd told him quietly. "I must pay for what I did." Then when he took her hand she'd winced. Her wrist was sore probably because Roxie had tried so hard to wrestle the gun from her and there was a scrape on her middle finger from where she'd scratched it trying to turn on the pin.

Then Dennis said he thought they should go to trial and he'd represent her but she said it wouldn't even be right to get off. She had taken a life.

"Give up apartment," Nelly wrote. "Turn off the telephone. Furniture? Clothes?"

She looked up. A smartly dressed Alvirah was at the door. "You look nice, Alvirah," she said admiringly. "Do you know what color the prison uniforms are? It's funny. Last night I was just lying awake thinking about things like that."

"Don't worry about prison uniforms," Alvirah told her. "It ain't over till it's over. Now I'm going to take you home in a taxi and I called Dennis and said that you are *not,* repeat *not* going near the district attorney's office or signing anything until I put my plan in action, starting with interviewing the heartbroken widow of the late Tim Monahan."

Roxie March Monahan debated about what to wear for her meeting with Alvirah Meehan. It was exciting to think of having a whole article written about her in the *Globe*. She'd loved the story in the *Post* but was sorry she hadn't had her hair done Monday the way she'd planned. It had looked a little stringy in the picture of her watching Tim's body being carried out. But on the other hand she'd been crying hysterically so maybe it was better that her hair was going every which way. Kind of rounded out the effect.

She glanced around. The junior suite in the Omni Park

Hotel was very attractive. She'd rented it the day of the shooting. The District Attorney's office had asked her to stay in New York for a short time until all the facts of the case were settled. They'd told her that Nelly was undoubtedly going to plea bargain so there wouldn't be any trial.

Roxie decided that she'd miss New York but she loved golf and in Florida could play it every day without worrying about rattling dishes for some dreary party. Catering was hell. God, she didn't think she'd ever cook so much as a string bean for herself again.

She smiled. She'd been wrapped in a warm glow of anticipation ever since that dumb-bunny Tim had handed her the ticket just as they went into the lottery office. Actually Tim wasn't that dumb. That first night when he'd showed her the winning ticket she'd offered to hold it for him. No way, he'd told her. He wanted to make sure that they were really compatible.

She'd been stuck with having to look at that dopey face every day, listen to him snore at night, see him plopped in that shabby recliner with a beer in his hand, act happy when he slobbered all over her with clumsy kisses. She'd earned every nickel of the *quarter of a million* bucks less taxes she had coming in every year for the next twenty years.

She held up the two black suits she'd bought in Annie Sez yesterday. One had gold buttons. The other, sequin lapels. Gold buttons it would be. The sequins looked a little too festive. Roxie dressed, put on her customary bangles and turquoise ring. She knew she didn't look fifty-three. She knew that with her blonde hair and snazzy figure she was very attractive. At last she had money and could afford clothes and travel.

It all added up to catching a really interesting guy for the first time in her life.

Thank you, Tim Monahan. Thank you, Nelly Monahan. Incredible the way I snatched victory from the jaws of defeat, Roxie exulted. Her one blunder had been to tell Tim the truth when he saw that the movers were leaving and his recliner was still squatting in the living room. She should have bluffed it out somehow. She certainly would have kept her mouth shut if she had known that Nelly Monahan would ring the doorbell seconds after she told Tim to go jump in the lake. As Roxie reshaped her lips, the phone rang. Alvirah Meehan was in the lobby.

"Our angle is to talk about how winning the lottery ticket has turned into such tragedy for you," Alvirah sympathized as she sat opposite Roxie a few minutes later.

Roxie dabbed at her eyes. "I'm sorry I ever found it in my makeup drawer. I came across it under a box of Q-tips and I'd just read an article about how a lot of people don't realize they have a winning ticket and never know they might have been millionaires. The number to call was listed so I laughed and said to Tim, 'Wouldn't it be a gasser if this was a lucky ticket?' "

Alvirah turned slightly so that the recorder in her sunburst pin wouldn't miss a word. "And what did he say?"

"Oh that silly darling said, 'Don't waste the phone call unless it's an eight-hundred number.' " Roxie squeezed tears from her eyes. "I'm sorry I did."

"You'd rather be catering, wouldn't you?"

"Yes," Roxie sobbed. "Yes."

Alvirah never used vulgar language but a familiar vulgarity almost escaped her lips. Instead, through gritted teeth she managed to say, "I have just a few more questions and then our photographer wants to take some pictures."

Roxie's sobs ended abruptly. "Let me check my makeup."

Mel Levine, the top photographer from the *Globe,* had his marching orders: Get good closeups of her hands.

Willy's oldest sibling, Sister Cordelia, did not like to be left out of anything. Knowing that Alvirah was involved with Nelly Monahan, the woman who had shot her husband, made Cordelia decide to pay an unannounced visit to Central Park South.

Accompanied by Sister Maeve Marie, the twenty-seven-year-old policewoman-turned-novice, Cordelia was ensconced in the wing chair in the living room when Alvirah arrived home. Since the chair was upholstered in handsome crimson velvet and Cordelia still wore an ankle length habit and short veil, Alvirah had the immediate and familiar thought that if a woman pope were ever elected, she would look like Cordelia.

"Cordelia just dropped by," Willy explained, his right eyebrow lifted. That was a signal he hadn't brought Cordelia up to date on their plans.

"I hope it's not an inconvenience, Alvirah," Sister Maeve Marie apologized. "Sister Superior felt you might need our help." Maeve had the slender diciplined body of an athlete. Her face, dominated by wide gray eyes, was strikingly handsome. Like Willy, her expression was saying, "Sorry, Alvirah but you know Cordelia."

"So what's going on?" Cordelia asked, getting straight to the point.

Alvirah knew there was absolutely nothing to do except to tell her the truth, the whole truth, and nothing but the truth. She sank down on the couch wishing she'd had time for a peaceful cup of tea with Willy before the visit. "We have to get Nelly off. It's my fault that she went to see Tim and I can't let her spend the rest of her life in prison."

Cordelia nodded. "So what are you going to do about it?"

"Something you may not like," Alvirah answered. "Brian wrote a screenplay for Mirage Films."

"I know that. I hope he can trust them not to put a lot of smut in it. What's that got to do with Nelly Monahan, poor soul?"

"On the day of the shooting, Mirage was filming a scene right outside the building where Tim Monahan and Roxie lived. We're going to try to make Roxie believe that the camera caught her twisting Nelly's hand and pointing the gun at Tim."

"You're going to fake it?" Cordelia exploded.

"Exactly. Brian got the producer to cooperate. Mel, the *Globe* photographer, took a lot of pictures of Roxie today. Besides that, we have pictures of her when Tim's body was being carried out. We've got to get a model who, in a blurry long shot, resembles Roxie. We'll dress her in the same kind of striped pantsuit Roxie was wearing and do a close-up of her grabbing Nelly's hand. I still have to talk Nelly into this but I'll manage."

Willy gave her an encouraging nod and continued the explanation. "Cordelia, we've already put a deposit on the apartment. The only furniture in the room was Tim's recliner and it's still there. The chalk marks where the body was lying are visible. I'll take Tim's part. I mean I'll stretch out on the floor by the recliner. Nelly said Tim was wearing a gray sweatsuit and moccasins."

Sister Maeve Marie's eyes were snapping with excitement. "When I was a cop we called that 'testalying.' I love it."

Willy looked at Cordelia. He knew Alvirah had every intention of carrying out her scheme. Even so it would help if Cordelia wouldn't try to throw a monkey wrench in the plans. Alvirah was worried enough about having set up the plan that got Nelly in so much trouble. When Cordelia didn't approve of a course of action she had an uncanny way of convincing you it was destined for failure.

Cordelia frowned momentarily and then her brow cleared. "God writes straight in crooked lines," she decreed. "When are we going to film?"

Alvirah felt a wave of relief. "As soon as possible. We've got to find an actress who can impersonate Roxie." As she spoke she was looking at Sister Maeve Marie. Like Roxie, Maeve was tall and had a good figure. Like Roxie, her hands were well-shaped with long fingers.

"I'm very glad you two came," she said heartily.

Two days later they were ready to close the trap. In the Christopher Street apartment where Tim Monahan had met his end, Brian was directing the action.

"Uncle Willy, just lie down there. We had to erase the chalk marks but we penciled in the outline."

Obediently Willy stretched out by the recliner.

The cameraman stepped aside and Brian peered through the lens then consulted the picture of the dead Tim that the editor of the *Globe* had managed to get copied by bribing an aide in the medical examiner's office.

"You don't look fat enough," Brian decreed.

"Good news," Willy mumbled.

The problem was solved when Brian took off his sweater and stuffed it under Willy's sweatshirt.

Nelly was standing in the corner. She was wearing the blue suit and print blouse she'd worn when she visited Tim and Roxie. In her purse she was carrying a gun that looked just like the one that she had taken from the boys the other day.

Only four days ago, she thought. It doesn't seem possible. She peeked over at Dennis O'Shea, who gave her an encouraging smile. He was such a nice person. In a funny way when he was around she felt so comfortable even in the midst of all this horror. It made her think of long ago when her mother and father used to sit together and just talk about this or that over dinner and then spend the evening reading or listening to the radio. *Amos and Andy*, she thought. That was their favorite program

She wondered if she could have a radio in her cell in prison. Last evening Alvirah and Willy and Dennis had come into her apartment together while she was sorting clothes to give to Goodwill and told her that they thought Roxie was the one who'd shot Tim and they needed her help proving it.

All night Nelly had slept fitfully. She dreamt about Tim and Roxie and her finger ached where she'd caught it on the pin. Then she woke up remembering she'd forgotten to give the pin back to Alvirah.

Then she glanced at Sister Maeve who looked unnervingly like Roxie. She had on a blonde wig and an exact copy of the striped suit Roxie had been wearing when she became the widow Monahan. An outsized turquoise ring reached the knuckle of her index finger. Acrylic bloodred fingernails accentuated her long fingers and liver spots had been painted on the backs of her hands. *Just like Roxie,* Nelly thought with a touch of satisfaction as she glanced down at her own smooth skin.

Sister Cordelia was watching the proceedings with her arms folded. She reminded Nelly of the nuns she'd had in parochial school, the kind who were very fair but could wither you with a glance if you stepped out of line.

That nice young man Brian was asking her if she was ready. When she nodded he said, "Go to the door, Nelly. Try to do everything just as you did it the other day."

She looked at Willy. "Then you can't be dead yet."

As he struggled to his feet she went to the door. "Roxie let me in," she explained. "Tim was sitting in his chair. I could tell he was very upset but I thought it was at me or maybe even because I had told him about being terminal. Anyhow I just walked past Roxie and went over to him and just blurted out that I wanted the truth before I died . . ."

"Do it," Brian ordered. "Maeve, you go to the door."

Nelly had rehearsed the speech she made to Tim so much that it wasn't hard to stand over the recliner and deliver it again. It wasn't hard to superimpose Tim's face over Willy's. But Willy looked concerned.

"You should start smiling," she instructed. "It was very mean of you but you shouldn't have smiled when I told you I was dying."

Oh my God, Alvirah thought. Maybe I'm barking up the wrong tree.

"But then I forgave you because right away you admitted that you'd switched the ticket." Nelly opened her purse. "And I almost fainted because I remembered I didn't have the pin on and I opened my purse and started fumbling for it like this and Roxie saw the gun." She paused. "Wait a minute. Roxie was yelling at Tim to shut up but when she opened the door for me she had just said something else to him."

"It's not important," Brian said quickly. "We're not doing audio."

Nelly felt as though she was watching the replay of a video tape. It was all coming back. She grabbed the pin at the bottom of her purse and like an echo she could hear Roxie scream about the gun.

"I let go of the pin and grabbed the gun and pulled it out and tried to show it to her. Tim jumped up. The gun went off. Tim yelled . . . what did he yell? . . . 'Nelly, don't go wacko. We'll split the ticket.' Then he dove for the floor."

He dove for the floor, Alvirah thought. He didn't fall. He *dove.*

It was all clear to Nelly. She thought she'd shot him and started to faint then felt a hand close on hers, her wrist being wrenched. That's why my wrist hurts. That was the way it happened. I'm sure of it now.

Tim had said something else, she thought. *What was it?*

She felt Sister Maeve twist her hand and point the gun down at Willy now acting out his part on the floor. *That was when I fainted.*

She let her knees cave in and sank to the floor.

"That was very good, Nelly," Brian said. "I can't believe we did it on a first take but I think we have it. We'll just play it back to be sure then hope to God Roxie won't see through the trick."

Nelly sat up. She reached for her purse and dug in it for the pin which she failed to return to Alvirah. "I wonder," she said.

Alvirah experienced that wonderful moment when instinctively she knew something important was about to happen. "What is it Nelly?" she asked.

"Just now it was as though I was hearing Dennis teaching me how to turn on the pin. He told me that I had to give it a hard snap with this finger." She held up the index finger of her right hand.

"And that finger has been bothering me since I was here the other day. Do you think I might have turned on the recorder just before I tried to show Roxie the gun? I never checked it. Do you think it might have picked up Tim's voice pleading for his life?"

"Saints preserve us," Cordelia breathed.

The recorder in the pin Alvirah had given Nelly was still turned on. The battery was dead, but Alvirah expertly took out the tiny cassette and switched it to her own pin.

Cordelia's lips moved in silent prayer as Alvirah turned it on. The sound began immediately. A shot, Tim's voice calling Nelly a wacko. Nelly saying, "Oh my, oh my, oh I'm sorry," then a harsh angry voice, Roxie's voice, "Tim, you bastard."

I forgot that, Nelly thought. *Nice language.*

And finally Tim's pleading, "Roxie, don't. Roxie, don't shoot me!"

Alvirah felt Willy's arm around her. "You've done it again, honey."

As a former policewoman, Maeve had insisted that with the weight of evidence, the district attorney should be brought in on the scam. One of his best undercover agents had posed as the cameraman who'd captured the shooting when they confronted Roxie.

It was a clean sweep. When Roxie saw the tape and heard the audio she'd immediately offered him whatever he wanted to sell it to her. Under his skillful questioning she admitted everything. Now she was under indictment and Nelly was vindicated and declared the rightful owner of the lottery ticket.

Two nights later Nelly insisted on cooking the celebration dinner for the six of them, Alvirah and Willy, Sisters Cordelia and Maeve Marie, and Dennis and herself.

Dennis had brought champagne. With moist eyes Nelly acknowledged their toast and then raised one of her own. "To all of you and to Brian. I'm sorry he has to be in Hollywood tonight what with the earthquakes they have every time someone sneezes."

"It's all so unbelievable," she said a few minutes later as she watched Dennis carve the succulent saddle of lamb she'd prepared with her own special recipe.

Tomato and onion salad, mashed potatoes, crisp green beans, flakey biscuits, mint jelly, warm apple pie. Nelly beamed as she accepted their compliments.

At nine o'clock Cordelia and Maeve got up to go. "I'll see you first thing in the morning," Cordelia ordered Willy. "Bring your toolbox. I've got a bunch of jobs for you."

"We're ready to go too. We'll drop you off," Willy told her.

"I'm not setting foot out of here until I help Nelly clear up," Alvirah announced firmly. Then she felt Willy's shoe tap her foot.

She turned. Nelly and Dennis were smiling into each other's eyes.

"It's time to go home, honey," Willy said firmly as he put his hands on the back of her chair.

Kitty and Her Sisters

Also by Maureen Lee

THE PEARL STREET SERIES

Lights Out Liverpool

Put Out the Fires

Through the Storm

Stepping Stones

Liverpool Annie

Dancing in the Dark

The Girl From Barefoot House

Laceys of Liverpool

The House by Princes Park

Lime Street Blues

Queen of the Mersey

The Old House on the Corner

The September Girls

Nov. 2016
RL - Good Reading

Kitty and Her Sisters

Maureen Lee

First published in Great Britain in 2006 by Orion,
an imprint of the Orion Publishing Group Ltd

A CIP catalogue record for this book
is available from the British Library.

Typeset by Deltatype Ltd, Birkenhead, Merseyside

Printed in Great Britain by Clays Ltd, St Ives plc

The Orion Publishing Group Ltd
Orion House
5 Upper Saint Martin's Lane
London WC2H 9EA

www.orionbooks.co.uk

The Fifties

Chapter 1

Bootle, Liverpool
1950

'I wonder why people still sing war songs?' I mused. ' "Roll Out the Barrel", "When the Lights Go On Again", that sort of thing. I'd've thought they'd want to forget the war, not be reminded of it, particularly at a wedding.'

My friend, Marge, just grunted. We were sitting by a window watching our Norah have her photo taken with her new husband, Roy Hall. Norah's going-away outfit was a pale-pink costume with a white hat, gloves, bag and shoes. Like me and my other sisters, Norah was neither tall nor short and had the same dark red hair, blue eyes and wide mouth. None of the four McCarthy girls were exactly pretty, but were often described as striking.

It was my opinion that Norah was wasted on Roy Hall, a most unattractive individual with heavily Brylcreemed hair and the sort of moustache sported by the late Adolf Hitler. He worked as a clerk with Bootle Corporation.

The wedding reception had reached the stage that I always thought of as 'half time'. Any minute now, Norah and Roy would leave for their honeymoon. Most of the food had been eaten, and what remained was spread on a table by the door for people to help themselves. Some of the older guests had already gone home, the smaller children had fallen asleep on their weary mothers' laps, while the older ones lounged around, looking bored out of their skulls while they waited for the activities to recommence.

'It stinks in here,' Marge said, holding her nose.

'I'm not surprised.' Layers of smoke floated beneath the ceiling, and the room smelled of stale cigarettes, beer and sweaty bodies. I saw my brother, Jamie, who was seventeen and should have known better, sneakily burst a balloon, making everyone jump. The pianist had disappeared, leaving an empty tankard in the hope it would be re-filled, and an unnatural hush had fallen on the scout hut where the sound of us enjoying ourselves had only recently threatened to bring down the walls and lift the roof. The double doors were wide open to the late-afternoon sunshine. It was June and had been a perfect day for a wedding.

'Your Norah should have worn a pink hat,' Marge remarked. 'I read in a magazine that you should never have more than three accessories the same colour.' Marge wore a smart tan linen suit with dark-brown shoes. Her hat, a tan beret, had been deposited in the cloakroom. The trouble with Marge was she always bought clothes a size too small so that the jacket was buttoned tight across her breasts and the skirt wrinkled on her thighs. As usual, her pretty face was plastered with make-up and her long brown hair had been permed to a frizz. I wished someone would tell her she looked like a tart – *I* didn't have the courage.

'It's a bit late now to inform Norah she bought the wrong colour hat,' I said. 'In a while, I'm going home to change out of me bridesmaid's dress. Things will liven up later and it might get ripped or someone will spill beer on it. Anyroad, I loathe the damn thing.' The dress was lilac slipper satin with puffed sleeves, a full gathered skirt ending in a double frill, and a sash that tied in a huge bow at the back. I'd got rid of the lilac picture hat, but still felt like a doll perched on top of a Christmas tree.

'You'll feel more comfortable in something of your own,' Marge said idly.

'I hope you're not saying that because I look desperately beautiful and you're madly jealous.' I grinned.

Marge contrived to look hurt. 'As if I would! Your Claire's already changed, but Aileen's still wearing hers.'

'Poor Claire. She didn't know she'd be expecting when Norah ordered the bridesmaids' outfits. The dressmaker had to let it out to accommodate the bulge.' The minute the photos were taken, Claire had swapped it for a maternity frock. 'And Aileen's only waiting for Norah to leave to change into something else.'

Marge gave me a nudge. 'Have you noticed Ada Tutty keeps staring at your Danny as if she'd like to eat him?' she said in a low voice. 'She's hardly taken her eyes off him all afternoon.'

I transferred my gaze to a rather mournful young woman clad in a frock more suitable for someone three times her age, who was watching my other brother with a look of longing on her plain face. Ada was the daughter of our next-door neighbour in Amethyst Street. I always felt dead sorry for her. 'She's mad on our Danny,' I said. 'Sundays, she waits by the parlour window until he leaves for Mass, then follows and kneels as close to him as she can. No matter what Mass he goes to, the very first or the very last, she's always there. It drives him doolally.'

'I quite fancy your Danny meself,' Marge confessed. My brother was currently flirting outrageously with a friend of Norah's. He was twenty-two and I could see nothing remarkable about him, but he must have had sex appeal because girls were attracted to him like flies to jam.

'Would you like me to tell him?' I offered.

'Jaysus, Mary and Joseph, don't you dare do such a thing!' Marge gasped.

'It'd be nice to have you for a sister-in-law, Marge.' We were both nineteen and had been friends since we started school together at five.

'It'd be the gear,' Marge agreed, 'but if you breathe a word to your Danny I'll never speak to you again.'

We moved our chairs to allow my ten-year-old niece, Patsy, who was wearing one of the bridesmaids' hats, to gather the confetti that had collected underneath.

'What are you going to do with that?' I asked.

'I'm keeping it for when *I* get married,' Patsy announced. 'I only want the silver bits, I like them best.'

'Why do little girls always assume they'll get married?' I wondered aloud when Patsy had gone.

Marge shrugged. 'Because it's what little girls do when they grow up.'

'Not all of them,' I argued.

'Only if a man doesn't ask them and they end up sad old maids.'

'What if a women *chooses* not to get married no matter how many men ask?' I felt rather put out by the idea that a woman without a man would automatically be sad.

'Then she'd be crazy,' Marge said flatly. 'No one in their right mind would be an old maid when they could have a husband. I want kids and you have to be married for that.'

'Does that mean you'd marry any old man just to get a ring on your finger?'

'As long as he didn't have a face like a horse and had a decent job.' She looked at me defiantly. 'Wouldn't you?'

'Not on your nelly, no.' I'd been out with plenty of chaps in my time, but there hadn't been one I'd wanted to spend a whole day with, let alone the rest of my life.

'Now you're talking like a soft girl, Kitty McCarthy.'

I couldn't be bothered arguing any more. 'Oh, look! Norah and Roy are coming in to say tara. Don't you think he's a drip?' Perhaps Marge was right in a way, because I was convinced our Norah had only married Roy because she was twenty-four and worried she might be left on the shelf when Peter Murphy jilted her after they'd been courting for three whole years. 'Me, I'd sooner be an old maid any day than marry a drip like Roy Hall,' I said defiantly.

After the newly married couple had made their goodbyes, Norah tossed her bouquet – Marge caught it, much to her delight – then departed in Roy's brother's van for the honeymoon in Cornwall.

Aileen came up. 'I can't wait to get out of this horrible frock, sis. I didn't like to before in case I hurt our Norah's feelings, but now I'm going to Amethyst Street to get changed. Mam and Dad went back a couple of minutes ago.'

'Did Mam seem all right?' I asked, alarmed.

'Fine,' Aileen said reassuringly. 'She said she just felt like a decent cup of tea and a little lie-down.'

'That's all right, then. Hang on a mo while I find me bag; I'll come with you.'

'It looks the gear on you – the dress, that is,' Aileen remarked as we strolled along Marsh Lane towards the house where we were born. Four years ago, Aileen had married Michael Gilbert and now lived in Maghull. She had a good job as an overseer in Wexford's Biscuit Factory on the Dock Road where Michael was head of Accounts. The first McCarthy to live in a bought house, she considered herself a cut above the rest of us.

'It looks nice on you, too,' I said loyally. 'And it would have looked nice on Claire if she hadn't been in the club. As it was, she looked like a badly wrapped parcel.'

'I wouldn't mind looking like a badly wrapped parcel if it meant I was pregnant,' Aileen said wistfully. She was desperate for a baby.

'Never mind, sis, it'll happen one day,' I promised recklessly. 'Have you noticed everyone's staring at us?' I was glad the shops had closed so there weren't as many people about as usual.

'I'm not surprised. I feel like a dog's dinner in this outfit. I was hoping Norah would pick silk or crêpe de Chine and a less sickly colour. Then we could've taken them up and worn them again. Now I don't know what to do with the stupid thing,' she finished in disgust. 'I can't think of a single thing I can make from it.'

'Pin cushions?'

Aileen rolled her eyes. 'Sometimes,' she said when we turned into Amethyst Street, 'I wander around my three-bedroom semi and wonder how ten of us managed to squeeze into one of these little terraced houses. In those days, the lavatory was at the bottom of the yard and we got bathed in a tin tub in front of the fire.'

'Yes, but things have improved since then.' Dad had fitted a bath and lavatory in the washhouse with the help of Danny who was a plumber. A door had been installed leading to the kitchen. The old lavatory had been removed and we now used the place to keep coal.

'Not before time,' Aileen sniffed.

'I'm dead sorry our Norah's gone,' I tried hard to sound sincere, 'but it means I'll have a double bed to meself for the first time in my life.'

'In other words, you're not sorry at all.' Aileen paused opposite a lamp-post over which a rope had been thrown; a little boy was swinging round and round, his eyes blissfully closed. 'I used to have some fun on that,' she said nostalgically. 'When we were little, me and our Claire had some terrible fights over who had first go on the swing.'

'Who usually won?' I hadn't been born until Claire was twelve and Aileen ten.

'Me. I was the smallest, but I had the strongest punch.'

All these years later, it was impossible to imagine my sisters, elegant Aileen and motherly Claire, involved in a fistfight.

We arrived at number twenty-two. Aileen put her hand through the letterbox and pulled out the key attached to a string. She unlocked the door and stepped inside, then turned to me, whispering, 'Mam's crying. It sounds like she's upstairs. Dad's with her.'

I made a face. 'I thought she was better. I haven't heard her cry for months.' We crept down the hall and sat at the bottom of the stairs to listen, our dresses floating around us with a breathy sound before settling in folds at our feet.

'I'm sorry, Bob,' Mam wept. 'I'm sorry if I'm spoiling the day for you, but ever since I woke up this morning I haven't been able to get our Jeff and Will out of me mind. They should have been at Norah's wedding and I kept seeing them among the guests. Like ghosts, they were, smiles on their dear faces, but whenever I looked again they'd disappeared. I managed to hold meself together for Norah's sake, but as soon as she left all I wanted to do was come home and have a good cry.'

'Cry as much as you want, Bernie, luv,' Dad said gently.

'I kept thinking, Jeff would be thirty if he were still alive and married to Theresa – those children of hers would have belonged to him. And Will would be twenty-seven. Oh, Bob!' she cried, 'I'll never get over losing me lads, not if I live to be a hundred.' The sobs tore at her frail body and her breathing was hoarse and wretched.

I felt an ache come to my throat. Tears were trickling down Aileen's cheeks. Then my sister held out her arms and we clung together at the bottom of the stairs as we listened to our mother weep her heart out.

When the war had begun eleven years ago in 1939, there'd been eight McCarthy children – four boys and four girls – but by the time it ended six years later, only two of the boys were left. The first to go was Jeff, only twenty-four when he was hit in the chest by a sniper's bullet as the Allies fought their way across Occupied France. We were still in a state of shock when Will, three years younger, had gone down with his ship in the icy waters of the Baring Sea when it was ripped apart by a torpedo, a present from the German U-boat lurking underneath.

Losing Jeff had been bad enough, but for Mam Will's death had been the last straw. She'd removed the crucifix that used to stand on the sideboard and every single holy picture and statue from the house, as if she'd given up all faith in God, although she still went to Mass and Benediction on Sundays. As the years passed, she hardly ate, and became thinner and thinner, weaker and weaker. Sometimes, I wondered if she was doing it deliberately, willing herself to die so she could join her sons, entirely forgetting she had a husband and six children who still needed her.

Lately, though, it seemed she was coming to terms with the loss of her two strapping lads. Perhaps it was the preparations for Norah's wedding that had taken her mind off it a little. But now Norah was married, did it mean it was all going to start again and we would have to continue watching our mother fade to nothing in front of our eyes?

'What exactly happened when they died, Bob?' Mam was saying in a thin, shaky voice. 'Did the bullet that struck our Jeff in the chest kill him instantly? Or did he lie there in agony before he passed away? And was it the torpedo that did for Will or did he drown when the ship sank? It gnaws away at me all day long. I've lived through their dying moments a million times.'

'There, there, sweetheart.' Dad's voice held a note of desperation. Perhaps he had no words of comfort left. He'd had no opportunity to mourn his sons, no one to make a fuss of him as he'd done of Mam. His remaining children had tried, but it wasn't enough. Only another parent could properly understand how he felt inside. I wouldn't have dreamed of saying it aloud, but I often wondered if Mam was wrong to unload all her misery on to our father when he already had enough of his own. Tragedies should be shared, not borne by a single pair of shoulders, however strong they might appear to be.

'I left my clothes in the front bedroom,' Aileen whispered, 'but I can't very well disturb them. I'll go back to the reception and get changed later.'

'So will I.' My clothes were in the bedroom I'd shared with Norah, but I thought it best not to venture upstairs just now.

When we got back to the scout hut, the atmosphere had livened up. Fresh sarnies had appeared, the pianist had returned – his tankard had been refilled – and he was playing a lively march for the children, who were involved in a game of musical chairs.

'It's like the war all over again,' Claire said disgustedly when we joined her. She looked dead tired. I wondered guiltily if it was her who'd had to make the sarnies. 'The bigger kids are throwing the little ones all over the place in order to reach a chair. My three are already out and they're not very pleased about it. Patsy's lost all her confetti, Colette's limping, and I'm sure our Mark didn't have a black eye when we left the house this morning.'

'You'd better keep out of the road in your condition,' I advised when my pregnant – and favourite – sister looked in danger of being mown down by a decreasing circle of frantic children waiting for the music to stop so they could fight their way to the chairs.

Claire backed away. 'I thought you both went home to get rid of them ghastly outfits?'

'We did, but Mam was crying upstairs and we thought we'd leave it till later,' Aileen said. 'Poor Dad, he sounds at the end of his tether.'

'Mam said she kept seeing Jeff and Will at the wedding like ghosts. Perhaps we should have guessed today would upset her,' I added.

'I don't want to know about it, not right now,' Claire said harshly. 'Me kids are all hurt in one way or another, me husband's disappeared and the baby's kicking the hell out of me. I've got enough to worry about. In fact, *I* wouldn't mind going home.' She looked close to tears. 'Oh, and you might like to know our Jamie's as drunk as a lord.' The youngest McCarthy was always getting into mischief of some sort. Claire turned away, muttering, 'Mam's not the only one who saw ghosts at the wedding.'

I had also thought about my brothers throughout the day, but didn't say so. Instead, I changed the subject. 'Have we got a prize for whoever wins at musical chairs?' I asked. The game was nearly over, there was only one chair left and a muscular-looking girl of about ten from the bridegroom's side of the family was competing with a weedy lad of indeterminable age whom I'd never seen before. He was exceptionally fast on his feet.

'If the girl wins,' Claire said threateningly, 'her prize will be a smack on the gob. She's the one who tripped up Colette and made her limp.'

Fortunately for the girl, the boy won, and he didn't seem to expect a prize – the applause and feeling of achievement were clearly enough.

I went to look for Marge and found her talking to Ada Tutty – she must have taken pity on the girl. 'Did you know Ada's going to night school to learn to speak French and Spanish?' she asked.

'Really?' I didn't know much about Ada other than she had a crush on Danny and had been in the year behind me and Marge at school. She was clever and had passed the scholarship, but her mother refused to let her go to secondary school, saying she couldn't afford the uniform. Ada was very small with a little pale face and thin pale hair – the sort of girl who was never looked at twice.

'I want to be an interpreter,' she whispered.

'Is there much of a call for interpreters in Bootle?' Marge asked. She winked at me from behind Ada's back, but I ignored it.

'No, but there is in London and abroad.'

'Are you thinking of going to work abroad, Ada?' I was impressed.

'I might.' Ada blushed, and her eyes flickered towards Danny. He was now flirting with a different girl, who was fluttering her eyelashes at him coyly.

'That's a marvellous idea.' I genuinely meant it, though got the distinct impression Ada wouldn't dream of going abroad if she could get her hands on our Danny. 'I wouldn't mind doing it meself. I wouldn't mind going to night school, either. I'd take English. At school, my spelling was hopeless and my grammar even worse. I'm not even sure where to put a comma.'

'What point would there be in that?' Marge demanded.

'Knowing where to put commas?'

'No, learning English, soft girl.'

'Well, I could write a decent letter for one thing,' I said stoutly.

'How many times a year do you write a letter, Kitty?'

'Two or three, and I'm reaching for the dictionary every other minute.'

Marge sniffed. 'You'd be better off taking cookery. At least it'd be useful. You're a hopeless cook.'

'Oh, no!' Ada's little plain face was suddenly transformed and she looked quite animated. 'There's plenty of time for Kitty to learn to cook, but writing letters – writing anything – is terribly important. You have to know how to express yourself and what words to use. I write poetry,' she added shyly.

'See!' I gave my friend a challenging look. 'I've never written a poem in me life.'

'And a fat lot of good it'd do you if you did.'

I would have liked to continue the discussion, but the pianist struck up the Gay Gordons and Liam, Claire's husband, asked me to dance.

'I hope you don't mind, but Claire's not up to it and I need the exercise,' he said, stamping his huge feet like a member of the

Gestapo. I liked Liam Quinn, a big, noisy man with brown curly hair, laughing brown eyes and an extrovert personality. He played football for Bootle Rangers, an amateur team, and he and Claire were extremely happy with each other.

'Claire said you'd disappeared,' I said accusingly.

'Just went round to a mate's house to listen to the cricket results on the wireless and have a quiet brew. By the way, 'case you're interested, North Korea has invaded South Korea. It said so on the news.'

'What does that mean?'

'Another war,' Liam said laconically. He twisted me round and we marched back the way we'd come.

'But it's only five years since the last one ended!'

'Don't I know it, Kitty. I was in the Lancashire Fusiliers, remember?'

'Will you be called up again? Will our Danny have to go? And what about Jamie? He'll be eighteen in December. Oh, this'll kill Mam,' I wailed.

'I dunno what's going to happen.' He shrugged. 'North Korea has the Soviet Union behind it, and America backs the South. This could be the start of the Third World War and we'll end up atom-bombing each other to bits. We'll just have to see. Come on, Kitty,' he urged as he tried to twirl my limp body around, 'it's like dancing with a sack of sawdust. I'd've been better off with Claire and she's six months pregnant.'

'I'm sorry, Liam, but I don't feel like dancing any more.' I walked off the floor.

'Oh, come off it, luv. I was exaggerating about the war.' He followed and grabbed my arm. 'It'll just be a storm in a teacup, that's all.'

He was still holding my arm when I went outside, where the sun was setting. It felt cooler. 'I didn't mean to upset you, Kitty,' he said contritely. 'I was exaggerating, like I said before.'

'But there *might* be a war. Oh, Liam, I *hate* wars.' I'd loathed sitting in the shelter listening to bombs explode all over Bootle, hated going to school next morning and seeing the empty spaces where houses had once stood and the empty desks of my classmates who'd lived in the houses and were now dead or injured. Most of all, I'd hated losing the brothers whom I'd loved with all my heart, then seeing my mother turn into an old woman almost overnight.

Liam took me in his arms, patted my back and said, 'There, there,' in the same tone my father had used to my mother earlier on. I was about to push him away, ashamed of appearing weak, when Claire appeared in the doorway.

'Should I divorce you now, Liam, for having an affair with me little sister, or wait until I've got more evidence?' she asked, smiling. She'd recovered her good humour.

'I just told Kitty some bad news I heard on the wireless,' Liam explained. 'She's taken it hard.'

'Trust you not to be able to keep your big mouth shut, Liam Quinn,' Claire said amiably. 'You can tell me the bad news tomorrow. I'm not in the mood for it right now. Come on, Kitty, luv, let's go in the kitchen and I'll make us a cup of tea.'

'I wonder if our Norah's reached Bridgenorth yet?' Claire said. She switched on the urn in the shabby kitchen and put two spoonfuls of tea in a giant metal pot.

'I'm not sure how far away Bridgenorth is.' Norah and Roy were staying the night there and carrying on to Cornwall in the morning.

'Neither am I.' Claire grinned. 'I don't envy her, sleeping with Roy Hall for the first time – or it might not be the first time, who am I to say? I can't understand why she married the chap.'

''Cos Peter Murphy jilted her, that's why.'

'Yes, but all she had to do was wait a while and someone else would've come along, someone with a bit more spunk in them who didn't look like death warmed up.'

'And have a moustache like Hitler's,' I added.

'And have a moustache like Hitler's,' Claire agreed with another grin. 'In fact, I can't understand why women are always in such a rush to get married.'

'You did when you were twenty,' I pointed out.

'Yes, but I had to, didn't I? Didn't you know that?' she said when my eyes widened in surprise. 'I thought the whole world did, or at least the whole of Amethyst Street. Our Patsy was born seven months after the wedding. Oh, Mam went round telling everyone she'd arrived early, but no one believed her.'

'*I* did,' I said indignantly. 'I expected to see this titchy little baby, but Patsy was quite big and I wondered what she'd have looked like if you'd gone the whole nine months.'

Claire laughed. 'Poor innocent little Kitty! Anyroad, not long after Patsy came along, Liam was called up and, instead of spending the next five years doing war work and having a good time with me mates, I was stuck in the house with a baby to look after. I love the bones of Liam, but I wish we hadn't had to get married when we did.' Her expression grew serious. 'Take my advice, Kitty, if you ever feel tempted to go with a feller, make sure you don't fall for a baby and end up having to marry him. It might not be someone like Liam Quinn you get stuck with, but a chap like our Danny, who I wouldn't trust any further than I could throw him. He'd make a terrible husband.'

'I'll remember that,' I vowed.

Of course, I didn't. The day came when I made the same mistake as Claire but, in my case, it turned out very differently.

The night wore on. Mam and Dad returned, both looking rather strained. Our Danny asked Marge to dance twice, and her face bore a triumphant smile as she whirled past in his arms. Me and Aileen agreed we couldn't be bothered to go home and change our frocks. No one mentioned the fact that North Korea had invaded the South – or was it the South had invaded the North? I'd never heard of Korea before and could have got it the wrong way round. Liam found our Jamie in a drunken sleep at the back of the scout hut. Claire told him to leave him there.

'Let him sleep it off, the daft little bugger. Serve him right if he wakes up in the middle of the night and everyone's gone home.'

'You're a hard woman, Claire Quinn,' Liam said, shuddering.

'Don't I need to be with an idiot like you for a husband?'

Liam looked at me, as if to say, 'What have I done wrong?'

Roy's mother exchanged blows with her husband, and my father had to separate them. An old lady fell asleep in the only lavatory and couldn't be budged until someone climbed over the door. Ada Tutty had to take Mrs Tutty home when she swore she was having a heart attack, but it turned out to be indigestion.

All in all, it was a typical Liverpool wedding and, apart from one or two hiccups, I quite enjoyed myself. It was the day I began to look very differently on life. Perhaps it was Norah getting wed to drippy Roy Hall, the things Claire had said about not marrying young, Marge going on about old maids or the way Ada had looked at our Danny, but it was on that day that I decided I wasn't willing to stay in my dead-end job until a fellow came along and rescued me. I would find another job, go to night school and be taught where to put commas. Oh, and I'd only get married to a man I was head over heels in love with. If I didn't meet one, then I'd be quite content to become an old maid, though I promised myself I wouldn't be sad.

I'd worked in the packing department of Cameron's Shoe Factory in Hawthorn Road since I left school at fourteen. I wrapped shoes in tissue paper, placed them in the right-sized box, and stuck a label on the end: Lady's Red Court, size 4; Gent's Grey Brogue, size 10; Child's Brown Sandal, size 1. The label also had a little drawing of the model inside and a reference number for re-ordering. It wasn't exactly an inspiring job, but I worked with three other women – Betty, Enid and Theresa. We got on well and had a good laugh.

Betty and Enid were both sixty if a day, and Theresa I'd known for years, long before I came to work at Cameron's, as she'd been engaged to our Jeff. They were going to get married when the war was over. I'd always admired her lovely serene face and smooth brown hair, which she still wore coiled in a bun at the back of her neck. She was now married to a chap called Barry Quigley and had two children, a boy and a girl. Her mother looked after them during the day.

'How did the wedding go?' she asked when I arrived on Monday. It looked as if Betty and Enid were going to be late.

'Fine,' I told her. 'I'm sorry you weren't invited, but Mam couldn't stand the idea of seeing you with the children. It would've reminded her too much of Jeff.'

'Perhaps I'd've been too much reminded of Jeff an' all,' Theresa said quietly. She'd never said anything, but I don't think she was very happy with Barry. 'Your mam wasn't the only one whose heart was broken when Jeff was killed,' she went on in the same tone. 'But you have to move forward, not live in the past and make everyone around you as miserable as sin. You know, luv, I shouldn't say this, but it's about time your mam came to terms with the fact that Jeff and Will are dead. Oh, I'm not suggesting she get over it, that'd be too much to ask, but it's not fair on the rest of you for her to keep on grieving so that it stays fresh in your minds, as if it only happened yesterday, not six years ago.'

I had already begun to have the same thoughts myself, but didn't have the opportunity to say so because Betty and Enid came in together, full of their weekends and also wanting to know about the wedding. I only told them the funny bits, like the old lady falling asleep in the lavatory, and our Jamie coming home in the early hours of the morning having woken up behind the scout hut with a terrible hangover and highly indignant at being left behind.

'I could've been murdered,' he'd complained when I went downstairs to see what the noise was, worried he'd disturb Mam.

'It would have served you right,' I told him, 'getting drunk at your age.'

The others, Theresa included, found this highly amusing, and the supervisor, Ronnie Turnbull, came to ask what was so funny.

'Your face,' Enid cackled, and we laughed even more as we continued to pack shoes and stick labels on boxes – Ronnie never had any reason to complain about our work.

As the hours passed and my arms began to ache, I remembered that I'd vowed to find another job. I'd spent five years in Cameron's – eight hours a day, five and a half days a week – and it wasn't exactly rewarding. I'd miss my mates, but there had to be more to life than packing shoes.

I discussed it next day with Theresa in the canteen when we were having our dinner, and explained how I felt.

'I've often wondered what you were doing here, Kitty. It's the sort of job where you only need half a brain. I do it for the money and Betty and Edna for the company. But you?' She smiled at me warmly and I desperately wished she'd married our Jeff and we were sisters-in-law. 'Unless you intend getting wed shortly, you'd be better off doing something more interesting.'

'Anything would be more interesting than what I do now.' I gave a dismissive sniff.

'Not necessarily, luv. At least we have each other for company so the time doesn't drag.'

'I suppose that's true.'

'It is true, Kitty, there's no suppose about it. There's some

Mondays I look forward to coming to work after a weekend at home. Me and Barry don't exactly get on.' She gave me a wan look.

'I'm sorry.' I put my hand over hers.

That night, I looked through the dozens of vacancies in the *Liverpool Echo*. I hadn't the experience for the ones I fancied, and didn't fancy any of the rest.

'Are you thinking of getting another job, luv?' Dad asked when he noticed the page I was reading. We'd just finished our tea. Danny was upstairs getting ready to go out – I've no idea what he did to himself up there, but he took ages and never came down looking any different apart from having put on a suit – and Jamie had his face buried in the *Wizard*. Mam was resting in the parlour.

'Yes, Dad, but there's none really suitable, least not tonight.'

'Well, you can look again tomorrow. Is there anything in particular you're after?'

'Well,' I leaned on the table and rested my chin on my hands, 'I wouldn't mind being an actress or a singer or a writer, but I can't act, I can't sing and I can't spell.'

Jamie lifted his head out of the *Wizard*. 'Ha, ha,' he sneered. He seemed to think it was my fault he'd been left behind at the scout hut.

'Have you got a big enough brain to read that comic?' I asked frostily. 'Or are you just looking at the pictures?'

'The *Wizard* isn't a comic, it's a magazine,' he retorted.

I stuck out my tongue. 'Ha, ha.'

Dad smiled at this exchange and it struck me how rare it was that he smiled. Suddenly, I wanted to throw my arms around his neck and kiss him, but he wasn't a demonstrative man and it might make him feel embarrassed. I was also struck by how ill he looked; his face was chalky and heavily wrinkled, and his eyes were dull. I felt the urge to cry. If anything happened to him, if he died, I didn't know what I'd do. He was our rock, strong and immovable, the person our family depended on more than any other. A docker all his life, he worked long hours in a job that required great strength, but the last six years had taken its toll and I couldn't help but worry if he was still up to it.

'Would you like me to make more tea, Dad?' I asked, swallowing hard. It was all I could think of.

'I wouldn't mind, luv. Ta.'

I went into the kitchen and was filling the kettle when Mam shouted weakly from the parlour. 'Bob, are you there?'

'It's all right, Dad. I'll go.' I hurried back to the living room and rested my hand on his broad shoulder, squeezing it gently. I glanced at Jamie and jerked my head in the direction of the kitchen. 'Make the tea,' I mouthed. He nodded.

'Where's your dad?' Mam whispered when I went in. She was lying on the settee with a blanket thrown over her. Her face was pale and her hair completely white. It was hard to believe this was the same woman who'd once been so pretty and full of energy that the girls in school had envied me having her for a mam.

'Our Jamie's about to make him a cuppa, Mam.'

'Ask him to come in will you, Kitty?'

I squeezed myself on to the edge of the settee. I could feel her legs against me, as thin as sticks. 'What is it you want? I'll get it for you.'

'I just wanted to talk to him a minute,' she said fretfully.

'Well, talk to me. As I said, Jamie's making him a cuppa. He's hardly been home from work an hour and he's dead tired.' I did my best to hold back the tears. 'I'm worried about him, Mam. He doesn't look a bit well.'

'Doesn't he?' I saw fear come to her eyes. She, more than anyone, would be lost without Dad.

I remembered what Theresa had said that morning and felt my sympathy swing wildly between my mother and my father. Mam couldn't escape from the trap of grief and my heart bled for her, but she was also keeping Dad inside the trap. I stroked her brow; it was hot and sticky. 'Paul Temple's on the wireless tonight, Mam. Why don't you listen to it? It'll do Dad good to have a nice peaceful evening. I'll go round to Reilly's and buy you some sweets, shall I?' I only had enough money for a couple of bars of chocolate, but they'd be better than nothing.

She managed the ghost of a smile. 'You're a good girl, Kitty. I'll do what you say.'

'Would you like a cup of tea an' all?'

'Indeed I would. In fact, I'll come in the other room and drink it with you.'

I helped her off the settee. Jamie had made the tea and Danny had come downstairs. We all sat around the table and it was almost like old times, though I felt as if we were treading on eggshells. I worried that one of us would say the wrong thing and Mam would dissolve into tears.

Later, I went to Reilly's and bought a bar of Cadbury's Caramel and a bar of Fruit and Nut, Dad's favourite. When I got back, Danny had gone, Jamie had re-buried himself in the *Wizard*, and Mam and Dad were discussing buying a new three-piece. 'We could go into town on Saturday afternoon and look around the shops,' Dad was saying.

Mam nodded. 'That'd be nice.'

I hoped she was being sincere, not just making the effort, but either way it was a good sign.

'You're late,' Marge said accusingly when she opened the door of the house in Garnet Street where she lived with her mam. 'The first picture will have already started.'

Marge was an only child, her dad having done a bunk before she was even born. It wasn't surprising considering Mrs King was the most horrible woman in the world, with a vicious temper and a habit of taking a swipe at anyone who came within range. Once, when we were little, she'd actually hit me, and my own mam had come round to Garnet Street and torn her off a strip.

I said I was sorry. 'Things were happening at home and I couldn't get away.'

'That's all right.' I was forgiven. 'Come on in, Kitty.'

'Is your mam home?' I asked nervously. I was still afraid of Mrs King.

'No, she's gone to the pub, so I've got the house to meself till closing time.'

'We can go to the pictures tomorrow.' *Bride of Vengeance* with Paulette Goddard and Macdonald Carey was on at the Palace in Marsh Lane and I was anxious to see it. Then I remembered I'd spent all my money on the chocolate and would have to borrow some.

'I can't tomorrow. It's Tuesday and I'm going out with your Danny, aren't I?' She gave an irritating smirk.

'I'd forgotten.' We went into the parlour, a dismal room that smelled dusty and unused, and sat on the lumpy settee. 'What about Wednesday?'

'OK. Where's Danny tonight?' she asked in an offhand way.

'I dunno.' I shrugged. 'He went out earlier.'

'Has he got a date with someone?' Her tone was slightly less offhand, almost anxious.

'I dunno,' I repeated, though was pretty sure Danny was going out with one of Norah's friends he'd met at the wedding – he probably had a date with the other one on Wednesday.

'I think he likes me.' She was looking at me, as if expecting me to say, 'He's mad about you, Marge,' but Danny never discussed his complicated love life with anyone.

'Everyone likes you, Marge,' I said instead, which was true. It probably applied to Danny, but he liked an awful lot of girls – too many, if the truth be known.

I continued to look in the paper for a job but, unless I was willing to work in a shop, swap one factory for another or become a cleaner, there was nothing I could apply for.

'You're getting awful choosy in your old age,' our Claire said huffily when the family came round to tea on Sunday and I told her about my predicament. She'd worked in Scott's Bakery before she'd married Liam.

'It's not that,' I tried to explain. 'I don't think I'm too good to work in a baker's, fr'instance. I'm just looking for something more interesting, that's all.'

'It was quite interesting in Scott's. Some of the customers were a scream.'

'Leave her be,' said Mam. 'If she wants to change her job, then let her.'

'She seems better,' Claire whispered when Mam went into the kitchen. Dad and Liam had taken the children to play in Stanley Park. 'Did she make this fruit cake?' I nodded. 'It's ages since she made a cake. It's the gear.'

'I said something to her the other day about Dad looking ill; I think it got through to her that she was wearing him out.' I only wish I'd thought to say something like that before. 'Yesterday, she and Dad went into town to look at three-piece suites.'

'Did they now?' Claire's eyes gleamed. 'If they get a new one, d'you think they'd let me have the old? I really fancy brown tweed like the one our Aileen bought from Maple's for her posh new house, but Mam and Dad's will do. Norah won't want it: she and Roy are in furnished rooms. Our suite was second-hand, or might have been third, when we got it ten years ago; now it's not fit for a tramp to use.'

'I'm sure she will.' Claire lived nearby in Opal Street in a house similar to our own. Liam was a labourer for one of the biggest landlords in Bootle, but he didn't earn much. She was jealous of Aileen and her 'posh new house', and Aileen was jealous of Claire because she had three children. People were never satisfied with their lot, but then neither was I, so who was I to talk?

I discovered the Workers' Educational Authority held classes in the Community Centre on Strand Road, so put my name down for English Grammar when the new term started in September. I felt very pleased with myself for taking the first step towards becoming the new Kitty McCarthy, though it was a month since the wedding and I was no nearer finding a job than I'd been then.

Mam and Dad had bought a new three-piece – oatmeal moquette – and Liam cheerfully wheeled our old one home on a handcart. Claire had given *their* old one away, amazed there was anyone willing to give it house room.

Norah and Roy had returned from their honeymoon. Norah looked quite pleased with herself so perhaps Roy was all right once you got to know him.

The war in Korea had hardly been mentioned, not surprising seeing as it was so far away, unlike the last one. Britain had sent troops, but the general opinion was no one would be called up. Dad always made sure Mam didn't hear the news on the wireless, so she knew nothing about it.

Marge had been going out regularly with our Danny at least twice a week and she gave the impression of being madly in love. Every time we passed a jeweller's she stopped to price engagement rings.

'It looks as if there's a chance I'll be your sister-in-law, Kit,' she'd said only the other day. We were on the ferry on our way back from New Brighton. It was all we could afford as it was Thursday, the day before we got paid, and we were both virtually skint. All we'd bought was a threepenny bag of chips to share between us.

'Just because you've been out with him half a dozen times, it doesn't mean he'll marry you.' I was watching the lights reflected in the River Mersey, the way they wobbled in the rippling waves.

'It's eight times, actually.' She looked smug.

'Eight times, then. Peter Murphy went out with our Norah hundreds of times before he jilted her.' Since Claire had pointed out what a terrible husband Danny would make, I wasn't sure if I wanted him and my best friend to get married.

Female required, 18–40 years, to help look after two small children Monday to Friday. Hours 9–5.30. £2.10.0d. References essential. Mrs F. Knowles, 12 Weld Road, Orrell Park, Liverpool.

I read the advert several times. It wasn't quite what I'd been after, but it would be a change and I liked children – at least, I liked our Claire's three. Mrs Knowles hadn't mentioned needing experience and Orrell Park was only a bus ride away from Bootle. The wage was five bob less than Cameron's and I'd have fares to pay, but it didn't put me off.

'What do you think of this?' I showed the advert to Jamie who was the only one around.

'With you looking after them, sis, those kids will be dead within a month,' he snorted.

'Seriously, though,' I insisted.

'I was being serious. Oh, all right!' He ducked when I hit him with the paper. 'Sounds dead boring to me. I wouldn't do it if they paid me twice that much, but I suppose it'd be better than packing shoes. Have you got references?'

'I can get one from Cameron's.'

Later, Mam and Dad said it wouldn't hurt to apply, so I sat at the table and wrote a letter in my very best handwriting, reaching for the dictionary more than once. I couldn't remember if there was one 'p' or two in apply, or whether birth was spelled with an 'e' or an 'i'. When I looked, it could be spelled either way, but the one I wanted had an 'i'.

When it was finished, I took it next door to show to Ada Tutty, along with the advert. 'Does this seem all right, Ada?' Her house was even more miserable than Marge's. Mr Tutty worked on the docks, like my own dad, and their two sons were long-distance lorry drivers, so it wasn't as if they were poor, but Mrs Tutty was a real money-grubber and preferred to keep the money under the mattress rather than spend it.

'Well, it's not too bad,' Ada said after she'd looked the letter over.

'What's wrong with it?' I felt hurt.

'Rather than saying "I want to apply" it'd be better to put "wish". And "Dear Mrs Knowles" sounds friendlier than "Dear Madam". You've missed the "h" out of school and the whole letter's one long paragraph when it should be split into three. Would you like me to correct it,' she asked kindly, 'so you could do it again? There's one or two other things that would look better put a different way. Fr'instance, you don't sign Miss Katherine McCarthy, but Katherine McCarthy, and put the "Miss" afterwards in brackets.'

'Thanks, Ada.' I hadn't bothered to look up 'school' as I'd thought I could spell it. 'It must be nice to be clever,' I said admiringly.

'It's not much use when you work behind the counter in a butcher's,' she said bitterly. 'I wish I could've gone to secondary school, but Mam said we couldn't afford it. She couldn't wait for me to go work and bring in some money.'

She scrawled all over the letter and handed it back. 'Is Marge King courting your Danny?' she asked casually. 'I've seen them out together a few times.'

'Marge thinks they're courting, but I doubt very much if our Danny's of the same mind.'

A reply to my letter came by return of post. F. Knowles (Mrs) requested that I attend for interview on Monday afternoon. Weld Road was a mere two minutes walk away from Orrell Park Station the letter informed me. I wondered what the 'F' stood for – Freda, Fanny, Fay, Florence? There'd been a girl in my class at school called Francesca.

I decided to take the whole of Monday off and not tell anyone beforehand except Theresa. If I got the job I'd give my notice in on Tuesday. If I didn't I'd say I'd been sick.

Monday, I put on my best cream frock, a straw halo hat Norah had left behind, and lace gloves I'd borrowed off Aileen; I had lace gloves of my own, but they were full of holes and needed mending. I parked myself in front of the mirror, put on some lippy, powdered my nose and stood back to examine the effect. I quite liked my face.

I could judge my looks better than most people could because my sisters and I looked very much the same: Claire's face was the plumpest, Aileen's eyes a paler blue than the rest of us, and Norah's hair a slightly darker red. I had the widest mouth – I could have sworn it was getting wider and one day it would reach my ears. I adjusted the hat on my short curls. Aileen and Norah wore their hair long, but me and Claire preferred it short; it was less trouble.

It was only half past twelve when I set off, and hardly one when I got off the bus by Orrell Park. It was a brilliant day, the sun shining hot enough to crack the flags. I found Weld Road straight away and identified number twelve – it was a three-storey semi-detached house with a long front garden. The grass was badly in need of cutting and the front door could have a done with a lick of paint. I was about to walk back as far as the shops where there was a Woolworths and I could buy a few things, when a small boy of about three, wearing only underpants, came hurtling round from the back of the house on a little three-wheeler bike. He pedalled like a maniac down the path and was about to enter the road through the open gate, when the front door opened and a woman came out.

'Oliver!' she called limply. 'Oliver, darling, please come back.'

I stood in front of the child. When it appeared he was intent on running me down, I leaped out of the way and grabbed the handlebars.

By now, the woman had reached the gate. 'Thank you,' she gasped. 'He wants to go and see his father. He's in Egypt at the moment – well, I got a card from there this morning, but he'll be somewhere else by now.'

I looked down at the child who was still trying to pedal the bike, despite my hold on the handlebars. He reminded me of a cherub, with black curly hair, rosy cheeks and a little pink mouth. His big eyes were almost as dark as his hair. 'You'll need more than a bike to get you as far as Egypt, Oliver,' I told him.

'Wanna see Daddy,' he said stubbornly.

'Then you'll have to wait until the next time he comes home.' I lifted up both Oliver and the bike so they were pointing the other way and he pedalled up the path and disappeared behind the house.

'I try to keep the gate latched, but the postman always leaves it open,' the woman said distractedly. I guessed she was in her forties – quite old, I thought, to have two small children; I took for granted it was Mrs Knowles. She wore slacks and a cotton blouse, no make-up, and her hair hadn't been combed in quite a while. I admired her fine bone structure, straight nose and beautifully moulded cheekbones. Her eyes were silvery grey.

She smiled at me wearily, said thank you again, and was about to return to the house when another cherub, a smaller version of Oliver, came tottering down the path completely naked.

'Robin! Oh dear God, he's climbed out of his cot and come down the stairs on his own,' she screamed. She scooped the boy up in her arms and rushed inside the house. I followed, latching the gate firmly behind me.

'Look,' I said loudly through the still open door, 'my name's Kitty McCarthy and I applied for the job of looking after the children. Would you like me to give you a hand?'

The woman was sitting at the bottom of the stairs, clutching Robin and looking moidered to death. The sweat glistened on her forehead and had begun to run down her lovely cheeks.

'You're early,' she said in a quivery voice. Robin chuckled and pulled his mother's hair.

'I know. I only came to make sure I knew where the house was, then I intended doing a bit of shopping until two o'clock, but Oliver came out . . .' I didn't go on, she knew what had happened then. 'Shall I put some clothes on Robin?'

'If you don't mind. They're in his bedroom at the back of the house.' At that moment I think she would have handed Robin over to the Loch Ness monster.

'Right.' I held out my hand. 'Come on, Robin. Let's get you dressed.'

Robin willingly took my hand and led me upstairs. The bedroom was a midden: clothes and toys were all over the place, and the sheets on his cot and the single, unmade bed where his brother must have slept could have done with a good wash. I found underclothes, a tiny pair of cotton trousers, a short-sleeved shirt and a pair of sandals, but socks were nowhere to be seen. While I was dressing him, he grabbed my hat and flung it to the floor, then looked at me challengingly, his eyes full of devilment and his little pink tongue sticking out.

'This isn't a game,' I told him severely. 'I'm not going to put it back on so you can pull it off again. Now, put your feet in these sandals. I'll ask your mam for socks when we're downstairs, otherwise your heels will get rubbed raw.'

Oliver came in and looked at me curiously, probably wondering who this strange woman was who had stopped him from going to Egypt and was now dressing his little brother.

'You look smart enough to get dressed by yourself,' I told him. 'Shall I sit here and watch while you do it?'

Five minutes later, I took them downstairs and found Mrs Knowles fast asleep in a huge kitchen, which looked as if a typhoon had just swept through it. Her head was resting on the table. I shook her arm and she came to with a start.

'Oh, I see you've got them dressed. How on earth did you manage that?' Without waiting for an answer, she went on, 'Thank you again. You'd better go now. I take for granted you don't want the job.'

'You haven't interviewed me yet.'

She looked at me, astounded. 'You're not still interested?'

'Nothing's happened so far to put me off.' I picked up Robin and sat him on my knee. He immediately grabbed my hair and I was reminded that I must collect our Aileen's hat before I went home.

'I interviewed three women this morning: one said all they needed was discipline and their bottoms smacked regularly, another that they should be locked in their rooms, and the third one had some airy-fairy notion about teaching them to dance and sing. "That'll keep them occupied," she claimed.' She dragged herself to her feet. 'Would you like a drink? I'm longing for a coffee. I haven't had one for hours. Robin had me awake at six this morning, which means I've been up seven hours and I've hardly done a thing.' She shook her head tiredly. 'I don't know where the time goes.'

'I'd love some coffee, ta.' The McCarthys weren't coffee-drinkers, but I enjoyed the occasional cup.

She ran water into a percolator while looking at me over her shoulder. 'You said your name was Kitty. I can't remember getting a letter from a Kitty.'

'I signed it Katherine, Katherine McCarthy.'

'Oh, yours was the nicely written one, beautifully set out. You work in a shoe factory, don't you?'

I preened myself, though it was Ada Tutty who should take credit for the letter. 'Yes, I took the day off to come here.'

'Would it be possible for you to start tomorrow?'

It was probably the quickest interview anyone had ever attended: she hadn't asked a single important question nor mentioned references. 'Not really. I have to give a week's notice. It'll still be a day short if I give it in tomorrow, but I doubt if anyone'll mind.'

She looked disappointed as she spooned coffee into the percolator and put it on the stove. 'It was the lady in the Post Office who suggested I get help with the children. Once I'd got the idea in my head, I wanted someone immediately. I'm amazed I hadn't thought of it before, but I suppose it just made me feel even more inadequate, the idea that I couldn't manage two small children on my own.'

Oliver had put his chin on the table and his dark, mischievous eyes were darting from me to his mother and back again. 'I'm a handful,' he announced.

'Oh, isn't that terrible?' Mrs Knowles groaned. 'I should never have said that in his hearing.'

'A *real* handful,' Oliver stressed, as if intent on making his mother feel worse.

'Darling, would you mind going into the garden and looking for your red ball? I've a horrible suspicion it might have been thrown into next door's garden and the lady will be terribly cross again.'

'The lady next door is a bitch,' Oliver said. 'We hate her, don't we, Mummy?' With that, he marched outside to look for the ball.

'It's in the shed,' Mrs Knowles confessed. 'I just wanted him out the way a minute while I explain my circumstances.' She cleared her throat. 'Both Eric and I – Eric is my husband – have been married before. My first husband was in the Navy and was killed in the first year of the war; Eric's wife died in the London Blitz.'

I made the appropriate sympathetic noises, which she acknowledged with a little nod.

'I met Eric in nineteen forty-four and we got married after the war ended. I was thirty-eight and he forty-three. We never really intended to have children – I have a son from my first marriage – but were pleased when I found I was expecting Oliver. I never dreamt,' she said with a shudder, 'that I would find looking after a baby so tiring. My doctor tells me I'm anaemic, which is why I have so little energy.'

'That's a shame.' Robin was standing on my knee, our noses pressed together. I removed his chubby hands from my ears.

'I don't know why I'm telling you all this, Kitty,' his mother said, sitting down. 'I've hardly known you five minutes and you already know my life story. I suppose I don't want you to think I'm one of those women who farms her children out to someone else because she can't be bothered looking after them. I try, I really do try, but I'm afraid, once Robin came along, that I just couldn't cope. My sister, Hope, has lived with me for the past year and she can't stand children. She tells me I'm an ineffectual mother.'

'They're very lively,' I remarked as Robin began to screw my nose off.

'Excessively so. They hardly sleep and are on the go all day long.' She got to her feet. 'The coffee should be ready now. Do you take milk and sugar?'

'Both, please. Would you like me to take the children for a walk in a minute so you can have a rest?' I'd noticed a big pram in the hall.

'That would be lovely. Thank you, Kitty. I haven't washed yet and I can't remember when I last combed my hair.' She ran her fingers through it, making it look worse. 'Lord knows what those women thought this morning. I'd meant to make myself respectable, but never found the time. Is it all right if I call you Kitty? My name is Faith, by the way.'

Faith and Hope! I wondered if there was a Charity, too. 'You're not from Liverpool, are you?' She hadn't even a trace of a scouse accent.

'No. I was born in Richmond on the outskirts of London. We came to live in Liverpool because it's where Eric's ship usually docks. He's captain of a cruise liner,' she said proudly. 'He usually sails between here and America, but at the moment he's going round the world.' She smiled cheerfully and appeared far less harassed than when I'd first arrived. 'Now, Kitty, I've told you all about myself. It's about time I knew something about you. Have you any brothers and sisters, for instance, a boyfriend? Oh, I do hope you're not likely to get married any minute and leave!'

I felt an inner glow. I haven't even started the job yet and she was already worried I might leave. It was *me* who was responsible for the cheerful smile. I liked Faith Knowles very much. Her children were little monkeys, but I was looking forward to taking care of them. I'd never looked forward to packing shoes.

I told her my life story – it sounded very uninteresting – then took the children for a long walk in the pram as far as Derby Park where I let them run around on the grass for a while. They behaved like wild animals who'd been released from their cages and I had a job catching them.

When I got back to Weld Road, Faith had washed, combed her hair and put on some make-up. She'd changed out of the slacks and blouse, and now wore a pretty flowered summer dress. She looked quite beautiful.

'It's the first time I've worn a dress in ages,' she cried. 'And I even managed to iron it.' She stared into the pram. 'They're both asleep,' she exclaimed. 'I can hardly believe my eyes: they never go to sleep during daytime.'

'They're both exhausted. I'll carry Oliver upstairs, shall I? We can leave Robin where he is.'

'I've got more coffee on the go for when you come down.'

We grinned triumphantly at each other, and I knew that me and Faith Knowles were going to get along just fine.

Chapter 2

I'd been in my new job for almost two weeks and loved every minute, but it seemed I was getting on Marge's nerves.

We'd been to the Forum in town to see *All About Eve*, starring Bette Davis and Anne Baxter, and were on our way home on the tram. I was describing Faith's huge parlour with its floor-length windows – possibly for the second, or even third, time – the equally large dining room, the cosy breakfast room. 'And I'm convinced our whole house would fit inside the kitchen,' I was saying when Marge broke in.

'I'm sick to death of hearing about Faith Knowles *and* her kids *and* her big house with five bedrooms,' she said. 'It's all you go on about. She can't exactly be up to much if she's incapable of looking after her own children.'

'She's forty-four,' I said defensively, 'and the children are a pair of little divils. I look upon Faith as a friend.'

'After only a week and a half?' Marge sneered. 'I thought *I* was supposed to be your friend.'

'People can have more than one friend.' I gave her a reassuring nudge. 'You're me *best* friend.'

'Am I?' She looked at me in a way I could only describe as pathetic and not a bit like Marge.

'What's wrong?' I asked. She'd been in a funny mood all night.

'Nothing.' She turned away, avoiding my eyes. 'I didn't go into work today,' she said to the back of the seat in front.

'Why not?' She worked in a dry-cleaner's on Strand Road.

'Didn't feel like it,' she said, shrugging.

'What did you think of the picture?' I asked after a long pause. 'I thought it was the gear, one of the best I've ever seen.'

'I dunno. I hardly concentrated the whole way through.'

We continued the journey in silence that I could have sworn was rather strained. When we got off the tram in Stanley Road, Marge said, 'Could you come back to our house for a mo?'

'Will your mam be there?'

'Not while the pubs are still open, no.'

'All right.'

It was raining, the sort of drizzle you can hardly feel but which soaks right through your clothes. We walked beneath our umbrellas in more silence until we reached Garnet Street. Marge unlocked the door of her house and led the way into the parlour, where she lit the gas mantel – unlike us, the Kings didn't have electricity.

'Can't you turn it up?' I asked. The dim glow made the gloomy room appear even gloomier.

'No,' she said abruptly. She sat heavily on the settee and the springs creaked in protest. 'I'm expecting a baby,' she announced, just as abruptly.

'Marge!' I was so shocked that I felt myself go cold. We usually told each other everything, but she'd never mentioned having slept with a man. 'Who's the father?' My voice shook.

'Your Danny.'

I went even colder. I knew Danny had had a whole army of girlfriends but, in my innocence, I thought all they did was have a good neck. As far as I knew, not a single one had fallen for a baby. 'You haven't been going out with him long enough to know you're pregnant.' I tried to keep the coldness out of my voice, but it didn't work.

'It's been seven weeks now, nearly eight. I've missed one whole period and I should've started another three days ago, but nothing's happened. I've always been regular, never so much as a day late.'

'Did you sleep with him the very first time?'

'We didn't *sleep* with each other, Kitty. We did it standing up in the entry behind Reilly's shop. And,' she went on angrily, 'there's no need to sound so critical. I didn't exactly force your Danny; he enjoyed it just as much as I did. And, before you ask, it was more than the once. We did it every time we went out.'

'I suppose now you expect Danny to marry you?' I'd thought I couldn't go any colder, but I did.

'He can't very well *not* marry me, can he?' She tossed her head and I was convinced I saw a glimmer of a smile on her over-made-up face. 'I'm having a baby and he's the father. You said at the wedding you'd like me for a sister-in-law.'

'Not this way, Marge.' The smile had made me feel suspicious. 'Did you set him up?' I demanded. 'Did you deliberately get pregnant so he'd marry you?' Danny had a good job as a plumber and didn't have a face like a horse, the two conditions she'd laid down as essential for a husband.

'How does anyone *deliberately* get pregnant? What a thing to say, Kitty McCarthy. I took a risk and so did Danny.' She jumped to her feet. 'It's not five minutes since you called me your best friend. I only told you because I thought you'd be sympathetic, that you'd understand, but now you're accusing me of all sorts of things.'

I stood up, too, and we faced each other across the dimly lit room. 'Understand what?' I cried. 'That you tricked our Danny into marrying you? You might well be me best friend, Marge, but Danny's me brother and I love him. I don't approve of some girl he hardly knows trapping him into marriage. And how can you be sure it's Danny's baby? For all I know, you could have been with all sorts of other men.'

'How dare you!' She raised her hand, as if to slap my face, but must have thought better of it. 'I was a virgin before I went with Danny. If you think I'm lying, ask him – *he* knows.'

'All right then, so I will.'

I stormed out of the house, slamming the door behind me. I'd forgotten about the rain and had left my umbrella behind. I passed Mrs King on her way home, but she was too drunk to recognize me. I wondered how *she* would react when Marge told her she was in the club.

Mam and Dad were on the point of going to bed when I got in. Both looked much better these days. Dad seemed less tired and I hadn't heard Mam cry in ages. I often worried that she waited until the house was empty before she let go, but there was no way of finding out. Jamie was in bed reading a book, I was told, and Danny was still out.

I said I'd just make myself a cup of tea and would be up in a minute, a deliberate lie because I wanted to talk to Danny. You never know, Marge might have been talking rubbish.

The tea made, I sat in front of the fire. It wasn't lit, but Mam always left it set – firelighter at the bottom covered with twists of paper, firewood and coal – just in case the temperature dropped unexpectedly. Then all she'd have to do was strike a match.

A fifteen-year friendship had just come to an end within a matter of minutes. I couldn't quite believe it. I'd always imagined me and Marge staying mates for ever. She was right to say I hadn't been sympathetic. Her pleased little smile had told me she was glad she was pregnant and that she was looking for congratulations, not sympathy. In a way, I felt betrayed. She'd been trying to get me on her side, I realized, knowing there'd be ructions later.

It was half past eleven when Danny came home, looking dead chuffed with himself, as always. In the meantime, I'd tried to read the paper, but it was a waste of time: the words meant nothing.

'Why are you still up?' he asked, surprised, when he saw me. His tie was undone and there was lipstick on his chin. I supposed he was quite attractive in a way: tall, like Jeff and Will had been, with reddish-brown curly hair, blue eyes and the same appealing smile. He was always smartly dressed, actually possessed *three* good suits. Dad and every other man I knew only had the one.

'I wanted to talk to you, that's why.' I came straight to the point. 'Marge King claims she's having a baby and that you're the father.'

Danny's face turned ashen. He closed the door and collapsed into an armchair. 'But she told me she was using something,' he stammered.

'Using what?'

'I dunno.' He stared at his feet. It wasn't the sort of conversation a man usually had with his sister. 'Whatever it is women use to stop themselves from getting pregnant.'

I'd been told they soaked a sponge in vinegar and shoved it inside them. It sounded such a revolting practice that I couldn't imagine doing it myself. 'Oh, Danny, luv,' I cried, 'what on earth got into you? And Marge, of all people. Did you forget she was me friend?'

'What's that got to do with it?' He wriggled uncomfortably. 'When a woman offers herself, there's hardly a man in a million who'd turn her down. Holy Mary, Mother of God!' he groaned, dropping his head into his hands. 'What the hell's going to happen now?'

'She expects you to marry her, that's what.' Now there was no doubt about it in my mind: Marge had definitely tricked my brother.

By now, Danny was looking panic-stricken. 'But I don't want to marry Marge King! I don't want to marry anyone, not yet. Me and a mate from work were planning on starting our own plumbing business. It means taking risks and I can't do that with a wife and kid to support.'

I wanted to say he should've thought of that before, but felt sorry for him. He'd acted like a fool and Marge had been too clever for him. If he'd had a bit more nous, he wouldn't have believed a word she'd said and would have taken precautions of his own – I'd seen used French letters in the back entries loads of times.

'What am I going to do, Kitty? Mam and Dad will do their nuts.' He sounded terrified.

'You've not got much choice, Danny. You'll have to marry her.'

'I could run away.' His bottom lip trembled at the thought.

'You could an' all, except it'd be a dead cowardly thing to do.' I felt a shred of sympathy for Marge at the idea of her being left to have the baby on her own. Her mother was bound to chuck her out and she'd have nowhere to go. 'At least Mam and Dad both like Marge,' I said. Though liking her was one thing: having her for a daughter-in-law when she'd *had* to marry their son was something else altogether.

I told Faith Knowles about it the next morning while we sat having coffee in the spotless kitchen. The house was unrecognizable from the one I'd first entered a few weeks ago. Faith cleaned and tidied, did the washing and ironing, indulged in leisurely baths, while I took the children for long walks or played with them in the garden. She was almost as unrecognizable as the house, looking years younger and always nicely dressed.

'I hardly ever feel tired since you came, Kitty,' she'd told me. 'You've made all the difference to my life.'

When the children were taking a long afternoon nap, exhausted after their exertions in the park, me and Faith gossiped over endless cups of coffee. It was a job made in heaven, being paid to gossip and drink coffee.

'It seems a shame you and Marge will no longer be friends,' she commented when I relayed the events of the night before.

'Would you still be friends with someone who'd behaved the way she did?'

'Probably not,' she conceded. 'I haven't got a brother, but if I had, I'd always put him first. Mind you, Kitty, you must admit that Danny should share some of the blame. Despite the fact Marge "offered herself", as you put it, he didn't *have* to accept. She didn't force him at gunpoint to make love.'

'"Making love" doesn't sound right when they did it in a dirty back entry.'

'Whatever it's called, wherever it was done, it's produced a baby, and now the baby must come first. He or she has the right to both a mother and a father. Don't you agree?' She looked at me keenly.

'I must admit I hadn't given much thought to the baby.' The fact that a real live human being was curled up in Marge's womb hadn't really sunk in yet.

'Have you told your mother yet?' Faith asked.

I shook my head. 'I've already interfered enough. It's up to Danny to tell our mam.'

'It will upset her dreadfully,' she said, making a face – she knew about Jeff and Will – 'Danny being forced into a shotgun wedding. Let's hope he can make it appear a happy affair, as if he and Marge had intended getting married all along, but now there's a baby on the way and they have to do it sooner rather than later.'

'That's not a bad idea.' I'd hardly slept the night before: worrying about Danny and Dad, but Mam most of all.

Oliver came into the room, sleepily rubbing his eyes. 'Can we play football, Kitty?'

'You forgot the "please", darling,' his mother informed him.

'Can we play football, Kitty, please?' the little boy repeated with an impish smile.

'As soon as I've finished this coffee. You go in the garden and look for the ball.' There were days when I wouldn't have minded an afternoon nap myself.

That night, for the first time in my life, I went to the pictures on my own. I wouldn't have called on Marge to save my life and had no intention of staying in because there was no one else to go with. I only went as far as the Palace in Marsh Lane to see *The Perils of Pauline*, which starred Betty Hutton.

On the way out, I came face to face with Danny. 'What are you doing here?' I asked. 'You look strange without a girl hanging from your arm.'

'I've given up on women,' he said glumly. 'I didn't want to stay stuck in the house, so I came with a mate. He's somewhere behind.'

The mate arrived, a smiling young man with red hair a much paler shade than my own, almost carrot, and about ten million freckles. His eyes were green and he was nearly as tall as Danny, who introduced us in the same glum voice. 'This is me sister, Kitty. Kitty, this is Con Daley. He's a mate from work.'

We shook hands. 'What's Con short for?' I asked.

'Connor,' he answered with a grin. 'What's up with your Danny? He's had a miserable gob on him all night long.'

'I've no idea,' I lied.

I tried to link Danny's arm, but he shrugged me away. 'Me and Con are off to have a pint,' he grunted.

'Can I come?' I pleaded. Going to the pictures by myself hadn't been all that enjoyable and I liked the idea of having company.

Danny looked as if he were about to tell me to get lost, but Con took my arm and tucked it inside his. 'It'll be a pleasure. You know, I'm amazed your mam and dad let a bobby dazzler like you out on your own.'

'I usually go out with me friend, but she's sick.' Another lie!

'Is she likely to be sick for long?' He looked at me gravely, but there was still a hint of a grin on his face. 'If she is, I'm willing to take pity on you and escort you to the pictures sometime – tomorrow, say. Or we could go to a dance, the Grafton or the Locarno.'

'I'd like that,' I said demurely. I wasn't lying now. He had a nice sense of humour and a terrific grin.

Danny came to life. 'Hey, that's my little sister you're talking to. You'd better treat her proper, Con Daley, or you'll have me to answer to.'

I couldn't help but think what a hypocrite he was considering what he'd been up to with Marge, who had no one to look out for her – no sisters or brothers, no dad, just a mam who spent most of her time in the pub.

We went to the Clarence in Marsh Lane and Con went to get the drinks – I'd asked for a shandy. As soon as he'd gone, I grabbed Danny by the chin and turned his face towards mine. 'Listen,' I said urgently, and told him what Faith had suggested earlier that day. 'You and Marge are to tell Mam and Dad that you're getting married soon. There's no need to mention the baby, they'll guess that for themselves as they know you've been going out with her for almost two months. Pretend you're really happy about it, that it's what you planned all along, and they won't be nearly so upset. Have you got that, Danny?'

'Yes.' He irritably knocked my hand away. 'I wish you'd keep your nose out of my business, sis.'

'But don't you think it's a good idea?' I wanted to shake him until his teeth rattled. 'It'll mean there won't be a horrible atmosphere at the wedding.' Marge would be all for it, knowing she wouldn't have our Claire, Aileen and Norah giving her filthy looks in church. I'd be the only one who knew the truth of the matter, not counting the happy couple, that is.

He flinched at the word 'wedding', sighed and stuffed his hands in his pockets. 'I suppose. I'll see Marge about it tomorrow; it's too late now.' Con came up with the drinks and Danny hissed, 'I'm still thinking of running away,' but I knew that this time it was him who was lying.

The next night, I went to the Locarno with Con Daley, who turned out to be a hopeless dancer but a great talker, so for most of the night that's all we did: sit in a corner and talk. I tried to count his freckles, but gave up after fifty and they were just on his forehead. He was twenty-two and had seven sisters and two brothers of which he was the youngest. Like me, he was a Catholic, and lived in Seaforth, no distance from Bootle. It turned out that he was the one Danny had been planning to go into business with. As far as Con was concerned, the plan was still on. I didn't like to tell him that Danny might have to pull out. It reminded me that right at this moment Marge and my brother might be telling my parents they were about to get married. I prayed that everything would turn out all right.

In between his frequent grins, Con could be quite serious. He had all sorts of opinions, about politics, for instance, and the rights and wrongs of the death penalty, things I'd never even thought about. I knew that last year a woman called Margaret Allen had been hanged in Manchester and Con thought it was quite disgraceful.

'But didn't she kill an old lady?'

'Yes, but then the State killed her,' Con said, his green eyes blazing. 'It was nothing more than judicial murder, making us just as bad as the original murderer.' He then launched into a tirade against the atomic bomb. I found it terrifying, and agreed with every word he said.

At eleven o'clock I asked if he would take me home, so he waltzed me across the floor towards the exit, though the band was playing a foxtrot. Halfway there, he blew on my hair. It wasn't what you'd call a romantic gesture, but I felt strangely moved and, for some reason, I slid my arm further around his neck and he slid his further across my back. We arrived at the exit in what could only be called a clinch and held hands on the tram all the way back to Bootle. Outside our front door, he kissed me softly on the lips. We arranged to go out the day after tomorrow, Saturday.

'We'll go somewhere and have a meal,' he promised.

I let myself in, feeling pleasantly dizzy. I wasn't in love, not a bit of it, but thought it seemed a likely possibility.

The light was on in the living room and I assumed Danny had waited up to tell me what had happened earlier, but when I walked in, to my astonishment, not only was Danny there, but Mam, Dad, Jamie and our Claire. Danny was sitting dejectedly at the table, looking as if he'd lost a pound and found a sixpence, Mam had been crying, Dad's face had sort of collapsed, as if all the stuffing had been knocked out of him, Jamie looked puzzled and Claire as mad as hell.

'What's the matter?' I asked. At first, I thought it was nothing to do with Marge, but something far worse.

Claire answered. 'Our Danny's only gone and put a bun in Marge King's oven,' she spat. 'She came round earlier in buckets of tears. Apparently, she'd told her mother who immediately threw her out, so where else could she come but here?'

'Where is she now?'

'Upstairs in your bed, luv,' Mam said shakily. 'You'll just have to sleep together until everything's sorted out.'

'You mean until she and Danny get married,' Claire snapped.

'But I thought . . . ' I glared at Danny. It wasn't supposed to have happened this way.

Danny hung his head. 'I was on me way to see her,' he muttered, 'but decided I needed a couple of pints inside me first. When I called at her house, no one was in. She was here instead.'

The lovely dizziness I'd felt before vanished, along with all thoughts of Con Daley. The feeling was replaced with seething fury. There'd been no need for Marge to tell her mother yet. I was convinced she'd done it knowing she'd be chucked out and could throw herself at the mercy of a much softer heart: in other words, my own mother's. If only she'd kept her big mouth shut, the situation could have been sorted out quite amicably, or at least not as bad as it was now. I wanted to run upstairs, drag her out of *my* bed and tell her all this to her face, but it would only upset Mam more.

'Did you already know about this, Kitty?' Claire demanded.

'Marge told me two days ago, but it wasn't my job to tell anyone,' I said haughtily. 'That was up to Danny.'

Claire looked as if she was about to give me a mouthful, but must have considered it would be unfair. Instead, she turned her anger on Marge. 'That girl is nothing but a slag,' she raged. 'You can tell just by looking at her. I wouldn't be surprised if she hasn't slept with every man in Bootle.'

'That's not true, sis,' Danny said quickly.

'How the bloody hell would you know?'

'How d'you think I'd know?'

Claire flushed. There was only one way Danny could have known and he couldn't very well spell it out in front of the family. I bet he hadn't said anything about Marge offering herself, and I admired him for not making excuses.

'Oh, I'm going home.' Claire leapt to her feet. 'I only popped in a minute to give Mam a recipe and I've stayed for hours. It's nearly midnight. Liam will think I've left him.' She left, slamming the front door with such force that it must have woken half the street.

Mam said, 'I suppose we'd better get to bed, Bob. Tomorrow, Danny will have to see about a licence and arrange to have the banns called. I suggest you get married on a weekday, son, when there won't be so many people in the church.' She gave a tearful sniff. 'You'll be the first of me lads to get married and I always thought it'd be very different.'

Danny waited until the bedroom door closed before bursting into tears.

Jamie said, 'I don't understand what all the fuss is about.'

*

When I walked along Weld Road the next morning, there was a black car in the drive of number twelve and Oliver was busily drawing faces on the bonnet with chalk. As I opened the gate, a woman came out of the house. 'You stupid, *stupid* child!' she shouted angrily. 'How dare you!'

'It's all right, I'll wipe it off,' I called.

The woman threw me a look that would have made a lesser person quail – but the only person who could make me quail was Marge's mam. This must be Hope, Faith's sister. She was five years younger and they were very alike, with the same classic features, though Hope's face was as hard as nails and her eyes were cold and unfriendly. She had an important job in a bank. Today she was wearing a smart black costume and black patent leather shoes with enormously high heels.

'I suppose you're Kitty,' she said now.

'I suppose I am.' I pushed past her. 'I'll just go indoors and get a duster.'

'It's about time he knew better than to do things like that,' Hope said when I returned and rubbed the chalk marks off.

'It's not done any harm,' I assured her. 'You won't do it again, will you, Oliver?'

Oliver was staring at the ground with his arms behind his back. He shook his head mutely. Hope had clearly upset him.

'What those children need is a good hiding,' she muttered as she got into the car and drove away.

I reached for Oliver's hand. We went indoors. Faith was coming downstairs with a fully dressed Robin. 'What's the matter, darling?' she asked Oliver in a concerned voice. 'You look very down in the dumps.'

Oliver's answer was merely a long shaky sniff, so I explained about the drawing on the car. 'But it came off straight away when I rubbed it.'

'Hope has a meeting in Southport this morning and she's going straight there. That's why she left so late. I thought I heard shouting. Was it Hope shouting at Oliver?'

I nodded and she looked troubled.

Later, I used the chalk to draw a hopscotch grid on the path, and Oliver and me played for a good hour until we were both fit to drop. Robin insisted on sitting in the squares, but we managed to play around him.

Halfway through the morning, Faith called me in for coffee – I'd drunk more coffee in her house than I'd done in my whole life. I left the children kicking a ball to each other and went indoors.

'Are you prepared to listen to a good long moan?' Faith asked when we were both seated at the table.

I said I was all ears and had something of my own to moan about when she'd finished.

'It's Hope,' she began. 'A year ago, she asked if she could come and live with me when she left her husband for some reason. I was only too pleased to let her. I said I wouldn't dream of charging her rent, so she lives here for nothing. The thing is, Kitty,' she went on, her perfect nose twitching with indignation, 'she's terribly impatient with the children – and with me, come to that, for not keeping them under control. I'd hate for us to have a row, but it really gets me down.'

'I'm not surprised,' I said understandingly. From what she'd said before, I already disliked Hope and now I'd met her I disliked her even more. 'It's *your* house, they're *your* children. She has no right to criticize.'

'I'm so pleased you agree. I was worried I was being unreasonable expecting her to fit in with us, rather than the other way round. She gets so cross when they wake her up at night. Poor Robin was inconsolable when he was teething.'

'I think she has a cheek. She hasn't had children, so what would she know about it?'

'Exactly!' Faith slapped her hands on the table and gave me a brilliant smile. 'Do you know, I feel much better having got that off my chest. Would you like more coffee? Then you can have your reciprocal moan.'

I made a mental note of 'reciprocal', having never heard the word before. 'It's Marge,' I said.

'I thought it might be,' Faith said darkly.

I described all that had happened last night and she made sympathetic clucking noises. 'Now Mam and Dad are really fed up – just when things were almost back to normal. Danny's as miserable as sin and me sister, Claire, is spitting tacks. She's bound to tell our Aileen and Norah, and they'll spit tacks, too. I'm not looking forward to the wedding: it's going to be dead horrible.'

'And you actually have to *sleep* with Marge?' Faith looked shocked.

'Until she marries Danny, yes,' I said resentfully. When I'd got into bed last night, Marge was crying quietly, but I ignored her. I'd hardly slept a wink.

'We have a spare bedroom on the top floor. It's for if my Charlie ever comes to stay.' Charlie was her son from her first marriage. He lived in Hong Kong. 'You can stay here, until everything's over, if you like,' she said generously.

'That's really nice of you.' I felt touched. 'But I'd feel as if I was deserting a sinking ship. It'd only make things worse for everyone at home.'

She patted my arm. 'I understand. You're a good girl, Kitty. If I'd had a daughter, I would have wanted her to be just like you.'

At first, it was standing room only in the McCarthy house that night. Claire and Liam came not long after we'd had our tea, then Aileen and Michael. Norah and Roy weren't far behind. They all crammed in the parlour along with Mam and Dad, Jamie, Danny and a red-faced Marge who hadn't been to work that day but had followed Mam around, saying over and over that she hadn't wanted to cause any trouble, a big fat lie if I've ever heard one.

Mam actually felt sorry for her. She warned me beforehand 'not to get on to the poor girl. It's Danny's fault as much as hers,' and had said the same thing to my sisters when they arrived.

Danny announced in a whisper that he'd got a licence, had been to the church about the banns and the wedding would be at ten o'clock on Wednesday, 12 September. 'That's the day me baby's due,' Claire said belligerently.

'That doesn't really matter, luv.' Mam was evidently trying to keep the peace.

'What do you mean, Mam, that it doesn't matter? It matters that I can go to me own brother's wedding, to me at least.'

'It's the first day we can legally get married, sis,' Danny said wearily. 'Would you rather I made it later?'

'Of course she wouldn't, Danny.' Mam turned to Claire. 'When I said it didn't matter, I meant we should get the wedding over with as soon as possible. By then, Marge will be almost three months pregnant. Do we want the whole world and his wife to know she and Danny had to get married?'

'You can always tell everyone the baby came early, like you did with our Patsy,' Claire said cuttingly. 'Honestly, Mam, all you bloody care about is appearances. I for one don't see why Danny and Marge have to get married. Why can't he just give her a weekly allowance to pay for the baby's needs?'

At this, Danny raised his head hopefully, Marge raised hers in alarm and Dad said, 'Appearances are very important to your mother, Claire. Marge and Danny are getting married as soon as humanly possible and that's all there is to it.'

'Well,' Liam said, rising to his feet and making for the door, 'now that's settled, I'm off to have a pint. Are you coming, Mike? Roy?'

'Can I come?' Jamie asked.

Liam was about to agree, but Dad intervened. 'You're not old enough, son.'

'I'll be eighteen in a few weeks, Dad.'

'It's more than a few weeks. You're not eighteen until December.'

'Oh, go on, Bob, let him,' Mam urged. 'It won't hurt. And why don't you go, too, luv? It'll do you good to have a little break, our Danny an' all. He won't want to be left alone in a house full of women.'

'I thought we were all here to have a big discussion,' Aileen said when the house was suddenly bereft of men.

'So did I,' Norah complained. 'I've hardly opened me mouth until now.'

'It was all sorted out much quicker than I thought,' Mam admitted. 'I'll make us all a cuppa, shall I? Come on, Marge, you can give us a hand.' Marge followed like a shot. Mam was her protector and she wanted to stay close. Perhaps she didn't trust the McCarthy girls not to tear her eyes out.

'You know what that means, don't you?' Claire said ominously.

'What what means?' Norah asked.

'What our Jamie said about being eighteen soon. It means he'll be called up to do his National Service. The Government is sending conscripts to fight in Korea. If our Jamie goes, it'll just about kill Mam.'

All of a sudden, the idea of Danny and Marge having to get

married melted into insignificance when we thought about our little brother having to fight in yet another war.

The wedding was a dead miserable affair. No one bothered to buy a new outfit. Marge wore the suit she'd got for Norah's wedding and I wore my best cream frock. There were no guests apart from the immediate family. Liam, Michael and Roy loyally took the morning off work to be with their wives. Claire was as big as a house, the baby expected literally any minute. Marge's mam had the gall to turn up, apparently mollified by the fact her daughter was marrying a McCarthy – our family was highly thought of in Bootle.

No one smiled, but quite a few people cried, Mam the most. Danny and Marge looked as if they were about to be hung, drawn and quartered. I wondered if she now regretted what she'd done. After all, it was a lousy way of getting a husband.

When we came out of the church, I glimpsed Ada Tutty hurrying away. She must have been watching the ceremony from the back.

We all went back to Amethyst Street for refreshments: just sarnies, a few cakes, sherry for the women and beer for the men. At midday, all those with a job to go to drifted away, including me, I'm pleased to say. Marge's mam was still there and would no doubt stay until she'd demolished the sherry *and* the beer.

I left thinking that when I came home, our Danny would be gone. Mam had found him and Marge a little flat over the confectioner's on the corner of Pearl Street. And in a few months, Jamie might also be gone, then I'd be the only one of the McCarthy children left. I didn't mind, but at the same time it felt terribly, terribly sad.

'It *is* sad,' Con agreed when I shared my feelings with him that night over curried prawns and rice in the Golden Moon, a Chinese restaurant in town. I had insisted on paying for the meal. Although he earned twice as much as I did, it made me feel cheap to let him pay for everything so, once a week, it was me who took him out. 'Your mam and dad will have always known that one day their kids would leave and they'd be left on their own, but it doesn't stop it from being sad. But at least they still have you for the time being.' He gave his infectious grin. 'Lucky old them.'

'Hmm.' I had a feeling he was a little bit in love with me and wasn't sure if I didn't feel the same. We got on really well, always had loads to talk about and his kisses when we said goodnight were getting more and more passionate. I responded just as passionately, and wished we could have said goodnight somewhere other than a shop or office doorway, somewhere quiet and comfortable where we wouldn't be disturbed. I wondered what Danny and Marge were doing in the little flat over the confectioner's where they had all the privacy in the world. Were they talking to each other? Would they actually sleep together in the big double bed?

Con reached across the table, and I had a little feeling of warmth when his hand rested on top of mine. 'Penny for them.'

'They weren't worth a penny.'

'Ha'penny, then.'

'They weren't worth that much either.' I smiled at him, fed up with feeling miserable. We'd established that certain aspects of life were sad, but there was nothing we could do to change them. 'I went to my first English class last night,' I reminded him.

'I'd forgotten all about it.' He looked suitably apologetic. 'What did you learn?'

'That an adjective is a descriptive word – actually, I knew that much, but I've never been sure what a verb is, or a noun or a pronoun.'

'And now you do?'

'And now I do, but I couldn't quite get the hang of adverbs and they didn't touch on commas.' I was very anxious to know about commas.

The nights were swiftly drawing in. When we came out of the restaurant it was pitch-dark and there was a nip in the air. We strolled down to the Pier Head to catch the tram. Con had his arm around my shoulders and I had mine around his waist. Halfway down Lord Street, he stopped outside a jeweller's and stared in the window.

'What are you looking for?' I asked.

'I was interested in the price of things.'

'What sort of things?'

'Engagement rings. There's this girl I know who I'm thinking of asking to marry me. What sort of ring d'you think she'd fancy?'

My head began to swim, the way it did when we kissed. 'I dunno,' I mumbled.

'Ah, come on, Kitty.' He squeezed my shoulder. 'I know nothing about precious stones other than you can get red ones, blue ones and green ones.'

'Most engagement rings have diamonds and they haven't got a colour. They're like glass.'

'Do you think she'd like a diamond ring?' His green eyes were sparkling, just like emeralds.

I shrugged and shook my head. 'I dunno,' I repeated.

'I wonder if she'd like one diamond, two or even three? And look, there's one over there with a stone shaped like a heart. What do you think of that, Kitty?'

I wanted to say something very important, but this was an elaborate, roundabout way of proposing and I knew it would hurt his feelings. I took a deep breath. 'Maybe you should ask the girl first if she wants an engagement ring. Me, I always think they're like when you see a piece of furniture in a shop and it's got a ticket on it saying "Sold: To Be Collected." Least, that's how I'd feel if I wore one.'

He looked at me with exasperation. 'Christ Almighty, Kitty McCarthy, you don't half talk daft.'

'They don't mean anything, anyroad, engagement rings,' I said sniffily. 'Peter Murphy bought one for our Norah, a lovely solitaire, but it didn't stop him from jilting her three years later. And he asked for the ring back.'

'You must be the most unromantic woman who ever lived. Here I am, asking you to marry me, and you throw my proposal back in me face.' His tone was light, but I could tell I'd hurt him.

'No, I didn't. I threw an engagement ring back in your face, that's all.'

'So, if I go down on bended knee and propose, you won't kick me or anything?'

'No, but don't you think it's a bit too soon?' I turned to him, put my arms around his neck and pressed my cheek against his. 'We've only known each other a matter of weeks,' I whispered in his ear. 'Let's wait a bit longer, at least six months, before we think about getting married. Why don't we forget about rings and promises and commitments, and just continue having a dead good time?'

'If that's what you want, but I'm worried I might lose you, Kitty.' His voice broke and for the first time in my life I felt the power of being a woman who was loved by a man. 'I've never met anyone like you before. I love you, Kitty. If I had my way, I'd marry you tomorrow, lock you up and never let you get away.'

I knew he didn't mean the words the way they came out, but they sent a little chill through me. But then I forgot everything because he'd begun to kiss me, right in the middle of Lord Street. People passed on either side, but we didn't care, just kissed and kissed until we came up for air, then ran until we came to the first empty doorway where we kissed some more.

I arrived home to find Mam all smiles for once. Liam had just been to say Claire had had her baby, a boy, and the birth had been as easy as pie. 'And she's calling him Robert, after your dad: Bobby for short. I'm going into hospital to see him in the morning.'

I promised I would go the next night. A birth and a wedding, both on the same day!

'Oh, and I nearly forgot, what with all the excitement: Norah came earlier to say *she's* expecting a baby. It should arrive next May.'

On Friday, Eric Knowles's ship docked in Liverpool and I met him for the first time. He'd been away for five months, the longest he and Faith had ever been parted. The day before, she'd had her hair set and bought a new frock: midnight-blue velvet with long sleeves and a circular skirt. I told her she looked very beautiful and would knock Eric's eyes out.

'I hope so. I always try to tidy the house and pretty myself up for when he comes home, not always successfully. It'll make a change for him to find the place all spick and span and his wife looking like the woman he married.' Her smile was dazzling. She was obviously very much in love with Eric. 'And Kitty, I'm so pleased you've offered to babysit for us. Hope positively refuses to, and it means Eric and I can go to the theatre or for dinner – or both!' She pulled a face. 'He's only home for a week, then he'll be off again, but next time it's only as far as America.'

'Do you mind if Con babysits with me?'

'Of course I don't mind. I know what it's like when you're courting and you've got nowhere to go. It was like that with Tom, my first husband. Eric and I had our own houses so there wasn't a problem, but Tom and I were always stuck for places where we could be by ourselves. I remember once that a friend of Tom's let us have his flat when he went away for the weekend, but his mother turned up and we had to leave: either that, or put up with the mother for two days.' She stood stock still, a half-smile on her face, a faraway expression in her grey eyes. 'Sometimes, I almost forget about Tom, yet he was the love of my life. I shall never love Eric half as much as I did him. It was young love, first love, the sort that only comes once.'

There was a photograph of Tom and Faith in the parlour – her name had been Collier then. It had been taken on the day of their wedding by one of the guests and was entirely natural, showing them running away from the church, hand in hand, mouths slightly open. Faith's veil had blown upwards in the breeze and they both looked very young and blissfully carefree. Thinking about it now, looking at Faith's wistful face, it made me want to weep.

There were more photographs in the parlour: of Eric and his first wife, of Eric and Faith at their wedding, of Faith's other son, Charlie, who looked very much like his father, some of Oliver and Robin. Eric was definitely the winner in the looks department. He was a small, dapper man, dark-haired and dark-eyed, and as handsome as a film star, whereas Tom was big, blond and ungainly, and his nose was too big for his face. Yet, going by the photos, I preferred Tom, who reminded me a little bit of Con and even more of my rock-solid father, the sort of person I would have trusted with my life.

Eric Knowles arrived in a taxi in the middle of the afternoon. Faith, her senses alerted, heard a car door slam and flew to meet him, quickly followed by the children, who were falling over themselves to get to the door first. I stayed in the kitchen, glad of a few minutes' peace. Faith would introduce me when the time came.

The time came about ten minutes later. The boys swept into the room along with a blushing Faith, and Eric not far behind. He wore a navy-blue uniform, embellished with lots of gold braid, and was slightly taller than I'd expected. His almost-black hair was greying at the temples, only serving to make him look even more handsome, like a matinée idol: Charles Boyer or Herbert Marshall.

'This is the young lady who has brought order out of chaos, darling,' Faith gushed. 'Kitty, dear, this is Eric, my husband.'

'I have a great deal to thank you for, Kitty.' Eric shook my hand warmly. I'd never seen such neat, white hands on a man before: the nails looked as if they'd been polished. 'Entirely due to you, I have my old wife back again. It's a long time since I saw her looking so lovely.' He kissed Faith on the cheek and squeezed her waist. 'It's really good to be home.'

To me, that sounded a bit offensive. Faith had two small children and a big house to look after, yet he expected to find her looking like a model.

'Kitty and her young man are going to babysit for us tomorrow,' Faith cried, 'and any other night we'd like to go out.'

Eric beamed and told me I was an angel sent from heaven and he didn't know how to thank me enough. He was extremely confident and sure of himself, as befitting the captain of a ship.

It was Faith who let us in the following night. She looked very glamorous in the velvet frock and a three-strand seed-pearl necklace with earrings to match. To my surprise, she seemed a bit down, though managed to smile when I introduced her to Con.

'I would have known you anywhere,' she said. 'Kitty told me you looked a bit like Van Johnson.'

'She's never told *me* I looked like Van Johnson,' Con said indignantly.

'Well, you do. Now, go and sit yourselves in the parlour and I'll make a drink. Oliver and Robin are fast asleep – let's hope they stay that way. Eric's booked a table in the George for eight o'clock, so we shall have to leave in a minute.'

I showed Con into the parlour but didn't stay. Instead, I followed Faith into the kitchen. 'What's wrong?' I asked.

'Oh, does it show?' She put her hands to her cheeks. 'I'm trying to act if I don't care.'

'Don't care about what?'

'That Hope is coming to dinner with us. She asked Eric, I suppose he didn't like to refuse.' She blinked furiously in an effort to hold back the tears that had welled up in her eyes. 'It's the first time in ages we've been out together, just the two of us, and I was looking forward to it so much.'

I felt like calling Hope every name under the sun, but all I said was, 'I'm awfully sorry, Faith.'

'So am I,' she said bitterly. 'The evening's been spoiled before it even started.'

Ten minutes later, the trio left in Hope's car, with Eric in the passenger seat and Faith in the back all on her own. The second the car disappeared, Con and I snuggled into each other's arms in the parlour, looking forward to a few hours on our own. I was telling him how Hope had ruined the evening when the door opened and Oliver came in, his face all shiny and scrubbed, his eyes full of mischief, and an absolute picture in his striped pyjamas. He giggled mightily and threw himself on top of us.

'Let's play football, Kitty.'

'I will do no such thing,' I said indignantly. 'Your mother promised me you were asleep.'

He giggled again. 'I was just pretending.'

'That was very deceitful, Oliver. In future, I'm going to tell Mummy to stick a pin in you, then you won't be able to pretend you're asleep.'

'Yes, I will,' he bragged. He turned to Con – somehow he'd managed to lodge himself between us. 'Who are you?'

'I'm Kitty's boyfriend, son.' Con rolled his eyes. 'Who are you?'

'My name is Oliver Knowles and I live here.'

'Don't you think you should go back to bed, Oliver Knowles? All over the country, little boys of your age are fast asleep.'

'But I'm not tired, Kitty's boyfriend.'

'I still think you should go back to bed.' I lifted him up, carried him upstairs and laid him on the bed. 'Now, go to sleep,' I said sternly, tucking the covers around him. 'Mummy will be very cross if I tell her you came downstairs.'

He closed his eyes, murmuring, 'No, she won't.'

I crept out of the room.

Con and I had only managed a single kiss when he came down again, this time accompanied by Robin. We decided to give up and hope they soon wore themselves out. To this end, Con gave them piggybacks around the room, we played Hide and Seek and Blind Man's Bluff, and raced each other around the settee. It was a good hour before their eyes began to look tired. I made them each a cup of warm milk and they reluctantly agreed to be taken to bed.

Back in the parlour, we both collapsed on to the settee in fits of laughter. 'Faith's evening wasn't the only one that was ruined,' I gasped. 'I'm worn out.'

'So am I, but not too worn out for this.' Con held out his arms. 'Come here, Kitty McCarthy.'

I sank willingly into his arms and we sat there, breathing hard, before we could find the energy to return to what we'd been doing when Oliver had come in. That night, Con touched my breasts for the first time and I felt as if I was on fire when he rubbed his fingers against my nipples. I shivered with pleasure and he whispered hoarsely, 'I love you, Kitty.'

'I love you, too, Con,' I replied in a shaky voice.

Minutes later, his hand was stroking my thigh, when we heard a car turn into the drive. The engine was switched off and a door slammed. I quickly fastened my bra and was buttoning my blouse when the front door opened and Faith came in. My blouse still wasn't fastened, but I doubt if Faith would have noticed if I'd had nothing on. Her face was creased in pain and her eyes were feverish.

'We had to come home early. I've got a splitting headache.' She put a hand to her brow as if to soothe it. 'I hope you don't mind if I go straight to bed.'

'Would you like me to bring you up some aspirin and a warm drink?' I asked.

'Thank you, Kitty, that would be lovely. Have the children been all right?'

'They've been fine,' I assured her. 'Not a peep out of them.'

'Good.' She swayed slightly as she climbed the stairs, a slim, elegant figure in midnight-blue.

Con came into the kitchen while I was waiting for the milk to heat in the pan, dipping my finger in it from time to time to make sure it didn't get too hot. He put his arms around me from behind and nuzzled my neck. 'That's very unhygienic,' he remarked. 'Lord knows where that finger's been.'

'I washed it beforehand.'

'I didn't notice.'

'Well, I did.' I leaned back against him and he began to stroke my breasts. Before I knew where I was, the milk had boiled over and I had to pour some away and fill it up with cold. I told Con it was his fault and ordered him to clean the stove while I took the milk and aspirins up to Faith.

Her clothes had been thrown on to a chair and she was already in bed in the half-dark room. For some reason, only one of the curtains had been closed, so I put the cup and tablets on the bedside table and went to close the other.

Faith sat up, emptied three tablets into her hand and swallowed them with a mouthful of milk. Then she slid back under the clothes and pulled them over her head, all without saying a word, not even 'thank you' or 'goodnight'.

I knew then for certain that, when she'd drawn the first curtain, she had witnessed the same sight as I had when I drew the second: her husband and her sister kissing passionately outside the front door.

I desperately missed Marge. I wanted to tell her what I'd seen when I'd looked out of Faith's bedroom window. We would have talked about it for hours, days even, trying to imagine what would happen next, what we would have done in the same position, and discussed the fact that I hadn't trusted Eric from the moment I'd seen his photo.

But, on reflection, I couldn't have brought myself to say a word. It was too private, too personal, too *awful* to relate to another soul, apart from Con on the bus on the way home, only because I was in a state of shock and couldn't quite believe what I'd seen.

'She seemed nice, Faith,' he said quietly.

'She *is* nice. She doesn't deserve a husband like him – or a sister like Hope.'

'What are you going to do?'

'Nothing – not unless Faith mentions it first.'

On Sunday afternoon, I went to the hospital again to see Claire and Bobby, the new baby. I took Con with me – it was about time he met my family. I could tell Mam and Dad liked him, and Claire, flushed and happy, regarded him slowly, from the top of his head right down to his toes, then gave a little satisfied nod, as if to say, 'You'll do.' Liam had met him before, and they shook hands as excitedly as if they'd just come across each other in the middle of the Sahara Desert.

Mam, Norah and Aileen were already there. What with Claire

having just had a baby and both Norah and Marge in the club, poor Aileen must be feeling very much out of things.

Then Marge came in with a bunch of chrysanthemums. There was a short, uncomfortable silence until Mam got up and gave her a warm hug and a kiss. Claire managed a polite, 'Thank you, Marge. They're lovely.' As for me, I stood on the other side of the bed and ignored her.

A staff nurse arrived, a real tartar with sprouting eyebrows and the suggestion of a moustache. 'Mothers are only allowed two visitors at a time,' she barked. 'The rest of you will have to leave and come back later.'

Liam, who never missed the opportunity to go to the pub, invited Con for a drink – 'To wet the baby's head.'

'You've already wet it about a hundred times,' Claire said curtly, but with a smile.

Marge said she'd only dropped in to deliver the flowers, and Aileen that she and Michael were having dinner with his mother and it was time she left. 'I'm not in the least looking forward to it,' she said nastily. 'All she ever does is criticize.' She never had a good word to say for her mother-in-law.

The staff nurse was still lurking in the ward, so I went to the nursery to have another look at Bobby, hoping she would have left by the time I went back. Half a dozen other people were peering through the nursery window when I arrived.

Bobby Quinn, six days old, was in the second row, sobbing his little heart out, his face so red that I was worried he was about to burst a blood vessel.

'Is he all right?' I asked a passing nurse, pointing to my latest nephew.

'They're all all right,' she said breathlessly. 'Some are hungry, some are tired, some want their nappies changing, but apart from that they're all fine.' She departed in a rush.

I looked doubtfully at Bobby. He didn't *look* all right. His fists were clenched as he beat hell out of the empty air and his little feet danced with rage. I wanted to rush into the nursery, pick him up and take him to Claire, but doubted if she would appreciate my gesture of concern.

'Bobby's fine,' said a voice. 'As soon as the visitors have gone, they'll give him to Claire and she'll change his nappy, feed him and give him a cuddle. Right now, he's just letting off steam.'

'How would you know?' I growled. Marge was standing next to me. She looked awfully sad and a little bit lost. She wasn't wearing make-up for a change and it made her appear much younger.

'I just do,' she sighed. 'This time next year I'll have a baby of me own. It'll be about six months old.'

'Did you think I didn't already know that?'

It was a while before she answered. 'I'm sorry, Kitty. You were right, I did play a trick on your Danny. I told him I was using something when I wasn't. But it was the biggest mistake I'll ever make in me life. He never talks to me, he doesn't touch me; we're like strangers to each other.'

I was watching Bobby again. It seemed to me his movements were getting slower. He was tiring himself out. All of a sudden, he stopped crying and fell asleep in front of my eyes, turning into a quite different baby.

'Who's the chap who came with you to the ozzie?' Marge asked.

'Con Daley. We've been going out together for about five weeks.'

'He looks nice – and he's dead fond of you. I could see it in his eyes.'

'I'm fond of him.' We moved out of the way to let two elderly women look at the babies. From their conversation, it seemed one had just become a great-grandmother for the first time.

Marge bit her lip. 'It's dead horrible to think you've been courting all these weeks and I've known nothing about it.'

'Whose fault is that, Marge?'

'Mine.' She nodded furiously. 'It's all my fault. I've made a terrible mess of everything. I've ruined Danny's life, not to mention me own. Your sisters hate me, I've lost you for a friend, and I've upset your mam and dad – I really love your mam, Kitty. She's one in a million.' She gave a long, shuddering sigh. 'If you must know, sometimes I feel like sticking me head in the gas oven. It'd be best for everyone all round.'

'It wouldn't be best for the baby,' I pointed out. 'And my sisters don't hate you.' But I knew they might if they discovered Marge had tricked Danny into getting married. 'They don't know the whole truth and they'll come round soon enough.'

She looked slightly relieved. 'I thought you'd told them about . . . you know.'

'Well, I didn't, and neither did Danny.'

'I suppose that's something. Oh, well, I'll be off now, Kitty. Tara.' She turned and walked away, the girl who only a few weeks ago had been my best friend in the world. From the back, I could see she'd lost a lot of weight – in her condition, she should be putting it on.

'Marge,' I called, and she twisted round so quickly that she stumbled. I darted forward and caught her arm. 'Why don't you come back in the ward for a while?' The staff nurse was bound to have gone by now.

Her eyes brightened. 'I'd love to. It's dead miserable in the flat. Weekends, Danny just disappears, I've no idea where.'

We walked back to the ward together. I didn't link her arm as I might once have done, but I'd taken the first step towards being friends with Marge again, though I knew we would never be such good friends as we'd been before.

On Monday, when I asked Faith if her headache was better, she just laughed it away.

'It had gone by the time I woke up next morning. I truly don't know what came over me, Kitty. I hardly ever get headaches, but we'd only been in the restaurant about an hour when my head began to throb really painfully. I stuck it out for quite a while, but in the end I felt I just had to come home. I offered to catch a taxi, leaving Eric and Hope to finish the meal, but they insisted on coming with me. Poor things,' she laughed, 'I completely spoiled their evening.'

As I recall, she'd already declared the evening spoiled before she'd even left the house, but she didn't mention Hope again, and told me Eric was going into town later, 'to do some shopping. The boat docked at all sorts of cities while on the cruise, but he rarely has time to go ashore.'

'Would you like me to look after Oliver and Robin, then you can go shopping with him?'

'That's awfully kind of you, dear, but I really don't feel like it.' She laughed again.

She was talking far too quickly and laughing for no reason at all. I longed to tell her that I had seen Eric and Hope kissing outside the house on Saturday night. She'd feel all the better for talking about it, but that was up to her.

Jamie's National Service call-up papers had already arrived. He was due to leave for a training course in Aldershot, Kent, on 3 December, two days after his eighteenth birthday. A big party was planned. All his mates from school and work would be invited, as well as the family. I got the impression Jamie was quite excited he'd been called up, but was doing his best not to let it show for Mam's sake. And it was for Mam's sake that no one so much as mentioned the words 'Aldershot' or 'National Service'. As for the war in Korea, as far as the McCarthys were concerned, we'd never heard of it.

All Mam talked about was the birthday party – the food, the drink and did we think it would be the sort of party where people would play games or just stand around and chat?

'I'll ask our Aileen if we can borrow their gramophone,' she said fussily. 'Her and Michael have lots of modern records: Frank Sinatra and Perry Como. It'd be nice to have some music in the background.'

We dreaded to think what would happen after the party when Jamie had to go away.

Chapter 3

I was nine and had been at school the day our Will left home for the Navy. Mam said he'd 'volunteered'. I hadn't known what that meant at the time. Jeff, older by three years, had waited nine months until he was called up and had joined the Army. He left on a Saturday. Lots of the neighbours came outside to wave goodbye. A little girl ran up and gave him a bar of chocolate, and a man chucked a packet of Craven A to him, though Jeff didn't smoke. The minute he'd disappeared around the corner, Mam and his fiancée, Theresa, rushed into the parlour for a good cry, despite thinking he wouldn't be away for long. The war hadn't ended in six months as everyone had predicted, but it was bound to end soon. No one had dreamed it would last six long years.

Will and Jeff were children when I was born, but I mainly remembered them as adults: two six-foot-tall men who sometimes behaved like little kids, wrestling each other to the ground, all quite good-humoured, not minding if me and Jamie joined in. They were very gentle with us.

Weekends, it was like a station in our house, what with Claire and Aileen's boyfriends, and Will and Jeff's girlfriends, all descending on the place together. Mam loved it. She was in her element, making endless pots of tea and cutting sarnies.

My big brothers had come home on leave occasionally until the time when they came no more. I think I was more upset for Mam and Dad than anything. I cried a lot. Everybody did, even the neighbours, particularly when Will's ship went down and my parents lost their second son.

Looking back, it all seemed very unreal, as if my brothers had never existed and it had all been a dream.

But Jamie wasn't a dream. Jamie was real. When he was born, I was only two and the baby of the family. All of a sudden, I discovered Mam's knee wasn't always available to sit on whenever I felt like it, because she was already nursing Jamie.

I could remember him learning to walk and the first time he'd managed to say 'Kitty'. I'd felt dead pleased because mine was the first name he'd learned after 'Mam' and 'Dad'. I knew everything about Jamie, things I'd never known about Jeff and Will. I'd watched him turn from a baby into a little boy and from a boy into an eighteen-year-old man. Not a single day of my life since I was two years old had passed that he hadn't been part of.

But today he was going away and I couldn't bear it. He was only off to do his National Service but, given the history of the McCarthy family, plus the fact there was a war on, it held more significance to us than it did to most people. The weather didn't help: the sky was like mud and it was damp and chilly.

Mam had had his best suit cleaned, Claire had bought him a new tie, Dad had polished his shoes, I'd helped pack his suitcase. He was wearing the watch Aileen and Michael had bought him for his birthday and, in his pocket, there was a leather wallet from Norah and Roy, along with one of the white handkerchiefs with a blue 'J' embroidered in the corner from Danny and Marge. It had come in a box of four.

'You look as if you belong in Burton's shop window,' Claire remarked when he was dressed in all his finery, looking dead smart and incredibly grown up, yet at the same time hardly more than a child. His face was still baby-soft and he only shaved once a week. He wasn't quite as tall as Danny – perhaps he still had a bit more growing to do – and not nearly so cocky. Mind you, Danny had had all the cockiness knocked out of him since he'd learnt that Marge was expecting his baby – he was too old for National Service. Jamie's hair was more brown than red. He hated having it cut, particularly since he'd been old enough to go to the barber's. Perhaps he thought the barber's hand might slip and cut off one of his ears, I don't know, but the only way of persuading Jamie to get his hair trimmed was to tell him he looked like a girl. Then he'd be off like a shot.

'I'll have to go in a minute,' he said.

'Are you sure you wouldn't like us to come with you into town, son?' Dad asked. He was catching the midday train from Exchange Station to London, then changing on to another train for Aldershot, where he would spend six weeks training to be a soldier. Upstairs, Bobby, now two and a half months old, began to cry, but Claire ignored him.

'No, ta. I'd feel daft, turning up with me mam and dad. But thanks for asking,' he added quickly, worried he'd hurt their feelings.

'Write to us as soon as you can, won't you, Jamie?'

'The very minute I arrive, Mam.' He picked up the suitcase and edged towards the door. 'Tara, everyone.'

I burst into tears. 'Don't think you're getting away that easily, Jamie McCarthy.' I flung my arms around him. 'Take care of yourself, luv.'

'Gerroff, sis.' He shrugged me away, but I could see he was close to tears himself.

'Come here, you!' Claire gave him a quick kiss and patted his face, and Dad pumped his arm and slapped his back. Mam just kissed him lightly on the cheek and held him briefly. Then we all went to the door and waved Jamie goodbye.

'Are you all right, Bernie?' Dad asked when we came back into the house.

'Yes, Bob. Don't worry,' Mam said in a voice that I could only describe as cold, 'I'm not going to cry, but if our Jamie doesn't come back then I shall kill meself.'

'It was horrible,' I wept. 'Really, really horrible.'

'She actually said she was going to kill herself?' Faith was horrified. I'd taken the morning off to say goodbye to Jamie, but couldn't stop crying all the way on the bus to Weld Road and still couldn't stop crying now. Poor Faith didn't know what to do with me. She'd put the light on in the kitchen because it was so dark outside and the children were playing Red Indians all over the house. For the first time, the noise was getting on my nerves.

'I can still hear it in me head. It sounded as if she really meant it.'

'Oh, dear! Look, I'll make you some coffee, very strong with loads of sugar. Perhaps that will help.'

I couldn't imagine anything helping, but I sipped the coffee slowly and by the time I'd finished, the tears had stopped. 'I'm sorry,' I sniffed. 'I'm here to look after Oliver and Robin, and I'm crying buckets in your kitchen instead.'

'Kitty, dear, as if I mind!' Faith said warmly. 'We're friends and that's what friends are for, to confide in when something awful happens. And haven't I told you enough about my own troubles in the past?'

'Even so,' I sniffed again, 'it's not exactly what you pay me for, is it?'

'I didn't pay you to make those lovely Indian headdresses for the children the other day, but you did. I don't pay you for all sorts of the kind things you do, Kitty, so please don't talk about payment again, or I shall get very cross.' There was a scream from upstairs and she said, 'That's Robin, it sounds as if he's fallen over.' I was halfway out of the chair, but she pushed me back. 'You stay there, I'll see to him.'

I heard her say, 'Oh, you poor darling, you've got a bump on your forehead. Let Mummy take you into the bathroom and bathe it. Then we'll go downstairs. Kitty's here now and she'll kiss it better for you.'

She was so patient with the children, who would have driven any woman spare. I liked her enormously, almost loved her in a way, and I dreaded the time coming when she discovered that Eric and Hope were having an affair. Or perhaps she already knew and was ignoring it for some reason, praying it would stop. For the umpteenth time, I wondered if she really had witnessed the incident outside her front door the night Con and I had babysat. She'd never mentioned it and neither had I. Maybe she hadn't seen anything, or maybe she had and put it down to the fact that they'd both drunk too much and that it meant nothing.

About six weeks ago, Hope had gone to Guildford to stay with an old friend from school called Emily Rowe. 'They were bridesmaids at each other's weddings and it's ages since they've seen each other, though they write and telephone all the time,' Faith told me. 'She's staying a whole fortnight. I must say I'm rather pleased about it. It means the children can make as much noise as they like while she's gone. She gets cross when they wake her early on Sunday morning.'

Hope left in the car the day before Eric returned to his ship. A few days later, Faith was in the bath and I was in the kitchen watching

Oliver and Robin colour in their magic painting books, when the telephone rang. I went to answer it.

'Is that Faith?' a woman's voice asked.

'She's having a bath.'

'Is it possible to speak to Hope? I just rang the bank and they said she's off sick. I was wondering what was wrong, that's all. This is Emily Rowe, by the way, Hope's friend.'

For a moment, I was flummoxed. I considered saying Hope was in hospital, but then Emily might want to know the name and it would mean more lies. In the end, I decided to tell the truth. It wasn't my job to protect Hope's back. 'Hope told Faith she was going to stay with you. If she's not there, I've no idea where she is.'

'Oh, Lord!' There was a horrified gasp at the other end of the line. 'Who is this I'm speaking to?'

'My name's Kitty. I help look after Faith's children.'

'Look, Kitty, would you mind forgetting we had this conversation? It seems I've put my great big foot in it. I've no idea what Hope's up to, but please forget I rang.'

'I already have,' I said, replacing the receiver. My mind was working overtime. Hope had left the day before Eric. If I'd had a hundred pounds, I'd've bet every penny that she'd gone with him on the ship to New York.

It was Tuesday and I had an English Grammar lesson that night. A comma, I had already discovered, separated words and phrases to create a pause. It was also necessary to put one between adjectives. For example: 'Kitty McCarthy has a big, wide mouth.' Last week we'd done apostrophes and exclamation marks, and we were now learning how to structure sentences. I'd learned it was wrong to say 'me and Con', and that it should be 'Con and I'.

At Norah's wedding, Marge had asked what use there was in learning grammar. All I knew was it made me feel better inside, even if I only wrote shopping lists (a comma was supposed to go between each item). Oh, and I was training myself to stop saying 'me' when I really meant 'my'.

Con was waiting for me outside the community hall. It had been a horrible day and now it was a horrible night. The pavements were wet, though it hadn't rained, and it was getting foggy. Nowadays, Con and I met every night. Sometimes, all we did was walk along the Dock Road as far as Liverpool then catch the tram home, or we sat in a pub for hours, Con with a pint of beer and me with a shandy. It was enough for us just to be together.

By now, we were hopelessly in love, but my brain had split into two halves. With one half, I was looking forward to us spending the rest of our lives together; with the other, I was dreading him proposing a second time. That half of my brain liked things the way they were – meeting every day, going into town to see the latest pictures, having a meal.

'Where shall we go?' he asked, linking my arm.

'Do you mind if we go back to our house? Our Jamie only went to Aldershot this morning and I'd like to be with Mam and Dad.' The atmosphere when we'd had our tea, just the three of us, had been frigid. Dad's face was tight and drawn, and Mam had hardly said a word. When she did, her voice was as cold as it had been when Jamie left. I'd felt mean leaving for my English class.

Con was the easiest-going man in the world. He just turned round and we headed for Amethyst Street. On the way, I told him what Mam had said that morning. His reaction surprised me. It seemed he wasn't so easy-going after all.

'That's a disgraceful thing to say!' he spluttered. 'Now your poor dad – your whole family – will be on tenterhooks for two bloody years until Jamie comes home. I hope you don't mind me saying this, Kitty, but your mother is dead selfish.'

'Selfish!' I'd always thought Mam the opposite of selfish, yet Theresa had said more or less the same thing.

'Selfish, thoughtless, whatever. Actually threatening to kill herself if Jamie doesn't come back?' He was shaking with rage. 'It's just not fair.'

I didn't answer, but thought of Dad's face when we'd had our tea. Con was right; it wasn't fair.

The fog was thicker by the time we reached Amethyst Street. I was about to pull the key through the letterbox, when the door opened and Claire came out.

'I've just been tidying Jamie's room, save Mam having to do it. It was like a midden in there. There's no one in. Our Aileen and Michael came round in the car to collect the gramophone and insisted on taking Mam and Dad out for a meal. There was no fog then, so Lord knows what time they'll be back. Michael only drives about a mile an hour in normal circumstances, so it could be sometime next week. Till then, you've got the place to yourselves.' She winked leerily. 'Don't do anything I wouldn't do. Tara.'

'Tara,' we both muttered. As soon as the door closed, I asked Con if he'd like a cup of tea.

'Afterwards,' he replied. To my relief, he was grinning again.

'After what?'

'This.' He took me in his arms and we shuffled into the parlour, where we sank on to the settee. We made love. It wasn't something I'd expected to happen, but it just did. I could have stopped him, easily, but I didn't want to. It hurt a bit at first, but I didn't mind. It was enough just to feel Con inside me, making me part of him and him of me.

When it was over, I didn't make the promised tea for quite a while. We just lay there, squashed together on the settee, thinking how wonderful it had been.

Con said, 'When on earth will we have the opportunity to do this again?'

I confessed I didn't know. 'Mam and Dad never usually go out at night, apart from Sunday when they go to Benediction.'

'My ma goes to a whist drive every Wednesday and Dad goes to the pub. Our Sheila still lives at home, but she's courting and hardly ever in. Even if she were, she wouldn't clat on us.'

Well, twice a week was better than nothing.

Jamie wrote regularly. He sounded homesick, but seemed to be enjoying himself. He didn't like drill, but going to the gymnasium was the gear. He was also learning to box. 'I'm quite good at it and might take it up professionally when I come home,' he said.

Faith had *The Times* delivered every day and I read everything I could about the war in Korea. To my horror, I discovered that the Chinese Army had joined in on the side of the North Koreans so the Americans and their Allies had to fight on two fronts. There was actually talk of using the atom bomb, and the threat of a Third World War. The British Prime Minister, Clement Atlee, flew to America to see President Truman to protest at the use of the bomb. Thousands of British troops had been sent to fight, mainly National Servicemen like Jamie. Those who'd already served their allotted two years had had their time extended. It was all far worse than I'd imagined and I felt dead ashamed of my ignorance.

At Christmas, Jamie came home for a few days, looking extremely fit and no longer babyish. He took Danny into the yard and showed him how to box, though the lesson quickly ended when Danny accidentally received a bloody nose.

Faith and the children went down to Richmond for Christmas to stay with her widowed mother – Eric wasn't duc home until the New Year and Hope was going to stay with her friend, Emily Rowe. 'That's twice in the space of a few months,' Faith remarked. 'She said Emily's a trifle depressed over something. Perhaps, if you've nothing better to do, Kitty,' she added casually, 'you could drop in now and then to see if the house is all right.'

As there was nothing I could think of that could go wrong with the house apart from it setting itself alight, I took this as a roundabout way of saying that me and Con could come whenever we liked, which is exactly what we did. We lied quite brazenly, refusing all invitations from both our families to come for a meal, saying I'd promised to go to Con's, while Con said he'd been invited to ours. It meant we hardly ate a thing over Christmas. Instead, we had an exhilarating time in the second-floor bedroom in Weld Road.

Always at the back of my mind was the awareness that Con wasn't taking precautions when we made love and that I stood a good chance of getting pregnant. Was I, I wondered, just sitting back and letting things happen until the decision was taken out of my hands and we'd *have* to get married? If so, which half of my brain did *that* idea come from?

The Knowleses returned from Richmond, and Jamie went back to Aldershot, half his training already completed. In another three weeks he would be a fully trained soldier, fit to fight in a distant war in a strange country where many British servicemen had already lost their lives.

Life returned to normal. The year turned into 1951 and I recommenced my English classes, looked after Oliver and Robin, and went out with Con. Over Christmas, we'd been spoiled. The snatched half-hour in the parlour in Amethyst Street while Mam and

Dad were at Benediction, and the slightly longer time on Wednesdays in Con's house in Seaforth, no longer seemed enough. Once again, he asked me to marry him and once again I turned him down, reminding him I'd asked him to wait six months before he proposed again.

I only half listened while he pointed out all the advantages of marriage, chief among them being the fact that we could make love whenever we felt like it. I didn't point out that it wouldn't be the same, that nothing could beat the excitement of doing it hurriedly, secretly, in a place where any minute we might be discovered, our hearts pounding whenever we heard footsteps outside that might mean someone was coming home. Or in Weld Road, where it had seemed a daring adventure. I wasn't totally sure if it had been what Faith meant when she'd asked me to make sure her house didn't come to any harm. When she'd returned she seemed to have forgotten all about it and didn't ask whether I'd been or not. Anyway, at the end of January, something happened, something so awful that I'd never forget until my dying day. It put all thoughts of getting married to Con and everything else completely out of my mind.

Jamie had finished his training and was sitting in Aldershot waiting to be told where he'd be sent next. Our Norah's blood pressure rose to an alarming level, so much so that she was worried she would lose the baby. She was ordered not to lift a finger and to sit with her feet up until after it was born. Roy, who I'd considered such a drip, turned out to be a brick, waiting on his wife hand and foot, bringing home flowers and little prezzies almost every day. I decided I liked him after all.

Oliver caught a chill and passed it on to Robin. I read to them until my voice grew hoarse and I would willingly have killed Goldilocks and the Three Bears, their favourite story, had they appeared before me in the flesh – or the fur, in the case of the bears.

The boys had been allowed downstairs for the first time in a week and were lying, one at each end of the settee in the parlour, looking very pathetic and hard done by. It was a crisp, winter day full of sunshine. I was reading *Jack and the Beanstalk* – it made a pleasant change – when the doorbell rang. Faith went to see who it was. Seconds later, she came in. 'There's a man to see you, Kitty.'

'Who is it?'

'I don't know, dear. It's not Con. He's come in a car. Here, give me the book; I'll take over.'

Michael was in the hall, hopping anxiously from one foot to the other, but Aileen's husband was the sort of person who always looked anxious about something. At first, it didn't quite click that he would only have come for a vitally important reason.

'Kitty!' He seized both my arms and shook them roughly, as if I were a piece of washing and he was trying to shake the moisture out. 'Kitty, I'm afraid your mother's very ill. She's been taken to Bootle Hospital and they think it might be a heart attack.'

'I'll come straight away.' I reached for my coat that was hanging on the rack. 'I'll just tell Faith.'

But Faith had already opened the parlour door. 'I couldn't help but overhear, Kitty. I hope your mother soon gets better. One of my uncles had a heart attack, but he completely recovered.'

'What happened?' I asked Michael when we were in the car. I felt quite calm. Mam hadn't exactly been laughing her head off when I'd left home earlier, but she'd seemed perfectly fit.

'What happened,' Michael said grimly, 'is that a telegram arrived—'

'A telegram!' A wave of nausea passed over me. *Jamie!*

'It wasn't for the McCarthys,' Michael went on, and I felt just as sick with relief, 'but the people in the neighbouring house, the Tuttys. There was no one in, so the boy knocked next door, wanting someone to sign for it. Your mother took one look and began to scream and scream.'

I imagined Mam opening the door to a uniformed boy with an orange envelope in his hand. She would have had the same thought as I'd had. *Jamie!* She'd had only two telegrams in her life, each informing her that she'd lost a son. What other reason could there be for a third than she'd lost another?

Michael squeezed my knee. 'Are you all right, Kit?'

'More or less.' I felt a bit like screaming myself.

'Anyway, the neighbours came out in force, but there was nothing they could do to stop her from screaming. She just kept on and on, tearing herself apart, until she collapsed, from exhaustion so they thought. Someone ran to get your dad, someone else fetched Claire. Then an ambulance arrived and took your mother to hospital; Claire phoned from there to ask if I'd pick up Aileen. She intended ringing Weld Road, but I said I'd collect you. It would've been rotten for you, having to catch a bus home.'

'Thank you, Michael,' I said gratefully. He was a thoughtful man, exceptionally kind, with a gentle face and pale, receding hair that made him appear older than thirty-seven. I liked him enormously, but he got on Aileen's nerves quite a lot and she never bothered to hide it, often berating him in public while Michael just stood there, not saying a word.

Some people, Claire for one and me for another, made fun of his pedantic ways and his inability to go fast in the car (we were proceeding towards Bootle at a snail's pace, though his hands were as tense on the wheel as someone driving at a hundred miles an hour). He continued to relate the happenings of the morning, determined not to be rushed. Danny's firm had given him half a dozen small jobs to do, so no one knew where he was, but they hoped to have tracked him down by now. Marge was on her way to the hospital, but Norah hadn't yet been told due to the state of her health: 'Your dad said to leave it unless it became absolutely necessary.' As soon as I was dropped off at the hospital, Michael was going back to Amethyst Street to look through Jamie's papers and see if he could find the telephone number of the barracks in Aldershot to request Jamie be allowed compassionate leave.

'Is it likely,' I asked, 'to be absolutely necessary? I mean, to tell Norah and have Jamie come all the way home?'

'I haven't spoken to the doctor, Kitty, but, according to your dad, your mother's condition is critical.'

It wasn't until then that the penny dropped. *Critical.* In other words, there was a chance that Mam might die.

The family were hidden behind a curtained off section in a corner of the ward: Claire, Aileen and Marge, and a breathless Danny, who'd only just arrived, and, of course, my father in his working clothes. There was an expression on his face, a look of resignation, as if he'd been expecting something like this to happen for years. Now it had, but he'd already lived through it perhaps a hundred times before.

'Hello, Kitty, luv.' He kissed me tiredly on the forehead. 'Your mam still hasn't said a word.'

I could hardly believe the person on the bed was my mother. I had a vision of the slim, red-haired woman who'd taken us to the shelter not long after the war had begun. Then, she had been pretty and full of life, always the first to start the singing, organize games for the children – not just the McCarthys. She would read to us, fairy stories, the sort I'd been reading to other children less than half an hour before. That was only a decade ago, yet to look at Mam now, with her parchment-coloured skin and sparse, white hair, it could have been twenty, even thirty years.

There and then I made a vow that, whatever happened to me in the years to come, however tragic, I would never, never allow it to ruin my life and the lives of those around me in the way it had done my mother.

I bent and whispered in her ear, 'Hello, Mam, it's Kitty.'

'She can't hear, luv,' said Claire. 'She can't hear and she can't speak, but her lips are moving all the time, as if she's talking to herself inside.'

'I wonder what she's saying?'

'I reckon it's something to do with Jamie,' Aileen whispered. 'She thinks he's dead. That's why she won't wake up, because she thinks Jamie's dead and she doesn't want to face it.'

Marge made a choking sound and began to cry. 'I don't want your mam to die, Danny. I'd miss her something terrible.' I remembered her saying, in another hospital, how much she loved Mam. *She's one in a million.*

To my astonishment, Danny put his arm around his wife's shoulders and pulled her towards him. 'She won't die, Marge. She may not look it, but Mam's as strong as an ox.'

A doctor, tall and beefy with sandy hair, came in, felt Mam's pulse and left without a word. Claire picked up the same white hand and began to feel for a pulse. 'I can't find it,' she muttered irritably.

'Let her be,' Dad sighed. 'Leave her in peace, there's a good girl.'

'All right, Dad,' Claire said obediently, and carefully laid Mam's hand back on the cover.

Michael arrived to say he'd found the telephone number of the barracks and that Jamie was being sent home. If *he* could get through to Mam, I thought hopefully, convince her that he was alive, then she was bound to recover.

All of a sudden, it was visiting time. People poured in, laughed, told jokes, swapped stories, and brought fruit and flowers that perfumed the ward. Smoking in the ward was forbidden, but the smell of cigarettes drifted in from the corridor. Then, just as suddenly, visiting time was over, and the people poured out with a chorus of 'taras' and noisy kisses, leaving behind only the faint aroma of flowers and smoke.

A nurse arrived accompanied by two doctors – the tall, beefy one, and a much older, distinguished-looking man with silver hair. Stethoscopes hung around their necks. The nurse asked if we would please wait outside while the patient was examined. 'Doctor Whiteside is a heart specialist,' she whispered. 'He's very well known in medical circles and has only just arrived.'

We hung around in the corridor, not knowing what to say. Marge said she needed to sit down; Danny took her to look for a chair. Claire and Aileen went in search of the Ladies', and Michael to see if anybody could provide us with a cup of tea, leaving Dad and I alone.

'You know, Kitty,' he mumbled, his voice so low I could hardly hear, 'I've always half expected something like this would happen. At work, whenever someone called me name, me heart would leap to me throat, and I'd think, "It's Bernie. She's done it at last, killed herself or been taken ill with the misery of it all."'

I held his hand. It was exactly as I'd thought. 'She'll pull through, Dad. As Danny said, Mam's as strong as an ox.'

He shook his head. 'I don't know where Danny got that idea from. Since your brothers died, your mam's been as weak as a lamb.'

Michael returned with a tray containing seven mugs of tea and a little bowl of sugar. 'They took pity on us in the kitchen,' he announced. He handed us a mug each then took the tray to look for the others.

Dad said, 'Our Aileen's got a good 'un there. I wish she wasn't always so short with him. I know he's a bit of a fusspot and not very exciting, but she'll never want for anything while she's married to Michael. It's a pity they haven't got kids; he'd make a great dad.'

Claire and Aileen came back and left again immediately to look for Michael and the tea. They were both desperate for a cuppa.

The ward doors swung open and the silver-haired doctor emerged. 'Mr McCarthy?' Dad confirmed this was the case with a little nod. 'I'm afraid your wife has suffered a massive heart attack. We've done all we can, but I doubt very much if she'll last the night. I'm sorry to be so blunt, but I thought you should be prepared.'

Dad nodded again, quite calmly. 'Thanks for telling me, Doctor. Can we go and sit with her now?'

'Of course.' He put a well-cared-for hand on the sleeve of Dad's old working jacket. 'I'm very sorry, Mr McCarthy.'

'So am I, but you see, Doctor, her heart was broken a long time ago, so I'm not all that surprised this has happened.'

The doctor glanced patronizingly at my father. I thought he was about to explain that a broken heart had nothing to do with a heart attack, but must have decided not to bother. He turned on his heel and went back into the ward.

By now, everyone had returned. Michael was despatched to fetch Norah. Claire expressed my own feelings when she said, 'Let's hope the shock doesn't harm her baby.'

Then we all went into the ward, drawing the curtains tight around us, making me feel as if we were in our own little world and nothing of any consequence was happening outside. There was just us, the McCarthys, waiting for our mother to die.

Bernadette McCarthy passed away at twenty-three minutes past nine, still talking to herself, until her lips stopped moving and her broken heart stopped beating forevermore.

'She's in heaven now with Jeff and Will,' Dad said quietly, placing a final kiss on the lips of his wife.

Jamie arrived about half an hour later. We'd decided not to tell him about the telegram. It might have made him feel somehow responsible.

Then we all went back to Amethyst Street. Con had called earlier and had been told Mam was in hospital. He was waiting for me on the front doorstep and could tell by the expression on my face that the worst had happened.

'I'm sorry, Kit.' He took me in his arms. 'So sorry.'

He'd called Mam 'selfish'. Perhaps she had been, I didn't know, but now she was dead and I felt as if I'd lost the dearest mother in the world.

Amethyst Street looked as if it had gone blind on the morning of Mam's funeral. Every single curtain was closed by the time the hearse arrived to collect the coffin from the parlour where it had lain for five days without the lid so everyone could see her peaceful face. Father Ryan had been every night to lead the prayers.

We walked behind the hearse – St James's Church was only a minute away – Dad erect and tall, bearing himself with remarkable dignity, Roy supporting Norah, who walked gingerly, her hands resting on her swollen tummy as if to protect the baby inside.

Marge was the only one who cried. The rest of us emerged from the Requiem Mass dry-eyed to examine the flowers and wreaths that were spread on the grass outside. There was a beautiful wreath from Faith, white lilies and ivy, another just as beautiful from Con's family, one from Cameron's signed by Theresa, Betty and Enid. There were flowers from every person I knew and some I'd never heard of. I shook dozens of hands, many of them belonging to strangers who'd read the notice in the *Bootle Times* and had come to pay their respects.

Every single one of them came back to our house for the refreshments that Claire and I had got up at the crack of dawn to prepare. We sang all Mam's favourite songs and it was like the Blitz all over again, until gradually people began to leave and there were only the McCarthys left.

Now we had to get on with our own lives – without Mam.

It turned out that the telegram that killed Mam was from Ada Tutty addressed to her mother. Apparently she'd left exceptionally early for work that morning, but instead of going to the butcher's, she'd caught the train to London. The telegram was to say that she'd left home and had no intention of coming back. It later turned out that she'd taken the money Mrs Tutty had been saving for years and kept under the mattress: £73.4.8d. according to Mrs Tutty, who'd written it down.

Norah's baby arrived early – *genuinely* early – at the end of March, a little scrap of a girl weighing barely five pounds. She was called Bernadette after Mam.

Marge was annoyed. 'If I have a girl, I was going to call her Bernadette,' she complained. 'Danny thinks it's a gear idea.'

'It won't hurt to have two Bernadettes in the same family,' I assured her. 'One can be shortened to Bernie.'

Her eyes brightened. 'I wouldn't mind which it was: Bernadette or Bernie.'

Marge appeared to be quite content these days. I don't know quite how it happened, but she and Danny were getting along just fine. In fact, when you considered that my sisters and brother were relatively happily married, I don't know why I had such an aversion to it myself, why I thought of marriage as the end of everything and the beginning of nothing.

It was about this time – April Fools' Day to be precise, making me realize what a fool I'd been – that I began to suspect *I* might be pregnant. I was five days late with my period. I'd been late before, but never more than a day or two. It was no use panicking and getting into a tizzy, I'd walked into the situation with my eyes wide open and it was nobody's fault but my own.

I knew I should tell Con straight away, so that we could be married as soon as possible. I don't know why I didn't. There were more signs. I woke up every morning with the strong sensation I wanted to be sick, though I never was. Yet the feeling I was having a baby hardened in my mind, until I knew for certain it was the case.

A few days later, Con asked me to marry him again. We'd just finished a meal in our favourite Chinese restaurant and had ordered coffee. 'Do you realize,' he said in a hurt voice, 'that it's long past that six-month deadline you set? I've been waiting for you to bring it up yourself, ask *me* to marry *you* for a change.'

'I'm sorry.' I looked at him, outwardly calm, but inside there was a storm raging in my breast. Now was the time to say, 'Yes. Yes, Con, I will marry you, and it'd better be soon because I'm having our baby.' But those words, the correct ones, refused to come. The words that did emerge from my lips were the opposite of what he wanted to hear. 'I'm sorry, Con,' I said again, 'but I don't want to get married, not to you or anyone. It'd be best if we broke up. I'm only wasting your time and you'd be better off with another girl.'

Con was stunned into silence. The waiter came with the coffee. I picked up my cup, bending my head to sip it so I couldn't see his stricken face.

'You don't mean that, Kitty?'

'I do,' I whispered into the cup.

'You're actually telling me to find another girl?' His laugh came out more like a bark. 'And where, exactly, would I find another girl like you?'

I looked at him directly, about to say, 'There's plenty around,' but it sounded too jokey. 'I don't know, Con, but one day you will.'

'I doubt that very much, Kitty. In fact, I don't doubt it, I *know* it. We were made for each other, darling. I've known that since the day we first met.'

He'd never called me 'darling' before, and it seemed a bit sad that he did so on our very last date. 'Then you were wrong, Con. I wasn't made for you else I'd want us to get married.' That sounded hard and I hadn't meant it to. I hated being responsible for the look of total desperation on his face, the hurt in his green eyes. It wasn't fair to treat another person so cruelly, particularly not one as honest and decent as Con, whom I truly loved, but not quite enough.

He began to plead with me, bully me, reason with me, but I stood my ground, though it was hard, particularly when he promised never to mention marriage again. 'Let's just continue with things the way they are,' he urged. 'I shouldn't have asked so soon. I was pressing too hard. After all, it isn't even a year since we met.'

Had it not been for the baby, I might have felt tempted to agree, but it would have only been prolonging the agony to break up in two, three or five years' time instead of now.

I shook my head. 'No, Con.'

The two words reduced him to tears. 'I love you so much, Kitty,' he wept. The people on the next table had begun to stare.

I got to my feet, picked up my bag, entirely forgetting I'd promised to pay for the meal. 'I know, Con,' I said gently. 'As I said before, I'm sorry.'

I was so sorry that I was weeping myself when I left the restaurant. Instead of walking down to the Pier Head and risking he would follow, I went up Skelhorne Street and caught the Ribble bus as far as Walton Vale, then the one I travelled on to and from Weld Road that went to Bootle.

That night, I cried myself to sleep. Had I just made the biggest mistake of my life by rejecting a fine man like Connor Daley? At some unearthly hour I woke up to a silent world and thought about the baby. I wasn't about to shame my family and become a talking point for the neighbours by staying at home, nor had I even considered getting rid of it – although it was said a woman in Ford

Street carried out abortions without charging a penny. No, I knew exactly what I was going to do about the baby.

Next morning, I telephoned my sister, Aileen, from Weld Road and asked if I could come and see her that night.

'Of course, sis. I'll be home by six. Michael might be a bit late, but we'll both be pleased to see you. Since Mam died, we hardly ever have visitors,' she continued in a complaining tone. 'Our Claire's always too busy, Norah's tied up with the new baby, Marge is on the point of having hers – it's already a week late – and I don't suppose poor Dad feels up to it.'

I promised I would come as soon as possible after six – I would have gone straight from Weld Road, but felt obliged to go home first for my tea as Claire came round every day to make it. I felt guilty that I hadn't been to Aileen's since I couldn't remember when, but it was a long journey to Maghull on buses that didn't run very often. In fact, Mam had only gone the occasional Sunday afternoon with Dad. Michael had always driven them home in time for Benediction.

All the roads on the small estate had been named after famous writers: Dickens, where Aileen and Michael lived, Thackeray, Austen, Galsworthy, Eliot. Trollope Road had been changed to Shakespeare when the residents complained it sent out the wrong message.

'Hello, stranger,' Aileen greeted me when she opened the door at almost half past seven. 'I was expecting you much earlier.'

'How can I be a stranger when we saw each other a few days ago at our Norah's?' I asked irritably.

'You're a stranger in *this* house,' she sniffed.

'Well, you shouldn't live in the back of beyond. I had to wait for a bus and it took ages getting here. Are you going to let me in or leave me standing on the doorstep all night?'

'Sorry, sis. Come in. Michael's in the garage doing something to the car; he'll be in in a mo.'

'Actually, I wouldn't mind talking to you by yourself first.'

Aileen looked at me curiously. 'Is something wrong?' she asked.

I shook my head. We entered what she referred to as 'the lounge', a long room with windows at each end and an orange fitted carpet.

The wallpaper was cream, patterned with tiny orange flowers, and the tweed three-piece was the colour of chocolate. Perched at exactly the same angle on each chair stood an orange velvet cushion, and one at each end of the settee, like identical twins. The box-like piece of furniture in the corner of the room was in fact a television, the screen hidden behind closed doors.

Aileen and Michael's house always depressed me. It was too new, too clean, too tidy. There wasn't a single smudge on the wallpaper, the carpet was spotless and the kitchen looked unused, with everything hidden in the numerous shiny white cupboards or the even more shiny refrigerator. Claire was dead envious of the refrigerator, not to mention the television, the gramophone, the car in the garage and even the garage itself, which could have been turned into an extra bedroom. Despite this, Claire, in her little house in Opal Street, was undoubtedly happier. Aileen always seemed discontented with her lot, something I'd always put down to her longing for a baby. I hoped what I'd come to say would change that.

I sat carefully in an armchair, doing my best not to disturb the cushion. I wasn't sure how to begin, but supposed it was best to start at the beginning and so I burst out with, 'I'm having a baby.'

Aileen's jaw dropped and she blinked furiously. 'Is it Con's?'

'Yes.'

'Oh, well,' she said dismissively, 'knowing him, he'll be only too willing to marry you, so there's nothing to worry about.'

'Except I don't want to marry *him*. He asked again last night. I turned him down.'

Her jaw dropped again, this time even further. 'Does he know about the baby?'

'No, you're the only one I've told.'

'Really?' She looked pleased. 'If there's anything Michael and I can do to help, Kit—'

I swallowed hard, knowing I was about to drop a bombshell. 'You can help by taking the baby, pretending to adopt it. I wouldn't want people knowing he or she was mine.'

'Kitty!' Her lips moved agitatedly, reminding me a bit of Mam on her deathbed. 'Kitty, you shouldn't say things like that. How on earth can you have a baby without everyone knowing?'

'I shall go away,' I said calmly. 'I don't want to be the talk of Amethyst Street, nor do I want to upset Dad or get an ear-bashing from our Claire. The baby won't start to show until I'm about four months gone. You can tell people you've started adoption proceedings, then come and collect it from wherever I am when it's born.'

'You make it sound so simple,' she said in a voice that trembled with emotion.

'It *is* simple,' I stressed. 'There's nothing complicated about it.'

'Isn't there?' She folded her arms. 'Then tell me, where exactly will you live for five whole months without everyone guessing why you've gone? Our Claire will clock on straight away, she's got a nose for that sort of thing. She'd make a good spy.'

'I thought of going to London.' If Ada Tutty could go to London, then so could I, though I had to confess that I hadn't yet come up with a convincing excuse to explain my long absence from Amethyst Street. 'I've got loads of time to think of something,' I assured her.

She still looked unconvinced. 'How many periods have you missed?'

'Only the one.'

'Only the one!' Now she was annoyed. 'I miss periods all the time, loads of women do. How can you possibly be sure you're pregnant when you've only missed the one?'

'I've never missed one before – and I feel sick in the mornings, too. Believe me, sis, I know for certain that I'm having a baby.'

'Oh, Kitty!' she cried. 'You're not yet twenty years old and you don't seem to understand the seriousness of this. You're actually offering to let me have your baby – your *baby*, Kit.' She made a rocking motion with her arms, as if she was already holding a baby in them. 'How do you know you won't want to keep it when it's born? Are you really willing to let another woman raise your child?'

'Only if the woman's you, Aileen.'

At this, she began to cry. I began to wonder if this was why I hadn't cared if I got pregnant, because I'd always known in my heart I could give the baby to Aileen and Michael, who wanted one so very, very much. 'It's hardly fair on Con, is it, Kitty?' Aileen said through the tears. 'After all, it's his child just as much as yours.'

I agreed it was most unfair on Con. 'But if he knew, he might object to me giving it to you and Michael.' I felt uncomfortable referring to my baby as 'it'.

Just then, Michael came in. Usually dressed so smartly, he looked strange in an old pair of trousers and a shirt with a frayed collar.

There was a streak of oil on his cheek and he wore only socks on his feet. Aileen wore slippers and I remembered, too late, that I'd forgotten to remove my shoes when I came in, which was a rule of the house. I hoped I hadn't made marks on the spotless carpet.

'What's the matter, love?' he asked, alarmed, when he saw Aileen's tears.

I immediately excused myself by saying I wanted to go to the lavatory. It wasn't a lie, as lately it seemed necessary to go every five minutes. That might have been another sign of pregnancy, I wasn't sure. I didn't want to be present while Aileen told Michael the reason for my visit.

I stayed in the bathroom for a good ten minutes, admiring the pale-green tiled walls and the pale-green plastic curtain hanging over the pale-green bath that was a shower as well. A knobbly mat, a much darker green, fitted snugly around the lavatory, and the lid had a cover to match. Our lavatory at home didn't even have a lid, let alone a cover.

'Are you all right up there, Kitty?' Michael shouted.

I returned downstairs. He was waiting at the bottom, holding out his arms, and I had never seen such a look of radiant happiness on a face before. 'Thank you, Kitty. Thank you, very much. You have just granted Aileen and me our greatest wish. We'll be grateful to you for the rest of our lives.'

I told Faith I would be leaving in about three months' time and explained why, omitting all mention of Aileen. 'I'm expecting a baby,' I said, 'but don't want any of my family to know, so I'll be living in London from July until November. When it's born, I shall have it adopted.'

She wasn't shocked, but expressed disappointment at the idea of losing me. From the matter-of-fact tone of my voice, indicating that my mind was quite made up, she didn't ask why I wasn't marrying Con or question me in any way.

'I shall be sorry to lose you, Kitty,' she said warmly, 'and Oliver and Robin will be bereft. They both love you very much.'

'I'll come back to Liverpool when it's over and work for you again, if that's what you want.'

'Hmm,' she murmured thoughtfully, even though I'd thought she'd jump at the chance. She was very quiet all day, and I began to worry she was shocked after all and didn't want an immoral character like me looking after her children.

Just before I left, she asked, 'Will you be staying with anyone in particular in London, Kitty?'

'No. I've no idea yet where I'm going to stay.' Michael was going to arrange my accommodation. He and Aileen had insisted on paying my rent and giving me an allowance while I carried their baby, and wanted me to live somewhere tranquil. 'What about a little cottage in the Lake District?' he'd suggested initially.

I groaned and said I'd be bored witless. 'I'd prefer London.'

'There'd be all sorts of distractions there, Kitty,' he said with a worried frown. 'I'd like to think you were taking things easy, not gadding about.'

'Oh, shut up, Michael,' Aileen told him. 'She's having a baby, not going on retreat. Our Kitty's got a sensible head screwed on her shoulders. She'll look after herself, won't you, sis?'

I promised faithfully that I would. I wouldn't have minded gadding about a bit, but not while I was pregnant.

At that point, the telephone had rung. It was Claire from the hospital to say that Marge had just given birth to a lovely baby boy weighing almost ten pounds. Aileen relayed the news: 'Claire said Marge looks so exhausted you'd think she'd just delivered half a ton of spuds, and Danny's over the moon. They're going to call him George after the King and they want you to be godmother, Kitty.'

A few days later, when Faith and I were sitting in deckchairs in the garden on a dazzlingly sunny April day and the boys sailed two tiny boats in an old tin bath that had been left in the garden shed, she told me she was leaving Eric. I was surprised, but not all that much.

'He and Hope are having an affair,' she said, making a face. I pretended to look shocked. 'Eric is a womanizer. It's something I've always known and was prepared to put up with while he confined his womanizing to the ship, but not when he gets involved with my sister. They must think I'm stupid,' she continued indignantly. 'As if I wouldn't notice them carrying on under my nose! I suspected as much, months ago, when we went to that dinner at the Adelphi. Hope was flirting with him madly, and later I saw them kissing outside my very own front door. Since then, there've been lots of little signs, not enough to accuse them of anything solid, until a few weeks ago when Hope cleared some things out of her room and put them in the dustbin. Later, I was about to throw away the potato peelings and saw a menu from Eric's ship, the *Adrienne*, for last Hallowe'en's Eve when Hope was supposed to be staying with her friend, Emily. She must have gone with Eric on his ship instead!' Her grey eyes, usually so mild, blazed with fury.

'You don't sound very upset,' I remarked. I said nothing about the telephone call from Emily Rowe that I'd promised to forget.

'I'm too angry to be upset. I thought about leaving there and then, Kitty, but to tell the honest truth, I didn't want to leave *you*. I'm more than twice your age, but you feel more to me like a sister than Hope ever has or ever will.'

Embarrassed, I muttered something about her feeling like a sister to me, though I already had three that I loved very much.

'When will you be going?' It would seem my job in Weld Road would soon be coming to an end.

She gave me a brilliant smile. 'The same time as you, dear. I shall go back to Richmond and you can come with me. It's the perfect excuse to give your family when you tell them you're leaving, that Faith is breaking up with her husband and taking you with her to look after Oliver and Robin. No one will suspect a thing, not even your sister, Claire, the master spy.'

Aileen and Michael thought it a marvellous idea, though Michael was worried I'd wear myself out looking after the children. 'You must find the time to sit with your feet up for a few hours every day,' he insisted.

I asked if he'd like to come and live in Richmond to keep an eye on me.

'I'm sorry, Kitty,' he said meekly. 'I know I'm being an old fusspot, but this is the most wonderful thing that's ever happened to Aileen and I; I'm terrified something will go wrong.'

I kissed his cheek affectionately. 'Nothing will go wrong, Michael. I feel perfectly fit and everything's going swimmingly, so stop worrying or we'll all be nervous wrecks by the time the baby's born.'

'Hear, hear,' Aileen cried.

In March, Jamie had been sent abroad, not to Korea, but to Berlin to join the British Army of Occupation of the Rhine where he stood no chance of being killed, at least not in battle. If the telegram hadn't arrived for the Tuttys next door, then Mam would have been alive to hear the news and see her two new grandchildren: Bernadette, such a tiny thing when she was born, but rapidly putting on weight, and big, fat Georgie, my godchild, who never cried – not even at his christening – and slept twenty hours a day. Claire was expecting again, and soon, Aileen would reveal that she and Michael were adopting a baby and that she, too, would become a mother in the not-too-distant future.

'It's almost as good as announcing you're pregnant,' she said, rubbing her hands together gleefully. She seemed so much more contented these days and had stopped being horrid to Michael.

In a few weeks' time, at the end of May, I would leave my teens behind and enter my twenties. Oliver had been thrilled to discover he would be four on the same day and we were having a joint birthday party in Weld Road.

All in all, the McCarthys had recovered well from Mam's death only three months ago. I thought about her all the time, we talked about her a lot, we missed her still, yet it felt as if a shadow had been lifted from the house in Amethyst Street and it had become a happier place in which to live. We no longer had to tiptoe about in case we disturbed Mam, and could say whatever we wanted without worrying it was the wrong thing. Dad had started to go to football matches with Liam and, a few nights a week, he went for a pint with his mates from work. Before, he wouldn't have dreamt of leaving Mam on her own. He'd recently begun to smile again, quite a lot.

It bothered me so much to think that the death of our beloved mother could actually make life better for the people left behind that one day I discussed the matter with Faith.

'In her own way,' Faith said soberly, 'your mother was very ill. If she hadn't recovered from your brothers' deaths after six years, then the chances are she never would. Her life was so sad. When someone who is suffering dies, it's almost an act of mercy because the suffering comes to an end and everyone concerned feels a sense of relief. Does that make sense?'

'Sort of.' Only sort of.

*

The night before my birthday, our Danny came round. He was on his way to the pub, he explained, but had just dropped in because he wanted to ask me something.

'Ask away,' I sang.

'Promise not to lose your rag, sis.'

'On my heart.' I put my hand over my heart as proof I wouldn't.

'I haven't spoken to Dad yet, I thought I'd talk to you first, but what would you say to me, Marge and Georgie moving in? Our flat's too small for two people and a baby, and there's loads of room here. Marge will look after the house, do the washing and make the meals. What do you say, sis?'

'There'll be no need for her to do my washing. I'd rather do me – *my* – own,' I said, and immediately felt ashamed. 'Actually, Danny, I think it's a marvellous idea,' I gushed in an attempt to make up for the trite remark. 'And it fits in really well with my own plans – Faith's about to leave her husband and I'm going to Richmond with her to look after the children.'

'You're not going to stay there, are you?' he asked quickly. He looked quite put out by the news.

'It'll only be for a few months while she settles in.' It hadn't entered my head that people, apart from Dad, would miss me. 'Oliver will be four tomorrow and he's going to nursery in September. Robin won't be much trouble on his own.'

'Good,' Danny said, pleased. 'Anyroad, I'll have a word with Dad about us moving in, see what he thinks. Oh, by the way, I met Con Daley the other day. He's started his own business, doing quite well at it, too. He asked after you.'

My heart missed a beat. 'What did you tell him?'

Danny shrugged. 'Can't remember, sis. I suppose I told him you were fine.'

I received a card from Con on my birthday. I reckon it must have been the most expensive in the shop with a padded satin panel surrounded by a lace frill containing a single rose. The printed message said 'Happy Birthday to a Loved One', and it was signed 'Con'. Once again, I wondered if I'd made a terrible mistake, but I couldn't reverse things, no matter how much I might want to. I was carrying a baby who no longer belonged to him or me, but to Aileen and Michael.

★

The party in Weld Road went extremely well. Oliver and I toasted each other with homemade lemonade, and he promised to marry me when he grew older.

'I shall remind you of that one day,' I joked.

'I shan't forget, Kitty,' he said gravely.

'You have two beautiful children, Faith,' I said, as we watched them slaughter each other with the tommy guns I'd bought – one each, so Robin wouldn't feel left out.

'I know.' She looked at them fondly. 'At first, I felt as if I'd given birth to two little monsters, but now I see them as just two exuberant little boys. I have Eric to thank for my children, if nothing else. He thinks the world of them and they do of him. I suppose I shall see a lot of him in Richmond – he's bound to want to visit.'

'Will your mother mind being landed with you, me and the children?' Faith and Hope had been born when their mother was in her thirties so she would be seventy-something by now.

'She won't mind a bit. Mother's not quite all there – it's nothing to do with age, she's always been a bit odd, though she's been worse since father died. Anyway, it's not her house, but mine. You see,' she went on in response to my look of surprise, 'when my father passed away in nineteen forty-two, Tom hadn't long been killed and I was a widow with Charlie to support. Apart from a hefty allowance for Mother, he left everything in his Will, including the house, to me, as long as I let Mother live there for as long as she wanted. Hope didn't get a penny: she'd just married Graham Sheridan who was incredibly rich and owned an engineering company. By the time the war ended he was even richer.'

'What's he like,' I asked, 'apart from rich?' I'd often wondered about Hope's husband.

'Ruthless, a real hard-headed businessman, but incredibly charming. He's about fifteen years older than Hope. You'll probably meet him, he often pops in to see Mother. Oh, Kitty!' She put her hands to a face that had suddenly drained of colour. 'I've just thought of something. Did Hope come to live with me because she'd fallen in love with Eric? Was it her intention to *steal* him from me? She would never explain why she left Graham. Oh, Kitty,' she groaned, 'what a fool I've been.'

'It hardly matters now,' I said comfortingly.

She sighed. 'No, I don't suppose it does.'

In the end, I left home a few weeks earlier than planned. It was almost a year to the day that our Norah had got married, a truly momentous year in which so much had happened. The reason for my early departure was that my English class came to an end and we decided to have a little party, but, when I put on my best cream frock, the buttons wouldn't fasten around the waist. I knew if I stayed any longer I'd start getting suspicious looks from Claire.

Faith was anxiously waiting for the word from me. She was finding it increasingly difficult to be civil to Hope, and to Eric when he was home, but wasn't prepared to tell either of them why she was leaving. 'I know I'm being a coward,' she said, 'but they'll only deny having had an affair and call me the biggest idiot under the sun for even thinking such a thing.' She squared her shoulders. 'No, I shall leave a note for Hope: *she* can tell Eric when he comes home.'

'He'll probably do his nut,' I remarked. 'Having an affair with Hope's one thing: living with her might not be quite what he had in mind.'

'That's just too bad,' Faith said with a shrug.

The house was rented, the furniture had come with it, and all she had to do was pack the clothes and the children's toys.

So, we left halfway through June on a humid, sunless day. Faith had ordered a taxi to Lime Street Station and it called for me first. Dad and Danny both gave me a sloppy kiss before they went to work – Danny and Marge were now living in Amethyst Street and the arrangement was working well. Later, my sisters turned up to see me off.

'Look after yourself, sis,' Claire cried, holding me close.

'Have a lovely time,' Norah said, as if I were going on holiday.

'Take care, Kitty,' Aileen whispered. 'Michael and I will be thinking of you all the time.'

'Good luck, Kit,' said Marge. I hesitated a moment before kissing her clumsily on the cheek.

The taxi arrived. I climbed inside and waved madly through the back window, until we turned the corner and I couldn't see Amethyst Street any more.

'Where are you off to, luv?' the driver asked. 'I mean, after I've dropped you off at the station?'

'A place called Richmond, it's just outside London. But I'm not going for long,' I said fiercely. I already felt homesick. 'I'll be back in a few months.'

Chapter 4

'Kitty, darling, have you seen my lilac handbag?'

'It's in the kitchen, Mrs Appleton. You brought it down to breakfast with you. Hang on a mo and I'll get it.'

'What a dear girl you are! I honestly think I would forget my head if it weren't screwed on. Didn't I tell you to call me Grace?'

'Yes, you did – Grace.'

I fetched the bag. It would have gone perfectly with the bridesmaid's dress I'd worn at our Norah's wedding. When I got back, Grace Appleton had disappeared from the hall where we'd just spoken and I found her peering through the window in the elegant parlour with its sage-green silk curtains and Chinese wallpaper.

'Mollie's late,' she complained. 'She promised to call for me at one. We're going to Harrod's for afternoon tea.'

I looked at the beautiful black lacquered clock. 'It's only just gone half past twelve.'

'Has it, dear?' she said vaguely. 'Then Mollie's not late at all?'

I confirmed this was the case and she sank into one of the huge, plush armchairs and immediately fell asleep.

From the back, Faith's mother could easily have been taken for a much younger woman. It wasn't until she turned around that she looked her real age, which was seventy-five. Today, she wore a lilac linen suit and a lace blouse with a frothy frill that hid her raddled neck. The face that emerged from the frill was deeply wrinkled and heavily made up. The various cosmetics were applied the minute she got up each morning and, as the day wore on, the lipstick would run into the fine lines around her mouth, the eye shadow would melt into the creases above her baby-blue eyes, and the powder would form clots on each side of her, by then, shiny nose. It never occurred to her to look in the mirror and carry out minor repairs.

She was incredibly absent-minded. Only yesterday, we'd passed each other on the stairs and she'd completely ignored me, yet an hour later she was calling me 'darling'.

Faith had warned me not to take any notice. 'She's the same with everyone, even family, as if she genuinely loses contact with the world from time to time. I think I told you it had got worse since Father died.'

'Perhaps when she loses contact with the world, her spirit's with your dad,' I suggested.

'What a lovely idea, Kitty! I've never thought of that before.' Faith looked quite touched. 'She and Father adored each other. They met in a music hall: she was a chorus girl and he was in the audience. He waited for her outside the stage door and courted her for ages before she would agree to marry him. Ten years ago, she could still do the can-can.'

Whatever was wrong with her, it didn't stop Grace Appleton from having loads of friends, many of them from her years in music hall. They called in their droves, often to find she was out when she'd said she would be in, or had gone to lunch or tea with someone else when she'd promised to go with them.

'Oh, well, that's Grace for you,' they would laugh, not a bit annoyed.

The children loved their grandma. Oliver would trace the wrinkles in her face, starting at her forehead and working right down to her neck. He and Robin liked living in Richmond in a house much bigger and grander than the one in Orrell Park. In the garden, apart from the magnificent display of colourful roses and other flowers, there were half a dozen mature trees, and I'd tied ropes to the strongest branches to make swings, and drawn stumps on one of the trunks so we could play cricket. We'd only been in Richmond ten days, but they were used to their father being away. Neither had asked where he was or when he would be coming.

As for me, I didn't like Richmond a bit, though I felt I might once I got used to it and stopped feeling homesick. After Bootle, the wide roads lined with large detached houses felt alien to me, not to mention the complete absence of children playing outside, women scrubbing the doorsteps, cleaning their windows, or just standing around having their daily jangle. It seemed strange having to walk miles to the nearest shop and not see a pub on every corner.

Each night, I cried into my pillow because I missed my family so much. I missed Dad and our Claire the most. Since Mam died, Claire had made an enormous fuss of me, as if she was trying to take her place, and I kept half hoping she would come bursting into the room, take me in her arms and insist I came back home.

But even if this most unlikely thing should happen, I would have to say no. It was July, the fifth month of my pregnancy, and the baby was starting to show. I was already wearing maternity clothes and was stuck in Richmond until the baby was born and I handed it over to Aileen and Michael. Only then could I return to Bootle.

Faith had loaned me a little eternity ring that Tom, her first husband, had bought her when he'd joined the Navy. 'I promised myself I would never wear it until he came safely home,' she said. 'As he never did, it's hardly been on my finger. It will do you as a wedding ring, Kitty.'

So I could be introduced to the many callers as a married woman, I was now Mrs Kitty McCarthy. My husband, John, had recently emigrated to Australia to look for work and somewhere to live. I would join him as soon as the baby was born. Faith thought it best I keep my real name to save confusion when letters arrived for me from home.

'Won't anyone notice that I don't get any from my husband in Australia?' I asked with a grin. I was rather enjoying the cloak and dagger aspect of my situation.

'Mother usually gets to the post first. Friends write to her from all over the world, and she won't notice where your letters come from, or if they have "Miss" on them, not "Mrs".'

All in all, there wasn't much to complain about in Richmond. The house was lovely, my bedroom was large and comfortably furnished – there was even a rocking chair by the window overlooking the back garden – Oliver and Robin were being their normal lively selves, and Faith seemed far more relaxed and happy. I was growing to like Grace Appleton, despite her erratic behaviour, I got on well with the cook, Mrs Hyde, and had long conversations with the cleaning lady, Maud, about films; she'd been to see *Gone With the Wind* fifteen times.

Once I stopped feeling homesick, everything would be fine.

*

Eric was due to return from New York the next day to be met by Hope, who'd tell him his wife and the children had left him. Faith was dreading he'd come racing down to Richmond, claim he was innocent of any wrongdoing and attempt to convince her the whole thing was a product of her over-heated imagination. She looked at me with scared eyes. 'What worries me, Kitty, is that I'll believe him.'

'You didn't imagine him and Hope kissing outside the front door, did you?' I asked sternly.

'I don't think so, no, but I do remember having an atrocious headache that night. I couldn't really see all that well.'

'Well, *I* didn't have a headache, and I saw them, too. I didn't say anything before because I didn't want to upset you.'

'Did you really? Oh, well, that's something. He can't possibly say I imagined it.'

In fact, Eric arrived in Richmond late that night, having returned to Liverpool earlier than expected. He caught the next train to London out of Lime Street Station and a taxi from Euston to Richmond, whereupon he hammered on the front door with his fists, waking the entire house.

Minutes later, he and Faith were ensconced in the parlour where a great deal of shouting was going on, nearly all of it from Eric. Grace, Oliver, Robin and I went into the kitchen and I made us all tea – it had been bought especially for me.

'I never liked him, you know.' Grace's face glistened with cold cream and she slid her blue eyes in the direction of the shouting. 'Such an obnoxious individual, not nearly good enough for you know who.'

'Are you talking about Daddy?' Oliver enquired. Both children were clearly upset. Robin had run into his father's arms, but had been churlishly pushed away.

'Not at all, darling. I'm talking about someone else altogether.' She turned to me. 'Had Nicholas, that's my husband, been alive, he wouldn't have liked him either.'

'Then who are you talking about?' Oliver demanded.

'A chap called Mr Hoskins who delivers the meat.'

'Why are you talking about him now when Mummy and Daddy are having a fight?'

'I really don't know, darling.'

We lapsed into silence. I knew it was a waste of time insisting the children went back to bed, and cursed Eric for having woken them in the first place. I suggested we play cards, something that normally they would have jumped at, but they weren't interested. Robin was close to tears, but Oliver looked more angry than upset.

The shouting continued, but was getting fainter now. Eventually, it stopped and Faith appeared in the doorway, accompanied by an uncomfortable-looking Eric. 'Daddy's going to stay the night, perhaps a few nights, we'll just have to see,' Faith said. 'And now,' she added, giving Eric a look that was a mixture of anger and contempt, 'he'd like to put his little boys to bed.'

Eric held out his hands to his sons. Robin ran to take one, but Oliver went to him reluctantly. 'Why were you shouting at Mummy?' he asked accusingly.

'Because I lost my temper, son, but I've promised Mummy never to do it again. I'm going to be a very good daddy from now on. Aren't I, darling?' he said to Faith.

'If you say so,' she muttered coldly.

'What's he done?' Grace asked after Eric had taken the boys to bed.

Faith sank into a chair with a sigh. 'Only had an affair with your other daughter, Mother.'

Grace didn't look the least bit surprised. 'Hope always wanted what you had. I might have known Eric wouldn't have the gumption to turn her down.' She sniffed disdainfully. 'You should never have married the man.'

'It's a bit late to tell me that.'

'I said it long before you married him, but you didn't want to hear.' Grace pushed herself to her feet. 'Now the drama's over, I shall continue with my beauty sleep. Graham's coming tomorrow to take me to a matinée in the West End – George Bernard Shaw's *Arms and the Man* – and I want to look my best.' She trotted out of the room.

'That's torn it.' Faith pulled a face. 'Graham is Hope's husband. I hope Mother doesn't mention Hope's been sleeping with Eric, or there could be another scene.'

'Where's Eric sleeping tonight?' I asked.

'In one of the spare rooms. Oh!' She looked at me askance.

'Surely you didn't think I'd let him sleep with me? I've given him complete freedom to see the boys whenever he wants, but that's as far as it goes.'

'Good for you,' I murmured.

'I think so, too.' She looked quite elated. 'In fact, I'm very proud of myself. I completely held my ground, positively refused to believe him when he tried to claim he'd never touched Hope. In the end he conceded that he had, but said it was all Hope's fault: she'd thrown herself at him and he couldn't resist.' She gave a little curt laugh. 'He swears he wants nothing more to do with her and begged my forgiveness. Then he had the nerve to ask me to come back to Liverpool, where Hope will be ordered to leave and he'll never so much as look at another woman for as long as he lives.'

'What did you say?'

'I said it didn't matter whether I forgave him or not and that I had no intention of living with him again. Then I told him to put the boys to bed and give them loads of kisses because he'd really upset them. As you saw, he meekly complied.'

'I'm glad it's all been sorted,' I said sincerely. 'Now you can get on with your life.'

'Yes, but not in the way I expected.' The jubilation had gone. 'I loved Eric. In a way I still do. I thought we'd grow old together, not split up in such an ugly way. I wonder if he loves me, too,' she asked herself thoughtfully, 'and really meant it when he said he'd never look at another woman?'

I confessed I had no idea and made us a drink, this time coffee.

The following day, Eric played with Oliver and Robin in the garden for hours, breaking off occasionally to make an enormous fuss of Faith, as if he wanted to convince his sons he was a great dad and his wife was making a big mistake by getting rid of such a perfect husband.

It was so sickening I couldn't bring myself to watch. Anyway, the heat from the midday sun was burning me to a cinder. I went indoors and sat with my feet up in my favourite room, the late Mr Appleton's study. It was one of the smallest rooms in the house, about twelve feet square, with a desk, two huge squashy leather chairs – one in front of the desk and one behind – a bookcase full of novels, another with reference books dealing with various aspects of the mind, reminding me that Mr Appleton had been a psychiatrist with a surgery in Harley Street. There was also a small cupboard I hadn't investigated. The pictures on the wall were mainly of snow scenes, and a fish in a glass case hung over the door, though why anyone would want a dead fish for an ornament was quite beyond me. Nothing could be seen from the window except a space of grass and the hedge separating the house from the one next door.

I was sitting in the chair behind the desk with my feet on the velvet-covered footstool underneath, an unopened book on my lap – *The Moonstone*, by Wilkie Collins; I was halfway through it – thinking about life and all its strange twists and turns, when the doorbell rang, and Grace shouted, 'I'll get it.'

Seconds later, she squealed with delight. 'Graham! Graham, darling, it's ages since I've seen you, *years*.'

'No, it isn't, sweetheart. I came at Easter, brought you a giant egg. Don't you remember?' The voice was loud and musical, the words almost sung. 'I heard you have those dear little boys staying with you. Where are they? I've brought them presents.'

'In the garden playing with their father.'

'Eric's here?' There was a burst of thunderous laughter. 'Has Hope managed to seduce the bugger yet? That's the only reason she left me and went to live in Liverpool.'

'Yes, she has,' Grace said primly. 'And it's no laughing matter, Graham. Faith's terribly hurt, the boys are upset and Faith's friend, Kitty, is staying with us. She's expecting a baby and last night's kerfuffle can't have done her much good.'

'Kerfuffle! What a lovely word, Gracie. Is Faith's friend, Kitty, married? Or was it Eric or some other bugger who put her up the stick?'

'What a nasty mind you have, darling.' Grace giggled. 'It was some other bugger. She likes to pretend she's married, but she's wearing the ring Tom gave Faith before he went in the Navy and the letters that come for her are addressed to "Miss". Me, I don't give a stuff whether she's married or not, but you, Graham, are not to repeat what I've just told you to a soul. If Kitty wants to make out that she's married, then it's up to her.'

My face burning, I reckoned Faith had seriously underestimated her mother's intelligence. As for Graham Sheridan, he sounded a proper idiot. He'd actually *known* his wife was after Eric!

'So, some rotten bounder has had his wicked way with our Kitty and left her to cope on her own?' he said now, and my face burned even hotter.

'Well, Kitty certainly doesn't give that impression. Look, darling, help yourself to a drink, why don't you, while I go upstairs and change out of these shoes. They're pinching dreadfully.'

'Can I have a dram of dear Nicholas's best Scotch whisky?'

'Of course you can, darling; you know where it's kept.'

Grace's high heels tip-tapped up the stairs, the study door flew open and Graham Sheridan burst in, stopping short when he saw me seated behind the desk, my face as red as a flame. I bet it wasn't often he was stuck for words, but he was now. He was a tall man, a few years younger than my father and reminded me of him a little with his broad chest and shoulders, though Dad would never have worn a pale-grey silk suit with a matching tie, a pink shirt and crocodile shoes. I had a feeling the outfit was in very bad taste. His head was as big as a lion and he had a mane of grey hair that looked as if it had been set in a hairdresser's, bushy eyebrows and a mouth even wider than my own. His small brown eyes twinkled at me in a friendly fashion.

'No one has had their wicked way with me,' I said, very slowly, very deliberately, leaving a slight pause between each word. 'The baby is my boyfriend's and he desperately wanted to marry me, but I turned him down. I'm coping on my own because that's what I prefer.' I felt the urge to stick out my tongue and say, 'So there!'

The man's reaction was more or less as I expected. He threw himself into the other chair and burst out laughing. He laughed so long and so hard that I felt the urge to join in. He was still laughing, his wide shoulders shaking, when he got up, opened the cupboard, took out a bottle and a glass, and poured a drink. He waved the bottle in my direction, but I shook my head. 'No, ta.'

In the chair again, he stopped laughing and said, 'I like you, Kitty – what's your surname?'

'McCarthy,' I snapped.

'I like you, Kitty McCarthy.'

'That's a relief.' His twinkling eyes were hard to resist. I was reluctantly beginning to like him, too.

'How old are you?'

'Mind your own business.'

'Do you know who I am?'

'You're Hope's husband.'

'Have you ever met my dear wife?' he enquired lightly.

I acknowledged that I'd met her a few times. 'But we didn't have much to say to each other.'

'I bet you didn't. Hope only deigns to speak to people who can be helpful to her. You, I suspect, were of no use at all, so she didn't bother wasting her breath.'

I nodded. 'I expect you're right.'

'I *am* right,' he said forcefully. 'I was married to her for eight years and know her inside out. I know she only married me for my money. I, in turn, only married her for her looks.'

'It can't have been a very happy marriage.'

'It was dire.' He laughed, though I could see nothing funny about it. 'We were both having affairs within a year.' He swallowed the whisky in a single gulp and poured another. 'Why am I telling you all this?'

'I haven't a clue. Perhaps I've got a kind face, or you realize I must have heard you ask Grace if Hope had seduced Eric and this is your way of explaining you don't care.'

'I don't care what you heard, nor do I care that Hope has managed to bed the sea captain. I feel sorry for Faith and her little boys, naturally, but she shouldn't have let the viper into the nest.' He played a tune on the desk with the fingers of one hand. 'I don't know why I told you that, either. I don't usually explain myself to anyone.'

'In that case, I'm stumped.' 'Stumped' was Oliver's favourite word.

'It must be your kind face, then.' Graham Sheridan studied me. Not to be outdone, I studied him. Faith had described him as ruthless. He didn't look particularly ruthless, yet he didn't look particularly kind, either. I suspected those twinkling eyes could quickly become hard, that he was a man determined to get his own way in everything, the sort of person who didn't suffer fools gladly. And he was obviously vain, judging by the clothes and the hair.

We finished sizing each other up and he asked, 'Why have you hidden yourself away in here?'

'I'm not hiding away, I'm reading a book.' I produced the volume and laid it on the desk. 'It's hot outside, Eric's looking after the children and my presence wasn't required.'

'How do you fancy coming to London with Gracie and me?' he enquired. 'She's bound to fall asleep on the way home, or go into one of her trances, and then I'll have you to talk to.'

'To the theatre?'

'The best seats will have all gone by now and you'd be stuck up in the gods. No, I'll drop you off in the West End and you can explore. Have you been to London?'

'Not yet, but I've been dying to,' I conceded. I felt quite made up by the invitation, flattered that someone like Graham Sheridan should want to talk to me, though wouldn't dream of letting it show. I considered myself every bit as good as he was, but as a conversationalist I had my limits. Why such a rich and successful businessman should want my company was a bit of a mystery, but he'd said he liked me and maybe that was the reason.

And I liked him, else I wouldn't have gone.

Graham's car was silver and as big as a bus. When we went out of the house, a tall, round-shouldered man wearing a smart lounge suit got out to open the door. Graham said graciously, 'Thank you, Fred.' Grace and I sat on the back seat; Graham perched on a little bucket seat opposite. Most of the way to London, Grace regaled us with stories of her days in music hall.

'I saw her once when I was a child,' Graham told me. 'I went with my ould dad. My mother had a fit when she found out. She said she didn't want me mixing with the lower elements of society, though she put it rather more plainly than that.'

'Cheek!' Grace expostulated. 'Us chorus girls were frightfully moral.'

'If I remember rightly, darling, you wore red frilly knickers and a black lace garter.'

'Only on stage. In my private life, I dressed like a nun.'

'Are you a Londoner, Graham?' I asked.

'Not just a Londoner, darling,' he answered proudly. 'I was born within the sound of Bow Bells, which means I'm a cockney through and through.'

'His family drank out of jam jars and ate with their fingers because they couldn't afford knives and forks,' Grace said sarcastically.

Graham gave her a reproachful look. 'I've never claimed to have been *that* poor, darling. We could afford cups and saucers and cutlery, even if nothing matched.'

Grace winked at me. 'He's a self-made man and can't stop going on about it.'

'If you continue being nasty to me, Gracie, I shan't talk to you any more,' Graham said, pretending to look hurt.

'Oh, darling, you know I love you to bits.' Grace patted his knee. 'Why my stupid daughter left you to go chasing after that smart-arsed Eric, I shall never know. You're more attractive by yards. There's more sex appeal in your little finger than there is in that man's entire body. If I were younger, I'd marry you myself.'

'We could have an affair?' Graham suggested.

'Do people have platonic affairs? I'm afraid I'm not up to the other sort.'

'In that case, we won't. I'm only interested in the other sort.'

I'd never heard people, particularly *old* people, speak to each other like this, and the conversation made me uncomfortable. I was relieved when Grace turned to me, but a bit put out by her question. 'Have you been smitten by Eric's charms, Kitty?' she asked.

'What charms?' I asked, genuinely puzzled.

For some reason, they both found this very funny and laughed like drains. They continued laughing about something or other until we arrived in London. I'd never seen such heavy traffic before in my life. The car inched its way along Regent Street – Graham told me the names of the roads – where the clothes in the windows of the big shops made my mouth water. We arrived at Piccadilly Circus, edged along Shaftesbury Avenue, and stopped in front of a theatre. We all climbed out.

'We'll meet you here, Kitty, in exactly two and a half hours' time,' Graham said in the commanding voice of a man accustomed to giving orders. 'Don't forget, we're in Shaftesbury Avenue and this is the Apollo Theatre.'

'I won't forget – sir.' I wrinkled my nose at him and he grinned.

'Have a nice time, Kitty.' Grace waved as they disappeared into the foyer.

They'd hardly been gone a minute when I was overcome by the heat. My hair felt as if it were on fire and the pavement was so hot I could feel it through the soles of my sandals. The sultry air and the choking traffic fumes were making it hard to breathe, added to which I suddenly felt incredibly tired. Because of Eric's appearance last night I'd lost several hours' sleep, and my legs were threatening to stop supporting me. What's more, I seemed to be in everyone's way. I was fanning myself with my hand, wondering which way to go, when a woman stopped and asked, 'Do you feel all right, dearie?'

'Not exactly,' I told her.

'You need to sit down. If you go down that way and turn left, you'll come to Leicester Square, and you can sit under the trees where it's a bit cooler. It's not a good day for someone in your condition to be in the Smoke.'

'The Smoke?'

'London, darlin'. That's what we call it: the Smoke.'

I thanked her, found Leicester Square and bought a bottle of ice-cold orange juice. I noticed that the square was virtually surrounded by cinemas. *The African Queen* with Humphrey Bogart and Katharine Hepburn was on, a film I'd promised myself I would see but which hadn't reached Liverpool before I left. I finished the drink, bought a ticket and entered the coolness of the virtually empty cinema. The film had just started and I enjoyed every minute, including the little nap I had halfway through.

I emerged two hours later and walked slowly back to Shaftesbury Avenue, feeling better, but not that much. The afternoon had shaken me. I was used to being in the best of health. The loss of a few hours' sleep wouldn't normally have affected me, nor would the hot weather, but now there was another human being growing inside me and it was taking its toll. I rather resented the idea of having to slow down and decided not to tell Grace and Graham that I'd spent the afternoon at the pictures. I wanted everyone to think of me as strong, not weak.

'Have you had a nice time, darling?' Grace asked when we met outside the Apollo Theatre. 'Did you go around the shops?'

'Just Liberty's.' It was the only name I could remember.

'You look pale, Kitty,' Graham said contritely. 'I shouldn't have asked you to come. I quite forgot it's always several degrees hotter in the centre of London than it is in the suburbs.'

'But I feel fine,' I lied.

'Then let's have something to eat. There's a very nice restaurant just around the corner.'

I had chicken salad, it seemed more sensible than anything hot, but refused the wine and stuck to water. When we came out an hour later, as if by magic, Fred was waiting for us with the car. As Graham had predicted, Grace fell asleep on the way home, and he told me about the play.

'Have you ever seen anything by George Bernard Shaw?'

'I've never even heard of him – and I've never been inside a theatre,' I replied.

'I hadn't heard of him when I was your age – whatever your age happens to be. You wouldn't tell me when I asked earlier.'

'I'm twenty.'

'You look younger, but act older. When the weather cools down a bit,' he said in his commanding voice, 'I shall take you to see one of his plays. There's bound to be one on somewhere in London.'

'Yes, sir.' I saluted. 'Anything you say, sir.'

It had been a funny old day, I thought later when I got into bed. Within minutes, I was dead to the world. When I woke the next morning, I realized it was the first night I hadn't cried myself to sleep.

I didn't mention Graham Sheridan the next time I wrote home – every few days, I wrote to one member of my family and told them to pass the letters around. There was something faintly disreputable about a man almost our father's age joking about red frilly knickers and having affairs. I didn't mention Eric coming home and making a scene, either. I'd never told them that Grace Appleton had been a chorus girl or that she occasionally entered another world and forgot who everyone was. My family must have thought I was leading an extremely dull life, as I only wrote about innocent things, like Oliver getting stuck up a tree – though not the fact I'd climbed up and rescued him, because Aileen and Michael would be bound to read the letter and start to worry I was doing too much.

I *had* been doing too much but, after my visit to London, I forced myself to do less. I still played cricket with the boys, but only if I could bowl from the spot: I wasn't prepared to run an inch. For the first time, I went to see a doctor, who examined me and pronounced me perfectly fit.

'Whereabouts in Australia is your husband living?' he enquired. He was an elderly man who looked close to retirement.

I'd been asked the same question several times before, so had my answer ready. 'Perth,' I replied.

'Do you want me to put your name down for the nearest maternity hospital, or will you be going private?'

'The nearest hospital, please.'

'Good. I don't approve of people who go private. We have a wonderful National Health Service: everyone should use it.'

The hot, humid weather continued throughout July and I was relieved when August arrived and the air became fresher. By then, Eric had been back twice, Graham Sheridan had taken me and Grace to Brighton for the day, and the baby was kicking the hell out of me, although I worried if it was still for too long. Had it died? I asked Faith fearfully once.

'Of course not, silly,' she laughed. 'He or she is just asleep.'

I'd got into the habit of resting my hands on my tummy so I could feel the little feet thrusting against my hands. This was my baby: mine and Con's. Sometimes, I couldn't understand why I was in this strange place carrying our baby and, preparing to hand it over to another woman, even if she was my sister. Why wasn't I in Bootle, married to Con, waiting for our child to arrive? All I could think of was that I didn't want to live like other people. I wanted something different, though had no idea what. One day, something truly spectacular might happen and I was unwilling to miss it because I was married.

Hope had moved out of the house in Orrell Park and was now living in Crosby.

'What's it like there?' Faith asked.

'Very nice, very respectable; she should like it.' As if I cared!

'She said in her letter to Mother that she feels very lonely.' She sighed. 'When we were young, we got on frightfully well. She was so sweet then. I never dreamt that one day she'd try to steal my husband. In a way I feel sorry for her because she's failed and she can't be very happy on her own, though it's entirely her own fault.'

Towards the end of August, on a lovely fresh day with the hint of drizzle in the air, Graham Sheridan took me to see *The Apple Cart* by the famous George Bernard Shaw. 'Did you like it?' he asked afterwards when we were seated in a restaurant that he'd boasted was one of the most expensive in London.

'I thought it was the gear,' I enthused. 'Dead funny.'

'Mr Shaw would have been pleased to receive such a penetrating review of his play,' Graham said with enormous sarcasm.

'Is he dead?'

'He died last year at the ripe old age of ninety-four. You should take up theatre reviewing for one of the London papers,' he continued in the same tone.

'I read somewhere that sarcasm is the lowest form of wit and the highest form of ignorance.'

'That's an extremely clever remark. You must write it down for me sometime so I can use it myself.'

'With pleasure.' I'd managed to work out why he liked being with me. It was because behind the loud voice and the jolly laugh, the expensive clothes and restaurants, the mountains of money, Graham Sheridan felt unsure of himself and faintly ill at ease. Somehow, he just missed being a gentleman, and remained an ordinary man like my father, except he'd come up in the world. Every now and again his accent would falter and he would mutter something in pure cockney like, 'Cor blimey!' With me, he could be completely natural. We came from similar backgrounds, I wasn't his employee and I didn't want anything from him. There was no tension between us and he enjoyed introducing an ignoramus like me to George Bernard Shaw and impressing me with posh restaurants.

The waiter came with two dishes of unappetising-looking black jelly. After he'd gone, I patted it with the back of my spoon. 'What's this?'

'Caviar. It comes from the roe of the Russian sturgeon.'

'Gosh! Is it what rich people eat?'

'Yes, in the same way as poor people eat pigs' trotters and jellied eels.'

'I've never even seen a jellied eel, but I love pigs' trotters. I haven't had any since I came to live in Richmond.'

'You're not likely to, either.' He delicately ate the caviar with a spoon. 'One of these days, you must come and have dinner in my flat and Fred will make you pigs' trotters like you've never had before, accompanied by bubble and squeak.'

'I thought Fred was your chauffeur?' I had a go at the caviar. It was OK, but nothing to write home about.

'He's also my cook, my valet and my housekeeper, all rolled into one. We've known each other since we were nippers. The First World War had only just started when we both joined up. We spent the next four years in the trenches.' His brown eyes grew misty. 'We saved each other's lives more than once. He and Hope loathed each other. She kept demanding I get rid of him, but I was having none of it. I told her I'd far sooner be rid of her.'

'I'm not surprised she had affairs with other men if you took that attitude.' I'm pretty sure Hope had hurt him badly, not because she'd slept with Eric, but because she'd fallen in love with him.

He appeared to be lost in thought so I took the opportunity of having a good look around. The ceiling of the restaurant was like the top of a wedding cake, all fancy scrolls and fluting and curly bits. Chandeliers glittered and so did the tables with their dazzling white cloths, silver cruets and fancy cutlery. My feet were almost hidden inside the thick carpet. Most of the guests wore evening dress. I had on a cotton maternity frock and felt like Little Orphan Annie beside so many heavily bejewelled ladies in their satin and velvet gowns. I had a feeling I wouldn't have been allowed in the place had I not been with Graham, who was exquisitely attired in a navy-blue silk suit, white ruffled shirt and bow-tie. He seemed to know all the waiters by name and had pre-booked one of the best tables, close to a little raised portion where a beautiful black woman in a sequinned dress was playing a grand piano and singing some of my favourite songs: 'Somewhere Over the Rainbow', 'Moonlight Becomes You', 'East of the Sun' . . .

I finished the caviar. A waiter smoothly removed the empty plates. Seconds later, another waiter arrived with the main course, roast wild duck, and I thought what a long way I'd come from Bootle.

Our Claire sent a letter to say she felt knackered – her next baby was due in ten weeks, about the same time as my own. 'I've told Liam that's my lot,' she wrote:

Five is enough for anyone. This isn't the old days when some women had a baby every year. Why don't you come for the chrissening, Kitty? Its only four hours on the train. Faith wouldn't mind you taking a day off, or does she expect you to work on Sundays?

Has Aileen told you her and Michael are adopting a baby? The mother hasn't had it yet so they don't know if it will be a boy or a girl. Lets hope Aileens prepaired to have her dead posh 3 peice suit full of sick and doesn't mind the house stinking of dirty nappys.

Jamie thinks he'll be home for Chrissmas. If only Mam were alive she'd be over the moon. Which reminds me – we think Dad might have a woman on the side. Her name is Edna Nelson and she is a widow. I felt a bit upset when I herd, but he was so paishent with Mam all those years, I suppose he deserves some happyness for a change.

Anyroad look after yourself Kitty. Try and get home for the chrissening if you can.

Lots of love

Claire

Apart from an urge to go through the letter with a red pen correcting the atrocious spelling and returning it to my sister with nought out of ten, it left me with mixed emotions. I also felt a bit upset to learn that my father might have become involved with another women, but also thought he was entitled to a bit of romance in his life.

I was now faced with the problem of trying to find a believable excuse for not going to the christening, but what bothered me most was what Claire had written about our Aileen. I recalled her perfect house with nothing out of place. Surely she and Michael wanted a baby too much to give a damn about vomit on the chocolate-brown three-piece and the immaculate orange carpet? I put my arms protectively across my stomach where the baby rested, quietly for a change, possibly fast asleep. Aileen's house was almost certainly the way it was because she *hadn't* had children. Once she had my baby, everything was bound to change.

Eric Knowles came to see his children, looking very sober and downcast. 'What's the matter with him?' I whispered to Faith as we watched him embrace first Oliver, then Robin, with the suggestion of tears in his eyes. I could have been invisible for all the notice he took of me.

'He misses them badly,' she whispered back. 'The house in Weld

Road must seem terribly miserable when he comes home and there's no one there. Then he has the long journey to Richmond to see his family.'

The next day, Eric asked if he could take the children to Regent's Park Zoo. When Faith agreed, he then requested she come with them. 'I'm not used to having the boys out on their own. I'm worried I might lose one,' he said, smiling sweetly. 'It'll be nice for us to go out together for a change.'

It was early when they left. I soon understood how Eric must feel in an empty house, because Grace went out soon after and it was Maud's day off, which left Mrs Hyde, who was busy in the kitchen and didn't like being interrupted. I moped about, hating the silence, too bored to do anything. It was one thing escaping to my favourite room when there were people to escape from, but the study held no appeal when I had the whole house, apart from the kitchen, to myself.

Grace came home mid-afternoon, looked at me strangely but didn't speak, and went straight to bed. The Knowleses didn't return until almost eight o'clock, by which time Mrs Hyde had gone home and tea was spoilt, but it didn't matter because they'd eaten in London.

'In an Italian restaurant,' Faith cried. I'd expected her to be fed up having spent the day with Eric, but she looked the opposite, quite starry-eyed. 'The children had spaghetti bolognese and loved it, didn't you, darlings?'

Oliver sat on my knee and described what spaghetti looked like. 'It's like bits of string, Kitty. You're supposed to wrap it round your fork, but mine kept falling off. Daddy had to chop it into little bits for me. I ate it with a spoon. Mummy did the same for Robin.' He nestled his head against my neck. 'Why didn't you come with us, Kitty? I missed you.'

'I had loads of other things to do, Oliver, that's why.' Even if I'd been invited, I would have refused. I'd have felt in the way, a gooseberry. I wondered why Faith had returned home looking so happy. A suspicion entered my mind, but I shrugged it away, tightening my arms around the little boy. Oliver was my favourite. Next week, he was starting nursery and looked good enough to eat in the uniform: maroon blazer, grey shorts, white shirt and striped tie. He was a gorgeous child with a lovely nature, and was utterly fearless. I remembered the first day we'd met when he was on his way to Egypt on his bike to see his father. Once, he'd been so busy waving a wasp away from my face that he hadn't cared it might sting his hand. When it did, raising a huge lump, he'd been very brave about it.

Eric, still trying to impress, had gone to water the garden. Faith took a sleepy Robin to bed, then returned for Oliver, but he buried his head further in my neck. 'I want Kitty to take me.'

'All right, darling.' She reached for the kettle. 'I'll make some coffee. When you come back, Kitty, I'd like us to have a little talk.'

The suspicion entered my head again. I bathed Oliver, put him to bed and began to tell him a story, but he fell asleep halfway through. I tucked the covers around him and went downstairs. The percolator was bubbling, giving off a delicious smell.

'There you are, dear.' Faith fussed around. I could tell from her face that she felt uncomfortable about what she was about to say. The suspicion returned for the third time and I soon discovered I'd been right all along: Faith and the boys were going back to Liverpool to be with Eric.

'It'd be silly not to,' Faith was saying. 'We both still love each other and he couldn't be more sorry about what happened with Hope. He misses me as much as he does the boys and admitted he'd been very weak. It was the biggest mistake of his life and he swore he'd never do anything like that again.'

'He said that before, months ago,' I muttered.

'Yes, but I didn't believe him then. Now I do. Oh, Kitty,' she cried, 'I hate leaving you, but you'll be all right here, won't you? Mother loves having you around. I'll pay you three months' wages, so you won't be short of money.'

'There's no need, thank you. I've plenty of money.' Michael sent a £5 postal order every week. 'When are you going?'

She looked uncomfortable again. 'Tomorrow. Eric's going to hire a car, a big one, so we can pack everything in. Then we'll be there to wish him goodbye when he goes back to sea.'

I nodded, my face expressionless, when what I really wanted to do was upturn the table, throw the chairs against the wall and shriek at the top of my voice that I wouldn't have been in Richmond if it hadn't been for her. Grace Appleton was all right, but she was out a lot of the time and more often than not asleep when she was home, not exactly the sort of person I would have chosen to spend the next ten weeks with. I appreciated Faith's first loyalty lay with her husband – though he hadn't exactly been loyal to *her* – but felt I was owed a bit of loyalty, too. Had I been in Faith's place and she in mine, I would have felt obliged to stay until the baby was born. Only then would I have gone back to Liverpool to be with my husband.

She was looking at me with concern. 'You're upset, aren't you, Kitty? But don't forget you offered to look after the children once you'd had the baby. By Christmas, we could all be back together in Weld Road and everything will be the same as it was before.'

'I don't think so, Faith,' I said soberly. 'Nothing will ever be the same.'

She'd badly let me down and I would never forget it.

It almost broke my heart to see Oliver and Robin leave after we'd had lunch the following day. They were inconsolable. Oliver clung to my legs, refusing to let go. 'Why isn't Kitty coming with us?' he screamed. Eric had to pull him away and carry him, sobbing, to the car.

A rather shame-faced Faith kissed me goodbye. 'I'm sorry, Kitty, but you know how it is . . .'

'Of course.' I waved and waved until the car disappeared, then went back into the house with Grace. I was about to vanish into my room for a good cry when she said, 'Now that Faith's gone, I shall telephone Hope and tell her she can come.'

'I beg your pardon?' I wasn't sure if I'd heard right.

'Hope has been longing to come home for ages, but couldn't very well while her sister was here. Not only is it Faith's house, but she'd slept with her husband.' She shook her head disapprovingly then smiled. 'Sometimes, Hope can be a very naughty girl.'

'And she's coming to live here?'

'In a day or so, yes, dear. I wonder where I left her letter with the telephone number on?' She wandered into the parlour. 'She might not be here for long. Things worked out so badly for her in Liverpool, I wouldn't be at all surprised if she doesn't try to persuade Graham to take her back.'

I sat on the bed, staring unseeingly out of the window. What on earth I was supposed to do now? I knew, as surely as eggs were eggs, that Hope would resent me living in the house. She hadn't liked me in Liverpool, but now she would like me even less because she was about to come home with her tail between her legs and I knew why. I thought it most unlikely that Graham would want her back.

Tomorrow, I decided, I would go to London, find a cheap hotel and look for somewhere to live. If the hotel was cheap enough, I might be able to stay for the next ten weeks, though I didn't fancy it a bit. But then I was booked into a hospital not far from Richmond and would have to find my way back when the baby was due.

I groaned and thought briefly about getting in touch with Michael. But he would only panic. No, I'd sooner manage on my own.

That night, I went to bed early, but not before I'd gone into the children's room and put away the clothes and toys they'd left behind. There hadn't been room in the car for everything, and Faith had said she would collect them next time she came.

'I might even manage to visit while you're still here, Kitty. That would be nice, wouldn't it?' she'd said.

'It'd be the gear,' I'd replied shortly.

Sniffing wretchedly, I picked up the little singlets and pants, made pairs out of the socks, folded the shirts and jerseys, and put them neatly in drawers. Robin had forgotten his favourite teddy bear. I'd post it to him tomorrow. He'd be lost without Teddy.

But not as lost as I felt without him and Oliver.

Next morning, I left the house early. When I looked for Grace to say tara, I found her sitting up in bed wearing a frothy pink bed jacket and eating breakfast – Mrs Hyde had already arrived.

'I'm feeling a bit off colour today,' Grace explained. 'It's all the excitement, all this coming and going. I'm really looking forward to having Hope to stay. Sometimes, I think I prefer my naughty daughter to the nice one. Are you all right, Kitty? You look a bit off colour, too.'

I assured her I felt perfectly fine, then trudged towards the station, my stomach stuck out like a battering ram, prepared to flatten anyone who dared approach. I hardly noticed when a car stopped on the other side of the road with a screech of brakes. A man leaped out, and a familiar voice shouted, 'Kitty! Where are you off to? Fred and I have come to rescue you.'

'Rescue me from what?' I asked stupidly as Graham crossed the road towards me.

'From my dear wife, from Grace, from Richmond.' His face split into a broad grin. 'She telephoned last night, Grace, to say that Faith had gone and Hope was about to climb on her broomstick and fly home, though she didn't use those exact words. Where were you going, Kitty?' he asked, serious now.

'To London to look for a hotel. I was going to collect my suitcase later.'

'I thought you might do something mad like that, that's why we came early. Come along, darling, get in the car and we'll collect your suitcase now. Grace won't mind, not when she'll have Hope in a day or so.'

'But where will I stay?'

'In my flat in Grosvenor Square. Fred's going to look after you.'

'Hello, ducky,' Fred said when I climbed into the car.

'Hello,' I said weakly. I'd never truly believed that every cloud had a silver lining, but I did now.

Graham's flat was on the top floor of an elderly building with a squeaky lift and a uniformed porter stationed in the hall to keep an eye on visitors. It had three spacious bedrooms, three reception rooms just as big, a black marble bathroom that I thought looked a touch sinister, a small study and a pokey little kitchen.

'This is where Fred reigns supreme,' Graham remarked when he showed me around. 'Don't you, Fred?'

'I like cooking,' Fred admitted grudgingly. He was a tall, lugubrious-looking man with a heavily wrinkled face, long narrow nose and drooping eyes, reminding me very much of a horse. Fred only spoke when he had to. At first, I'd thought Graham rude when we were in the car as he never included Fred in the conversation, until I realized he preferred to be with his own thoughts rather than engage in idle chit-chat. 'Would you like a cup of tea, ducky?'

'I'm dying for one,' I exclaimed.

'Why don't you unpack your suitcase while I make it?'

My two frocks and one coat looked pathetic when hung in the wardrobe that was big enough to sleep in. The rest of my things fitted in a single drawer. It was a man's room, with grey walls and dark furniture. The coverlet on the bed was grey with black stripes. I was sliding the suitcase under the bed when Graham appeared in the doorway.

'Everything OK?'

'Yes. Why does that building across the square have flags outside?'

'Because it's the American Embassy. This is one of the best addresses in London,' he said boastfully. 'Anyone who's anyone lives in Mayfair.'

'Did Hope live here with you?' There was no sign of a woman's touch.

'Only if there was a reason for us to stay in London. She preferred the house in Surrey. It's much bigger and has beautiful grounds.'

'You've got *two* homes!'

'I have three. I also have an apartment in the South of France: Monaco.'

'Lucky old you, though it seems a bit pointless. You can only live in one at a time.'

'True, Kitty, true,' he agreed with a grin.

I was really happy during the weeks I spent in Graham's flat in Grosvenor Square. I still missed Oliver and Robin, but was enjoying myself too much to brood about it, and didn't mind being left on my own on the days when Fred drove Graham to one of his factories in Middlesex, Essex and the west of London in a place called Acton.

'He's semi-retired, but likes to keep the management on its toes,' Fred, who had turned out to be quite a chatterbox once I got to know him, explained. 'He always turns up on a different day so they never know when to expect him. Sometimes, he goes back again the next day, so they can never relax.'

During the war, all three factories had produced armaments. The Acton one still did, but the others had converted to less lethal, everyday products such as refrigerators and washing machines in Middlesex and motorcycles in Essex.

'The guv'nor's got his fingers in an awful lot of pies,' Fred told me. He often boasted about his employer, almost as much as Graham boasted about himself. 'He owns a couple of newspapers and magazines, a string of small hotels in Scotland and a department store in Bristol, yet, when we were nippers, we'd hardly a penny to scratch our arses with.'

'Did you mind him becoming so rich and successful? Graham told me you'd known each other all your lives.'

'Nah!' Fred shook his head dismissively. 'He's offered me all sorts of important jobs in the past, but I turned them down. I ain't got no head for business. It wasn't until me wife, Elsie, died, that I came here. I'd worked in this chop-house off the Old Kent Road, and it was what I was used to, cooking and cleaning. Poor old Elsie, she was an invalid a long while, so I was a dab hand at washing and ironing, too. The guv'nor paid for me to have driving lessons so I could cart him around. I like me job, ducky, I wouldn't change it for the world.'

'That's how I felt when I looked after Faith's children, though I knew it wouldn't last for ever, that one day they'd start school and I wouldn't be needed any more.'

'You could do much better than look after other people's nippers, ducky.' He jerked his head at my stomach that was growing bigger by the day. 'What's going to happen to yours when it's born?'

'I'm letting my sister have it. She and her husband can't have children.'

'Does the kid's father go along with that?'

'He doesn't know I'm having a baby.'

Fred frowned. 'Isn't that a bit high-handed, ducky? Surely the geezer has a right to know he's about to become a dad?'

I wrinkled my nose and mumbled a reply. Fred was spot-on. Con was entitled to know, but it was much too late to tell him now. Who knows what would happen if I did? And I couldn't possibly disappoint Aileen and Michael.

If the weather was nice and the men were out, I'd go for a stroll around Hyde Park, which was only a minute away and looked beautiful now that autumn was upon us and the leaves had started to fall, forming a crunchy golden carpet. On dull days, I wandered around Selfridges and Derry & Toms. The cost of virtually everything was well beyond my means, but there was always C&A Modes where the prices were more reasonable. I bought a smart black leather handbag there – I had a passion for handbags and already had four. I felt a bit like Graham with his houses, as I knew I could only use one bag at a time.

Graham, Fred and I became very close. When I went to bed, Fred would bring me a mug of cocoa and sit on the side of the bed while I drank it. Then Graham got into the habit of coming in and sitting on the other side. I didn't feel the least bit uncomfortable about it. We just talked and talked for ages, until my eyes began to blink with tiredness and they'd both leave, Fred taking the mug to wash in the little kitchen where he made the most delicious meals: pigs' trotters with bubble and squeak was my favourite, followed by fresh fruit salad for pudding.

Sometimes, Fred and I went to a matinée at the pictures, leaving Graham buried in his study, bringing himself up to date with his various enterprises and harassing the management on the phone. Even when I grew very old, I never forgot going to see *Easter Parade* with Fred, and our poor imitation of Fred Astaire and Judy Garland as we danced our way home.

One night, as they were sitting on my bed, Graham said, 'We'll really miss you when you go, Kitty. You've brightened up the lives of two rather miserable old men. We've loved having you. I've talked it over with Fred and we'd like you to stay after the baby's born.'

Before I could think of a reply, Fred said, 'We'd like it even better if you kept the baby, ducky. Neither me or the guv'nor were lucky enough to have kids. It'd be the bee's knees having a baby around – and it'd have two dads.'

'Think about it, Kitty,' Graham said warmly. 'One of the reception rooms could be turned into a nursery.' He patted one of my feet under the clothes, Fred patted the other, and they left, leaving me feeling stunned and totally confused, but with pleasant images of taking the baby for walks in his or her pram through Hyde Park on lovely sunny days, or cold winter ones when the grass and the trees were full of snow.

But no! Putting aside the fact I would be badly letting down my sister, it would be too easy. I doubted if I would ever again get on with two people as well as I did with Graham and Fred, but, whether I stayed with the baby or alone, it would be like copping out of the real world. And I'd sooner be in charge of my own destiny, not dependent on others. One of these days Graham and Hope might get back together just as Faith had done with Eric, and where would I be then?

She arrived, my little girl, on a rainy Sunday afternoon in November, a few days earlier than expected. Graham had booked me a room in a private maternity hospital in Chelsea. I rang and cancelled the one in Richmond. Fred rushed me there in the car. Before leaving, I telephoned Aileen in Maghull to tell her the news. Tomorrow, she and Michael had planned to come down to London and stay in a hotel so they would be present for the birth, but Michael said they'd come straight away.

He must have really put his foot down for a change. They arrived about six hours later while I was still in labour, by which time it was dark and the curtains were drawn in the room where I lay alone, counting the minutes between contractions. Fred had wanted to stay, but I'd insisted he go home. Every now and then, a young nurse with blonde hair came to check if I was all right and tell me I was doing fine.

Aileen clutched my hand. 'I can't believe it's happening, really happening. Any minute now, I'll be a mother and Michael will be a dad.'

I think I smiled, but wasn't sure. I saw my sister and her husband through a thick mist and their voices were more echoes than real. It wasn't that I was in pain, more a belief that this was all a dream and soon I would wake up, find myself back in Amethyst Street, and nothing would have changed: Mam would still be alive and I'd be going out with Con.

The nurse returned and I heard a disembodied voice ask Aileen and Michael to leave. Suddenly, my bed was being wheeled along a corridor into a brightly lit room, where another disembodied voice, this time a man's, asked how I was feeling. The first voice said, 'She's out of it, Doctor. I doubt if she can hear you.' I could hear all right, I just couldn't answer because this was only a dream.

I snapped out of the dream the very second my baby was born. It hardly hurt at all. I opened my eyes, heard it yell, saw that the doctor was holding a real, live baby and realized with a jolt that it was mine.

'You've got a little girl, Mrs McCarthy,' the doctor said jubilantly. 'What are you going to call her?'

'I haven't decided on a name yet.' I was leaving that to my sister.

The nurse lifted me to a sitting position and the doctor placed my daughter in my arms. She was wrapped in a fluffy towel. 'You can hold her for a minute, then Nurse will clean the pair of you up.'

'Thank you.' The tiny body of my little girl felt warm and solid against my own. Her legs shifted and her feet pushed against my arm, as if she were enjoying the freedom of being able to move at will. I couldn't tell the colour of her hair as it was dark and sticky and needed to be washed. She yawned, showing an expanse of pink gums. Her eyes opened and looked at me vacantly. They were very blue, but all newly born babies have blue eyes. I examined her miniature hands, the nails like pearls. I had no idea how I felt – it was something I couldn't have described to save my life – but it seemed little short of a miracle that this perfect little girl had been curled up inside me for nine whole months until she decided to come out. Now she was no longer dependent on me for survival, someone else would be responsible for that.

The nurse took her away and I felt a terrible sense of loss. Another nurse, much older than the first, bathed me and changed my nightdress. Then I was taken back to my room where Aileen and Michael were waiting. They both jumped to their feet. 'What did you have?' they asked together. Neither seemed interested to know how *I* was, just my baby.

'A girl,' I said shortly

'A beautiful little girl weighing eight pounds, six ounces,' the nurse emphasized. 'I'll bring her in shortly.'

'About a name, Kitty,' Aileen said excitedly when the woman had gone. 'We'd like to call her Eve, if that's all right with you.'

'I think Eve is a nice name.'

'Eve Bernadette Gilbert,' Aileen breathed, her eyes glittering with emotion. Michael put his arm around her shoulders and gave them a squeeze: I badly wanted someone to do the same to me.

A girl in a white overall came to ask if I'd like supper. I said I was starving. She left and the older nurse returned carrying Eve. Aileen stepped forward, holding out her arms, a look of greed mixed with longing on her face. The nurse either didn't notice or ignored her, and gave Eve to me. 'Doctor thinks you should try to breastfeed,' she said.

I told her I wouldn't be breastfeeding and would she please

prepare a bottle. She went without saying a word, but I could tell she disapproved.

'You look much better after a good wash,' I told Eve. 'And you've got fair hair!' The hair was creamy yellow, without a trace of Con's ginger and my red. 'I wonder where that came from? You're a very pretty baby, Eve Bernadette Gilbert.'

'Can I have her?' Aileen said in a taut voice.

'Not yet.' At that moment, I hated my sister with all my heart. I took a long look at my daughter, knowing this would be the last time I would hold her as a baby. When I went back to Bootle, I would ask Aileen to keep out of my way, tell her never to expect to see me in Maghull. It would hurt too much, yet I hadn't expected to give a damn. As Mam would have said, I'd just made a rod for my own back and it was no more than I deserved.

I sighed and handed my baby to Aileen.

I left hospital the next morning. The rain was heavier than it had been yesterday. A nurse I'd never seen before yelped when she came into my room and saw me on my feet, fully dressed. 'You're supposed to stay in bed for five days,' she gasped, 'and spend another five convalescing.'

'I feel very well and I'm going home,' I told her.

'You're not taking the baby, surely? I don't think that can be allowed.'

'I'm not taking the baby, no. You're to keep her for as long as necessary, then let my sister have her. She and her husband will be along shortly.' With that, I picked up my bag and left.

I took a taxi back to the flat in Grosvenor Square. To my relief, no one was in. I made tea, then lay on the bed for an hour – I realized I wasn't quite as well as I'd just claimed. I felt as if I had been pushed through a mangle and my stomach hurt. After I'd rested, I wrote a long letter to Graham and Fred, saying I would miss them just as much as they would miss me, but that I felt I had to move on. I thanked them for their generosity and love, and promised to remember them all my days.

Then I packed my suitcase, caught a bus to Euston Station, where I bought a ticket to Liverpool, and went home.

The Sixties

Chapter 5

'I think that's everything, Mrs Tyler,' I said. 'Two dozen nappies, two bottles and a couple of spare teats, baby clothes, including rubber pants and a shawl, and iron tablets for yourself – you should take one three times a day with food.'

'I won't be wanting the bottles, Nurse. As you can see, I'm breastfeeding.' The woman looked down at the tiny baby sucking greedily at her sagging breast. His name was Ronnie.

'According to the hospital, Mrs Tyler, your Josie's only nine and a half months old; you can't feed two babies at the same time.' I took for granted she'd been feeding Josie herself until she'd had Ronnie – breast milk was the cheapest baby food and lots of women fed their children until they were as much as two or three years old. 'The bottles are for her. She's old enough to drink fresh milk and I've brought a pint with me. It should be plenty enough for today and tomorrow. Give her half milk, half warm water to start in case it upsets her tummy.'

'Thank you, Nurse, I'm very grateful.'

She didn't look particularly grateful. No one liked accepting charity and some people resented it, Olive Tyler for one, though it was her husband she should resent for impregnating her within weeks, possibly days, of her having the latest child. A pale, shapeless woman with sullen eyes, she looked a good fifty, yet was only thirty-three. So far, she had given birth to twelve children, three of which had died.

I didn't bother pointing out that I wasn't a nurse, only looked like one in my plain blue cotton frock and navy cardy. As Hilda had pointed out, it would be entirely lacking in sensitivity to visit poverty-stricken women dispensing charity while dressed up to the nines.

'Is there anything I can do for you, Mrs Tyler, while I'm here?' I asked. 'Feed Josie, perhaps?' It must be Josie who was screaming her little head off upstairs. Two tiny boys, wearing only dirty singlets, were sitting beneath the table sucking furiously on dummies – I wondered if they'd eaten today – and she had another boy under five, although I could see no sign of him; perhaps he was among those playing in the street. The rest were at school, at least so I thought until a girl of about twelve came downstairs with Josie in her arms. The baby had stopped crying, but was whimpering pathetically. My heart bled for her.

'If you show me how to make the milk, Nurse, I'll feed her,' the girl offered. I asked her name and she replied, 'I'm Peggy. I'm the eldest and I stayed home from school to help me mam.'

I picked up a bottle, a teat and the milk, and we went into the kitchen. It was filthy, the window too dirty to let in the glare of the August sunshine. I itched to scrub the place from top to bottom, but had two more mothers to see that morning and there wasn't the time. Anyway, Hilda wouldn't approve. 'You always get too involved,' she chided. I felt the kettle: it was still warm and contained a small amount of water. I prepared the bottle, gave it a good shake and handed it to Peggy. 'She should be fed three or four times a day until she starts on solids.'

'I gave her tea on a spoon while Mam was in the ozzie and she liked it fine,' the girl said.

'I'm sure she did, dear, but Josie's only a baby and she needs more than tea to build her up.' I wouldn't be surprised if Josie wasn't back on tea before the day was out, nor to learn that Peggy spent more time at home helping her mother than she did at school. 'That reminds me, try to make sure your mother takes the iron tablets. She needs building up, too.'

Peggy nodded obediently. 'All right, Nurse.'

I wondered if Mrs Tyler had once been as pretty as her daughter. Peggy had lovely brown eyes and hair to match. Somehow, in the midst of all the filth, she managed to keep herself very clean, though her frock was frayed under the arms and hadn't been ironed.

She put the bottle in Josie's mouth and the baby began to suck hungrily. Before leaving the kitchen, I noticed a couple of pairs of cotton shorts hanging on the rack. They felt dry, so I took them into the living room and persuaded the boys to let me put them on. Their mother gave me a glowering look and I realized I'd outstayed my welcome.

'Would you like me to come back tomorrow?' I asked.

It was Peggy who answered. 'If you wouldn't mind, Nurse. Five little 'uns are a lot for Mam to manage.'

I agreed to come at the same time, thinking it was Peggy who seemed to do all the managing. She came with me to the door, Josie in her arms still sucking the bottle. I was outside when she said in a low voice, 'Is there any way of keeping me dad off me mam? He was at her again last night when she was hardly back from the ozzie. Before you know it, she'll be in the club again.'

'Not that I know of, Peggy,' I answered regretfully. It was an awful question for a girl so young to ask but, other than killing the man, I couldn't think of a single way to help.

It was hard to believe, I mused, as I drove away from the Tyler house in the brilliance of a perfect August day, that, in the second half of the twentieth century, such poverty existed, not just in Liverpool, but in cities all over Britain. It wasn't as bad as I remembered as a child – a few years ago Child Benefit had been introduced which was an enormous help – but pockets of poverty still remained and a lot of women had Hilda Foxton to thank for the parcels of clothes and nappies similar to the one I'd just delivered to Mrs Tyler. Until today, she'd been missed because Ronnie was the first of her babies to be born in hospital. The others she'd had at home and Hilda hadn't been informed.

I'd met Hilda Foxton almost nine years ago on the day I'd left London and returned to Liverpool, a day that remained as clear in my mind as if it were only yesterday. It was less than twenty-four hours since I'd given birth to Eve and I'd felt sick when I got on the train: when it started, the motion made me feel even worse. The rain drummed on the roof and the scenery looked as bleak as my heart. I had a horrible feeling I was about to give birth to another baby and desperately wished I'd stayed in hospital. I groaned and crumpled sideways on to the seat – fortunately it was empty. Even more fortunately, I was in a corridor train and the only other person in the compartment, a middle-aged man reading *The Times*, ran outside and yelled for a doctor. I could hear his voice getting fainter and fainter as his search continued further down the train. A woman came in, put her hand on my forehead and told me I had a temperature. 'I have some tea in a flask, lovey. Would you like a cup?'

I shook my head. I had no idea what I wanted other than to die. Then Hilda appeared in the doorway. 'I'm not a doctor but I am a trained nurse,' she announced loudly in a dead posh voice. 'What's wrong with the girl?'

The first woman answered. 'I've no idea other than her forehead's awfully hot. I just offered her some tea, but she refused.'

'Water, she needs water. Would you kindly get a glass from the restaurant car?' The woman hurried away and Hilda knelt beside me. 'Do *you* know what's wrong, young lady?'

I was too frightened not to admit the truth. 'I had a baby yesterday and now I feel as if I've just had another.'

'It's probably the after-birth. Let's have a look.' She pulled down the blinds, lifted my skirt, dragged off my pants, and said, 'I was right. The after-birth consists of the placenta, the umbilical cord and other membranes. It's said it's good for roses, did you know that?'

'No,' I said weakly. I already felt better knowing I was in capable hands. Hilda grabbed *The Times* the man had left and used it to scoop up the bloody mixture that I'd thought might be a baby.

The woman returned with the water. Hilda gave her the paper and told her to put it in a rubbish bin. 'If you can't find one, just chuck it out the window. It'll do the countryside good. Now, young lady, I take it you have plenty more sanitary towels with you?'

'There's a whole packet in my suitcase.'

My suitcase was yanked off the rack, the towels were found and Hilda looped two on to my sanitary belt. She advised me to have a bath the minute I got home, adjusted my clothes, took hold of my hands and gently raised me to a sitting position, then sat on the seat opposite.

'How do you feel now?'

'Fine.'

'Don't be ridiculous, girl,' she said derisively. 'You can't possibly feel fine: a trifle better than before, maybe, but not fine. Here, drink this water. What's your name?'

'Kitty McCarthy,' I said meekly.

'I'm Hilda Foxton and, as I said before, I'm a nurse and a qualified midwife. You should be confined to bed, not flitting around on trains the day after you've had a baby. You're very irresponsible, Kitty McCarthy. Say if I hadn't been around, what would you have done then?'

'Died?' I suggested. The glimmer of a smile crossed her haughty face.

I studied her as I sipped the water. She was fiftyish, extremely tall and thin, and wore wire-rimmed spectacles perched halfway down a nose that looked as sharp as a razor. Her mouth was as thin as the rest of her and her chin ended in a point. She wore a grey suit that I reckoned had cost an arm and a leg long before I was born, and a mouldy fur coat that smelled of mothballs. But, at that moment, the only thing that mattered to me was the compassion that shone from Hilda's rich brown eyes. She might sound like a sergeant major, but she turned out to be the kindest and most generous person I would ever meet in my life.

'You wouldn't have died,' she snorted, 'but you'd have been removed from the train at Stafford and carted off to the nearest hospital. How would you have liked that?'

'I'd've hated it,' I confessed.

'Where's the baby?' she asked, taking me by surprise. 'The one you had yesterday.'

'It's a long story.'

She folded her arms and settled herself in the seat. 'We have plenty of time. The train won't arrive in Liverpool for another two hours.'

There was a tap on the door and Hilda opened it a crack. It was the man who had gone to look for a doctor. He took his bowler hat and briefcase from the rack and said mildly, 'I think I left my newspaper behind.'

'Someone threw it out the window,' Hilda barked.

'Oh! Oh, I see.' The man scurried away, too intimidated to ask why.

I told Hilda my story: we'd reached Crewe by the time I'd finished.

She said, 'You're a very foolish young lady. You'll regret what you've done for the rest of your life. Still,' she shrugged, 'it's done now and there's no going back. What's more, you can't go home in your condition. You look an utter wreck and your family will be worried sick. What you need is some time in bed to recover your strength. If you wish, you can come home with me; Dorothy will look after you.'

'Who's Dorothy?'

'My friend. She's a nurse, too. You won't be the first girl in your position she's cared for.'

Hilda's house was in Everton Valley. A hundred years before, its situation had been one of the best in Liverpool – her grandfather had traded in cotton – but the area had deteriorated since and now the bricks were black with smoke, the servants had gone to work at more salubrious addresses and Hilda's was the only house in the row that hadn't been turned into flats. It had five floors, ranging from a dark, damp basement, which had once been a kitchen, to a spacious attic.

Hilda and Dorothy slept on the first floor. More often than not, the other bedrooms were occupied by women like myself during the week when I'd been nursed back to health by plump, homely Dorothy. As soon as I felt better, I'd returned to Amethyst Street and received such a warm welcome from my family that I dissolved into tears. When I'd left six months ago, it had felt rather like a game, but now I felt wretched for having deceived them and told so many lies. I couldn't stop thinking about my baby. But, as Hilda had said on the train, there was no going back, and the lies would stay lies and the deception remain undiscovered for quite a few years.

I met Claire's new baby, a little girl called Katherine, who'd been born a week before Eve. 'She's named after you, but we're going to call her Kate so there won't be any confusion.'

A few days later, Aileen and Michael came back from London with Eve. I managed to be out when they brought their 'adopted' daughter to see Dad, and hoped no one would notice that I always avoided my sister's child. I'm pretty certain no one ever did. Seeing her would have been too painful.

Jamie came home for Christmas, our first without Mam. It should have been a sad occasion but four babies had been added to the McCarthy clan that year, something to celebrate rather than mourn. Aileen was too busy with Eve to come to Amethyst Street and I made excuses not to visit her in Maghull.

Christmas over, Jamie went back to Berlin and I announced I was starting a new job.

'And where would that be, luv?' Dad asked. He was still keeping Edna Nelson hidden from us, but Liam said he often saw them together in the pub.

'I'm going to work for a lady called Hilda Foxton in Everton Valley. She's a nurse. She's not married and started a charity years ago that provides women with all the basic necessities needed when they have a baby – if they're too poor to buy them themselves, that is. And she does other things, too,' I went on animatedly. 'Sometimes, she has women and babies staying in her house while she finds somewhere proper for them to live, or pregnant girls without a husband whose mams have chucked them out.'

Dad looked impressed. 'This Hilda woman sounds like she's got a big, kind heart, but where does all the money come from, Kitty? Can she afford to pay wages?'

'She can, but not much.' I made a face. It would be a long time before I would be able to buy new clothes and I'd have to restrict my visits to the pictures. 'Hilda used up her own money a long time ago and now she relies on donations from good Samaritans as she calls them.'

'Seeing as you seem to have a sensible head on your shoulders – for most of the time, at least,' Hilda had said when I'd been about to leave her house, 'why don't you come and work for me? Dorothy's always needed here, and nowadays I have so much paperwork to deal with that some nights I'm at work in the office until midnight. If I had someone to make the visits, life would be so much easier.'

I jumped at it, despite the paltry wages. I remembered how hard it had been to find an interesting job when I'd longed to leave Cameron's and knew I'd never have another opportunity like this. I learned to drive Hilda's ancient Morris Minor, which was pitted with rust and rattled when it turned a corner.

Nine years later, it would be hard to say I loved my job – I came face to face with too much misery for that – but I felt I was doing something worthwhile, though was inclined to get too involved. I'd just promised Peggy Tyler I'd go back tomorrow when all that was expected of me was to deliver the parcel, then disappear out of the Tylers' lives.

The next lady on my list was Mrs Christine Mason, aged forty-two, who lived in a middle-class road in Allerton. I wondered why she was in need of charity, and soon discovered the reason, as Mrs Mason was still hurt by the way she'd been treated by the father of her child. She was a good-looking woman, nicely dressed, who didn't give the impression of being easily fooled. The words came pouring out in a torrent. I suppose there weren't many people she could confide in – perhaps I was the first.

'My husband was killed during the war not long after we were married. He was a schoolteacher like me. I never dreamt I would get married again, but then I met Ray.' Her lips twisted bitterly. 'He was so charming. I believed him when he said he'd fallen in love with me. Maybe, without realizing it, I was lonely because, before I knew it, *I* was in love with him and was thrilled when I found I was expecting a baby – my husband and I had intended to start a family after the war. There, there, sweetheart.' The baby on her shoulder gave a loud burp, and the woman smiled. 'It's such a relief when she brings up her wind.'

'She's a lovely baby,' I remarked. 'What's she called?'

'Eliza. It was my mother's name.' She winced. 'I can't imagine what Mum would say if she could see me now.'

'What happened with Ray?' I really should be getting on, but didn't want to leave until I'd heard the whole story.

'Him!' she snorted. 'Oh, as soon as I told him I was expecting, he ran a mile. It turned out he was already married but, by then, he'd managed to swindle me out of all my savings for some mythical business venture. Later, I found all the little expensive ornaments my mother had left had been taken, as well as my pathetic amount of jewellery.'

'Did you call the police?'

She shrugged. 'I thought about it, but felt ashamed of having been made such a fool of. I had to resign from my teaching job and go on the dole, though it's not nearly enough to live on. I ended up pawning things like my best clothes and some of the furniture to pay the rent and other bills. Lord knows how I'm going to manage now. There's hardly anything left to pawn, and no way can I work while I've got Eliza. Do you get dole when you've got a baby?'

'I've no idea, but when I get back to the office, I'll ask Miss Foxton. There might be other benefits you're entitled to.' She wouldn't get Child Benefit as it only commenced with the second child.

'You've been very kind,' Christine Mason said. She gestured at the things spread on the table. 'I've been using towels for nappies. I've been wondering what else I could pawn to buy new ones.'

'Tell me something,' I said as I got to my feet to leave. 'If it weren't for Ray, you wouldn't have Eliza: would you sooner have met him than not?'

The woman thought hard for a long time, then her face brightened. 'I'd sooner have Eliza any day. Oh, I'm so glad you asked that question. It's sort of put things in perspective. Despite the hardship, she's the best thing that's ever happened to me – and I've got that swine, Ray, to thank for it.'

My final visit that morning was to Mrs Martha O'Donnell, a cheerful soul whom I'd called on twice before when she'd had babies. The latest was a boy called Seamus, who was fast asleep in a cardboard box in front of the fireplace where a small fire burned. The room was shabby, but immaculately clean. Mrs O'Donnell had been in the middle of washing the floors when I arrived, and answered the door with a mop in her hand.

'I don't really need all this stuff, dearie,' she exclaimed when I unpacked the parcel. 'It'd best if you let some other woman have 'em. I've got nappies left over from our Paddy, and some of his clothes, too. As you can see, I've still got his shawl.'

'I'm sure Seamus would like some nice new things.' The shawl he was wrapped in had been washed so many times it had acquired the texture of a carpet.

'I suppose he would an' all, wouldn't you, darlin'?' She looked fondly at her son.

'How are your other boys, Mrs O'Donnell?' She had seven, and the eldest was fifteen.

'They're all fine,' the woman sang. 'Our Sean started work last month and gives me every penny of his wages, unlike me ould fella who spends most of his on the ale. Would you like a cuppa, dearie? I was just about to make one for meself.'

'I'd love one, ta.'

We sat and chatted for about half an hour. Mrs O'Donnell was looking forward to the day when all her boys were at work and would support her. 'Then I can tell me ould fella to go and piss up his kilt. I won't be needing him any more.'

All in all, it had been a very satisfactory morning, though I'd taken twice as long as I was supposed to. When I left Mrs O'Donnell's house in Toxteth, I turned the car around and headed for Bootle. Tuesdays and Thursdays, I had dinner in Amethyst Street; Marge would be expecting me.

When I returned from London all those years ago, Marge had already been pregnant with her second baby. As soon as Elizabeth came along, I realized the house in Amethyst Street wasn't big enough for us all. I didn't mind moving out as Hilda had already offered me her attic. It was a vast room with a window at each end and my own lavatory, though I had to share the bathroom with Hilda, Dorothy and anyone else who might be staying.

So, I left home again, but this time no one minded, me included. After all, I would only be living a few miles away in Everton Valley, not some faraway place where I would feel homesick.

Since then, Marge had had a third baby named Angela, and now all three were at school. She and our Danny seemed happy enough, but I often wondered if they'd have been happier had they married because they'd been in love.

'That smells nice,' I shouted when I went in.

Marge was in the course of setting the table in the living room. 'It's scouse. I got some brown sauce especially for you. No one else likes it.'

'Goody.' I rubbed my hands. 'I'm starving.'

'You're always starving, Kitty. I can't understand why you don't put on more weight.'

'What do you mean *more* weight?' I said indignantly. 'I haven't put on *any* weight.'

'I know,' Marge said gloomily. 'I just have to *look* at a cake and I put on another pound.' Marge hadn't exactly let herself go, but she didn't do much to make herself look nice, either. These days, she hardly bothered with make-up, and her hair looked respectable, but that was about all. She wore a pinny over her clothes and her big toe poked through a hole in one of her slippers.

'Don't look at them then – cakes, that is.'

'That's easier said than done,' she sighed.

'Where's Dad?'

'Still at work: he should be home any minute.'

Dad had retired from the docks, but he was still hale and hearty and had felt restless at home with nothing to do, so had found himself a part-time job in a little sweet and tobacconist's in Marsh Lane where he worked from eight till one. Our Claire was convinced he was having a relationship with the woman who ran the place, Margaret Gill. It was a long time since he'd been seen with Edna Nelson, but his name had been linked with a half a dozen other women over the years. He'd never brought them home. Maybe he was worried his children would see them as a replacement for Mam and would be hurt, though I doubted it.

The back door opened and he came into the yard, seventy now, but as straight-backed as ever. His hair was silver and just as thick. I jumped to my feet and gave him a kiss.

'Hello, Kitty, luv.' He twisted my ear. 'That's a nice smell, Marge. It can only be scouse, me favourite. Will our Danny be home for his dinner?' He eased himself into a chair.

'He might or he might not, he wasn't sure. There's plenty in the pan if he deigns to turn up.'

I glanced at Marge. The words were said more harshly than necessary. Her face was surly when she went to fetch the meal. I praised it to the skies, saying no one could make scouse like she could. Dad said, 'Hear, hear.' He banged the table with his knife and Marge was smiling by the time we finished.

The meal over, Dad went to the pub and Marge and I into the kitchen to wash the dishes.

'What's up?' I asked.

Her head was bent over the sink and she didn't look at me. 'What do you mean?' she mumbled.

'Have you and our Danny had a fight?'

'No, and we're not likely to because he's never here to fight with.' She turned on me, eyes blazing. 'I'll tell you what, Kitty, I'm fed up to the teeth with men, your Danny in particular, and your dad an' all. I've got three kids and a house to look after, and no one ever thinks to give me a hand. The minute they've eaten, they're off to the pub where they sit all night with their mates, while I'm left to wash the dishes and put the kids to bed, by which time I'm too worn out to do anything except go to bed meself. If this is what married life's about, then you can keep it.' She began to wash the dishes, slamming the plates on to the draining board until one cracked and she muttered, 'Bugger!'

'It's only cracked a bit,' I said as I dried it. 'It's still usable.'

'I don't half envy you, Kitty. You've got a decent job and the rest of your time's your own.' She glared at me. 'What the hell are you smiling at? Me, I can't see anything so funny about it.'

I hadn't realized I was smiling. 'I'm sorry, but I was remembering the conversation we had at our Norah's wedding.' It had stuck in my mind ever since. 'You said a woman would be crazy not to get married and that if they didn't, they'd end up sad old maids. You called me a soft girl for not agreeing with you.'

'Well, I agree with you now. All right?' she said belligerently.

'All right, Marge,' I said gently. 'Look, let's leave the dishes and have another cup of tea, but I'll have to go shortly. Hilda will be wondering where I am.'

'I envy your Claire an' all,' Marge said when we were in the living room with the tea. 'She's got five kids, but she's a bundle of energy, forever coming round with cakes and stuff she's baked.' She sniffed wretchedly. 'I envy every bloody one, not just you and Claire, but your Norah and Aileen, too. Mornings, Roy fetches Norah a cup of tea in bed and hardly goes near the pub, and Aileen went back to work once Eve started school and she has a woman in to clean her house.'

At that point I said I would have to go, but not before I'd suggested that we went to the pictures one night. I often went alone and rationed myself to once a week – my wages had increased over the years, but not by much. '*Indiscreet*'s on in town with Cary Grant and Ingrid Bergman,' I said. 'It's a lovely romantic comedy and might cheer you up a bit.'

'Oh, Kitty!' She looked at me soulfully. 'It's ages since I went to the pics, and I'd love to, but after what I've just told you how do you expect me to get away?'

'Get ready while Danny's having his tea, then just announce you're going,' I said bluntly. 'If he wants to know who'll look after the kids, tell him *he* will. He can't very well refuse, can he?'

'No. Well, no, he can't. Oh, can we go tomorrow?' she cried, clapping her hands gleefully.

'Tomorrow it is,' I said, adding grandly, 'I'll collect you in the car.'

When I got back to Everton Valley, I found Hilda in her office seated in front of an ancient typewriter and surrounded by masses of paper. She had stopped nursing in her forties due to back trouble but, like my father, had found life boring without something to do. By then, she had inherited the family wealth and began to give the money away to worthy causes.

'But writing cheques didn't exactly keep me occupied,' she told me, 'so I decided to start a charity of my own. I'd delivered enough babies to know that some poor women were obliged to use rags for nappies and there was no chance in the world of them affording proper clothes for their little ones. At first, I took the parcels into hospital, but the women were so desperate for money they were selling them to better-off mothers. For all I know, they might still sell them, but it's not so likely if they're delivered to their homes once the baby's born.'

Hilda's charity was called M.A.B. It stood for Mothers and Babies. Every day, she wrote dozens of letters encouraging people to send donations, typing furiously with two fingers, her head bent over the typewriter so that her nose almost touched the keys. She also wrote articles for newspapers and magazines describing what the charity did. If ever anyone deserved a medal, it was Hilda Foxton, and if I had my way she'd be given one tomorrow.

'I've got some bad news for you, Kitty,' she announced now in her loud, penetrating voice. 'I've had a letter from a solicitor in London: your friend, Graham Sheridan, died a few weeks ago.'

'Oh, no!' I hadn't seen Graham since I left London, but we'd corresponded regularly and sometimes he'd telephone for a chat.

'Don't be sad, girl,' Hilda said. 'It happens to us all in the end.'

'I know, but it's still sad. I wonder what will happen to Fred?'

'From what you've told me, I should imagine Fred will be well taken care of.'

I frowned. 'Why did a solicitor write to tell you that Graham was dead?'

'Because he's left us five thousand pounds in his Will, that's why.' Hilda waved the letter exultantly in my face, which wasn't exactly tactful seeing as how I was so upset. 'That's the biggest donation we've ever had. Enough to give you a rise in wages, for one thing.'

'Oh, but I couldn't possibly take it!'

'You can and you will, dear. No, don't argue,' she commanded when I opened my mouth to protest. 'You're working for peanuts and it's not right. I couldn't afford to pay you more, but now I can. After all, another pound a week is only a fraction of what your friend left, and he wouldn't have known we existed if it hadn't been for you.'

I tried to telephone Fred, but there was no answer from the flat in Grosvenor Square, so I wrote a letter instead. The rest of the afternoon was spent looking after a little girl called Rosa whose mother was in hospital about to give birth to her second child.

'She's only nineteen, poor lamb,' Dorothy explained. 'Her husband's working away somewhere, and she didn't like leaving Rosa with the neighbours. They're a very rough crowd and she doesn't trust them, so she brought her to us.' Dorothy's voice was as soft and gentle as Hilda's was loud and abrasive. They'd worked together for years and Dorothy had come to live with her friend when she retired and had been forced to leave the nurses' home where she'd lived all her adult life. Everything about Dorothy was round: her face, her figure, her kind blue eyes.

Rosa was two, very talkative and forward for her age. She wore a dress that came down to her ankles and would have fitted a child of five. We played with dolls together, I read her stories, she helped me make a cake for tea and I took her for a walk, thinking all the time about my own little girl who'd been the same age the first time I saw her after giving her to my sister in London on a rainy November day.

It had been another November day. The sky was full of grey clouds but, so far, it hadn't rained. I'd taken the afternoon off work to go to Maghull with Claire and Kate. Eve, my daughter, was having a party for her second birthday. I went because Claire had asked me and because I knew I couldn't avoid seeing Eve for the rest of my life. While I ached to, I also dreaded it.

'I offered to make a birthday cake,' Claire said on the bus on the way there – she'd refused to let me drive her, saying she didn't trust me or the car – 'but Aileen said she was going to *buy* one.' Her voice rose indignantly. 'Have you ever heard of such a thing, actually *buying* a birthday cake?'

'Well, it would seem some people do.'

'Aileen's got more money than sense. Did you know that Michael's been promoted? He's been made a director of Wexford's, whatever that means.'

'Dad told me. He's very fond of Michael.'

'Michael's OK, but he's dead boring. So's our Norah's Roy. Liam's a scally, but he's anything but boring.' She waved at the new, boxlike houses we were passing. 'They look like coffins. I'd sooner live in Bootle with Liam any day than one of them places.'

'Liam will be pleased to know that,' I remarked.

'Oh, he already knows, Kitty.' She sighed happily. 'The longer we're married, the more we love each other. With some couples, it's the other way round. Kate, will you sit still a minute? Have you got ants in your pants or something?'

'No, Mam, wasps,' Kate sniggered. She was a typical McCarthy: blue-eyed and red-haired.

'Will you listen to the child?' Claire said. 'Barely two years old and already cracking jokes. Your dad'll never be dead while you're alive, young lady. I think we get off at the next stop. Come on, Kitty.'

Aileen's house looked exactly the same as it had done the last time I'd seen it. The chocolate-brown suite and the orange carpet looked as good as new and nothing was out of place. A standard lamp with a fringed shade was switched on, and there was a smaller lamp on the sideboard, making the room look warm and cosy on such a dull day. There was no sign of Aileen, but our Norah was already there with Bernadette seated on her knee. Although she'd been born prematurely, Bernadette had quickly made up her weight and was a perfectly healthy little girl, but Norah and Ray treated her like an invalid, terrified she might catch something, and taking her to the doctor's if she so much as sneezed. The poor child was spoiled rotten, showered with toys and plied with food. If Norah and Ray weren't careful, their daughter would soon become *un*healthily chubby.

Our Jamie's German wife, Lisa, had also arrived. They'd got married in Berlin and we'd missed the wedding. Lisa was genuinely beautiful with flaxen hair and eyes exactly the same shade of brown as Aileen's suite. She was heavily pregnant and her baby was due on Christmas Eve. Jamie had emerged from his National Service without a scratch on him and without going anywhere near Korea. The war had limped to a halt with neither side declared the winner: thousands of lives had been lost in vain.

My eyes swept the room for my own little girl. There were three other women there, strangers, all smartly dressed, who must be friends of Aileen. At the far end, five small girls were leaping up and down like jack-in-the-boxes and laughing shrilly. I couldn't tell if they were just excited or playing a game but, somehow, I just knew straight away that none were mine. Kate ran to join them, Bernadette struggled to get off her mother's knee and Aileen came into the room. 'Where's Eve?' she asked.

Norah said, 'She went upstairs. I think she was frightened by the noise.'

'I'll go and fetch her. The trouble is she's not used to company.'

Aileen left and Claire whispered, 'The trouble is she never normally invites other kids to play with the child. She's too worried they'll harm her bloody house. Eve's just another acquisition, like the telly and the posh three-piece. And have you noticed Marge isn't here? Aileen considers her too common to meet her posh friends.'

I could hear Aileen returning downstairs, saying, 'There's nothing to be frightened of, darling. They're just little girls, friends, who've come to play with you on your birthday.'

'Am I two, Mummy?' a small voice piped.

'Yes, darling, you're two. Later, we're going to have a cake with two candles and you can blow them out while everyone sings "Happy Birthday".' Aileen laughed when she came in. 'She was playing with her dolls. Look, Eve, your Auntie Claire's arrived and Kate.' When she saw me, her face changed and she gave me a wary look. 'I didn't know you were coming, Kitty.'

'Claire asked me. Anyroad, I thought it was about time I did.'

Aileen nodded. 'It probably is,' she said evenly.

She moved away, and I watched Kate draw Eve, her cousin, into the crowd – she was a generous, big-hearted child, Kate, just like her mother. Eve still hung nervously back. She turned her head to look for her mother and her eyes caught mine. To my astonishment, her face lit up and she smiled, as if she knew me, or perhaps she just liked me at first sight. I smiled back, Kate nudged her, and the children joined hands and began to dance in a circle singing 'Ring-a-ring-a-roses'. When they came to 'we all fall down', Eve collapsed with a giggle and looked at me again. I was still smiling.

I don't suppose she was any prettier or better dressed than the other girls in their party frocks – Eve's was blue taffeta with rosebuds around the sleeves and hem – but she was *my* little girl and in my eyes she looked the prettiest of the lot. Her hair was still the colour of butter, her eyes had stayed blue and there was something vulnerable about her little, heart-shaped face that made me want to weep. She didn't have the same confidence as Kate and the other children. It made me feel angry because I knew that if *I'd* kept her she wouldn't look like that. Then I hated myself because I hadn't *had* to give her to Aileen.

You make it sound so simple, she'd said to me a million years ago in this very room when I'd offered to give her my baby. *Are you really willing to let another woman have your child?*

Only if the woman's you, Aileen, I'd replied.

Now, it was as if I was blaming my sister for taking her, as if I somehow expected Aileen to read my mind and bring up my child in exactly the same way as I would have done myself.

The game finished. Eve came and pressed herself against my knees. Close up, I saw her eyes were the colour of bluebells, the lashes thick and gold. 'Hello,' she said.

'Hello, Eve, I'm Kitty.'

'I'm two today. It's my birthday.'

'Are you having a nice time?'

'Yes.' She nodded gravely. I was about to pick her up and hold her on my knee, but Aileen came and led her away. She didn't look at me. I think she was worried I'd do something awful, like announce to the room that Eve was really mine. 'Come along, darling. We're going to play another game.'

The afternoon was torture, yet I didn't want it to end, even though it was tearing me apart. *Eve's just another acquisition*, Claire had said. Was that really the case? I hated thinking so badly about my sister, and wished with all my heart that I hadn't been so careless with my little girl, that I hadn't handed her to Aileen as if she were one of Hilda's parcels. Had I kept her, I would have managed somehow. Then she wouldn't have had such a timid look on her dear little face, and our Claire would have made the birthday cake.

I had to carry Rosa home from Stanley Park when she complained she felt tired – I must suggest to Hilda that we get an old pushchair or a pram to keep in the house for occasions like today.

Rosa had seemed as light as a feather when I first picked her up, but it wasn't long before I felt as if I were carrying a sack of coal. My pace slowed, the little girl fell asleep on my shoulder and my thoughts returned to Eve . . .

Since the party on her birthday, I'd seen her exactly four times: once at Christmas, the second at our Norah's when I'd gone to see her one Sunday afternoon and found Aileen and Eve already there. The third time was when Patsy, Claire's daughter, had got married at St James's Church, and the fourth a mere few weeks ago when Claire and Liam threw a party for their twentieth wedding anniversary. Eve was now eight and she'd smiled at me, as if I was someone very familiar, not a woman she only met every few years. Her face still bore the same nervous expression she'd had when she was two, and she seemed to lack the feeling of certainty about her place in the world that I'd had at the same age. She was growing fast, looking almost gawky with her long, slim legs and thin arms. This time, Aileen didn't snatch her away when she came to talk to me. Perhaps by now, my sister felt more sure of herself.

I looked searchingly into Eve's blue eyes and asked what her favourite lesson was at school.

'Writing,' she replied seriously. 'I like writing stories and poetry. I like making things rhyme.'

'You sound to me like a very clever little girl,' I said admiringly. 'I enjoyed doing things like that when I went to school.' Eve went to a private school and would emerge far better educated that her real mother. *She* wouldn't have to go to night school to learn where to put commas.

'Would you like me to write *you* a poem, Kitty?' she asked.

I said I'd love it, which was the God's honest truth. 'What will it be about?'

Her brow puckered. 'I don't know. What would you like it to be about?'

'Flowers?' I suggested. 'A crazy daisy and a silly lily.'

She looked at me astounded, then began to laugh. It was a loud, almost raucous laugh coming from such a slight body, and very catching. Dad began to laugh, too, and so did Marge who was sitting nearby. Then our Aileen did no more than slap my daughter hard on her bare arm, saying brusquely, 'Be quiet, Eve! Stop making a show of yourself. Everyone's looking.'

'She was only laughing, luv,' Dad said crossly. 'It's hardly worth a slap. You did some dead awful things when you were eight, but no one laid a finger on you.'

Aileen went red. 'I'm sorry. I'm just not feeling very well tonight. I'm sorry, darling.' She tried to take a stony-faced Eve in her arms, but the child shrugged her away. I was wondering if I dared take hold of her myself, when she spied Michael across the room watching the situation with narrowed eyes and went to him instead. Aileen left the room and I heard her run upstairs.

Dad shook his head. 'Our Aileen's too hard on that kid by a mile. She expects her to behave like a lady when she's only a child. I wonder what the real mother would think if she knew Eve had been given a crack just for laughing.'

I was on my way into the yard to cool down because I couldn't remember having felt so angry, but had to pass through the kitchen where Claire was cutting more sarnies. 'I just heard the contretemps in there,' she said, tossing her head in the direction of the living room. 'Aileen's having an affair, that's the reason her nerves are so on edge. Michael knows and they're daggers drawn.'

'How the hell did you find that out?' There seemed to be nothing in the world that our Claire didn't know.

'I'm friendly with this woman who works at Wexford's. *She* told me,' my sister said smugly. 'Apparently the chap, the one Aileen's having the affair with, is a bit like Montgomery Clift and Rex Harrison rolled into one. In other words, dead sexy, and as different from Michael as chalk from cheese. His name's Steve something, he's a bit younger than Aileen and he's married with a couple of kids. I don't know about him, but with her it's probably just a middle-aged fling – she's fast approaching forty. Michael's more Donald Duck than Rex Harrison.' Claire stopped making the sarnies and said thoughtfully, 'She's probably enjoying the excitement of having a decent screw for a change. Once she's had enough, everything will go back to normal.'

'It's a bit hard on Michael though, isn't it?'

'More than hard, it's dead cruel. Still, he loves her and although he might be boring, he's too nice to bear a grudge.'

I slowly digested this information, wondering what effect it would have on Eve, but knowing there was nothing I could do about it. 'Does she often slap Eve like that?' I asked.

'Nah – well, I don't think so. I'm not in a position to say for sure, though I know she's inclined to nag a lot. You know the sort of thing: don't speak until you're spoken to; children should be seen and not heard; take your elbows off the table and your hands out of your pockets.' Claire snorted loudly. 'I could never understand the last one. I mean, what are pockets for except to keep your hands in?' She remembered the sarnies and began to slice them in half with manic energy. 'Don't worry, Kit. Aileen loves Eve to bits and wouldn't dream of hurting her. It's just that at the moment her nerves are raw.'

When Claire told me not to worry I should have been suspicious that she knew more than she let on – it would have been understandable for me to be concerned for Eve, but not worried. It wasn't until a few weeks later that I discovered that Claire had known the truth all along.

Dorothy had the tea ready when Rosa and I got back to the house, and I discovered we had another temporary guest, who was considerably older than the ones we'd had so far.

I quickly learned that Cecily Hunter was sixty-two, childless, and had been a loyal wife to Mr Hunter for forty-one years. He was a chartered accountant and a member of Liverpool Chamber of Commerce. Cecily was nicely dressed in a cream jersey frock and her hair, more grey than brown, looked as if it had recently been set at the hairdresser's. The only remarkable thing about Cecily was that her face had been beaten to a pulp. Both of her eyes and her nose were bruised and badly swollen, and she had a cut on her chin that Dorothy had already dabbed with iodine. There was blood on the front of the cream frock.

It turned out that Mr Hunter had arrived home for lunch, discovered his wife was out, so waited until she came home and gave her a good hiding. Cecily said he hardly ever came home for lunch so there was no reason why she should have stayed in. The beating had shaken her, but otherwise she seemed remarkably calm. 'It's happened countless times before,' she told us in a voice that throbbed just a little. 'Whenever something goes wrong at the office or in some other part of his life, he takes it out on me. This time I decided I'd had enough. I was due at a bridge party this afternoon, but I had to let my partner down. My cleaner had told me about this place, so I wondered if I could stay here until my face heals, then I shall do something I should have done years ago: leave James and find somewhere else to live. I shall pay you, of course.'

'There's no need for that, dear,' Dorothy told her. 'We're a charity. It's what we're here for.'

'Then I shall make a donation to your charity,' Cecily insisted. 'I have plenty of money, but if I was as rich as Croesus there aren't many places I could go with a face like this.'

Dorothy didn't say it was the first time we'd had a battered woman on our hands. We'd had women with the occasional black eye or bruise, the result of a casual punch from their husbands, but never one who'd been as badly beaten as Cecily. I'd never dreamt that wife-beating went on in middle-class homes. You learn something new every day, I reflected gloomily.

Cecily slept in the room below mine and I was woken in the middle of the night by the sound of her weeping. She was *really* crying – loud, hoarse, wretched sobs that came from deep down inside her. I contemplated going down to comfort her, but reckoned Cecily would sooner be left to cry alone. From now on, she'd have to do everything else alone. She had no children, no relatives, no close friends. 'I think that's why I never left James,' she said not long before she went to bed, 'because I was scared of being on my own.'

Things always seem worse in the middle of the night than they do in the daytime. Before long, I was worrying that I'd end up in the same position as Cecily when I was sixty-two. I had plenty of relatives, but I couldn't exactly count Marge as a close friend and, to all intents and purposes, I had no children. It was a depressing thought, but when I woke the next morning, it didn't seem to matter in the least.

*

The next day was as busy as usual. The first thing I did was go to see Mrs Tyler, taking another pint of milk for Josie. Peggy let me in. I wondered if the girl got any schooling.

'Mam and the little 'uns are still in bed,' she told me. 'Ronnie kept everyone awake half the night crying, but I managed to get the bigger ones off to school.' Josie had enjoyed the milk but, she said regretfully, it had all gone by teatime and she'd had to give her tea.

'Tea without milk?' I asked.

'Yes, Nurse,' Peggy conceded. 'Me dad only likes tea with milk in and he used the last.' The girl looked uncomfortable, as if she considered it her fault. I realized I was heaping too much responsibility on her young shoulders. It wasn't her job to make sure Josie was properly fed, and it wasn't mine either. As far as the Tylers were concerned, my business with them should have ended yesterday. I told Peggy she was a marvel for doing all she did, gave her the milk and helped clean the kitchen. Then I went to deliver my next parcel, my connection with the Tyler family over for good – or so I thought.

When I got back to Everton Valley, I found Cecily Hunter in the office typing away. I was admiring the way her fingers skimmed over the keys when she paused. 'I used to type for James when we were first married and he started a business on his own,' she said. 'I thought I'd give Hilda a little break: her back's hurting and she's lying down.'

'Do you feel up to it?' I asked. Her face was still swollen and the bruises had turned a vivid shade of purple.

'Not really, but I like to keep busy. It takes my mind off things a bit.' I remembered then that I'd heard her weeping during the night. 'You have another woman upstairs: she arrived this morning. She's heavily pregnant and has been living in a room somewhere, but the landlord threw her out because he didn't want a baby in the house. She didn't mention a husband. Dorothy's looking after her. Rosa's somewhere around.'

'I'd better give her a hand.' Before leaving the office, I rang the flat in Grosvenor Square again in the hope of speaking to Fred, but the phone at the other end rang for ages and no one picked it up. By now, he should have received my letter. I was looking forward to a reply.

The new woman turned out to be a prostitute of about forty with hard eyes and a ravaged face. Her name was Sally Reilly. 'I told him,' she was raging when I went in, 'I told the bastard I wasn't keeping the kid. I told him someone else could have it. How am I supposed to look after a bloody baby in a shitty room like that? Most of the time, there's no hot water and it's bloody freezing in the winter.' She burst into tears. 'I ask you, how's someone like me supposed to look after a baby?'

'You can if you want to, Sally,' Dorothy said softly. 'Think about it. If you decide to keep your baby, we'll find you a place where no one will complain. If you'd sooner have the child adopted, then it's entirely up to you. The decision is yours and yours alone. In the meantime, you're free to stay here.'

'I wouldn't make much of a mother, would I?' the woman sniffed.

'I can't possibly pass an opinion on that. You might make an excellent mother or an appalling one, I wouldn't know.'

'Once you see your baby, you might want to keep it,' I blurted out. Dorothy frowned and shook her head. We weren't supposed to pass opinions or put pressure on women to act in a way we would have acted ourselves. I mouthed 'sorry', went to look for Rosa and found her sitting on Hilda's bed reading her a story.

'Well, not exactly reading,' said Hilda. 'She's describing what she thinks is happening from the pictures, aren't you, darling?' Rosa nodded. 'The stories have taken on a completely different meaning than the author intended.'

A few days later, Sally Reilly went into hospital and gave birth to a healthy baby boy that she decided to keep. Hilda found her a tiny flat in Grove Street in a house where there were already a number of children and the landlord didn't mind another. 'I just hope she doesn't go back to her old trade,' she said with a sigh.

Rosa's mother returned to collect her. She'd had another little girl and was looking forward to having the family back together. 'My husband's coming home this weekend and he can't wait to see the new baby,' she said.

Cecily Hunter's face was gradually healing. She asked if I would mind going back with her to Calderstones to collect her clothes and a few other things. She was still wearing the frock with bloodstains on the front – they had refused to come out even when scrubbed –

and had been sleeping in her underclothes because she didn't have a nightie. 'I'm just worried James might be there. We'll catch a taxi there and back – if you're prepared to come, that is.' She managed a painful smile. 'I doubt he'll beat the two of us up.'

I was only too willing: it would make a change from my usual duties.

Cecily's house was very similar to the one in Richmond except that the furniture was more modern and the decoration brighter. 'I spent years making this place look nice,' she said as we went upstairs, 'but it holds no warm memories. I shall be glad to see the back of it.'

The bedroom was papered in pink with a pattern of silver flowers, and the curtains were the same. I hadn't known you could get curtains to match wallpaper. The bedroom suite was pale grey, the same shade as the carpet. Cecily remarked that she'd often spent weeks hunting down things for the house. 'There's a lovely turquoise-blue vase downstairs that took ages to find. It goes perfectly with the curtains and I remember how triumphant I felt when I found it.' She sat abruptly on the bed. 'It seems so trite now after living in Hilda's for barely a week. Hilda's is a home: this is merely a house. Nothing good ever happened here.' She sighed. 'I'll get the suitcases out of the loft. Perhaps you could start folding the clothes, Kitty? They're in that wardrobe over there. James keeps his in the smaller one.'

I removed a heap of clothes from the wardrobe, threw them on the bed and began to fold the tweed costumes, sensible skirts and blouses, and plain frocks. I was removing a hyacinth-blue crêpe evening dress when Cecily staggered in with two large suitcases and told me to put it back. 'I can't visualize wearing an evening frock again.'

'You can give it to Dorothy,' I suggested. 'She's handy with a needle and she could probably make two little frocks out of it.'

'Then we'll take it,' Cecily said quickly. 'I'm quite good with a needle myself so I can give her a hand.'

'I thought we'd carry the coats over our arms, they'll never fit in the suitcases.'

Cecily said thoughtfully, 'I don't really need so many coats and I was going to leave some behind, but I suppose Dorothy could make use of them, too. Some of your ladies might be grateful for a nice, warm coat.'

In the end, we took everything and had to stagger downstairs, the suitcases packed solid with clothes. We left them in the hall, then went back for the coats and the carrier bags containing smaller items.

The taxi was waiting outside. We were halfway down the path when Cecily said, 'I've just thought of something.' She dropped the suitcase and went to speak to the driver. A few seconds later, he drove away, and Cecily returned, saying, 'I paid him off. I have my own car in the garage. We'll go in that and you can use it instead of the near-wreck you have now.'

'You're giving us your car?' I gasped.

'Yes, it's a Mini, almost new. It will do as my donation. I find your charity very . . . *inspirational*, Kitty,' she said earnestly. 'You, Hilda and Dorothy are the kindest people I've ever known. I've reached the grand old age of sixty-two without having done a single thing faintly comparable to the wonderful things you do.' Her still-bruised face shone with an expression of joy that I found very touching. 'But it's not too late,' she cried, 'I can start now. Tell me, you have four spare bedrooms in the house. Do you ever have all four occupied?'

I shook my head. 'I can't recall a time when we did.'

'Then do you think Hilda would let me live with you? I can help with the typing and the cooking. It's a long time since I cleaned my own house, but I'm sure I'll remember how. I wouldn't want paying. What do you think, Kitty?'

'Me? I'd love you to stay, but you'd have to discuss it with Hilda first.'

When we got back to Everton Valley, Hilda said another pair of hands would be very welcome. Later, I helped Cecily put away her clothes in the old, chipped wardrobe and the wobbly chest of drawers, thinking how drab the room was compared to the one with the pink and silver wallpaper. Yet I doubted if there was a woman in Liverpool as happy as Cecily was right then.

Three months passed and, according to Claire, Aileen was still embroiled in an affair. 'The woman I know from Wexford's – her name's Mildred Sweeney by the way – said her and this Steve chap don't bother to hide it any more. The other day his wife came and created a scene in Aileen's office, shouting at her to keep her filthy hands off her husband. I feel dead sorry for Michael,' she said soberly.

'How's Eve?'

'I wouldn't know, Kit.' Claire shrugged. 'I haven't seen hide nor hair of Aileen, Michael or Eve in ages. Last week, I spoke to Michael when I rang to invite Eve to our Kate's birthday party on Sunday, but she didn't turn up. Next week, Eve will be nine, but I've no idea what's happening.'

A few days later, another girl a few years older than Eve came to me for help and, for a little while, I forgot all about my daughter.

It had been an unusual, highly emotional morning. The bell had rung at about half past six and, when Dorothy had opened the door, she'd found a baby boy only a few hours old on the step. He was warmly dressed in good-quality clothes, but there was no sign of whoever had left him. After Dorothy had made sure he was all right, I'd driven her and the baby to the maternity hospital in Oxford Street, while Hilda telephoned the police. She was still waiting for them to come when we got back a few hours later.

'There's someone to see you, Kitty,' Hilda said. 'She refuses to talk to anyone else and wouldn't even tell me her name. I've put her in the living room where there's a nice, warm fire. She looks very distressed, poor child.'

'It's a child?' For a moment, I thought it might be Eve, but if she were in trouble, she'd go to her granddad or our Claire, not me. I don't know why, but I wasn't all that surprised when I found my visitor was Peggy Tyler, wearing a cotton frock and a coat that was much too short. She jumped to her feet and I saw her eyes were red-rimmed and her sallow cheeks sunken. She looked more like an old woman than a girl of twelve or thirteen. 'Hello, Nurse. I knew where you lived because you left a card with the address on that time you brought the nappies and stuff for me mam. I hope it's all right to come.'

'Of course it is, Peggy.' I smiled warmly, hoping to put her at her ease. 'Is something wrong with your mam? Let's sit down, love, and you can tell me all about it.' I nudged her towards the settee.

'No, Nurse, it's not me mam. It's me.' She began to cry. 'I think I'm having a baby. I feel sick all the time, the way Mam does when she's expecting.'

Jaysus, Mary and Joseph! I felt myself go very cold. 'Who's the father, Peggy?' I asked gently.

'I can't tell you. Me mam'd do her nut if she found out. She doesn't know I'm here, either. I told her I was going to school.'

'I won't tell your mam, I promise.' I took a deep breath. 'Is it your dad, luv?'

The girl nodded reluctantly. 'I try to push him off, honest I do, but he won't let me.'

'Has he done it more than once?'

She nodded again. 'Him and Mam had a fight, you see. She told him she wasn't having any more kids and to keep away from her or she'd kill him.' She grabbed my hand. 'I don't like it, Nurse, it's horrible.'

I was no good at this. I didn't know what to say, other than to curse Mr Tyler to high heaven and call him every name under the sun, though I managed not to do it out loud. 'Look, Peggy,' I said after a while, 'I'm not a nurse, but there are two ladies here who are. Would you mind letting one of them examine you to make sure you're pregnant? While they do, I'll make some tea. Have you had any breakfast today?' The girl looked as if she hadn't eaten in days.

'No, Nurse. I can't remember when I last ate anything.'

'I'll do you boiled eggs and toast. You sit there a minute while I fetch one of the ladies.'

Hilda was in the office and I told her what had happened in as few words as possible.

'I'll check the child,' she said. 'You know, Kitty, there are some men who should be castrated. In fact, I'd enjoy doing the deed to Mr Tyler myself.'

I was waiting outside the door with the eggs and toast when Hilda came out. 'She's definitely pregnant. I asked if she wanted the baby and she shook her head until it nearly came off, so I'm going to abort it. Take those eggs away and give the kitchen table a good scrubbing. Don't look so shocked, Kitty. I've done it before. That's why I stopped nursing, not because of my back, but because I was dismissed for aborting the foetus of an eleven-year-old girl who'd been raped by her brothers. Yes, brothers,' she repeated when I looked even more shocked. 'All three of them.'

'What are we going to tell Mrs Tyler?' I asked later that afternoon as Hilda drove like a maniac along Scotland Road towards Kingdom

Street where the Tylers lived. It was already growing dark and a fog was descending on the city making everywhere look hazy.

'That Peggy's had an accident.'

Peggy was tucked up in bed in the house in Everton Valley and wouldn't be back on her feet until tomorrow. Her father's child no longer existed.

'What sort of accident? She's bound to ask.'

'I don't know,' Hilda said irritably. 'I'll have thought of something by the time we get there.'

'Your daughter fainted in the street, Mrs Tyler,' she announced after a girl not much younger than Peggy had shown us into the Tylers' house. A fire burned in the grate, but it was mainly bits of wood and wouldn't last five minutes. 'Someone sent for an ambulance and she was taken to hospital where it was discovered she was suffering from malnutrition – that's lack of food. Apparently, she hadn't eaten in days. She's being kept in overnight and will be back home tomorrow. I suggest you keep her in bed for a few days.'

'But will she be all right?' The woman looked wretched. Everything was too much for her and the news about Peggy was a further blow. Her house was a midden: there were children everywhere and one of the little boys lay fast asleep under the table. It didn't seem to have crossed her mind to wonder what I was doing there.

'She will be if she has some rest. Why hasn't she eaten, Mrs Tyler? Is there food in the house?' Hilda was being unnecessarily brusque, I thought.

'There's bread and jam.' The woman limply waved her thin hand. 'We've all just had bread and jam.'

'That's totally inadequate for growing children,' Hilda said crossly. 'Tell me, what will your husband have to eat when he comes home from work?'

The woman stared at the floor. 'Boiled spuds and stewing steak. Bert insists on a hot meal.'

'Does he now? Well, what's good enough for Bert is good enough for your children, too.'

Anger flashed across the woman's face, but disappeared as quickly as it had come. 'And where's the money supposed to come from to buy stewing steak for us all?' she asked listlessly.

Hilda had an answer for everything. 'You have nine children, Mrs Tyler. By my reckoning, you should receive around four pounds a week in Child Benefit, well enough to buy proper food.'

Mrs Tyler's gaze returned to the floor. 'Yes, but Bert takes it.'

'Child Benefit can only be cashed by the mother. How does Bert manage to get his hands on it?'

'He makes me sign the form on the back and cashes it himself, then he gives me thirty bob for the housekeeping. By the time I've paid the rent, there's not much left for food.'

'And I suppose Bert keeps the rest as well as his wages!' Hilda's fierce expression melted and she smiled a smile that could have broken a dozen hearts. 'Dear Mrs Tyler,' she said warmly, 'you have so much to put up with, but your children didn't ask to be born. Now they're here and you must put them first and Bert second.' A toddler crawled into the room wearing only a nappy and rubber pants – it could only be Josie. Hilda picked her up. 'What a beautiful child! You have a lovely family, Mrs Tyler. You must feel very proud of them.'

'Well, yes, I do,' Mrs Tyler gulped, glancing round at the assortment of skeletal children who had gathered around Hilda, no doubt fascinated by her posh accent and strange clothes. Today she wore a narrow skirt that reached her ankles and the mouldy fur coat she'd had on when we first met on the Liverpool train; all these years later, it looked even mouldier. 'Yes, I do feel proud of them,' Mrs Tyler repeated.

Hilda addressed the children. 'I take it you all help your mother around the house?'

'Yes, we do, miss,' the older children chorused, though it didn't quite ring true.

'What would really help is if the big ones dressed the little ones before they went to school and got them ready for bed at night. Promise me you'll do that from now on.'

'Ooh, *yes*, miss.'

'Good! You never know, if Santa Claus is watching, he might bring you sweets at Christmas.' Hilda handed Josie to the nearest child, patted a few heads and announced, 'I shall leave now. It's been very nice meeting you, Mrs Tyler. Goodbye, children. I shall come and see you again soon. Oh, I nearly forgot. Who's willing to go and buy fish and chips for tea?'

'Me, miss, me.' Half a dozen hands shot up. Hilda chose the one that reached the highest.

'What's your name?'

'Alan, miss.'

'Buy half a crown's worth, Alan.' She put a coin in the boy's hand. 'And hurry back in case they get cold.'

'Ta, miss.' Alan raced out of the house at the speed of light.

Hilda put two more half-crowns on the sideboard. 'Later on, Mrs Tyler, perhaps you'd like to send a couple of the lads out for a bag of coal.'

'You were a bit hard on Mrs Tyler at first,' I remarked when we were back in the car. The fog was thicker now and I was dreading driving home with Hilda, who didn't seem to feel the need for caution at the wheel.

'I know,' she said abjectly. 'I hated doing it, but it was the only way of getting through to her. The poor woman's brain is numb with misery. I think I did manage it by the end.'

'Why don't you start the car?' I enquired when Hilda seemed quite content to sit hugging the steering wheel, her chin resting on top.

'Because I'm waiting for Mr Tyler to come home. I'd like a word with him.'

Quite a few men walked down the street. Each time I tensed, waiting for one to stop outside the Tylers' house. Alan came rushing home with a huge parcel of fish and chips. The fog got even thicker and I felt as if I were slowly freezing to death, when a small, weedy individual with a drooping moustache approached. He produced a key and was about to open the door, when Hilda leaped out of the car, calling, 'Mr Tyler?'

'Who wants to know?' the man replied in a surly voice.

'I do. You stay there, Kitty,' she commanded when I went to open the door.

I ground my teeth, unable to hear a word, as Hilda went up to the man and poked him hard in the chest. She was half a head taller and I was amazed that Mr Tyler was such a puny individual. I'd been expecting someone tall and powerful.

Hilda continued to poke him in the chest and he kept backing away until they were almost lost in the fog. She returned about ten minutes later, huffing and puffing, and started the car. I asked what she'd said to him.

'I told him incest was a crime and if he dared lay a finger on Peggy again – or any of his other children – I'd have the law on him and he could go to prison for at least ten years. Then I told him that tomorrow it was my intention to warn the staff in the Post Office to call the police next time he tries to collect the Child Benefit that should go to his wife.' Hilda shook herself and said in a disgusted voice, 'He's one of those loathsome little men who make up for their inadequacies by making life hell for their families. But,' she went on as the wheels of Cecily's Mini screeched around a corner and we nearly crashed into a tram, 'I put the fear of death in him and he won't do it again.'

I felt quite lucky to get back to Everton Valley all in one piece. It had been an upsetting day and I was looking forward to having something to eat followed by a quiet read. But I'd hardly been in a minute when Cecily informed me there'd been a phone call from my sister, Claire, who wanted me to call back as soon as I came in.

'She only rang a short while ago. She said it's urgent.'

I groaned. I wasn't in the mood to make a phone call but felt I had no alternative except to ring Claire immediately – she and Liam had recently had a telephone installed.

'Kitty!' Claire said tensely. 'I thought you should know that our Aileen's having Steve's baby and they've run off together, God knows where. Michael hasn't been to work in days and I've no idea what's happened to Eve.'

I was dead tired and nothing was making sense. What did Claire think had happened to Eve? She could only be with Michael. 'Why are you telling me?' I asked.

'Oh, Kitty, luv. Eve's your daughter and I'm worried sick about her. Lord knows what sort of state Michael's in or what he'll do. I was about to go to Maghull meself, but it's dead foggy here and it'll take ages on the bus. I thought you could pick me up – we'll go together.'

Suddenly, everything became clear and I no longer felt tired. 'I'll come straight away,' I said crisply, and slammed down the phone.

Chapter 6

I was a good driver. I never went too fast or too slow and always obeyed the Highway Code. Heavy traffic didn't bother me, nor did the rain, but I'd never driven in such thick fog before. The journey to Maghull was a nightmare. For much of the way, I had no idea where I was and just followed the lights of the car in front. Familiar landmarks were shrouded in fog. I seemed to stop and start a thousand times until, by some miracle, I recognized I was in Bootle and drove through the murky streets until I reached Opal Street. I stopped outside the Quinns', sounding the horn. Claire came out straight away and got into the Mini. 'You took your time,' she complained.

'I like driving in the fog so much I came the long way round,' I said acidly.

We hardly spoke on the way to the Maghull. A few times, Claire tried to start a conversation, but I told her to shut up. I had to concentrate, particularly during a long stretch of road where there were no lights and I was scared we'd end up in a ditch. We reached Maghull, found Dickens Road, but I couldn't see the house numbers. Claire got out to look while I crawled along until she waved at me to stop. I emerged from the car with my arms trembling, my legs wobbling and my head feeling as if it were stuffed with cotton wool.

'The lights are on, but the garage is empty. Michael must be out in the car,' Claire said. She rang the doorbell.

I still couldn't understand the hurry. Eve was my child and there was nothing in the world I wouldn't do for her, but while Aileen splitting up with Michael was worrying, it was hardly my concern. I couldn't very well insist on taking Eve back, upsetting her even more and removing the only member of Michael's family that he had left. It would be too cruel.

A comfortable, grey-haired woman answered the door. It turned out that her name was Susan Mercer and that she was the regular babysitter; Claire had met her before. She let us in immediately, remarking what a terrible night it was.

'We were just passing,' Claire said, 'and we thought we'd pop in and see Aileen and Michael.' In view of the fog, this seemed a most unlikely thing for anyone sane to do, but Mrs Mercer accepted it without question.

'Mr and Mrs Gilbert are both out,' she told us. She clearly knew nothing about the break-up. 'Mr Gilbert rang at teatime and asked if I'd babysit Eve. Mrs Gilbert is away, he didn't say where.'

'Of course!' Claire slapped her brow dramatically – she'd never been any good at lying. 'I'd forgotten our Aileen had gone away. So, Eve's upstairs, is she?'

'That's right.' The woman looked at Claire, as if to say, where else would she be? 'Last time I looked, she was fast asleep.'

'My sister and I are going to stay until Michael comes back, so you can go home if you like, Mrs Mercer.'

'Are you sure?' She looked doubtful.

'Absolutely certain.' It was obvious Claire wanted rid of the woman, but didn't like to be rude. 'In view of the weather, it would be best if you left now before it gets worse. Have you got far to go?'

'I only live round the corner in Thackeray Road.'

'Tea, tea, tea!' Claire gasped when Mrs Mercer had gone. 'I desperately need a cup of tea. No, ten cups, one after the other.'

We went into the spotless kitchen. 'It looks as if no one lives here,' Claire said disgustedly as we stared at the bare, white surfaces. 'I wonder where she keeps things? I can't even see a bloody teapot.'

I said I was going upstairs to take a look at Eve and left her to find things on her own.

My little girl lay on her side with her arm curled over a rag doll that had seen better days. I could only see part of her face and it looked terribly pale. I wondered if she'd had to listen to an awful lot of rows since Michael had discovered his wife was having an affair. It was only then I remembered Claire had said that our sister was expecting her lover's baby – it could only be Michael's fault that she hadn't conceived before. It was hard to imagine how he must be feeling. Eve's eyelids began to flutter madly and she uttered a little cry, but didn't wake. I didn't dare touch her, just whispered, 'Goodnight, sweetheart,' and went downstairs.

Claire had managed to hunt everything down and I went into the living room to find tea and a packet of Garibaldi biscuits on a table in front of the electric fire – it had imitation coals that didn't look even faintly real. For the first time, I noticed the brown three-piece had been replaced by a lovely blue velvet one, and the carpet was cream instead of orange.

'I'd give me eye-teeth for a suite like this,' Claire remarked. She was already ensconced in one of the armchairs. 'Mind you, my lot would have it in tatters within a week.'

'Perhaps now you can tell me why we had to come rushing over here like maniacs,' I enquired. 'Eve's fast asleep in bed and Michael will be home in a couple of hours. What did you expect to find?'

Claire looked embarrassed. 'Mildred Sweeney said Michael looked suicidal. I read in the paper the other week about this chap down south whose wife went off with another feller and he did no more than suffocate their two kids and hang himself on the landing.'

'You're a soft girl, Claire Quinn,' I said mildly. At least her heart was in the right place. 'How long have you known Eve was mine?'

'Since you came back from London. I could tell you were pregnant before you went away, and when you came home and Aileen turned up with Eve at about the same time, I just put two and two together and made four.'

'Who else knows?'

She shrugged. 'No one else has ever said anything. I've never mentioned it to a soul, not even Liam. Once he's got a few pints down him, he can't be trusted to keep his gob shut. I take it Connor Daley's the father?'

'Yes. You should have been a detective: you're better than Sherlock Holmes.'

'I know.' She preened herself, but then her face became serious. 'I wish you'd confided in me though, Kitty. You must have felt awful being pregnant without a single member of your family around.'

'Oh, I didn't mind a bit,' I said airily, quite forgetting how homesick I'd been at first. 'I enjoyed being in Richmond with Faith and the lads.' I'd never told them about Graham and Fred and the flat in Grosvenor Square, only because Aileen and Michael would have worried had they known I was living with two elderly men. Fred had collected my letters from Richmond.

'What happened to Faith?' Claire enquired. 'I've often meant to ask.'

'Oh, she and the lads came back to live with Eric in Liverpool, but they didn't stay for long. In no time, she found out he was having an affair with a stewardess on the ship, so she left him for good.'

I'd only been back in Liverpool a few weeks when I'd visited the house in Orrell Park. Oliver and Robin had been so pleased to see me it had brought a lump to my throat, but Faith had been a bit distant. I think by then she'd already discovered Eric was being unfaithful again. The next time I went, the house was empty. I'd felt deeply hurt that Faith hadn't let me know they were leaving. Not long afterwards, Graham wrote to say they'd all turned up in Richmond and that Hope was looking for somewhere else to live.

'She actually had the nerve to ask if I would have her back,' he wrote, 'but I told her Fred and I preferred to be on our own. She called us a pair of pansies, but what do I care?' I had imagined him chuckling as he scribbled the letter.

'What are you thinking about?' Claire asked.

'Nothing much.' I sighed and went to fetch more tea.

We spent the next few hours in a mainly silent world. Every now and then, a car would crawl by, or there'd be muffled footsteps outside. Claire kept lifting the curtain to see if the fog had lifted, but each time swore it was getting thicker. She rang Liam to say she had no idea what time she'd be home; I rang Hilda in Everton Valley to tell her the same thing. I turned on the television, but quickly turned it off again in case it woke Eve. Anyway, we'd sooner chat. We talked about Mam and the way things had been before Jeff and Will were killed and the way things had been afterwards.

'It's an awful thing to say, but she used to get on me nerves a bit, Mam,' Claire said sombrely. 'It was more what she was doing to Dad than anything.'

'Con thought she was selfish,' I told her.

'Liam met Con a few months ago. That plumbing business of his has really taken off. He's got three staff and you often see his adverts in the *Echo*. You should have stuck with him, Kitty, but it's too late now. He married a girl from Walton Vale and they've got a couple of kids.'

'I know, our Danny told me. He's really fed up they didn't go into business together, but he couldn't afford to take a risk when he had to marry Marge. And I shouldn't have stuck with Con,' I went on, annoyed that she thought I should have married him just because he'd become a successful plumber. 'I love my job and I'm perfectly happy as I am.'

'Has it made you happy watching your sister bring up your daughter?' Claire asked thinly. 'Me, I couldn't have stood it for five minutes. But then I couldn't have given one of me kids away to save me life.'

'I didn't realize it would hurt so much until I did it,' I confessed, 'but by then it was too late.' I remembered the way Aileen had stood by my bed with her arms outstretched, waiting to take my baby from me. Now she was having a baby of her own and didn't want mine any more.

'It's nearly midnight,' Claire muttered. 'I wonder where the heck Michael is?'

Michael arrived almost an hour later, so drunk he could hardly walk. We heard the car crash into something when he drove into the garage, and I had to let him in when he unsuccessfully struggled to open the door with his key.

'I've just destroyed the lawnmower,' he announced in a slurred voice when he limped inside. 'Aileen will kill me, that's if I don't kill her first,' he added with a macabre grin. He didn't seem to notice that there were two women when he'd left Eve with only one. I honestly don't think he recognized Claire and I.

'Come on, luv, let's get you to bed.' Claire took one of his arms and hooked it over her shoulder, signalling me to do the same. Together we managed to drag our usually perfectly dressed, perfectly sober brother-in-law upstairs. He reeked of alcohol, had lost his tie and must have fallen over because his trousers were plastered with mud. For some reason, his shoelaces were undone. We reached the landing and Claire paused. 'I think we'd best put him in the spare room and we'll sleep in the double bed. We can't go home and leave him in this state. I'll have to ring Liam again.'

We let Michael gently down on to the single bed: his shoes fell off in the process. Claire pulled off one leg of his trousers, I pulled off the other, and we managed to remove his jacket without too much difficulty.

'Take a look in the airing cupboard for something to put over him, Kit,' Claire whispered. 'We should've taken off the bedding before we laid him down.'

I found two thick blankets. By the time we'd covered him, he was fast asleep. Before returning downstairs, I looked in on Eve: she was still lying in the same position, her arm over the doll.

Claire was in the kitchen about to put the kettle on. 'I've just found some cocoa. I'll make us a cup, then we'd better get to bed. I feel dead sorry for that poor bugger.' She nodded towards the stairs. 'We're going to have to rally round Michael over the next few months, give him our support. He's just had his whole world turned upside-down.'

But none of us had the opportunity to rally round Michael. When I woke the next morning, the fog had gone and so had he. Claire was already up and I found her in the living room, a letter in her hand. 'Michael left this on the table,' she said. 'It's addressed to you, but I've already read it.'

'Then perhaps you could tell me what it says.' Any other time, I would have pointed out she had no business reading my letters.

'You'd better read if for yourself.'

'Thanks,' I said sarcastically. The handwriting was surprisingly neat considering the state he'd been only a few hours ago. It read:

Dear Kitty

I'm going away, I've no idea where. I need to escape from the hell my life has become this last year. I'm leaving Eve with you – who better to look after her than her own mother? I don't know when, or even if, I shall ever come back. The house belongs to me and me alone. I bought it with a legacy from my father: my wife doesn't own a single brick and one day soon I shall have it transferred to Eve. I shall continue to pay her school fees and arrange for the bank to send a monthly allowance to settle the bills. I'm leaving the car and hope your own insurance covers you to drive it. If Eve asks after her daddy, tell her I love her more than life itself, but I had to go away for the sake of my sanity.

God bless you, Kitty, and thank you for the gift of my darling daughter who has given me so much happiness.

Michael

'Jaysus!' I whispered, close to tears. 'I'd like to punch our Aileen into the middle of next week.'

'Me, too,' Claire echoed. 'The poor bugger must've walked all the way to the station.' She sighed. 'I suppose you'd better wake Eve and tell her what's happened. If I were you, I'd say her dad's only gone for a while: you never know, he might be back in a few months. Then I'll get the bus home and see to my lot. Our Patsy's expecting to go into hospital any minute to have the baby. As for you, you can't very well go to work, you've got too much thinking to do. And by the way, you'd better hide Michael's letter and keep it in case Eve would like to read it when she's older.'

I *did* go to work, though much later than usual. I insisted Claire wake Eve rather than me, she was a far more familiar figure, and I waited downstairs until she appeared, looking forlorn and a trifle lost and even taller than I remembered, in her navy-blue gymslip, white shirt and striped tie. I was relieved that, despite hearing about Michael, she'd decided to go to school.

I kissed my own daughter for the first time in my life and said, 'You could do with some proper stockings, luv.' Her three-quarter-length socks were already slipping down her legs.

'I know. Mummy says I'm too young to wear a suspender belt, and garters make my legs numb.' She had hardly any trace of a Liverpool accent. 'Auntie Claire said that Daddy's gone away for a while and you're going to look after me until he comes back. Mummy's already gone because she found a man she likes much better than Daddy.' She gave a pathetic sniff. 'I wonder if she'd have taken me with her if she'd known Daddy was leaving, too.'

I grimaced, wondering what on earth had prompted Michael to say such a thing. Maybe he'd got to the pitch where he no longer cared what he said. 'What would you like for breakfast, love?'

'Cornflakes, please. Did Daddy say where he was going?' she asked anxiously.

Claire came bustling in. 'No, but it can't be very far. Now, Eve, how do you get to school? Did your dad take you in the car?'

'No, Marian Caffrey's mother picks me up. She brings me back, too, and I stay at their house until Mummy and Daddy come home from work. She'll be here in fifteen minutes. Would you tie the ribbons on my bunches, please? They're in the drawer beside the fridge. Mummy always puts a fresh ribbon on every day. She doesn't like them to be creased.'

I opened the drawer and found several ribbons wound neatly in rolls. 'There's green, yellow and white. What colour do you fancy?'

'White, please.'

I was about to take a handful of hair and tie a ribbon round it, but Eve said, 'Mummy always parts my hair down the middle first.'

There was a comb in the drawer. The silky hair was parted and the ribbons neatly tied, while Claire poured cornflakes into three bowls. Then we sat down to breakfast.

Mrs Caffrey arrived dead on time. By then, Eve was in the hall wearing a navy-blue coat and a velour hat, a satchel slung over her shoulder. I kissed her again and waved tara from the door. Mrs Caffrey gave me a little wave back. I wondered if she'd ask Eve who I was when she got in the car.

'Phew!' Claire was washing the dishes. 'That girl's holding herself in so tight that any minute she'll bust a gut. Once the tears start, she'll probably cry for a week without stopping for breath.' She looked at me sideways. 'Are you going to tell her you're her mother, Kit?'

'I wouldn't dream of it,' I said, shocked. 'She might not even know she's adopted. Do you know if Aileen told her?'

Claire shrugged. 'I haven't a clue. It's the sort of thing she'd have confided in me once, but after she married Michael, me and Aileen didn't stay as close as we'd been before. I think she considered she'd joined the middle classes and left the rest of us McCarthys behind. Look, luv, would you like me to come back again tonight and give you a hand, like?'

'No, ta,' I said firmly. 'I've got to learn to manage on me own. Anyroad, if your Patsy has the baby, she'll be wanting her mam.'

'In that case, I'll be off in a minute. Have you any idea what times the buses run?' I told her there was no need to get the bus, I'd give her a lift on my way to work. 'But you need to sort yourself out, Kitty,' she protested.

'I can sort meself out in me head while I'm working. I'm not going to sit here on my own all day and slowly go mad.'

*

Now I had my daughter to myself, but it had happened so suddenly and in such an unpleasant way that, for Eve's sake, I'd sooner it hadn't happened at all. She had grown up thinking Aileen and Michael were her parents, but now both had gone and I was expected to become her mother and father rolled into one, yet we were strangers to each other. I knew nothing about her. I didn't know her likes or dislikes apart from English being her favourite lesson and that she enjoyed writing poetry. Did she mind having tea with the Caffreys every day – an arrangement Aileen must have come to when she returned to work – or would she sooner come straight home and have tea in her own house? Should I even ask? Or should I just let things stay the way they'd been with Aileen and Michael, causing as little disruption as possible?

There was also my own job to consider and I felt dead selfish because I didn't want to give it up. I'd never worked regular hours. Living on the premises meant I was available twenty-four hours, most days of the week, although I took the occasional evening off to go to the pictures, lately with Marge. Many times in the past I'd got up in the middle of the night when there'd been a crisis, but now I would have to drive to and from Everton Valley every day and be back in Maghull for when Eve came home. And what would happen during the school holidays? Come to that, what had Aileen done with Eve during the holidays? Farmed her out to someone else? Well, I had no intention of doing any such thing. So, what *would* I do?

While I wouldn't dream of comparing my situation with Michael's, his life wasn't the only one about to be turned upside-down.

'Bring her with you,' Hilda said crisply when I told her what had happened and the problems I now faced. 'How old did you say she is?'

'Almost nine, which reminds me, I'd better start organizing a party, that's if she wants one.' She might not be in the mood.

'Nine isn't too young to learn how the other half lives. She can help deliver the parcels, lend Dorothy a hand. You said she's inclined to be a bit nervous and it'll do her all the good in the world, make her feel useful and grown up.'

'Do you really think so?' I tried to imagine how I would have felt had I done things like that when I was nine. Perhaps Hilda was right.

'She won't break up for the Christmas holidays for a while yet. In a few weeks, once you're used to each other, bring her in one Saturday. Tell her you'd like her to see where you work.'

'Oh, Hilda,' I said gratefully. 'You're a genius, you really are.'

Hilda sniffed and said I was talking rubbish. 'I've taught myself to think in a straight line. Other people see obstacles where there aren't any.'

'It means I won't be able to help during the night.'

'No, but Cecily will. Kitty, my dear girl,' Hilda put a claw-like hand on my arm, 'you'll be sadly missed, but we'll manage without you. Anyway, it's about time you had a life outside this place. See, I'm thinking in a straight line again.'

It was a strange day. I had nothing to deliver, there were no women apart from ourselves on the premises and Cecily had the typing up to date. Dorothy disappeared into the kitchen to begin a mammoth baking session, Cecily set about the task of polishing the banisters, Hilda went shopping and I busied myself tidying up my attic room, wondering if I would ever live there again. I packed my clothes and a few books in the suitcase I'd brought with me almost nine years ago, ready to take home, though it would take some getting used to, regarding Aileen's house as 'home'.

When I arrived 'home', I drew the curtains in the living room, and switched on the lamps, the fire and the telly, so the room would look cosy when Eve came in. The house felt warm and the radiators were hot when I touched them – they must switch on by themselves, I thought vaguely. I had no idea how central heating worked. I'd never had to look after a house before, and I was a lousy cook. Until now, other people had done the cooking for me. I could just about manage beans on toast and Welsh rarebit. Oh, and I could boil an egg.

The kettle was on and I was spooning tea into the pot, when the front door opened. I went to look. Eve was standing with her back to it, an expression of such misery on her face you'd think she had the weight of the entire world on her shoulders. She hadn't noticed me and I felt a surge of anger at Aileen and Michael for putting themselves first and reducing my little girl to such a state. She sighed, dropped her satchel, kicked off her shoes, took off her hat and coat, and put everything away in the cupboard under the stairs.

I put on my broadest smile and went to greet her. 'There you are, luv.' I gave her a brief hug and an equally brief kiss, not wanting to overwhelm her with affection that she might resent. 'What sort of day did you have at school?'

'All right,' she said dully. Her blue eyes regarded me warily. I reminded myself that I wasn't the person she wanted to see when she came home from school.

'Did you do English? I remember you telling me it was your favourite lesson.'

'We have English three times a week, but not today. We had Art. I like Art, but we had Needlework and Arithmetic.' She frowned. 'I'm a *bit* good at Needlework, but no good at Arithmetic, and we were given loads of homework.'

'I'll help you with it later, if you like?' I offered recklessly. I'd been no good at it either, but at least I'd done it until I was fourteen.

'Thank you – do I call you Auntie Kitty or just Kitty?'

'Oh, just Kitty, please. Now, why don't you go and sit down while I make you a drink? What would you like? And would you like something to eat while I'm at it? I know you've just had your tea, but you might have room for another mouthful.' It was another reckless offer, as I had no idea what was in the larder.

'I'd love something to eat. I'm starving. Mrs Caffrey only gave us sandwiches. They're having company later and she was in the middle of making a great big dinner.'

I swallowed hard and said cheerfully, 'Let's see what there is, shall we?'

'The tins are in the top cupboard behind the door and the fresh stuff is in the fridge,' Eve informed me.

I opened the fridge and we studied the contents: four sausages on a plate, some cooked ham, a half-empty tin of beans and the same of tomato soup, cheese, butter, lard, a tray of eggs and two pints of milk. 'Is there anything there you fancy?' I asked.

'Can I have anything I like?' she asked hopefully.

'Anything at all.'

'Then I'd like the sausages, the beans and a fried egg, please.'

'And what would madam like to drink while I'm making it?'

To my pleased surprise, she managed the ghost of a smile. 'Milk, please, but I'll just go upstairs and change out of my uniform. Did you know the television's on in the lounge?'

'Yes, I put it on for you. You can watch while I make the food.'

'But I haven't done my homework,' she said with a note of reproof in her voice. 'Mummy doesn't let me watch until it's done.'

I didn't like to remind her that Mummy was no longer around. 'Well, *I* don't mind, so it's up to you whether you watch or not.'

At this, she nodded thoughtfully and went upstairs. She came down wearing a jersey and skirt. Later, I took in the milk and felt slightly exultant when I saw she was watching telly. That's one in the eye for our Aileen, I thought. She's hardly been gone five minutes and I've already encouraged Eve to break one of her rules.

'Can I watch *Bootsie and Snudge?*' she asked. 'It's on later. I usually go to bed before it starts, but all the girls in my class are allowed to see it.'

'If you like. What time do you normally go to bed?'

She wrinkled her nose. 'Half past seven, but,' she added hastily, 'I'm never tired.'

I tried to remember what time I'd gone to bed when I was her age, but recalled the war was on and people went to bed at all sorts of unearthly hours, sometimes not at all if an air raid lasted all night. 'I suppose half past eight will be early enough from now on, later at weekends when you don't have to go to school.' I remembered it was Friday so tonight would be a late one.

At this, Eve looked so delighted that I began to worry it was wrong to let her do things she hadn't been allowed to do before. Yet I could see no reason for such an early bedtime, nor did it seem fair to stop her watching telly before her homework was done. *Who better to look after her than her own mother?* Michael's letter had said, so from now on, as long as it didn't upset her, I'd treat my daughter as I would have done had I brought her up myself.

She didn't seem to care that the sausages were burnt and the egg fried too hard – the beans were perfect as I'd stirred them regularly and none had stuck to the pan. I made myself a ham sarnie. Eve produced two beautifully ironed linen serviettes out of a sideboard drawer, and we sat at the table to eat. Her table manners were perfect and she ate daintily, if rapidly, as if she were genuinely starving.

'Why did Daddy want *you* to look after me?' she asked when she had finished. It was an obvious question, one she was bound to ask. I should have had an answer prepared and I imagined the cogs in my brain going into overdrive as I tried to think of one.

'I'm not sure. Maybe it's because I'm the only one of Mummy's sisters who isn't married with a family and he thought I'd be best.'

She considered this for a while. 'Maybe,' she said, not very positively.

'Auntie Claire's already got five children,' I went on.

'Auntie Norah's only got one,' she pointed out. 'Mind you, I don't like their Bernadette much. Mummy said she's spoiled.'

I explained this was only because Bernadette had been a tiny, very delicate baby and Norah and Roy had worried she might die. 'They've never quite got over it. They still treat her as delicate even though she's a big, bouncing nine-year-old.'

'She's fat,' Eve said bluntly.

'That's not Bernadette's fault. It's because she's given too many sweets and cakes.' I had a brainwave. 'I know why your daddy asked me to look after you: because I'm the only one who hasn't got a house and it meant I could come and live with you in this one. You wouldn't have liked moving to a different house, would you?'

Her head drooped like a flower and she said sadly, 'No. I'd sooner everything had stayed the same and Mummy and Daddy were still here.'

I had no answer to that. I suggested she turn off the television while she did her homework. Together we managed to work out the complicated long divisions and subtractions. She told me that Daddy had been really good at Arithmetic: 'But he called it Maths.' I sensed that she'd been closer to Michael than she'd been to Aileen.

We watched *Bootsie and Snudge* – I'd never seen it before and found it a scream – and she went to bed shortly afterwards. I went up to tuck her in and found her lying with her arm around the doll. Her pink lips were tightly pursed, as if she was doing her best not to cry.

'What's your dolly called?' I asked.

'Gloria,' she said in a small voice. 'It's my favourite name.'

'It's a lovely name.' I bent and kissed both her and Gloria. 'Look, sweetheart,' I said softly, 'you must feel dead upset about everything's that happened and you might feel better if you had a good cry.'

She gave me a strange look. 'Mummy said brave girls don't cry.'

'Then I can't be very brave because I cry all the time.'

'Do you really?' Another strange look.

I nodded furiously. 'The least little thing makes me cry. My friend Marge and I went to the pictures the other week and we cried all the way through – and all the way home as well.' The film was *Summertime* with Katharine Hepburn and it had been so *sad.*

'Do you mean Auntie Marge who's married to Uncle Danny and lives with Granddad?'

'That's the one.'

'*She* cries?'

'Everybody cries at one time or another, luv. I've seen Auntie Claire and Auntie Norah cry loads of times.' I'd also seen Aileen cry, but didn't mention it.

'So it's all right to cry?'

'Perfectly all right,' I assured her.

She gave a little satisfied grunt. 'I wanted to cry when I first came to bed, but now I don't any more.'

'That's all right, too.' I pulled the clothes over her shoulders and gave her and Gloria another kiss. 'Goodnight, sweetheart, I'll see you in the morning.'

'Daddy used to call me sweetheart,' she said in a sleepy voice.

By the time I'd reached the door, she was well away, and I went downstairs and cried my heart out.

The family thought it very odd that Michael had designated *me* to look after his daughter.

'I would have looked after her with pleasure,' Norah said indignantly when she found out.

'She could have come here,' put in Marge.

'Will you be able to manage all right, Kitty, luv?' my father asked when I took Eve to Amethyst Street for Sunday dinner on our first weekend together. 'You haven't had any experience with kids.'

'I deal with them almost every day in my job,' I told him. 'I'm managing fine. Eve and I have really taken to each other.'

'Well, let's hope we see more of her from now on,' Dad said. 'I'm dead fond of the kid, but Aileen didn't bring her round all that often. She didn't like Marge,' he added in a whisper. 'Considered her dead common.'

'Well, she's really enjoying herself now,' I remarked. 'Eve, that is.

She's never played in the street before.' I'd watched from the parlour window when she first went out. Marge's three were playing football with a pile of other children. Eve had hung back at first, reluctant to join in, until the ball had landed at her feet. She'd looked at it, bemused, for a few seconds, before kicking it with all her might and scoring a goal with her very first shot. There'd been a loud cheer and suddenly she was one of the gang. I'd felt a glow of pride and the urge to have a little weep.

Dinner over, Claire arrived with Kate and announced she'd become a grandmother. 'Our Patsy had a little boy weighing just over eight pounds at about two o'clock this morning. She's calling him Jay after some actor in *The Lone Ranger*. I always thought Jay was a horse, but apparently not.'

'I'm an aunt,' Kate said proudly. 'Hello, Eve. I didn't know you were here. Why didn't you come to my party? I was nine.'

Eve went pink. 'I'm sorry, but I didn't know you were having a party.'

Claire was talking to Dad, but it seemed that, on top of her other talents, she had the ability to listen to several conversations at the same time. She said, 'I rang and told your dad, luv, but he must've forgotten about it.'

'I'm sorry, Kate,' Eve said again.

'It wasn't your fault,' Kate said kindly. 'Come on, I'll teach you how to play two balls. Our Patsy can play with three, but now she's had a baby she probably won't do it any more.' They ran off together and Claire gave me a conspiratorial wink, I'm not sure why.

Norah, Roy and Bernadette arrived, followed not long afterwards by our Jamie, Lisa and their baby, Isobel, now ten months old and as beautiful as her mother, who was already pregnant with her second child. I hadn't realized how much I'd missed these family gatherings while I'd lived in Everton Valley. There'd been nothing to stop me coming, but I'd always felt reluctant to leave in case there'd been a crisis. Hilda had been right: it was about time I had a life outside.

On Tuesday, Eve would be nine. She'd specifically requested *not* to have a party. 'I don't like them. At least, I don't like mine. Everybody keeps looking at you and you have to smile all the time and pretend to be enjoying yourself, even though you're not.'

'In that case, you won't have one,' I promised, 'but we can't let your birthday pass without doing something to celebrate. How about I collect you from school and we go to the pictures? Better still, if we left it till Saturday, we could shop for your present and have tea first.'

'Could we go to Southport?' Eve's eyes lit up like two blue stars. 'I like Southport better than Liverpool.'

'Southport it is. I'll find out what pictures are on.' I was already looking forward to it.

I'd left the Mini in Everton Valley for Hilda and Cecily, and was now using Michael's Ford Consul, which was twice as big and used twice as much petrol. On Tuesday, Eve's birthday, I put the car in the garage, closed the doors and was rooting through my bag for the keys to the house, thinking I must remember to put the car keys and the house keys on the same ring, when a woman climbed out of a large gleaming black car parked in the road, and came towards me. She wore the biggest and longest fur coat I'd ever seen, and I could smell her perfume yards away.

'Who are you?' she demanded aggressively. 'And why are you using my son's car?'

'I'm Kitty McCarthy, Michael's sister-in-law. You must be his mother.' I'd entirely forgotten Michael had a mother. Mrs Gilbert and Aileen hadn't got on, I recalled. What Michael's feelings were I had no idea, but he hadn't mentioned her in his letter.

'Where's Michael?' she asked in a voice that was only slightly less aggressive. 'What's going on? It's ages since I heard from him and I rang Wexford's today and was told he'd left. And where's Eve? I've brought her a birthday present.' She held up a George Henry Lee carrier bag.

'Eve will be home from school any minute. As for Michael . . . look, you'd better come in and I'll explain.' It was freezing outside. I opened the door and switched on the lights and the fire. 'Would you like a cup of tea?'

'Not until I've had an explanation as to the whereabouts of my son.'

I hunched my shoulders and spread my hands. 'I've no idea where Michael is. He just went away. He didn't say where he was going or when he'd be back.' In the light, I could see Mrs Gilbert was visibly shaking, not with anger, but because she was deeply upset. She was a handsome woman with dark grey eyes and a regal nose. Her eyebrows were thick and black, contrasting oddly with her perfectly waved silver hair.

'But why? Why did he go away? And where's his wife? Where's,' she paused, then almost spat the next word, '*Aileen*?'

Oh, Lord! She mustn't have been told about the affair. I said, 'Why don't you sit down and take off your coat? It's warm in here.'

She removed her coat and threw it on to the back of a chair, but it slid off with a hissing, slithery sound, as if it had a life of its own, landing in a furry heap on the floor.

I explained what had happened, using as few words as possible, because I wanted to get it over and done with before Eve came, finishing, 'As soon as my sister, Claire, found out that Aileen had gone off with this chap, Steve, we came rushing round to make sure Michael was all right.'

'And was he?' she asked hoarsely, her eyes bright with anguish. Michael was her son and he'd been badly hurt. It was clearly as painful as if Michael had still been a child, not a man in his forties.

'Not really. He was out when we arrived: Eve had been left with a babysitter. When he came home he was drunk, so we put him to bed and decided we'd better stay the night. By the time we woke up next morning, he'd gone. He left a letter saying he wanted me to look after Eve.'

'Can I read it, the letter?'

'I'm afraid I threw it away,' I said steadily. I didn't want her to know I was Eve's mother.

'Did it mention me?'

'Not that I recall.'

'In other words, it didn't. Oh, dear God!' she wept. 'Poor Michael. My poor, dear son.'

The front door opened and I said urgently, 'Mrs Gilbert, please don't let Eve see you like this. She's been coping well since it happened and I'd sooner she wasn't upset.'

'I won't upset her, don't worry.' She wiped her tear-streaked face with the back of her hand. I went into the hall where Eve was hanging her coat behind the cupboard door and told her she had a visitor.

'*I* have?'

'*You* have. Come and say hello.'

'Happy birthday, darling,' Mrs Gilbert sang when we went into the living room. 'I've brought you a present.'

'Hello, Gran,' Eve said shyly. I couldn't tell whether she was pleased to see her grandmother or not. She accepted the carrier bag that Mrs Gilbert proffered and took out a pretty blue quilted dressing gown. 'It's lovely, Gran. Thank you very much.'

'Lovely enough to deserve a kiss?'

Eve politely kissed her cheek. 'Thank you, Gran,' she said again.

'Aren't you having a party for your birthday, darling?'

'No. On Saturday, Kitty and I are going to the cinema in Southport instead.' A note of excitement had entered the young voice. 'We're going shopping and having our tea first.'

'That sounds marvellous, Eve. I hope you enjoy yourself – your*selves*.' Mrs Gilbert nodded in my direction.

I admired her for putting on such a good show when she was so upset over Michael.

Eve went upstairs to get changed. I disappeared into the kitchen to make tea, and discovered all the dishes I'd left in the sink that morning had been washed, dried and put away, along with the teapot, tea caddy, sugar basin and all the other things I'd left out because I couldn't be bothered putting them away myself. I remembered Aileen had employed a cleaner who must still be turning up and was therefore responsible for turning a perfectly normal kitchen into this bare, clinical room. Later, I noticed the beds had been changed and the carpets vacuumed, there wasn't a speck of dust to be seen anywhere. Next week, I'd leave a note telling the woman not to come again, but to let me know how much she was owed. From now on, Eve and I would do the cleaning between us.

Mrs Gilbert appeared in the doorway. 'She seems fine, Eve. You and she get on well together.'

'Do you think so?' I was dead chuffed.

'Although it's not at all surprising; you're her mother, aren't you?'

I was in the act of pouring water into the kettle, but was so startled that the kettle slipped and water splashed all over my skirt. I turned off the tap and listened in case Eve was on her way.

'It's all right. I heard her go in the bathroom. She won't be down for a little while.'

'What on earth made you say that?' I asked, flustered. 'Did Michael tell you?'

'Michael didn't say a word. No, I guessed straight away, the minute you came into the room together. It's the way you look at her.' Her rather stern face melted into a smile. 'You love her, I could tell from your face, and not many aunts love their nieces to that degree. You even stand the same way, with your hands clasped behind your back and one foot almost at right angles to the other.'

I finished pouring water into the kettle, switched it on, searched for the teapot and the caddy, all without speaking. 'I hope no one else guesses,' I said eventually. 'My sister, Claire, is the only one who knows – oh, and the women I work with. It's not myself I'm worried about, but I don't want Eve finding out. She's had enough shocks lately. She wasn't officially adopted, I didn't sign any forms or anything. I'm not even sure if she knows Aileen and Michael aren't her real parents.'

'She doesn't. Michael said they weren't going to tell her until she was older. I argued she'd be better off knowing right from the start, but your sister bit my head off, as usual.' She shrugged. 'You're not at all like your sister, Kitty. Do you mind if I call you Kitty?'

'Well, it's my name, isn't it? Of course I don't mind.'

'You must call me Muriel. Aileen never did. I was still Mrs Gilbert after she'd been married to Michael for over sixteen years. Well,' she said, 'it's nice to have met you and lovely to have seen Eve again, but I'll get out of your way and let you get on with things.'

'But you can't possibly go without a cup of tea! In fact, stay for a meal. I'm not sure what we're having. Eve's already had tea at the Caffreys', but she's still hungry when she gets home. I let her pick what she wants out of the fridge, not that there's much in there. I'm terribly disorganized,' I explained. 'I've never had to buy food before, let alone cook it. I'm slowly learning, with the emphasis on the slowly.'

'I'd love to stay for a meal, thank you,' Muriel said. She looked so pleased that it was bordering on the pathetic.

Eve came in and opened the fridge. We both watched as she put her head on one side and checked what it held, which wasn't much. 'Can I have a bacon sandwich, please?'

'Your wish is my command, luv. Go and sit down; I'll bring it in a minute.'

'Is there enough bacon for me to have one, too?' Muriel asked. I couldn't help but wonder if she'd ever eaten a bacon sarnie before and if she was just trying to be accommodating.

'There's a whole pound, plenty enough.' I felt extremely efficient.

Fifteen minutes later, the three of us were sitting round the fire munching bacon sarnies and watching *Sooty and Sweep*. Later, Muriel and I sat talking quietly about nothing in particular while Eve did her homework. She finished just in time to see *Hancock's Half-Hour* before she went to bed.

'Do you like your gran?' I asked, as she snuggled under the bedclothes with Gloria.

'I like Granddad McCarthy best. He's my favourite granddad in the world, but I like Gran, too.'

'Do you really mean that about your gran, or are you just being polite?'

She giggled. 'I really mean it. She hardly ever came to our house before and we only went to hers at Christmas, but I liked her tonight.'

'That's good.'

'Why is it good?'

'I don't know, it just is.' I quite liked Michael's mother as well.

I went downstairs and found Mrs Gilbert – Muriel – washing the dishes. 'There's no need for that,' I protested.

'It's no bother. Someone's got to do it and it may as well be me. It might make up a little for how rude I was when I arrived. I just didn't know what to think when you drove up in Michael's car. I was already worried stiff after being told by Wexford's that he'd left the company. When I saw a strange woman driving his car, I began to wonder if something terrible had happened and he'd been murdered.' She sighed wearily. 'Something terrible *has* happened, but at least he's still alive.'

'I'm sure he'll get in touch with you soon,' I said soothingly.

'I hope so. We used to be so close, Michael and I.' She stared through the window at the dark, November sky, a faraway look on her face, the dishes forgotten. 'His father died in France in the final year of the Great War when Michael was four. He was our only child. We'd never had the opportunity to have more. I married Hugh in nineteen thirteen, and the war started the following year.

Hugh volunteered. I never saw him again – and he never saw Michael.' She looked at me. 'Do you already know all this?'

'Only that Michael never knew his father; he told me once.'

'He was such a sweet little boy,' she said, her face softening with the memory. 'When Hugh first went away, my father insisted I come and work for him. He sold office supplies wholesale: stationery, ink, reams of paper, that sort of thing. We had, still have, our own little outlet in Liverpool, but we mainly dealt with big firms. It was only so I wouldn't mope and feel lonely stuck at home with a baby. I'd take Michael with me. He'd toddle up and down the aisles between the shelves of stationery, as good as gold. As he grew older, he'd help check the stock with me. We became a partnership, a team. Even when he was eighteen and went to university, he always came home at weekends to see his mum.'

'That sounds just like Michael,' I murmured.

'Doesn't it?' She smiled proudly. 'Of course, I knew it wouldn't last, that one day he'd get married and I'd no longer be the most important person in his life. He didn't have many girlfriends, he was too shy for that, so I was pleased when he met Aileen at Wexford's and they fell in love. I don't really know how things went wrong.' She ran her hand distractedly through her silver hair. 'I didn't *mean* to be possessive, but perhaps I was. He meant so much to me: I couldn't stop caring for him at the drop of a hat. Perhaps I fussed too much, insisted on him wearing a scarf when it was cold, that sort of thing. Whatever it was, Aileen seemed to think I was trying to hold on to him, yet all I wanted was for Michael to be happy. The atmosphere when we were together grew frostier and frostier. There was nothing I could say that she didn't apply a different meaning to. If I said her hair looked nice, she'd take this as inferring that most of the time her hair *didn't* look nice. Then she'd tell Michael I'd said something offensive, and he'd ask me to be nicer to her. In the end, I realized *she* was the possessive one.'

'It must have been awful for you.' I felt shocked. I hadn't known my sister could be such a bitch.

'It was.' She remembered the dishes and began to wash them again. 'I shouldn't be complaining to you like this. After all, Aileen is your sister, but I was worried she'd said things and you might have a bad opinion of me.'

'I didn't have a very good one,' I said truthfully.

'Do you still feel the same now?'

I was wondering why she was looking through the window, not at me, until I noticed both our reflections were as clear as if we were in front of a mirror and it was my reflection she'd addressed the question to.

'No.' I shook my head and said no more.

'Then do you think it possible for me to play some small part in Eve's life?' she said eagerly. 'I've not seen much of her, but I love her just the same. I could look after her if you wanted to go out.' She paused and bit her lip, as if she'd said too much. 'I hope I don't sound too pushy.'

'Not at all. I'm sure Eve will be pleased to get to know her grandmother. And I will too,' I added, smiling.

We had a great day out in Southport. I bought Eve a silver charm bracelet for her birthday and a white *broderie anglaise* blouse for myself. For tea, we had fish and chips followed by sherry trifle, and then went to see Jerry Lewis in *The Bellboy*. I'd considered inviting Muriel along, but it seemed too much too soon, so I'd asked her for a meal a week on Sunday instead.

It seemed almost a miracle that Eve had adapted so easily to the disappearance of Aileen and Michael from her life, but I discovered this wasn't exactly the case the next time I went to see my father.

By now, it was the first Saturday in December and the shops were decorated for Christmas. I'd taken Eve to Liverpool to buy presents for her friends at school, stopping on the way at the house in Everton Valley. I'd already told her all about my job and what it entailed, and had been thrilled to bits when she'd asked if she could see where I worked.

When we went in, Dorothy kissed her, Hilda shook her hand in a terribly grown-up manner and Cecily gave her a pound to buy herself a Christmas present. She met Chrissie and her three-year-old daughter, Nuala, who'd come to stay with us the day before. I explained that the bandage around Nuala's arm covered the spot where her father had stubbed out his cigarette. Eve looked very grave.

After she'd bought the presents for her friends, we had a turkey dinner in Owen Owen's and she said she'd like to spend Cecily's pound on a doll for Nuala. Dinner finished, she bought a large celluloid doll dressed like a fairy in the toy department and delivered it to Everton Valley on the way home. Nuala was having her afternoon nap, but Chrissie looked pleased enough for both of them when Eve presented it to her, blushing slightly.

'Would you like to come to work with me over Christmas, luv?' I asked when we were back in the car. 'There's all sorts of useful things you could do.'

'Oh, Kitty, I'd *love* to,' she breathed. 'Will Nuala be there?'

'I'm not sure. Hilda might have found her and Chrissie somewhere else to live by then.' I felt doubly pleased that I wouldn't have to arrange for Mrs Caffrey or Susan Mercer to look after her during the holidays.

'Are we going home now?' she asked.

'Not yet. I bought a cardy in town for Patsy's Jay, I never got round to buying a prezzie when he was born. I'll call in at Amethyst Street and you can stay with Granddad while I nip round to Auntie Claire's with the cardy. Is that all right with you, sweetheart?'

'It's fine,' she replied, sighing blissfully. She'd never said anything, but I had the feeling she led a much more interesting life nowadays than she had with Aileen.

For once, the house was empty except for Dad. Marge, Danny and the children had gone to a carol concert at St James's Church.

Dad held out his arms and Eve ran and sat on his knee, showering his face with kisses. 'Your face is awfully rough, Granddad,' she complained. 'It hurts a bit.'

'Sorry, luv,' Dad said, stroking his chin, 'but I need a shave and I was leaving it until tonight when I went out. I wasn't expecting a pretty young lady to kiss me before then.'

She looked at him coquettishly. 'D'you think I'm pretty, Granddad?'

'As pretty as a picture, luv – no, even prettier.'

'You're only saying that.' Nevertheless, Eve looked flattered.

I nipped round to Claire's and found her house stuffed with children of various ages. 'I ain't nothing but a hound dog,' Elvis Presley was complaining in the parlour.

'Am I supposed to give this lot their tea?' Claire asked despairingly. She was in the kitchen, arms folded, as if she didn't know which way to turn. 'I don't know who half of them are.'

'Make them sarnies,' I suggested, 'and perhaps they'll go home.'

'If I make them sarnies, it might tempt them to stay. Liam's playing football, so Lord knows what time he'll be home to give us a hand. I told him it was time he gave it up at his age, but he still thinks he's twenty-one.'

I said I'd only come for a minute to deliver the cardy for Jay, else I'd have given her a hand myself. 'I've left Eve with Dad.'

'Our Patsy's coming round later; I'll give it to her then. It seems she's having a problem breastfeeding. I don't know what she expects me to do about it.'

'Give her some advice, I suppose.'

'I suppose.' She sighed and looked harassed. 'I know what I'll do.' She undid the pinny. 'I'll come back with you to Dad's. If anyone wants something to eat, they can make it for themselves and at least I'll have somewhere to sit.'

The minute we opened the door, Dad came out into the hall and put his finger to his lips, 'Shush!' he whispered, 'Eve's asleep. I had to lay her on the sofa in the parlour when me arm began to grow numb.'

'Asleep!' I crept into the parlour where Eve lay with her thumb in her mouth, her face red and swollen. I crept out again and closed the door. 'Has she been crying, Dad?'

'She cried enough to water the Sahara Desert, luv. I don't know what started it.' He looked bewildered and a bit shaken. 'She was sitting on me knee and just began to cry for no apparent reason, as far as I could see. I just patted her back, gently like. People say it doesn't hurt to have a good cry, so I just left her to it. After a while, she stopped and went asleep.'

'I wonder why she did that?' I felt really worried. 'I'm sorry if it upset you.'

'It didn't upset me, luv. Anyroad, it'd hardly be your fault if it did. It surprised me a bit, that's all.' His tough old face was troubled. 'Poor little mite. I could kill our Aileen for going off and leaving her – and Christ only knows what Michael's going through. Have you heard from him yet, Kitty?'

'No. I don't really expect to, at least not for a while.'

'He's the salt of the earth, Michael. No man could've had a better son-in-law. It's just not fair the way he's been treated.'

Claire announced she was about to make a drink, but I grabbed her arm and shoved her into a chair. 'Every time I talk to you, you're standing in front of a sink. Sit down, *I'll* make the drink.'

Eve was her usual, talkative self in the car on the way back to Maghull. I wanted to ask her why she'd cried, but decided it was best to let her broach the subject herself. But she never did. It was almost as if she'd forgotten about the incident, or perhaps she thought she'd dreamt it. But it happened again just after Christmas when Marge and I took the children to see *The Wizard of Oz* and Eve asked if she could stay with Granddad instead. It was as if he was the person with whom she could let go without feeling embarrassed. I felt a bit hurt that she didn't like to cry in front of me, but although I deliberately left her alone with my father a few more times, she didn't cry again. It had just been her way of grieving for the loss of the two people she'd thought were her mam and dad and, from now on, I thought hopefully, she would accept and grow to love her Auntie Kitty as much as she'd loved them.

It seemed to happen overnight, the way Liverpool changed from being a city like any other in the British Isles to one of the most famous in the world. The reason could only be put down to four young men who called themselves The Beatles, a basement club in Mathew Street called The Cavern, and a new type of music known as rock 'n' roll.

Liverpool groups dominated the music charts and every lad I knew was nagging his parents for a guitar. Our Claire's eldest, Mark, started a group, The Termites. None could play an instrument and the noise they made was painful, but Claire and Liam had every faith that one day they would become famous. Eve spent every penny of her pocket money on records, and the house rocked to the sound of Gerry and The Pacemakers, The Three Jays, The Searchers and, of course, The Beatles.

Marge and I went to The Cavern one night, just to see what it was like, but we were thirty and everyone else was at least ten years younger. We felt out of place. 'We're part of a lost generation,' I moaned. 'Too young to have taken part in the war, and too old to enjoy The Cavern.'

'Still,' Marge sighed, 'as long as we can tell our grandkids we saw the place. Shall we leave and go to the pictures instead?'

We went to see *The Apartment* with Jack Lemmon and Shirley Maclaine. It was very touching, but I found it hard to concentrate. For the first time in my life, I felt old, on the outside looking in. All sorts of exciting things were happening in the world that I could no longer be part of, though when the Liverpool Poets became famous for their *avant garde* poems, I joined a poetry group and we met at each other's houses once a month and self-consciously read our work aloud. I asked Eve if she'd like to contribute, but she'd lost interest in poetry.

The years slid inexorably by. Eve was ten, eleven, twelve . . . She didn't exactly refuse to attend the private senior school where most of her classmates were going, but asked if she could please go to the William Morris Comprehensive, which was only a short walk away from Dickens Road. 'The girls are much nicer and they don't have to learn Latin and daft stuff like that. They do cookery and learn to type as well.'

'And there's boys there, too,' I said with a smile.

'I like boys,' she admitted frankly, 'but the only ones I know are my cousins and their friends.'

I had worried about her going to another single-sex school. The role of women was changing – not that I'd noticed, but I'd read about it in the papers. Women were becoming more assertive, demanding equal pay for equal work. They could see no earthly reason why some jobs were regarded as the prerogative of men.

Eve was allowed to attend the school of her choice. I didn't say I'd sooner she learned Latin rather than cooking and typing, thus ruining all chance of her becoming a doctor, for instance, but ensuring she'd make a good housewife with a menial job in an office in between.

Anyway, the comprehensive school was free and Michael's monthly payments had suddenly stopped a few months before. I couldn't possibly afford the high fees demanded by the public school. Muriel Gilbert had become a good friend and I knew she would be only too willing to help – she was a wealthy woman and often asked if I was in need of cash, but I always refused. I was glad I didn't have to ask her to pay for Eve's schooling.

I couldn't help but wonder what had happened to Michael. He'd never been in touch with me, or his mother. He could be anywhere in the world. There'd been no word from Aileen, either. Even Claire, with her contact at Wexford's, hadn't the faintest idea of our sister's whereabouts.

'Mildred Sweeney's convinced she went to Australia,' she told me once.

'What makes her say that?' I asked.

'Nothing. She just feels it in her water.'

Life continued, pleasant but uneventful, though earth-shattering events were taking place outside the confines of my comfortable little world. Late one afternoon, a week after Eve's twelfth birthday, I turned on the television to discover President Kennedy had been assassinated in a place called Dallas in Texas. I wept, I don't know why. Perhaps it was because, unlike most politicians, he'd seemed so genuinely nice and sincere. A year later, America appeared to be on the verge of another war, this time in Vietnam, another country that, like Korea, I'd never heard of.

I'd told Eve about Will and Jeff and the telegram that had killed her grandma. 'She thought it was to say Jamie was dead, but it turned out to be for next door.'

'Oh, Kitty, that's awfully sad,' she said sombrely. 'I bet Granddad was upset.'

'We all were,' I assured her.

We were very close, Eve and I, more in the way of sisters than mother and daughter. I conscientiously attended all the school events: the concerts, the speech days and sports days. I had a few boyfriends, but none was as serious as the relationship I'd had with Connor Daley, who remained the only man I'd ever slept with. Would things have been any less pleasant, less eventful, had I married him? I often mused. I would still have gone to Amethyst Street to see my father every Sunday, and to the pictures with Marge once a month. And Eve would still be my daughter, though I could well have had more children by now. I was still waiting for something spectacular to happen that I would have missed had I been married, but I seemed destined to wait for ever. Or perhaps that was just an excuse and I wasn't the marrying kind.

*

Eve bought her first lipstick and became very particular about what she wore. At fourteen, she was taller than me by about three inches with long, slim legs that were shown off to perfection in one of the new fashioned mini-skirts. I bought one for myself, but never had the courage to wear it outside the house, worried I'd look like mutton dressed up as lamb. Because mini-skirts looked grotesque with a suspender belt and stockings, tights came into being, so women no longer had to suffer the torture of metal suspenders pressing against their thighs.

Claire said Liam had forbidden her to wear tights because they weren't remotely sexy. 'Or at least he tried,' she reported. 'I told him to get stuffed. If he fancies suspender belts all that much, he can have my old ones with pleasure. Me, I'm sticking to tights. They're a million times more comfortable.'

And so it continued, my pleasant and uneventful life, until 1966 when three things happened: I lost my job, my father died and Eve discovered that I was her real mother.

Chapter 7

Hilda had stopped the parcels years ago, not because the nappies and clothes were no longer needed, but because we didn't have the time. Nowadays, the house in Everton Valley was full to capacity with the wives and children of violent men who'd turned to us for shelter. It wasn't that men were becoming more violent, but it had gradually seeped through to women that their husbands had no right to treat them as their own personal punchbags.

No one was turned away even if all the bedrooms were occupied. They slept in the living room, or Dorothy gave up her own room and slept on a camp bed with Hilda, until they could be found alternative accommodation.

Often I would arrive in the morning and find a couple of policemen present because some irate man had discovered the whereabouts of his family and hammered on the door in the middle of the night screaming for them back. On two occasions men broke in the back way and each time Cecily had been physically assaulted when she tried to stop them from flinging open doors in search of their already bruised and battered families.

The noise was relentless. Children slid down the banisters and played on the landings. Despite the injuries they'd suffered at the hands of someone much stronger than themselves, it didn't stop some of the women from inflicting similar injuries on their children – or on other women's children if they felt so inclined. Fights frequently broke out, but Hilda flatly refused to tolerate aggression under her own roof. Her attempts to keep the peace frequently resulted in her being treated to a shower of abuse from the very people she only wanted to help.

'It's not their fault,' she would claim afterwards. 'It's just that it's all they've ever known, poor things: violence and abuse. Most of the women are grateful for what we do.'

Nevertheless, Hilda and Dorothy were over seventy and Cecily wasn't far off. I felt guilty that I slept peacefully in Maghull, leaving them to cope with the trauma of running the shelter. I wasn't surprised when one day Hilda announced that she'd had enough.

'I never thought I'd say this, Kitty, but things are getting too much for me. I'm selling the house and buying a little bungalow in Formby for Dorothy and me,' she told me in the office during a rare quiet moment. 'I think we have both earned some peace and tranquillity in our declining years. There are so many books I would like to read and programmes on television I would like to see. And Dorothy has hobbies she would like to pursue, but hasn't the time.'

I noticed for the first time how frail and stooped Hilda looked, how tired her eyes were, and recalled the day I had first met this kind, vivacious woman on the train to Liverpool less than twenty-four hours after I'd had Eve. I said tearfully, 'I can't imagine life without you and Dorothy.'

'You'll manage, dear,' she assured me with a smile, 'and there's a good chance you won't be out of a job. Another charity based in London is purchasing the house and it will remain what it has become, a shelter for abused women. They have some very rich donors and intend to employ permanent wardens, a day one and a night one. The rest of the staff will be volunteers who'll work four-hour shifts. I have already suggested you for the day warden and I'm sure they'll jump at the chance of having someone so experienced.'

'Thank you, Hilda.' I felt relieved that I wouldn't have to look for another job. 'What's happening to Cecily?'

She smiled again. 'Cecily is going back to Calderstones to look after her husband who is very ill and in need of constant nursing. I doubt if it will be for long,' she added drily. 'Anyway, dear, next month, March, a woman from the new charity is coming from London to get the feel of the place, as it were. Her name is Millicent de Silva, she sounded very nice on the phone, and I'm sure you and she will get on like a house on fire. She'll be staying a week, at the end of which Dorothy and I plan to move to our bungalow overlooking the Mersey, where we shall watch the waves lap on to the beach, think about the house in Everton Valley and wonder how you are getting on.'

★

Millicent de Silva was an attractive, terribly well-spoken women of about forty with sleek black hair parted in the middle and coiled in a bun at the nape of her slender white neck. She wore a smart black-and-white striped suit with a crisply starched blouse underneath, and looked as if she'd just stepped out of the pages of a fashion magazine. Hilda designated me to show her around. At the present time, we had three women and nine children living on the premises.

It was dinnertime and the first room we went into was the kitchen where three of the children and their mother, Sheila, were seated at the table while Dorothy ladled out a mouth-watering stew.

'Hello, Kit.' Sheila gave me a nod. She sported a whopping black eye and her arm was in a sling – fortunately, it was only a sprained wrist.

'Hello, Kit,' the children echoed.

'Hello, everybody.' I patted the children's heads. 'How are you feeling today, Sheila?'

'Well enough to give that fucking husband of mine what for if he was around,' Sheila growled. 'I'd like to empty that pan of fucking scouse over him.'

'It's not scouse, dear,' Dorothy pointed out. 'It's Scotch broth.'

'Whatever it is, I'd like to blind the bugger with it.'

'Sheila's been with us for three days,' I told Millicent when we were back in the hall. 'Her husband hasn't been in work for years and he takes it out on her and the children. Hilda's applied for a council house for them, but I don't know how long she'll have to wait. Shall we go upstairs?'

I knocked softly on the first door we came to at the top. 'Are you and the kids up yet, Edie?'

The door opened a crack. 'I'll be down in a mo,' a voice whispered. 'I'm dying for a cuppa, but the kids are still asleep. It was long past midnight by the time our Tommy dropped off.'

'Well, there's always tea in the pot, luv,' I whispered back. 'Just help yourself. Edie only arrived late last night,' I explained to Millicent when the door closed. 'She has four small children. Her husband came home from work in a terrible rage. He was swinging the baby around by his ankles, threatening to throw him against the wall, but Edie managed to rescue him and flee the house with the other kids. They'd been wandering the streets for hours until the police found them and gave them our address. We think she'll go back to her husband eventually. She said it was the first time he'd ever done such a thing.'

'I see.' Millicent nodded, her face expressionless. 'You have a very relaxed attitude here.'

'We have to. The families have been through terrible times – it takes a lot of courage to leave home, however awful it is.' A lump came to my throat. 'Me, I think they're terribly brave. I admire them very much.'

'I see,' she said again.

I showed her Sheila's room with its untidy jumble of beds, creaky old wardrobe and chest of drawers, then took her up another flight of stairs. 'Only one of these rooms is occupied at the moment. Anne Jones has two lovely children. Her husband is an electrician who suffers from attacks of severe depression but refuses to see a doctor. During the last attack, he almost strangled her so she had no alternative but to leave. Every day, she takes the children for long walks in the pushchair. I've no idea what's going to happen to them.' Anne's room was impeccably tidy, the beds were neatly made and there was not an article of clothing in sight. 'There's an attic upstairs,' I went on. 'I lived there for years. When I left, Cecily moved in, but now she's leaving there'll be an extra room.'

'I see,' Millicent de Silva said for the third time. 'Thank you for showing me around, Kitty. Now I'd like to discuss the financial side of things with Hilda.'

It was an awfully strange five days. Millicent was staying at the Adelphi, the best hotel in Liverpool, and came every day dressed up to the nines in a different outfit. Hilda let her have the run of the place and I often came across her making notes on a pad. I couldn't quite make her out and kept hoping she would offer me the job of day warden, but so far it hadn't been mentioned. On Friday, the volunteers arrived and she showed them around. They seemed terribly posh, but then so was Hilda, who had the biggest, kindest heart in the world.

Hilda and Dorothy disappeared into their rooms whenever they had a spare minute to pack their things ready for Formby, while Cecily returned to Calderstones after a great deal of emotional hugging and kissing and promising not to lose touch.

'Of course we won't lose touch,' Hilda said gruffly. 'You and

Kitty must come and see us. Come at Easter – Easter Sunday – and Dorothy will make a scrumptious tea, won't you, Dottie, dear?'

'I can't wait,' Dorothy assured us.

'Easter Sunday it is.' Cecily looked delighted. After more hugging and kissing, she left. The house felt even stranger without her and I hated to think what it would be like when Hilda and Dorothy had gone, too.

As expected, Edie went back to her husband after he'd apologised profusely and promised never to do it again – a promise I'd heard before, but wasn't always kept – Sheila was allotted a council house in Huyton and Anne Jones went to live with her mother in Portsmouth, while her husband agreed to have medical treatment for his depression. Their rooms were only empty a matter of hours before being occupied again and I missed the arrival of Ivy Glaister, our oldest resident yet. Ivy was over eighty and full of beans, despite having half her ear sewn back on in the hospital before being sent to us in the early hours of the morning.

'It was our Albert what done it, me brother,' she said. 'Running round the house with a razor like a flamin' madman, he was. I ain't going back home till he's been put in the loony bin. The Bobbies are sorting him out today.'

Millicent de Silva called me into the office late on Friday afternoon, saying she'd like us to have a little talk. She seated herself behind Hilda's desk and said, 'I expect you know Hilda recommended you for the post of day warden?'

'She did mention it, yes,' I muttered. I noticed how beautifully made up her eyes were and wondered if I'd suit eyeliner.

'I'm very sorry,' she said kindly, 'but after watching you at work I am unwilling to go along with her recommendation. To be blunt, I find you over-familiar with the women and you allow them to be over-familiar with you, when you should be cool and detached. You are also too emotional, empathizing with their problems, making them your own. Instead of being a figure of authority, you become their friend.'

I felt myself go very hot. 'But they've already run away from a figure of authority,' I argued, 'and it's the last thing they want. They *need* a friend, someone who understands how they feel and what they've been through.'

'I couldn't possibly disagree with you more, Kitty, but it would be a waste of both your time and mine to discuss it any further.' She handed me an envelope in a gesture of dismissal. 'Here are two weeks' wages in lieu of notice. Hilda and Dorothy are moving into their new house tomorrow, so there'll be no need for you to come again. As from tomorrow, the new staff will take over. I shall act as day warden until we find somebody suitable.'

I found Hilda in her bedroom where she and Dorothy were sitting on the bed looking very glum.

'She hasn't given you the job, has she, dear?' Hilda cried when she saw my face was probably the glummest of the lot. 'I didn't say anything, but I thought there was a chance she might not. You're too nice, not strict enough. She doesn't approve of us being on first-name terms with the women. In fact, she doesn't approve of anything we've done.'

'She's one of those frightfully posh, extremely wealthy women who take up charity work to fill in their time and make them feel good about themselves,' Dorothy said disgustedly. 'Look at this!' She handed me a sheet of paper. 'It's a list of rules.'

'Rules!' I read the list with a mixture of anger and amazement. The women were expected to be up by eight, have their breakfast by nine, then carry out their allotted tasks. Lunch was at twelve-thirty, dinner at six – between these times the kitchen was out of bounds. Lights out was half past ten, after which complete silence was expected. There was to be no swearing, children weren't allowed to play on the stairs and alcohol wasn't allowed on the premises. The last was the only rule Hilda had made. 'What does she mean by "allotted tasks"?' I enquired.

'Cleaning, I suppose.' Hilda sniffed dejectedly. 'It sounds more like a prison than a shelter.'

'No wonder she wants wardens day and night,' I snorted. 'Liverpool women will never stand for it. She'll have a rebellion on her hands the first week.'

I arranged to meet Hilda and Dorothy in Formby the next morning to help them unpack, and then I went home, jobless for the first time in my life apart from the short time I'd spent in Graham's flat in

Mayfair, which you couldn't really count because I'd been expecting Eve.

Eve didn't arrive home at her usual time and I remembered she was staying late for the debating society that had just been formed. Tonight, they were discussing the pros and cons of vivisection. I cursed, because I badly wanted to moan to someone about what had happened and Eve was the obvious person. I rang our Claire instead.

Kate answered and informed me her mam was out. 'She went into town with Auntie Norah and she's not back yet. Our tea's going to be awfully late,' she complained, as if she expected me to do something about it.

It meant it was no good ringing Norah, and I couldn't speak to Dad or Marge because they didn't have a telephone in Amethyst Street. In desperation, I rang Muriel Gilbert, who listened sympathetically to the whole story and agreed Millicent de Silva sounded an out-and-out bitch.

'What are you going to do for money?' she asked.

'Oh, I'll manage,' I said confidently. 'They gave me two weeks' wages in lieu of notice. I'm bound to have found another job by the time it runs out.'

'Don't forget that to all intents and purposes Eve is my granddaughter and it was my son who deserted her. I shall be very cross if I find you've been reduced to pinching and scraping and didn't ask for help.'

I promised faithfully I would tell her if there was any danger of us starving to death or being taken to court for non-payment of bills.

'Good,' she said. 'Oh, and if you can't find a job, Kitty, I know of one that's likely to fall vacant any minute.'

'What sort of job?'

'In a shop, *our* shop, the little stationer's I told you about in North John Street.' Muriel and her brother, Paul, whom I'd never met, had inherited their father's business. 'You won't believe this,' Muriel continued, 'but Robert MacKendrick, who manages the place, was actually a friend of my father's. Dad would be well over ninety if he were alive, so Robert can't be far off that himself. I think it's his intention to die on the premises, but I've told him I'm not having it. Anyway, I've talked him into retiring at Easter. The job's yours if you want it, Kitty.'

'I'll think about it,' I promised, but hoped that's all I'd have to do.

After working for fourteen years in a refuge, I rather hoped to find more interesting work than in a shop.

I sighed and trudged upstairs, looking forward to a long soak in a hot bath. I emerged from the rapidly cooling water half an hour later feeling much better about myself, but the good feeling cooled as rapidly as the water when I caught a glimpse of my towel-wrapped figure in the full-length mirror on the landing.

Why hadn't I noticed before that my hair was such a mess and I looked a good forty when I was only thirty-four? I closely examined my face for the first time in years. Bits of it had sagged and there were lines running down from the side of my nose to my chin – or would have, except I no longer seemed to have a chin. Where had it gone? I patted it frantically until it appeared; it was due to my posture that it had sunk into my neck. I'd forgotten how to stand up straight. I stood up and immediately looked better. Gingerly, I let the towel drop and, to my dismay, discovered I had a spare tyre. Now that I was about to look for a job, it wouldn't be a bad idea to smarten myself up. I'd got into the habit of throwing on my oldest clothes when I went to work and not bothering with make up. I touched my toes, relieved that I could still reach them. Tomorrow, I'd have my hair cut and styled, and I'd do exercises every day until I got my figure back. Then I'd buy some new clothes.

A few weeks later my hair looked better, I was gradually losing the spare tyre, had bought a frock from C&A Modes – navy-blue, A-line, barely reaching my knees – and was convinced I looked fantastic, yet no one was prepared to offer me a job. I'd written to every charity in Liverpool and a few beyond – beautifully written letters, the grammar perfect – but it appeared my years with the shelter didn't count when I didn't have a single qualification to my name.

In the end, I contacted Muriel to say I'd take the job in her shop, my heart in my mouth, worried it might have already gone.

'Would you be able to start the Tuesday after Easter?' she enquired.

'Yes.' I tried not to sound as miserable as I felt.

'Shall we meet in the shop at around half past eight? It's ages since I've been there and I suspect Robert has neglected the place dreadfully. It's been losing money for years, yet it's in an ideal position and could make a mint in the right hands.'

'What's happened to Robert?'

'I persuaded him to go back to Scotland. He has brothers there. They must be a very hardy, long-living family.'

'So, who's been looking after the shop?'

'No one, dear, it's closed. I was waiting for you to find a job before I took on someone else, so you'd have the shop to fall back on if you were unsuccessful.'

'Oh, Muriel,' I said emotionally. 'You're so *kind*.'

On Easter Sunday afternoon, I had tea with Hilda and Dorothy. The bungalow was surrounded by a rocky wall and situated on the very edge of Formby Sands. We sat on easy chairs in front of the picture window, watched the Mersey chop and churn, and ate cucumber sandwiches and an assortment of Dorothy's delicious cakes: Easter biscuits, Swiss fingers dipped in chocolate icing, coffee whirls, pineapple cream tarts . . . My mouth watered just looking at them.

'I've made two simnel cakes for you and Cecily to take home,' she informed me.

'She's been in her element for days,' Hilda chuckled.

Cecily had left her husband with a neighbour for the afternoon. 'He hasn't got long to go. I desperately wish I could care more, but whenever I hold his hand I can't help but remember the times he used it to punch me.'

'I hope he appreciates what you're doing for him,' Hilda barked.

'Oh, I think he does. Sometimes he looks at me and I can see something in his eyes, as if he's asking me to forgive him. Perhaps I will have by the time the end comes.'

We watched the sky grow darker and the water take on a silvery hue. A man walked by throwing stones for his dog, followed by a couple, strolling arm in arm. They must have gone too close to the incoming tide, because the woman suddenly screamed and the man laughed as he dragged her away.

'It's lovely and restful here.' I snuggled further into my chair. 'How are you getting on with all those books you wanted to read, Hilda?' She appeared much less exhausted since she'd retired.

To my surprise, she pulled a face. 'Not so well. To tell the truth, I find things a bit *too* restful. I'm bored. I miss the refuge and the women, never knowing what was going to happen tomorrow or the next day.'

'You probably need a few months to wind down,' Cecily suggested.

'Possibly, but I'm thinking of taking up bridge and joining the Women's Institute. In September, I shall go to night school and take something that will exercise my brain.'

'Before you know it,' Dorothy said, 'she'll be as busy as ever.'

I told them about the job I was starting the day after tomorrow and they promised, if ever they needed ink or a writing pad, they'd come and buy it from the shop in North John Street.

The shop was barely ten feet wide and I reckoned it hadn't been treated to lick of paint since the year dot when it had been done a dark, dismal brown. There were more bare patches than paint and the name 'Ainsworth's Stationery' in gold was barely legible. (Ainsworth was Muriel's maiden name.) I must have passed it loads of times, but hadn't noticed it before, which wasn't surprising seeing as the window was used, not to display items for sale, but to store them. Dusty boxes were piled on top of more dusty boxes, and the dust looked too thick to have accumulated since Robert MacKendrick had gone to Scotland. This dust was as long-lived as him and his brothers.

'There's a lavatory at the back that probably needs cleaning,' Muriel told me while she showed me around – it took less than a minute – 'and a sink and a gas-ring for boiling water so you can make yourself a cup of tea whenever you want.'

The lavatory stank to high heaven, the gas-ring was encrusted with soot and the tiny sink looked as if it might once have been white; added to which, the floor needed scrubbing, the wooden counter was crying out for a good polish and the window was too dirty to see out of. I wouldn't have been surprised to learn the telephone was the first one ever made, along with the till.

'If I'd known it was in such a state, I'd have done something about it before,' Muriel said, wrinkling her nose. 'I'd better leave it closed another week and get someone in to clean it from top to bottom and have the front painted.'

'*I'll* do it,' I announced. 'The cleaning, I mean, not the painting.' I was fed up sitting at home twiddling my thumbs, and noticed a brown overall hanging behind the door to the back of the shop that I could wear over my frock. 'Tell me where I can buy cleaning stuffs around here and I'll get started straight away.'

'Are you sure, Kitty?'

'It'll do me good. Might even finish off my spare tyre. If I get the paint, will you arrange for someone to do it as soon as possible?'

'Are you about to clean the *Queen Mary*, luv?' the man in the basement hardware shop close to Exchange Station enquired when I reeled off the list of cleaning materials I required: Vim, Harpic, a window leather, a tin of polish, half a dozen dusters, a scrubbing brush and Brillo pads. Muriel had given me the money.

'Are you sure there's nothing you've forgotten, like?' he said when everything was spread on the counter.

'Yes, a floor cloth. Oh, and some disinfectant with a nice smell: pine, if you've got it. I'll be back tomorrow for paint. Have you got a bright red?' Muriel hadn't specified a colour.

'I've got pillar-box red. Would that do?'

'Pillar-box red would do fine, thanks.'

I spent the entire day scrubbing and scraping. I had to return to the hardware shop to buy a bucket for the water to clean the windows, a feather duster to get the cobwebs off the ceiling, and a small ladder. The man offered to carry the ladder for me. Apart from window-cleaning, it would be useful for the top shelves that were beyond my reach and had clearly been beyond Robert MacKendrick's reach, as they were empty apart from the inevitable dust.

'How's it going?' the man asked on the way.

'I'm slowly getting there. At least the place smells nice.'

I cleaned the windows inside and out, and was giving the inside a final polish, when a young man poked his head around the door and asked, 'Are *you* for sale?'

I fluttered my eyelashes. 'A million quid and I'm yours.'

'Give me ten minutes while I pop round to the bank.' He grinned and I grinned back. He was rather nice, about twenty-five, wearing a dark suit, a dazzling white shirt and striped tie. 'Seriously—'

'I thought you were already being serious?'

'*Seriously*, is Ainsworth's opening up again with you in charge or are you just the window-cleaner?'

'I'm in charge *and* the window-cleaner.'

'Has old Robert gone to meet his maker?'

'No, he's gone to live with his brothers in Scotland.'

'Wow!' He looked impressed. 'Will I be able to buy stationery off you tomorrow?'

'We're open for business, so you can buy it today, except you'll have to wait while I look for it.'

'Tomorrow will do. I want five reams of white foolscap and five reams of flimsy. No, make that one ream of each, and then I'll have an excuse to come in for the next five days. Bye – what's your name?'

'Kitty.'

'Bye, Kitty.' He winked. 'I'm Kieran, by the way.'

'Tara, Kieran.'

He stuffed his hands in his pockets and walked away whistling 'Love Me Do'. I felt quite chuffed at the exchange, and began to wonder if Millicent de Silva had done me a favour by not wanting me as day warden in the shelter, where the only men I'd ever met were wife-beaters or policemen. I finished the cleaning singing 'Love Me Do' at the top of my voice.

Next morning, I was faced with the problem of what to put in the window. The shelves that went up to the ceiling on three sides of the shop were now packed with reams of paper all clearly marked, as were the boxes containing black, blue, red, lilac and green ink. I knew exactly where to find the carbon paper, the fountain pens, the ordinary pens, nibs, pencils, shorthand notebooks and all the other stuff that people in offices used, as well as the things they didn't, such as confetti, birthday cards, tissue paper in a variety of colours, children's crayons, sketch pads and felt pens.

In the end, I contented myself with putting the non-office stuff in the window, arranging it casually, with a sketch pad in the middle, open on the first page, on which I had scrawled in big, bold letters, 'We don't just stock stationery.'

'Very artistic,' Kieran said when he came in. 'A ream of white copy paper and a ream of flimsy, please, and can I have a receipt to show the boss?'

'Won't he wonder why you're wasting time buying paper in dribs and drabs instead of all in one go?' I asked while I struggled with the ancient till.

'Probably, but he's also my dad and won't mind.'

'What does your dad do?' I asked curiously.

'He's a solicitor. So am I, but he gets all the interesting cases and all I get is the dross.'

'Poor you!' I said with mock sympathy as I handed him the receipt.

'See you again tomorrow.' He left with a cheery wave and I buried myself in the office supplies catalogue Muriel had given me the day before for when I wanted to re-order. It sold everything, from desks to duplicators. After a while, I added something else to the sketch pad in the window: 'Don't forget, you can buy your office furniture and machinery through us.' Muriel had said the shop could make a mint in the right hands and I was determined to prove that my hands were the right ones.

Half an hour later, the man arrived to do the painting and by the end of the day Ainsworth's Stationery was bright red instead of dingy brown and the name was painted in black. I'd also served ten satisfied customers, made a list of the new opening times and stuck it behind the door – I would no longer be closed for lunch or on Wednesday afternoons, but would only open from nine to twelve on Saturdays.

Millicent de Silva *had* done me a favour. This job was fun and, although working in the shelter had been extremely worthwhile, after fourteen years I reckoned I deserved some fun for a change.

'If you'd like to earn a bit of extra pocket money,' I said to Eve, 'you can look after the shop on Saturday mornings.'

'How much would I get?' she asked eagerly.

'Seven and six an hour. That's twenty-two and sixpence for three hours, but you'd have your fares to pay out of that.' I'd earned less than that in a week when I'd first started at Cameron's Shoe Factory.

'I travel half-fare so that wouldn't be much. It means I'll have more than a whole pound to myself. And I can meet my friends in town as usual. Oh, Kitty!' Her blue eyes shone. 'I'd love to.'

'I thought you might.'

After six weeks in the shop, I'd learned that most offices were closed on Saturday and business was very slow. Some of Eve's friends had little jobs – washing dishes in pubs, delivering papers and the like. They spent their money on clothes, more clothes and make-up.

Her life was pretty much the same as mine had been at fourteen, except she and her friends had more pocket money. Muriel slipped Eve a pound every now and then, and I pretended not to notice. Even when Marge and I had gone to work, our wages went straight to our mothers and we were handed back a few bob for ourselves. We'd wander around the shops in Stanley Road on Saturday afternoons – Woolworths where nothing cost more than a tanner was the favourite – whereas Eve and her friends went into town and roamed the big department stores. They had coffee in the Kardomah while me and Marge had shared a threepenny bag of chips. I doubt if they had a better time than we'd had, but I envied their youth and the fact that they had their entire lives ahead of them. I just hoped Eve wouldn't make the same mistakes Marge and I had.

Cecily came to buy cards announcing the death of her husband.

'I suppose I feel sad,' she said over a cup of tea – I gave tea to all my relatives and friends – 'but not all *that* sad. I'm going to sell the house in Calderstones and buy something smaller, then travel the world. There's all sorts of exotic foreign countries I'd like to visit.'

Hilda and Dorothy bought a writing pad each and two bottles of ink – lavender and green – and Dorothy came alone one day to buy a Parker fountain pen for Hilda's seventy-third birthday. Hilda had joined the Women's Institute and taken up whist as well as bridge, she informed me. 'And she's going to take politics and current affairs at night school. She's so busy I hardly ever see her.'

'Do you mind?' I asked anxiously. It would be awful if Dorothy felt lonely.

'Not a bit. She can be a pest if I'm engrossed in some intricate embroidery and she won't shut up. I've just started a big tapestry of the Battle of Trafalgar. It's likely to take years.' Dorothy gave a sigh of satisfaction.

Later the same day, a young woman opened the door wanting to know if we sold birthday cards. 'I meant to buy one in W.H. Smiths, but forgot and don't feel like walking all the way back.' I confirmed we stocked cards and she asked if it was all right to bring the pushchair in. 'Some shops refuse to have them.'

'Of course it's all right.' I came around the counter and held open the door. 'Your little boy might be frightened if he wakes up and finds his mummy's disappeared. I see he's already playing football.'

The child, about a year old with a stack of blond curls, wore a miniature Everton kit. 'What's his name?'

'Gary.' She laughed. 'If he doesn't become a professional footballer and play for Everton when he grows up, I think me husband will kill himself.' She put her head on one side. 'Haven't I seen you somewhere before?'

'I was just wondering the same thing.' We stared at each other. I had a feeling she was connected with the refuge. 'You're Peggy Tyler!' I gasped after a while. Hilda had aborted her father's baby on the kitchen table. I hoped she wouldn't feel uncomfortable about us meeting again and was relieved when her pretty face broke into a smile.

'It's Peggy Spencer now, and you're a nurse – I can't remember your name.'

'Kitty McCarthy, though I never was a nurse: people just assumed it. And now you're married with a baby!' I was really pleased that life appeared to have turned out well for Peggy. From her happy face, I could tell she hadn't been scarred by the disgusting thing her father had done to her. 'How's your mother these days?'

She smiled again. 'You'd never recognize Mam if you saw her,' she said proudly. 'She really pulled herself together after our dad walked out. Now all the kids are at school and she's got a part-time job. I'll tell her you were asking after her; she'll be dead pleased.'

'Your father left?' I wasn't all that surprised.

'It wasn't long after the lady from the refuge came to the house – I can't remember her name, either.'

'Hilda Foxton,' I supplied.

'Me, I wasn't there, but our Lillian told us about it afterwards. From that day on, Mam seemed to change, and so did our dad.' Her eyes glowed as if the memory still gave her pleasure. 'It was as if the boot was on the other foot. Anyroad, one morning he went to work and never came back. Nobody cared,' she added laconically.

I bet they didn't. I offered her a drink, but she said there wasn't time, that she had to get home and start on the tea, but would I mind if she and Gary dropped in next time they were in town?

I said I'd love to see her again, and she was already on her way out before we remembered the birthday card.

Our Claire and Norah often dropped in for a chat and a cuppa, and some of my customers hung around for so long I half expected a search party to come looking for them. It was hard to believe that stuffy-looking Mr Manning who worked in insurance had spent the war years fighting Rommel in the North African desert, or that pale Mr Swanson, a solicitor's clerk who walked with a limp, had flown a Spitfire in the Battle of Britain when he was only eighteen. I learned that Miss Mary Sutcliffe, secretary to an accountant, had lost her fiancé in a car accident thirty years before. 'We were both twenty-one' she said, 'and I've never met another man I wanted to marry.' I felt tempted to offer everyone a cup of tea, but worried I'd end up with a restaurant on my hands. At any rate, the takings had increased threefold since I'd taken over, and Muriel was thrilled to bits.

'What on earth are you doing in town?' I exclaimed one lovely sunny afternoon in June when the bell on the door rang and my father entered the shop.

'Just came to see how you're getting on, luv.' He settled in the chair on the other side of the counter and took a good look around. 'It's nice here. Cosy. Interesting, too, with all those boxes. I suppose you know what's in every one?'

'Every single one, Dad. Just say if you want some paperclips or a stapler and I'll get them for you in a jiffy.'

'I don't know what a stapler is, luv, and I've never had much use for paperclips.' He looked at me proudly. 'Our Claire told me you're the only one in charge. I suppose that makes you the manageress.'

'I suppose it does,' I conceded, 'though I haven't got any staff under me, unless you count Eve who works here on Saturdays.'

'Even so, you're a clever girl, Kitty, running the place all on your own. It looks dead complicated to me.'

'Not really,' I said modestly. 'You're looking well, Dad.' He was going on for eighty, but was the picture of health: his face was pink from the sun and his eyes were bright and full of vigour.

'I feel it, luv. I feel it.' He straightened his broad shoulders, as if to prove how strong and well he felt. 'Later, I think I might go for a sail across the Mersey, just to New Brighton and back. Me and your mam used to do it when we were courting and hard up for a few bob. Sometimes, you could sit on the ferry for hours on end, just sailing back and forth, if they didn't come round to check the tickets.'

'That'll be nice, Dad.' I looked out of the window where the glittering sun was making the pavements shimmer. 'In fact, I wish I could come with you.'

'I wish you could too, luv. It'd be just like going with your mam – you're most like her than any of me other girls.'

For a moment, I was tempted to close the shop and go with him, but I was the 'manageress' and should know better.

He stayed a while longer to finish his tea, then got to his feet as nimbly as a man half his age, and kissed the tip of my nose. 'Well, I'll be off, Bernie, luv.'

'Tara, Dad.' He'd called me by Mam's name for the first time ever. It made a lump come to my throat and I wanted to cry, but lumps came to my throat at the drop of a hat and I was forever wanting to cry for no earthly reason.

It was about four hours later that Dad was found on the New Brighton ferry sitting on a bench in the bright sunshine, his body already stone cold. His big, stout heart had just given up and his death was as peaceful and serene as a death could be. He'd probably been thinking about Mam, perhaps she'd even called to him to come and join her and our Jeff and Will in the heaven where they were bound to be.

His children were bereft. Our father had been there for us all our lives: now we felt like ships that had lost their moorings and were adrift in a wild, dangerous sea. The lads, Danny and Jamie, cried unashamedly. Us girls clung together, Eve and Marge, too. Even Lisa, Jamie's wife, was deeply upset by the loss of the father-in-law she had grown to love.

The funeral was held on another sunny day in June and it seemed as if the entire population of Bootle had come out to mourn the loss of the highly respected, dignified man who'd been our father. He was buried in the grave with Mam.

'Together again at last,' Claire whispered when his coffin was laid on top of that of his wife.

Life went on. It *had* to go on. No matter who died, no matter how dear or how indispensable they'd seemed to your very existence, life still went on. It seemed no time before everyone was back at work, doing what they'd been doing before Dad died, going to the pictures, even laughing after a while, though it was a long time before the McCarthys stopped feeling slightly adrift, as if something terribly important was missing from our lives and would never be replaced.

Eve, our Claire's Kate and Norah's Bernadette had all been born the same year. Whenever I met my sisters, we discussed the girls' futures. When she left school, Kate wanted to work in one of the new boutiques that were springing up all over the place.

'She's started making her own clothes,' Claire bragged. 'She's very good at it, too, can even turn a collar, or whatever it is you do with collars. Apparently, it's very complicated.'

'Our Bernadette wants to go to university and become a teacher,' Norah said.

Me and Claire exchanged glances. We knew this wasn't true. Bernadette wasn't exactly the Brain of Britain. It was Norah and Roy who wanted her to go to university and become a teacher. Unlike her cousins, who were at a comprehensive school, Bernadette attended Seafield Convent, only because a coach had been employed to get her through the 11-plus. Now another coach was preparing her for O-levels. I'd like to bet Bernadette would sooner work in a boutique with Kate.

'Eve has no idea what she wants to do when she leaves school,' I sighed. She was fourteen and would start her final year next September, but whenever I tried to bring up the subject of her future, she'd say airily, 'We'll just have to see, Kitty,' usually adding the favourite of the week

'I'd quite like to be a ballet dancer,' she said when I'd raised the matter again on Sunday.

'You've never had a single lesson,' I pointed out. Last time, she'd wanted to join a circus, before that to hitchhike around the world. Nursing had been the favourite for a while, and becoming an air hostess had lasted a good fortnight. 'You need to make up your mind soon.'

'I might never make up my mind. I might do loads of different jobs and then get married.'

That shook me a bit. 'Do you really want to get married?'

She was lying on the settee with her legs draped over the arm and managed a sort of shrug. 'I don't know. Mum and Dad didn't exactly set a good example, did they?'

'Not exactly.'

'Most of the girls at school want to get married.' She balanced a shoe on her big toe and let it fall to the floor.

'It doesn't mean *you* have to.'

She raised her head. 'Are you putting me off?'

'No. I just don't think marriage should be your sole ambition. You should only marry when you fall in love with a man you want to spend the rest of your life with.'

'Why didn't you get married, Kitty?' The other shoe fell.

'Because I've never met a man I wanted to spend the rest of my life with.'

'You're not unhappy, are you?'

I raised my eyebrows. 'Do I look unhappy?'

'No, you look fine.' She regarded me keenly with a slight smile on her face. 'You don't look as happy as Auntie Claire does when she's with Uncle Liam, but you look happier than Auntie Marge does all the time. She and Uncle Danny don't like each other, do they?' She was clearly quite perceptive for a fourteen-year-old.

'They probably like each other,' I explained. 'They have their ups and downs, but they're not in love.'

'Then why did they get married?'

It wouldn't hurt if she were told the truth. 'Because they had to, that's why. Given more time, they'd probably have married quite different people.'

'Have you ever been in love, Kitty?' She rolled on to the floor and began to kick her long, slim legs into the air.

'I thought I was once, but I mustn't have been because I refused to marry him.'

'What was his name?'

The conversation was getting dangerous and I'd had enough of it. 'Mind your own business,' I told her. 'It's Sunday afternoon. Why aren't you out playing tennis or something?'

'It's too hot. I'm waiting for Charlotte and Penny to come. We're going to sit in my bed and talk about who we'd like to marry.' She grinned and I threw a cushion at her. She caught it, her face becoming serious. 'You know, Kitty, sometimes I'm almost glad Mummy and Daddy went away and you came to live with me.'

There was a knock on the door and she scrambled to her feet like a gazelle and went to answer it. I sat there, flushed and pleased. It was quite the nicest thing she'd ever said to me.

★

In no time, Christmas was upon us. I decorated the window of the shop with lengths of tinsel, fake holly and coloured lights, filling it with ideas for presents: fountain pens and propelling pencils in fancy boxes; leather writing cases; crystal inkwells; diaries of all different sizes. Kieron, who I'd learnt was married as well as being an outrageous flirt, bought a desk diary for his father. By Christmas Eve, the window was almost empty.

'You've done wonders, Kitty,' Muriel said admiringly when she arrived just before midday, closing time, and announced she was taking me to lunch. 'Assuming you're not in a rush to get home?'

'I'm not, and I'd love lunch, ta. It's been dead busy this morning with people buying last-minute presents.'

'How much did you take?'

I opened the till and stared at the contents. 'I'm not sure, fifty or sixty pounds, I guess. Shall I count it?'

'There's no need, dear. Put the whole lot in your handbag. Paul and I would like you to have it as a Christmas bonus.'

'But I couldn't . . .' I began.

'You can and you will.' Her expression brooked no argument. 'We're so pleased with the shop. It was like a little beacon of light when I came round the corner today, brightening up dull old North John Street no end. Paul passed it the other night and was extremely impressed.'

'Am I ever likely to meet Paul?' I enquired.

'I doubt it. He's a crusty old bachelor and his only interest in life is chess – he was on his way to his chess club when he passed the shop.'

'That's something I could have sold as presents,' I said thoughtfully, 'chess sets. I could have put one in the window with the pieces set out on the board.'

'Kitty, dear.' She linked my arm. 'It's almost Christmas, the shop is about to close and I positively forbid you to think about it until it opens again in three days' time.'

'I was wondering if I should have a sale in the New Year.'

'You do whatever you like.' She turned the 'Open' sign on the door to 'Closed'. 'Come on, there's a taxi outside waiting to take us to the Adelphi where I've reserved a table for two. And if you mention the shop while we're eating, I shall scream.'

★

We missed Dad over Christmas, but he'd have been the first to tell us to stop moping and have a good time, though none of us fancied having our dinner in Amethyst Street, which had become a family ritual. We had it our Claire's instead, then transferred to our Norah's for tea.

On Boxing Day, I went to see Hilda and Dorothy, and took Muriel with me. Eve had expressed total disinterest and gone to see a friend.

Hilda had received a letter from Cecily with instructions to let me read it. 'To save her having to write the whole thing twice,' Hilda said. I'd done the same thing when I'd lived in Richmond.

Cecily was in California, having discovered that the exotic foreign countries she'd always longed to visit were full of poverty, disease and insects 'as big as rabbits and even *snakes*!' The letter went on: 'I'm not as adventurous as I thought. At least California is clean and people speak English, even if it's with an American accent. I have met a delightful Canadian gentleman called Max who is showing me around. The other day, I could have sworn I saw Clark Gable drive by in a yellow, open-topped limousine.'

'She couldn't have,' Hilda growled when I read that bit aloud. 'Clark Gable died in nineteen sixty.'

'How on earth do you know that?' I asked, amazed. 'Surely it wasn't part of the course on politics and current affairs?'

'She reads the newspapers from cover to cover every single day,' Dorothy said. 'She knows everything. She'll quote you last week's football results if you're interested.'

'Not particularly,' I said hastily.

Before leaving, Muriel made arrangements to return on Saturday to make up a fourth for bridge. 'Dorothy's so sensible and Hilda's so interesting,' she said on the way back to Maghull. 'I'm glad you introduced us, Kitty.'

'Kitty!' Eve yelled the minute she came through the front door. 'Where's my birth certificate?'

'It's in a big brown envelope in the right-hand sideboard drawer with all the other important papers.' I deserted the sponge cake I was making and went into the hall where she was taking off the red coat she'd got for Christmas – it exposed most of her thighs and hadn't an ounce of warmth. 'What do you want it for?'

'To get a passport for the weekend in Paris at Easter.' The school was arranging it for pupils taking O-level French.

'Today?' It was four o'clock on New Year's Eve and I doubted if the passport office would be open. I'd closed the shop at one, having had only a single customer all morning.

'Of course not today,' she said impatiently. 'I just wanted to make sure I had one. Penny's mother can't find hers anywhere and she's had to send away for a replacement.'

'Yours is quite safe, I can assure you. Check if you like.' It was the sort that didn't give the name of the parents, just that of the child and where it was born. I returned to the sponge cake I intended taking to Amethyst Street that night where I would see in the New Year with the rest of the McCarthy clan, the adults, that was. Most of the children, Eve included, had parties of their own to go to. I was gearing up for Eve to ask why she'd been born in London and trying to think of a reply, when she came into the kitchen bearing, not her birth certificate, but a letter that I didn't at first recognize.

'This is from Daddy,' she said in a strange, stiff voice.

I felt my blood turn to ice. I had completely forgotten Michael's letter had been in the envelope. Why had I kept it?

'It hasn't got a date, but he obviously wrote it the day he left. It starts "Dear Kitty" and says, "I'm leaving Eve with you – who better to look after her than her own mother?" ' She held the letter to her breast, hugging it, and looked at me. Her eyes were huge and full of tears, yet they were also accusing eyes, angry. 'Are you my mother, Kitty?'

'Yes,' I whispered. I felt as if all the organs in my body were moving to a different place.

'Why didn't you tell me?' She crumpled the letter into a ball and threw it in my face. '*Why didn't you tell me?*' she screamed.

'I don't know,' I said helplessly.

'Would you *ever* have told me?' She was still screaming and every bit of colour had drained from her face.

'I don't know that either. You thought Aileen and Michael were your mam and dad. I was worried it would upset you to find out the truth.'

'Upset me? Ha!' she sneered. 'They both went away, left me behind. Why should I be upset to discover I didn't belong to them, but to *you*?' She was silent for a moment and her face worked, her lips moved, as if she was working something out in her head. 'But you, *you* must have given me away because you didn't want me. I bet you weren't too pleased when you got me back.' She burst into tears and ran into the living room. I followed. She'd thrown herself full-length on the settee, her face buried in a cushion, sobbing for all she was worth.

'Sweetheart.' I knelt beside her and put my arm around her shoulders. 'Sweetheart, it wasn't like that at all.'

'Then what *was* it like?' Her voice was muffled by the cushion. 'If you wanted me, why did you give me to your sister?' She struggled to a sitting position, roughly dislodging my arm. 'Tell me everything,' she demanded. 'Start at the beginning and tell me everything. I've a right to know,' she said belligerently when I must have looked reluctant. 'Who's my father? What's his name? Is he the man who wanted to marry you, but you refused because you didn't love him?'

'I'll tell you, but I'd like to make some tea first.'

She grabbed my skirt. 'No! Tell me *now*.'

If I couldn't have tea, I'd have sherry. I'd bought a few bottles for Christmas and what was left was on a tray on the sideboard with some glasses. I filled a glass almost full; my hand was shaking and my heart was beating far too rapidly. I sat down and drank half the sherry in one go. It didn't make me feel the slightest bit different.

'I was twenty,' I began, 'no, nineteen, when I met your father. His name was Con, Connor. He was a friend of Uncle Danny's. We got on really well, but when he proposed, I turned him down. I suppose,' I said thoughtfully, 'that I did love him in a way, but I had a thing about not getting married. I still have.'

'If you felt like that, you should have made sure you didn't get pregnant,' Eve said primly.

'I know.' I drank more sherry and this time my head began to swim. 'But I enjoyed taking the risk, you see. It was dead exciting and I knew I could always marry Con if it came to it. Better still, Aileen and Michael badly wanted children and I could give the baby to them.' I leaned towards her and said earnestly, 'When I realized I was expecting you, I didn't think of you as a person, just this anonymous baby growing in my tummy. When I told Aileen, she and Michael were so excited, as if I was presenting them with the Holy Grail. It felt really good.'

'Good,' Eve echoed. I waited for her to say something else, but she just sighed and looked at the carpet.

'Anyroad, apart from Aileen and Michael, I didn't tell anyone in the family I was expecting. I went to live in a place called Richmond with Faith Knowles – she knew, obviously. I've told you about Faith, haven't I?'

'The one with the two little boys?'

'That's right, though they'll be men by now – well, almost. It still didn't seem real, not until the end when you were born and they put you in my arms.' I smiled, remembering. 'You were so sweet, so tiny, so precious. I didn't want to let you go, but Aileen was standing with her arms outstretched, saying, "Kitty" in an urgent voice as if she resented every second I had with you. I hated her then. I've hated her ever since, though it was hardly her fault.'

'So you wish you'd kept me?' There was a tremor in her voice.

'More than anything on earth, sweetheart.'

We looked at each other and, for the briefest of moments, I thought everything was going to be all right, but she turned away, saying contemptuously, 'It was all a game to you, wasn't it? You could marry my father, give me to your sister: it didn't bother you whatever you did.'

She was right. I'd been breathtakingly irresponsible, playing with her life, never putting her first. 'I'm sorry,' I said weakly.

'It's a bit late to be sorry now.' The way she said it! So grown up, so cutting. In the short time since she'd read Michael's letter, she'd changed from a child into a woman.

'I've been sorry for years. I told you, the minute you were born I wanted to keep you so much it hurt.'

'Huh! It can't have hurt all that much, else you wouldn't have given me away.'

'I didn't know what to do. I felt so weak – I'd only just had you – and I felt torn between keeping you and disappointing Aileen and Michael.' It sounded awfully lame.

'And you didn't give a fig for *my* feelings,' she said scornfully.

'You were a tiny baby only a few hours old. Look, Eve,' I said patiently, 'I wasn't exactly giving you to the wicked witch of the north. Aileen and Michael had a lovely house, and plenty of money, and they'd been trying for a baby since they got married. I knew they could give you a far better life than I ever could, that they would love and care for you as if you were their own.'

'That's rubbish and you know it.' She had an answer for

everything. No matter what excuse I came up with – and they were excuses – she demolished it. Where had she acquired that talent? Was it a talent? 'What it boils down to, Kitty,' she said like a teacher summarizing a lesson, 'is that you had sex with my father because it was exciting, but when it resulted in a baby, instead of getting married like any normal woman, you got rid of me in a way that made you feel good. I'm surprised you didn't have an abortion,' she finished bitterly.

'It never crossed my mind.' I felt tired, sick and tired. I'd drunk too much sherry too quickly. 'Look, love, I've said I'm sorry. What else d'you want me to do?'

'Nothing. Absolutely nothing.' She got abruptly to her feet and left the room. A minute later, her bedroom door slammed, making me jump. Music filled the house – I'd let her take the gramophone upstairs. It was so loud I could hardly think. I made the longed-for tea with double the amount of leaves, stirring them madly when I added the water. I drank a cup, leaning against the sink, then noticed the sponge cake still in the bowl. I put it in the fridge, then I looked at the clock: half past five.

An hour later, music still blared out upstairs and I'd drunk a second pot of tea. It was about time I started getting ready. I'd promised Marge I'd be early and help set out the food, but I didn't move from the chair where I seemed to be stuck. I wasn't in the mood for a party.

The music stopped and Eve came running downstairs, entering the room breathless, eyes blazing. 'What did my father have to say about you giving me away?' she demanded hoarsely.

Dear God! It was about to get worse. 'He didn't know about you.'

'He didn't know? You didn't tell him? Doesn't he know he's got a daughter?' The questions came out like bullets from a gun.

I put a hand on my forehead, as if it had just been hit. 'No.' I licked my lips nervously.

She laughed, but there was nothing nice or funny about it. 'You're the end, do you know that, Kitty? The absolute end. What's his name? His other name?'

'I can't tell you.' I shook my head so hard it made me dizzy.

'Why not?'

'Because he's married now and has children: two, I think. I don't want you going near him. It wouldn't be fair after all this time. Look, luv, shouldn't you start getting ready for your party?'

She completely ignored the question. 'You're the last person to talk about being fair.' There was that sneering look on her face again. 'Did Granddad know I belonged to you?'

'No one in the family knew except our Claire, only because she guessed. Hilda and Dorothy knew, and your gran. She guessed, too.'

'Gran knows and she didn't tell me?'

'I reckon she didn't think it was her business to. Look, Eve,' I tried to stand, but my head felt as if had turned upside-down and I fell back in the chair. 'Look, sweetheart, I was sorry when Aileen and Michael left, but really thrilled when I realized I was getting you back—'

She interrupted before I'd had a chance to finish. 'How could you be getting me back when you'd never had me in the first place?' She turned on her heel and went back upstairs, but this time there was no music.

Marge telephoned some time later – a phone had been installed in Amethyst Street after Dad died – wanting to know why I was late. I told her I was sorry, but I didn't feel well and wasn't up to a party. She promised to phone after twelve and wish me a Happy New Year. 'You're not likely to be in bed, are you? I mean no one goes to bed before midnight on New Year's Eve, no matter how sick they are. Just think, it'll be nineteen sixty-seven next time we speak. How the years fly by, eh?'

'They do indeed.' I couldn't wait for it to be 1967, or 1968, come to that, by which time Eve might have forgiven me.

No one had ever hurt me as much as my daughter. It came as a shock to discover the power children had to break their parents' hearts. Had I thought it would work, I would have gone down on my knees and begged her forgiveness, but I suspected it would only make matters worse. The best thing would be to leave her to get used to the idea of me being her mother in her own good time.

I spoke to her in a normal voice, asked how she was getting on at school, where was she going that night, had she enjoyed herself? Her answers gradually became less curt, her tone softer, she began to ask my opinion on things again. But it was never the same as it had been before: we didn't get on nearly as well as mother and daughter as we'd done when she'd thought I was her aunt.

She left school at Christmas, only weeks after her sixteenth birthday, not waiting to take her O-levels the following summer, and went to work as a copy-typist in an office not far from the shop. I tried to insist she take the exams, but it was a waste of time, making me feel that I'd lost the right to influence her decisions. I'd lost *her*.

The following summer, when her friend, Penny, left school, she informed they were going to live in London. 'We're hoping to get jobs in Carnaby Street where all the fashion shops are,' she said excitedly. I didn't even try to stop her.

She wrote about once a month: long, rambling letters describing the marvellous time she and Penny were having, the parties they'd been to, the weird people they'd met, the various jobs they'd had, mainly waitressing, and the clothes they'd bought. She sent a photo of her and Penny in front of a shop in Carnaby Street. They wore ankle-length frocks, shawls and wavy straw hats decorated with flowers, and were accompanied by two young men dressed in antique military uniforms.

'What do they look like, eh?' Claire marvelled when I showed it to her. 'You'd think they were two old grannies and the lads had just fought in the Battle of Waterloo. They both look dead gormless. Liverpool lads would never dress so daft.'

'That's true.' Liverpool was no longer the centre of the universe. The Cavern had closed, the rock 'n' roll groups had disbanded or gone to live in the capital. The action had moved on and London was now the place where everyone wanted to be.

It was Claire who, at my request, had told the family that I was Eve's mother. She reported that no one had seemed terribly surprised, though she was glad she hadn't had to tell Dad because he'd have been hurt. Marge said later that it all fitted in with the strange life I'd led, the strange jobs I'd had and my strange friends, such as Hilda and Dorothy.

I protested I could see nothing strange about my life, my jobs or my friends, but Marge said, 'That's because we were cast in a different mould, Kit.'

★

Eve had only been gone a week when I'd had an unexpected visitor. It was Saturday, one of those lovely, sunny winter days that would normally have made me glad to be alive, except I'd come home from the shop feeling low and dispirited. I'd known who my visitor was before I opened the door because there was a van in the drive with 'Connor Daley, Plumbing & Heating Services' painted on the side. My heart did a double cartwheel.

'Hello, Kitty.' He grinned. I saw the same old Con, solid and dependable, with the same red hair and millions of freckles. He wore jeans, a check shirt and a navy anorak. He'd never used to dress so casually, but then men hadn't in the days when we were courting. His face glowed with health and wealth, and he had the look of a man who'd made a success of his life.

'You've hardly changed, Con.' The years fell away and it felt as if it were only yesterday that we'd last met – in a Chinese restaurant in Lime Street, I recalled – and I'd told him I didn't want to see him any more.

'Neither have you, except you're a bit thinner.'

'Am I?' I stood aside to let him in. His arm brushed against mine and I felt an unwelcome and entirely unexpected twinge of desire.

I took him into the living room, told him to sit down and offered him tea.

He refused, saying, 'I'll hardly be staying a minute. I expect you know what I've come to see you about?'

'I have a suspicion.' Eve must have tracked him down. I'd told her his name was Connor, that he was a plumber and a friend of our Danny's. All she'd had to do was probe a bit and she would have got the answer she was after.

'Our daughter came to see us just over a week or so ago: Eve. She's a pretty girl, but not a bit like either of us.' He leaned back in the chair and crossed his legs. I noticed he wore soft leather boots that looked as if they'd cost the earth.

'I hope she didn't come to your home.' Surely Eve wouldn't have been so thoughtless?

'No, she came to the office and asked to speak to me alone. It came as a shock, I must say. Why didn't you tell me, Kitty?' he asked gently.

'I don't know.' I licked my lips. 'I really don't know.'

'Yes, you do. It was because you thought I'd insist on us getting married. And you'd no right to give her away even it was to your sister. *I'd* have had her. Me mam would have welcomed a baby in the house. And June, my wife, isn't the sort who'd mind if I'd had a kid by a previous relationship. In fact, I told her about Eve and she'd like to meet her.' He shook his head. 'I'll never understand you in a million years, Kitty. You seem to do everything the wrong way around.'

'I don't think I understand myself, Con,' I whispered.

He slapped his knee. 'Y'know, I think I'd quite like a drink after all. Tea or coffee, I don't mind.'

I had opened the fridge to get the milk when the tears came. I don't know why. I hadn't felt like crying, but they just poured down my cheeks, making tiny puddles on the tiled floor. I didn't think I'd made a sound, but for some reason Con came out and took me in his arms.

'Oh, Kitty,' he said. 'Oh, Kitty.'

I buried my head in his shoulder and continued to cry. 'I don't know why I'm doing this,' I said brokenly.

'I don't know why either, but I feel like crying, too.' He stroked my hair. 'Lost dreams, I suppose. Lost hopes.' He tightened his arms. 'I know I shouldn't say this, Kit, but I've never stopped loving you. June's a smashing girl, but she's always been second-best.' He pulled my hair until we were facing each other and kissed me on the lips. My head began to swim, yet at the same time I was aware that what we were doing was monstrously wrong. I pushed him away at exactly the same time as he pushed me.

'We'd best forget about that drink,' he said gruffly before he fled from the house. I stayed where I was, standing in the middle of my drying tears, and listened while the van's engine started. Con backed out of the drive, and drove away into the crisp November sunshine.

'What was that all about?' I asked myself, bewildered.

I wasn't the sort of person who could stay miserable for ever. I had my health and strength, I loved my job and my family. I convinced myself that Eve was doing no more than thousands of young people did nowadays: having an adventure. It was the sort of thing she might well have done had she been living with Aileen and Michael.

About every three months, she descended on the house like a whirlwind: tall and lovely, smelling of flowers, her face vivid with make-up, shocking the neighbours with her outlandish clothes and bizarre hairstyles – not that I gave a fig what the neighbours thought.

It was autumn, only a few weeks off her eighteenth birthday, when she wrote to say she was getting married: 'To Rob Horton. He's the one standing beside Penny in that photo I sent. I'm bringing him home the weekend after next: his mum and dad are coming, too.' There was a PS, just two words: 'I'm pregnant.'

I imagined her sticking out her tongue, saying, 'See! *I'm* getting married. Unlike you, *I'm* not giving my baby away.'

The Seventies

Chapter 8

1970

I wanted to kill my daughter when I discovered she'd asked Con to give her away. It was a relief that he didn't bring his wife to the wedding and an even bigger relief when he left after making a nice little speech. It meant we hardly had a chance to speak to each other and that suited me right down to the ground.

Two weeks before, Eve had brought Rob and his parents to meet me. I cleaned the house from top to bottom, got new sheets for the double bed in case they wanted to stay the night, ironed things that had never been ironed before, and bought a bunch of very expensive chrysanthemums to put in the window. Had our Aileen chosen to return that day, even she would have been impressed.

Mrs Horton didn't even try to be polite. Dyed-blonde, fiftyish and shaped like a barrel, she wore heavy spectacles with zebra-striped frames studded with what looked like diamonds. She couldn't have given the gleaming house a more disdainful look had it been a pigsty. Instead of being offended, I'd felt the urge to laugh. Her accent was so posh it would have put the Queen to shame.

Her husband was as different from his wife as chalk from cheese. Small and pixie-like with pointed ears and a jolly red face, he was working class and proud of it. He told me to call him Barney and presented me with a bottle of whisky. 'Irish malt, the best there is,' he crowed. I offered him a glass and he accepted with alacrity.

'Would you like some, Mrs Horton?' I enquired politely. 'Or would you prefer tea or coffee?'

'Is the coffee percolated?'

'No, I'm afraid it comes straight out of a jar.'

'Then I'll have tea.'

Rob was clearly infatuated with my daughter. His adoring eyes followed her every move as she flitted around the room wearing an assortment of old-fashioned clothes that could only have been bought in a second-hand shop. He wore a maroon velvet suit and a floppy grey bow-tie, and looked as gormless in the flesh as he'd done in the photo, though he was extremely handsome, with long thick black hair that reached his shoulders and hung in a fringe over his sleepy brown eyes. He spoke in a lazy drawl, though his accent wasn't as cut-glass as his mother's. I discovered later that he was a dealer in modern art.

Eve followed me into the kitchen. 'Isn't she a scream?' she hissed.

'You mean your future mother-in-law?'

'Yes. Barney's OK, but Mrs Horton is the biggest snob who ever lived.' She continued to hiss. 'They live in this big, posh house in Hampstead, and she thinks she's the bee's knees because they've got pots of money. They haven't had it for long: there are two other sons, much older than Rob, and their wives are quite ordinary, but when Rob came along, they could afford to send him to public school and she wanted him to marry into society, not some cheap tart like me.'

'You're never a tart!' I gasped, shocked to the core. 'You're a very well brought-up young lady.'

'Mrs Horton doesn't think so.'

'Well, Mrs Horton will be told to go jump in the lake if she says anything like that to me. Where does their money come from?'

Eve's face split into a grin. 'Crime!'

'*Crime?*' I choked.

'Barney has a scrap yard somewhere in Essex, but Rob says he's really a fence.'

'And the wife of a fence has the cheek to call you a cheap tart?'

Eve nodded and collapsed into giggles. 'Like I said, she's a scream. She's had elocution lessons, but when she loses her temper, she forgets and swears like a trooper and her posh accent goes out the window.'

'Is that the sort of family you really want to marry into, sweetheart?' I asked seriously.

Her reply was just as serious. 'I'm marrying Rob, not his mum and dad, and he's very sweet. He loves me with all his heart and really wants us to get married.' She smiled dreamily. 'That's what I really need, to be loved and wanted.'

From the way she spoke, you'd have thought she'd never been loved and wanted in her life.

There was a spate of weddings at about the same time: Eve, the first McCarthy to get married in a registry office – she'd given up religion since moving to London, she told me; followed by our Claire's eldest, Mark – *he'd* given up his rock 'n' roll group – who married a girl from Kirkby called Veronica; and, to Norah and Roy's horror, their precious Bernadette married a chap called Johnny Kelly after revealing she was three months' pregnant. Johnny had been on the dole since he left school.

'We had so many hopes for her,' Norah wept, 'but she refused to go to university and now she's having a baby by some work-shy wastrel who hasn't a penny to his name. Children!' she said bitterly. 'What would you do with them, eh?'

'Don't ask me.'

At least Rob had money and his own flat off the King's Road in Chelsea, one of the best addresses in London, according to Eve. I remembered Graham saying the same about his flat in Mayfair. I'd told Eve the house in Maghull belonged to her if she wanted it: 'If you read that letter, *the* letter, through to the end, Michael said he was transferring the house to you, though I never heard if he did.'

Eve smirked. 'And what would happen to you if Rob and I wanted to live here?'

'I'd find somewhere else to live, naturally.' Easier said than done, I thought grimly.

'Oh, don't be daft, Kitty. As if I'd chuck you out of house and home. And the last place I want to live is Liverpool. I'd sooner be in London any day.'

So, off she went and I was left alone in the house in Maghull. I'd been alone before, but I'd always anticipated that one day she would come back and settle down. But now she was a married woman about to start a family and she'd gone for good.

Holly Horton, weighing just over eight pounds, was born the following April. Rob telephoned and announced in his sleepy voice that he'd just become a father.

'How's Eve?' I asked.

'OK, I guess,' he said vaguely.

Eve wasn't having her daughter christened, so Muriel and I went down to London for the day to see the new baby when she was three weeks old. Muriel was her great-grandmother in a sort of way. As for me, I'd become a grandmother at the age of thirty-nine. I wasn't exactly glad there wouldn't be a christening, but it was a relief to know we wouldn't come face to face with the charmless Mrs Horton.

The Chelsea flat was like a modern art gallery. Muriel and I rolled our eyes at each other when we entered the vast living room and saw the ghastly paintings covering virtually every inch of the walls. I recalled that Rob was a dealer in modern art. Perhaps these were the ones he'd been unable to sell.

Eve took us to the nursery where a wide-awake Holly lay in a pine cradle lined with ruched white satin.

'Oh, she's beautiful,' I breathed, taking in the mop of black hair, the deep-blue eyes and sweet little face with rosy cheeks. 'She's got Rob's hair, but your features, Eve.' I wondered if her eyes would stay blue.

'You can pick her up if you like,' she said generously.

We all went into the living room where we sat amidst the garish paintings and I nursed my granddaughter in my arms, her tiny body warm against mine, conscious of the beating of her heart and the slight movement of her legs, just as I had when I'd held her mother for the one and only time. 'You're dead pretty, you are,' I said softly, touching her little round chin. I wanted to hold her for ever, but remembered Muriel and gave the baby to her with a feeling of enormous reluctance.

'She's gorgeous,' Muriel murmured, and I think I saw tears in her eyes.

Eve was in her element. Her taste in clothes had changed for the better: grey flannel slacks, a long white silk blouse and strappy sandals with high heels. Holly was the perfect baby and hardly cried at all, she told us proudly. They had a live-in *au pair*, Francine, who took her for walks, did the washing and babysat whenever they wanted to go out.

'In fact, we can go for a meal now and leave Holly with Francine,' she sang. 'There's this lovely Italian restaurant just around the corner. We eat there all the time.'

'I'd sooner stay with Holly,' I said, glancing at the baby and wishing Muriel would give her back. 'After all, we've come all this way to see her, not visit some posh Italian restaurant.'

Eve grinned. 'You're always so down to earth, Kitty. We'll stay in and ask Francine to make us omelettes. Go and rouse her, Rob, there's a dear. She'll be in her room.'

Rob had been hovering around the edge of things, hands pushed into the pockets of his jeans, hardly saying a word. He seemed glad to be given a task to do. He returned to say that Francine was about to start the omelettes and that he had an appointment with some chap in Bond Street and had to go out for a while.

'That's good,' Eve said with a relieved sigh when the door closed. She didn't go on to say what was good about it and I thought it a bad sign that she was pleased to be rid of the husband she'd only had for a matter of months. I wanted to ask if she was happy, but it seemed a cheek. She *looked* happy enough, but I felt it was all an act, that she wanted to prove to me she'd done the right thing by marrying the father of her baby.

On the train home, Muriel fell asleep and I was left to my own thoughts. I wished Eve lived in Liverpool so I could see Holly all the time as Claire did her grandchildren, and as Norah would when hers was born. I hoped Eve wasn't working Francine too hard: she was only seventeen and had looked terribly tired. I worried about Eve and Rob's marriage, and if Eve could bring herself to tell me if things were going wrong. Then I worried about Muriel, who woke up just before we reached Liverpool complaining she felt sick.

'I think I must be getting a stomach bug or something,' she said.

'Perhaps it was the omelette. There might have been a bad egg in yours.'

I put her in a taxi when we reached Lime Street then walked down to Exchange Station to catch the train to Maghull. The phone was ringing when I opened the door. It was Claire, who stood in for me in the shop during the holidays and whenever I needed a day off. She'd only rung, she explained, to say everything had gone fine that day and ask what Holly was like.

'She's beautiful, really beautiful. I wanted to bring her home with me.' I'd tell her my suspicions about Eve and Rob some other time, otherwise we'd be talking till midnight.

She rang off. I'd barely reached the kitchen to put the kettle on for a longed-for drink, when the phone rang again. I picked it up and gave the number through gritted teeth.

'Hello, who is this speaking?' enquired a soft, Irish voice.

'Aren't I suppose to ask *you* that?' I asked rudely.

'Oh, sorry. I'm Mary Brady and I was just looking through an old diary of Michael's and found this number. Are you a relative of his?'

My heart missed a beat. 'Michael? Michael Gilbert?'

'That's right. Oh, I'm doing this all wrong, aren't I? I should have said his name was Gilbert.'

'I'm Kitty McCarthy, his sister-in-law. What's happened to Michael? Is he all right?'

'No. I'm awfully sorry, but Michael died two days ago.' The voice was unnecessarily apologetic: it was unlikely to be her fault Michael had died. 'I rang in case whoever it was would like to come to the funeral. He never mentioned relatives, but I knew he was bound to have some. And I was right, wasn't I? It's in three days' time, the funeral, on Friday.'

'Where?'

'Belfast. He lived with us in a little hotel called Buckles on the Falls Road. It's at ten o'clock, so you'd have to come the day before. You can stay in the hotel, there's plenty of room.'

'What did you say your name was?'

'Mary Brady. I was Michael's . . . friend.'

My manners returned. 'Thank you, Mary. It's kind of you to ring. I'll see you some time on Thursday. Oh, and I'll be bringing Michael's mother with me.'

'Bring anyone you like: they'll all be very welcome.'

Michael was *dead*. I'd thought about him so many times over the years, him and Aileen. I should have asked Mary Brady how he died, but I could do that on Thursday. She'd paused before she said 'friend', as if they'd been more than that. I hoped so. She'd sounded nice and I'd been very short with her, yet if she and Michael had been more than friends she'd be terribly upset.

The thoughts chased each other around my tired brain. Who should I phone? Muriel, obviously – she'd be terribly upset, too. Our Claire, not just because she'd want to know, but I'd have to ask her to look after the shop again. Eve? I wasn't sure about Eve. For a long time she'd thought Michael was her father and I recalled she'd seemed fonder of him than of Aileen. But it was only two weeks since she'd had Holly and she might feel obliged to go to the funeral. No, I'd tell Eve *after* the funeral. If she was annoyed, it was just too bad.

I got wearily to my feet, went into the hall and dialled Muriel's number. While it was ringing, I remember she'd felt ill when we got off the train. I put the receiver down. I'd ring tomorrow when she'd probably be feeling better.

Claire was shocked by the news. 'I used to make terrible fun of him – remember how slow he drove the car, like a snail? But he was a really nice chap. Our Aileen needs her arse smacking for the way she treated him.'

A memory surfaced, of the night Mam died. I was standing in the hospital corridor with my father. '*Our Aileen's got a good 'un there,*' he'd said. '*She'll never want for anything while she's married to Michael.*'

'And I'll look after the shop for as long as you want, Kit,' Claire was saying. 'I really love it there, and I think I've finally got the hang of decimal currency. I'll do it Saturday morning, too, save you having to rush home. You know what Irish wakes are like: they go on for ever. And while you're in Belfast, buy a wreath from me and Liam. I'll give you the money when you get back.'

Next morning, I telephoned Muriel, but there was no reply, nor in the afternoon when I called from the shop. Tomorrow, I planned for us to catch the ten o'clock ferry to Belfast and it was vital I got in touch with her soon. She lived in Woolton on the south side of Liverpool – Maghull was in the north – and I was wondering whether to catch a bus to Woolton when the shop closed, or go home on the train and drive over there tonight. I never used the car for work, it was much quicker and less hassle on the train.

I was in two minds as to what to do, when it struck me that if Muriel wasn't answering the phone, she was unlikely to answer the door. I began to panic, visualizing her in bed, seriously ill and unable to contact anybody. I was about to close the shop and go haring over to Woolton in a taxi – I'd break in, if necessary – when I remembered she had a brother, the mysterious Paul whom I'd never met, but who lived only a few roads away from his sister.

I found Paul Ainsworth's name in the telephone directory. The receiver at the other end was picked up straight away, as if he'd been sitting with it on his knee. He didn't give the number, just said, 'Hello.'

'This is Kitty from the shop,' I said. 'I'm sorry to disturb you, but I'm worried about Muriel. She doesn't seem to be answering her phone.'

'She's in hospital, dear.' He spoke like Laurence Olivier in a lovely mellifluous voice. 'She had her appendix out last night and will be out of action for a while. Is there a problem with the shop? Can I help in any way?'

'It's nothing to do with the shop.' I told him about Michael. He gave a sharp intake of breath. 'I'm going to the funeral and I thought Muriel would want to come with me.'

'Oh, she would have, she would have, dear.' His voice trembled slightly. 'Oh, how awful about Michael. Muriel will be terribly upset, but I won't tell her until she's out of hospital. He was such a dear little boy, Michael,' he reminisced, 'so obedient and cheerful, always with a smile on his face. If it's not too much trouble, perhaps you could buy a wreath for him. Take the money out of the till and write on the card, "With love from his mother and Uncle Paul." '

Belfast reminded me of Liverpool with its docks and long streets of little terraced houses. Dad used to call it Titanic Town, because it's where the ship was built. The air smelt the same, a mixture of salt and smoke. There were plenty of British troops about, all armed, reminding me there was virtually a civil war going on.

I caught a taxi to Buckles Hotel, a narrow three-storey building on the busy Falls Road. The front door was a work of art, comprised entirely of tiny stained-glass windows, each with a different flower. It was slightly ajar and, when I pushed it open, I came face to face with about a dozen men who were gathered in the foyer clutching their ale – or it might have been Guinness, I wouldn't know the difference. A counter with a sign that said 'Reception' was unattended. The men looked at me with interest, though some of the looks weren't exactly welcoming. One man actually stood in front of me, as if to block my entrance, but another, intimidatingly tall and as bald as a coot, said gruffly, 'Ah, I bet you're here for Michael's funeral, are you not?' I confirmed I was, and he went on: 'Mary said she was expecting two of yis, not just one.'

'His mother couldn't come, she's in hospital.'

'And you're his cousin? I think Mary said it was a cousin who was coming.'

'No, I'm his sister-in-law. Michael was married to my sister.'

'Ah, so Michael had a wife, after all. We often wondered. Well, in you go, Michael's sister-in-law. Mary's in the bar.' He pushed a door behind him and held it open: I had to duck underneath his arm to get in. 'Mary thought you might arrive about now and she'll have the kettle on.'

There were about a dozen people in the bar, which was larger than I'd expected. The bottom half had been covered with heavily embossed paper that looked as if it had been painted with treacle, and the top a dreary beige. The solid wooden tables appeared to have been planted there along with the benches on each side, and the wooden floor was uncarpeted, the boards worn away in places from the tread of thousands of feet. The bar occupied a corner at the far end and the woman behind smiled as I approached.

'Hello, I'm Mary Brady. I expect you're Kitty McCarthy?'

I smiled back, remembering how rude I'd been when she'd phoned. 'I'm afraid Mrs Gilbert couldn't come. She's had her appendix taken out and she doesn't even know about Michael yet.'

'Ah, that's a terrible shame.' We shook hands and I tried not to look at the birthmark on Mary Brady's face: a port wine stain covering her ear and left cheek, stopping short of her pretty, snub nose. She looked about forty, with short brown hair cut urchin-style and dark-green eyes. There'd been a girl at school with a similar blemish, though somewhat smaller, and she'd used to wear her hair loose on one side so it fell over her cheek. Mary had made no attempt to hide her birthmark.

'Would you like a cup of tea now, Kitty, or would you prefer a little glass of the hard stuff, or maybe some lemonade?'

'Tea, please.'

'And would you like to drink it out here or in the kitchen, or in your room maybe?'

'Out here would be nice.' A few of the people there were women, so I wouldn't feel out of place.

'I'll go and make it. Sit at that table nearby and I can talk to you while I've nothing to do: we'll be closing soon. By the way, Michael's in the office if you'd like to take a look at him while I'm making the tea. It's through that door; save you going through the foyer and being gawped at by that crowd of eejits out there.'

I almost laughed with disbelief when I saw the body lying in a coffin in a dark stuffy room, which held a single rusty filing cabinet, a desk and a typewriter older than the one that Hilda used to have. The body wasn't Michael's. This man had grey, receding hair, and a salt-and-pepper beard. There was a gold hoop in his left ear. I couldn't think of a reason on earth that would have persuaded the Michael Gilbert I'd known to grow a beard or wear an earring. The Michael I'd known had had soft white skin and small delicate hands.

I took one last look at the body before reaching for the door – and paused. Above the woolly beard, the man's skin was soft and white, and the hands crossed peacefully on his chest were small and delicate. I blurred my eyes and tried to ignore the beard. It *was* Michael. He was even wearing a well-cut pinstriped suit, the sort he had favoured.

The door opened and Mary Brady came in. 'What happened to him?' I whispered. I felt agitated. 'He's changed so much.'

Mary answered in a normal voice. 'He was clean-shaven when he came to stay with us. It was only going to be for a couple of nights, but it became a couple of weeks until in the end he never left. He used to help behind the bar, do the cleaning, that sort of thing.'

'Michael *cleaned*?' I gasped. 'But he was an accountant back in Liverpool. He had a really important job.'

'Did he now? Well, I'm not surprised,' Mary said calmly. 'He'd do me da's books for him in a jiffy, whereas it'd take me da weeks. I don't know whether he was happy being an accountant in Liverpool, but he was happy with us. He was a very popular man, Michael. Everyone's coming to his funeral.'

'Something happened,' I muttered. 'His wife, my sister, Aileen, went off with another chap: she was having his baby. That's why Michael left.'

'Did he not have children of his own?' She was obviously keen to know about Michael's past life.

'An adopted daughter, Eve. I've been looking after her. She got married last year and has just had a baby.' I returned to the coffin and touched the cold face. 'Why did he grow a beard?'

'It made him feel one of the boys. The earring was a bet. No one thought he'd do it, but he did.'

I still hadn't asked the most obvious question of all. 'How did he die, Mary?'

'It was a road accident.' She sighed. 'He went out last Saturday morning to get the bread and stepped in front of a bus. He died two days later. I don't think the driver's stopped crying yet. He's not the only one, except I cry inside.' She bent and kissed Michael's white forehead. 'Why, oh, why, didn't you look where you were going, Michael, me darlin'?'

'I'm so sorry,' I said softly. 'Though I'm glad he had you.'

'I'm glad we had each other for more than ten whole years. I'm having him buried in Milltown Cemetery in the same plot as me mam. Me and me dad will join him when the Good Lord decides it's time.' She sniffed and took my hand. 'Come along, Kitty. I've made the tea. After you've drunk it, I'll show you to your room. You might like a little lie-down for a while. After all, you've had a long journey all the way from Liverpool.'

'I'd like to order three wreaths if it's not too late.' One from Claire and Liam, one from Muriel and Paul, and one from me.

'It's not a bit too late. You can do it on the phone. There's a florist's no distance away where we ordered our own flowers. If you give me the money, I'll pay when they're delivered in the morning.'

I woke a few hours later to the sound of music: a piano, a violin and loud singing. It was half past eight and the sun was still shining outside. I got up, washed my face, powdered it and put on some lipstick. Apart from the clothes I was wearing – a white blouse, flowered skirt and blue cardy – I'd only brought a black frock and jacket for the funeral. I had no idea whether I'd leave as soon as it was over, or stay for the wake and leave on Saturday. Claire had promised to hold the fort in the shop for as long as necessary, so there was no need to hurry home. I tried to shake the creases out of my skirt, combed my hair and went downstairs.

The foyer was packed, the bar was packed, the noise was deafening and the air was thick with cigarette smoke. I pushed my way through the crowds towards Mary, whose head I could glimpse at the end of the room, along with that of an older man with a halo of silver hair. Mary smiled when I arrived and said something I couldn't understand. The man shook my hand and I guessed she'd just introduced me to her father. I think she asked if I'd like a drink and I shouted, 'White wine, please,' just in case. Perhaps her ears had become accustomed to the noise, because she poured a glass of wine, but refused to take the money.

I sat on the edge of a bench on an otherwise crowded table. Everyone smiled and I got the impression they all knew I was Michael Gilbert's sister-in-law and wanted to make me welcome. I relaxed and listened to the songs I knew so well because I'd sung them hundreds of times before at parties and wakes: 'The Red Velvet Band', 'The Wild Colonial Boy', 'The Leaving of Liverpool' . . .

There was a piano against the wall opposite being played by a man with long black untidy hair whose face I couldn't see, just his broad back and his hands flashing up and down the keys. The violinist was little more than a teenager, small and fair-haired with a wispy beard, his face shining with perspiration as he put all his heart and soul into the music. The tall man who'd opened the door for me was standing next to the piano, singing so loudly that his hard voice could be heard above all the others. His eyes and face were hard, too. I thought I wouldn't like to get on the wrong side of him or his friends, the ones who'd given me such menacing stares when I'd arrived that afternoon.

The music came to a sudden end, the violinist wiped his brow with his sleeve, and the pianist stood and turned around. He was only young, in his early twenties, tall and slim, wearing jeans and a white shirt open at the neck. His eyes were dark and he was beautiful in the way men sometimes are while remaining wholly masculine. When he smiled, as he did now, my heart turned over, I can't think why. He spoke and the man with the hard face handed him a drink, as if he'd said, 'I'm thirsty.' He took a few mouthfuls, smiled a second time and once again my heart tugged, or twisted; it did something. I couldn't understand what was happening to me. I felt stupid and clumsy. Wine was dripping on to my knee and I put the glass on the table with an unsteady hand. When I looked back, the young man was staring at me thoughtfully and our eyes met for what seemed like for ever, but was probably only a few seconds before I looked away.

I stared at my feet until the music started again, but when I raised my head, a different man was playing the piano and there was no sign of the dark-haired, dark-eyed man who'd played such havoc with my heart.

The smoke was stinging my eyes and the noise was giving me a headache. It was time I went to bed. I finished the wine, waved to Mary and her father, and went through the door that led to the office. I wanted to say goodbye to Michael for the last time.

By now, it was dark in the room and I didn't bother searching for the light. The coffin looked as if it were suspended in mid-air and all I could see were Michael's white face and his crossed hands. 'I wonder what our Aileen would say if she could see you now?' I whispered, rubbing my cheek against his cold one. His beard felt soft and silky. 'Goodnight, my dear Michael, and goodbye.'

My room was on the second floor, small and snug, with an old-fashioned iron bedstead and a thick feather mattress. I hadn't bothered to lock the door and was surprised to find when I opened it that the light was on: it had been daylight when I'd left and there'd been no need for a light. I entered cautiously and got the shock of my life when I saw the young man who'd affected me so strangely sitting on the bed.

'Hello, Kitty.' His dark eyes danced. He got to his feet and, to my intense astonishment, took me in his arms. 'Fancy seeing you here!' He kissed my forehead, my nose and both my cheeks, then laughed at my bewildered face. 'You don't recognize me, do you? I saw you staring earlier and assumed you had.'

'I was wondering where I'd seen you before,' I lied, not wanting him to know I'd been staring for quite another reason.

'It's Oliver, Oliver Knowles.'

'Oliver!' I breathed. I threw my arms around his neck. 'Oh, Oliver! How on earth could I possibly have recognized you? It must be almost twenty years since we last met. You were only four.' I reminded myself that I used to bath him, change his clothes, dry his tears, cuddle him. It seemed only natural that we should embrace when we met again, but I really shouldn't be enjoying it quite so much. 'Where on earth did you learn to play the piano like that?'

'I had lessons when we went back to Richmond for good; Robin did, too.'

'How are Robin and your mother?' I loosened my arms around

his neck and rested them on his shoulders. His hands slipped down to my waist and he began to swing me slightly as we talked.

'They're both fine. Robin teaches at a school up your way, Preston. He got married last year – his wife had twin boys a few weeks ago. 'Fact, Mum's thinking of moving up north so she'll see more of them. Gran died ages ago and the house in Richmond is much too big for her.'

'I hope they'll be better behaved than you and Robin were. You were a pair of little divils.'

He grinned and his eyes sparkled with the same old mischief. 'You didn't seem to mind. You were patience itself.'

'I couldn't bring meself to be cross with you, I loved you both too much.'

'I loved you, too, Kitty. If I remember rightly, I vowed I'd marry you when I grew up.' He lifted my left hand off his shoulder and examined it. 'And now, here I am, all grown up,' he said soberly, 'and you haven't got a ring on your finger.'

I went hot and cold in quick succession, but told myself he was only joking. I was wondering what to say in reply, when there were footsteps on the stairs and he dropped my hand and slid the bolt across the door.

'Why did you do that?' I asked.

He put his fingers to his lips and whispered, 'Shush!'

I shushed. He waited until the footsteps returned downstairs before he spoke again. 'You must promise not to tell anyone you knew me before,' he said urgently, clutching my arm. 'My name isn't Oliver Knowles, it's Jack O'Donnell. Please don't ask why, Kitty, because I can't tell you.'

'I don't want to know why.' It didn't need much imagination to assume whatever he was doing was dangerous. Those men he'd been with in the bar . . . I shivered and sat on the bed. 'I hope you're being careful, Oliver.'

'As careful as I can be, but just think,' he went on, sitting beside me, 'I'd known Michael for over a year and all that time there was a connection between us – you! Now, I can actually remember him coming to the house to take you to hospital when your mother was ill.'

'You've been doing this for a year? Sorry,' I muttered when he raised his eyebrows. 'I didn't mean to ask a question.'

'Let's talk about you for a change.' He leaned against the iron bedhead and patted the pillow beside him. I shuffled along on my bottom and we sat companionably together, hugging our knees. Outwardly, I was calm, but inside I was struggling with a whole host of emotions. I still felt overwhelmingly attracted to the young man who'd been playing the piano downstairs, despite discovering he was Oliver Knowles whom I'd first looked after when he was just a three-year-old and I'd been nineteen.

'I remember when we first met,' I said. 'You were on your way to Egypt to see your father on your little three-wheeler bike.'

'I remember – you tried to stop me from going.'

'I *did* stop you.' I chuckled for no reason and he linked my arm.

'What happened to your baby? I remember you grew very fat and Mum said it was because there was a baby growing inside your tummy. I felt jealous because I wanted the baby to be me!'

'I had a little girl. Her name's Eve. My sister, Aileen, who was married to Michael, brought her up.' I didn't like to say I'd given her away. 'Then Aileen left Michael, and Michael left Liverpool, and I looked after her. Now she's married and lives in London. In fact, she had a baby about the same time as Robin's wife, so you became an uncle and I became a grandmother at about the very same time.'

'You're never a grandmother, Kitty!' he protested, his face a picture of amazement.

'I am indeed.'

'Well, you're the prettiest, youngest-looking grandmother I've ever met in my life.' I've no idea why learning I had a grandchild should prompt him to kiss me, but kiss me he did, full on the lips for quite a long time, and I felt as if I were drowning, drowning, drowning in the soft feather mattress. I knew I should push him away and say something stern, like, 'Don't be so silly, Oliver.' But I didn't want to. I wanted him to keep on kissing me, keep on undoing my blouse and kissing my breasts, sliding his hand underneath my skirt, touching me, touching me . . .

He slid inside me and my body arched to meet his. Oh, God, oh God, oh God! It was so wonderful, so truly, deeply, *fantastically* wonderful. I was shivering, shaking, shuddering, as if my entire being was trying to grasp at something even better that was just slightly beyond my reach. Then I caught it, I reached it, and it was even more wonderful than anything I'd felt before. The feeling faded, like the last grains of sand trickling through an hourglass, and I collapsed like a balloon and Oliver collapsed on top of me.

There was a long silence, until he said in a satisfied voice, 'I've always wanted to do that.'

'That can't be true,' I panted. I was still breathless. 'You were only a small child when we knew each other before.'

'It *is* true. I always wanted you to hold me, cuddle me, stroke my hair. I got angry when you did the same things to Robin. It was you who I wanted to put me to bed, bath me. I used to have wet dreams because of you,' he said accusingly, biting my ear.

'How old were you then?'

'Can't remember.' He bit my other ear. Then he sighed and said, 'I'll have to go. I've already been away too long and they'll wonder where I am.' He climbed off the bed and began to straighten his clothes.

'Where do they think you are now?'

'I said I was going for a walk to clear my head, but they still don't trust me, not completely. I went out the front door and came in again through the back.'

'Now you'll have to go out the back and come in the front?'

'That's right.' He zipped up his jeans, buckled the belt around his waist, ran his fingers through his untidy hair and looked at me. 'When can I see you again, Kitty? I've *got* to see you again.'

'I can stay tomorrow night.' It would be easy to end up like Michael and stay for the rest of my life.

'Not here. It's too risky; for me, that is. I'll find somewhere else and let you know at the funeral.'

'All right.' Mary would think it very odd, me moving to another hotel. I'd have to pretend I was going back to Liverpool. Thank goodness Muriel hadn't come with me. I shouldn't be pleased she'd had to have her appendix out, yet I was. 'But I thought we weren't supposed to know each other?'

'We're not, but someone's bound to introduce me to Michael's sister-in-law. If they don't, I'll introduce myself.' He cradled my face in his hands and kissed me hard on the mouth. 'I'll see you at the funeral, Kitty.'

And with that, he was gone.

The church was packed for the Requiem Mass. The sun shone through the stained-glass windows, the colours dancing on Michael's coffin with its cross of white lilies. I recognized quite a few faces from the bar last night, including the hard-faced men Oliver had been with – and, of course, there was Oliver himself, wearing a cheap suit and a black tie. My heart began to race at the mere sight of him. Most of the women were dressed in black. Mary wore a thick veil over her face, hiding the disfiguring birthmark and making her look mysterious and very lovely.

The priest referred to Michael as 'our good friend' and 'our comrade', and I wondered what my mild-mannered brother-in-law had been up to in Belfast. How strange and unpredictable life was. Had Aileen not left him, he would still be an accountant, living in the house in Maghull, and growing older, cleaning the car on Sundays, discussing whether it was time they bought a new carpet or painted the front door a different colour or where they would go on holiday next year. Eve might not have gone to London, wouldn't have met Rob Horton, wouldn't have a baby called Holly. She might be married to someone else or not married at all. And my own life would have been vastly different in so many ways, the main one being I wouldn't have come to Belfast to Michael's funeral and met Oliver Knowles again.

The wake was a lively affair. There was plenty to eat and drink. As Michael's sole relative present, I was made a particular fuss of. Everyone wanted to shake my hand and impress upon me what a fine boyo Michael had been, the very best, who'd mended their electricity when it broke and didn't charge a penny, or fed their dog and taken it for walks the time they'd gone to England to see their Davy. He'd gone on messages for old Mrs McCready when she was stuck in the house with the terrible 'flu, and was always willing to drop what he was doing and take them to the doctor or the dentist in the Bradys' old van if they didn't feel up to walking.

'He'll be sadly missed,' I was told over and over again.

'Hello, I'm Jack O'Donnell,' a voice said in my ear about halfway through the afternoon. I turned to find Oliver standing behind me and felt a blush come to my cheeks.

'How do you do, Jack?' We shook hands. His grip was warm and strong. 'Did you know Michael well?'

'Not as well as most people here, but he was a decent guy and we'll all miss him. I've booked a room in your name in the Continental Hotel in Great Victoria Street,' he went on in the same conversational tone. 'Take a taxi. I'll see you there at around half past seven. When are you going back to Liverpool, Kitty?'

'On the six o'clock boat,' I said loudly. I looked at my watch and saw it was almost four. 'In fact, it's about time I started getting my things together.' We shook hands again. I told him it had been nice to meet him.

I didn't like being underhand. In fact, I hated telling Mary that I was leaving, when I was doing no such thing, but transferring to another hotel. But it meant I'd see Oliver again and I didn't care. I was in love, properly in love, for the first time in my life, and quite prepared to tell a million lies.

It became awkward when Mary offered to take me to the ferry in the van. 'It'll save you a few bob,' she insisted when I protested I'd sooner phone for a taxi when she was so busy attending to the bar. 'The bar can do without me for half an hour or so. Me da's perfectly capable of managing on his own.'

We hadn't had much chance to be alone together and I realized she wanted to talk about Michael and Aileen. What was Aileen like? Was she pretty? What sort of house had they lived in? Had Michael really had such a good job?

When I told her he'd been a director of the company he'd worked for, she pursed her lips and gave a little whistle. 'Would you fancy that now! He never said anything about his past. What a pity it is that his poor mother couldn't come to the funeral. What did you say her name was?'

'Muriel, she's lovely. She'll be devastated when she finds out he's passed away, but pleased when I tell her he made so many good friends in Belfast. It was a lovely funeral, Mary.'

'A lovely funeral for a lovely man,' she said softly. 'Michael will be sadly missed.'

'That's what everyone said.'

We came to the dock. Mary and I kissed, promising each other we would meet again.

'You must come and have a proper holiday in Belfast. I'll show you the sights.'

'And you must come to Liverpool and meet Muriel. She'd love that.'

She handed me a worn brown envelope. 'These are Michael's papers. There's a Will in there – at least, it ses so on the envelope, I haven't opened it – and his passport, well out of date. I think he intended travelling around the world, but only got this far. Oh, and the old diary where I found your telephone number.'

I thanked her, got out of the van, praying she wouldn't wait for me to go inside the terminal before she drove away. Just in case, I stood on the pavement and waved madly until she started up the van, continuing to wave until it was out of sight. I gave a sigh of relief, went over to a row of taxis and asked to be taken to the Continental Hotel.

The Continental was very grand, with a dead posh foyer full of dead posh people. I registered and was informed the room had been reserved for an indefinite period and to let them know the night before I intended to leave. I entered a lift that was so quiet it hardly seemed to move before it stopped at the fifth floor. The thickly carpeted corridor was as silent as the grave. I found my room, number fifty-five, and as soon as I went in, I dropped everything on the floor, removed my jacket and lay spread-eagled on the double bed.

In a minute, after I'd rested, I'd call Paul Ainsworth to see how Muriel was and tell him about the funeral. After that, I'd have a long hot soak in the bath and wait for Oliver.

It felt as if there was electricity, not blood, running through my veins. I throbbed all over, my feet ached, and my neck was stiff. I couldn't keep still, yet was doing my best to relax. The last two days had been desperately strange, the strangest of my life: finding out about Michael, meeting Oliver, the funeral . . . The events chased each other around my brain. I was glad about Michael, not that he was dead, but because he'd had a good life since leaving Liverpool.

Meeting Oliver had been the strangest thing of all. I couldn't quite get my head around the fact that last night the little boy I'd looked after so many years ago had made love to me – and I could hardly wait for it to happen again.

It *did* happen again, not many hours later. I'd not long emerged from the bath and was still in my petticoat, when there was a knock on the door and I opened it to Oliver, wearing the suit he'd had on at the funeral, though he'd removed the black tie. He gave a whoop, grabbed me in his arms and we sort of danced across to the bed and made love. It was even better than the night before. There wasn't the same rush and we could be more leisurely about it, draw it out, until I wanted to scream because the sensations I was experiencing were almost painful, yet at the same time mixed with delight.

'Wow!' Oliver murmured when it was over. 'That was even better than I imagined when I was three.'

'I never realized you were such an incredibly sexy little boy,' I said lazily.

He grinned. 'I tried to hide my passion for you, that's why.'

'I have to confess I didn't nurse the same passion for you, though I loved you far more than I did Robin.'

'Poor Robin! He didn't know what he was missing.'

'He wasn't missing anything. I always made sure it didn't show.' I sat up, feeling extremely thirsty. 'Shall we order some tea from room service?'

'There isn't time. I have to leave in half an hour and I want to make love to you again before I go.' The look in his eyes made my insides turn to water. 'You can order the tea then.'

'But I thought you were staying the night?' I felt bitterly disappointed.

'I daren't, Kitty, me darling.' He began to stroke my breasts and I forgot my disappointment, forgot everything except Oliver and what he was doing to me. We made love again, this time hurriedly, but just as passionately.

'Can you stay again tomorrow?' he whispered in my ear.

'Yes,' I said promptly. Nothing in this world would have made me refuse.

'It's Saturday, no work to go to. I can get away for longer.'

'What sort of work do you do?'

'I make coffins. There's been quite a few required in Belfast of late.'

Later, I watched him get dressed, marvelling at his beauty and his manliness, his long limbs and broad chest. Muscles rippled on the little chubby arms that had once curled around my neck.

'Why daren't you stay the night?' I asked.

'Because I can't be away too long. I told you last night, they still don't trust me.'

'Who are the "they" you keep talking about?'

'You're an intelligent woman, Kitty. I'm sure you've guessed that already.' He looked at me sorrowfully. 'You're asking questions I can't possibly answer.'

'I'm sorry,' I said abjectly. 'I'm being dead nosy.'

'And I'm sorry I can't be more open with you, but it's all frightfully hush-hush and I can't tell a soul. Mum doesn't know, nor Robin. No one.'

He was in the Army! According to films I'd seen, 'frightfully hush-hush' was an Army expression. He'd infiltrated a group of terrorists and was spying on them, a perilous thing to do. Dear Lord, please keep him safe, I prayed.

After he'd gone, I ordered tea and a sarnie from room service, and spent the rest of the night watching telly or reading the novel I'd brought to read on the boat. I went to bed early, but not before calling room service again and asking to have breakfast sent to my room. It seemed sensible to keep a low profile in the hotel. Someone who'd been at Michael's funeral might work here and I didn't want it getting back to Mary that I was still in Belfast in case it harmed Oliver in some way – I couldn't think in what way, but it was best not to take the chance.

I didn't fall asleep for ages. This was only my second night in Belfast, but it felt more like the hundredth. My life in Liverpool belonged to a different world: only this life was real. But it wouldn't last for ever. Soon, I would have to return to Liverpool. I went to sleep wondering if I would see Oliver again after he'd stopped being a spy and had resumed *his* old life?

I was just finishing breakfast when the telephone rang. 'Good morning, Kitty. I just wanted to make sure you were awake.'

'I'm wide awake and sitting by the window with a cup of coffee. It's a lovely day again.'

'I wish we could go for a walk,' he said wistfully. 'You'd love the Botanic Gardens.'

'I don't want to go for a walk. I want you. Get over here immediately, Oliver, or there'll be trouble like you've never known before.'

'I'm already here. I'm in the foyer and I've brought some wine.'

I hung up, went outside and put the 'Do Not Disturb' sign on the door.

I'd never known a day like it before and never would again, just me and Oliver in a hotel room in Belfast, making love, drinking wine, sleeping, talking, watching TV, then making love again. We showered together and sat by the window, draped in towels, lazily watching people in the street below, feeling sorry for them because they weren't *us*.

'What dull, humdrum lives they must lead,' Oliver remarked.

I agreed. 'They're missing so much.'

He kissed me and said casually, 'Maybe one day, when I'm Oliver Knowles again, we could get married?'

I caught my breath. 'Maybe we could, darling.' I meant it with all my heart, though in my head I had the strongest feeling it would never happen.

'Do you really mean that? You're not just saying it?'

'I said it because I meant it.' I stroked his face and remembered that we shared a birthday. In a fortnight, I would be forty and he would be twenty-four. The age difference didn't bother me, but it might trouble him once he'd had time to think about it. 'I'd love to be your wife, but let's wait until you're Oliver Knowles again and see how you feel about it then.'

'I'll feel exactly as I do now, loving you with all my heart and soul, wanting you to be my wife, wanting us to be together.'

'I know you will.' I took him in my arms and pressed his head against my breast, threading my fingers through his long, untidy hair. 'You must feel very lonely in Belfast.'

'I do. Meeting you has restored my sanity, even if only for a little while.'

'Come with me,' I whispered, taking his hand and leading him to the bed. The towels fell away. I pushed him down and stroked his beautiful body, every inch of it. When I'd finished, I knelt over him, he slid inside me and we journeyed to heaven, returning speechless with wonder and falling asleep in each other's arms. When I woke a good hour later, he was getting dressed.

'I have to go,' he said. 'Will tomorrow be our last day?' He looked as if he was about to cry.

I nodded, wanting to cry, too. Tomorrow was Sunday: if I didn't go home soon, people would start to worry, and I couldn't ask Claire to look after the shop for ever. 'I'll catch the last boat.'

'I'll bring champagne with me,' he promised when he kissed me goodnight.

'That would be the gear, Oliver.'

I cried when he left, wondering how I would get through the next day and, when we said goodbye, if it would be for ever.

The church bells woke me from a strange dream. I'd been on the ferry and Oliver was there, but we'd never managed to come face to face. I kept seeing him disappear around corners or halfway up stairs, yet when I followed, I couldn't find him. I'd turn away, disappointed, only to see him going through a door, but when I entered the same door, there was no sign of him. I woke up feeling unsettled and anxious about something I couldn't quite put my finger on – perhaps it was because I knew I was about to miss Mass for the first time in my life. I was pleased when the telephone rang. It could only be Oliver, and it was.

'How do you fancy champagne with your breakfast?'

'Very much.'

'I'm in the foyer and I'll be up in a minute.'

There was a knock on the door: it was the waiter with breakfast on a trolley. I poured the tea, my unsettled, anxious feeling gone. If yesterday had been good, then today would be even better, even though it was bound to end sadly. I lifted the lid on the platter of bacon, eggs and sausages. There was enough for two and plenty of toast.

I sat in the window in my nightie, sipped the tea and wondered why Oliver hadn't come. Perhaps the lifts had broken down and he was using the stairs. I threw on some clothes and ran along the corridor until I reached the lifts. One stopped and a woman got out and wished me good morning.

'Good morning,' I replied. The door to the stairs was adjacent to the row of lifts. I pushed it open, and stood at the top. 'Hello,' I called, but no one answered and no one came. Back in the corridor, I caught a lift down to the foyer, but there was no sign of Oliver there. I knew at once that something truly dreadful must have taken place.

I stayed in the room all day until it was time to leave for the last boat to Liverpool. In the long hours I spent lying on the bed, I imagined my darling Oliver being bundled out of the hotel into the back of a car, but my imagination refused to go any further. I didn't want to think, couldn't bear to think, what might have happened to him next.

Chapter 9

Eve rang early one morning at the end of May to wish me happy birthday. 'You're forty,' she reminded me, as if I didn't know. 'Getting old.'

'So are you,' I pointed out. 'We all are.'

'Oh, don't!' I imagined her giving a delicate shudder. 'I don't ever want to be forty.'

'You're not the only one, but the only way to avoid it is to die first.'

'You don't seem in a very good mood for your birthday. What's the weather like up there? It's dull and drizzly here.'

I looked out of the window and sighed. 'It's dull and drizzly here.'

'Did you like the handbag?'

'Yes! I'm sorry, I forgot to thank you. It's lovely, just the sort I like.' She'd sent a beautiful red leather bag with loads of pockets.

'That's all right,' she said airily. 'Are you having a party?'

'No, I'm going to dinner in town with Claire, Norah and Marge.' Claire had offered to throw a party, but I'd refused. 'And I was in a perfectly good mood until you reminded me I was getting old.' This wasn't true. I'm not a moody person, but the world had seemed a very dark place since I'd returned from Belfast last month. It still was. 'Anyroad, how's Holly?' My granddaughter was now six weeks old and I'd only seen her the once. 'I'd like to come and visit one day soon.'

'Holly's thriving, and you can come as soon as you like. When's it likely to be?' Her tone was offhand, but I sensed she was anxious for me to come. I was pleased in a way, but sorry if it was a sign she and Rob weren't getting on.

'How about Sunday? I'll drive down.' I'd have to invite Muriel, but reckoned she'd say no. The operation, plus the news about Michael, had taken a lot out of her and she wasn't her old self by a long chalk.

'See you then, Kitty.' She rang off.

The dinner was a bit flat. It was my fault: I couldn't get into the swing of things. There were few laughs and too many awkward silences that even Claire, with her usual exuberance, was unable to fill. The food was excellent, but I couldn't stop reflecting how much my sisters and my friend had changed, as if I was only just noticing that, like me, they'd aged. I was aware of Claire's sprinkling of grey hair – not surprising since she was fifty-two – Norah's drooping mouth – she'd been down in the dumps since Bernadette had got married – and the non-existence of Marge's waistline – she ate too much.

I drove home wondering why you were supposed to feel happy on your birthday. At what age did you stop feeling glad you were a year older and wish you were a year younger? Twenty-nine, I decided, when you realized this time next year you'd be in your thirties and life was getting shorter.

'What the heck . . .' I muttered when I stopped outside the house and saw the lights were on inside and a bright yellow Mini was parked in the drive. I went in to find a carrycot and a large suitcase in the hall, and Eve in the lounge. She was wearing a hideous geometric-striped frock and nursing an irritable Holly.

'I didn't know you'd passed your driving test?' was all I could think of to say. The last I'd heard she was taking lessons.

I was treated to a dazzling smile. 'I haven't, but I can drive perfectly well. The instructor said I'd taken to it like a duck to water.'

'You mean you drove all the way from London and you haven't passed your test?'

'Yes,' she said proudly, as if she'd done something enormously clever. 'I just took the L-plates off. Why are you carrying two handbags?'

'I got the white one off our Norah for my birthday.' I sat down with a bump. 'What are you doing here?' I got up again and took the crying baby off her knee. She felt far too hot. I removed her fine woollen shawl, put her over my shoulder and rubbed her back. 'There, there, sweetheart,' I cooed.

'It's my house, isn't it? Daddy – Michael – confirmed he wanted me to have it in his Will. I'm not exactly trespassing.'

'No one's accused you of trespassing, Eve. I merely asked why you were here.' She looked so cocky my hand itched to slap her face. Since she'd left home, my feelings for her had changed. She was no longer the shy, awkward little girl who'd cried herself to sleep on her granddad's knee and made my heart ache, but an arrogant young woman who got on my nerves rather a lot. I loved her as much as ever, but the mother–daughter relationship seemed far more healthy and normal nowadays.

'I've left Rob,' she said dramatically, throwing back her head and making her long silver earrings dance. 'I've only just realized what a shit he is. He's supposed to be an art dealer, but all he does is buy paintings off art students for peanuts, then sell them at a huge profit.'

'It's called capitalism,' I said tartly. 'It happens every time you buy something from a shop.' Holly had stopped crying and was in the process of emptying her bowels.

'Whatever it's called, it stinks.' So did Holly.

'And the realization that Rob's a shit only hit you today? There was no mention of leaving him when you called this morning.'

'Well, actually, Kitty,' her face went pink, 'Rob's father, Barney, was arrested this afternoon and charged with receiving stolen property, and Mrs Horton came charging round to stay with us claiming she'd be scared living on her own. But worse than that – that's if there could be anything worse than living under the same roof as my mother-in-law – I'm worried Rob might be involved. Sometimes, he sells antiques as well as paintings and I've no idea where they come from.'

It would appear she had no intention of 'standing by her man' as the song went. And what a charming family she'd married into. 'Does that mean you're home for good?'

'I suppose it does. Do you mind?'

I raised my eyebrows and gave a nonchalant shrug. 'Would it matter if I did? After all, as you just reminded me, it's *your* house.'

She went pink again. 'I didn't mean it like that; you know I didn't. This is your home for as long as you want. Can I have something to eat? I'm starving.'

'You can either make it yourself or change Holly's nappy, one or the other.'

'I'll make the food,' she said with alacrity. 'I don't know how to change nappies. Francine, the *au pair*, always did it.'

'You'd better learn quick,' I said sharply. 'I don't intend making a habit of it.'

'Well, you certainly didn't make a habit of changing *mine*,' she retorted just as sharply, as she left the room and started to bang things around in the kitchen.

I'd asked for that, I thought ruefully. 'Where are the nappies?' I shouted.

'In that bag on the settee.'

I laid Holly on the floor and rooted through the bag, but could see no sign of nappies, until I realized the packet of cotton wool pads, like giant sanitary towels, were the type that were used once, then flushed down the lavatory. I'd heard of them, but never seen them before. 'Do you always use the disposable sort?' I shouted again. 'Aren't they very expensive?'

'*Very* expensive, but the towelling ones have to be *washed*.'

'Oh, dear,' I said to Holly who'd woken up and was regarding me with wise blue eyes. 'We can't have Mummy *washing* your nappies, can we?' Holly kicked her feet in agreement. 'Let's take you upstairs and I'll change you in the bathroom.'

I had to flush the lavatory three times before the dirty nappy went down. In future, they'd be put in the bin. It'd smell to high heaven, but better than having blocked drains.

When I returned downstairs with a sweetly scented Holly – I'd sprinkled her bottom liberally with talcum powder – Eve was at the table eating beans on toast. 'Is that all you could find?' I asked. 'There's loads of food out there.'

'It's all I could be bothered doing. I've lost the knack of cooking.' I couldn't remember her having had it. 'We mainly ate out, and Francine did the cooking at home.'

'Does Holly need feeding?'

'There's a bottle and a tin of formula in the bag. The instructions are on the side. Perhaps you can get it ready while I eat.'

'Did Francine usually do that, too?'

'Yes,' she said belligerently, 'but I always gave Holly the bottle.'

'That's good to know.'

She choked on the beans and spluttered, 'If you're going to say things like that all the time, Kitty, I'll go back to London.'

I looked at her and grinned. 'Would I be worse to live with than Mrs Horton?'

'I don't suppose so, no,' she said, grinning back, much to my relief.

I was glad she was home, I thought, when I got into bed. It gave me a good feeling to know my daughter was in the room next to mine, and my granddaughter fast asleep in her carrycot in the spare. Eve's old cot was in the loft: I'd fetch it down in the morning. It would probably need a new mattress. I fell asleep wondering if I bought one in town tomorrow, would it be possible to carry it home on the train? It made a pleasant change from the dark thoughts I usually had these days.

The wretched, heart-rending wail woke me at precisely half past three. I lay there for a while, unable to work out what the sound was, until I realized it was Holly crying. I waited for Eve to see to her, but when it appeared that wasn't going to happen, got up and walked like a zombie on to the landing. Eve had actually had the nerve to close her bedroom door! No doubt, poor Francine had seen to the baby during the night. Holly was the perfect baby, Eve had boasted when Muriel and I had gone to see her, but Holly could have been the worst baby in the world and her mother wouldn't have known. I was beginning to wish she'd brought Francine with her.

'What's up with you?' I whispered to my granddaughter. She stopped crying and looked at me pleadingly. I wasn't sure if the look meant she was hungry or needed a change of nappy, so thought I'd better see to both. I changed the nappy, made the bottle and gave it to her sitting up in bed. 'Your mother will have to pull her socks up,' I told her as she sucked contentedly. 'If she thinks I'm going to take over the role of *au pair*, she's got another think coming.'

As soon as she was back in the cot and fast asleep, I opened Eve's door as wide as it would go. She was as still as a corpse, only the slight movement of her chest indicating she was still alive. If Holly woke again, I wanted to make sure her mother would hear.

*

She appeared while I was having breakfast on what was another dull, drizzly day. She hadn't washed her make-up off the night before, and there were dark smudges under her eyes. In her skimpy cotton nightie, with her blonde hair all tousled, she looked like a street urchin, like the pathetic waifs who'd come to Hilda's house in Everton Valley. I'd forgotten just how long her legs were. 'You should have stayed in bed,' I told her. 'I was going to bring you up a cup of tea before I left.'

'Left!' Her mouth fell open. 'Left for where?'

'For work. I manage a shop, remember?'

She looked dismayed. 'But you're not going today, surely?'

'I can't think of any reason why I shouldn't,' I said crisply.

'But I can't manage Holly on my own,' she cried. 'I need you here. She's likely to wake up any minute and I won't know what to do.'

'I'll ring your Auntie Claire in a minute and ask her to come round. She'll sort you out. It's a pity you didn't breastfeed Holly. It's far less trouble than bottles.'

'You didn't breastfeed me,' she said sulkily.

'Well, I can't make it up to you now by breastfeeding your daughter.'

To my horror, tears came to her eyes. 'Do you have to be so flippant about everything?'

'Best to be flippant than get angry and upset every time you point out what a useless mother I was.' I wouldn't have minded a good cry myself.

'I'm sorry.' She sniffed pathetically. 'Although you *were* a useless mother.'

I conceded I'd been an absent mother rather than a useless one, and said I was sorry, too. 'We seem to be scoring points off each other all the time. Perhaps we should make a vow to be nice to each other from now on?'

She nodded. 'I'll go along with that.'

As an indication of how nice I could be, I told her to sit down, poured her a cup of tea and offered to go to work late. 'I'll wait until Claire comes – it'll give you time to have a shower and something to eat – and I'll show you how to change a nappy. It's dead easy with the disposable sort. Will you be able to afford them from now on? I mean, will you get an allowance from Rob?'

'Not if he has to go to prison with his dad. But we have loads of money in our joint account. I can use that.'

'You won't if Rob gets to it first. If I were you, I'd go to the bank as quickly as possible, start a new account of your own and transfer the money into that.'

She wrinkled her nose. 'It seems a horrid thing to do.'

'But sweetheart,' I reasoned, 'you have Holly to look after. You'll need money for her, and for yourself. You're entitled to what's in the account. Do you love Rob? Are you worried about hurting him?'

'I don't give a shit about Rob,' she said bluntly. 'I never loved him, but he loved me and that seemed enough. He'd been pleading with me to marry him for ages, but the minute I did, he went right off me. Well, not the minute,' she conceded, 'but not long afterwards. He stopped talking to me and went out with other women. He was *unfaithful*!' She seemed more outraged than upset. 'It was as if I no longer mattered now that I was his wife. If it weren't for that, I'd've stuck by him if he went to prison. It's what wives do, isn't it?' She looked at me with huge, moist eyes.

'Oh, Eve!' I reached for her hand. 'I wish you'd told me this before.' I felt outrage that she'd had to put up with such behaviour at such a young age.

'I imagined you saying, "I told you so." You advised me only to marry someone I wanted to spend the rest of my life with. I didn't think that far ahead when I married Rob.'

'I would never have said such a thing!' On reflection, there was a good chance that I might have. 'Would you like some toast, sweetheart?'

'Yes, please, Kitty.' Her bottom lip quivered.

After I'd made the toast and another pot of tea, I telephoned Claire, who promised to drop everything and come straight away. I had no idea how the McCarthys would have managed without her kind heart. Despite her own large family, she was always available in a crisis. 'The older kids get, the more trouble they are,' she declared. 'Poor Norah and Roy don't know whether they're coming or going. They've got Bernadette, the baby and that lazy bugger of a son-in-law living with them. The house is a tip, Bernadette never stops crying and neither does little Debbie, and all the so-called son-in-law does is lounge around, eating them out of house and home and watching telly.'

'It's not that bad here,' I said thankfully, 'but I think *my* so-called son-in-law might possibly end up in jail quite soon.'

It was a relief to enter the quiet shop. Someone had put a note through the door saying, 'I thought you were supposed to be OPEN!' I tore it up, not caring if I'd lost a regular customer. I didn't care about a lot of things these days: how I looked, if I ate, what I said. I'd been horrible to Eve last night, not the least bit sympathetic. I cared about *that*. She'd seemed so irresponsible, running away from her husband after only a few months, not giving the marriage a chance. Now I knew differently, but she really should have got to know Rob better before she married him.

I put the kettle on, sold a box of ballpoint pens, made tea, answered the phone: yes, we did stock raffle tickets; no, we didn't close for lunch. I put the receiver back, picked it up again straight away and dialled a number. A soft, beautifully modulated voice said, 'Hello, Faith Knowles speaking.'

I hung up. It was the fourth time I'd done it and I still didn't know why. It was as if hearing his mother's voice was the next best thing to hearing Oliver's.

When I arrived home at the end of the day, Claire had gone, but Muriel was there. Eve and Holly were having a little nap, she informed me. 'Your sister had to leave, so Eve rang and asked if I'd come.' She looked terribly pleased to be wanted. She'd made a cheese and egg flan and boiled some new potatoes for tea. Earlier, she told me, she'd taken Holly for a long walk while Eve had caught the train to Walton Vale. 'She had to go to the bank and seems to have lost the keys to her car.'

'They're not lost, they're in my bag.' The car had been left unlocked, the keys in the ignition. Anybody could have stolen it. 'She hasn't taken her driving test, yet she drove all the way from London.' I was still shocked. 'I took them with me so she couldn't use it.'

Muriel tut-tutted. 'It's a good job you did, dear. Young people, they can be very daring, though Michael was always extremely cautious about everything. He never took chances.' Since her son had died, she spoke about him a lot. She was looking much better today and it turned out she'd telephoned Mary Brady and arranged to stay in Buckles the weekend after next.

'I'm so looking forward to it,' she said now. 'We can share our memories of Michael.'

'They'll be very different memories,' I warned.

'I know that, Kitty, but I think it will do us both good.'

Eve came in wearing white sandals and a fetching red frock with a halterneck. 'Holly's still asleep. Is tea ready? I'm starving.'

'Everything's prepared, I'll put it out.' Muriel hurried into the kitchen.

'You're always starving,' I remarked.

'Do you mind?' she asked frostily.

'Of course I don't. I'm pleased you have a healthy appetite. Shall we set the table for Muriel?' I nearly added, 'unless you've lost the knack', but remembered I'd promised to be nice.

'I rang Penny earlier,' Eve announced. 'She's back from London for good. We sort of lost touch after I got married. Would you mind babysitting Holly tomorrow night so we can go to a club or something?'

'I don't mind, no.' I could see my life was about to be turned upside-down and inside-out. I'd arranged to go to the pictures that night with Marge to see *Butch Cassidy and the Sundance Kid* for the second time. Marge wasn't sure whether she fancied Paul Newman or Robert Redford the most. I'd call later and change it to the night after.

Society was breaking down, or at least the McCarthys' little part of it was. Lisa left our Jamie and went back to live in Berlin with their two children. As quick as a flash, Jamie turned up in Amethyst Street with a new girlfriend – Claire was convinced she was an old girlfriend and the reason why Lisa had left.

Norah and Roy threw their son-in-law out and told him not to return until he'd found work and could pay his way. Bernadette was bereft, but didn't go with him.

Then Claire's son, Bobby, the adorable baby I'd seen in hospital only days after he was born, now a handsome twenty-one-year-old, was revealed to be having an affair with a married woman almost twice his age.

'What's the world coming to?' Claire shrieked. 'Morals have gone right out the window. Thank the Lord Mam and Dad aren't alive. This would kill them for sure.'

I pointed out that she and Liam had had to get married, so had our Danny and Marge, and I'd had Eve. 'We were just as immoral, but these days things are more open and honest. I like it better this way.'

'Oh, you would,' Claire said shortly. 'You've never swum with the tide.'

I was about to swim against the tide again. Claire always claimed she could tell from a woman's face if she was expecting a baby, but so far she hadn't guessed I was three months pregnant with Oliver Knowles's child.

'Hello, Faith Knowles speaking.'

'Faith! You'll never guess who this is: Kitty, Kitty McCarthy. Do you remember me?'

'Kitty! As if I could ever forget you!' Faith said warmly. 'What a lovely surprise to hear from you after all this time. How are you, dear?'

'Very well, thanks. What about you?'

'I'm well, too, thank you, Kitty. I felt a little odd rattling around this big house on my own – Mother died a long while ago – so I put it on the market and it's just been sold.' I imagined her in the big hall where the phone was kept on a little carved table next to a tapestry chair, the sun streaming through the window making the polished wood floor gleam. It was August and the entire country was basking in a heat wave.

I licked my dry lips. 'And how are the boys?'

'Robin got married last year to a lovely girl called Alice. Their twin sons, Jeremy and Stuart, were born around Easter time. They really are adorable, Kitty,' she said proudly. 'You'd love them.'

'I'm sure I would. What about Oliver?'

There was a pause. 'Oliver's here with me.'

My head reeled. I didn't know what to say. I licked my lips again and thought of something. 'The reason I phoned, Faith, is I'm coming to London on Sunday in the car. I thought I might pop in and see you.'

Another pause. When she spoke again, her tone was polite rather than warm. 'It would be nice to see you again, Kitty. In fact, I've been looking for a property your way – Robin lives in Preston and

I'd like to see more of the twins. I've had details of a house in Southport I quite fancy. I'll show them to you when you come. We used to be so close,' she went on wistfully, 'almost like sisters. It was Eric's fault we stopped being friends. Still, that's all water under the bridge now, isn't it?'

I said, at least I think I said, and it came out more like a mumble, that we could be friends again when she moved to Southport. She asked what time to expect me tomorrow – I hadn't realized Sunday was tomorrow – and I said about midday. With that, we rang off.

The trees in the back garden were taller: I could see them soaring over the roof when I walked down the path at ten to twelve. I'd left Maghull early, just after seven, as I had no idea of the way: the road map that had belonged to Michael didn't make sense.

'It's way out of date,' Eve said. 'There's a new motorway, the M1, that isn't shown. Would you like me to come with you?' she asked kindly, as if she was talking to an old woman who'd never looked at a map in her life, let alone a road map. 'I could leave Holly with Muriel and be your guide.'

'No, ta. I'll manage.' I would have loved to have her as a guide, but this was a journey I had to make on my own.

'What's wrong with this Faith person anyway, that you have to drive all the way to Richmond in such a hurry?'

'There's nothing wrong – well, not much. It's just that she badly needs my advice about something so I offered to go and see her.' I appreciated her concern, but wished she'd stop asking questions. I'd had to offer an explanation as to why I was about to disappear for the day and had stuck as close to the truth as I could.

She made a list of the towns and villages I would pass through and the numbers of the roads, instructing me to keep it on the seat beside me. 'But don't study it while you're driving. Find somewhere to stop first,' she added.

'Yes, Eve,' I said meekly. She'd only passed her driving test a month ago, but obviously considered herself an expert compared to me, who'd been driving since not long after she was born.

I managed the journey with relative ease, no doubt due to Eve's directions – I'd tell her so when I got back – and now, here I was, ringing the bell, waiting for Faith to open the door, knowing that Oliver was somewhere inside, and he would tell me why he hadn't come to the hotel room in Belfast, why he hadn't tried to track me down since it would have been a relatively simple thing to do.

Faith answered the door and threw her arms around me. 'Why oh why haven't we done this before?' she cried. She held me by the shoulders. 'You've hardly changed from the young girl who came to see me in Orrell Park all those years ago – how many is it? Twenty-one?'

I conceded that it was. 'You've hardly changed either, Faith.' I remember how much I'd envied her perfect bone structure. Now she was in her sixties and there were fine lines beneath her eyes and around her mouth, but her neck was smooth and slender, with no suggestion of a double chin. She would remain a lovely woman until the day she died. She wore a simple white cotton frock that showed off her tanned arms.

'Come in, dear, come in. I'll just make us a drink for now: we can have lunch later. Would you prefer tea or coffee?'

'Coffee, please.' We'd always drunk coffee in the past, never tea.

'Let's have it in the kitchen. It's lovely and sunny out there, much nicer than that stuffy old dining room. Try to ignore the mess: I've been turning out the loft. You wouldn't believe the stuff I found up there.' There were packing cases in the hall, books piled on the stairs, heaps of bedding tied with string. All I was interested in was Oliver, but there was no sign of him.

'Now sit down, Kitty, and tell me every single thing that's happened since the last time we met.' Faith put a mug of coffee in front of me, shoved a plate of fig biscuits in my direction and sat at the other side of the table prepared to listen. For all her affability, I could tell it was mainly for my benefit, that she was upset about something. Her long slender hands were trembling, so much so that when she'd put the coffee down some had spilled on to the white cloth, yet she hadn't noticed.

Nevertheless, I told her everything, starting with Hilda and Dorothy and the house in Everton Valley, and finishing with Eve leaving Rob and bringing Holly to live with me in Maghull, condensing the entire history of my adult life into a few hundred words that took only minutes to relate. Something prompted me not to say Michael's funeral had been held in Belfast, but that was the only thing I left out.

'So, you're a grandmother,' she gushed when I'd finished – Faith had always gushed when she was nervous. 'How incredible! You look so young, yet we both acquired grandchildren at around the same time. By the way, Hope has a whole horde of step-grandchildren. You won't know, but she married a widower with five children not long after Graham died.'

'What happened to Fred?' I asked suddenly. 'I wrote to him loads of times, but he never answered.'

'Graham left Fred his apartment in the South of France, Monte Carlo, I think it was – is. Fred moved out there straight away. For all I know, he may still be there, living the life of Riley.'

There was still no sign of Oliver. I was about to ask after him – was praying he hadn't deliberately gone out when he knew I was coming, that he wanted to avoid me – but then Faith said, 'I'll take you to see Oliver. He's in the garden.' She got to her feet. I followed unsteadily. My heart felt as if it was twice, three times, its normal size as it hammered noisily away in my breast.

A chair in which was sitting an achingly familiar figure had been placed beneath the large, shady elm tree that Oliver used to climb when he was a small boy. I'd had to climb up and rescue him more than once, even though I'd been expecting Eve. Two things struck me: Oliver didn't turn his head when his mother approached; and the chair was in fact a wheelchair with a catheter hooked on the side.

'Oliver, darling.' Faith knelt on the grass, took one of Oliver's hands and pressed it to her cheek. 'There's someone to see you. Remember Kitty? Remember she used to look after you and Robin when you were little? Look, darling, here she is.'

But Oliver's head remained perfectly still. The parched grass made a crunching noise as I walked across and stood in front of the wheelchair, feeling sick to my stomach when I saw the dead eyes in Oliver's gaunt, expressionless face. His shaven head was covered with a faint bristle of black hair.

Faith had begun to weep. 'They kneecapped him,' she said in a harsh whisper, 'then they beat him with baseball bats until they'd knocked all the sense out of him. He can't hear, he can't walk, he can't understand anything. All that's left is a shell of my lovely son.'

'How did it happen, Faith?' My legs still felt unsteady, but I managed to kneel beside her and take Oliver's other hand. It felt unnaturally cold. I shivered. The branches of the tree shivered, too, and little bright sun-patches danced on the grass.

'He joined the Army – Captain Knowles. I was so proud of him.' Tears were running down her cheeks, but she didn't bother to wipe them away. 'Since he left university, he'd been very restless, showed no sign of settling down, not like Robin who went to Teacher Training College: he'd always wanted to teach. Oliver started half a dozen jobs, but always gave them up, claiming he was bored. I was relieved when he joined the Army; a career at last, I thought.' She gave a melancholy smile. I put my free hand on her shoulder and squeezed it.

'He was sent to Belfast,' she continued, 'and I knew straight away that something odd was going on. I had to send his letters to a box number. He hardly ever wrote back, never explained anything. Then this happened . . .' She stopped for a few seconds, unable to go on. 'I can only guess the reason for it; the Army didn't offer a proper explanation.'

'Shouldn't he be in hospital?'

'He usually is. This is the first weekend he's been allowed home. The doctors thought it would do him good, being in a familiar place with his mother.'

'Do you think it has?' I gripped Oliver's hand hard, pressing my thumb against his palm, but he showed no reaction. I remembered the way the same hand had stroked my body, touched me . . .

'I don't know,' Faith wept. 'I can't tell. Sometimes I think his eyes show a flash of recognition, or his mouth moves in a smile, but it's probably just my imagination. I want it to happen so much. So much,' she repeated. 'So very, very much.'

'*Will* it happen?' I asked, wanting to know everything there was to know about my beloved Oliver. 'I mean, he'll get better, won't he, one day?'

'The doctors think there's a fifty-fifty chance he'll snap out of it, but there's been permanent damage to his brain and he might never again be the Oliver we used to know.' She gently placed Oliver's hand on his knee and sat back on her heels. 'Would you like a drink, Kitty? An alcoholic one? I'm ashamed to say I've been drinking a lot since this happened – taking after Mother, I suspect – and have acquired a taste for brandy, but there's plenty of other drinks inside.'

'A small sherry would be nice,' I said, just to be sociable.

She got to her feet with a sigh and went indoors. I kissed Oliver softly on the lips. 'Sweetheart, it's Kitty. We met again in Belfast, remember? You were playing the piano in a hotel called Buckles and afterwards you came up to my room and we made love. You told me you'd always loved me, ever since you were a little boy, and we made love again and again in a different hotel. Can you remember how wonderful it was, Oliver, my darling? You asked if I would marry you one day and I said yes, that I would. Well, now we can get married, if it's what you want. Oh!' I groaned. 'Speak to me, Oliver, say something, anything. Just speak to me.'

'That's what the doctor said we should do.' Faith had returned with a drink in each hand. 'Talk to him. I must have dredged up every single solitary memory over the last two days, but I may as well have talked to that tree for all the use it's done,' she finished bitterly.

'It's bound to take time.'

'I suppose,' she said in a hopeless voice.

'Don't give up, Faith,' I pleaded. 'Does Eric know what's happened? After all, he's Oliver's father.' She needed someone to support her at a time like this. I couldn't see Hope being of much use, and Robin lived hundreds of miles away in Preston and had a family of his own to care for.

'Eric!' Her shoulders twisted, as if she found the name repugnant. 'The last I heard of Eric he was living with a woman half his age and had started another family. I haven't the faintest notion of how to get in touch with him. Robin telephones daily, and Charlie's in Hong Kong. He never married and sends long sympathetic letters, as well as telephoning once a week, but he has a very important job in a bank and can't come rushing home at the drop of a hat.' Charlie, I recalled, was the son from her first marriage whom I'd never met.

'Will you be bringing Oliver with you if you move to Southport?' I asked.

'Oh, yes. There's a hospital in Chester that will have him and bring him home for weekends.' She looked thoughtfully at her son. 'I suppose he *has* improved a little since I first saw him. His head used to droop, but now he's able to hold it straight. The doctors say he's physically very fit, so that should help.'

'I'm sure it will.' I wanted Oliver to get better more than anything in the world.

I suggested we ate lunch outside, 'right in front of him. And bring that portable wireless I saw in the kitchen and play it very loud. We'll *make* him notice us, even if it's only in his mind.'

She dissolved into tears again. 'When you rang yesterday, I was about to tell you not to come, but then I remembered how good you'd been with him and Robin. I'm so glad you came, Kitty. You always seemed to know what to do.'

I stayed until the ambulance came at about six o'clock and took Oliver away. At some point in the afternoon, Faith asked the real reason why I'd come to London. 'You were coming anyway, weren't you, not just to see me?'

'Eve left most of her clothes in the flat in Chelsea. She's rather anxious to get them back, particularly the winter ones, but doesn't fancy coming face to face with her mother-in-law. I offered to collect them for her.' Only the last sentence was a lie. Eve really was anxious to retrieve her leather coats and thigh-length boots, and other things she couldn't possibly afford to replace, at least not like with like. 'But,' I said to Faith, 'it's not all that important. I can always collect them another time. I'd sooner stay with you and Oliver.'

By now, I was three months pregnant and supposed it was time I told everyone. To my astonishment, Eve burst out laughing. 'You,' she said in a choked voice, 'are the weirdest mother anyone could possibly have. Fancy having an illegitimate baby at your age! And who's the father? I've never even seen you with a man.'

Marge merely grinned. 'Congratulations, Kitty. Who's the lucky feller?'

'Oh, Kitty!' Norah sighed. 'You're not married and I'd've thought you'd know better than to get pregnant at your age. Have you no shame?'

I had to concede that I hadn't.

Our Claire was tearing her hair out because I flatly refused to reveal the identity of the father. 'Ah, come on, Kit, you can tell me,' she said coaxingly.

I still refused. It was a secret I'd resolved to take with me to my grave.

Hilda and Dorothy were quite blasé about it. They'd seen enough during their long, eventful lives and nothing could shock them any more. Dorothy offered to knit baby clothes: 'White, so they'll do whether it's a boy or a girl. What would you like, Kitty, dear?'

'I don't mind,' I said airily, though I badly wanted a boy, another Oliver.

I told Faith the next time I went to Richmond – it was obvious by then – and all she said was I seemed to be making a habit of getting pregnant every twenty years.

Muriel was the only one to disapprove. I could tell by the way her lips tightened when I gave her the news. She didn't say anything, so I left her to get used to the idea of her own accord.

I was twice as old as when I'd had Eve. This time I went to see a doctor straight away. He examined me and pronounced me to be as healthy as a horse, but suggested I come and see him immediately if I had a problem. He wanted me back in month, anyway. 'So I can keep an eye on you. Oh, and I see on your card you're down as Kitty McCarthy, Miss. Can I have your married name?'

'I haven't got one,' I said cheerfully. 'I'm still Kitty McCarthy, Miss.'

Two months later, on a cold, breezy day in October, Faith moved to Southport. I went to see her the same night to help sort things out in the pretty, three-bedroom bungalow with a large, mature garden and roses around the front door.

Robin was there. He was only two when I last saw him, but we hugged and kissed and he swore he would have recognized me anywhere. 'And I seem to remember you were pregnant when we lived in Richmond. Oliver and I thought you were growing fat, but Mum said you were expecting a baby.' Oliver had told me the same thing in Belfast.

'Well, *I* wouldn't have recognized *you*!' He wasn't quite as tall as Oliver, not quite so handsome. He showed me photographs of his twins; I said they looked just like him.

'They're bringing Oliver to Chester tomorrow,' Faith told me. 'He's coming home for two days at the end of next week.'

I promised I would be there. 'Has he made any more progress since I saw him last?' I'd been to Richmond twice since my first visit and was convinced I could see an improvement. I hoped it wasn't just wishful thinking on my part that he seemed more alert, that his eyes weren't quite so dead.

'Yes!' Faith said, glowing. 'He can drink through a straw, so doesn't have to be fed intravenously any more, and he looks much more like himself since his hair's grown.' She didn't see anything strange about my interest in Oliver's welfare, but seemed to find it perfectly natural that I would be concerned about the little boy I'd loved so dearly in the past.

'What are you going to do about money when you have the baby?' Eve asked one morning when we were having breakfast. 'You'll have to give up the shop. I still have plenty in my account, but it won't last for ever. I should get maintenance when the divorce goes through, though I don't know how much: it depends on Rob's financial situation.' She was divorcing Rob on the grounds of adultery. Barney's trial was set for December and, as far as she knew, Rob hadn't been accused of any crime. 'Perhaps the antiques he sold were above board and he's completely innocent, or perhaps Barney's protecting him. Either way, I'm not going back. I've had enough of Rob Horton.'

I groaned. 'I've been wondering how I'll manage without a job myself.'

'Aren't you entitled to something called Maternity Leave?'

'For six weeks before the baby's born and six weeks after. Our Claire's offered to fill in for me: she likes the shop and the money comes in useful, but I can't see me taking over again with a small baby, can you?' I groaned again.

'It's no use complaining, Kitty,' Eve said with a grin. 'It's your own fault for getting pregnant by the invisible man. What if I looked after the shop and you looked after Holly?' she added casually.

'*What?*' I screeched.

'You heard. By then, Holly will be almost eleven months and she's already as good as gold.'

'She'll have started crawling by then and she'll have to be fed, her nappies changed, bathed.' I listed the things on my fingers. 'Who'll do the washing? Who'll clean the house? And please don't say you will, Eve, because I know darn well you won't. I'll be worked off me feet,' I finished indignantly. Actually, it wasn't such a bad idea: plenty of women managed to look after two babies at the same time.

'We can do the housework together at the weekend – Auntie Claire will give us a hand.'

'Do you seriously think I'd ask her? Anyroad, what makes you think Muriel will agree to you looking after her shop?'

'I can wrap Muriel around my little finger,' Eve said with a smirk. 'She'll let me do anything I want.'

I promised to think about it, knowing in the end I would agree.

Eve was longing to meet Oliver. 'It sounds so romantic,' she sighed, 'like that film *Random Harvest* with Ronald Colman and Greer Garson. It was on television the other week. They fell in love and got married, but he had an accident, lost his memory and forgot all about her, so she became his secretary and he fell in love with her all over again.'

'There's nothing romantic about Oliver, sweetheart,' I said sadly. I recalled seeing *Random Harvest* with Marge when we were about fifteen: we'd cried our eyes out. 'He hasn't just lost his memory, his brain is damaged. He can't walk or feed himself.'

'Yes, but he's getting better, isn't he? You said so last time you went.' I agreed that was the case and suggested she came with me the next time I went to Southport. According to Oliver's doctors, the more people he met the more stimulated his brain would be.

November turned out to be one of those dreary months when the sun never seemed to shine and the sky was always grey. It rained almost every day and was raining the Sunday I took Eve to Southport to meet Oliver. Holly lay on the back seat in her carrycot, gurgling away as she played with her feet. She was a pretty, easy-going little girl, with her father's straight black hair. Her eyes had turned a lovely golden brown.

The bungalow was cosy and warm. Faith had got rid of the big, old-fashioned furniture from her old house, and bought smaller items to suit the smaller rooms. Oliver was in the lounge in his wheelchair in front of a blazing fire. Faith's embroidery frame lay on the cherry-red settee and the standard lamp emitted a rosy pink glow. The room was scattered with little Victorian tables and there was a pretty writing bureau on one of the flower-sprigged walls.

'Visitors, Oliver,' Faith said in a loud voice as she showed us in. Oliver's head moved, only slightly, in our direction. His eyes wavered, but it was impossible to tell if he could see us or not.

I crossed the room and kissed his cheek. 'I've brought my daughter to see you, Oliver. Her name's Eve.' He was looking better, I was sure of it, like a man slowly waking after a long, deep sleep. I half expected him to blink and say, 'Where am I?'

'Hello, Oliver,' Eve said shyly. 'It's nice to meet you. Kitty's told me such a lot about you. This is Holly, my little girl. She's seven months old. Would you like to hold her?'

I gasped when Eve put the baby on his knee. Faith said sharply, 'No!'

'It's all right, I won't let her go.' Eve left her hand firmly on Holly's plump waist, but there was no need. I gasped again when Oliver's arms curled around the tiny girl and he looked down at her *and smiled.*

'Oh, my God!' Faith collapsed on the settee.

But the miracle wasn't over yet. Eve pressed her hands against Oliver's cheeks and put her face close to his. 'This is Holly, Oliver. Holly.' And Oliver's mouth opened and he said falteringly, 'Hol . . . *ly*.'

'And I'm Eve. Eve, say it after me, Oliver: *Eve*.'

'Eve,' Oliver said, very slowly, 'Eve.'

'There, that was very clever.' Eve sniffed and burst into tears.

'I don't know what came over me,' she said later when we were having tea on our knees in the lounge. Holly was fast asleep in her carrycot, and Oliver had dozed off in the chair. 'As soon as I saw him, I went all funny, dizzy almost, and I just knew if I concentrated hard enough I could *will* him to do things. My hands were tingly, as if there was power flowing through them, into Oliver's brain, so that he knew what I wanted him to do.'

Instead of being pleased with herself, she seemed very subdued and shaken by what she had achieved. 'Can I come and see him again tomorrow?' she asked.

'I'm afraid he won't be here,' Faith said. She regarded my daughter with a certain amount of awe. 'The ambulance will be coming for him in an hour or two. But I'll ask the hospital if he can start coming home midweek: Wednesday, say. You're more than welcome to come then. I'm sure his doctors will be impressed with the progress he's made today. Thank you, Eve.' Her eyes shone with a mixture of gratitude and tears. 'Thank you so much for what you've done for Oliver.'

★

'Kitty?' Eve said sleepily on the way home.

'Yes, sweetheart?'

'Remember what you said about not marrying a man you didn't want to spend the rest of your life with?'

'I remember, yes.'

'Well, the minute I saw Oliver Knowles, I knew he was the one I wanted to spend the rest of *my* life with.' She sighed contentedly. 'As soon as he's better, I'm going to marry him.'

I'd lost all interest in the shop. I ran it as efficiently as ever, kept the place fully stocked, changed the window display regularly and was already geared up for Christmas with scores of special gifts. But when I locked the door on Christmas Eve, it would be for the last time. Claire would take over until I'd had my baby and felt well enough to look after Holly. Then the key would be handed to Eve.

November had come to its miserable end and December had brought sun and clear blue skies. I sat behind the counter on what had been an unusually slow morning, looking out on to the sunny street, thinking about Eve and Oliver.

Oliver was improving rapidly. He still couldn't walk, but that was due to the kneecapping and he would walk again with time.

Although his speech was hesitant, his vocabulary was growing, and he could recognize people and remember their names. But his life before the vicious beating remained a complete blank. For the second time, he learned that Faith was his mother and Robin his brother. And I was a friend.

'A very old friend, darling,' Faith informed him. 'Kitty used to look after you and Robin when you were little.'

And Oliver had smiled at me, a sweet, generous smile, but there wasn't even the faintest recognition in his eyes that we'd once been lovers as well as friends. I felt certain then that I'd lost him.

'His doctors think he might permanently block out the memory of his time in the Army,' Faith said, 'seeing as it was so frightful and ended the way it did. It's called a defence mechanism or something.'

By now, Oliver spent more time at home than in the hospital, and every day he was home Eve went to see him.

'She's a truly remarkable young woman, your daughter,' Faith said in a voice thick with emotion. 'She has committed herself totally to

Oliver getting better. He's so fond of her and Holly. Oh, Kitty, wouldn't it be wonderful if they fell in love?'

'Wonderful,' I'd replied. 'Truly wonderful.'

I rested my elbows on the counter and put my chin in my hands. I didn't know whether I was living in a dream world or a nightmare. I was actually jealous of my own daughter yet, at the same time, pleased that she and Oliver were getting on so well. I wasn't a selfless person, I wanted Oliver for myself, but he would never again be the man I'd known in Belfast, the man I'd fallen head over heels in love with after a single glance. That Oliver was dead and would I, could I, love the new Oliver quite as much as I'd done the old? His baby gave me a hefty kick. I patted him gently and told him to stay still, that I was thinking about his father.

In the end, I realized I had no alternative but to let events take their course. If Fate had decreed my life would go a certain way, there was nothing I could do to change it.

Although I didn't find the shop half as fascinating as I'd once done, it was a wrench to leave. Like all jobs, it had provided a timetable: getting up and coming home at regular hours, knowing that Saturday afternoons were my own and that I could get up whenever I pleased on Sundays, as long as I didn't miss Mass. I thought I'd feel lost without my timetable, though no doubt my baby would provide a new one when he came.

On my final day, a Saturday, Muriel arrived to take me to lunch. I'd been forgiven for getting pregnant and she asked how I was feeling.

'Big!' I patted my stomach. 'Awfully big.'

When lunch was over, she presented me with a long, slim velvet box containing a beautiful gold watch. 'It's from Paul and me,' she said, 'in appreciation of all you've done for the shop. You've turned it into a little gold mine.'

'It's been a pleasure. I've enjoyed every minute.' I slid the gold band on to my wrist. It fitted perfectly. 'Thank you, Muriel – and thank Paul for me. I shall treasure it for ever.'

'I've also bought a little gift for Claire. She's so obliging and friendly. You know,' she said ruefully, 'I wish I'd got to know you all when Michael and Aileen married. You've made such a difference to my life. I shall always be grateful.'

*

Perhaps it was just me, but I found Christmas exceptionally boring. We all went to dinner at Claire's, had tea at our Norah's, spent Boxing Day evening in Amethyst Street with Marge and Danny, and everyone came to Maghull one night for a party. On each occasion, we ended up singing the same old songs, telling the same old jokes and digging up the same old memories. But we were bound to each other by a mixture of love and blood, and I couldn't imagine Christmas being any other way.

Hilda's brain was as sharp as ever, but she was becoming increasingly immobile. 'Old age is taking its toll,' she remarked cheerfully on New Year's Eve when I went to visit. Her eyes were as bright as buttons in her wizened face. 'My bones are turning to chalk and beginning to crumble, or something like that. I switch off when the doctor reels off all my ailments: I'd sooner not know.'

'She refuses to take her medicine,' Dorothy said accusingly.

'And I will continue to do so, Dottie, dear. I intend to die when my body decides it's time, not gobble hundreds of pills a day to keep me going. It's not natural.'

'I thought you were supposed to be a nurse,' I said. 'Is that how you used to treat your patients?'

'I left it to the patients to decide whether to take their medicine or not.' She threw a dark glance at her friend. 'Unlike some nurses I know.'

'I pray she goes before me,' Dorothy said when she showed me out. 'If I die first, she'll have to go into a home and she'll hate it.'

I shuddered. 'Oh, stop talking about dying. It's depressing.'

'I'm sorry, dear,' Dorothy said abjectly. 'Here's you carrying a new life inside you, and all we've talked about is death. We're at opposite ends of the pole, aren't we?'

Eve had deserted the McCarthys over Christmas, and spent most of her time with the Knowleses. It had been late when she and Holly returned home on Christmas Day. Oliver had remembered what mistletoe was for and had kissed her when they sat down to dinner, she told me, eyes shining like stars in her excited face. And now that he could walk with the aid of crutches, Faith had taken him shopping and he'd bought Eve a necklace, actually chosen it himself.

'Isn't it pretty?' She held the necklace out for me to see: pink quartz stones in a silver setting.

'Very pretty,' I agreed.

'And he bought Holly a doll dressed in green and red velvet – the colour of holly. It's in my bag, I'll show you in a minute. Oh, and there's a present for you. I think it's a scarf. He bought Faith and Alice scarves. And he wore the pullover I got him all day.' She paused for breath. 'He said to thank you for the book and he'd start reading it when he went to bed. Faith's sent you something and so has Robin. Oh, Kitty!' she gasped. 'I've had the most marvellous day, the best of my life.'

'I'm so glad, sweetheart.' I felt genuinely glad and green with envy, both at the same time.

Jake McCarthy made his painful way into the world just before midnight on 14 January 1972. I had no way of knowing whether it was as painful for him as it was for me, but when he emerged he was screaming blue murder, taking over from his mother who'd just left off.

'Bloody hell,' I gasped. 'That didn't half hurt.'

'You made that obvious, Mrs McCarthy,' the midwife smiled as she lifted up my red, crinkly, screaming son.

'I'm afraid I'm not the sort to suffer in silence. Is he all right?' I asked anxiously.

'Well, he's got a fine pair of lungs on him, that's for sure, and everything's there. It's a beautiful little boy you've got here. What are you going to call him?'

'Jake.'

'Is that short for Jacob?'

'No, it's short for Jake.' It was a question I'd be asked numerous times in my life. I always gave the same answer. 'Can I hold him?'

'For a minute, then we'll clean the pair of you up.'

I seized my baby son and held him against my breast. He looked terribly angry, but had stopped screaming, thank the Lord. 'Hello, Jake,' I whispered. 'My name's Kitty and I'm your mother. You've got a sister called Eve and a niece called Holly who can't wait to meet you. Least Eve can't, Holly's too young to know she's just had an uncle.'

'D'you think he took all that in?' the midwife asked.

'Oh, yes,' I assured her. 'He listened intently, didn't you, Jake?'
Jake didn't exactly nod, but he looked interested and his anger was subsiding.

'You're one of the daftest mothers we've ever had,' the midwife opined.

'You don't know the half of it,' I told her.

I examined my baby. His brow was broad, his chin firm, and he had inherited the wide McCarthy mouth and Oliver's black hair. Right now, his nose was just a little button, but that would change. He had a fine pair of shoulders on him and was exceptionally long. 'You're going to be very tall when you grow up,' I told him – the midwife had gone so there was no one to eavesdrop on our conversation – 'just like your father.'

Jake punched the air in acknowledgement of this fact.

'I take it you're not going to give this one away,' Claire said acidly when she came to see me the next morning. Jake was asleep in a cot beside my bed. She studied him closely in the desperate hope that she could guess the identity of his father.

'I've no intention of making the same mistake twice,' I replied, just as acidly.

'I should hope not. Is Jake short for Jacob? Isn't that a Jewish name?'

'It's short for Jake and I don't give a stuff whether it's a Jewish name or not.'

'He's lovely,' she said sincerely.

'I know.' We smiled at each other.

'He looks more like a month old than a few hours.'

'He's twenty-two inches long,' I said proudly. 'And he weighed nine pounds, three ounces.'

'Are you going to breastfeed?'

'Just try and stop me!' I was going to do everything for Jake that I hadn't done for Eve. This time, there wasn't a woman standing by my bed with her arms outstretched wanting to take my baby from me. This time, my baby would be all mine, and I intended to enjoy every minute with him.

Of course, I didn't, at least not every minute. He was a lovely baby, very intelligent – well, *I* thought so – but there were times when I felt like killing him, particularly when he woke twice in the same night asking to be fed. 'You,' I told him more than once, 'are the most demanding baby in the world. D'you think I'm made of milk or something?' He was barely six weeks old yet I could visualise him in his twenties waking me in the middle of the night for cups of tea and sarnies.

Eve wasn't much help. She and Holly went to see Oliver virtually every day. Anyroad, she was terrified of Jake, who was so big and fierce compared to her own dainty baby. I really missed our Claire, but she was too busy looking after the shop to come and see me.

The health visitor suggested I supplement the breast milk with a bottle. 'I don't think you have enough milk to satisfy him. Don't forget, you're not as young as you were.'

'Who is?' I asked irritably.

She ignored this. 'He needs two mothers: one for night and one for day. To put it bluntly, he isn't getting enough to eat.'

After she'd gone, I burst into tears at the idea that I was an inadequate mother who'd been starving her child. 'I'm useless,' I wept.

Eve, who was about to leave for Southport, came to see what the noise was. I told her what the health visitor had said.

'You're not to blame yourself, Kitty,' my daughter said sternly. 'He's a big baby and he needs big feeds. When Holly was tiny, Francine used to give her a bottle at night.'

'That's only because you were too lazy to get up and feed her yourself,' I sniffed.

Eve agreed. 'Having money makes you lazy. You pay people to do all the nuisance things.' Her face brightened. 'Talking of money, now that the divorce has been finalized, any minute now I should hear from my solicitor how much maintenance I shall get off Rob.'

Poor old Barney, Rob's father, was in a prison somewhere serving the first of a five-year sentence. Whether his son was guilty of any sort of crime we would never know but, if he was, he'd got off scot-free.

The letter from the solicitor arrived early the following week while both babies were fast asleep. I was enjoying an unusually quiet and peaceful breakfast.

Eve screamed when she read it, terrifying the life out of me and waking Jake. She burst into the kitchen, waving the letter. 'Two hundred and fifty pounds a month for me, and twice that much for Holly. Oh!' Her face paled and she looked agitated as she read the letter further. 'It says here that Mr Horton reserves the right to have contact with his daughter at some future date. Cheek!' she spat. 'He hasn't shown the slightest interest in her so far, not even so much as a phone call to ask how she is.'

'It just said he "reserves the right". It probably doesn't mean anything,' I assured her. 'I expect his solicitor thought it wise to put it in.'

'Do you really think so?' She chewed her lip, still agitated.

'I *think* so, I don't *know* so.' I edged towards the door. Jake's cries were reaching a crescendo. I reckoned he was ready for two breasts and a bottle.

'Say if I refused the money, would he still retain the right to see Holly?'

'Almost certainly.' I wasn't exactly an expert on divorce law and was anxious to get to my child before he burst a blood vessel. 'That and the money are two completely separate issues. Anyroad, sweetheart, you'll need the money in the not-too distant future. Only the other day, you were saying you didn't have much left in the bank.'

She gave me a coy look. 'That might not matter any more.'

I stopped in my tracks. 'What do you mean?'

'Remember the first time I met Oliver and I said I wanted to marry him when he got better?'

'I do remember, yes.' I swayed unsteadily on my feet and grabbed the doorknob for support. 'Has he proposed?'

'No, but I'm going to propose to *him*.' Her eyes danced. 'I only decided yesterday. I talked it over with Faith and she thinks it's a great idea.'

'Is he in a fit state to accept?' Now it was *me* who was agitated.

'Do you really think I'd ask if he weren't?' she said in a hurt voice.

'I suppose not, but if you'd asked my opinion, I'd've suggested you waited until he got the idea first.'

'Well, it's a good job I asked Faith and not you.' She stuck out her tongue.

I went upstairs to see to Jake. I picked up his hot, heaving body, and told him there was a good chance that *my* daughter was about to marry *his* father. 'But we'll just have to pretend we don't care, won't we, son?'

Oliver accepted Eve's hand in marriage. Once again Connor Daley was called upon to give his daughter away in a registry office, this time in Southport. On this occasion, Con brought his wife, June. He'd told me once she wouldn't have minded him having a child by a previous relationship, but she seemed to mind a great deal meeting that child's mother.

It was a beautiful, balmy day in May, the sun bright and warm in a cloudless blue sky. Eve looked dazzling in a cream costume with a short pleated skirt and an outsize cap made from the same material. Her cream shoes had high heels and platform soles, making her almost as tall as Oliver. She carried a posy of miniature cream roses. Her cousin, Kate, the only bridesmaid, looked gorgeous in buttercup yellow.

By now, the bridegroom could manage with the aid of a walking stick, though his movements were stiff and awkward. His hair was cut militarily short and I wondered if he would ever remember that he'd once worn it long. He clearly adored Eve, his happiness evident for all to see, his face set in a familiar childish grin. I had the awful feeling that it was Oliver the child getting married, not Oliver the man.

I'd made a real effort to look nice for the wedding. Faith had gone to London to buy her outfit, and Hope was coming and was bound to turn up in something frightfully smart and expensive. I'd spent the last three months dressed like a tramp, my face a stranger to make-up. I was worried I'd have to attend the wedding in the same state, but our Claire rode to the rescue and offered to look after Jake one Saturday afternoon when she finished in the shop so I could buy an outfit suitable for the mother of the bride. Eve had offered to pay. 'It can be your birthday present,' she'd said.

It was a lovely, liberating feeling wandering around the shops on my own yet at the same time it felt strange, as if I wasn't a whole person and had left an important part of me behind: I wanted to rush home and fetch it. In the end, I bought a long pale-blue chiffon dress dotted with white daisies from Owen Owen's. It had a stand-up collar, long sleeves that ballooned out at the elbows and a very slimming bias-cut skirt. I went on to buy a white boater hat trimmed with more daisies, short white gloves and a titchy white handbag that I'd probably never use again. I vaguely remember Marge once saying that you should never have more than three accessories the same colour, so managed to find a pair of peep-toe sandals with moderately high heels that were exactly the same blue as the dress.

So, I didn't let my daughter down when she married Oliver Knowles. I didn't even cry, though I badly wanted to. It was almost a year to the day that I'd met a quite different Oliver in a hotel called Buckles in Belfast. For a short time, we'd been lovers, but now my lover was my son-in-law, and nobody could have a better reason for crying than that.

Faith and Eve had paid for the reception between them – Con had insisted on paying for the cars and the flowers. It was held in a dead posh hotel in Southport and we had a sit-down meal: fresh salmon, salad, new potatoes, followed by cherry gateau and buckets of wine. A rather subdued group of musicians played romantic songs – 'When I Fall in Love', 'I Only Have Eyes for You', 'Night and Day' – but they could hardly be heard above the sound of people talking and the clatter of dishes. Claire had taken Jake off my hands for as long as he was willing. As the parents of the bride, Con and I were seated next to each other, while June, his wife, was designated to a lower table next to our Norah on one side and Liam on the other. When we were introduced, she'd been cold to the point of rudeness, and she was throwing me so many baleful looks that Con couldn't help but notice and felt obliged to apologize.

'She wasn't expecting you to be quite so gorgeous.'

'I'm sorry about that.'

He winked at me – like every other adult in the room, me included, he'd drunk too much wine. '*I'm* not.'

'Don't say things like that, Con,' I chided, though felt flattered and pleased on top of the whole host of other things I felt that day.

'Can't help it, Kit.' He sighed.

'What's wrong?'

'Marriage going through a bad patch, that's all.' He sighed again.

'All marriages go through bad patches. It'll work itself out eventually.'

'How would you know? You've never been married. What happened with that little chap's dad?' He nodded at Jake, who was perched on Claire's shoulder taking everything in. 'Did *he* propose and you told him to go screw himself like you did with me? Does *he* know he's got a son?'

I said the first thing that came into my head. 'Jake's father's dead.'

'Jaysus, Kitty!' He winced. 'I'm sorry.'

'So am I.' I noticed June was giving us daggers and was about to suggest we spoke to our neighbours rather than each other, when Robin, the best man, banged the table to ask for quiet, and the speeches began. I think I must have dozed off. By the time they were over, I couldn't remember a single word.

Halfway through the afternoon, Eve and Oliver left for their honeymoon in Jersey, the musicians revealed themselves to be heavily into rock 'n' roll and everyone settled down to having a really good time, apart from me, who felt as miserable as sin. I reclaimed my son – he seemed genuinely pleased to see me – and wandered around the hotel until I found a quiet corner where I could sit and think, making myself feel even more miserable as a result.

'Never mind, son,' I told Jake. 'We can go home soon, though the house will be awfully quiet without Eve and Holly.' They wouldn't be coming back. For their wedding present, Faith had bought the newly married couple a house in Ainsdale. Me, I'd got them an electric kettle and a toaster to match.

But, in my experience, life was never predictable. It turned out that the house in Maghull wasn't quiet for long. Before the month was out, another woman and her child had taken Eve and Holly's place.

Chapter 10

Eve and Oliver came home from their honeymoon after a week. Oliver was still under the care of the doctor and had been advised not to stay away too long. It only confirmed my opinion that he should have waited until he was completely better before he married Eve. But I was no expert on matters medical, or anything else I could think of, so wasn't entitled to an opinion.

I thought about them a lot, though, Eve and Oliver, while they were away. In the cold light of day, I thought about them making love, going to sleep and waking up together in the same bed, looking out of the window of their hotel as Oliver and I had done when we'd stayed in a different hotel, saying how sorry we were for the people outside because they weren't *us*. Yet I didn't feel a thing: no envy, no desire to be in Eve's place, nothing.

The feeling lasted a good five minutes and was replaced by one of insane jealousy. I still wanted Oliver, I still loved him, but there was nothing I could do about it except get used to the fact that he was married to my daughter and what we'd had during those short, sweet days in Belfast, we'd never have again.

The house had been unnaturally quiet, but I was surprised to find I didn't mind. Jake no longer woke in the middle of the night. I had a few visitors and the weather continued to be balmy – June wasn't far away and summer was almost upon us. The hedges were thick with May blossom, the neighbours came out in force to mow their lawns for the first time this year and everywhere smelled of cut grass. My own lawn remained uncut and scattered with buttercups and daisies. I couldn't wait until it was warm enough to take Jake to the sands in Formby – I could see Hilda and Dorothy at the same time.

Life stretched ahead, peacefully and uneventfully, in a way it never had before. I received just enough money from the State to live on and wished I felt more content.

I worried, sometimes, about the shop. Claire had looked after the place since December, but she'd never wanted permanent, full-time work. She had children and grandchildren who needed her, and was longing to leave, but didn't like to let Muriel down. Now that Eve had re-married, she was no longer interested in the job. I knew Muriel would sooner not employ a stranger, and racked my brains trying to think of someone who could take over, but Marge already had a part-time job in a pub and our Norah claimed she just wasn't up to it: the business with Bernadette had knocked all the stuffing out of her.

Still, the shop was no longer my concern, and I was glad when the daughter of one of Muriel's friends agreed to look after the place. I had a baby to care for and he occupied most of my free time, along with attempting to keep the house clean and tidy.

Over the last few weeks, a miracle had occurred, and Jake was no longer a cross, demanding baby, but a sunny, happy individual who smiled all the time.

'It must have been three-month colic that made him so bad-tempered,' Claire said. 'He still had a cob on him even after the health visitor said he wasn't having enough milk.'

'Stuff and nonsense!' Hilda scoffed when I told her. 'There's no such thing as three-month colic.'

I didn't give a damn what the reason was for Jake's first tempestuous few months, just pleased that when I opened my eyes in the morning I usually found him wide awake in the cot beside my bed, chuckling to himself and trying to reach the mobile strung overhead. It was time he slept by himself, but I wanted to decorate the spare room first, buy new curtains, a nursery lamp. I kept putting it off because I'd miss him too much if we no longer shared a room. When he saw me, he'd kick his legs and crow with delight. It was his way of saying, 'Good morning, Kitty.'

'Good morning, Jake.' I'd pick him up and we'd lie on the bed together for a few minutes while I told him what a marvellous little chap he was, then I'd give him a feed and he'd cup my breast in his hands as if it were a bottle. Sometimes I wanted to cry because it moved and thrilled me so much.

This was how my days were spent, watching my baby, marvelling when he did things for the first time, like grabbing his rattle and shaking it, enthralled by the noise, rolling on to his tummy, raising his body on his hands like a little seal, turning his head when he heard my voice. Muriel had bought him a baby chair, similar to a deck chair, but with a springy metal frame. I carried my child around the house so he could watch while I made the bed, worked in the kitchen or watched television – he did his utmost to grab the characters on the screen, while trying to drown their voices with his own loud, incoherent babble. I'd end up watching Jake rather than the telly; he was ten times more entertaining.

By now, he'd grown a head of thick, sooty black hair just like Oliver's. He had the same brown eyes, and I was convinced he had Oliver's features, but perhaps that was only because I knew Oliver was his father. Our Claire, the well-known detective, hadn't noticed, and if *she* hadn't, nobody would.

I lay in bed very early one morning, listening to Jake's light breathing and wondering what to wear when we went to see Eve and Oliver who were having a housewarming party that afternoon. They'd just acquired a puppy and a kitten, Bootsie and Smudge, and I was longing to see them. I wondered if I could wear my blue dress, but it seemed far too grand. My denim skirt, I decided, and a white cotton jumper. Then I remembered Jake had been sick on the jumper and it had yet to be washed. I'd have to look for something else.

The sun glimmered around the edge of the curtains: it was going to be another lovely day. There was a knock on the front door and I groaned, crawled out of bed, grabbed my dressing gown, struggling into it as I went downstairs. It would almost certainly be the postman with a parcel or something to sign for.

But instead of the postman, a weary, rumpled woman with grey hair was standing outside, accompanied by a boy of about twelve. 'Yes?' I asked sleepily. The boy smiled, the woman gave me a bad-tempered glare.

'Is that all the welcome I get?' she said angrily.

'I beg your pardon?' I blinked, tempted to slam the door in her face.

'It's Aileen, your sister. What the hell are you doing in my house, Kitty? And where's Michael?'

*

'*Your* house?' I gasped after she'd pushed her way in and we were standing facing each other in the hall. The boy had stopped smiling and looked upset. 'What d'you mean, *your* house? You'd think you'd just popped out for half an hour and I'd taken over in your absence. You've been gone for twelve years, for God's sake.' Twelve and a half to be precise.

'Where's Michael?' she demanded again, almost as if she expected him to appear out of thin air and welcome her back with open arms.

'Michael's dead,' I said bluntly, not prepared to pussyfoot around and tell her in a more gentle fashion. 'He died just over a year ago in Belfast.'

She burst into tears. Perhaps I should have been gentler with her. The boy threw his arms around her neck. 'Don't cry, Mum, don't cry.' He must be the child she'd been expecting when she went off with her lover: I couldn't remember his name.

'I thought he'd still be here,' she wept. 'I couldn't imagine him ever leaving this place.'

'Well, it didn't hold many happy memories for him, did it?' I made my tone slightly softer, more for the boy's sake than Aileen's. 'He left the day after you did.'

She sniffed. 'What was he doing in Belfast?'

'Living with a woman called Mary Brady. I met her at the funeral. Look, you'd better sit down and I'll make some tea.'

I put the kettle on, raced upstairs and threw on some clothes, pleased to see that Jake was still asleep. Downstairs again, the kettle was boiling. I made the tea and took it on a tray into the lounge. My sister and her son were on the settee. She was smoking and he was holding her hand and regarding her worriedly with his young eyes. Aileen was two years younger than Claire, but looked much older, her hair completely grey and her face weather-beaten and heavily wrinkled. She was dressed in an assortment of clothes that had seen better days, the hem of her frock hanging inches below a brown belted coat with frayed buttonholes. Her shoes were down at heel, and her tights were crinkled around her ankles. She wasn't even faintly recognizable as the sleek, stylish Aileen I used to know.

Her son was much better dressed in jeans, T-shirt and a tan anorak. His training shoes were new. 'What's your name?' I asked him with a smile.

'Ben.' He responded with a smile of his own. He was a fine-looking boy, deeply sunburned, with fair, curly hair and the McCarthys' blue eyes and wide mouth.

'Do you take sugar in your tea, Ben?'

'Two teaspoons, please.' His voice was firm and he had an accent of some sort.

'He's probably hungry,' Aileen said. 'He hasn't eaten since we were on the plane. It landed in Heathrow last night and we went straight to Euston. The last train to Liverpool was about to leave, so there wasn't time for even a snack. We've been hanging round Lime Street Station for the last few hours waiting for the buses to run. I couldn't afford a taxi.'

'I'll make you something to eat in a minute, Ben,' I promised. 'Perhaps you'd like to look in the fridge and see if there's anything you fancy. The kitchen's at the end of the hall.' Ben left with alacrity, and I said to Aileen, 'The plane from where?'

'Australia,' she said tiredly. 'It's taken us a good two days to get here and we're both worn out.'

'What happened to . . . ?' I still couldn't remember his name.

'Steve.' She shrugged, and her shoulders almost collapsed with the effort. 'Steve McSherry. He left us years ago. I managed on my own for a while, but I felt so homesick and longed to come back to Michael and the house. I had a job, but the wages weren't up to much and I was ages saving up for the fare.'

'Did you truly expect Michael to be here after all this time?' I couldn't believe she was so arrogant, so absolutely sure of Michael's love, that she felt she could just come back and take over from where she'd left off.

'I *made* myself believe it,' she said hoarsely. 'It was thinking of Michael that kept me going.'

'Did you feel like that before Steve left, or afterwards?' Ben apart, there wasn't much I liked about my sister.

'Afterwards,' she whispered. 'Oh, Kitty!' Her voice rose to a cry, almost a howl. 'You don't know what it's like to be in love, *really* in love, to love someone the way I loved Steve. It takes over your whole life. You can't think of anything else.' Her voice returned to a whisper. 'When he left, if it hadn't been for Ben, I would have killed myself.'

I knew what it was like to be in love, but not in the way she'd just described. It made her sound a little bit mad. I said I'd better make Ben something to eat and asked if she wanted something herself.

'A sandwich will do. I couldn't possibly eat anything cooked.'

Fifteen minutes later, Ben was tucking into a heap of fried food and Aileen had removed her coat and was nibbling a cheese sarnie. I was about to make more tea, when I heard Jake give a little impatient cry. I raced upstairs to fetch him.

'Have you been wondering where I was, sweetheart?' He kicked his legs in welcome and I picked him up and held him against my heart. Aileen's return worried me, frightened me almost. What was going to happen now?

She looked stunned when I came back into the room with a baby. 'Who does that belong to?' she asked sharply.

'He's mine. His name's Jake, he's just over four months old.' I resented my precious child being referred to as 'that'.

'Are you married? You're not wearing a ring.'

'I'm not wearing a ring because I'm not married.'

Ben looked up from his food and grinned. 'He's a great kid.'

'So are you,' I told him, returning the grin.

Aileen had already lost interest in Jake. She lighted another cigarette and said, 'That reminds me, where's Eve? I forgot to ask about her.'

'I'd noticed,' I said pointedly. 'Last month, Eve got married for the second time to a super chap called Oliver Knowles. She has a little girl, Holly, who's one year old. They've just moved into a house not far from here in Formby.'

'Oliver Knowles?' She frowned. 'The name rings a bell.'

'He's one of the little boys I looked after in Orrell Park.'

'Of course!' Her face cleared. 'She's done well for herself, then.'

'Extremely well.' I left the room saying I was going to make Jake's bottle. I'd breastfeed him later when I felt less anxious. In the kitchen, I put him in his chair. He gave a little squeak and waved his hands when he saw me take the already made-up bottle out of the fridge and put it in a pan to warm. 'Are you hungry?' I asked, and he squeaked an emphatic 'yes'.

I heard Aileen go upstairs, her heavy shoes clumping on each step. The lavatory flushed, but it was a while before she clumped back down.

'The house is a tip,' she said, coming into the kitchen. She must have been inspecting the bedrooms. She glanced around the room, which was an even worse tip. 'You've really let this place go.'

I came to the swift conclusion that she was genuinely mad. 'I don't think that's any of your business, Aileen,' I said coolly.

'I think it is, Kitty.' She gave me a hard look. 'I know I went away, left Michael—'

'And Eve,' I interjected.

She took no notice. 'Michael was my husband, we never divorced, so legally the house is mine. I have no idea why you're here and don't expect you to leave, at least not straight away, but Ben and I need somewhere to live and this is all we have. I noticed Michael's car is still in the garage. Later, I'll drive into town and collect our luggage from Lime Street Station. From now on, you and Jake can sleep in the spare room until you find somewhere else.'

I sprinkled the contents of the bottle on the back of my hand. It felt just right. 'Come along, Jake,' I cried, picking him up and carrying him into the lounge. Ben was scraping his plate. He sat back, looking satisfied. 'That was fantastic, Auntie Kitty.'

'Call me Kitty,' I said.

'OK, Kitty.'

'There's tea made if you'd like to help yourself to a cup. And you'll find biscuits in the tin, the striped one with the red lid.'

'Thanks.' He departed for the kitchen in a rush, taking the dirty plate with him.

I settled in the corner of the settee. Jake was straining for the bottle held tantalizing out of his reach. I placed the teat in his mouth and he began to suck greedily, as if he hadn't been fed for a week. I hoped he wasn't conscious of the way my heart was thumping loudly in my breast with anger, fear and loathing for the woman who claimed to be my sister.

'About what I just said, Kitty—' She'd followed me into the room and was in the course of lighting another ciggy.

'About what you just said, Aileen. Firstly, the house doesn't belong to you. It belonged to Michael and he left it to Eve. There's a letter in the sideboard he wrote the morning he left – I'll show it you in a minute. I can't quite remember how he put it, but I think he said you don't own a single brick. Secondly, the car's insured in my name and you're not to touch it. Finally, the reason I've been living here for the last twelve years is because Michael asked me to look after Eve.' Jake stopped sucking and was looking at me intently. Somehow, it had got through to him that I'd worked myself up into a lather. 'It's all right, sweetheart,' I whispered, giving him my biggest smile. 'Mummy's fine.' He began to suck again, but keeping his eyes on my face.

Aileen began to cry again. 'I'm sorry,' she whimpered. 'I would never have thrown you out. It's Ben I'm concerned about. The last few years have been really tough for him.'

'They were tough for Eve when you walked out.'

'I didn't think about her, or Michael.' There was despair in her voice. 'All I could think about was Steve. I didn't care how much I hurt people.'

'You obviously feel the same way now. You didn't care how much you hurt me and Jake.'

'I didn't mean it,' she sobbed.

I sighed and suggested she lay down for a while. 'In Eve's room,' I said firmly. 'You might feel better after a rest.' I certainly hoped so.

She nodded obediently. 'I've hardly slept for two days.' I watched her retreating figure. I was still unable to connect this Aileen with the sister I used to know.

I asked Ben if he'd like to rest, but he claimed not to feel the least bit tired and said he'd sooner go for a walk, 'to see what Liverpool's like. I didn't see much of it from the train.'

'This is Maghull, not Liverpool. You mightn't be able to find your way back.'

He said that Maghull would do for now, so I wrote my address on a slip of paper and insisted he take it with him. 'Just in case you get lost.'

'Thanks, Kitty.' I suspected he wanted to get out of his mother's way. It was obvious they cared for each other, but Aileen can't have been the easiest person to live with since Steve left. I watched him walk down the road, tall and confident, a son to be proud of.

I crept upstairs to make sure the door to Eve's room was closed, crept down again and picked up the telephone. If the cord was stretched, it just about reached inside the lounge. I put Jake on the floor so he could roll around, and rang our Claire. 'You'll never guess what's happened,' I said in a hushed voice when she answered.

'I won't even try, Kit.'

'Our Aileen's back and she's brought her son with her. Oh,

Claire,' the words came tumbling out, 'she's really weird. Steve's dumped her and I think she's lost her mind.'

'Jaysus, Mary and Joseph!' Claire screeched. 'Where's she been all this time?'

'Australia.'

'Me friend, Mildred Sweeney, had a feeling she'd gone to Australia, didn't she? She could feel it in her water. What's the son like? He'll be about twelve, won't he? And what do you mean, she's really weird?'

'*Really* weird, unbalanced, not quite with it. She only wanted to chuck me and Jake out, saying it was *her* house. Of course, I told her it wasn't, that it belonged to Eve. Oh, and her son, Ben, is lovely, very grown-up for twelve. Hold on a minute.' I put the receiver on the floor and managed to reach Jake just in time to stop him from trying to take a bite out of the chair leg. He was at the stage when he put everything he touched in his mouth, but I drew the line at a chair. I put him back into the middle of the room and picked up the phone. 'It was Jake,' I explained. 'He was just about to eat the furniture.'

'Your voice is all shaky, luv. Has Aileen upset you?'

'You can say that again. She looks awful, too, like a hundred-year-old female tramp.'

'Where is she now?'

'Asleep.'

'Right! Well, Kitty, you go and make yourself a nice cup of tea and stop worrying. I'll catch the next train to Maghull. I should be with you within the hour.' The line went dead.

Aileen was still asleep when Claire arrived exactly an hour later. Ben had returned home and they took to each other immediately – everyone liked our Claire. While she nursed Jake, Ben told us about life in Australia. It sounded very interesting, but I wished he would go out again so we could talk about his mother instead.

The time eventually came for me to get ready for Eve and Oliver's housewarming, yet still Aileen slept. 'Of course you should go,' Claire cried when I said I'd better phone and say I wasn't coming. 'We'll be here for your mum when she wakes up, won't we, Ben?'

'Yes, Auntie Claire,' Ben agreed, very adult.

'Would you like me to make you something to eat, luv?'

'Yes, please.'

He was eating another gargantuan meal by the time I was ready to leave. I was glad to escape the terrible atmosphere the house had acquired since Aileen had arrived. Claire came out while I strapped Jake into the car seat. 'Well, this is a turn-up for the books,' she said.

'Isn't it just? I hope she's awake by the time I come home. The tension's killing me.'

'I'll rouse her in a minute, take her some tea and find out what she's up to.'

I kissed her cheek and swore I didn't know what I'd do without her.

The house had been built at the end of the last century. The bricks were rosy-red, the windows latticed and the front door was made of thick panels of ancient oak joined together with black metal strips. Lichen crept across the grey-tiled roof and the leaves of the apple trees mingled with each other in the back garden, forming a lacy, shady cover.

Oliver let me in, a neat and tidy Oliver, wearing grey flannel trousers and a well-ironed check shirt. 'I see you're managing without a stick,' I smiled as he gave me a dutiful kiss.

'Only in the house, but I'm coming on.' He spoke in the polite, respectful tone of a man addressing his mother-in-law. 'I drove the car the other day.'

'Not in the house, I hope.'

'Of course not.' His shocked expression changed to one of bashfulness. 'Sorry, that was a joke, wasn't it? My brain still works rather slowly. It takes its time recognizing when people joke. Hello, Jake.' He poked his son in the tummy; Jake rewarded his daddy with a coy smile. 'Everyone's in the garden, Kitty. Would you like a drink: hot or cold, alcoholic?' He waved his hands. 'Whatever.'

'Orange juice, please, or lemonade: something long and cold. I've brought bottles for Jake.'

I walked through the house into the sun-blessed garden. Faith, a vision in flowered chiffon – making me wish I'd worn my blue dress – was seated on a deck chair, while Robin and Alice lounged on the grass watching the twins who'd just started walking. Holly could walk, but preferred to crawl, as she could go much faster. She chuffed like an engine in and out of the trees, followed by a watchful

Eve. We waved to each other. The scene reminded me of an Impressionist painting. It would probably be called something like *The Housewarming* or *Afternoon on the Grass*.

Bootsie and Snudge were taking turns chasing each other in and out of the house. Bootsie was a Scottish Terrier, as black as night, and Snudge a lovely marmalade colour. They were clearly already the best of friends.

Faith clapped her hands when I appeared with Jake. 'So many babies! Isn't it lovely? And the best thing of all is I don't have to pick them up when they cry or drag myself out of bed at night to feed them.' She held out her arms. 'Can I hold him for a minute?'

I placed Jake on her knee; he immediately seized her pearl necklace and put it in his mouth. 'Oh, God! It might snap and he'll swallow some,' she cried. I managed to rescue the necklace all in one piece. She took it off and I advised her to remove her earrings, too. 'Oliver and Robin were just the same,' she remarked. 'Everything went straight into their mouths.'

Oliver brought my drink and went to relieve Eve, who came and gave me a hug. 'He couldn't love her more if she were his own child. Isn't it wonderful? Everything's wonderful.' She sighed blissfully. 'I'm so happy, Kitty.'

'I'm glad, sweetheart.' I meant it with all my heart.

'Don't you feel well or something?' She gave me a searching look 'You're awfully pale.'

'Something's happened. I'll tell you later.'

'No, tell me now. Let's go in the kitchen. I need a drink like yours.'

The kitchen was rather old-fashioned with a deep sink and an unnecessarily large boiler. Eve intended having it modernised at some time in the future. She poured herself a glass of orange juice. 'So, what's happened? It's obviously upset you.'

'Aileen's back.'

'Shit!' She made a face. 'What does she want?'

I nearly told her not to swear, but it was no longer my job to monitor her language. I described the events of the morning, finishing with the fact that Aileen was probably still fast asleep and that I'd left Claire in charge of Ben

'Shit!' she said again. 'I suppose I'll have to go and see her. I'll take Holly, but not Oliver. What are you going to do, Kitty?'

I shook my head, so hard that I felt dizzy. 'What are *you* going to do? It's your house, Eve. It's up to you whether she stays or not.'

'Oh, for God's sake, Kitty,' she said irritably. 'For all intents and purposes, it's *your* house for as long as you want it. I'll never live there again. *This* is my house, the one where I live with Oliver and Holly.'

She looked through the window to where Oliver was giving Holly a piggyback on the grass, and I imagined her thinking of the idyllic years that lay ahead with her husband and daughter, and no doubt other children in the course of time. 'It's up to you what you do about Aileen,' she said.

I left early, too agitated to enjoy myself, and drove back to Maghull with Jake fast asleep making little bubbly noises. I arrived home to find Claire watching telly in the lounge. All the windows were open and there was no sign of Aileen and Ben.

'Have they gone back to Australia?' I asked hopefully.

'No chance, luv.' She turned the telly off. 'I sent Aileen to the shops to stock up on food. Ben's gone with her. He seems to need a meal an hour, and your fridge is like Mother Hubbard's cupboard. Oh, and I had to give her the money. It would appear she's virtually skint.'

'What am I going to do with her, Claire? I know it's Eve's house, but she said it's up to me.'

'Sit down and I'll tell you her life story. It might help make up your mind.'

'I'll take Jake upstairs first.' I put Jake in his cot and, on the way back, went to the fridge for orange juice, but found it had all gone. I had water instead.

Claire patted the space beside her on the settee. I sat. She cleared her throat, as if she were about to give a lecture, and told me about the twelve years our sister had spent in Australia.

'They stayed in Melbourne for the first five years, then Steve fancied something more adventurous so they went to live in the Outback, whatever that may be, and he worked for a sheep farmer. A few years on, he started having affairs. Aileen thinks he'd have left her then if it hadn't been for Ben. More years passed, and he *did* leave for a woman half Aileen's age. The farmer chucked her and Ben out, so she lost Steve and her home in a matter of weeks.

According to her, she went grey overnight – I've heard that can happen, but I didn't believe it until now.'

'Oh, Lord,' I sighed.

'Yeah, I know.' Claire gave a wan smile. 'It makes you feel dead sorry for her, doesn't it? Anyroad, she went to work as a sort of housekeeper for another farmer. He treated her like dirt, gave her all the filthy jobs to do, but she stayed until she'd saved enough for the fare home. Somehow, she managed to convince herself that Michael would still be living here and he'd be willing to have her back. I wouldn't exactly say she's gone completely round the bend, but she's definitely on the way.'

'I suppose I'll have to let her stay, if only for Ben's sake.' The thought made me dejected. 'And for her sake, too.'

'She's our sister, after all,' Claire said half-heartedly. 'The McCarthys have always stuck together.'

'Apart from Aileen,' I pointed out. 'She left without even saying goodbye.'

'She was besotted with Steve, that's why.' Claire got to her feet and muttered something about staying till Aileen and Ben came back, then she'd go home. 'If you're wondering why all the windows are open, it was to let out the fog. She smokes like a bloody chimney.' She chuckled. 'It's funny, in a way. When she used to live here, she made it a rule never to let anyone smoke in the house.'

'I'll make the same rule.' I felt even more dejected. I hated rules.

Aileen stayed with us for a year. She dyed her hair red, but it looked false and unnatural, nothing like the lovely red it had been when she was younger. The clothes she'd left behind still hung in the wardrobe in the spare room where I'd put them twelve years ago, and she had them altered, the hems taken up or let down.

There was no need to make a no-smoking rule, because she gave up straight away. Perhaps she needed the money for the expensive creams she massaged on her face and neck. As far as I could judge, they didn't remove a single wrinkle, though she was gradually beginning to look more like the sister I remembered. She went to work in a hotel in Southport in charge of the laundry. The wages weren't up to much, but they paid for her and Ben's keep, and left enough to put in the bank. She never said what she was saving for, but I often noticed her writing figures in a little notebook and adding them up.

I don't think a night passed when she didn't cry herself to sleep, loudly and passionately. At first, I'd crept into the bedroom to ask if there was anything I could do, but she told me curtly to go away, so I stopped asking, though found it impossible to sleep until the crying stopped.

There was no way of telling what this was doing to Ben. He started at the local comprehensive where Eve had gone, and seemed happy there. He was a likeable child – good at football, even better at cricket – and quickly became popular. But he too heard his mother cry herself to sleep at night and it must have had some effect on him, even if he didn't show it. His numerous cousins did their best to make him feel at home; Liam, who'd given up playing and was now a spectator, took him to a football match every Saturday afternoon. He and Eve became very fond of each other, and he went to see her at least once a week. Eve visited Aileen a few times, but the woman who'd once been her mother looked at her as if she were a stranger and hardly spoke.

Our Claire and Norah came as often as they could, more for my sake than Aileen's. 'To lighten the load,' as Claire put it. I truly felt as if Aileen was a burden I would have to carry until something happened and she left.

Marge didn't come at all. 'I wasn't good enough for your Aileen before,' she declared. 'She didn't want to know me then and I don't want to know her now.'

I'd be surprised if Aileen noticed who came and who didn't. She was cold and aloof with everyone, me included, despite us living in the same house. I found myself doing all sorts of things in the garden that I'd never done before in order to avoid my sister, who seemed to have lost the art of conversation and spent most of her time staring into space, no doubt thinking about Steve McSherry. I felt desperately sorry for her, but she made it plain she didn't want sympathy. All she wanted was a roof over her and Ben's head, not a friend, even if it was her sister.

Two other people who didn't come at all were our Danny and Jamie. I found it upsetting that they made no attempt to see her. I couldn't stop thinking about Amethyst Street when Mam and Dad had been alive, and how close we'd always been. It would appear the McCarthys were coming apart at the seams and would never be close again.

In September, Hilda died. She'd been watching television and Dorothy had been busy with her tapestry of the Battle of Trafalgar – it had taken years to do and was almost finished. 'The programme changed,' she told me later, 'and a game show came on. After a while, I thought to myself, why on earth is she watching that? She hates game shows. I said, "Would you like me to change the channel, Hilda?" but she didn't answer. She'd passed away in the chair. It was the way she'd have liked to go, given the choice.'

'You must feel devastated, Dotty,' I said softly. We were sitting in the room that looked out on to the Mersey. Children were playing on the sands and paddling in the sparkling water, their shrill cries audible in the quiet room. Somewhere in the distance, a dog barked.

'I do, but I'm glad she went first,' Dorothy said bravely, though the sadness in her eyes made me want to weep. 'She'd never have stood it in a home.' She gave the ghost of a smile. 'And the home would never have stood her.'

'Will you still live here?' I asked.

'Oh, yes.' She gave another joyless smile. 'She left me everything in her Will, the house included, on condition that when I died it all went to charity.' She glanced around the room, full of Hilda's things, indications of her busy and, until recently, active life. 'You'll sort things out for me then, won't you, Kitty? Make sure everything goes to the right place. The library would probably be grateful for the books and there's bound to be some poor souls who'd appreciate the furniture. A solicitor will look after the sale of the house.'

I promised I'd see to it all, but added, 'That won't be for a long time yet.' Despite her advanced years, Dorothy looked remarkably fit and healthy. 'You'll have time to do another half-dozen tapestries before I have to sort things out.'

'That reminds me,' she looked at me shyly, 'I'd like you to have my tapestry, dear. I'll have it finished before the week's out.'

'Oh, Dottie!' Tears came to my eyes and I gave her a hug. 'I can't think of anything in the world I'd like more.'

Considering all the people Hilda had helped over the course of her long life, only a pathetic few attended her funeral: Muriel, our Claire

– who'd only met Hilda a few times, but had admired her immensely – Eve – who remembered her well from the days when she'd come with me to the house in Everton Valley – a few neighbours, an elderly man from the golf club Hilda had joined, and an attractive fiftyish woman wearing a smart grey costume who looked vaguely familiar. Peggy Tyler – Spencer now – who was expecting another baby, sent a wreath. Cecily hadn't been heard of for quite a while; I hoped she'd settled down with the charming Canadian gentleman called Max.

The vaguely familiar woman approached when the short service was over. 'Hello, I was wondering if you'd be here. You're Kitty, aren't you? You won't remember me, but you came to my house once with one of Miss Foxton's parcels. I lived in Allerton then and I'd just had my daughter, Eliza. My name was Christine Mason, but I remarried a few years later and it's Gregory now. When I saw the notice of Miss Foxton's death in the *Echo*, I felt I just had to come to the funeral.'

'I remember you well. I was wondering where I'd seen you before.' She'd been a schoolteacher, I recalled, who'd lost her husband during the war and had fallen in love with a man who'd done a bunk when she'd told him she was pregnant. I was deeply touched that she'd come to Hilda's funeral, and liked her warm smile and friendly manner, as well as the fact that, despite her expensive clothes, she wasn't ashamed to admit she'd once been in desperate need of charity. 'How is Eliza?'

'She's fourteen now, incredibly pretty, and doing well at school. I actually had another baby at the grand old age of forty-five: a little boy called Peter. Fortunately, I'd married by then and could afford to buy my own nappies,' she finished with a smile.

'Would you like to come back to the house for something to eat?' I asked.

'I'd love to, but as soon as Peter started school, I went back to teaching and I only took the morning off.'

We walked back towards the cars. Dorothy had only ordered one for herself and the neighbours. The rest of us had come in our own. Christine Gregory opened the door of a red Mercedes that looked as if it had just been collected from the factory, and got inside. 'Bye, Kitty.' She gave me a little wave.

'Tara, Christine.' I climbed into Michael's Ford Consul, which was showing its age and unlikely to pass its next MOT, and followed the funeral car back to the house that now belonged to Dorothy, thinking, as I so often did, about how strange life was and how easily fortunes could change.

Hilda had been in her grave barely a week when Dorothy passed away one afternoon just as peacefully as her beloved companion. I wondered if her heart had broken, if she hadn't wanted to go on living without Hilda.

I'd taken to calling every day until she got used to living on her own. The back door was unlocked when I arrived and I was greeted by the smell of something burning. When I opened the oven there was a tray of little black cakes on each shelf.

'Dorothy,' I called. 'Dottie, where are you? Your cakes have burnt.'

I found her lying on the bed, fully dressed, as if she'd decided to have a little lie-down until the cakes were done. I shook her plump shoulder several times in an attempt to wake her, but it was no use. Dorothy was dead and I'd lost two of the best friends anyone could possibly have had.

There were even fewer people at Dorothy's funeral than at Hilda's. Only me and a few neighbours came to say goodbye to the kind, generous woman who had spent her entire adult life caring for the poor, the sick and the dispossessed.

Afterwards, me and our Claire spent a busy two weeks sorting out the house, accompanied by an irritable Jake who was teething. Books were carted to the library, and the clothes, ornaments and bedding to a charity shop. Another charity sent a van for the furniture.

It was Claire who made me burn the dozens of private letters we found, the diaries Dorothy had kept, the faded photographs of strangers in old-fashioned clothes smiling, or scowling, at the camera. Me, I'd wanted to keep them.

'What for?' Claire demanded. 'The people in the photos mean nothing to you, and you can't very well read the letters or the diaries, they're private. They'll just lie around your house getting older and older, and Eve'll end up having to sort them out when *you* die.'

'But these things were an important part of Hilda and Dorothy's lives,' I wept. 'I feel as if I'm burning *them*.' Nevertheless, I threw another bundle of letters on the fire, curious to know who they were from and what they said. Jake stopped complaining about his teeth and watched, fascinated, as flames shot up the chimney.

'Don't be daft, girl. When I die, I don't want me family drooling over a pile of old tat. As long as people remember me with warmth in their hearts, that's all I care. Look!' She handed me a black-and-white postcard-sized photo. 'I bet that's Hilda and Dorothy just after they qualified. You can keep that.'

'It *is* them,' I whispered. Two young nurses wearing starched caps and striped frocks photographed from the waist up, one taller than the other by at least six inches. Hilda's face was the most recognizable, thin and full of life, the skin scrubbed to a shine. An already plump Dorothy was smiling demurely. 'They had a good life,' I murmured.

'And a peaceful death,' Claire said. 'You can't ask for much more than that. Now, what are we going to do with that ghastly thing?' She waved at the tapestry still on its frame. It measured about four feet by two and showed the Battle of Trafalgar at its bloody height: ships lurching in a stormy sea; guns exploding; Lord Nelson, a patch over his eye, in the throes of death on the deck of the *Victory*; and the poor sailors blown overboard swimming desperately for their lives.

'It's mine,' I said. 'Dorothy gave it me. She only finished just before she died. I'm going to have it framed and hang it over the fireplace at home.'

'Our Aileen's already depressed enough. That'll only depress her more. Couldn't Dorothy have done something a bit more cheerful, like a nice bunch of flowers or a bowl of fruit?'

'This took far more skill,' I said defensively. But on second thoughts, the tapestry was unlikely to raise anyone's spirits. I'd hang it in the hall where it was less likely to be noticed. I hoped Dorothy wouldn't mind.

Christmas came and we went through the usual routine: dinner in Amethyst Street, tea at Norah's, a party at Claire's. There was no sign of our Jamie – no one had seen him for months – and Aileen refused to leave the house, claiming she felt too tired. She wasn't exactly in a party mood when everyone came to mine on New Year's Eve and she went to bed hours before Big Ben announced the arrival of 1973.

We kissed each other dutifully, wished each other a Happy New Year, and sang 'Auld Lang Syne'. It all seemed rather flat, I thought, wishing Jamie were there and Aileen had stayed downstairs.

The telephone rang: it was Eve. She and Oliver had preferred to spend the night in their new house by themselves. She wished me a Happy New Year and announced she was expecting a baby. 'He, or she, should arrive mid-July. Oliver's thrilled.'

'So am I,' I told her. 'Congratulations, sweetheart. Wish Oliver a Happy New Year for me, and Holly, too. Is Oliver looking forward to starting work?' Oliver had been getting very restless with nothing to do all day. It had come as a relief when the doctor pronounced he was fit enough for work, as long as the job wasn't too taxing. An ex Army officer who dealt in antiques had offered to take him on as an assistant in his shop in Formby. I had a sudden, quite unexpected vision, of the wild, bright-eyed young man playing the piano in Buckles. *That* Oliver wouldn't have touched the job with a bargepole.

'He can't wait!' Eve said fervently. 'He starts the day after tomorrow, though I'll be terribly lonely all day without him. Is it all right if I come and see you when he leaves for the first time?'

'Since when has there been a reason to ask?'

The news about the baby had made me feel better. I went upstairs and wished a sleeping Jake a Happy New Year. As Ben had taken over the spare room, Jake still slept in the cot beside my bed. I sat down and rested my chin on the side of the cot. 'In two weeks' time, you'll be one year old,' I told him in a whisper, 'and charging around the house like a maniac.' He could already totter across the room and had attempted to climb the stairs more than once. I'd ask Claire if Liam would put a gate there.

As if by magic, Claire came into the room and sat beside me on the bed. 'Are you all right?' she whispered. 'You looked a bit downcast earlier.'

'I was wishing our Jamie had come and Aileen hadn't gone to bed. But I'm all right now,' I assured her. 'That was Eve on the phone, she's expecting another baby.'

'Babies!' Claire breathed. 'I'll have a couple more grandchildren by the time summer comes. Whenever I'm feeling low, I think about the babies. It cheers me up no end.'

'When do you ever feel low?' I snorted. 'You're the happiest person I've ever known.'

'I'm like you, luv.' She squeezed my arm. 'I don't want people to grow old or die, meself included. But common sense tells me we can't live for ever. The world would be an awful crowded place if we did. I missed Jamie tonight, too, and our Aileen, but that's another thing we can't expect to happen, for the McCarthys to stick together until the end of time. Jamie's got his own life to lead. He's a divorced man on the lookout for another wife, and that's more important to him than us. As for Aileen, all she can think about is that bugger, Steve.'

Jake stirred and uttered a series of little grunts. I put my hand on his forehead and shushed him back to sleep, while downstairs everyone began to sing 'When Irish Eyes are Smiling'. I waited a minute to make sure it hadn't disturbed Jake before going down to join them. The front door opened and Ben came in – he'd been to a party in the next road – and the singing stopped so we could all wish him Happy New Year.

All of a sudden, I felt glad to be alive and began to sing at the top of my voice. Happy New Year, Kitty, I wished myself.

In May, our Aileen left the way Michael had all those years ago, in the middle of the night, leaving merely a note to explain why, though a much shorter one. I found it on the table when I went downstairs to make the first pot of tea of the day.

'Dear Kitty,' it said, 'I'm going back to Australia to look for Steve. Please take care of Ben for me. Love, Aileen.'

'Jaysus!' I muttered, and woke Ben to tell him. At first, he seemed a bit shaken, but otherwise took the news quite calmly.

'She's been saving up for the fare ever since we came,' he explained. 'I always knew she'd go back one day.'

'Did she tell you that, love?'

He shook his head. 'No, but she really loved my dad. She'd never have left Australia if it hadn't been for me.' He looked at me anxiously. 'Will it be all right for me to stay?'

I ruffled his hair. 'Of course! What a silly question to ask.'

I felt sorry for Aileen, but relieved that she had gone. The atmosphere in the house improved without her dark presence. And it meant Jake could have his own room at last. Or so I thought.

Our Norah had always been the quietest of the McCarthy sisters. She was five years older than me and it was she who'd taken me to school on my first day – by then, she was in the top class at St James's Junior and Infants. She always made a point of searching for me at playtime to make sure I was all right, and brought me home when school finished for the day, holding tightly to my hand as if she was worried I would escape and, more often than not, Marge hanging on to her other hand.

For most of the time, Norah's face bore a wistful, slightly pensive smile. She never had a tantrum, shouted or picked a fight. While Claire, Aileen and I behaved like prima donnas, making a huge fuss if we didn't get our own way, Norah would be lost in a daydream, the noise going over her head.

She was twenty-one when she met Peter Murphy and fell head over heels in love. Three months later, they got engaged. Three years later, he jilted her for a girl called Emily who worked in the cloakroom at the Adelphi. Everyone expected Norah to fall to pieces, but in no time at all she married Roy Hall, and we told each other she was marrying on the rebound, that Roy was a drip and it would never last. But Roy had turned out to be the best of husbands. They'd bought a little terraced house in Seaforth not far from the shore and close to where Con used to live. Norah had never needed to work and seemed perfectly content to stay at home and look after Roy and their treasured Bernadette.

Both Roy and Norah were gutted when Bernadette married Johnny Kelly, who'd never done a stroke of work in his life. Since then, he was on and off the dole like a yo-yo and Bernadette had had a second baby. They lived in a council flat off Stanley Road.

'We had so many dreams for her,' Norah moaned. 'We imagined her becoming a teacher or a doctor, something really grand. We'd've been so proud.'

I was surprised when Norah turned up in Maghull one day, quite out of the blue. It wasn't a bit like her. If Norah wanted to see someone, she usually telephoned beforehand to make sure it would be convenient.

'You've had your hair cut!' was the first thing I said. She was wearing jeans and a T-shirt for the first time in her life and looked quite girlish. 'It's taken years off you.'

'I know.' She ran her fingers through her short, red curls, barely touched with grey. 'Roy always preferred it long, but this is so much more convenient.' She followed me into the kitchen while I put the kettle on.

'Does Roy mind that you've had it cut?'

She tossed her head and the curls shook. 'I haven't discussed it with him. I don't give a fig if he minds or not.' This was a rather bolshie statement coming from Norah, who'd always been a very docile wife. 'I'm leaving Roy,' she added with another toss of the head. 'That's why I'm here, Kit. I want to know if I can move in with you for a while. I could have the room where our Aileen slept.'

The news was equivalent to being knocked down with a feather. 'What's brought this on?' I gasped.

'I dunno,' Norah said vaguely. 'I think it's because our Bernadette's gone and there's nothing left for us to talk about. I should never have married Roy. I did on the rebound after Peter Murphy jilted me.'

I looked at her in astonishment. 'That was almost a quarter of a century ago. Has the penny only just dropped?'

'The penny dropped a long time ago, Kit, but what could I do?' She spread her hands helplessly. 'Roy was a good husband. Trouble is, he was only a good husband because I was a good wife. I let him make the rules, staying at home when I'd sooner have got a job, never wearing trousers and keeping me hair long because it was the way he liked it, but now Bernadette's left and I'd like to spread me wings a bit, except Roy's dead set against it. He claims,' she added indignantly, 'that these jeans make me look like mutton dressed up as lamb.'

'But that's ridiculous, they look great on you.' Never, in all the years she'd been married, had she said a word against Roy – until now. I'd always thought she was perfectly happy. 'But what do you mean, spread your wings a bit?' I asked suspiciously, wondering what she was about to get up to in the bedroom. It had only been empty a fortnight and I'd already bought wallpaper patterned with little red engines and puffy white clouds to convert it into a nursery for Jake.

'I'm not sure,' Norah said, vague again. 'I'd like to get a job, take driving lessons, go to night school and learn to cook exotic foreign meals, maybe start my own restaurant one day. I suppose I'm fed up being Roy's wife and Bernadette's mother, and fancy being meself for a change.'

'Oh, Norah!' I threw my arms around her. 'Of course you can stay, but not in Aileen's room. I was about to decorate it for Jake, but he'll have to share with Ben – I'll buy bunkbeds – and you can have the spare. Did you want to move in today?'

Norah shrugged. 'Today, tomorrow, next week, it really doesn't matter. I'll help you decorate, if you like.'

'I'd like that very much.' I'd never wallpapered before and was worried I'd make a mess of things.

It turned out Norah had never wallpapered before either and we made a mess of things between us. But when the room was finished, it hardly seemed to matter that the fronts of the little red engines didn't always match up with the backs and some of the clouds looked a bit cockeyed. I bought bunkbeds – Norah insisted on paying half – and two weeks later she moved into the spare, by which time she'd got a job taking the money in a self-service garage on Southport Road. I think the manager must have taken a fancy to her, because he picked her up every morning at half past eight, brought her home again at six and was teaching her to drive in the dinner hour.

During the day, I was inundated with calls from Roy wanting to know if she was all right. 'There was no need for her to leave, you know, Kitty. I must have told her that a hundred times, but her mind was made up and nothing I said would change it.'

'She seems OK,' I said whenever he rang. It didn't seem fair to tell him Norah was having the time of her life and thoroughly enjoying her newly found freedom.

Eve telephoned at about three o'clock in the afternoon on a sparkling July day to say she'd just had her first contraction and would I mind having Holly for a few days? 'Faith offered to take her, but she's a bit off-colour at the moment and I thought you wouldn't mind.'

I said I'd love to have Holly and offered to drive over and fetch her.

'It's all right,' Eve said. 'I'll bring her over myself on the way to the hospital.'

'You're never driving yourself to hospital while you're in labour!' It seemed a mad, irresponsible thing to do.

'I've only had a single contraction, Kitty,' she said airily. 'I'll be fine.'

'Why don't you let me take you?' I urged.

'In that old heap of yours? No, thanks.' With that, she rang off.

'You're about to become an uncle again,' I told Jake. 'I wonder if it'll be a niece or a nephew?'

He looked up from the plastic telephone on which he'd been carrying on a mysterious conversation with himself and smiled at me benignly. 'Uncle,' he said. 'Uncle, uncle, uncle.' He must have liked the sound of the word.

'Holly will be here in a minute.'

'Holly, Holly, Holly.'

'Do you have to repeat everything three times?'

'Times, times, times.' He collapsed, giggling, on to the floor.

We played word games until a horn sounded. I ran outside to collect Holly and save Eve getting out of the car. 'How do you feel?' I asked.

'Wonderful,' she said sarcastically, and drove off before I could say another word. Indoors again, I called Oliver, who told me he was about to leave for the hospital. 'Eve said to wait until I finished work, but I refused.'

We both agreed that Eve was too independent for her own good. He promised to telephone as soon as there was any news. 'I might call on you if it's not too late and say goodnight to Holly.'

Norah came home at six and I told her about Eve.

'I wish we'd had more children,' she said wistfully. 'All our love and affection was concentrated on Bernadette. We were wrong to expect her to go to university and become a teacher or a doctor, though it's a bit late in the day to think that. She just wasn't up to it, poor girl. Parents have no right to organize their children's lives. They should be left to make their own decisions.'

'Ben wants to go to university,' I said. 'Earlier, when he came home from school, he was wonderful with Jake and Holly. He sat them on the floor and taught them how to count up to ten. It's strange,' I mused, 'that he's so well adjusted and sensible considering the life he's led. I mean, both his mother and father walked out on him.'

'It's more than strange, it's a miracle.' Norah yawned and stretched her brown arms: if the garage had no customers, she sat outside in the sun, and had acquired a lovely tan. 'I think I'll have a shower before I eat. Did Roy ring today?'

'Twice this morning. I told him you were OK.'

'I'm more than OK, I feel marvellous.' She looked like a cat that had just eaten an entire jug of cream. 'I never realized life could be so much fun.'

Everyone else had gone to bed and the television was on without the sound while I waited for the ten o'clock news to start, when Oliver rang to say Eve had had another girl. 'We're calling her Louisa. She's lovely,' he said with a throb in his voice. 'Eve said to tell you she feels great.'

'Congratulations, Oliver,' I said warmly. 'I'll go and see her tomorrow.'

'How's Holly?' he enquired.

'Fast asleep at the foot of Jake's bed. They had a marvellous time together.'

'Good. Look, Kitty, is it all right if I drop in on you for a while? I don't fancy going home to an empty house. I'll never sleep the state I'm in, I'm much too excited.'

'Of course, Oliver. I never go to bed before midnight.'

'I'll be with you soon,' he promised, 'after I've said goodnight to Eve.'

I turned up the sound on the television, switched on the lamps and closed the curtains on what had been a lovely day – and was likely to be just as lovely tomorrow, judging by the red gashes in the navy-blue sky. Now my daughter had another daughter of her own! I half sat, half lay on the settee, ignoring the news, thinking about Eve and the various stages she had gone through: so tense and anxious when we'd first lived together, but gradually developing into a self-possessed young lady. I recalled how angry she'd been when she'd discovered I was her mother, the giddy years in London, getting married to the gormless Rob Horton. But now those unsettled days were over and she was happily married to Oliver Knowles. The day of the housewarming came to mind, of Eve looking out of the window at Oliver and Holly, me wondering if she was visualizing the idyllic years that lay ahead.

Oliver arrived earlier than expected. Eve had been asleep when he'd gone to say goodnight, so he'd left immediately, he explained when he came in, dark eyes shining, jacketless and without a tie, reminding me a little of the Oliver I'd met in Buckles. I kissed him on the cheek and congratulated him again.

He collapsed in a chair. For the first time since I'd seen him in a wheelchair in his mother's garden in Richmond, he looked fully alive, as if all his senses were working. He beamed at me. 'I can't get over the fact that I'm a father.'

'You'll get used to it,' I assured him. 'Would you like a drink, a proper one, to toast Louisa?'

'The doctor forbade me to drink because of my tablets, but what the hell!' he said recklessly. 'It's not every day something like this happens. What have you got?'

'There's a bit of whisky left over from Christmas, some gin and loads of sherry, but Oliver,' I protested, 'I'd sooner you didn't drink if you're not supposed to.'

'A single whisky won't hurt. I've no intention of staying teetotal for the rest of my life.'

'Just a little one then.'

'What's this?'

I was pouring out the drinks – whisky for Oliver, sherry for me – and turned to find his eyes fixed on the television on which the announcer was summarizing the day's news. 'What's what?' I asked.

'A bomb exploded in Belfast. One of the psychiatrists I saw told me I'd been posted to Belfast when this happened,' he touched his head, 'but I can't remember a thing about it. You've been there, haven't you, Kitty?' His gaze turned to me. 'Eve said you went to a funeral. She reckons we must have been there at around the same time.'

I handed him the whisky. 'Here's to Louisa,' I said, raising my glass.

'To Louisa,' he said absently. 'When were you in Belfast?'

I'd hoped to change the subject from Belfast. 'I can't really remember. About two years ago, I think. I was only there a few days.'

'They tell me I was there for a year. One day, when I feel more up to it, I might go back and see if anything jogs my memory.'

'Is that such a good idea? Perhaps some things are best left forgotten.'

He shook his head. 'Oh, no, Kitty. You've no idea how frustrating it is to have whole chunks of your life missing. Some days, the memories come pouring in and I have difficulty sorting them out, putting them into context. It's like someone opening a blind – what are they called, the ones that have slats you pull open with a string?'

'Venetian blinds.'

'That's it. Every now and then, the blind opens another fraction and I remember more. I write it all down in a notebook before I go to bed and Eve reads it next morning. But I won't be happy until the blind's completely open and I've remembered every single thing.' He swallowed the whisky in a single gulp and asked if he could have another. 'I won't take a tablet later to help me sleep,' he said when I looked reluctant. 'I feel really keyed up tonight, Kitty. Another drink won't hurt.'

'Oh, all right, but don't blame me if it makes you sick.' The whisky I gave him barely covered the bottom of the glass. Upstairs, one of the children gave a little cry. I couldn't tell if it was Jake or Holly. The sound must have disturbed Ben, as the mattress on the top bunk made a crunching noise when he turned over.

Oliver grinned. 'I wouldn't dream of blaming you for anything, Kitty. I'll tell you something I remembered: my fourth birthday party. We were in Orrell Park and I vowed I'd marry you when I grew up. I wrote it down and when Eve read it she thought it terribly sweet. But I've told you that before, haven't I?' he said, frowning. 'Haven't I, Kitty?' he insisted when I didn't answer.

I still didn't answer, just shrugged and looked vague. Alarm bells were ringing in my head. He'd said it to me in Buckles when we were sitting on the bed in my room.

'But I couldn't have done. I haven't seen you in a fortnight and it only came back to me the other day.' He frowned again and I could see a pulse beating in his forehead. 'Yet I can hear it, hear my voice saying the words. Then I lifted your hand – why did I lift your hand? And I said . . . I said . . .' His hands were balled into fists, the knuckles white, making a sharp, cracking noise as he beat them together. Perspiration dripped from his brow in the effort to make his damaged brain work. 'I said, "And now here I am, all grown up, and you haven't got a ring on your finger." Why did I say that, Kitty?'

'Oliver,' I cried, unable to stand his expression of bewilderment and pathos as he tried to make sense of the words, 'you're drunk and you're imagining things. I think you should go home this minute.' But he couldn't possibly drive while he was in such a state. I jumped to my feet. 'I'll phone for a taxi.'

'No!' he said frantically. He got up and began to walk around the room. 'I don't want to go home. All sorts of things are coming back to me. Who's Jack O'Donnell? The psychiatrist wanted to know if I could remember Jack O'Donnell, and it's there, on the brink of my mind. There was a funeral, was it *his*? I was in a church with a coffin. I can see it quite clearly. Whose funeral did you go to, Kitty?'

'I'm going to make you some very strong coffee.' In the kitchen, I leaned against the sink, closed my eyes and took a long, deep breath. I desperately wanted Oliver to get better, for Eve's sake as well as his own, but he would never do that until he'd recalled all the missing pieces of his life. I should be helping, not hindering him, yet there were certain memories I'd sooner stayed forgotten.

He came into the kitchen, leaned against the frame of the door and said in a low, angry voice, '*I* was Jack O'Donnell, and *you* were at the funeral. Why the hell haven't you told me that before, Kitty?'

'I don't know,' I whispered.

'Eve said you'd gone to a relative's funeral,' he pressed. 'Someone called Michael.'

I gave in. I couldn't refuse to answer any more of his questions. It just wasn't fair. 'Michael was my brother-in-law. He was married to my sister, Aileen. When they split up, he went to live in Belfast. They looked after Eve until she was nine.'

'What was Michael's other name? Eve didn't say.'

'Gilbert,' I muttered.

'Michael Gilbert. Why would I be at Michael Gilbert's funeral? I know I was working under cover for the Army because they told me, but nobody seems to know the details. Either that, or they're keeping them to themselves. How come we were at the same funeral, Kitty?' He grabbed my shoulders and shook me hard. '*Tell me.*'

'You were involved with a group of terrorists.' I did my best to keep my voice steady and calm. 'They – and you – used to drink in a hotel called Buckles on the Falls Road where Michael lived.'

'With Mary Brady!' The words were expelled in a rush. 'I feel as if a snake's crawling into my head.' He beat his forehead with his fist. 'Mary Brady's father owned the hotel. I used to play the piano there and, one night, I turned around and I saw you. *That's* when I told you I'd vowed to marry you when I grew up, later on upstairs.' His face reddened and then he flinched. 'We *slept* together. Christ Almighty, Kitty,' he groaned, 'you should have told me that before I married Eve.'

I closed the kitchen door, worried someone would hear. 'No, I shouldn't, Oliver, because it didn't matter any more. It was over and done with, part of the past.'

'Part of *our* past.' He began to walk again, up and down the small room, banging the wall at one end, the door at the other. 'I loved you. I asked you to marry me and you said yes. Perhaps I still love you, I don't know.'

'You love Eve now,' I said steadily. 'She's your wife and you have a child together.' I wanted to bite off my tongue the very second the words were out, because Oliver stopped walking and looked at me with glazed eyes.

'Do *we* have a child together?' he asked hoarsely. 'Is Jake mine?'

I felt too numb to do anything else but nod. I turned away to hide my scarlet face and poured water into the kettle, washed two mugs and spooned coffee into them, tried to remember if Oliver took sugar, but couldn't.

'What are we going to do now?' he asked after a long silence.

'Nothing,' I said firmly. 'Absolutely nothing, just carry on as normal, as if we'd never met in Belfast. It's all over and done with. You must never mention it to a soul – *I* haven't. You're married to Eve and you have a family. Your responsibility lies with them.'

'But what about you?' he cried. 'What about Jake?'

'Me and Jake are doing fine on our own, thank you.'

There was another long silence. Then Oliver said, 'It's all coming back to me, like watching a film. I'd brought champagne to have with our breakfast. I rang you from the foyer of the hotel, but when I turned round there were two of them behind me: Sean Doyle and Joe McMurphy.' He was speaking very fast, as if worried if he didn't get the words out quickly he'd lose track, forget what he wanted to say. 'Before I knew where I was, I was thrown into the back of a car and they drove out of Belfast. They dragged me out and beat me around the head with baseball bats. I was too far gone to feel the bullets they shot into my knees.'

'Was it because of me you were found out, Oliver?' It would have looked very suspicious had they discovered he knew Michael's sister-in-law.

'It was nothing to do with you, Kitty. Their side had people working undercover, same as ours. Someone, I'll never know who, grassed on me. I was followed to the hotel that morning . . .' He shrugged. 'I've told you what happened then. But it's what happened before that concerns me.'

'What do you mean?'

'The days we spent together in that hotel. Christ Almighty, Kitty, I'd never known anything like it before – or since, come to that.' His eyes narrowed and the look on his face sparked off memories that I'd far prefer to forget. It was the same look he'd had when we were about to make love. 'It was bloody marvellous. How can we forget the things we did to each other?'

'Because we have to, Oliver.' I forced myself to sound angry. 'Because I'm sixteen years older than you and you're married to my daughter and she's just had your baby. Because we just had a fling, that's all. It meant nothing to either of us and you must never mention it again, not to me, not to anyone.' I stamped my foot. 'Never, never, never.'

With that, I went to phone for a taxi. It arrived within a few minutes and took him to Formby. During those minutes, neither of us spoke.

Chapter 11

Our Jamie got married for the second time in August. His new wife, Barbara, was divorced with two children and not nearly as pretty as Lisa, his first wife, and the children weren't half as nice as the ones Lisa had taken back with her to Berlin.

'He's getting a second-rate wife and second-rate kids, all because he couldn't keep his trousers buttoned while he was married to Lisa,' Claire said disgustedly. 'But that's men for you. The world would be a much happier place if the good Lord hadn't provided them with willies.'

The McCarthys were inclined to agree with the first part of this statement, if not the second: we'd all liked Lisa very much and weren't too keen on Barbara.

The marriage took place in a registry office and Jamie only invited his immediate family: Claire and Liam, Danny and Marge, Norah and Roy, who were still a couple despite being separated, and me. The ceremony was short and rather business-like: afterwards, we went into town and had lunch in a private room over a restaurant in London Road. I wore the long blue dress I'd bought for Eve and Oliver's wedding, and Claire said I looked far more like a bride than Barbara did in her grey linen suit.

The meal over, we shook hands with Barbara's unsmiling mother and her equally unsmiling sisters and their husbands – perhaps our Jamie compared badly to Barbara's first husband – and went about our various ways: Claire and Liam to look at beds – their old one was falling to pieces – Norah, Roy and Danny back to work, leaving me and Marge wondering what to do with ourselves.

'That wedding was even worse than mine and Danny's,' Marge remarked, linking my arm. She was much more contented these days. Her children were working and living in Amethyst Street so money wasn't a problem, and she'd resigned herself to the fact that Danny spent half his life in the pub. Some nights, she even went with him. 'Let's go to the pics,' she said. 'It'll be quite like old times.'

These days, there were hardly any cinemas left in Liverpool, but *The Godfather* with Marlon Brando was on at the Odeon. We emerged almost three hours later feeling quite elated and agreeing it was the best film we'd ever seen.

'Our lives are so dull in comparison,' Marge remarked with a sigh.

'I'd sooner lead a dull life than be married to a member of the Mafia,' I said with a shiver. 'They actually cut the head off a *horse*!'

'Shall we go for a drink?'

'Sorry, Marge, but I left Jake with Eve and promised to collect him ages ago. She'll be doing her nut. Holly's been playing up since Louisa arrived, I think she must be a bit jealous, and Louisa is like Jake: she never sleeps.'

Louisa was four weeks old, a pretty baby with her mother's blonde hair and a little pointed face. She looked delicate, but was as strong as an ox, kicking off the bedding contemptuously, however tightly it was tucked around her.

'She doesn't like to be confined,' Eve said tiredly.

I'd told Louisa she'd be sent back to where she came from if she didn't watch it, but she took not a blind bit of notice and continued to treat her bedclothes as if they were a prison from which she was determined to escape.

'Where have you been?' Eve enquired listlessly. I'd arrived in Formby long after I'd promised. The floor was littered with toys and Eve was wearing jeans and one of Oliver's shirts, her hair uncombed and her face devoid of its usual make-up. Louisa lay in her carrycot, wide awake, and thinking deeply about something. Bootsie and Snudge were sitting together on an armchair: even they looked fed up.

'Marge and I went to the pictures when the wedding feast was over, but it turned out to be a really long film. I'm sorry, sweetheart,' I said. 'Has Jake been a pest?' My son was clinging to my legs. I sat down and hauled him on to my knee. 'Have you missed me?' I enquired.

His brown eyes, just like Oliver's, danced with mischief. 'No,' he cackled.

'Jake's been very well behaved,' Eve said, 'but Holly's really getting on my nerves. The very second I sit down she wants to climb all over me.' She sniffed dejectedly. 'I put her to bed early and she cried herself to sleep. I expect that's only made matters worse.'

'Well, the poor child is probably feeling neglected with a new baby in the house. She might think Louisa's come to take her place.' I wanted to tell her she should be making an extra big fuss of Holly, not putting her out of the way, but she didn't look in the mood for advice from her mother.

'Where's Oliver?' He should be home by now, but there was no sign. I was glad: we hadn't met since the night Louisa was born and I'd sooner avoid him for as long as possible.

'He's in Wales buying antiques. Apparently, he now finds working in the shop boring. *He's* really getting on my nerves, too.' She looked on the verge of tears. 'One minute he's an invalid, next he's a bundle of energy. I wanted the kitchen renovating and he's decided to do it himself. He made a start last night and the place is just a shell. I intended getting proper kitchen-fitters in, but he won't let me. I telephoned Dad this morning and he's agreed to do the plumbing. He's coming first thing in the morning to take a look at things.'

'Dad?' I raised my eyebrows.

'Dad, otherwise known as Connor Daley,' she said cuttingly. 'The man you told me was my father.'

'Oh, yes, Con. It threw me a bit when you said Dad.' I'd forgotten she saw Con from time to time.

She rolled her eyes in exasperation. 'Honestly, Kitty, you are a truly hopeless mother. It's a wonder I don't have all sorts of complexes and personality defects because of you.'

'I'm sorry,' I said meekly. I knew she didn't mean it. My defects as a mother were a bit of a joke between us, if a rather black one.

'And so you should be. What are you going to tell Jake when he wants to know who his father is?'

'I don't know. I'll cross that bridge when I come to it.'

'Dad said you told him Jake's father was dead. Is that true?'

'Yes and no.'

'What sort of an answer is that?' she snapped. 'He's either dead or he isn't.'

I said I'd sooner not discuss the matter and asked if she'd like a drink. 'Tea or coffee?'

She shrugged. 'Coffee.'

'Then I'll tidy up and you can do something with yourself before your husband comes home. You look as if you've been dragged through a hedge backwards.' I put Jake on the floor and got to my feet. He held on to my skirt and followed me into the kitchen, which looked as if it had been hit by a bomb. Units had been torn from the wall, a stack of bricks supported the sink and half the wallpaper had been scraped off.

'Nice, isn't it?' Eve said from the door. 'How am I supposed to do the washing and make the food in this dump? I don't know what's got into Oliver, I really don't. He can't keep still a minute.'

'It's disgraceful,' I spluttered. 'Absolutely disgraceful. I wish you'd shown me this earlier: I wouldn't have dreamt of leaving Jake with you. I'll take the washing home and tomorrow you must spend the day with me – and every day from now on until this place is cleared up.'

'When it comes right down to it, you can be quite a decent mother, Kitty,' Eve said with the suggestion of a smile.

'Where are the cups and saucers, or has Oliver smashed them, too?'

'In that box in the corner. The coffee's in the fridge with the milk. I've no idea where the sugar is, but neither of us take it, so it doesn't matter.'

'Well, at least he's left the fridge intact,' I muttered as I opened the door.

When I arrived home, our Norah and Ben were sitting on the settee watching *Are You Being Served?* It was one of my favourite programmes and I was sorry I'd missed it. Jake ran across the room and snuggled between them with a little satisfied grunt. I remembered his father doing the same thing when Con and I were attempting to do a bit of courting in the house in Orrell Park, Faith having gone to the fateful dinner with Eric and Hope.

As soon as I'd put Eve's washing in the machine, I looked up Connor Daley's number in the telephone directory. There were two: one for his office, the other for his home. I rang the office first, just in case he was there, though it was unlikely at such a late hour. To my surprise, he answered.

'It's Kitty. I didn't expect you to be there,' I said.

'Hello, Kitty.' He sounded faintly amused. 'If you didn't expect me to be here, why did you ring?'

'I thought I'd give your office a try before I called you at home and June answered. I didn't want to cause you any embarrassment.'

'That's very thoughtful of you, Kitty, though you weren't always so thoughtful.' He paused a few seconds to let this sink in. 'What can I do for you, or is this just a social call?'

'Are you busy? I'm not interrupting anything important, am I?' He might be doing the books or preparing an estimate.

'You are, actually, something very important. I was about to peel the tab off a can of lager, but that can wait. Fire ahead, Kitty.'

'It's about Eve. Oliver's gone mad and wrecked the kitchen. She said you'd agreed to do the plumbing.'

'True, very true,' he agreed in the same amused tone. 'She called this morning.'

'Can you do the whole kitchen, Con? The units and everything?'

'If you ask nicely, yes.'

'I'm asking as nicely as I can.' He didn't sound exactly sober. I wondered how many cans of lager he'd drunk.

'How soon would this need to be done?'

'As quickly as humanly possible.'

'Correct me if I'm wrong, but are you being an interfering mother-in law?'

'Yes, but Eve's got Holly and a new baby to look after, and the kitchen's a complete and utter wreck.'

'What's got into Oliver?' He was serious now.

'He's feeling better, more his old self, and looking for things to do, energetic things. He probably genuinely intends to do up the kitchen, but doesn't realize what a big job it will be.'

'He sounds a bit of an idiot to me. Anyroad, I promised Eve I'd come first thing tomorrow. Will you be there?'

I supposed I'd better. 'Yes. Don't mention I rang, just offer to do the whole kitchen. I'm sure she'll agree. Con?'

'Yes, Kitty?'

'Why are you all alone in your office drinking beer at this time of night?'

'Because it's a vast improvement on doing it at home. Tara, Kitty. See you tomorrow.'

Ben was on his holidays and only too willing to accompany Jake and I when we set off for Formby first thing the next day. Con had arrived a few minutes before us. I was glad Oliver's car wasn't there: he must have gone to work.

Eve was still in her dressing gown, and she and Con were in the kitchen examining the mess Oliver had made. 'He's drawn up plans and intends to build the new units himself,' Eve was saying when I entered the back door. 'Oh, hello, Kitty.' She seemed pleased to see me. 'I wasn't expecting you.'

'I thought I'd come and hear what Con had to say.'

Con gave me a brief nod. 'Is Oliver a carpenter, luv?' he asked Eve.

'No,' Eve said indignantly. 'He's never done anything like this before.' I nearly said he'd made coffins in Belfast, but realized just in time it was something I wasn't supposed to know.

'I think he might have bitten off more than he can chew,' Con said with admirable diplomacy. 'He needs to know about plastering, too, not to mention plumbing, tiling, wiring, decorating and one or two other things.' He moved around the kitchen, tapping walls, stamping on the floor, turning the taps on and off, apparently deep in thought. He looked solid and comfortable, a man to trust. What on earth was wrong with his marriage? I wondered. 'Eve, luv,' he said at last, 'would you like me to take on the whole job for you? If I pull out all the stops, put my entire crew on it, I could have it done within a week. There won't be time to have the units made to measure, we'd have to buy them in kits, but with a bit of ingenuity I can make everything fit. If it's left to that husband of yours, it won't be finished for months, if ever.'

Eve's face was a picture of sheer delight. 'Dad! You're a wonder, you really are. But what about your other customers? Won't you be letting them down?'

'You're me daughter, luv,' Con said gruffly. 'You come first and me other customers second. They'll just have to wait, won't they?'

He reminded me of my own dad, the way he spoke, and it crossed my mind what a terrible thing I'd done depriving Eve of a father like Con for most of her life. I hoped she wasn't thinking the same thing. Con said he just happened to have a catalogue of units in the car and she could choose the ones she liked. 'I'll go and fetch it, do some measuring up, then drive over to Kirkby Trading Estate where they make 'em.'

'Will Oliver mind you taking decisions over his head?' I asked Eve when Con had gone. If he did, it would be my fault for interfering.

'I don't care if he does or not,' Eve said hotly. 'I rang Faith last night and told her about the kitchen. She said she wasn't surprised seeing as how he seems so much better: he's always been very impetuous. She suggested I ask Dad to do the whole kitchen, but he suggested it first, so there was no need. If Oliver makes a fuss, at least I'll have his mother on my side.'

'And your own mother, too,' I assured her.

The kitchen proved a turning point in a number of lives. It was the reason for the first of Eve and Oliver's many rows and why Con and I became friends again, though this time our relationship was platonic.

Each day, after he'd finished work, he would call in at Maghull and give Eve a report on the day's progress, though a phone call would have done, or Eve could have judged the progress for herself when she reached home. I reckoned Con only came because he was lonely.

As soon as Eve and the children had gone, I'd make him a meal – Jake was in bed by then – and afterwards we'd play cards with Norah and Ben, watch telly, or the four of us would just sit and talk. Norah had always liked Con in the days when we'd been more than friends, and he and Ben got on just fine.

When the kitchen was finished, I suggested to Con he drop in for a meal any time he happened to be in the vicinity. 'You'll always be welcome,' I told him.

'I could happen to be in the vicinity almost every day, Kitty,' he said, his green eyes twinkling in a way I remembered well. 'Are you worried about me?'

'Yes,' I said bluntly. 'I don't like the idea of you spending so much time in your office drinking yourself to death. What's wrong between you and June?'

'Nothing you could put a finger on,' he said with a shrug. 'We just started getting on each other's nerves. She claimed I worked too hard and she hardly ever saw me. I can't remember what I told her, but we just kept going downhill until we could hardly stand the sight of one another. Last time we spoke civilly, we discussed getting divorced. I'm expecting to hear from her solicitor any minute.'

'What about the children?'

'They'll stay with June. I'll buy meself a little house somewhere, keep on working, and Philip and Marian can come and see me at weekends. It's strange, you know, Kitty,' he said thoughtfully, 'but I feel closer to Eve than I do to them. Perhaps it's because she appreciates having a dad more than they do.'

I just winced and didn't say a word. I was amazed that neither he nor Eve seemed to bear me a grudge for the crimes I'd committed against them. In fact, they genuinely appeared to like me.

In September, Ben went back to school and Norah signed up for an evening class in French cuisine. There'd been no suggestion of her finding somewhere else to live. We enjoyed each other's company. I felt guilty for hoping she wouldn't go back to Roy.

Our Claire met her friend, Mildred Sweeney, who was still at Wexford's where Aileen and Michael had worked, and who told her Steve McSherry was now back in Liverpool. 'Apparently, she heard it on the grapevine, but what about our poor Aileen, eh? She's still in Australia probably looking for him everywhere. If only there was some way of letting her know. Does she keep in contact with Ben?'

'She sends him postcards every now'n again, but they never give an address.' Only the postmarks revealed where Aileen happened to be at the time.

'Bugger! I usually say a little prayer for her every night before I go to bed. From now on, I'll say two. Should we tell Ben his dad's home?'

'I think his dad should tell him that himself, don't you? Ben will only be upset if he doesn't come to see him.'

Eve and Oliver were still fighting over the kitchen. It seemed the units Eve had chosen were inferior to the ones *he* would have built, and the cooker was in a most inconvenient position. Nor would he have chosen to cover the floor with linoleum, but had intended to lay real stone tiles.

'I think it looks fantastic,' I said the first time I saw the new kitchen. The units were a lovely golden pine with antique black handles, and the ones on the walls had leaded windows with lights underneath. The ugly boiler had been replaced with a much smaller one and the linoleum had a pattern of dark russet tiles. The room looked warm and inviting, particularly when compared to my own austere kitchen.

'I think it's fantastic, too, but Oliver never stops pointing out how much better it would be if he'd done it,' Eve said resentfully. 'I asked Dad to put the cooker in the corner, it's safer there, and the linoleum is almost half an inch thick. It cost the earth and is much warmer than stone. I would have hated stone.'

'Stone would have been very cold,' I agreed. 'Can't Oliver be persuaded to build a shed in the garden to keep himself busy? Or do some digging, plant some trees or chop some down?'

'He already has plans for the garden. He's designing a gazebo and he's going to make swings and a treehouse for the children.' She laughed, taking me by surprise. 'He's driving me wild, but in a funny way I don't mind. Before, it was like having a child for a husband; that's why I wanted us to get married, so I could mother him. Now I want to kill him, but he's much more exciting to live with.'

'That's a relief. I've been worried about you two.'

'There's no need. For a while, I was worried, too, but everything's working out just fine.'

I only hoped Oliver felt the same.

September was almost out when I received a letter from Ben's form teacher, Yvonne Harris, requesting my approval for him to take two O-levels, Maths and English, the following June: 'By then, he will be fourteen, two years younger than he would usually sit them, but Ben is an exceptionally clever young man and we'd very much like to see how he gets on.'

'How do you feel about it?' I asked Ben.

'I'd really like to do it, Kitty,' he said with enthusiasm. He was an extremely mature young man for thirteen. Since he'd come to live with us, he'd grown rapidly and was now almost six feet tall. His voice had broken almost overnight and he could easily have been taken for sixteen, eighteen at a pinch. It was a shame Aileen was missing such an important part of her son's life, the years when he passed from being a boy into a man.

'Are you the only pupil taking O-levels early?' I asked. I wouldn't want him to feel an oddity.

'There'll be nine of us altogether: five girls and four boys. Is it all right if I go to tea with one of the girls on Sunday?' he asked casually.

'Of course it's all right, Ben.' I'd been wondering when he'd acquire a girlfriend, a good-looking chap like him. 'What's her name?'

'Samantha Whelan. She started school the year before me, so we didn't meet until the headmaster asked us into his study to talk about O-levels. Afterwards, she invited me to tea. I quite like her,' he said offhandedly, but from the look on his face I could tell he liked Samantha Whelan very much.

It would seem Samantha felt the same. The following day, Mrs Whelan telephoned to say in a dead posh voice that her daughter had talked about nothing but Ben for days. 'She's had crushes before, but never like this, and they're usually on someone unattainable, like George Best or Paul McCartney.' There was a slight pause before she said, 'I take it I can rely on Ben to be sensible?'

'I don't quite know what you mean.' I knew exactly what she meant and felt annoyed at the suggestion that Ben might take advantage of a vulnerable young girl.

'I think you do, Mrs McSherry. Samantha's not very sophisticated: she's never had a boyfriend before.'

'Ben's never had a girlfriend – and isn't Samantha a year older than him? I'm sure he'll behave responsibly and I trust Samantha will do the same. Oh, by the way, I'm not Ben's mother, but his aunt: my name's Kitty McCarthy.' I rang off. She was only protecting her daughter as any mother would, but I'd resented her tone. You'd think Ben was a Casanova who seduced women at the drop of a hat, not a thirteen-year-old schoolboy about to go to tea with his first girlfriend.

Norah was practising her culinary skills. Every Sunday, she'd make a three-course meal that had us banging the table for more. My own favourite was onion soup for starters – called *entrée* in France – followed by *coq au vin* and *crème caramel*.

The family were invited two at a time to sample our sister's recently discovered talent for making mouth-watering meals: Claire and Liam; Danny and Marge; Jamie and Barbara. Sunday dinner quickly became the main event of the week, with everyone clamouring to be invited again.

'When are you going to ask Eve and Oliver?' Norah queried one day. 'I'm surprised you haven't invited them before.'

I mumbled something about Eve being busy with the new baby, but the truth was that I'd managed to avoid Oliver for months. I took for granted he was doing the same. So far, Eve didn't appear to have noticed, but I couldn't put it off for much longer. We couldn't go for the rest of our lives and never meet.

'I'll ask them to come next Sunday,' I promised. 'Anyroad, you haven't invited your Bernadette and Johnny.'

Norah grimaced. 'Only because if Johnny finds out there's a gourmet dinner going free every Sunday in Maghull, we'll never see the back of him. Why don't you ask Con at the same time as Eve and Oliver?'

'I'd sooner invite him the week after.' I didn't fancy having dinner with the fathers of both my children at the same time.

Gone were the grey flannels, the ironed shirts and the polished shoes. Oliver turned up in a polo-necked jumper, jeans and a shabby suede jacket that must have lived in his wardrobe for years. He was growing his hair long and it curled around his ears and on to his sunburned neck. His hands bore the cuts and scars acquired from hard physical work – he was halfway through building a garage on the side of the house. He hardly glanced at me throughout the meal and never once spoke to me directly, though he paid a lot of attention to Jake, who was sitting in his high chair, enjoying the food and the company, and giving us the benefit of his opinion from time to time.

He was seriously considering giving up his job in the antique shop, Oliver told us during the main course – *boeuf au vin rouge* – and going into business making garden furniture. He enjoyed working with his hands. 'It's so much more satisfactory than selling mouldy antiques.'

'What do you think about that?' I asked Eve. Faith had taken the children for the day and she seemed happy to have left motherhood behind for a few hours. She looked extremely elegant in black flared velvet slacks and a red silk top, and was beautifully made up.

'I'm all for it if it means he'll leave the house alone. I'm fed up with the sound of hammering and sawing all day long. It's like living on a building site.' She smiled brilliantly at her husband, as if to say she didn't *really* mind. She'd been in love with Oliver when they married, but it had been a gentle, caring love; now she was crazy about him. I could tell from the way she looked at him, the glow in her eyes.

'Why don't you go back in the Army, Oliver?' Ben enquired.

'They'd never take me, Ben,' he said regretfully, as if he'd given the matter some consideration. 'They'd consider me damaged goods.'

'Would you really go back in the Army after what happened? You were nearly killed.' That was me sticking my oar in.

'Yes,' Oliver said shortly. 'It's not likely to happen again.'

'True,' I conceded. 'Next time they might kill you properly.'

'Oh, Kitty, don't!' Eve put her hands over her ears.

'Who'd like more beef casserole?' Norah asked.

There was a chorus of 'me' from everyone except Eve who said she was going on a diet. 'I could hardly fasten the zip on these trousers. I must lose some weight.'

'Mum, I want to wee-wee,' Jake bellowed, as if he wanted the entire world to know.

'Oh, all right,' I said impatiently, 'but I thought I asked you to wee-wee before we sat down to dinner?'

'I did, Mum, but nothing came.'

'I'll take him.' Oliver scooped Jake out of the high chair, threw him over his shoulder and carried him upstairs, Jake squealing with delight.

A few minutes later they returned; this time, Oliver had Jake tucked under his arm like a parcel. He set him on the floor and they boxed each other for a while, until Oliver clutched his jaw and cried, 'Ouch! That really hurt.'

The meal continued, with Jake glancing apprehensively at Oliver from time to time.

I said, 'He's worried he really hurt you, Oliver. Will you please tell him you're all right?'

Apparently, this involved Oliver kneeling by the chair and rubbing Jake's hand over his chin to prove there were no broken bones. I caught my breath: they were so alike I was amazed no one seemed to have noticed, but perhaps the incongruity of Oliver being Jake's father was too absurd for anyone to contemplate. 'I'm fine, son. I was just pretending, but you've got a mighty punch on you all the same.' They shook hands and Oliver looked at me directly for the first time. 'The boy needs a father to play with. All sons deserve to have a father.'

Eve gasped. 'Oliver! What a rude, insensitive thing to say!'

My hair felt as if it were standing on end. I was terrified by the thought of what Oliver would say next.

Fortunately, Norah remembered that our Jamie had been a champion boxer in the Army. 'He talked about taking it up professionally when he left, but he never did,' she said. 'By then, he'd married Lisa and must've given up on the idea.'

The conversation continued in a normal vein until the meal finished. Norah cleared the table and I was about to go after her to help with the dishes, but Eve got there before me, Ben went upstairs to study in the bedroom and I was left alone with Oliver and Jake, who seemed to find it necessary to climb on to his father's knee and have another boxing match. I kept waiting for Oliver to apologize for his rudeness, but when no apology seemed forthcoming, I said in a low, gritty voice that made my throat quiver, 'Don't you dare say anything like that again, Oliver. What are you trying to do? Ruin things for everyone?'

'It's true,' Oliver said steadily. 'Boys need their fathers.' Jake had stopped fighting and was examining his dad's gold watch.

'You know why Jake doesn't have a father,' I hissed. 'It was an entirely unnecessary remark.'

'But Jake *has* got a father. Me! I had a right to be told before I married Eve.'

'And what would you have done then?'

He gave me a look that sent my blood pressure soaring. 'Married you instead.'

'Oh, don't be daft, Oliver Knowles,' I snorted, struggling to stay calm. 'Before you married Eve, you had no idea who I was apart from her mother. Imagine if I'd announced out of the blue that you were Jake's father. That would have put the cat amongst the pigeons, wouldn't it?'

'Stuff the bloody pigeons.' His dark eyes were hot with anger. 'It was your duty to say something. You had no right to keep quiet.'

'Stop this, Oliver,' I said, putting all the strength of my own anger and desperation into the words. 'Stop it this minute. It's horrible to talk like that when Eve's only in the next room. She's your wife and she loves you. She's also my daughter and I love her more than words can say. I will not have her hurt, do you hear?' I threw him a black look. He regarded me sullenly. 'Our lives have gone a certain way and that's the way they'll stay. Now, I'm going upstairs to lie down for a while: you've given me a headache.'

But I didn't have a headache. I just wanted to get out of his way.

The older you get, the more people you know who die. A few weeks before Christmas, Muriel, who'd been very frail for months, went into hospital with pneumonia and never came out again. I felt awful: I hadn't seen much of her lately, though I had a whole list of excuses, from the car playing up, to concern about Jake wrecking her lovely house.

Muriel had been the nearest thing to a grandmother Eve had ever had and she was terribly upset. But what upset her most was that Oliver refused to attend the funeral. 'I told him how much she meant to me,' she said when we emerged from the crowded church – Muriel had clearly had a great many friends – 'but he said he had an appointment he couldn't possibly miss.'

'Some people can't stand funerals,' I soothed. She would never know that it was due to me that Oliver hadn't come. When I'd spoken to Paul, Muriel's brother, on the phone, he happened to mention that Mary Brady was coming from Belfast. She and Muriel had become very close. Oliver was working out his notice in the antique shop and I'd called straight away to tell him.

'It'd be best if she didn't see you. It could get back to those thugs who nearly killed you and they might come to Liverpool and finish off the job.'

'You're right,' he said soberly. 'Thanks for letting me know.'

'Don't mention it.'

Muriel had remembered Eve and the children in her Will. There were trusts for Holly and Louisa and £10,000 for Eve. She also left me a thousand, for which I was tearfully grateful. I immediately sold the Consul, amazed that anyone was willing to give good money for it, and bought a second-hand Morris Marina in exceptionally good condition.

Eve's inheritance would remove the anxiety she felt about Oliver giving up his job. 'He gets a good pension from the Army, so we wouldn't starve, but we'd have found it hard to manage without his salary. He has to buy more equipment for the business, and advertising costs the earth.'

'Wouldn't Faith be willing to help?' I asked.

'She'd be only too pleased, but Oliver refuses to take a penny off her. He won't even let me use the money I get from Rob for Holly. He makes me put it in the bank for when she grows up.'

I raised my eyebrows. '*Makes* you?' I wouldn't have let a man make me do anything and would have expected my daughter to feel the same.

'Yes, *makes* me. He's so masterful nowadays, Kitty.' She giggled and looked coy. 'I quite like it.'

I could barely stop myself from being sick.

Another Christmas, but this year Marge and Danny were going to a hotel for their dinner. 'I hope no one minds, but Danny won the dinner in a raffle and we thought it would make a nice change,' Marge said apologetically.

Claire thought it would also make a nice change if they went to their Patsy's: she'd been inviting them for years and was fed up with being turned down. Norah's Bernadette hadn't been feeling well lately and Norah felt obliged to spend the day with her, Johnny and the children. 'Roy's going,' she said with a sigh. 'It's going to be really horrible.'

Jamie and Barbara were having dinner in her parents' house, Ben was having his in Samantha's, and Con was going to stay with one of his sisters in Manchester. 'So it looks as if it's just going to be you and me, kiddo,' I said to Jake, who looked at me uncomprehendingly. 'I don't know about you, but I don't mind a bit.'

But Eve wouldn't hear of it. 'Of course you must come to ours,' she insisted when she discovered Jake and I would be on our own on Christmas Day. 'Faith's coming, and Robin, Alice and the twins have been invited to tea. It means the entire family will be there.'

‘Oh, all right,’ I said, a trifle grudgingly. ‘I’ll come and watch Oliver being masterful.’

I was glad I went: it turned out to be a wonderful day. We’d agreed not to open the presents until Jake and I arrived, and it was lovely listening to his and Holly’s squeals of excitement as they opened theirs under the tree. Louisa sat on Faith’s knee, waving her arms at the twinkling, star-shaped lights.

I was thrilled to bits when I opened Faith’s present to me, a bottle of Chanel No 5, something I’d always yearned for but could never afford, and felt slightly ashamed that all I’d bought her was a pair of leather gloves that I’d got half-price in the summer sales.

‘Oh, what a lovely jumper!’ I breathed when I opened the parcel from Eve and Oliver. It was a sort of apricot colour with glass beading around the neck and the cuffs.

‘Oh, Kitty, it’s a sweater, not a jumper,’ Eve chided. ‘Jumper’s terribly old-fashioned, it really dates you. And you must stop saying slacks when you mean trousers. Do you like the colour? Oliver thought it would tone well with your hair.’

‘I love the colour – I love the sweater.’ I resisted the urge to stick out my tongue.

I felt really proud of my daughter that day for putting on such a good show. The house positively dripped with decorations, the tree looked like something out of a fairytale, and the food was delicious.

‘That’s nice,’ I remarked when we sat down to dinner, pointing to the centrepiece: a slice of tree-trunk as big as a dinner plate, heaped with fir cones, little sprigs of holly and a red candle in the centre, the whole thing sprayed with puffs of silvery snow.

‘I made it,’ Eve said proudly.

‘When Oliver starts his business, you could sell that sort of thing at Christmas.’

‘That’s a marvellous idea, Kitty.’ She turned to Oliver. ‘Isn’t it, darling?’

‘Marvellous,’ Oliver agreed. ‘If you have any other bright ideas for the business, Kitty, you must let us know.’

I tried to work out if there was a double meaning to his words, but couldn’t detect one. ‘I will,’ I promised. I couldn’t have faulted his behaviour today. He was giving Eve his undivided attention and being very courteous to me.

The afternoon was spent lazily digesting the food, sipping drinks and watching the children play with their new toys. Jake had been given a pair of boxing gloves and was again using Oliver as a punchbag.

At five o'clock, Robin, Alice and the twins arrived, and it was time to open more presents. At that point, Faith produced a camera and took everyone's photo in a variety of formations: I posed in front of the tree with Eve, did the same with Eve and Alice, and again with Jake. I helped Eve lay the table and came to tell everyone the meal was ready just in time to hear Faith say she'd used up the entire film.

Later on, the children by now in bed – apart from Louisa who positively refused to sleep – we played Charades, my favourite game, the Archdeacon's Cat and Trivial Pursuit, after which we had supper and I announced it was time I went home while I still had the energy left to drive.

Eve came out with me to the car while Oliver went upstairs to fetch Jake. 'It's been one of the best days I've ever known.' I gave her a hug and a kiss. 'Thank you, sweetheart.'

'We're so lucky, having a family, plenty of money and a lovely home,' she said soberly.

I gave her another hug. 'I hope you'll always be so lucky, Eve.'

She nodded. 'So do I, but I'm terrified my luck will change. It's odd, but it comes from being so happy with Oliver and the children. It makes me worry the happiness can't possibly last, that the luck's bound to run out one day.'

'You must stop thinking like that,' I scolded. 'The best thing to do is take each day as it comes and try not to think about the future except in a positive way.'

'That's easier said than done, Kitty. Oh, here's Oliver with Jake. I'll go inside; it's freezing out here.'

I opened the rear door of the car and Oliver strapped a sleepy Jake in his seat. 'Thank you,' I said politely. 'I was just saying to Eve, it's been a lovely day.'

'It's been great,' he said gruffly. He stroked Jake's cheek and gently kissed his forehead. 'Goodnight, son.'

I drove home, wondering if the greatest danger to Eve's happiness lay in her husband.

*

On Boxing Day morning we had a visitor. Ben answered the door and came into the kitchen where I was helping Norah prepare another one of her exotic meals, to say his father had arrived and wanted to talk to him. 'I had to ask him in, he's in the lounge.'

'Do you want to talk to *him*, Ben?' The boy looked upset, which wasn't surprising, seeing as he'd thought his father was on the other side of the world.

'I suppose I'll have to,' he said grudgingly.

'Would you like me to be there with you?'

'No, thank you, Kitty, I'd sooner there were just the two of us.'

'Shall I bring in some tea?' I was anxious to have a look at Steve McSherry, the man for whom our Aileen had given up everything important in her life.

'Yes, please.'

I quickly made a pot of tea and a couple of ham sandwiches, put four mince pies on a plate, arranged everything on a tray, and took it into the lounge, leaving the door open so Norah could take a peek.

Steve McSherry was still handsome in a seedy sort of way. Although badly in need of a shave, it didn't detract from his raffish good looks, but I reckoned he wouldn't have them for much longer – his eyes were beginning to droop and his cheeks starting to sag. His receding hair, more grey than brown, was tied in a ponytail that looked much too thin and faintly pathetic. He wore a pair of well-worn jeans and a baggy jumper – *sweater* – full of snags. I vaguely remembered our Danny having a belted overcoat when he was about twenty, but they'd been out of fashion for years. I could only suppose Steve McSherry's came from a charity shop.

'Hello,' I said brightly. 'I'm Kitty, Aileen's sister.'

He leaped to his feet. 'How do you do, Kitty? It's nice to meet you.' I hadn't realized he was Irish: he still had the accent, as well as a boyish smile. We shook hands and he held on to mine for a fraction longer than necessary, as if he was trying to charm me as he'd done Aileen. 'Thanks for looking after my boy here. You're doing a fine job with him, I must say. I'm not sure if he isn't as tall as his ould dad, even taller.'

'There's no need to thank me for anything, Mr McSherry. It's a pleasure having him and I don't know what Jake – that's my son – would do without him.' I noticed Ben was looking extremely uncomfortable, and I quickly left.

Norah and I did our best to listen to the conversation without actually eavesdropping, but all we could hear was muffled voices, so we gave up.

I was surprised when, a mere fifteen minutes later, the front door slammed, and I found Ben standing alone in the middle of the lounge, glowering.

'Has your dad gone already?' I said. 'Me and Norah thought we'd ask him to stay to dinner.' We'd both felt very sorry for the chap, despite him being a terrible rogue. 'What exactly did he want?'

'To know if there was enough room for him to come and live with us. When I told him there wasn't, he only wanted me to come and live with *him*. It seems he's got some grotty bedsit and the Council would be willing to house him if he had a child.' He quivered with rage. I'd never known Ben be angry before and it wasn't a pretty sight. 'I didn't know, but he's been back in Liverpool for months and can't get a job. He's just had a lousy Christmas and saw me as an answer to his problems, at least some of them. I told him to go away, and that I never wanted to see him again.'

I looked out of the window. Steve McSherry was shuffling slowly down the road, shoulders hunched, the picture of dejection. 'But he's your father, Ben, your own flesh and blood. Don't you feel at least a shred of pity for him?'

'None at all,' Ben said shortly. 'He deserted one family for Mum, then he deserted her for some other woman. He doesn't deserve pity; he doesn't deserve anything.' I was pretty sure I could detect tears in his eyes, but I doubted if they were for his father. 'I don't give a damn what happens to him. He can rot in hell for all I care.'

'I heard that,' Norah whispered when I returned to the kitchen. 'Remember you once saying Ben seemed so well adjusted and sensible considering the life he's led? Well, that's not true, is it? It's made him really callous. I could never bring meself to be like that with me own father, no matter what he'd done.'

'Neither could I.' I felt worried for Ben. With such an unforgiving attitude, he wasn't likely to lead a very happy life.

'The resemblance between them is remarkable,' Faith was saying. 'If I didn't know better, I'd swear Oliver and Jake were related in some way. They look almost like father and son in that photograph.'

'I don't see it meself,' I mumbled. I stared at the photo in my hand, of Oliver with Jake on his knee on Christmas Day. I'd been setting the table while most of the photos were taken and had missed this one. Had Oliver deliberately asked his mother to take it? Did he *want* the truth to come out? 'I suppose there is a bit of a likeness,' I admitted. It would be silly to deny it didn't exist when Jake was gradually turning into the double of the little boy I'd prevented from riding to Egypt over twenty years ago. 'Jake's father was a similar type to Oliver: he had the same colour eyes and hair.' I wasn't sure how that rated as a lie, or whether it was a lie or not, but I'd hated saying it. I was beginning to deeply regret the day that Oliver Knowles had recovered his memory.

'Oh, well, that explains it.' Faith smiled. 'Would you like a copy of the photo? That's the reason I brought them, so you can pick the ones you'd like copied.'

'Yes, please, and some of the others, too. I'll make some coffee, then go through them again.'

Oliver, I remembered after Faith had gone, was looking after the children while Eve went to the sales in Southport. She'd asked me to go with her, but I hadn't wanted to take Jake and there was no one to look after him, Norah having gone back to work and Ben to do an O-level project with Samantha. I sat Jake on the floor with a drawing pad and a set of felt pens, asked him to draw a picture and went into the hall to telephone his father.

'What are you trying to do to me?' I asked the minute Oliver answered, not prepared to beat about the bush. 'What are you trying to do to Eve, your children? Why did you have your photo taken with Jake so everyone could see the resemblance between you to such an extent that your mother actually said you looked like father and son?'

'Did she?' He sounded taken aback.

'Yes, she did,' I said angrily.

'I just wanted a photo of us together, that's all.'

'And it didn't cross your mind that it would only draw attention to how alike you and Jake are?'

'No, Kitty, honest,' he said in a small voice.

I didn't know whether to believe him or not. 'Oliver,' I said, 'what happened in Belfast, well, we weren't being unfaithful to anyone, so no one was hurt, but Eve would be badly hurt if she found out. We have to make absolutely sure she never does. Do you understand that?'

'I'm not a child, Kitty,' he said huffily. 'Of course I understand.'

'Then why is it I get the feeling that you don't? It's almost as if you *want* people to find out, that you're deliberately dropping clues in the hope they do.'

There was a long pause. Eventually he said, 'I think you're right. I should never have married Eve. It was too soon after the beating and I wasn't myself. She asked me, Mum was all for it and I didn't have the will to refuse.'

I sighed. 'I told her she should wait until you were better.'

'Well, she didn't,' he said bitterly. 'Now I feel trapped and desperately want to escape. That must be why I'm dropping clues; I'm looking for an escape route.'

'An escape route to where?'

Another pause. 'To you, Kitty: to you and Jake.'

'Oh, Oliver,' I breathed. 'Please don't.'

'I can't help it.' His voice broke. 'It's all I can think about, the days we spent together in Belfast.'

Jake was tugging at my leg. 'I've done a picture, Mum. See!' I looked down. He'd drawn what could only be a giant gooseberry with eyes, nose and a mouth. 'Very good, sweetheart,' I whispered. 'I'll have a proper look in a minute.'

'Shall I draw something else?'

'Please.' He trotted back into the lounge, a sturdy little figure in his denim overalls and red sweatshirt. I felt a rush of love that made me want to choke.

'Was that Jake?' Oliver asked.

'Yes, he's drawing pictures.'

'So is Holly. She's doing the Christmas tree. It's quite good.'

'And life could be good if only you'd let it, Oliver. Only the other day Eve was saying how lucky she was having you and the children. Can't you at least try to feel the same?' I pleaded.

'Tell me something, Kitty – promise you'll answer honestly and I promise never to drop another clue or mention Belfast again: if I was free, would you marry me?'

I cupped my hand over the phone, as if worried someone would overhear. 'Yes, Oliver,' I said softly.

'Do you love me, Kitty?' His voice was harsh.

'With all my heart.'

'That's all I wanted to know.' The line went dead.

I felt better for admitting it and I think Oliver felt better for knowing. The subject was never mentioned again and he threw himself into his new garden-furniture business. For my forty-third birthday, he built a small gazebo in the garden where I sat and watched Jake play, and Ben and Samantha went to study.

In August, Ben's O-level results arrived. He'd received high grades for both subjects, a remarkable achievement for someone only fourteen: his photograph was in the *Crosby Herald*. I cut it out to keep for when Aileen came back.

As a reward for Ben's hard work, I booked a chalet in a holiday camp on the Isle of Man for him, Jake and I. I'd never had a proper holiday before, usually using the time to catch up on the housework or tidy the garden. When Norah heard, she asked if she could come with us. Then Claire found out and asked if it would be all right if she and Liam came, too. Marge rang to say she and Danny wouldn't mind a week away. In the end, the McCarthys sailed *en masse* to the Isle of Man for a week-long party. I kept expecting our Jamie to turn up, but he never did.

Almost a year after my telephone conversation with Oliver, just before Christmas, Eve had another baby, a lovely little girl called Caroline. In the month that followed, Jake turned three and started playgroup. It nearly broke my heart to leave him. I could hardly tear myself away, but Jake needed playmates his own age – he was already on a seesaw with another boy and had forgotten all about his mum. I hurried home for a good cry followed by about ten cups of tea and a glass of sherry.

That was the year all three of Marge and Danny's children got married and they were grandparents by December. Marge went through a sort of metamorphosis and emerged two stones lighter, her hair dyed blonde and with a wardrobe full of dead smart clothes. She and Danny joined a Latin American dancing club and made loads of new friends.

Con's divorce came through and he started going out with a woman named Isobel for whom he'd installed a new bathroom. 'I'm not getting married, Kit,' he told me. 'I've had enough of marriage. One was enough to last me all me life.'

I don't know what Isobel did to change his mind, but she managed it somehow. Six months later, Norah and I were guests at their wedding.

Norah no longer went to classes in French cuisine and had instead become the instructor. She'd given up her job in the garage and, when she wasn't teaching, she was preparing *saumon au Cresson, moules gratinées, porc aux haricots, crêpes Suzette*, and other incomprehensible but otherwise extremely delicious dishes to deliver to people who were expecting guests to a dinner they'd pretend to have cooked themselves.

And so the month flashed by and became years. I'd find myself putting up the Christmas decorations when it seemed no time since I'd taken them down. Jake started school; Ben and Samantha went to university in Norwich; our Claire and Marge had five more grandchildren between them; I discovered several grey hairs and hid them with an auburn rinse; Oliver's business prospered and he took on two assistants – I thought of him every time an IRA bomb went off and wondered if the hard men I'd met in Belfast had been behind it.

I got a job as a morning receptionist in a doctors' surgery in Waterloo – it was only a few stops away on the train. I stood in in the evenings if someone was off: otherwise, I helped our Norah if she had a big meal on that night. By now, the annual holiday in the Isle of Man had become an institution, though sometimes Jake and I were the only ones who went.

In 1978, Eric Knowles drowned off the coast of Cornwall. Faith only found out when she read the notice in *The Times*. She didn't go to the funeral. A year later, the country acquired its first woman Prime Minister, Margaret Thatcher.

In no time at all the eighties were upon us and the seventies had become just a memory.

The Eighties

Chapter 12

New Year's Eve

I'd offered to babysit for Eve and Oliver on New Year's Eve: they were going to a dinner dance in Southport with friends. Faith would be there and I was quite looking forward to it. When I told Claire, she thought it an incredibly dull way of seeing in the new decade.

'You're getting old before your time,' she said severely. 'Me and Liam are going to a party at our Patsy's. You and Jake can come, if you like.'

'I can't, I've already promised Eve.' Perhaps I *was* getting old before my time. If so, I didn't care.

I arrived with Jake just as Eve and Oliver were leaving. The lounge was criss-crossed with silver chains, and the lights on the tree flickered on and off in the dimly lit room. Logs snapped and crackled in the grate behind a gleaming brass fireguard; Bootsie and Snudge lay in front, a little mountain of black and ginger fur. The scene would have made a perfect Christmas card.

Jake made a beeline for the piano in the dining room and began to play 'Chopsticks'. Faith was upstairs, Eve told me, supervising the girls while they put on their nightclothes. 'I've told them they can stay up until midnight, but only if they get ready for bed first.'

'You look extremely smart,' I said. 'Is that a new frock?' It was silvery blue with shoelace straps and fitted her long, slim body as tightly as a stocking.

'Oliver bought it me for Christmas. Isn't it gorgeous?' She did a little twirl, then patted her lean hips. 'You don't think I'm putting on weight?'

'Not at all. In fact, you could with a bit more flesh on you: you're much too thin.' She was preoccupied with her weight, for ever on a diet.

'Oh, Kitty, don't!' She shuddered. 'I can't stand the thought of being fat. Doesn't Oliver look handsome in his evening suit?' Oliver rolled his eyes in embarrassment.

'Very handsome.' If the truth be told, he looked good enough to eat. He was thirty-two and glowed with health, his clean-cut features lean and as brown as a berry from working outdoors. I felt a rare stab of envy, imagining how wonderful it would be to spend the evening in his company, and later in his arms when we danced together. Perhaps I wasn't getting old, after all.

Faith came downstairs with the shiny-faced girls, as pretty as pictures in their frilly nighties and dressing gowns. 'Hello, Kitty.' Faith kissed my cheek. She was seventy-three now, an elegant, still-beautiful woman with pure silver hair and perfect bone structure.

Louise and Caroline ignored me and scampered into the dining room to see Jake, who was playing 'Chopsticks' for the fifth or sixth time. I brought him over every Thursday afternoon for piano lessons with the girls, but it was a bit of a waste of time as we didn't have a piano at home and he couldn't practise. Holly gave me a hug. 'I'm glad you've come, Kitty.'

'I came especially to see you, sweetheart,' I whispered. While I was sure Eve and Oliver loved Holly as much as the other girls, I always got the impression she felt slightly out of things. She'd been part of Eve's life before she'd met Oliver, and Rob had made no attempt to contact her. Yet with her dark hair and dark eyes, she looked far more like Oliver's daughter than her half-sisters, who'd inherited Eve's pale golden locks and blue eyes.

Faith wandered off to make coffee, and Eve and Oliver left for the dinner dance. 'Have a lovely time,' I shouted, as Oliver opened the car door for Eve who was draped in a white fur wrap that belonged to Faith. She could easily have been a film star on her way to the Oscars, I thought proudly. Oliver walked around the car to the driver's side and opened the door, a look of such utter misery on his face that it made my heart ache. For years now, he'd seemed quite happy with my daughter, but in that one moment it seemed this wasn't the case.

'Do you think Oliver looked a bit downcast tonight?' Faith asked when she came in with the coffee. Holly had gone to join the others in the dining room.

'A bit,' I felt bound to admit.

'Perhaps he's not looking forward to the evening as much as Eve. Most men aren't interested in social events, getting dolled up and that sort of thing. Eric never minded, he liked showing off and flirting with other women, but Tom, my first husband, hated it.' She looked at me, her lovely face troubled. 'You know, Oliver's never been the same since that incident in Belfast. The doctors said he might never completely recover. He still takes tablets for depression, but I think it's something more than that.'

'Such as?'

'I shouldn't really say this – after all, Eve is your daughter – but I think he might have been involved with a woman in Belfast and he's still pining for her after all this time.'

'What on earth makes you say that?' I gasped.

She shrugged elegantly. 'I don't really know. Perhaps it's because I'm his mother – can't you tell when there's something wrong with Jake that he hasn't told you about?'

'I suppose I can, yes.' Only a few weeks ago he'd had a fight with a boy at school and I could see from his face when he came home something was wrong. It was two days before the truth came out. 'Are you suggesting that Oliver and Eve shouldn't have got married?' The logs in the grate shifted. We both jumped. I picked an extra large log out of the basket and threw it on top. Bootsie raised his head, peering at me groggily. I patted him and he went back to sleep.

'No, no, of course not.' Faith looked flustered. 'Oh, now I've offended you, haven't I? Eve is perfect for him. Oliver couldn't possibly have a better wife. Perhaps it's just the dance, or old memories resurfacing, the way they do on nights like this. I don't know about you, but I always find New Year's Eve rather sad.'

Before she could say another word, the girls and Jake came rushing into the room demanding to watch television. The set was turned on and Faith didn't broach the subject again.

We spent the rest of the evening watching telly, singing carols and playing games, until Big Ben chimed in the New Year. Jake and the girls became very excited. It wasn't just a new year, but a new decade. 'It's nineteen eighty,' Louisa squeaked. They ran around the room shouting, 'Nineteen eighty, it's nineteen eighty.'

'What it is to be young,' Faith said with a wry smile. 'When you reach my age, you can't help but wonder if you'll still be alive when the next year comes along, never mind the next decade.'

*

Norah had spent the evening at Bernadette's and had had a lousy time, mainly because Roy had turned up with a woman. 'A real floozie,' she said indignantly on New Year's Day when we were getting pleasantly squiffy on sherry in front of the horrible electric fire with its pretend coals. Jake had stayed overnight with the girls in Formby. Eve had promised to bring him home after lunch. 'She wore a ton of make-up and her fingernails were painted bright purple. They were at least an inch long.'

'Why should you care?' I said witheringly. 'You walked out and left him, how long ago is it – six years?'

'I *don't* care,' she raged. 'It's just that, if I'd known he was going to bring a woman, I'd have taken a man.'

'What man? There isn't a man you could have taken.'

'I know.' She collapsed in the chair like a pricked balloon. 'If I join a singles club, will you come with me?'

'Not in a million years, Norah,' I said, even more witheringly. 'There's about twenty women for every man and it'd be really degrading. If you're so keen on having a man, go back to Roy. You're still married to him and he'd dump the floozie like a shot.' Roy still rang occasionally to ask how she was and always sent flowers on her birthday.

'I don't want to go back to Roy,' she said sulkily. 'I'm perfectly happy living here with you and doing me cooking.'

'That's good, because I'm perfectly happy having you, so why do you want to join a singles club?'

'Because a man would prove useful occasionally,' she sniffed. 'Like last night, for instance. I felt like a gooseberry on me own.'

'There's nothing to be ashamed of being on your own. You should feel proud of it. You're saying to the world you don't need a man, thanks very much.'

'Oh, you!' she said disgustedly. 'You're not like other people. I'll never understand why you didn't marry Con Daley. He's one of the nicest men I've ever known and he'd have made a smashing husband. Why didn't you, Kit?' she asked curiously.

I thought hard before answering. 'I loved Con,' I said eventually, 'but I felt as if I'd be burning all my bridges behind me if we got married. It meant I'd miss the chance of something really stupendous happening one day.'

'And did something really stupendous happen?' She was even more curious now.

'I met Jake's father.'

My sister's eyes were like saucers. 'Why didn't you marry him?'

'It wasn't possible,' I said shortly.

'Was he already married?'

Perhaps the sherry was loosening my tongue because I came as close as I'd ever done to revealing the truth. I managed to hold back just in time. 'I've told you as much as I'm prepared to, Norah.'

'Meanie! You've got me all agog.' She pouted and refilled both our glasses. 'So, all that stuff about being proud to be on your own is only because you couldn't marry Jake's father?'

'I suppose it is,' I admitted, 'but I didn't go rushing out and join a singles club, did I? I couldn't have him, I didn't want anyone.'

'Would you mind if I joined one?'

'Mind?' I laughed. 'Why should I mind? It's your life and if you want to join a singles club it's up to you.'

We were sprawled in the chairs, too drunk to make lunch, when Eve arrived with Jake. 'I always loathed that fire,' she said, making a face at it. 'The coal looks nothing like coal. Why haven't you bought a new one?'

'Couldn't afford to,' I said laconically.

'It smells.'

'There's dust inside, that's why,' I explained, 'and there's no way of cleaning it.'

'This house could do with modernising from top to bottom.' She glowered at the walls, as if she'd like to knock them down there and then. 'The kitchen's horrible, the bathroom's out of date and the central heating came out of the ark. It could also do with double glazing.'

'I'll arrange to have all that done tomorrow.'

'Seriously, Kitty, Michael bought it in nineteen forty-something.'

'Nineteen forty-six,' Norah chipped in. 'It was one of the first houses built in Liverpool after the war. It's thirty-four years old.'

'And it looks it,' Eve said grimly. 'I'll have a chat with Oliver, see what he thinks about having the place done up.'

'Oliver won't want to do the kitchen, will he?'

Eve grinned. 'No, I'll ask Con. You could have a kitchen like mine.'

I sat up, suddenly interested. Until then, I'd hardly been taking things in. 'I'd *love* a kitchen like yours.'

'Then you shall have one,' Eve said grandly.

Over the next two months the house was a tip. The green bathroom suite was torn out and replaced with a lovely cream one. Pine units, just like Eve's, were installed in the kitchen, along with a built-in oven, washing machine and fridge. The horrid grey floor tiles were ripped up and cherry-red ones laid in their place. I gave a little cheer when the smelly fire was carried outside and placed in a skip. The new one had life-like flames that sprang up at the touch of a switch.

It was great to see Con again. I asked if he was happy with Isobel and he wrinkled his nose. 'Oh, Con, it's not gone wrong again!' I cried.

'It's not entirely wrong, Kit, but it's not entirely right either.' For a moment he looked old and tired. Then he pulled himself together and said with his familiar grin, 'I guess I just wasn't made for marriage, though I reckon I'd've been happy with you.'

'I doubt if it would have worked for me, Con,' I said gently.

'No, well, there you go. Life's not perfect, at least not for most people. I know that now, but it took a long time to sink in and I was pretty miserable in the process.'

'Are you miserable now?'

'Half and half,' he said cheerfully.

Because of the state of the house, Eve offered to have a party for Jake's eighth birthday. I asked if he could invite a few friends from school.

'Of course,' she replied, unaware what she was letting herself in for until the day when half a dozen boys arrived and tore around her garden, chased Bootsie up and down the stairs – Snudge wisely hid under one of the beds – dropped crisps on the carpet and trod them in, and spilled lemonade on the best tablecloth.

'You shouldn't have used your best tablecloth,' I told her when she complained.

'I wasn't expecting a horde of savages,' she snapped. 'Little girls are far better behaved.'

'Your little girls seem to be enjoying themselves,' I pointed out.

By now, the girls had become as savage as the boys and were chucking clumps of grass at each other.

'The boys are a bad influence, that's why.'

Things calmed down when Oliver arrived home early and organized a game of cricket. 'We used to play cricket when *he* was little,' I said as I watched with Eve from the window. 'I'd draw stumps on a tree. I was hopeless with the bat, but quite a good bowler. When I was expecting you, all I did was bowl from the spot because I couldn't run any more.'

'God, how strange!' Eve murmured.

'What's strange about it?'

'That you played with Oliver when you were expecting me and we ended up marrying each other. I mean, at the time it must have been the last thing you'd thought would happen.'

'The very last,' I concurred.

'I also find it strange,' she continued in an even tone, 'that you and Oliver don't seem to like each other nowadays.'

I gaped. 'What on earth makes you say that?'

'You're always very cool with each other. It's quite noticeable.'

'I like him very much. When we played cricket all those years ago and I'd known the baby I was carrying would marry Oliver Knowles, I would have been extremely happy about it. Does that make sense?' It seemed a very confused statement.

'Perfect sense. I hope it's true and wasn't said just to please me.' Just then, Oliver leaped into the air and caught the ball at what seemed an impossible angle. He'd always been an expert catcher. Eve said, 'I love my girls, but I wish one had been a boy for Oliver's sake. He would have loved a son. I think that's why he's so fond of Jake. he looks upon him as a son. Oh, by the way,' she turned to me, 'we bought Jake a chopper bike for his birthday It's in the garage. That's why Oliver came home early, so he could give it to him personally. At Christmas, Jake said he'd love a bike, but he wasn't going to ask his mum because she couldn't afford it.'

'Are you crying, Mum?' Jake asked when we drove home from the party.

I suppressed a sniff and surreptitiously wiped the tears from my eyes. 'No, sweetheart,' I lied. 'I think I might be getting a cold.'

'Can I go for a ride on me bike when we get home?' The chopper was in the boot.

'It's too dark, Jake. You'll have to wait until tomorrow.'

'It's got a lamp on the front.'

'Has it?' I hadn't noticed. 'All right, you can ride up and down the pavement a few times, but I'll follow behind in case you fall off.'

'OK, Mam,' he said contentedly. Unbeknown to him, I began to cry again because everything was so mixed up and terribly sad.

Easter arrived and Marge telephoned on Good Friday, her voice thick with excitement. 'You'll never guess who's here.'

'By here, do you mean there in your house?'

'No, next door.'

'It can only be Ada Tutty. She's come home to bury her mam.' Mrs Tutty had died a few days ago at the grand old age of eighty-nine. Mr Tutty had gone to meet his maker a long time ago and their lads hadn't been seen since the funeral. The same could be said for Mrs Tutty who rarely left the house these days. A social worker called occasionally and the neighbours did her shopping.

Marge gasped. 'I didn't think you'd guess in a million years.'

'I'm not stupid, Marge. You'd only need half a brain to know who you meant.'

'Oh, all right, clever clogs. Anyroad, she'd like to see you.'

'Has the ugly duckling turned into a swan?'

'No, but she's different.'

'Different in what way, apart from being thirty years older?' I'd be forty-nine next month and Ada was about a year younger.

'You'll see when you get here.'

Ada Tutty opened the door wearing jeans, a loose cotton shirt and woven leather sandals. Her remarkably youthful face was sunburnt and devoid of make-up, her hair short and badly cut – I wouldn't be surprised if she'd chopped it off herself without the aid of a mirror.

'Hello, Kitty,' she said crisply. 'You've hardly changed. I'd've recognized you anywhere. Come in, I'm just clearing out Mother's things, so I'm afraid the place is a bit upside-down.'

'You've hardly changed either, except you've lost your Liverpool accent.' In fact, she'd changed a lot. I knew what Marge had meant when she said she looked different. When I followed her down the hall, she didn't creep like the little mouse of old, but carried herself with an air of authority that made her appear taller.

'Excuse the smell,' she said in the same crisp voice. The house stank of dust and age and hadn't been decorated since the year dot. The living-room curtains were little more than threads and the linoleum largely holes. Plastic bags, full to brimming with old clothes and cracked dishes, were heaped on the floor. Ada gave one a kick. 'These are for the bin men.'

I said, 'I'm sorry about your mother.'

'So am I.' She sat on a chair by the rickety table and indicated for me to do the same. 'She led a lousy life. I've no idea what she did with herself in this place. She obviously didn't clean it, and there's no radio, television or books. I reckon all she did was count her money – there was over four thousand pounds under the mattress in her room. By the way,' she flashed me a brief smile, 'that money I took when I left, I paid back within a year. I've been sending money ever since, but it must have gone straight under the mattress. That's how the Social Services got in touch with me, from my letters. I flew home straight away.'

'What have you been doing with yourself all this time, Ada?' Whatever it was had done her good: she oozed confidence. Despite this, I sensed she wanted me to know how her life had gone since she'd run away from Amethyst Street. It was the telegram she'd sent that had killed Mam, I remembered ruefully, though she could hardly be blamed for that.

'I worked in London for a while,' she began, 'went to night school, learned how to speak French and Spanish, and got a job as an interpreter with the United Nations in Rome.'

'I remember you saying you wanted to be an interpreter,' I murmured. I already felt envious. I'd never been out of the country, unless you counted the Isle of Man and Belfast.

Ada shrugged disdainfully. 'It got boring after a while, so I went to work for a charity in Africa. I've been with them ever since. We're in Ethiopia at the moment where there's been a famine followed by a war: next year, they expect a drought. I run an orphanage.' Her face softened. 'Poor kids, they're always the first victims when things go wrong.'

'I've seen them on television,' I said, 'little babies trying to suck their mother's empty breasts, flies crawling all over them.'

'And what did you do about it, Kitty?' Her eyes flashed a challenge.

'Well, nothing,' I stammered. 'What could I possibly do?'

'Write to your Member of Parliament, write to the papers, raise money, take stuff to the Oxfam shop, put a poster in your window.' She ticked the things off on her fingers. 'It's disgraceful the way the West just sits back and allows these terrible tragedies to happen. As long as their own bellies are full they don't give a damn about the rest of the world. And it's such a rich world, too,' she went on, her voice mounting in anger. 'Did you know, in some countries they plough the grain back into the earth, worried there might be a glut and prices will fall? In Europe, there's a butter mountain – a *mountain*, Kitty – yet no one thinks to pass it on to people who haven't seen food since God knows when.' She fished through a capacious handbag. 'Look, there's our orphanage. A reporter took this a few weeks ago.'

She gave me a black-and-white photograph showing a long, wooden building with about fifty poorly dressed, extremely thin children of various ages standing outside, every single one grinning widely at the camera. Ada stood in the centre with a tiny baby in her arms. 'They're the lucky ones,' she said. 'Most of the kids are left to fend for themselves.'

'You're doing a wonderful job, Ada,' I said limply. She'd made me feel utterly worthless. My own life seemed pathetic beside hers. 'If you let me have a poster, I'll put it in my window. Perhaps I could have a coffee morning and raise funds for your charity.'

'I'll have head office send you half a dozen posters and you can distribute them to your friends and neighbours. Any money you make would be very welcome, Kitty. We're always short of cash. Can you knit?'

'Not very well.' I was beginning to wonder if there'd been any point in my having been born. I'd worked for Hilda's charity, but it was a long time ago and had been more by accident than design. Not only that, there was a whole world of difference between Everton Valley and Ethiopia.

'Head office will send you a simple pattern for a baby's cardigan with the posters. Just odds and ends of wool will do. Most people can make one in a night.'

I gulped. 'I'll give it a try.'

She rooted in the bag again and took out a packet of rolling tobacco. 'Do you smoke?' I shook my head. 'It's my only bad habit,' she said, expertly rolling a ciggie. 'I don't drink, I don't eat much and all my clothes are second-hand. Ah, that's good!' She took a long puff. 'Marge tells me you have two children: a boy and a girl.'

I was glad she'd changed the subject and I no longer had to feel guilty for not running an orphanage in Africa or knitting baby cardigans in my every spare minute. She also seemed more human with a ciggie in her hand. 'Eve's twenty-nine this year: Jake's only eight.'

'Did you marry anyone I knew?' She screwed up her eyes and put her small head on one side like a bird. 'If I recall rightly, you were courting a young man with ginger hair when I left.'

'That was Connor Daley, Eve's father. But I never married, Ada. I'm still Kitty McCarthy.'

'And I'm still Ada Tutty.' We grinned at each other. 'Mind you, I never told anybody this, but I used to be really keen on your Danny. I'd've married him like a shot if he'd asked.'

I didn't tell her the whole street had known. 'Are you glad or sorry that he didn't?'

She gave a deep, throaty laugh. 'I'm amazed you asked that question, Kitty. It's no reflection on your Danny, but if we'd married I'd still be living next door, our children would have grown up and I might even have joined a dance club.' She shuddered. 'Oh, no, I've enjoyed every minute of my life and don't regret a single thing.'

We parted friends. She gave me her address in Ethiopia and I promised to write. She refused an invitation to dinner the following night. 'Our Norah's become a fantastic cook,' I informed her.

'Sorry, Kitty, but I have too much to do. It's mother's funeral on Tuesday morning and that only leaves three days to have the house cleared – I've still got to get rid of the furniture. And I've loads of letters to write and phone calls to make: Marge has offered to let me use her phone.'

'I work mornings in a doctors' surgery and it'll be dead busy after the holiday, so I won't be able to come to the funeral, but let me know if you need a hand with the house.'

She gave another of her attractive laughs. 'I wouldn't expect you to give up a minute of your Easter in this filthy hole. No, I can manage on my own. I've had far worse things to cope with in my time, but thanks for the offer, Kitty.' She came with me to the door. When it closed, I could hear her singing as she returned to the squalor of her mother's house.

Ben was twenty, six feet two inches tall, with a mop of blond hair and boyish good looks – a perfect specimen of manhood. He and Samantha Whelan were obviously made for each other. They'd been in love for almost seven years since they were virtually children and planned to marry when they finished university the summer after next.

But love, no matter how perfect it seems, never runs smoothly. When he came home for the summer holidays it was obvious from Ben's long face that something was wrong. I asked straight out what the matter was when I cornered him in the gazebo after he'd mooched about the house for a couple of hours, hardly saying a word or eating a thing, and not even noticing that it was vastly different to the house in which he'd stayed at Christmas.

'Nothing,' he said shortly.

'Don't lie to me, Ben. If your face were much longer, your chin would scrape the ground. Is it Mrs Whelan?'

Samantha's mother hadn't approved of the match right from the start. It was nothing to do with Ben himself, but she hadn't wanted her daughter – her only child – to settle for the first boy who came along. 'I married my first love,' she told me bitterly on one of the rare occasions we met, 'and it was the biggest mistake I ever made in my life. I would have preferred Samantha to have a good time before she settled down, "play the field" I think it's called.'

'The worst thing you can do is try to separate them,' I said. 'It'll only make them more determined to stay together.'

She took no notice of my advice, but made things as difficult as she could for the young couple, to no avail – at least so far.

'It's nothing to do with Mrs Whelan,' Ben said. There was a suggestion of tears in his blue eyes.

'Then what is it, Ben? You can tell me now or you can tell me later. I'm bound to find out sometime.'

He glowered at me. 'Samantha's expecting a baby.'

I'd thought it something much worse, that Samantha had met someone else, for instance. 'Oh, well, that's not the end of the world, is it?' I said comfortingly. 'Don't they have crèches at universities these days?'

'Yes, but I wanted to do a Ph.D. after I get my degree. I've been offered a place at Cambridge, but how on earth can I do that with a wife and baby to support?' His sullen face had turned red with anger.

'Does that mean you want Samantha to get rid of the baby?' I felt my own anger mount.

He went even redder. 'Yes, but she refuses. It's all she talks about, that damn baby. We hadn't planned to have a baby for years. She wanted to go into publishing, become an editor. You can commute to London from Cambridge.'

'If you make Samantha have an abortion, Ben,' I said slowly, 'she'll never forgive you. Oh, you could still get married and live in Cambridge, but she'd bear a grudge for the rest of her life, however much she loved you.'

Ben got to his feet, towering over me, and stood in the doorway. 'Why is it no one ever puts *me* first?' he shouted. 'My dad walked out when I was ten, then Mum left and now Samantha's doing the same, putting the baby first.' He looked lost and hurt, as well he should be as far as his parents were concerned. But I recalled how unforgiving he'd been with his father. Now he was in danger of being just as callous with Samantha.

'But that's what *you* should be doing, Ben,' I cried, 'putting the baby first. He or she should come before everything and everyone. It's *your* baby, not just Samantha's. You're its dad. You'll manage somehow in Cambridge. As for your mam and dad, you're not the only one they didn't put first, are you? Don't forget Steve walked out on his other children when he went off with your mum, and she deserted Eve and Michael. They're two very selfish people – and you'd be taking after them. In fact, you'd be even worse if you forced Samantha to have your baby killed for the sake of your career.'

He stared at me, horrified. 'Is that the way you look at it, Kitty?'

'It's the only way to look at it, Ben.'

His shoulders drooped and he had the grace to look ashamed. 'I didn't think about it like that before.'

'Samantha must love you very much. Most girls in the same position would have told you to get lost – *I* would.'

'Would you?'

I nodded furiously. 'If you love her as much as she apparently loves you, I wouldn't mention the word abortion again. She's twenty-one, old enough to know her own mind, and she thinks what she's doing is right – for you, her and the baby. Be happy for her and pretty soon you'll be happy for yourself.'

'That sounds like the sort of thing you read in a birthday card.' He smiled for the first time since coming home. He returned to his seat and stared at his size twelve shoes, while I stared at the hedge that needed trimming and the grass that needed cutting, a task I loathed, mainly because it took for ever to start the petrol lawnmower. I'd ask Ben to do it when his mood improved. He said, 'I suppose you think I've been acting like an idiot.'

'I'd put it more strongly than that: idiot's too mild.'

He winced. 'What should I do now, Kitty?'

'Apologize to Samantha for one thing. You must have made her very unhappy.'

Once again, he began to study his shoes, as if they could provide a solution to his problems. 'Maybe we should get married now before the baby's born, not wait until next year.'

I smiled with relief. The shoes had come up trumps. 'That's not a bad idea. The McCarthys haven't had a wedding for a year or two, so it'll be a real treat.'

'I'll ring Samantha now, see what she thinks.' He began to walk towards the house, paused and turned back. 'I really *do* love her, you know, Kitty. I'm glad I talked to you. It's made me look at things in an entirely different way.'

I followed him into the house. He was already dialling Samantha's number, so I went into the kitchen and closed the door, for the first time in my life not wanting to eavesdrop on a private conversation.

'Did you find out what was wrong with him?' Norah asked. She was rolling out the pastry for a pear and hazelnut flan – *tarte aux poires* – Ben's favourite pudding.

'Yes, I'll tell you all about it later. How long does it take to make a wedding cake?'

'It should be made well beforehand but, if it's an emergency, I can do one in a couple of days.' Her face lit up. 'Is it for Ben and Samantha?'

'I really hope so.'

The door opened and Ben burst in. 'We're going to get a special licence first thing in the morning.' He kissed my nose. 'Thanks, Kitty. Would you like me to collect Jake from school?'

'He'd love that, Ben.'

'Whatever you said obviously did him the world of good,' Norah remarked when Ben had gone.

'So it would seem.' I wouldn't have minded having someone like me to talk to whenever I encountered problems in my life.

Ten days later, the McCarthys turned out in force for Ben and Samantha's wedding, young as well as old, though it was a weekday and most people were supposed to be at work. Even our Jamie and Barbara came. Perhaps it was because it was a long time since we'd all been together in the same place and a wedding was the ideal opportunity for a reunion, as well as an excuse for the women to buy new outfits.

Claire looked dead pretty in a rose-pink suit. Norah, never very adventurous, had bought a plain navy frock and a white hat. I didn't crack on that my turquoise shift came from the Oxfam shop and that I had put aside the money I would have spent on a new one to send to Ada next time I wrote – I had the whole family knitting cardies and my two coffee mornings had raised almost £30. Marge had gone in for a yellow frock with a flouncy skirt and dark-green shoes, gloves, hat and bag.

'Someone told me once you should never wear more than three accessories the same colour,' I told her. 'You should have bought a yellow hat.'

'Well, I don't know who told you that,' Marge said indignantly, 'because it's rubbish.'

'You did, actually, at our Norah's wedding.' I thought she'd be impressed by my feat of memory, but she wasn't in the least.

The wedding was held in St Peter and Paul's Church, Crosby, on a gloriously sunny July day. Mrs Whelan had phoned to say she wouldn't be coming. 'I'm too upset about the wedding and the baby. It isn't what I had planned for my Samantha.'

'It's fatal to make plans for your children, Mrs Whelan. Best to let them go their own way and just pray they'll do the right thing.' That sounded terribly sanctimonious and I wished I hadn't said it. Mrs Whelan clearly felt the same.

'Should I ever need advice from you on being a parent, *Miss* McCarthy, I'll ask for it,' she snapped.

'Will Mr Whelan be coming?'

'I've no idea. He's away at the moment. We don't talk to each other much nowadays. He might turn up or he might not.'

Mr Whelan, a good-looking man in his forties with a sweet smile, must have decided he didn't want to miss his daughter's wedding. On the day, Samantha walked down the aisle on her father's arm. She wore a simple pale-blue calf-length frock with a wreath of forget-me-knots on her long straight hair. As yet, there was no sign of the baby she was expecting.

The only other guests on the bride's side of the church were two elderly great-aunts and a middle-aged couple – the woman turned out to be Mr Whelan's sister.

It was a simple ceremony, very touching, with most people aware of the abnormal life Ben had led. Now he was taking on a wife and would soon have a family of his own.

The ritual over, we turned to leave, only to see Mrs Whelan seated at the back of the church crying her eyes out. 'I couldn't miss seeing her get married, could I, Ron?' she wept as her husband hurried towards her.

'Come along, Beth, darling.' He put his arm around her shoulders and led her from the church. Until then, I'd stayed dry-eyed but, for some reason, this little scene moved me to tears. I was crying buckets by the time we got outside.

There hadn't been much time to organize a reception. Despite the trauma of Jake's party earlier that year, Eve had bravely offered to have a marquee erected in the garden because, as she said, 'I'm terribly fond of Ben and I'd like him to have a wedding he'll always remember.'

Norah and I had slaved for days into the early hours making bite-sized pizzas, miniature sausage rolls, vol-au-vents with six different fillings, cheese straws, a variety of cakes and a two-tier wedding cake decorated with little pink roses. The top tier would be put away for the baby's christening. The food was set out on tables at the far end of the marquee for guests to help themselves. Eve had refused to let me have a collecting box for Ada's charity, saying it just wasn't done at a wedding. Soft music came from a record-player in the corner: a group of aging rock 'n' rollers was expected later for us to dance to.

They were friends of a friend of Liam's and had been quite famous in their day.

I was in the kitchen making yet another pot of tea, when Mrs Whelan came in to apologize for being so melodramatic. 'I made a real show of myself, didn't I? And you're right, Miss McCarthy, you shouldn't make plans for your children. The tall blonde girl, the one whose house this is, I understand she's your daughter?'

'Yes, her name's Eve. And I'm Kitty, by the way.'

'My name's Beth,' she said shyly. 'Eve's a credit to you. You must be very proud of her.'

'Oh, I am,' I assured her. 'All I ever wanted was for her to be happy, and the same goes for Jake, my little boy. Some people say that happiness is the wrong thing to want for your children, but I can't think of anything more important in life than that.'

'You're right.' She nodded. 'I hope Samantha will be happy with Ben.'

'I hope so, too.' I wasn't too sure. Ben's attitude to life was too hard for my liking; I hoped there wouldn't be problems in the future.

'Ron and I would like to pay for all this.' She waved her hand towards the marquee. 'After all, the bride's family are expected to organize the wedding, and I – we – haven't done a single thing. I'll send a cheque in a day or two.'

I was pleased to hear it: the food had cost a small fortune. 'Thank you very much.'

She left and Oliver came in. 'I'm looking for a can-opener,' he said. 'There's one in the cutlery drawer.' He opened the drawer and searched through it. 'I've found it.'

'That's good. It's very kind of you to have the marquee in your garden, Oliver.' I hadn't had a chance to thank him before.

'It was Eve's idea, but I was only too glad to go along with it. Ben's a nice lad and he's had a tough time. It's all going very well, don't you think? The reception, that is.'

'Extremely well.'

We smiled politely at each other and he returned to the marquee. The next people to arrive were Norah and Liam, who came in together. 'Liam's got something important to say to us,' Norah announced.

'Have we run out of beer?' I joked.

'No, it's something more serious than that.' Now sixty-three, Liam's brown hair had mostly disappeared and what remained was grey, but he had the bearing and posture of a much younger man and was still the life and soul of any party. He and Claire were as much in love as they'd ever been.

'Is there anything more serious than running out of beer?'

'Yes, Kitty, I'm afraid there is.'

I was struck by his sombre tone: it wasn't often Liam sounded so grim and I wished I hadn't joked. 'I'm sorry, Liam. What's wrong?'

'It's Claire,' he said bluntly, his voice wobbling slightly. 'She's got a lump in her breast and refuses to see a doctor. I was wondering if you two could persuade her to go.'

We stared at him, horror-struck. 'Oh, my God!' Norah cried.

'It might be benign,' I said quickly, refusing to believe there could be anything seriously wrong with my sister.

'And it might not, Kitty, luv. She needs to see a doctor to find out.'

'We'll drag her there, won't we, Norah?' Norah didn't respond, too shocked for words. 'We'll take her tomorrow, even if we have to knock her unconscious first.'

'Let's hope there'll be no need for that. Just try and convince her how much I – how much we all – love her and need her.' He broke down completely. 'I don't think I can live without Claire,' he sobbed.

I flung my arms around him. 'Don't worry, Liam. You won't have to. We'll make sure she sees a doctor. There'll be nothing to worry about, you'll see.'

'You're good girls, the pair o'yis. I'm sorry to have spoilt the wedding for you, but I had to talk to someone.' He shambled towards the door, muttering to himself like an old man. 'Claire refuses to discuss the matter. She just tells me to stop being an idiot and walks out the room.'

'You shouldn't have spoken to him like that,' Norah said when our brother-in-law had gone. 'You're not God. How can you possibly know everything's going to be all right?'

'Because it is.' I stamped my foot. 'Our Claire won't die. I won't let her.'

'You can't stop her, Kitty, luv. If the Good Lord decides it's time for Claire to go, then there's nothing we can do about it.'

'How dare you talk about her going – *dying*,' I yelled. 'The lump might be benign – the vast majority are. I know – I work in a surgery, in case you've forgotten.'

Norah sighed heavily. 'I just hope you're right, Kitty.'

Chapter 13

Since the day of Ben and Samantha's wedding, our family had shifted out of the light into the darkness. None of us had ever been seriously ill before. The worst I'd ever had was 'flu, Norah was prone to the occasional bout of bronchitis and our Danny was cursed with an ingrown toenail that sent him limping to the chiropodist every so often. We all had our own teeth, even if there were a few gaps here and there. It therefore came as a terrible shock when our Claire's lump turned out to be malignant.

I'd nagged, badgered, wheedled, threatened, told her she wasn't being fair to Liam, her family, herself, that she was irresponsible, silly and a coward. 'If *I* were in your shoes and refused to see a doctor, you wouldn't stand for it,' I shouted. I made three doctors appointments that she didn't keep. In the end she gave in and attended the fourth, 'If only to get you off me back.'

Her doctor sent her for a mammogram that showed the lump and, a week later, she went for a biopsy. On the day the pathologist's report came through, she phoned me at the surgery. 'I've got cancer,' she said in a gritty voice. My heart dropped like a lead balloon to the pit of my stomach. 'Are you happy now, Kitty? If it weren't for you, I'd never have known.'

'But now you can have it treated,' I cried.

'I don't want to have it treated. I'd sooner have been left alone. Say if I have to have me breast taken off. What will Liam think of me then?'

'Liam won't give a damn as long as you're still alive.' I wished she were there in the flesh so I could shake some sense into her.

'How would you know?'

'I know Liam and I know how much he loves you.'

She began to cry. 'I don't feel a bit brave about it, Kitty. I'm dead scared if the truth be known. I'd like to keep it from the kids.'

'You can't. It's much better to tell them rather than they find out from someone else.' I'd read so many leaflets that I knew the right way to deal with every conceivable situation. 'Have you told Liam?'

'No, I'll tell him when he comes home from work.'

'Are you in the house alone?'

'Only for now. I'm going to do a bit of shopping in a minute. I'm out of flour. I'll speak to you later, Kitty.' She rang off.

I telephoned Norah and gave her the news.

Norah's attitude to our sister had been completely the opposite of mine. She had thought Claire should be left to make up her own mind about treatment and that I should stop interfering.

'But Liam *asked* us to interfere,' I had argued. 'He pleaded with us. I've no intention of letting him down.'

'We're talking about Claire's body here, not Liam's,' Norah had said doggedly. 'The decision to be treated should be hers and hers alone.'

'What will happen now?' she asked when I told her the pathologist's report had arrived to confirm Claire had cancer.

'She'll be sent to see a specialist and he'll decide what has to be done next. Look, Norah,' I said, 'I don't know when I'll be home; as soon as I finish work I'm going to see her.' She'd be back from the shops by then. 'She'll be in the house all on her own and someone should be with her.'

'What makes you think she'll want to see *you*? You're too pushy by a mile, Kitty. In fact, you're a bully. *I'll* go and see our Claire. *I* won't lecture her and tell her what to do. We'll just sit and have a quiet talk. I'm sure that's what she'd prefer.'

'Oh, all right,' I said reluctantly. All I wanted was for my sister to get better. I didn't want our Claire to *die*.

It was all I could think about. My mission to save Claire occupied my mind to the exclusion of everything else. I insisted on going with her when she saw the specialist. It was me who took her hand when he informed her that a mastectomy was her only option. 'The cancer has spread too far for a lumpectomy, Mrs Quinn. I'm afraid your left breast will have to be removed. Even then, we might not catch the malignancy in total. Additional treatment will almost certainly be necessary.'

'What sort of treatment, Doctor?' I asked.

'Chemotherapy,' was the reply.

Claire wept as I drove her home. 'I'll lose me hair,' she sobbed. 'I think I'd sooner lose me breast than me hair.'

'Well, at least your hair will grow back.' They were cold words of comfort, but the best I could think of.

The operation would take place in three weeks' time. That night, she told the family, and they rallied round as I knew they would, terrified they were about to lose their mam. Her sons- and daughters-in-law were just as supportive. From then on, the house was always full to bursting with people who'd come to keep Claire company. Barbara, our Jamie's wife whom we'd never particularly liked, turned out to be a true friend with the rare ability to listen while Claire talked about her fears. Me, I kept interrupting with non-stop advice. Liam was useless, always on the verge of tears, Claire would end up comforting him, rather than the other way around.

Our Norah kept out of the way. 'Claire needs space, not a house full of old misery-guts. She said someone insists on following her to the lavatory, as if they expect her to fall down the pan or something, and the other day, their Patsy actually said the Rosary out loud and everyone joined in. It made Claire feel as if she were already dead. If she wants me, she knows where to find me.' They went to the pictures together a couple of times, to see *Annie Hall* with Diane Keaton and Woody Allen, and Burt Reynolds in *Smokey and the Bandit*.

There was one person who didn't put in an appearance at the house: Marge. I went round to Amethyst Street to demand why.

'I've been busy,' she said lamely. 'Come in.' She looked like a ghost, her face covered with a white clay mask. For some reason, she was wearing a flame-coloured dance frock inside out. I noticed there were pins in the darts around the waist: she must be taking it in.

'Busy doing what?'

'Things.' She waved her arms. 'All sort of things.'

'Such as smearing your face with slime and altering your frock?'

She tossed her head. 'There's a cha-cha competition tonight, me and Danny have entered, and I want to look me best.'

'I'm sure that's of great importance.' I hadn't come with the intention of being cross: it just came over me. Perhaps it was the sight of the flame-coloured frock. Did I feel envious because I secretly wanted to join a dance club? 'You might like to know Claire's noticed you've not been and she's very upset.' That was an outright lie. Claire hadn't noticed: if she had, she wouldn't be the least upset. *I* was the one who was upset. 'She's having a mastectomy next Monday.'

'In that case, I'll go and see her after we've had our tea.' Marge snipped off a needle and thread that hung from one of the darts. 'I *do* have a reason,' she said coolly, 'a genuine one, but it's something you'd never understand. You're too hard, too strong. You haven't time for people like me.'

'What do you mean, people like you?'

'Weak people. I'm weak, Kitty: you're the opposite. The reason I haven't visit Claire is because I was too scared. It makes me worried for my own . . . I can't think of the word.'

'Mortality?'

She gave a little nod. 'That's it, mortality. I want nothing to do with cancer. Oh, I know it's not catching, but I don't want to kiss anyone with cancer. I don't want to touch them. I've cried for your Claire, cried a lot, and prayed, too. I've lit candles in St James's almost every day. But I'll go and see her tonight. I feel awful, upsetting her when she's so sick.'

I sat down in a chair with a bump. 'I'm sorry,' I whispered.

Marge looked at me, bewildered. 'For goodness' sake, Kitty, what's wrong with you? One minute you're blaming me for not seeing Claire. Next minute you're sorry. Sorry for what?'

'For everything.' All of a sudden, I felt completely exhausted. 'I don't know if I'm coming or going, Marge. All I can think about is our Claire. Oh, and it wasn't her who was upset: it was me.'

'You're taking it too hard, luv. You're wearing yourself out. If you carry on like this, you'll make yourself ill.'

I couldn't understand why she was being so nice when I'd just been so horrible. And I didn't feel strong, not in the least, but as weak as a kitten if the truth be known. 'Actually,' I said, 'it's not just Claire I'm worried about. If you have a sister with breast cancer, it doubles the chance of getting it yourself. Even worse, it puts Eve at risk. Oh, Marge,' I wailed, 'I sometimes wish I didn't work in a surgery. You find out all sorts of things you'd sooner not know.'

*

Faith Knowles rang on Saturday morning to invite me to dinner that night. 'I know it's a bit short notice, but I have a surprise for you and I thought it might take your mind off things for a few hours.'

'It's kind of you, Faith, but I don't think I'd be very good company at the moment.'

'All you'll have to do is sit and listen and we'll talk to you.'

'Oh, all right.' Faith was right, I was badly in need of a break.

'Let's say seven o'clock for half past, then. And do come in a taxi, Kitty, otherwise you won't be able to have anything to drink.'

I lay in a warm, scented bath, doing my utmost to relax, conscious of the tension leaving my body, my breathing becoming easier, my shoulders less stiff. Every now and then, I'd let in more hot water when it began to feel cold. An hour later, I climbed out, feeling like a new woman – almost – washed my hair and put it in rollers. I hadn't forgotten all my worries, just temporarily pushed them to the back of my mind. Marge was right: if I carried on the way I was, I'd end up having a nervous breakdown.

I set up the ironing board to press the blue dress I'd got for Eve's wedding. 'Is that what you're wearing?' Norah commented. 'It looks really nice on you.'

'It's years old, but I've hardly worn it. It always makes me feel really glamorous.' The iron glided easily over the soft material. The house seemed exceptionally peaceful. Jake was sprawled on the floor in front of the television watching snooker. The subdued voice of the commentator and the click of ball hitting ball was almost mesmerizing.

'I wonder what the surprise is Faith mentioned?' Norah murmured.

'I haven't a clue. She talked about "we", so there'll be at least one other guest.'

'Perhaps she's bought you a prezzie, Mam.'

'She'd hardly invite me to dinner to give me a prezzie, Jake.'

My hair dry, I backcombed it vigorously to make it look thicker and made up my face with extra care. I'd thought long and hard before booking a taxi. It was expensive, but it would be nice to have a proper drink for a change and, if I went by train, Faith's house was a long walk from Southport Station. In the end, Norah talked me into it and the taxi duly arrived at half past six.

Since the wedding, I'd been too preoccupied to notice what was happening in the rest of the world. As the taxi carried me towards Southport, I was surprised to note the leaves on the trees were beginning to turn gold, and realized it was September. The driver asked if I minded if he opened a window. 'It's a bit fuggy in here. Me last fare was a smoker.'

I said I didn't mind a bit. I leaned back in the seat and listened to the birds exchanging their last bit of gossip of the day, and breathed in the evening smells: the scent of flowers, the hint of a bonfire, the salty tang of the distant river.

'We're here, luv.'

I opened my eyes. The taxi had stopped outside Faith's house and the driver was smiling at me over the seat. I'd fallen asleep!

'Have a nice night, luv,' he said when I paid him.

I wished him the same and pushed open the gate. Faith's garden comprised neat lawns on either side of the concrete path that led to the front door, each lawn surrounded by a narrow border of flowers that looked pretty at first glance, but on closer inspection, revealed themselves to be in a state of decay. The flowers were slowly dying, as we all were, I thought bleakly. A wave of depression swept over me, so fierce I could hardly breathe, and my eyes were seeing everything through a grey mist that I couldn't blink away, however hard I tried. I couldn't hear a sound, not a single sound, not even from the birds. For a moment, I feared I was the only person left on earth. I really didn't want to spend the evening with Faith. I'd sooner be in my own house with Jake. Right now, my son was the only person I wanted to be with. I needed to touch him to retain my hold on reality, because I could no longer count on my sisters. Jake was keeping me alive. I returned to the road in the hope I could recall the taxi, but there was no sign of it.

'Kitty!' Faith opened the door wearing something grey and filmy. 'I thought I heard a car stop.'

I forced my face into a smile and tried to think of something to say. 'Isn't it a lovely evening?' My voice sounded as if it belonged to someone else.

'Beautiful. It'll soon be autumn, my favourite season.'

'Mine is spring.' I ached for it to be spring. If it were spring, I would feel quite differently about everything.

'Come in, darling. You look cold, but you haven't brought a cardigan. I'll find you something of mine.'

'Thank you.' I was shivering. I went into the dining room where the French windows were open and the table was set for three. Was the third guest the surprise? If so, who could it possibly be? I prayed it wouldn't be Hope.

My senses were on fire and I was aware of a horrible smell coming from the garden: the sweet, sickly scent of dying flowers. I went outside, the mist still clouding my eyes, and examined a pink cabbage rose that had lost its bloom. The sight made me want to cry and I imagined Claire's breast being the same, full of pretty, pink petals that had started to turn rotten. 'You've got cancer,' I said aloud, and buried my face in the flower.

'I beg your pardon?' said a voice.

'The flower's got cancer.' A man had come into the garden behind me. I could only see him through a blur: a big, blond, ungainly man of about fifty with a nose too big for his face. In my present state, I didn't find it odd that he looked familiar, yet I knew for certain we'd never met before.

'Which flower has cancer?' he asked.

'This one – and that one.' I pointed to another fading pink rose. 'They all have.'

'I've never thought of it that way before.' He shoved his hands in his trouser pockets, peering at the roses with interest. 'That flowers get sick before they die.'

'We all get sick and then we die. Some flowers are plucked and they die earlier than the others, just like people.' Like my brothers, Will and Jeff.

He appeared impressed with this – I was impressed enough myself. 'Have you always looked at nature in this way?'

'Normally, I never look at nature in any way at all. I know nothing about it. It's just that my sister recently discovered she has cancer and I'm being dead morbid about everything, particularly tonight.'

He put his hand on my upper arm and led me back into the house. The hand was very large and warm. I was sorry when it was removed so he could close the windows behind us. 'I take it you're Kitty McCarthy?' he said.

'That's right.' I examined his face: the slightly bent nose and thin, sensitive lips. His eyes were grey with little shreds of silver. It was a nice face, gentle, and I liked it immediately. He was conventionally dressed in fawn, gabardine trousers and a cream shirt, with no tie. 'I can't guess who you are, yet I recognize you from somewhere.'

'I'm Charlie Collier.'

'Charlie! Of course, you're Faith's son by her first husband.' He'd lived most of his adult life in Hong Kong. 'I've seen your father's photograph loads of times. You're awfully like him.'

'So people say who knew my dad.' His eyes searched the room for the photo.

'It's on the mantelpiece in the lounge,' I informed him. 'There's also one of you, but you only look about fourteen.'

Faith came in with a fluffy blue stole. 'I searched for something that went with your pretty frock. This goes perfectly.' She smiled at me affectionately as she draped the stole around my shoulders. 'I see you've made each other's acquaintance. We've known each other for thirty years, Kitty, yet this is the first time you and Charlie have met. He's taken extended leave from the bank so he's staying for quite a long time, aren't you, darling?'

'Yes, Mum: six months.' He rocked back on his heels, smiling fondly at his mother.

'Hong Kong will be handed back to the Chinese in the not-too-distant future and he wants to get out before it happens, so he's looking to buy a house in the vicinity for when he retires.'

Charlie shook his head. 'Only bits of that are true, Mum. You're right about Hong Kong, but I will have left my job long before it's returned to China. We get chucked out of the bank at sixty,' he explained, 'so I've got another eight years to go. I'm looking to buy a property in the vicinity for when that happens, but I'm not going to retire.'

'What are you going to do?' I asked.

'Build a model railway,' he said instantly. 'I shall get a place with a loft and spend all my time up there, just appearing now and then, a mere shadow of my former self.'

'You're already a shadow of your former self, darling.' Faith tapped his shoulder disapprovingly. 'You look as if you haven't eaten in months. I've noticed you fasten your belt two notches tighter than you used to. I hope you haven't been playing too much rugby.'

'I'm getting on a bit for rugby, Mum. I haven't played for years.'

He had the build of a rugby player, but didn't look remotely tough enough to charge into a scrum.

'Then I bet you've been working much too hard.' Faith turned to me. 'This is the first time in ages he's had time to come home.'

Charlie raised his eyes to heaven and muttered, 'Mothers!'

Faith began to bustle around, asking what we wanted to drink, telling us to sit down, wanting to know if the wrap was warm enough. 'Charlie, get the drinks, there's a dear: I won't be long with the starter.'

I offered to help, but she wouldn't hear of it and disappeared into the kitchen. I sat down while Charlie saw to the drinks. He asked if I would like a cherry in my martini, and I said yes.

'Before,' he said, handing it to me, 'you said you felt very morbid about everything, particularly tonight. Do you feel any better now?'

'The feeling's gone.' I put my fingers on my forehead as if the feeling could be touched. 'It just disappeared without my noticing.' My eyesight was quite clear.

'That's good.' He smiled at me warmly, though it might have been sympathetically. He'd probably considered me more than a little bit daft when he found me in the garden having a conversation with a rose.

'Charlie, darling, will you light the candles on the table, please?' Faith called. 'There's a lighter on the sideboard.'

There were three red candles in a silver candelabrum. 'You know what she's up to, don't you?' Charlie said with a knowing look as he lit the first candle.

'Getting us dinner?'

'No, she's matchmaking. She thinks you would make me an ideal wife, look after me in my old age as brilliantly as you looked after Oliver and Robin. I've never had a wife, you see, and she worries about me.' He sniffed pathetically, but it was followed by a little chuckle.

I wriggled uncomfortably. 'I wish you hadn't told me that. It makes me feel embarrassed.'

'I thought it best you knew.' He had to concentrate hard on the final candle that refused to light. 'She's going to suggest you help me look for a house and I don't want you to refuse because you're worried I'm chasing you. I can read her mind like a book; she thinks it's a good way of getting us together.' The candle burst into flame.

'At last!' he murmured. 'The thing is, Kitty, I would really appreciate your help with looking for a property if it keeps Mum out of the way. She'll try and talk me into something quite unsuitable: she thinks all men want to live by golf courses in a house that's very plain and functional and easily cleaned.'

'And you want a different sort of house?'

'In Hong Kong, I've lived for years in a flat that's plain, functional and easily cleaned. I'd like a place that's a touch eccentric for a change. I don't expect a priest's hole or an inglenook fireplace, just something a bit out of the ordinary.'

I said I would be quite pleased to help him look, and promised to keep a straight face later when Faith suggested it.

Claire's mastectomy was carried out without a hitch. She emerged from hospital three days later to find her house full of chrysanthemums and people who'd come to welcome her home. Liam fetched her back in a taxi – in her absence, as a surprise, he'd painted the parlour a nice warm yellow.

'He thinks I'm cured,' she whispered to me. 'They all do.'

'Aren't you?' I'd prayed so hard that the operation was the last thing she'd have to endure that I'd been confident she'd be free of cancer from now on.

'It depends on the report on my breast tissue – I can't remember what it's called: it begins with a "p".'

'The pathology report.'

'It'll come in a few days. Remember what the specialist said, Kitty, that I might need more treatment if all the negative cells haven't been removed?'

'You mean the positive cells.'

'Do I?' She looked very wan and pale as well as incredibly brave. I felt terrible for having called her a coward and wanted to hug her, but hugs were out at the moment: they were too painful. 'You know,' she said tiredly. 'The hospital gave me some sleeping tablets and I'd love to go to bed, but it'd only hurt everyone's feelings.'

'To hell with other people's feelings, Claire; the only feelings that matter are yours.' I went to look for Liam. He was in the kitchen taking cans of beer out of the fridge, all set for a party. I told him Claire wanted to lie down. He shoved the cans back, shooed everyone out of the house and virtually carried his treasured wife upstairs.

'How is she?' Norah asked when I got back to Maghull. She hadn't joined the welcoming committee on the certain assumption that when Claire wanted her, she would call.

'Well, she's just had a major operation, so she's bound to be tired. She's lying down. Liam's the only one with her.'

'Faith rang earlier. She said this Charlie chap is taking everyone to dinner in Southport, including Eve and Oliver, and Robin and his wife. You're to let her know as soon as possible if you'd like to go so they can book another place.'

'I don't think I'll bother, not tonight.' I wouldn't be able to stop thinking about my sister lying in the quiet bedroom of the quiet house that had once been the noisiest in the street. I wondered if Liam was in the room with her, lying beside her, holding her hand, watching her sleep.

A few days later, Charlie Collier picked me up from outside the surgery. This time, he wore jeans, trainers and a blue sweatshirt. He looked well-scrubbed and healthy – almost handsome in a tough, rugged sort of way. At Faith's suggestion, we were going to look at a house.

'How's your sister?' he enquired when I climbed into the hired car, a maroon Ford Sierra.

'Very down, but trying hard not to show it.' I blinked away the tears before they had a chance to fall. 'She's recovering well from the operation, but the pathology report arrived yesterday. To cut a long story short, she's got to have a course of chemotherapy.'

He revved up the engine and inched into the traffic. 'I knew someone who had chemotherapy. It really takes it out of you. It's a case of the cure being worse than the disease.'

'Was the treatment successful?'

'No,' he said in a clipped voice.

'I'm sorry. Was it a friend of yours?'

'Rather more than that.'

There was something in his tone that told me he wouldn't welcome any more questions so I didn't pry, though I badly wanted to. He'd never married, but it didn't mean he hadn't had a love life. I hadn't married either but, although my love life had been limited, it was quality that mattered, not quantity, and the result had been two lovely children.

'Where is the house?' I asked.

'Birkdale, right by the golf course.' He made a face. 'Despite that, it looks interesting, so I thought I'd take a look. Mum said you were an expert on houses and I should take you with me.'

'I don't know anything about houses,' I snorted, 'apart from living in them. I've never *bought* a house, so I won't know what to look for. Your mum's having you on.'

'Well, as you know, Mum has other plans for us. Apparently, you're an expert on an awful lot of things, not just houses.'

We both laughed, and I thought it was rather nice to have Charlie for a friend. We both knew where we stood, so there was no tension. Neither of us was trying to make a good impression on the other. I wasn't worried he'd make a pass, or hoping he would. Anyroad, according to Norah who'd joined a singles club and had become quite knowledgeable about such things, men in their fifties were only interested in women much younger than themselves.

'They're after the twenty- and thirty-year-olds,' she told me indignantly. 'Me, I'm only fit for an old-aged pensioner: an *old* old-aged pensioner.' She was seriously thinking of giving up her search for a man as an occasional escort and concentrating on her cooking.

I asked Charlie if he'd enjoyed the dinner in Southport a few nights ago. He said it was good to see his half-brothers again. 'They're so much younger than me and I didn't see much of them when they were small. I feel more like their uncle than their brother. I managed to get home for Robin and Alice's wedding, but I'd never met Eve before. She's a lovely young woman and the kids are great. She and Oliver seem very happy together.'

'They are.' Well, Eve was.

We drove in silence for a while, which wasn't the least bit awkward. We'd almost reached Birkdale when he said, 'I understand you knew Eric Knowles.'

'Only a bit: I didn't like him much.'

'Neither did I,' he said darkly. 'That's when I went abroad, right after the war when he and Mum got married. I was only sixteen. First, I went to Australia, it seemed the place to go in those days, and

I wandered around picking fruit for a few years. It was a wonderful life, but I got restless and made my way to Tibet.'

'Tibet! I've never met anyone who's been to Tibet.'

'Well, you have now. I became a Buddhist and might have stayed if the Chinese hadn't invaded. By then, it was nineteen fifty, I was twenty-two, and reckoned it was time I moved on. I ended up in Hong Kong and got a job in a bank.'

I laughed. 'From Buddhist to banker, that's quite a big move.'

'In some ways, I rather wish it was the other way around. I was a much nicer person when I was a Buddhist than a banker.'

'You're quite nice now,' I assured him.

'I must remember to tell Mum what you just said: she'll think we're making progress.' He braked. 'I think this is the place. It's called Miranda Lodge.'

He'd stopped outside a square, yellow-bricked detached house set amidst a large plot where man-sized weeds mingled with mature trees. The slate roof glistened in the late September sunshine and the name, Miranda Lodge, was painted on a board above the door. 'The garden could do with a good pruning,' I remarked, 'but I really like the house. It looks as if it's grown there with the trees.'

'According to the estate agent, it's about a hundred and fifty years old and has been empty since the owner died a few years ago.' We got out of the car, and crunched up the pebble drive towards the front door. 'His wife was already dead, they had no children and there was a problem with the Will. It's taken all this time to sort out, so the place is only just on the market. The agent assures me there's dozens of desperate house-hunters ready and waiting to snap it up and I'm fortunate to be given the first opportunity.'

'Aren't you lucky?' I said cynically.

'You obviously don't think much of estate agents.'

I raised my eyebrows. 'Does anyone?'

He raised his. 'How many have you met?'

'Not a single one, but there was a survey in the paper: I can't remember whether it was them or politicians who came last. Have you got the key?'

'Of course I have the key, Miss McCarthy. I wasn't about to break the door down.'

The door opened on to a narrow, dusty hallway. It was uncarpeted. I remarked that the floorboards looked well preserved. I stamped on them hard and was relieved when they didn't give way. 'There's no sign of rot.' I entered the room on my right. 'This is lovely and big.' It was about fifteen feet square with windows overlooking the front and side of the house and an attractive Victorian fireplace. I pointed out a patch of damp in one of the corners. 'You'd need to have that seen to.'

'Will it be a major job?' He didn't look very concerned.

'It depends what the reason is. The bricks outside might just need pointing.'

'I thought you weren't an expert on houses.'

'I'm not, it's just common sense. Eve had the same problem with her house.'

'That's all right then,' he said easily. 'I'm off to examine the loft. According to the agent, it's vast and sounds exactly what I'm after for my railway. I'll leave you to look round the rest of the place. Let me know what you think.' He bounded up the stairs two at a time. I continued with my inspection.

There were four rooms on each floor, all the same size, all with two aspects. The ancient kitchen was squeezed in what appeared to be a lean-to shack at the rear. The bathroom had clearly been a bedroom in which a rusty bath, a sink and a lavatory had been added at some time. I could hear Charlie moving around in the loft. 'What's it like up there?' I shouted.

'Vast, like the agent said,' his muffled voice replied. 'I could probably get miles of track up here. Come on up and see for yourself.'

'What, and climb this ladder?' A mangy rope-ladder dangled from the open trapdoor. 'It'd never stand my weight.'

His head appeared in the aperture. 'It stood mine.' His face looked very young and boyish, as if he were excited at the thought of playing with his trains.

'I'm not risking it,' I said firmly. 'Anyroad, you're full of cobwebs and I'm terrified of spiders. I'll have a quick look around the garden. I'd sooner not be here when you climb down that ladder, but give us a shout if it breaks and you need an ambulance.'

We got back in the car, hungry, thirsty and very hot. 'Do you fancy lunch?' he asked. 'I could have a wash in the Gents'.' The water in the house had been turned off.

'I'd quite like a sarnie and a long, cold drink.'

'What's a sarnie?'

'A sandwich. I want to be back by half past three for when Jake comes home from school.'

'We can just about manage it if we eat the sarnies quickly.' He took one last look at the house before he drove away. 'Anyway, expert,' he said, 'what did you think of Miranda Lodge?'

I coughed importantly and began my report. 'I liked it very much. I particularly liked the big rooms, but it needs quite a lot of money spending on it. The kitchen's useless and the whole thing needs tearing down and a new one fitted in one of the rooms at the back. Oliver could help: he likes tearing kitchens to pieces. I'll explain that some other time,' I said when he appeared nonplussed. 'You'll need a new bathroom, too, and the whole place wants decorating throughout and central heating installed. You won't need them, but I'd leave those lovely fireplaces in the bedrooms.'

'Hmm!' he said thoughtfully. 'What about the garden?'

'It was once very pretty. It's just overgrown, that's all. There's loads of lovely trees, rhododendron bushes and other plants I don't know the names of. I'm hopeless at gardening. It takes me all my time to cut the lawn – it needs doing now,' I said with a sigh. 'It's probably too big for you to look after by yourself, as you'll be too busy with your trains. Once it's sorted, you'll probably have to have a gardener in at least once a week.' I only wished I could do the same.

'Hmm!' he said again. 'There's a pub ahead. Let's stop there for half an hour.'

'Should I buy it then, the house?' he asked when we were settled in the corner of the almost-empty pub with our sarnies, my lemonade and Charlie's pint of lager.

'Don't ask me,' I gasped, horrified. 'You didn't even look at it properly. You should get a survey, make sure it hasn't got any serious faults.'

'Such as?'

I shrugged. 'I don't know. It might be in danger of falling down, or have death-watch beetle or there could be something wrong with the drains. Anyroad, people don't buy the first house they see. They usually view loads before making up their minds.'

He raised his eyebrows questioningly. 'Even if the first house they see is exactly what they want?'

'It's quite a large house for someone on their own,' I said lamely.

'They might be planning on getting married and having a big family.'

'In that case, it'd be perfect.' He'd better convey that to his mother, the matchmaker, so she could fix him up with a woman considerably younger than me. I was approaching fifty, past the age when I could supply him any sort of family, big or small.

He dropped me off outside the school and refused an invitation to come back for a drink, saying he'd like to show the house to Faith while he had the key. 'She'd be hurt if I made an offer without her seeing it.'

I felt, quite unreasonably, annoyed that I wouldn't be viewing any more houses as I'd quite enjoyed it. I also felt extremely pleased the next day when Charlie turned up and offered to cut the grass.

'You sounded as if you weren't exactly looking forward to it and I thought it would be practise for when I have my own house.' He'd made an offer, it had been accepted and, before long, Miranda Lodge would be his. 'But only if it passes the survey,' he added when I gave him a worried look.

When Jake arrived home, the grass had been cut and Charlie was sprawled in the gazebo with a glass of Norah's homemade lemonade. I stopped admiring the freshly trimmed lawn and introduced them, 'Charlie, this is my son, Jake. Jake this is Mr Collier, Oliver's big brother. He lives in Hong Kong.'

'Hi, Jake, call me Charlie.' Charlie smiled as they shook hands.

'Is it very hot in Hong Kong?' Jake enquired.

'Extremely. Too hot sometimes.'

'I don't exactly know where Hong Kong is,' Jake said regretfully.

'Have you got an atlas?'

'It's in the house.'

'I'll come with you and show you Hong Kong. I'm urgently in need of more of your Auntie Norah's lemonade.'

'Is he staying to dinner?' Norah hissed when I entered the kitchen.

'I don't know, I haven't asked.'

'Well, ask quickly, and I'll start making something nice.'

'Everything you make is nice, Norah.'

'Then something *extra* nice.' She lowered her voice. 'Are things likely to get serious between you two? If you don't want him, I wouldn't mind having him for meself.'

'Charlie and I are just good friends,' I told her. 'You can have him if you want, but you must be prepared to give him lots of babies.'

Norah's face fell. 'Oh, well. It was just an idea.'

Claire's hair fell out after the second bout of chemotherapy. 'If it's making me better, I don't mind,' she said stoutly on one of her good days. No one was allowed to see, only Liam: she wore a turban indoors and out. The treatment made her feel nauseous, she had sores in her mouth and had completely lost her appetite.

I went to see her every day after I'd finished in the surgery, to find her curled up in a chair, looking incredibly tiny and very ill. She coughed incessantly. My mind often went back to the Claire of old. One incident particularly stuck in my mind. It was the year before the war began and I was playing in Amethyst Street with my skipping rope when Claire came strolling towards me on the arm of a young man I'd never seen before. He was tall and muscular, very handsome, and was wearing what was clearly his best suit: dark blue with a grey stripe. Claire had on her pink frock with cap sleeves and a flared skirt, a belt notched tightly around her slim waist – she was only nineteen. A little white cocked hat was perched like a bird on her dark-red hair, which she wore long in those days. Her cheeks were pink and I wondered why her eyes were shining quite so brightly. I felt very proud of my sister that day. When she saw me, she stopped and said, bursting with importance, 'Hello, Kitty. This is Liam Quinn. We met the other day on the New Brighton ferry. Liam, this is me sister, Kitty.'

'How do you do, Kitty?' Liam removed his hat.

I replied, very grown up, 'I'm very well, thanks. How are you?'

Now, more than forty years later, on what was clearly one of the bad days, Claire whimpered, 'I don't want to die, Kitty. I can't stand the thought of never seeing Liam and me kids again.'

'I won't let that happen, sis,' I whispered. It was a foolish thing to say, but it was all I could think of.

'It hardly seems fair,' I said to Charlie one night. We had continued to see each other regularly. Faith was convinced our 'courtship' was coming along nicely. 'Claire's never done harm to anyone. She's one of the kindest people who ever lived. Why should she get cancer and not me? I'm a bitch. I'm always hurting people's feelings.'

'Life *is* unfair,' Charlie said sadly. 'Good fortune is shared out most erratically. Some people get more than their share, some less.'

'I think I've had more. I've been very happy for most of my life.'

'By the way, I met Eve's father the other night: Connor Daley. He's putting a new kitchen and bathroom in Miranda Lodge. Eve insisted I use him.'

'I hope you don't want to know why I didn't marry him,' I said quickly, 'because I'm not sure myself. Every time someone asks I come up with a different reason.'

'I wouldn't have dreamed of asking. By the way, *I* don't consider you a bitch and you haven't hurt my feelings. At least, not so far,' he added with a grin.

I was like a pendulum swinging between Claire on one side and Charlie on the other. 'I'm glad you came home when you did,' I said to him another time. We were having dinner in a hotel in Southport, which had become our favourite, and had reached the coffee stage.

'Why's that?' he asked lightly, waving away the waiter who was about to pour cream into his coffee. I wished I had the willpower to do the same.

'Well, you take me out of myself. We're always too busy to talk to each other in the surgery and, apart from Faith, you're virtually the only person I know who isn't family. With them, the only topic of conversation is our Claire. Not that I mind,' I added hastily. 'I don't mind a bit. I'm glad everyone cares, but you help to make it bearable.'

'Good. Strangely enough, you're doing the same for me, helping to make something bearable.' He stared into the coffee. I could tell his thoughts were very far away. 'That's why I came home, because I couldn't stand another minute of Hong Kong. I only intended staying with Mum until I'd found a house, then I thought I might go to the States and South America, travel around a bit. But the minute I met you I decided to stay for the whole six months. You're good for me, Kitty.'

'We're good for each other,' I said.

*

It was one of the coldest Decembers I could remember. Christmas arrived in a flurry of snow, but this year, there was no question of the McCarthys not spending it together. We were all aware that it might be Claire's last Christmas on earth. On Christmas Day, Norah and I went early to the house in Opal Street to make the dinner, after first dropping Jake off at Eve and Oliver's where he'd have a far better time with the girls.

Claire, the master detective, knew quite well what was in our minds. We were just finishing the meal when she lost her temper. 'I'm fed up with people looking at me as if they'll never see me again,' she shouted. 'I'm getting better, I can feel it in me bones. I'll be around next Christmas, just you see, by which time I'll have all me hair back and I'll be dancing in the streets.'

'But you hardly ate a mouthful of your dinner, luv,' Liam complained.

'I only eat fruit nowadays: I'd've thought people would have noticed by now, particularly you, Liam Quinn, seeing as we live together under the same roof. Fruit's far better than roast spuds soaked in gravy. And who made the stuffing? It's as hard as a bloody rock.'

'I did,' I confessed.

'Then you should've let our Norah do it. She knows how to cook.'

'I wanted to,' Norah sniffed, 'but she insisted.'

'Only because I wanted to do my share,' I said huffily.

Marge joined in. 'Personally, I quite like hard stuffing. It's easily sliced.'

'I prefer it crumbly,' Danny said.

I think the entire family might well have joined the argument over stuffing had there not been a knock on the door. Liam went to see who it was. He reappeared a minute later accompanied by a stylish woman, beautifully made up, with glamorous silver hair and wearing an expensive fur coat – think it might have been sable, but I'm as ignorant about fur as I am about plants.

'It's Aileen,' Liam announced. 'She's come to wish us Merry Christmas.'

'Merry Christmas, everyone,' Aileen said with a confident smile. She screamed when she saw Claire. 'My God, sis! You look at death's door. What's with the turban? Seems to me I've come home just in time.'

Men just don't understand women. They disappeared sharpish to the pub, every single one, when we all started screaming at each other – well, the McCarthy sisters did. Barbara had never met Aileen before, and probably wondered what all the fuss was about, and Marge looked downright sour: she'd never liked Aileen for the very good reason that Aileen had made it obvious she didn't like her.

'Where the hell have you been all these years, Aileen?' Claire croaked after we'd all stopped screaming, Aileen had been introduced to Barbara, been informed that Ben, her son, was married and his wife was expecting a baby any minute, and Claire had indignantly denied she was anywhere near death's door. 'I'm getting better,' she said firmly, and I was inclined to believe she was right.

Aileen had plonked herself in a vacated chair. She opened her patent leather handbag, removed a gold compact and powdered beneath her eyes: they'd grown rather watery when she'd heard the news about Ben. 'I've been in Australia, that's where.'

'But Steve McSherry came back years ago,' Claire protested. 'Me and our Kitty wanted to write and tell you, but we didn't have your address.'

'Oh, Steve.' Aileen shrugged carelessly. 'I can't remember when I last thought about him. Four years back, I married this really nice chap, Vernon Cartwright: he has his own brewery just outside Canberra.' Vernon mustn't be short of a few bob if her coat was anything to go by. It was a big improvement on the last time she'd turned up looking like a tramp.

'Has he come home with you?' Norah enquired.

'No. He's getting on a bit, Verne, and isn't up to the journey, but he didn't mind me coming home to see my family at Christmas.' She treated us to a magnificent smile. 'I've got presents for everyone. In fact, I'll give them to you now.'

'It's been a funny old day,' I remarked to Norah on the way home. 'Fancy Aileen turning up like that! I was beginning to think we'd never see her again.'

'I've reached the conclusion that all the McCarthys are nuts – at least, the women are, if not the men – and Aileen is the nuttiest of the lot, with you a close second. She goes away for years, then comes back expecting everything to be the same. Did you see what she bought me? A bikini! I'm fifty-five years old and she expects me to wear a bikini,' she finished in disgust.

'Maybe older women do in Australia.'

'Huh! What did she give you?'

'A nightie. It's OK, but a bit short. I'll let Eve have it. But didn't Claire look great in that diamanté necklace and earrings?'

'She looked dead beautiful,' Norah said tenderly. 'You know, I really do think she's getting better. She *sounded* better, the way she tore Liam off a strip.'

We spent a few minutes in silence, thinking about Claire, until I asked if she'd like to be taken straight home, or come with me to Formby to pick up Jake. 'I'll probably end up staying an hour or so. I can't very well just walk in and straight out again.'

'I'd sooner go home, if you don't mind, sis. I might try on the bikini: give meself the fright of me life.'

I loved my daughter's house at Christmas. Faith opened the door and announced they'd only just finished tea. 'The girls were getting a bit tetchy, so they've gone to lie down for a while, Jake's watching television, and Oliver and Eve are washing the dishes. Next Christmas, I shall buy them a dishwasher.'

'I'm sure they'd appreciate that.'

'I entered the lavishly decorated room, feeling disappointed that there'd been no mention of Charlie. I'd expected him to be there and so was delighted to see him on the settee with Bootsie on one knee and Snudge on the other. Jake was on the floor watching *The Snowman*. A childish voice was singing 'We're Walking in the Air'. Faith asked after Claire, then popped upstairs to make sure the girls were resting. Dishes rattled in the kitchen accompanied by gales of laughter.

'Hiya, Mum.' Jake grabbed my ankle as I walked past.

I knelt and kissed his rosy face. 'Have you had a nice day, sweetheart?'

'Smashing. We had a snowball fight this afternoon. Holly pushed a snowball down my neck, so I pushed one down hers and we had to change our clothes. Did you have a nice day, Mum?'

'It was weird rather than nice.'

'I got some fantastic prezzies.' He sighed blissfully. 'There's some under the tree for you.'

'I'll open them later. Hello, Charlie.'

'Hello, Kitty.' He looked as pleased to see me as I was him.

'I like your sweater.' It was egg-yolk yellow with a turtleneck and made him look like a newly born chick.

'Nice, isn't it? I got it from Mum.' He winked, eyes dancing merrily. Every few years, he'd told me, Faith bought him a yellow sweater for Christmas. It was his least favourite colour. 'Thanks for the picture. It was a lovely surprise. It'll look great over the mantelpiece in Miranda Lodge. I've put your present under the tree. It's a handbag. Mum said you liked handbags, so I let her choose.'

'Thank you.' I could do with another bag. 'And you said you liked Picasso. I only wish I could have bought the original, but I didn't have a few million pounds to spare.'

'The original deserves to be in a museum where everyone can see it. A print suits me fine. By the way, this morning, I went to see how the house was getting on and found Con hard at work on the bathroom.'

I groaned 'On Christmas Day! Poor Con. This marriage has turned out as bad as his first. I'll phone him in the morning, invite him round.'

Bootsie gave a little grunt and Charlie fondly stroked his thick black fur. 'I'm going to get a cat and a dog when I take up residence in Miranda Lodge.'

'That won't be for ages.' Another eight years to be precise, when he turned sixty.

'It'll be sooner than you think.' He gave me a smile of pure happiness. 'I like it here so much I've decided to take early retirement. I shall go back to Hong Kong as planned, hand in my notice, and expect to be home permanently by next Christmas.'

'But that's marvellous news,' I cried. 'I bet Faith is pleased.'

Faith came into the room, having got the gist of the conversation. 'I'm as pleased as punch. For the first time in my life I'll have my three sons living nearby. I can hardly wait to see Charlie in his lovely new house.'

'I can hardly wait either, Mum.'

I couldn't help but wonder if *I* was the reason Charlie wanted to be home. The news had created a warm, tingly sensation in my breast. I imagined him, me and Jake living in Miranda Lodge, and knew with a certainty I could no longer deny that it was what I wanted more than anything in the world. His eyes met mine and I got the distinct feeling that he felt exactly the same.

Eve and Oliver emerged from the kitchen with their arms around each other. Oliver gave me a friendly nod and Eve sang, 'Hiya, Kitty, I didn't know you were here. What sort of day did you have?'

'It was weird rather than nice,' Jake told her.

'That sounds fascinating, you must tell us about it later.' She seemed particularly bubbly tonight. 'Now you're all here, I want to make an announcement. I'm having another baby. Oliver's thrilled to bits, aren't you, darling?'

'Thrilled to a million bits,' Oliver said jubilantly. He grabbed Eve's face in both hands and kissed her soundly on the lips. Faith clapped, Charlie whistled and I could tell that Oliver had fallen in love with my daughter – at last. From now on, I would just be his mother-in-law. It was exactly the way I wanted it to be, though there would always be a shred of regret that my life hadn't followed an entirely different course.

Aileen decided to stay in Liverpool until Samantha had her baby. Verne wouldn't mind, she said: 'All he wants is for me to be happy.' There being no room for her in my house – thank goodness – she stayed with Claire and Liam, being a damn nuisance, according to Liam. She threw the newspaper out before he'd had a chance to read it, and he could never find the *Radio Times*. 'The house is spotless, not a thing out of place,' he moaned, 'but it doesn't feel like home any more.'

In January, Ben returned to university and Samantha stayed in Crosby with her parents to wait for the baby to be born. It arrived a fortnight later, a gorgeous little boy called Jasper – a horrible name to inflict on a child, in my view. Ben came racing home from Norwich to see his son, having found a house for his small family to live in. Aileen had offered to help with the rent and cried her eyes out at the christening. Another fortnight later, the young couple went back to Norwich with Jasper, Aileen went back to Australia with the promise not to be a stranger any more, and Liam breathed a noisy sigh of relief.

*

Claire continued to improve. In February, I accompanied her to the hospital for her final chemotherapy treatment. It was a relatively painless procedure: she just sat in a chair while a cocktail of drugs was administered by a drip into the veins in her wrist. I stayed with her and we chatted. She said she couldn't understand Samantha leaving Jasper in a crèche while she continued with her degree: 'Meself, I just couldn't do it.'

I was about to say, 'Neither could I,' when I remembered I'd actually given one of my babies to my sister. If only it were possible to go back in time and change things! I wondered how many times in my life I'd wished that?

We discussed Aileen. 'Will we ever see her again?' I wondered.

'I reckon so. She was upset that she wasn't here when Ben got married. With her, it's a case of out of sight, out of mind. Either that, or she thinks time stands still in this country when she's away. I got the impression Verne's not long for this world. When he goes, she'll probably come home for good.' She sighed contentedly. 'I'll be glad if she does: it'd be nice to have all the McCarthys back in Liverpool again.'

'That's how Faith feels about Charlie.'

Claire gave me a piercing stare: I felt convinced she was reading my mind. 'Is it serious with you and Charlie?'

'Yes,' I mumbled. 'At least, it's serious with me and I'm convinced it is with him, but he hasn't said anything. He hasn't even tried to kiss me.' I grimaced. 'The thing is, when we first met we came to a sort of agreement that we'd only ever be friends.'

'In that case, *you* say something.' She gave me a little shove with her free hand. 'You've never been backward in coming forward, Kitty. Maybe he's just shy or he thinks you're not interested. When's he going back to Hong Kong?'

'Next month: March.'

'If he hasn't proposed before then, I suggest you propose to him.'

The treatment finished, I drove her home. She was excited, knowing that she'd never have to have chemotherapy again: 'From now on, the only way to go is up and I already feel halfway there.'

We were now into our third month of Arctic weather and it was getting hard to imagine a world without snow. It gathered in clumps in the corners of the windscreen, blocking my view, despite the fact that the wipers were going so fast they made me squint. The driving took all my concentration, and I hardly spoke. We'd almost reached the Dock Road when I made some remark about the foul weather and was surprised when Claire didn't answer. I thought she'd gone to sleep, but when I looked, her mouth had fallen open and her face had turned an ugly shade of grey.

'Claire!' I braked. The car behind hooted angrily, and the driver shook his fist as he overtook. Other cars sounded their horns. I was holding up the traffic, an unforgivable offence.

I shook my sister gently, but she fell sideways and her head hit the side of the car. I screamed, '*Claire!*' but there was no response.

I can't remember driving back to the hospital, but I must have managed it somehow. Claire was rushed into a ward and a nurse asked me dozens of questions that I think I answered coherently. Doctors came, I was shooed outside, where I waited, petrified my sister was dead, or at least about to die.

A nurse approached. 'She's reacted badly to one of the drugs she had this afternoon. Chemotherapy can sometimes be a bit of a hit and miss affair.'

'Will she recover?'

'We'll just have to see,' the nurse said enigmatically. 'Has she got a husband?'

'Yes.'

'Perhaps it wouldn't be a bad idea to get him here, and the rest of her family. There's a telephone just along the corridor.'

I rang Liam at work and he came about an hour later. It might have been more, it might have been less; when I looked at my watch it didn't make sense. Not long afterwards, Patsy arrived, followed by Claire's other children, and I felt in the way. I went outside again and hung about in the corridor. No matter how much I loved my sister, her husband and children came first.

It was time I rang Norah – I should have done it before. She sounded agitated when she answered. 'I've been worried sick about you, Kitty. I thought you might have had an accident in this weather. I've been ringing Claire, but there was no reply.'

'We're back at the hospital.' I explained what had happened. 'I don't know what to do,' I said helplessly.

'Come home,' she said instantly. 'I'll make me way to the ozzie on the train. I'll let you know if there's any developments. Are you fit to drive?'

'I'm OK,' I said, but I was shaking all over. 'Tell Jake I'll be there in about an hour.'

'Don't worry about Jake. Charlie's here. Apparently, you'd arranged to have an early dinner in town before going to the theatre. I made him something to eat and Jake's had his tea. Hang on a mo, Charlie's making signs.' There was a pause and she said, 'He's going to drive me as far as the station.'

I'd forgotten all about my date with Charlie. I drove carefully back to Maghull. There'd been no change in Claire when I left the hospital. Charlie and Jake were standing on the step when I parked the car on the drive. 'Jake recognized the sound of the engine,' Charlie said. 'Liam rang only a minute ago. He said Claire had just opened her eyes: she's conscious.'

I burst into tears. 'Thank God for that.'

He put his arm around my shoulder, Jake took my hand and they led me indoors. It made me feel precious and dearly loved. 'There's tea made, Mum,' Jake said. 'Shall I pour some out?'

'Yes, please, sweetheart. It's been a truly awful day.' Jake went to fetch the tea. 'It's such a relief to be home,' I said to Charlie as I sank into a chair. 'My mam always said, "There's no place like home," even if she'd only been gone a few hours.'

'Are you warm enough?' he asked fussily. 'Would you like the fire turned up a bit?'

'I'm OK, thanks.'

Jake brought the tea and said Charlie had been helping with his homework. 'It was grammar. I told him you were good at grammar.'

'I'm brilliant at grammar,' I said boastfully. 'I went to night school for a whole year because I had no idea where to put commas.'

'Good for you,' Charlie said with a smile. 'By the way, I ordered a lawnmower today. It's like a little tractor: you just have to sit on it and drive. Cutting the grass in Miranda Lodge will be a doddle.'

'You lucky divil!' I gasped. 'I'm green with envy.'

'I thought you would be.' His blue eyes twinkled. 'I might drive over once a month and cut your grass for you.'

'I wish you would,' I said with a heartfelt sigh.

'Can I have a go on it, Charlie?' Jake demanded, face aglow.

'That might be a bit dangerous, Jake, but you can come and watch. I'm just as anxious to have a go on it as you.'

Norah telephoned to say Claire was almost her old self again, if very weak. 'They're keeping her in hospital overnight, but she's concerned about you, sis, and wants to know how you are.'

'Tell her not to worry.' I glanced through the door at Charlie and Jake seated in front of the fire. It was a sight that made me feel extraordinarily happy. 'I'm fine now I'm home. What about you? Will you be coming soon?'

'I'll just wait a while with Liam, then I'll come.'

'See you, sis.'

Jake went to bed at half past eight. 'Do you like Charlie?' I asked as I tucked him in.

'You know I do, Mum. I've told you before. Can I read for a while?'

'You know you can, I've told you before.'

We grinned at each other. I patted his head and went downstairs. Then, before I could have second thoughts, I threw back my shoulders, marched into the living room and said in a rush, 'Why don't we get married, Charlie? I love you and I know you love me. It seems stupid not to.'

I had expected him to look surprised, but not thunderstruck. He recoiled in the chair, his mouth moved, but no words came until he managed to stammer, 'But I thought you understood, Kitty. I made it plain from the start that we would only be friends.'

'But that was months ago. I feel differently now. Don't you?' I said challengingly.

'Of course I do.' His embarrassment was almost painful to watch. 'I like you enormously, Kitty, but I'm sorry, I don't want to marry you.'

'Is it because I can't have children?' I demanded angrily. I was being unreasonable, but I'd been unreasonable all my life. 'You said once you might want to get married and have a big family, in which case it was very wrong of you to lead me on.'

'Kitty, my darling girl, that was a joke. It was a sick thing to say. Afterwards, I wondered how on earth I could have brought myself to say it.' He got to his feet and began to pace around the room, plainly distressed. 'I haven't been leading you on. I thought we were friends, good friends, the best friend I've ever had. I'm deeply flattered that you love me, but I'm afraid I don't love you back, at least not in the way you want.'

'It's the woman you knew in Hong Kong, isn't it? The one who died of cancer? You're still in love with her.' I knew I'd just made the biggest blunder of my life, but was unwilling to admit it even to myself. If I persisted, I was convinced Charlie would come round to my way of thinking.

'It wasn't a woman who died – at least, not quite a woman. It was my daughter, Jennifer. She was only sixteen.' The words were spoken quietly in a voice full of pain.

'Oh, *God*!' Everything inside me shrivelled. What had I done? Only forced Charlie into telling something that he'd sooner have kept to himself or he'd have told me before. 'Oh, God, Charlie, I'm so sorry.' It was only a few hours since I'd wished I could go back in time and change things, but I'd never wished it as much as I did then. Just five minutes would have done. 'I don't know quite what else to say,' I mumbled, longing to sink through the floor.

'Then don't say anything, Kitty.'

'I'll make some tea.' If I couldn't sink through the floor, at least I could disappear into another room.

Charlie caught my arm. 'No, Kitty, stay. I'd like you to know everything. It's best that you should, because when I come home from Hong Kong for good, I'll be bringing someone with me.'

'Jennifer's mother?' I whispered.

He nodded. 'We'd been having an affair for years, almost twenty. Her husband knew, but didn't care, though he refused to divorce her – he's a member of the Government out there and didn't want the scandal.' He sat down with his back to me, staring into the fire. 'In a way, we didn't mind. We rented a little flat that no one else knew about and met as often as we liked. Jennifer lived there with her nanny.' He slapped the arm of the chair with his open hand. 'Eighteen months ago, Jenny died: it was leukaemia. Life hardly seemed worth living any more. Imelda and I just drifted apart. On the anniversary of Jenny's death, I realized I needed a break from Hong Kong and came home.'

'Oh, Charlie, that's so sad,' I cried. 'But why didn't you tell me about Jennifer before?'

He turned and looked at me straight in the face. 'Because I didn't want you to know, that's why. I didn't want people making a fuss and feeling sorry for me. And I didn't want people asking questions or *not* asking questions, worried they'd hurt me. Would you have been so open about Claire had you known I'd lost a child to cancer?'

'No.' I would have kept lots of it hidden.

'It helped with my own pain, the way you confided in me.'

I crept across the room and sat in the other chair. Now I was more ashamed than embarrassed. 'You always act first and think later,' Mam used to say. Well, I certainly had tonight. Charlie's face was tight with grief and it was my fault. I said, meaning it with all my heart, 'I'm glad Imelda's coming to live with you in Miranda Lodge, Charlie.'

'She wrote to me at Christmas. She's divorcing her husband and wants us to live together, properly this time.' His eyes glistened and I recalled how happy he'd been on Christmas Day. 'I telephoned and we decided we'd had enough of Hong Kong: that's why I'm retiring early.'

And I'd thought it had been because of me!

'Don't say anything about Jenny to Mum, will you, Kitty? It'd only upset her. I might tell her later, once Imelda's here.'

'I won't breathe a word to a soul.'

Neither of us said anything for a long time, just stared into the fire at the dancing flames and the coal that looked so very real. I spoke first. 'I'm sorry about tonight, Charlie. I just don't know what got into me. I suppose it'd be best if we never saw each other again.' I'd squirm at the memory for the rest of my life.

'That would be difficult, Kitty. Your daughter is my sister-in-law. We're part of the same family. Anyway,' he smiled for the first time, 'I *want* to see you again. I meant it when I said you were the best friend I'd ever had, and I'd like you to make a friend of Imelda. She's likely to feel very strange after spending most of her life in Hong Kong.'

'I'll do my best.' I really would. 'Can I tell you something, Charlie?'

'Anything, Kit,' he said warmly, and I knew things would be all right between us, though it would take a while.

'You must also promise to not tell anyone. It's something I've never told a living soul before.'

'It won't go further than this room.'

'Oliver is Jake's father. We fell in love, had an affair before he met

Eve.' I don't know why I felt the need to tell him. Perhaps I just wanted him to know he wasn't the only person with a secret past.

'Wow!' He looked impressed. 'Does Oliver know Jake is his?'

'Oh, yes, he knows, but it's all in the past and he loves Eve. I hope and pray she never finds out. Neither of us were being unfaithful, but I have a feeling she would never forgive me or Oliver, that it would ruin their marriage.'

'I somehow doubt that, Kitty, but it's probably best not to risk it.'

'Would you like some tea now, Charlie?' I felt more comfortable now that we had opened our hearts to each other.

'Do you have cocoa?'

'Yes, would you like some?'

'Dearly. Mum never has any. The first thing I shall buy when I move into Miranda Lodge is a tin of cocoa.'

Charlie had gone. I'd insisted he leave when I saw it was snowing again. He had a long drive back to his mother's house. It had been a relief to see him go. It meant I could breathe more easily while I wallowed in my shame. Norah still hadn't come home.

I went upstairs. Jake was asleep, but I just wanted to see him, touch him, convince myself that he was there. Downstairs again, I stood by the window and watched the snow fall relentlessly on to the garden at the back, smothering the lawn, making giant snowballs of the bushes and turning my small portion of the earth into an alien, almost terrifying place. The view was as dreary and desolate as my heart.

I pressed my forehead against the window and cold tears trickled down my cheeks. I loved Charlie, but Fate had decreed we could only be friends, and who was I to argue? Frankly, I was fed up with Fate interfering in my affairs. Charlie was just one of the many mistakes I'd made in a life full of mistakes: Con, Eve, Oliver . . .

Con! I was transported back to the Chinese restaurant in Lime Street when I'd told him I never wanted to see him again. He must have felt as I did now: gutted, miserable, unable to believe that someone he loved so dearly didn't love him back. Yet, unlike Charlie, I hadn't had a genuine reason. I'd just been playing with Con's feelings. He hadn't deserved to fall in love with someone like me.

I closed the curtains with a flourish, shutting out the snow. The view wouldn't always be so dreary and desolate, and neither would my heart. Very soon, the sun would shine, the snow would melt, the grass would grow, leaves would appear and flowers would bloom. And Claire would get better.

I rubbed my hands together. I couldn't wait.

The front door opened: Norah was home.

I hurried into the kitchen to make a pot of tea. I honestly don't know what I would have done without my sisters.

Chapter 14

August, 1981

'Are you all right, luv?'

'I'm fine, thanks, Liam.' Claire, relaxing in a deck chair in her sister's garden, the sun warm on her face, stretched out her bare legs and stared at them thoughtfully. They weren't a bad pair of legs for a woman of sixty-two: nice and brown, with the suggestion of a shine, and still a reasonable shape. There were no swollen veins, despite having had five children. She waved away a wasp that was threatening to land on her knee.

'Are you all right, Claire?' Faith was smiling down at her. She appeared to be wearing a white, fluffy cloud and reminded Claire of the Queen Mother.

'I'm absolutely fine, thank you,' Claire replied patiently. She would have liked to tell Faith to sod off and leave her alone, and all the other people – her husband, her children, her friends and neighbours – who persisted in asking if she was all right a million times a day, when she'd been feeling better for months. She still had to attend hospital for checks, but the signs were she'd make a full recovery.

Her hair was growing back at last. She touched it. The prickly spikes had become tiny curls and she no longer looked like a female sergeant major or a prison warden. The hair was a pretty shade of silver and she was very pleased with that, as well as her legs. In fact, she felt pleased with herself altogether, mainly because she was still alive.

Norah dropped on to the grass beside her. Her sister wouldn't ask how she was. Norah seemed instinctively to know how she felt. She said, 'You look lovely, sis. You really suit pink.'

'It's what I got for Ben's wedding.' Claire smoothed her skirt. It looked like linen, but had something in to stop it from creasing. 'I thought I'd get dolled up seeing as I was coming to a garden party. I've never been to one before.'

'It's a lovely day for it.' Kitty's garden wasn't much to write home about, but it smelt nice. The hydrangeas were in full bloom and the sun glinted on the bright green leaves, making them look as silver as her new hair. Liam had come the day before to cut the grass – perhaps that's what the nice smell was. The Quinns didn't have a garden, just a backyard, and Claire was ignorant about such things.

Jake and Holly were playing on one of those swing-a-ball things; she quite fancied having a go. If Liam protested, she'd give him a mouthful, insist the exercise would do her good, that she was fed up being molly-coddled.

What she *really* fancied was a cup of tea, but didn't like to ask, not now she was feeling so well. She'd never liked people dancing attendance on her. The truth was the deck chair was extremely comfortable and she felt quite lazy. Perhaps someone would offer to fetch one, she thought hopefully. It wasn't quite the same as asking.

'Oh, look! Here's Eve with Zack,' Norah cried, as Eve entered the garden, as slim as a whip in a lovely emerald-green frock, carrying the new baby in her arms. Oliver followed proudly behind.

'I haven't seen him yet.' Claire craned her neck, but all she could see was a bundle of white. 'I expect she'll bring him round in a minute. What's he like?'

'Faith showed us some photos of Oliver when he was a baby and Zack's the spitting image of his dad: very dark, really lovely.'

Claire had always thought that Jake was the image of Oliver, still was, but the likelihood of their Kitty having had an affair with Oliver Knowles was so far-fetched it was hardly worth thinking about. She ground her teeth. It really bugged her that Kitty refused to reveal the identity of Jake's father. She said, 'I wonder how Eve manages to keep so slim? Every time *I* had a baby, me stomach hung down as far as me knees for months: hers is as flat as a bloody pancake.'

'She really works at it,' Norah explained. 'She does exercises every day and eats like a rabbit, nothing but leaves.'

'Leaves!'

'You know, lettuce and stuff, watercress, the occasional tomato. Our Kitty's really worried about her. She's so scared of putting on weight, it's become an obsession. Kitty's thin enough herself, but she eats like a horse.'

'Since I started to feel better,' Claire said with a sigh, 'I've got an obsession with food. If I'm not careful, I'll end up as big as a house.'

'You'd be miserable if you got fat.'

'I know, but I'm miserable when I'm hungry.'

'Then you'll have to choose between the two. Me, I'd go for the hungry.'

Claire laughed. 'That's a funny way for someone to talk when they're about to open a restaurant.'

'I don't care if the clientele get fat, I'm only thinking about you. Would you like to see the menus?' Norah scrambled to her feet. 'They only came back from the printers yesterday. They look really good. They're printed in French.'

'If there's any tea going in there, I wouldn't mind a cup,' Claire called after her.

Liam came and plonked himself in the place Norah had just vacated, a can of beer in his hand. 'If you've come to ask if I'm all right,' Claire said in a gritty voice, 'I'll pick up this deck chair and wrap it around your neck.'

'I bet you would an' all.' He grinned and her heart turned over. It wasn't long since they'd started making love again and it was better than it had ever been. Sometimes, she wondered if she wasn't the luckiest woman on earth having Liam Quinn for a husband. She remembered how gutted he'd been when she was ill and gave his neck a little stroke. He seized her hand and kissed it. 'I love you, Claire.'

'And I love you, Liam.' Perhaps it was because the sun was in her eyes, but he looked exactly the same as when they'd met on the New Brighton ferry a lifetime ago. A ball landed on her knee, one of those big colourful bouncy ones. She picked it up and threw it back to Louisa, one of Eve's little girls, who came running after it.

'I'm sorry, Auntie Claire, I hope it didn't hurt,' Louisa said primly.

'I'm not a piece of rare china, luv. It didn't hurt a bit. Here, throw it again and this time I'll catch it.' They played catch for a few minutes, until Claire said, 'You'd best go back now and play with your sister.' Not for anything would she have admitted that throwing the ball was making her left armpit ache. Occasionally, she even had a pain in the breast that wasn't there. Liam told her she looked better without it. 'I never liked that one as much as the other,' he'd said.

Norah reappeared with the menus and a mug of tea. 'I'll give our

Kitty a hand with the food in a minute. She's overwhelmed in there.'

Claire took the tea with one hand and a menu with the other. 'They're nice, luv. Oh, I see there's a translation underneath so people will know what they're ordering. What do you think, Liam?'

'Very smart.' Liam nodded. 'Very smart indeed. When's the place opening, Norah?'

'The first of October, but the day before I'm inviting all the family, as a rehearsal, like. I'm calling it La Bohème.'

Claire was studying the menu, already trying to decide what she would order. 'Well, I wish you every success, Nor,' she said warmly. Faith had put up the money to buy a little run-down shop off Lord Street in Southport, an ideal place for a restaurant. She'd never considered Norah had the spunk to take on such a risky business venture, and really admired her sister's nerve. Everyone, Liam included, had helped to do the place up; it now looked genuinely French, with red-and-white gingham tablecloths and a nightlight in a red bowl on each table. If the restaurant took off, Norah planned to move into the empty flat upstairs, to save travelling to and from Maghull every day.

'If you need a waitress at lunchtimes,' she said, 'I wouldn't mind putting in a few hours.' She glared at Liam, daring him to protest. If she let him, he'd wrap her in cotton wool for the rest of her life. Oh, but it was lovely that he cared! That so many people cared.

Eve and Oliver stopped in front of her with the new baby. 'Hello, Claire, how are you feeling?' Eve enquired.

'Fine,' Claire said automatically. She put the tea on the grass and struggled to get up, but seemed to be stuck.

Oliver leapt to her rescue, but Eve said, 'Don't move. I'll give him to you, it's easier.' She laid the baby in Claire's arms. 'He's in a bit of a grumpy mood today.'

'He's enormous,' Claire gasped. 'Has he been lifting weights or something? He's got shoulders on him like a bodybuilder.'

'He weighed almost ten pounds at birth,' Oliver said boastfully.

Eve winced at the memory. 'It didn't half hurt,' she complained.

'Well, you've got narrow hips, haven't you?' Zack was a perfect replica of Jake. Claire distinctly recalled going to see him the day after he was born and remarking on his size. Her brain went into overdrive. Kitty had already been pregnant when the Knowleses appeared back on the scene, so Oliver couldn't possibly be the father. Damn! She wondered if there was any chance they might have met before? She chucked Zack under his round, firm chin and could have sworn he gave her a filthy look. Jake had been a bad-tempered little bugger for the first three months, too. 'He's lovely.'

'I'll take him away, I don't want to tire you.'

'Holding a baby won't tire me, luv,' Claire protested, but the baby was removed all the same.

Norah went to help Kitty with the food and Liam to get another beer. Claire retrieved the tea: it had a wasp inside, struggling for its life. She emptied the remainder on the grass. 'If you're going to do that again,' she said as it flew away, 'you'd better learn to swim.'

Danny and Marge were practising the rumba, or it might have been the samba, in the gazebo. Claire was trying to persuade Liam to join the dance club. There were so many things she wanted to squeeze into the rest of her life – dancing was just one of them. Kitty had offered to teach her to drive.

She waved to Connor Daley when he entered the garden. She'd always liked him. He came and flopped down beside her. 'To save you asking, I feel fine,' she said quickly. She chuckled. 'I ran all the way from Bootle and I might well run all the way back.'

'Well, you certainly look fine.' Con grinned.

Claire felt like kicking their Kitty twice around the block for not marrying the chap. He would have made a fine husband. She understood he was about to get divorced for the second time.

'Kitty didn't say she'd invited you,' she said.

'That's because Kitty didn't: Eve did,' he said dryly.

'I'm sorry about your marriage breaking down, Con.'

'So'm I. Trouble is, I keep marrying the wrong woman, only because the right one wouldn't have me.'

She could tell he felt especially dejected otherwise he wouldn't have spoken so frankly. 'I think our Kitty must have her head screwed on the wrong way round,' she opined.

'Ah, so *that's* the reason she turned me down.' Con smiled, but it didn't quite reach his eyes.

Kitty chose that particular moment to come outside, clap her hands and announce the food was ready. 'I was going to set it out in the garden,' she shouted, 'but there's too many wasps around. It'd be best if we ate indoors.'

Beside her, Claire heard Con give a little, breathy sigh. Kitty looked particularly lovely today, reminding her of Mam when she was young and full of life. You'd never guess she was fifty. Her figure was so youthful and her face was hardly lined. Her red hair gleamed in the bright sunshine and she wore lipstick to match. She really suited that violet frock, too: sleeveless with a stand-up collar and a row of little pearl buttons down the front.

'She got that frock in a charity shop and added the buttons herself,' she told Con. 'The original ones were as big as half-crowns and looked horrible.' She would never get used to the fact that half-crowns no longer existed, along with sixpences and threepenny bits. She couldn't recall when she'd last seen a farthing.

Con just grunted and asked if she'd like to go indoors. 'In a minute,' she said. She'd wait for Liam to help her out of the chair. 'You can take this with you if you're going.' She handed Con the mug.

'Would you like a refill while you're waiting?' he asked.

'I wouldn't say no, but make sure the mug's washed first. A wasp's been for a swim in it.'

Marge and Danny emerged from the gazebo. Marge looked like a flamenco dancer, in a bright-red frock with a tiered skirt and earrings as big as chandeliers. 'Are you all right, Claire?' she called.

'I'm fine, thanks. I'll be in in a mo.'

All of a sudden, the garden was empty except for her, and Claire, usually so brave, shivered with fear. Being alone had never bothered her before, but nowadays it terrified her. Once Liam had gone to work, she did a few jobs around the house, then waited for one of her girls or daughters-in-law to call. If no one had arrived by half past ten, she caught the train to Maghull and spent the day with her sisters. It was why her legs were so brown: she'd lazed away the summer sunbathing in this very garden.

She felt relieved when Kitty came out again. 'Con said you wanted tea. Why don't you come inside? I've just made a fresh pot.'

Claire sniffed. 'I was waiting for Liam to help me out of this bloody chair. He only went in for a beer.'

'He's got the beer and now he's watching sport on telly.'

'What sort of sport? The football hasn't started yet.'

'I dunno what sort.' Kitty shrugged. 'It's men doing something with a ball: hitting it, kicking it or throwing it. I didn't notice. Come on, I'll help you out of the chair.'

'I'm scared it'll fold up on me. Tell Liam to come, that'd be best.' Liam would pick her up by the waist like a doll.

'Now you're being ridiculous.' Kitty seized Claire's right hand, put her other hand behind her neck, and helped her to stand upright. 'There! That didn't hurt a bit, did it?'

'No, Kitty,' Claire said meekly. Sometimes, she wondered if she would have got better without Kitty chivvying her. Kitty had just flatly refused to let her die. She dreaded to think what would have happened if the chemotherapy had failed. Her sister would have been as mad as hell and gone looking for another cure, or even invented one herself.

'I got a letter from our Aileen yesterday,' Kitty said as they strolled towards the house. 'She's coming to Liverpool again at Christmas.'

'I know.' Claire pulled a face. 'I got a letter, too. She wants to stay with us. Liam's doing his nut. She's a bugger to live with: if I so much as lean forward on the chair, she grabs the cushion and plumps it up.'

'I'm sorry, Claire, but I'm afraid I can't help. All our bedrooms are occupied.'

'There's no need to sound so smug about it.'

The contrast between the brilliance outside and the darkness of the house was so great that, at first, Claire could hardly see. Her eyes cleared and she saw Faith in the kitchen dispensing wine. She refused a glass. 'I take a ton of tablets a day and I'm not supposed to drink alcohol,' she said regretfully.

'I hope you're allowed to eat; there's loads of food in the lounge.'

'It's all I seem to do.'

'Well, you need building up after what you've been through.'

Kitty had commandeered her an armchair. Claire loaded a plate with an assortment of tasty morsels, her mouth already watering. By now, the children had returned to the garden with their food, regardless of the wasps, the men were noisily watching television at one end of the room and the women had collected at the other. Zack, the centre of attention, had just had his nappy changed and appeared much less grumpy than the first time Claire had seen him.

Faith came to join them. Kitty insisted she take her chair and sat on the arm of Claire's, draping her arm across her sister's back. They discussed the babies they'd had and their various eating and sleeping habits.

'I breastfed Charlie,' Faith remarked. 'In those days it was frowned upon to give babies a bottle, but I couldn't manage it with Oliver and Robin.'

'Jake needed two mothers,' Kitty said. 'I nearly died when the health visitor said he wasn't getting enough to eat.' She shuddered. 'I still feel guilty about it.'

'I breastfed all mine,' Claire said boastfully.

Marge said she had, too. 'I had so much milk I could've started me own dairy.'

Bernadette had been so delicate that Norah hadn't had the chance to feed her herself. 'They gave her bottles straight away. My milk had dried up by the time she came out of hospital,' she said sadly, and everyone clucked sympathetically.

Eve had already started giving Zack a bottle at night. 'So he can get used to it. I hate breastfeeding, it plays havoc with your figure.'

'Huh!' Kitty snorted.

'Is that a bracelet Zack's wearing, Eve?' Marge asked. 'I've only just noticed.' Claire hadn't noticed the bracelet either.

'A woman called Mary Brady sent it: she was a friend of Michael's and we met at Muriel's funeral. She's awfully nice and we've exchanged Christmas cards ever since. I told her last year I was expecting a baby and she sent this.' Eve touched the little silver band clamped around Zack's plump wrist. She glanced at her mother. 'You met her, didn't you, Kitty? Not just at Muriel's funeral, but at Michael's in Belfast? She's nice, isn't she?'

Kitty's reply – 'Very nice indeed' – was almost drowned by the roar from the other end of the room: someone must have scored a goal or hit a six. Even so, Claire was aware Kitty's words had come out rather stiffly and idly wondered why. Perhaps she hadn't liked Mary Brady and was just being polite.

Eve continued. 'Actually, Michael died while Oliver was in Belfast, so he and Kitty were there at the same time, but they never met.'

'Belfast's an awfully big place, Eve, so it's not surprising.' Not only was Kitty's voice stiff, but her body was, too. Claire could feel the tension in the arm lying against her back. She took a deep breath, her brain went into overdrive and everything became wonderfully clear. She remembered Kitty had stayed in Belfast for four whole days. She'd been expected back in Liverpool on either the Friday or the Saturday, but hadn't arrived until late Sunday night. Oliver *was*

Jake's father! She just *knew* it. They'd had an affair. It wouldn't have bothered their Kitty that Oliver was almost half her age.

'Are you all right, Claire?' Faith asked worriedly. 'You've gone terribly red.'

Kitty leapt to her feet. 'I'll fetch some water.'

'You feel awfully hot, luv.' Norah stroked her brow.

'Perhaps you should lie down a minute,' suggested Marge.

Eve wondered aloud if she was having a hot flush, 'Whatever that is, but I know older women have them.'

'I'm perfectly all right,' Claire insisted. *She knew! She knew!* Many were the times she'd lain in bed wondering who on earth could be Jake's father. And now she knew! She would never tell anyone, certainly not Kitty, but the question would no longer gnaw at her soul. It would have been nice to know if Oliver was aware Jake was his son, and if Eve knew, too, but that was just the icing on the cake and she could live without it.

The hours crept by, the air grew cooler, shadows inched across the grass. The dishes had been washed, the food put away, and Eve and Oliver had gone home because the girls had tired themselves out and Zack was starting to grumble. Faith went to help put the children to bed. The television was turned off and Liam, Danny and Con departed for the pub, taking Jake with them. 'But he's only nine,' Kitty had protested.

'That don't matter, Kit,' Liam said easily. 'We'll sit in the garden and he can have lemonade and a packet of crisps.'

'*Please*, Mum!' Jake's face twisted agonizingly when his mother looked about to refuse.

'Oh, all right,' she said, 'though it seems wrong to let a child of nine go to a pub.'

'There'll probably be loads of other children there,' Claire assured her.

'Even so,' Kitty sniffed, 'you're to bring him back well before closing time.'

Now there were only the sisters and Marge left. The house seemed unnaturally quiet. Norah asked if they'd like a drink and something to eat: 'There's loads of food left.'

Kitty said, 'Claire never says no to a cuppa,' as if she were in the habit of refusing herself. Norah left for the kitchen and Marge followed to give her a hand.

'Why didn't you invite Con to the party?' Claire demanded as soon as she and Kitty were alone.

Kitty raised her eyebrows. 'He was here, wasn't he?'

'Yes, but he said Eve had invited him.'

'I intended to, but Eve asked him first. She sees more of him than me.'

'That's a pity. He still loves you after all this time. His life's a total wreck, and you know whose fault that is, don't you?' Claire geared up for the attack. 'I can't understand why you didn't marry him. But not only did you turn him down, you didn't even tell him about Eve. You behaved disgracefully, Kit, and you don't seem to give a damn.' That sounded a bit over the top, but she didn't care.

She half expected her sister to react angrily. Instead, Kitty muttered, 'I'm very fond of Con, I always have been. I know I treated him badly, but it's a bit too late to make up for it now.'

'It's never too late to make amends, luv.' She wanted to say, 'To hell with it, girl, why don't you and Con get married? He'd jump at the chance and you'd be company for each other in your old age. After all, our Norah might leave soon and Jake won't live at home for ever.' But it would be fatal to say something like that to Kitty. She'd regard it as demeaning to marry someone just for the company, though Claire could think of a dozen worse reasons.

To her surprise, Kitty burst out laughing. 'Next minute, you'll be suggesting I propose to him. You did with Charlie Collier, remember?'

'And did you?' Claire had often wondered, but hadn't liked to ask.

'No, and it's a good job I didn't. He was already in love with someone else.'

'I thought you were mad about him.' She'd definitely given that impression.

'Only a bit and it didn't last for long.' Kitty waved her hand dismissively.

Marge came in with the tea. 'I heard that last bit. I didn't know you'd been keen on Charlie Collier, Kit. He seemed OK, but didn't he play with trains? Danny said it was a case of retarded development.'

'You mean you and Danny have been discussing my affairs?' Kitty pretended to be outraged.

'Of course,' Marge said cheerfully. 'We discuss you all the time. Danny always ses you should've married Connor Daley.'

'That's what *I* was just saying,' Claire put in quickly. Every little helped.

The sun was beginning to dip behind the houses at the end of the garden and the birds had set up a racket in the trees.

They reminisced about the old times, as they often did when the four of them were together. Remember when Mam did this, when Dad did that, when Jamie went off to do his National Service.

'He and Barbara didn't come today,' Kitty said sadly, 'though I invited them.'

'Perhaps they didn't think it all that important.' Claire had missed their little brother, too. 'But Jamie's a McCarthy and he'll always turn up when he's really needed.'

The men returned just after nine, Jake stuffed with self-importance after his first visit to a pub. 'I had two packets of crisps, Mam, and a Pepsi. Uncle Liam let me have sip of his beer.' He pulled a face. 'It was horrible.'

'Well, let's hope you always find it horrible, luv,' Claire said grimly, 'so you don't end up a drunkard like your Uncle Liam. He's sunk more beers than most people have had hot dinners.'

Liam didn't look remotely offended – Claire would have been upset if he had – and suggested it was time they went home. She conceded she felt dead tired. 'But it's been a lovely day, Kit, I've really enjoyed meself. And the food was fantastic, Norah.' She kissed them both and gave them an extra hard hug, so hard that it hurt her arm.

Danny said if they hurried there was time for him and Marge to catch an hour or two at the dance club.

'I'll have to go home first and get changed,' Marge wailed, but Danny insisted she looked fine as she was.

'I suppose I'd best be going,' Con sighed.

'Why don't you stay a bit longer, Con?' Claire suggested. 'Our Kitty won't go to bed for hours yet.' She glared challengingly at her sister. 'Will you, Kit?'

Kitty rolled her eyes and agreed she wouldn't. 'I'd like that, Con, if you can spare the time.'

Con said casually he'd quite like to stay, thanks, and Claire tried not to appear as triumphant as she felt.

Jake had collapsed on to the settee and was already half asleep.

Kitty ordered him to bed immediately. Norah announced she wouldn't mind having an early night. 'I'm exhausted,' she cried, stretching and yawning extravagantly both at the same time. She winked at Claire, who nodded approvingly. Norah had already cottoned on to what she was up to. Everything was going to plan.

Less than an hour later, Claire was sitting up in bed, sipping the cocoa Liam had made, while he sat beside her reading the *News of the World*: he only read the sports pages and hadn't a clue what was going on in the rest of the world.

'It's been a smashing day,' she said.

'Smashing,' he agreed, not taking his eyes off the paper.

She wondered what Kitty and Con were talking about. There were times when people refused to acknowledge what was directly underneath their noses. Kitty was stubborn and foolhardy, and Claire hoped it wouldn't be too long before the penny dropped and she realized she'd be crazy not to marry Con. Claire was quite determined that she would. She'd get Marge on her side, suggest she invited the couple to the dance club whenever they had an open night, and tell Norah to make sure they sat next to each other at that dinner she was planning in her new restaurant, La something; she should have asked for a menu to show the neighbours.

'What colour do I suit best?' she asked Liam, who still had his nose buried in the paper.

'Eh?' He didn't look up.

'I asked what colour suits me best?'

'Oh, er, black, luv.'

'I can't wear black at a wedding,' she said scathingly.

'Whose wedding?' She'd caught his attention at last.

'Our Kitty and Con's. I'd like to buy something new. Turquoise would make a change.' She couldn't remember having had anything turquoise before.

Liam looked hurt. 'Con didn't mention he and Kitty were getting married when we were at the pub.'

'That's because he doesn't know yet. Neither does our Kitty.' But, by the time she'd finished with them, Claire didn't have the slightest doubt that the McCarthys would have a wedding before the year was out.

She could feel it in her water.